Drumindor

Drumindor is a work of fiction. Names, places, and incidents are either products of the author's imagination or used fictitiously. Any resemblance to actual events, locales, or persons, living or dead, is purely coincidental. In accordance with the U.S. Copyright Act of 1976, the copying, scanning, uploading, and electronic sharing of any part of this book (other than for review purposes) without permission is unlawful piracy and theft of the author's intellectual property. If you would like to use material from this book, prior written permission can be obtained by contacting the author at **michael@michael-j-sullivan.com**. Thank you for your support of the author's rights.

Drumindor © 2024 by Michael J. Sullivan
Map © 2024 by Michael J. Sullivan
Interior design © 2024 by Robin Sullivan
Limited edition cover design © 2024 by Sarah Sullivan
Regular edition cover design by Deranged Doctor Designs
The Blue Parrot illustration © 2024 by Sarah Sullivan
Nightime in Tur Del Fur illustraion © 2024 by Sarah Sullivan
Tur Del Fur sketches © 2024 by Michael J. Sullivan
All rights reserved.

Limited edition: 978-1-943363-49-0
Regular hardcover: 978-1-943363-71-1

Published in the United States by Riyria Enterprises, LLC
Learn more about Michael's writings at **michael-j-sullivan.com**.
To contact Michael, email him at **michael@michael-j-sullivan.com**.

2 4 6 8 9 7 5 3 1

First Edition October 2024
Printed in China

RIYRIA ENTERPRISES

For Lady Macbeth, who lived a lonely life of abandonment before coming to us, and who for a time found happiness in our home.

Tragically, she disappeared, and we thought we'd never see her again. A week later, unexpectedly and against all odds, she managed to return, and she died in the arms of the one she loved the most.

We'll forever miss you, Mackie.

About the Book

HE PLANNED TO OBLITERATE AN ENTIRE CITY.
HE THOUGHT NO ONE COULD STAND IN HIS WAY.
BUT HE HADN'T HEARD OF RIYRIA.

When a master craftsman dwarf is fired and threatens retaliation, the rogues-for-hire enterprise known as Riyria is commissioned to stop him. Traveling to the paradise resort of Tur Del Fur, the two are granted a lavish allowance that, along with an easy task, promises to turn a job into a vacation. Everything would have been perfect except that the disgruntled worker's last name is Berling, and the targets of his wrath are the legendary towers of Drumindor.

Welcome to the fifth installment of The Riyria Chronicles, from Michael J. Sullivan, the *New York Times* and *USA Today* bestselling author. This is the eleventh book starring the cynical ex-assassin Royce Melborn and the idealistic ex-mercenary Hadrian Blackwater. While part of a much larger tale, this novel is written such that you can enjoy it even if you've not read any of the other books in the series. But for those who are fans of the pair, it's been over six years since we last saw them, and we're hoping you'll be pleased to be reunited. Either way, we hope you enjoy this adventure!

Contents

About the Book — *vii*
Author's Note — *xiii*
The Cycle Project — *xvii*
Reading Buddies — *xxi*
Map of Elan — *xxiv*

Chapter 1:	The Last Berling	1
Chapter 2:	The Affair	7
Chapter 3:	The Visitor	19
Chapter 4:	The Stagecoach	34
Chapter 5:	Trouble with Bubbles	49
Chapter 6:	Kruger	60
Chapter 7:	Tur Del Fur	75
Chapter 8:	The Blue Parrot	98
Chapter 9:	Flaming Peacocks	113
Chapter 10:	Fish and Birds	127
Chapter 11:	Millificent LeDeye	141
Chapter 12:	The Search Begins	153
Chapter 13:	Auberon	165
Chapter 14:	The Missing	179
Chapter 15:	Lady Constance	184
Chapter 16:	The Admirer	197
Chapter 17:	The Casino	212
Chapter 18:	As Rain Falls	227
Chapter 19:	Footsteps in the Dark	243
Chapter 20:	Under the Fancy Fin	252
Chapter 21:	Raising the Dead	258

Contents

Chapter 22:	The Locked Door	270
Chapter 23:	The New Deal	281
Chapter 24:	The Diary of Falkirk	293
Chapter 25:	Exodus	306
Chapter 26:	The Last Night	316
Chapter 27:	The Cave	330
Chapter 28:	The Last Ship Out	342
Chapter 29:	Scram Scallie	353
Chapter 30:	The Crown Jewel	372
Chapter 31:	Fate Lends a Hand	386
Chapter 32:	Can You Hear Me	395
Chapter 33:	The Climb	400
Chapter 34:	The Bridge	413
Chapter 35:	The Wall	428
Chapter 36:	The Big Room	438
Chapter 37:	Chain Reaction	447
Chapter 38:	Full Moon Rising	455
Chapter 39:	A Different Dawn	463

Afterword	*473*
Sullivan's Spoils	*479*
Of Gods and Men	*481*
About the Illustrations	*495*
About the Author	*497*

Author's Note

When I finished The Riyria Revelations series back in 2010, I was ready to put Royce and Hadrian and the entire world of Elan behind me. It was a single story after all, not a life's calling. By now, you've likely heard how my wife, Robin, complained that she wanted more time with the love of her life — Hadrian — and how she did not appreciate me standing between them. She wanted more, but I had no intention of enabling her love affair with another man. However, while Orbit was in the process of ramping up for the re-release of The Riyria Revelations, I was required to take down my self-published versions. This resulted in several months when I had no books available for sale. Robin felt this was a marketing blunder, and she aimed to fill that gap with a short story — one intended to promote the re-issued series. In this way, she coaxed me into writing "The Viscount and the Witch." I wrote it because I felt it made for a decent self-contained event: how Royce and Hadrian met Albert Winslow, which occurred in the second year of their partnership. It felt like the start of a novel, which got me thinking about writing the rest of the tale.

At the time, the new novel I had been working on, *Antithesis,* was failing miserably, so I began writing *The Rose and Thorn*. Note: the officially released title, *The Rose and **the** Thorn,* was decided by Orbit for reasons I'll never fully understand or agree with, but it wasn't something I had a say over. In any event, before finishing that book, I realized it was stupid to write about the second year without showing the first. I felt I had no choice but to write Riyria's origin story. I set *The Rose and Thorn* down and wrote *The Crown Tower,* then came back and finished the book that I had originally started. My wife was happy, even if Orbit was not—they don't like prequels and would have tried to talk me out of writing one if they had known that's what I was spending my time on. Those who know me realize that discussion wouldn't have gone well.

After completing these two novels, I was free to leave Elan and the fantasy genre behind and move on to other types of writing—for, you see, I never planned to be a fantasy author.

Except I wasn't free of Elan. Not yet.

I felt obligated to tell the truth about Elan's backstory and began a six-book series, The Legends of the First Empire (another set of prequels), which Penguin Random House was eager to publish. However, by the scheduled release date for *Age of Myth*, over four years would have passed since the last Riyria book. And according to the new contract with Penguin Random House, I wouldn't be allowed to publish another Elan book until their books were released. This would have been in 2021, making it close to a full decade after *The Rose and Thorn* that anyone would hear from Royce and Hadrian again. That would have been far too long. Then Robin got the idea that I could publish a new Elan book *before* the contract started.

"How fast can you write a new Riyria story?" she asked.

The answer, it turned out, was sixty-eight days. *The Death of Dulgath* was published in late 2015, just a few months before *Age of Myth*.

After I finished writing The Legends of the First Empire, and while I was waiting for those books to be published, I toyed with the idea of a set of "bridge books" to span the enormous gap of history between Legends and Riyria. This would later become The Rise and Fall series, but, working on that would once more mean a long time between Riyria tales, so I took a break and wrote *The Disappearance of Winter's Daughter*. Then because of a policy change at Penguin Random House (requiring that they retain audio rights, which we had already sold), we weren't able to license the final books in The Legends of the First Empire to Penguin. What's more, the division broke awkwardly (four with them and two with us). Given that that particular series is more akin to two closely related trilogies, Robin managed to regain rights to *Age of Legend* and tip the scales back to a three and three combination. The happy byproduct of that renegotiation made it possible to publish *The Disappearance of Winter's Daughter* in limited release as early as 2017.

What this all boils down to is that the last Riyria book was published six years ago. Given this, would it be worth the time to write another? Was anyone still interested in Royce and Hadrian? Did anyone care?

As it turned out, I had posed this question in several prior books and listed my email address to obtain the answer. Several people took the time to write. Here is some of what they said:

> *"I have heard you say in introductions to your books that you want to know if we want more. I just wanted to tell you: Yes! More Royce and Hadrian, please."*

> *"Your books with these characters are tremendous! You asked if readers want more to let you know. I want more!"*

> *"So, I just finished Death of Dulgath and I'm confident I could read 100 more Hadrian and Royce adventures."*

> *"I'm just wondering if there are any more recent adventures for Hadrian and Royce? Miss those guys."*

There are hundreds of others along these lines, which made me think that maybe . . . possibly . . . it was time to write another.

There was an additional factor influencing the writing of this novel. Readers who had just finished The Legends of the First Empire series and the three books of The Rise and Fall were a bit stressed out. The stakes had gotten higher, the drama more . . . well . . . dramatic. And there were more than a few heartbreaks along the way. They longed for a respite and asked for something fun, something more "slice-of-life," something that didn't include world-ending stakes or the death of a beloved character. What they longed for was a good old-fashioned Riyria holiday. Now, I never write in response to readers' desires. I have always only written the stories I want to read — best that way, really. Writing for other people would make my time at the keyboard a labor instead of a joy. Except . . .

There is *one* person who has the power to sway me. And she wanted — no needed — a little happiness brought back during some trying times. So that's what I set out to write, a little book that appealed to my wife's desire to just spend some time with two characters that she loved: Royce and Hadrian.

Problem is, these two can't help themselves. Trouble has a habit of finding them.

Here then is *Drumindor*, another story that many already know the end to, which began as a fun, carefree romp, which somehow grew into so much more, something wholly unexpected, and something I hope you will enjoy.

But before you start, I have an announcement . . . please stay tuned.

Michael J. Sullivan
September 2024

The Cycle Project

With the completion of The Rise and Fall series and now *Drumindor,* some of you have asked, "What's next?" And you haven't just inquired, I've received suggestions.

Some of you want to see a story about the First War, others the early years of Royce and Hadrian. Although after the release of *The Rose and the Thorn*—after seeing how Royce used to be in the *old days*—I'm seeing fewer requests for that. By far the top request, however, has been for a post-Riyria Revelations book or series. To understand why I've resisted this idea, you first need to know how I write my books.

I am not a fan of stories that start out fantastic and then quickly run out of steam with each added installment. Usually, this happens because the author puts all their "best stuff" up front to gain an audience. I don't do that. When I started writing The Riyria Revelations, I didn't think *any* of them would be published, so I wasn't concerned about making a "big splash" with my initial offering. Instead, I saved all the juicy stuff for the end. As a result, the last book in that series has been the best—by design—mostly because it was the culmination of everything that came before. Knowing I couldn't top that, I wasn't about to try.

The entire notion was incomprehensible. How could I raise the stakes higher than they were? How could I make the climax more dramatic? The series-long plotline had been satisfied, and there was simply no way to top *Percepliquis*. In order to do that, I would need a larger, profounder, over-arching plot: something with even greater stakes, more characters, and a bigger bang at the end. Without knowing it, what people were asking me to do would require nothing less than creating a whole new series devoted to the forming of the world and the Novronian Empire. Then it would be necessary for me to write another series linking those books to the Riyria stories. And somehow in doing all that, I must nurture a growing desire — no, a desperate need — on the part of the readers to see how it all turns out.

And that, dear friend, is just crazy.

A good case could be made that I am not altogether sensible because, of course, that's exactly what I did when I spent a decade writing The Legends of the First Empire and The Rise and Fall series. This effort, that culminated in the publication of *Farilane* and *Esrahaddon,* launched a new contender for the most requested suggestion that has rocketed to the top spot: the desire to know what happens to Turin.

In one sense this was good, as that was the point after all, to establish a hunger in my readers for something greater. But it's also like getting everyone's attention by grabbing the microphone at a wedding. The audience expects you to say something worth hearing, and as it turns out, laying the foundation was the easy part of this challenge.

The obstacles were overwhelming. I would need to invent new content and seamlessly marry it to aspects of Elan previously known only to myself. I also had to tie up twenty books in a comprehensive bow, all while maintaining the established rules and laws of my world — meaning I couldn't cheat. These preestablished, load-bearing walls that can't be relocated or removed, would hinder, if not entirely prevent, me from creating my be-all, end-all masterpiece that could challenge *Percepliquis* for the top spot. Because of this, I didn't know if what I hoped to do was even possible.

When facing such an insurmountable task, I did what any normal person would do in my situation. I formed a committee of highly skilled experts in the world of Elan and ordered them to deliberate on the feasibility of contemplating such a project. This became The Exploratory Committee, and given the necessary requirements to sit on such an esteemed advisory council, TEC became a committee of one — me.

On February 23rd of the year 2022, TEC entered the research and development room, and the door was nailed shut. For more than two and a half years the committee has deliberated in secrecy. Recently, however, there have been some leaks — both good and bad. Perhaps the worst is that "The Project" cannot receive a green light until all the required books have been written. I don't like promising something I ultimately can't deliver, so I won't. The best news is that "The Project" has been officially renamed: The Cycle. This wouldn't have happened if the committee didn't have a high degree of confidence in the outcome because giving something a name has the power to breathe it into existence.

Since *Drumindor* may very likely be the last novel I publish for a number of years, we won't be able to have these little chats for some time. As such, I want to leave you with a means of checking up on the process of The Cycle Project. You can do so by visiting our webpage or by joining the discord server (see links and QR codes below). Through these outlets, we will endeavor to keep you up to date with any significant developments.

Website: **bit.ly/the-cycle**   Discord: **bit.ly/cycle-discord**

Reading Buddies

While reading or listening to a Michael J. Sullivan book, have you ever finished a chapter or a scene and wanted to talk with someone about it only to realize you didn't know anyone else reading the book? Have you found yourself dying to share a theory? Needing a question answered? Or just plain mad as hell about the death of a beloved character and wanting someone who would listen, understand, and sympathize? Well, thanks to discord, there is just such a place (see links and QR codes on the next page). From there, you will find individual channels for each of Michael's twenty novels based in Elan. And to make it easy to find, we've temporarily relocated the Drumindor channel to the top. From there, you can interact with other Sullifans as you read without having to worry about spoilers. Also in the Drumindor channel you will find:

- **news:** for announcements on production and release information. Michael may also post events he's going to or cities he's traveling to.
- **author-free-zone:** a channel where you can discuss matters you don't want to be seen by Michael or Robin Sullivan.
- **ask-michael-or-robin:** a channel where you can pose questions to the author or the "woman behind the books" for anything non-writing related such as book orders.
- **typos:** if you see an error in the book, report it so that future versions can be improved.
- **end-of-the-book-discussion:** a place where spoilers can't exist because everyone there has finished the entire story.

And if you're looking to interact with other diehard Sullivan readers, there is also a lively and popular Riyria server: a site launched and operated by fans of Michael's books. He often visits this site with news, announcements, or merely to answer questions that befuddle the minds of readers. You can access it from the link and QR code below.

Oh, something else you might enjoy. For those who would like to know more about Elan and the stories, there is the wonderful YouTube channel called Riyria Explained (see link and QR code below). You will find deep dives into popular topics there but tread lightly. While its creator is careful to avoid—or at least warn—about spoilers, there are many of them to be found there.

Elan Discord: **bit.ly/elan-discord**

SCAN ME

Drumindor Discord: **bit.ly/dru-start**

SCAN ME

Riyria Discord: **bit.ly/riyria-discord**

SCAN ME

bit.ly/riyria-explained

SCAN ME

Works by Michael J. Sullivan

THE LEGENDS OF THE FIRST EMPIRE
Age of Myth • *Age of Swords* • *Age of War*
Age of Legend • *Age of Death* • *Age of Empyre*

THE RISE AND FALL
Nolyn • *Farilane* • *Esrahaddon*

THE RIYRIA CHRONICLES
The Crown Tower • *The Rose and the Thorn*
The Death of Dulgath • *The Disappearance of Winter's Daughter*
Drumindor

THE RIYRIA REVELATIONS
Theft of Swords (*The Crown Conspiracy* • *Avempartha*)
Rise of Empire (*Nyphron Rising* • *The Emerald Storm*)
Heir of Novron (*Wintertide* • *Percepliquis*)

STANDALONE NOVELS
Hollow World (Sci-fi Thriller)

SHORT STORIES IN ANTHOLOGIES
Unavowed: "The Storm" (Fantasy: The Cycle)
Grimoire: "Traditions" (Fantasy: Tales from Elan)
Heroes Wanted: "The Ashmoore Affair" (Fantasy: Riyria Chronicles)
Blackguards: "Professional Integrity" (Fantasy: Riyria Chronicles)
Unfettered: "The Jester" (Fantasy: Riyria Chronicles)
When Swords Fall Silent: "May Luck Be with You" (Fantasy: Riyria Chronicles)
Unbound: "The Game" (Fantasy: LitRPG)
Unfettered II: "Little Wren and the Big Forest" (Fantasy: Legends of the First Empire)
The End: Visions of the Apocalypse: "Burning Alexandria" (Dystopian Sci-fi)
Triumph Over Tragedy: "Traditions" (Fantasy: Tales from Elan)
The Fantasy Faction Anthology: "Autumn Mist" (Fantasy: Contemporary)
Help Fund My Robot Army: "Be Careful What You Wish For" (Fantasy: Contemporary)

STANDALONE SHORT STORIES
"Pile of Bones" (Fantasy: Legends of the First Empire)

Online map: https://bit.ly/drumindor-map

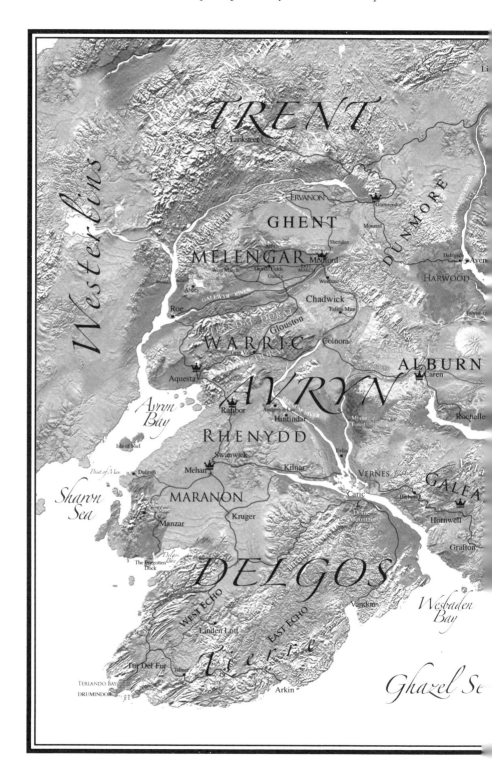

Drumindor

RIYRIA CHRONICLES BOOK 5

———◆●◆———

NEW YORK TIMES AND *USA TODAY* BESTSELLING AUTHOR

MICHAEL J. SULLIVAN

CHAPTER ONE

The Last Berling

"I'm sorry, Gravis," Lord Byron said in his most sympathetic tone, which he knew from experience was not up to such a task, "but I regret to deliver the unpleasant news that you are being let go."

The dwarf in front of Lord Byron stood before the grand desk, looking horribly out of place in the lavish office.

Lord Byron thought, *He'd look out of place anywhere, I imagine.*

Not quite three feet tall, the dwarf had hair that came to his knees and a beard that brushed the floor. His eyebrows, which grew on a pronounced ridge, appeared like a pair of neglected hedges whose gardener had died a century ago. These brows cast a brooding shadow on his face. Taken as a whole, Gravis Berling seemed little more than a hairy haystack with a pair of pitiful eyes.

But then again, they're all like that, aren't they?

"I don't understand, sir," Gravis said, his voice the traditional deep dwarven groan of grinding rock.

Lord Byron didn't know much about dwarfs despite employing a tiny army of them. Like everyone, he'd heard the legends, the jokes made at public houses, and he'd witnessed the depictions at theaters where they were always villains.

Dwarfs certainly looked the part. Small and hairy, they scurried about in the dark, completely at home underground where no reasonable person would ever go. Rats were the same way, and as such, they induced fear and loathing. People who weren't revolted were often the type to see small furry things as cute, such as the lady who tries to care for a hurt squirrel or raccoon. But dwarfs were neither. Nor were they so simple a thing as inconvenient rodents. Dwarfs were dangerous, their size misleading. Lord Byron had once seen a dwarven miner crush a rock with his bare hand. Armed with pickaxes, Gravis's brethren could cut through stone as if it were high grass. Not only were they frighteningly strong, but the entire race also possessed the endurance of wolves and the longevity of tortoises. Some stories claimed dwarfs lived as long as five centuries. Lord Byron had reason to believe there was truth to these tales as Gravis himself was easily over a hundred. The years showed in the gullies of his face, the deep valleys beneath those downtrodden eyes, and the brittle gray in all that hair. Some legends even put forth the notion that the diminutive race was not born of flesh and blood but rather crafted from stone. This was why their voices possessed that unpleasant grit and the reason why dwarfs had no feelings.

"What do you mean, *let go?*"

Lord Byron frowned, disappointed at the response. *He's pretending to be ignorant. I did hope it wouldn't go this way. But then I also hoped the gout in my left toe would clear up.*

"As of this moment," Lord Byron explained, "you are no longer an employee of the Delgos Port Authority Association."

The dwarf narrowed his eyes, bristling those awful brows. *They look like woolly bear caterpillars with their fur up. Do caterpillars do that? Raise their fur? Is that why they call them woolly bears? I doubt it.*

"What's that mean, sir?" Gravis continued with what appeared to be a charade of ignorance.

Lord Byron fought the urge to roll his eyes. It had been a long day, most of it taken up dismissing more than two dozen dwarfs. He could have had the foreman do it — regretted a bit now that he hadn't — but he believed in doing things the proper way. Delgos was a republic, not a monarchy. A worker had the right to hear such news directly from his employer.

"It means you no longer work here, Gravis. You will receive your final recompense at the door as you leave."

The dwarf continued to stare as if he no longer understood the Rhunic language. They sometimes did that, feigned ignorance while muttering something in their native tongue.

"But . . ." Gravis looked around the office. "I *don't* work here. I work at Drumindor, sir."

Lord Byron had expected that the old engineer would be a problem. Gravis Berling had been with the Port Authority longer than anyone, longer than even Lord Byron. And then, of course, there was the whole family name issue. It was said that a certain Andvari Berling—an ancient dwarf—had designed and overseen the building of the fortress. Lord Byron wasn't at all certain this was true, but it could be. *Anything could be, couldn't it?* Gravis certainly thought it was possible, and in the old engineer's mind, Drumindor was *his* property—the ancient fortress *his* inheritance. This was why Lord Byron had insisted that the old engineer was to be the last brought to his office. He knew the meeting would be unnecessarily quarrelsome and draining. He looked forward to consoling himself afterward with a cup of tea and a long walk along the bay. Nothing helped clear the head like salt-sea air and a hot cup of salifan, especially with a squeeze of fresh lemon. A cup of tea absolutely required fresh lemon, or what was the point?

Lord Byron didn't like scenes or disturbances of any sort. He was a proper man who woke each morning at sunrise, always put on his left shoe before his right, and never went outside without hat and gloves. Order was the proper way of things and routine the heart and soul of order. People like Gravis were . . . messy. Handling him was very much like clearing a clogged drain with a bare hand. And, if pressed on the matter, Lord Byron would admit to a certain personality flaw regarding the propensity to procrastinate when it came to anything expected to be disagreeable. Informing Gravis Berling that he would no longer be allowed to care for his beloved Drumindor after more than a century was undoubtedly going to be unpleasant.

Lord Byron took an exasperated breath before stating what he was certain Gravis was well aware of but pointedly pretending to be oblivious to. "Drumindor *is part* of the Delgos Port Authority Association, Gravis. Why are you being so obtuse?"

Perhaps it was his use of *obtuse* that caused it. Lord Byron doubted the likes of Gravis had a clue what the word meant. But whatever the reason, the dwarf appeared to stop listening. Despite his small vocabulary, Gravis had gotten the message. Perhaps it just took a bit of time to penetrate all that hair. "I've worked there all me life. I . . ." The dwarf stroked his beard, eyes shifting about in a vague panic.

Lord Byron had witnessed similar mannerisms in men walking to the gallows. Gravis was noticeably terrified as any person would be when faced with a very sudden end to what had been a long life.

"I never had any children," Gravis confessed, as if this were some great crime. He sounded suddenly short of breath. "I'm the last of the Berlings — the *last*. There's no one left in me clan. I . . . I have no family, except me wife, and she . . ." He hesitated as if a new and terrible thought had walked uninvited across the threshold of his mind. "My Ena, she's sick! The poor lass. She's been ill for some time, getting worse, too. How will I . . . Without me job, I'll be asked ta pay rent on that shack of ours. If I lose it — I got nothing. There's no place that will hire me, not now, not at my age." He looked at his hands as if they had betrayed him. "What'd I do wrong, sir? I swear ta your god and mine that I'll make it right. I will. I'll do anything. Please. Please."

Lord Byron had expected the question. They had all asked it, and he had answered the same way each time. "It's not anything *you* did, Gravis. The Tur Del Fur Administration Triumvirate has determined that, given the recent lawless disturbances, continuing to allow *your people* to operate Drumindor is . . . well, it's a threat to city security."

"What disturbances? And what do you mean about a threat to security?" Gravis looked lost. "The Berlings — built Drumindor, sir. This — this whole bay was uninhabitable before Andvari Berling arrived. I'll tell you what's a threat, sir — *not* having a Berling take proper care of the old gal. That's dangerous, that is. Letting me go — as you call it — that's irresponsible, unsafe, and *absolutely a threat to this city's security*."

"I am aware of your —"

"Mount Druma used to erupt all the bleeding time, spewing clouds of ash and poison gas and letting loose streams of lava. This lovely little bay was a toxic death trap a'fore we built Drumindor!"

"Yes, I fully understand—"

"And then there were the pirates, the Dacca and the Ba Ran. They used to ravage these coasts! If it weren't for *my people*, there'd be no Drumindor, no Tur Del Fur, no Port Authority Association or Administration Triumvirate! If it weren't for *my people*, this office would be in a smoking crater of molten rock! All your lovely little shops, cafés, taprooms, and theaters wouldn't exist."

"It's not my decision, Gravis."

"You're the president of the Port Authority Association!" The grind of gravel rose to the roar of a lion. "Ya just said Drumindor is part of the bloody DP-double-A."

"Yes, but I don't run the country. This decision was made by the Triumvirate. If you have a problem, take it up with them." This was Lord Byron's shield. He had never thought of it that way until witnessing Gravis change from the wandering wizard of wheels and levers into something more frightening. Once more, Lord Byron remembered how that miner's bare hand had crushed a rock like a clod of dirt, and for a moment, he felt afraid. Gravis's hands, old as they were, might still possess power beyond mortal man.

"Aye, you're right. It's not up to you. Not even up to the Unholy Trio. Even if they wanted to, they can't change the way men think," Gravis said in resignation as he looked at the polished floor and shook his head. "It's the same as always, isn't it? We thought the republic would be different. No kings, no emperors, no church. Just free folk minding their own business. But it's still the same. It's always the same." He looked up sharply and fixed Lord Byron with a piercing glare. "I should be the one firing you—all of ya. Drumindor is mine, and none of you deserve her. You can't understand her language, and ya don't even know how she works." He paused and thought a moment as if another idea—a horrible one—came knocking. "But I do."

Gravis Berling glared up at Lord Byron, and a smile appeared under all that hair, an awful, terrible smile. "Aye, that's right, I know her *very* well."

"You need to leave now, Gravis," Lord Byron said. "And remember, if you try to return to Drumindor, you will be arrested."

Gravis nodded and started toward the door. Then he stopped, and without looking back, he said, "If I return to Drumindor, sir, there won't be anything left to arrest, nor anyone left to arrest me."

Long after the dwarf was gone, Lord Byron stared at the empty doorway of his office, those final words echoing. They continued to haunt him, as did the coming of the full moon.

CHAPTER TWO

The Affair

After waking and finding Royce Melborn standing in the dark at the foot of her bed, Lady Lillian Traval's eyes went wide, but she didn't scream. Had she, Royce would have slit her throat in an instant, not so much out of necessity, but reflex. He was there to kill her anyway, but the woman's self-restraint bought the lady an extra pair of seconds. She made the most of them.

"Wait!" she said. The single word was urgently cast, but the volume was low, practically a whisper, as if the two were together in this endeavor rather than predator and prey.

Royce was so impressed he did as she asked. He had the luxury. The Traval Estate was practically vacant. Lady Traval had no children or pets, and her husband was away on business. As a precaution, she'd even gone so far as to send all the guards and servants away. Lady Traval and Edmund wanted to be alone, and as such, the lovers had the entire place to themselves. Royce couldn't have had an easier execution to perform. Lillian could have shrieked for hours, alerting no one other than Edmund, who lay fast asleep on his stomach beside her. The young baron was no more a threat than the pillow he lay upon. Royce's two victims were prone on the mattress, helpless in the lady's lavish bed chamber. Bright moonlight revealed the sheen of sweat on bare skin. Both lay naked, wrapped just as much in each other as in the tangled bedsheet.

Curiosity was what made Royce delay, and this came in two parts. The first was how this pampered wife of a noble shipping magnate had maintained her wits at such a moment. The second was the anticipation of what she might say next.

What can she say?

He expected to be disappointed. She would likely claim something to the effect of *You can't do this!* despite the obvious truth of the situation. Royce had heard such words on those few occasions where his target had had the opportunity to speak. Nevertheless, she had surprised him with her quiet restraint. That didn't happen often. He felt she'd earned at least one sentence, even if it wouldn't make a difference.

It did.

"I can pay more," Lady Traval said.

Well played, and in only four words.

Edmund stirred. "What? You're *paying* me now?" he asked merrily in between sleepy breaths. "Have I become your trollop?"

"Shut up, you idiot!" Lillian snapped, still in that carefully quiet voice.

"What makes you think you can pay more?" Royce asked.

At the sound of his voice, Edmund rolled over and peered into the dark. It took a second before . . . "Novron's ghost!" the Baron of Sansbury screamed. Luckily for him, the lady of the house had already entered into a negotiation sufficiently intriguing to grant a stay of execution for both.

"Because I know my husband," Lady Traval replied, as if Edmund didn't exist. "He's cheap. I guarantee that I can pay twice what he offered."

"Who is this?" Edmund glared at Royce. "Lilly, what are you two talking about?"

"Oh, Eddie, please do be quiet, or you'll get us both killed."

"Killed?" The young man's eyes threatened to fall out as he looked first at her then Royce.

"Twice as much?" Royce asked. "Are you being literal or just flamboyant?"

"I'm not sure," Lady Traval replied. "What is the life of a noble adulteress going for these days?"

Royce suppressed a smile. He had never met Lady Lillian Traval before, but he'd known of her for years. She had the distinction of being Riyria's first official client. While Royce was not normally sentimental, it still counted for something that she paid promptly and well. Her husband, by contrast, was indeed cheap. The lady had paid fifty tenents for the recovery of one earring, while in return for the double murder of his wife and her lover, Hurbert Traval was only willing to part with . . .

"Thirty," Royce replied.

"Gold, I hope," she said, sounding disappointed but not surprised.

"Yes."

"Is he really here to kill us?" Edmund asked. "Did your husband —"

"Silence, Edmund! Damn you! I'm trying to save our lives, you foolish boy!"

The baron cringed, whimpered, and pulled up the sheet. Edmund Wyberne, the eighth Lord of Sansbury, was pretty, pale, and pathetic. The lad was wealthy and still in his teens but always as morose as a man with a noose around his neck. His father had died only a few years ago of consumption—the White Death—leaving Edmund an enormous inheritance, including the illness that left him frail, pale, and inexplicably attractive to women. Apparently, ladies had a penchant for corpses.

"Sixty it is then," Lillian declared.

"You have it here?"

"I do."

"Wait! You can't trust a hired murderer!" Edmund wailed from behind the armor of the damp bedsheet that he held to his face. "What's to stop him from killing us, stealing your money, then collecting his reward from Hurbert?"

Lady Traval rolled her eyes. "If he does that, my husband will know he stole it, and that will be . . . well, bad for business. Won't it? No one would ever hire him again if news got around, and it certainly would *get around*. Gossip as spicy as this will spread through the gentry like water on a flat stone."

"Are you serious?" Edmund exclaimed. "You expect —"

"But if I *give it*," she said, her eyes on Royce, "I will provide an excuse for where the money went. I'll have to or admit to my husband I'm cheating on him, which your presence painfully proves he suspects. I trust you were not hired to simply kill me, but engaged to slit my throat *only if* you found me with someone in my bed tonight?"

Royce nodded.

"So, you can simply report I was alone, can't you? You'll have done your job — as far as my husband knows. After he pays, you'll walk away with three times as much money as promised. And no blood on your clothes, no need to look over your shoulder tonight. What do you say?"

Royce walked out the front door of the Traval Estate and through the moonlit, snow-blanketed gardens, feeling both pleased and oddly out of sorts. He had been prepared for a night of old-fashioned mayhem, a return to the long-neglected craft that defined him. Royce felt a tarnish had built up on his talents over the last few years of partnering with Hadrian Blackwater. The man had succeeded in stifling Royce's art, but this night was his chance to scrape off the rust and get back into shape. To his delight, Hadrian, who found the idea of killing a woman too repugnant, had opted to stay in the nearby port town of Roe. If Royce believed in gods, he would have declared this to be a sign. While not *exactly* looking forward to the killing — Royce took no more pleasure in murder than a butcher does when lopping off the heads of chickens — he did relish the anticipation of a certain return to normalcy.

Royce hadn't felt like himself in quite some time. He suffered bouts of longing for the old carefree days of blood and butchery. Back then, everything was simple; everything made sense. Now, nothing did.

I'm obviously sick, and the illness goes by the names of Hadrian Blackwater and . . . Gwen DeLancy.

Royce thought this was what it must be like for a wounded wolf who had been taken in by an ignorantly helpful family. They meant well enough, but a wolf is supposed to be wild, and the family wouldn't understand how all their feeding and petting could ruin the animal. With too much domestication, the poor wolf would forget how to survive on its own.

This evening should have been my night back in the wild. Free of their influence, enjoying a boy's night out, except . . . It's as if the universe itself is aligned against me and allied with them. Soon there will be no more place for my old self. What a sorry state.

Royce exited through the stone archway, officially leaving the garden and the Traval Estate behind. He took a moment to close and relock the iron gate.

"Where 'tis our book?" a voice asked.

In an instant, Royce ducked, dodged, pulled his dagger, and cursed his laziness. He searched for his assailant among the shadows of barren trees cast by the moon on the snow-covered road that led to town.

The man wasn't hard to find. Dressed in a tattered gray cloak, he stood along the path just outside the gate. Long red hair, mustache, and a pointed beard leaked out of the hood and wreathed a face even paler than Edmund-the-Baron-at-Death's-Door. He displayed no visible weapon. His arms remained limp at his sides.

"Wait not, so desperate am I. Produce it now, and rid me of my cursed dread." The voice was raspy and strange.

Back in the estate, Royce saw a light appear in Lady Traval's bedroom window. First floor, front-facing, the expensive glass was perfect for a snooping eavesdropper, or worse, a spy.

Too late for a random caller or wandering minstrel, he's here for a reason. He's either a very unfortunate busybody, or he works for Hurbert Traval.

Royce assumed the latter and was surprised the old baron had the intelligence to send a shadow to keep watch over his assassin. As impressed as Royce was, he couldn't let it go. He needed to warn the shipping magnate not to play games with Riyria.

Besides, his dagger, Alverstone, was already in his hand, and this was his *boy's night out.*

The man didn't so much as flinch when the dagger slid into the side of his throat. The neck offered all the resistance of a stewed carrot, and the white blade passed through until it pushed out the hood on the far side. The victim crumpled.

Royce studied the man for a moment, making certain he was indeed dead and that the corpse wasn't in any way familiar. Then he left the body where it lay.

As Royce walked on, two things bothered him.

First, if this was Hurbert's spy, why give himself away? And what an odd way to do it. *Where 'tis our book?* Royce pondered this a moment, concluding the obvious. He'd misheard. The man had a bit of an accent, and likely didn't say book at all. He probably said, where is the bok or boche, something in another language like Calian or maybe Alburnian. That's what his accent sounded like. Bok might be the Calian word for money, or gold, or something. Perhaps, after witnessing the deal Royce had made with Lady Traval—and knowing that Royce was carrying a bag of gold—the spy planned to double-cross Hurbert and blackmail the blackmailer.

This line of reasoning made perfect sense, assuaging his concerns—except for the second thing, which was a bit harder to reason away. Royce had just stabbed a man in the neck, making certain to sever the big artery, only . . .

Where is the blood?

Usually, such a murder resulted in a brief gush. Years of practice had taught Royce to anticipate the spray. He had moved to the side to avoid the mess. This usually worked, though he always got some on his blade hand. But this time, his knuckles came away clean. Such a thing was not inconceivable. After all, the dagger had done all the messy work. This, too, would have satisfied him except . . . Royce looked at Alverstone and, with the aid of the moon, saw the gleam of a clean white blade.

Royce found Hadrian in the village, drinking at the Pickled Pig's Foot. This wasn't a hard guess. As far as he knew, it was the only tavern in the entire seaside town of Roe—possibly the only one in the entire province of Oakenshire—and when Royce had left Hadrian, he had looked to be in a drinking mood. The shabby stucco-and-thatch public house was perched on a hill just up from the wharf, where it had a view of the ocean that was marred only by a couple tiers of roofs and a forest of chimneys.

Since it was past midnight, no other patrons remained inside, and the look on the tavern keeper's face as Royce entered suggested the owner had been hoping Hadrian would leave before anyone else wandered in. Despite the name, the

Pickled Pig's Foot was not an unpleasant place. Given the damp winter's night, the interior of the tavern provided a welcome warmth of seasoned wood and the cozy glow of resting embers.

Royce offered the tavern keeper an artificial smile, which was reflected back.

"What can I get you?" the apron-endowed, hair-deficient man asked without a lick of enthusiasm.

"Nothing, thanks. I'm not staying. Just here for him." Royce pointed.

As expected, this elicited a genuine smile.

Hadrian sat in the back corner near the fireplace, behind a table filled with empty mugs and a candle's melted corpse.

"I wasn't gone *that* long, was I?"

Hadrian looked up with a grimace. He had several days' worth of stubble and eyes that belonged to a much older man. "Enjoy yourself, did you?"

Royce glanced over at the owner, who was pretending not to notice them as he wiped a clean counter. Having only three people there was good, but it was also bad because, without other patrons, the place was utterly silent.

Hadrian followed Royce's line of sight and said, "Oh, right. Don't want to say too much in front of old Oscar, do we?" Hadrian burped and wiped his mouth. "That's Oscar, by the way. He owns the Pickled Pig's Toe . . . Foot . . . whatever." Hadrian stared off into space for a second, his mouth hanging open, then he asked, "Why is it that these places always have such disgusting names?" He looked at Oscar, who couldn't help but hear every word. Hadrian was drunk and therefore louder than normal.

"Sorry, no offense intended," Hadrian went on, "but honestly, is that the best you could come up with? Did you really think passersby would be so captivated by the promise of a severed pig's foot floating in a vat of brine that they would find it utterly impossible to pass your door without popping their head in to experience the promise? Why not just name it the Stinking Turd? Bet that would pack 'em in even more, right?"

"He's drunk," Royce apologized as he walked to Hadrian's table.

"Yeah, I know." Oscar wiped his hands. "You're heading out though, right? I'd kinda like to lock up."

"Just give us a second." Royce sat down.

"Yeah, give us a second, Oscar," Hadrian said. "My business associate needs to bring me up to speed on our latest project — likely wants to gloat. Do you want to gloat, Royce?" Hadrian put a hand to his mouth. "Oops. You think Oscar heard your name? That's bad, right?"

"This is why it's never a good idea to drink," Royce said.

"No? Wait, I thought you . . . you like wine, don't you?"

"I like Montemorcey, but it's incredibly rare, and when the source of your vice is almost nonexistent, it's an easy habit to keep in check."

Hadrian nodded. Then he pursed his lips, turned, and shouted. "Hey, Oscar! Got any of this rare Monty Mousey wine?" Hadrian's brow furrowed. "Wait, I think I got that wrong. How do you say it?"

"Don't carry wine," Oscar replied. "And I thought you were leaving."

"We are," Royce said, getting to his feet and welcoming Hadrian to do the same if he were capable.

"I wasn't asking for a bottle," Hadrian said, using the table to push himself up. "I was just curious. Don't need to be so touchy. For a guy who owns an alehouse named the Pickled Pig's Foot, you're awfully quick to push paying customers out the door."

"You've been here for *six hours*. Unlike some people, I have a life."

"Yeah, but . . . wait . . ." Hadrian stood with one hand still on the table, steadying himself as his eyes shifted in deep thought. "Pigs don't have feet — do they?" He first looked at Oscar, then at Royce. "I mean, they've got hooves, right? They're like horses, sort of, except that pigs' hooves are cloven. It's like they have two toes, but they aren't toes, not really. And since a pig has two toes and a horse has none, why are they both hooves?" He looked at each man in turn once more. Neither Oscar nor Royce said anything. "You know what I mean. But the point is, no one talks about horses' *feet*, right? No one says they're going to put a shoe on a horse's *foot* — even if that makes more sense. I mean, shoes go on feet. No one puts a *shoe* on a *hoof*. That's just so strange."

Royce grabbed Hadrian by the strap of his baldric and hauled him forward. "Did you pay?" Royce shook his head at his own stupidity. He turned to Oscar. "Did he?"

Oscar nodded. "Handsomely. If not for that, I'd have tossed him out hours ago. My wife is going to be furious."

"Oscar is going through a bad time right now," Hadrian said. "His wife is acting like a harpy. Tell him, Oscar."

"He'll tell me next time," Royce said, hauling Hadrian to the door. "Maybe he'll even have some mousey wine then."

"Yeah, that would be good. Do that, Oscar. Get some mousey wine for my friend for the next time."

The bracing cold of the winter night stiffened Hadrian, and his face crimped into a tight grimace, not unlike if Royce had slapped him. "By Mar! It's freezing out here! Let's go back in."

Oscar slammed the door shut and threw the bolt.

"Geez, Oscar, that was rude. I thought we were friends!" Hadrian yelled at the closed door.

"You'll need to be a little louder if you want to wake the *entire* village," Royce explained.

"Oh, you're a funny guy, aren't you? Did you tell Lady-what's-her-name a joke, too? Did she laugh, or couldn't she because her throat was slit?" Hadrian shifted unsteadily as he eyed Royce. "You don't even have any blood on you. Is that the mark of a professional, or did you wash up in her basin before leaving? And was it just the poor woman, or did you kill her dog, too?"

"Lady Traval doesn't have a dog." Royce pulled him over to where their horses waited.

Hadrian snorted a laugh. "Well, not anymore she doesn't. Chucked it out an upper-story window, did you?"

"There was no dog, Hadrian. Now, do you want help getting on your horse, or do you need to vomit?"

Hadrian stopped to ponder this perplexing riddle, then shook his head and pointed across the street. "Nah, I'm okay. My horse is in the stable over—"

Royce handed him Dancer's reins.

Hadrian looked up into the face of his horse. "Dancer! How'd you get here?"

"By Mar! How much ale *did* you drink?"

Hadrian once more stared off into space as he stroked the white diamond on Dancer's forehead.

Royce shook his head. "Never mind. I get it — it was *a lot*. Get on your horse. Let's go."

Hadrian managed to climb aboard Dancer after only three attempts. During this complicated operation, the horse remained rooted like a tree on a calm day, as if this wasn't the first time for either of them.

Royce thought that Dancer, being sober, would be capable of following Royce, but Hadrian, being drunk, couldn't be trusted not to interfere, so Royce attached a lead to the ring on Dancer's halter. Hadrian either didn't notice or didn't care.

"Did it get colder?" Hadrian complained, absently letting go of the reins to pull his wool cloak tight. "Feels colder. You know, winter is like a pretty woman who talks about a lot of nothing. They're nice at first: fun, different, beautiful even, but after a while . . ."

Hadrian picked up the reins and became fascinated by the knot that bound the ends.

Royce waited. "After a while, what?" he asked.

"Huh?"

Royce shook his head. "Forget it."

"I'm just saying that winter lasts *waaaay* too long. Aren't you tired of winter, Royce? Everything is cold. Cold and dead. As dead as Lady-what's-her-name."

"I didn't kill her."

"Come again?"

"Lady Traval. I didn't kill her."

Hadrian didn't say a word for several minutes.

"I would have told you sooner had I known it would shut you up."

"Why didn't you kill her?"

"I couldn't go through with it. She was a helpless woman with big, pleading eyes, and I just couldn't bring myself to take the life of an innocent —"

Hadrian fell off his horse.

He hit the snow on his back and grunted in pain. It took him a second, then he rolled to his feet with a miserable groan and looked up at Royce with the most incredulous set of drunken eyes. "Are you serious?"

"Of course not, you idiot. She offered me more money to leave her alive. I just wanted to hear what you'd say. That looked awfully painful, by the way." He grinned. "Ground's frozen, isn't it?"

"Yes, on both counts."

Hadrian climbed back into the saddle on the first try this time, leaving Royce to suspect the bracing cold and the fall had helped to sober him a bit.

On they went, up the river road that followed the bank of the Galewyr. The sides of the river were frozen, but a dark line of moving water cut through the center and made the ghostly sound of rain on long-lost leaves.

"It's still good news," Hadrian said.

"Absolutely. We made triple the money without *doing* anything other than taking a winter ride."

"*We?*" Hadrian shook his head. "That's *your* money."

"We're still partners, and the gold is clean. Not a drop of blood on it. You can spend the coin proudly." Royce considered mentioning the other fellow who also did not appear to have a drop of blood, but Hadrian was too drunk and too happy for Royce to ruin the improved mood. They had a long ride back to Medford, and the only thing worse than a happy-chatty Hadrian was a depressed-chatty Hadrian.

They rode for a while in silence.

"What?" Royce finally asked.

"I didn't say anything."

"I know. That's the problem."

"I was just thinking that four years ago, you wouldn't have offered to share the money—wouldn't even have told me about it. I also doubt you'd have let her live. You'd have taken her money *and* killed her."

"Four years ago, we weren't partners—not really. And leaving Lady Traval alive makes logical sense. No wisdom in killing a paying customer."

"Uh-huh, uh-huh." Hadrian nodded. "And the Royce Melborn I first met, even the one of only a couple years ago, would never have asked 'What?' because I was silent. The old Royce would have considered it a blessing. You've changed. You were once an animal, a wild thing really, but now . . . now you're practically domesticated, aren't you? You've become a tame beast, haven't you, Royce?"

"If you weren't drunk, I'd kill you."

"I'm gonna tell Gwen."

"Do not tell Gwen."

Hadrian laughed.

"I hate you when you're drunk."

"That's strange."

"How so?"

"Because that's why I drink . . . to stop hating myself."

CHAPTER THREE

The Visitor

After a good night's sleep and breakfast at the Silver Pitcher Inn, Hadrian felt decidedly better. Not that he had been feeling much pain the night before — even after falling off the horse, which he only barely remembered — the mild hangover didn't bother him. A little headache was nothing compared to how he'd felt on the way to Roe, which was downright nauseated. He and Royce had been hired to murder a woman in her own bed, and Hadrian couldn't think of anything more distasteful, aside from perhaps butchering small children who slept in their mothers' arms. He refused to be party to the killing, but Royce had accepted the job.

It had been a lean year, but the project wasn't taken because of the money. Hadrian had volunteered to clean stables and share his pay if Royce turned the contract down; he refused. Royce *wanted* to kill the woman. Not her in particular, anyone would do. Hadrian didn't know all the details, but he did know that Royce, who had been a thief all his life, had achieved the status of assassin in the criminal guild known as the Black Diamond. While abhorrent to most people, Royce's position was a highly respected occupation within a certain slice of the population, and he took pride in his work.

However, since the two of them had teamed up four years ago, Royce hadn't had much opportunity to ply his trade. They mostly made their living with theft. Not that they cut purses or picked pockets. Instead, they stole for others.

Contracts for jobs were arranged by Royce and Hadrian's associate, Albert Winslow. Being a viscount, he moved in affluent circles. They stole baubles for ladies and ledgers for businessmen, intercepted letters, spied on spouses, and planted evidence for blackmail. On only two occasions had they come close to contracted murder. In Dulgath, they were hired to *advise* on how to *perform* an assassination. But less than a year ago, they had received a true murder contract. Royce had been hired to kill everyone associated with the death of Genevieve Winter. The problem, as it happened, was that Genny was still alive. Royce had been teased with a dream job only to have it snatched away. This, Hadrian believed, had instilled an itch that Royce felt a growing desire to scratch.

In many ways, Royce was an exceptionally talented artisan whose greatest skill was underutilized. Hadrian understood this sense of wasted ability. He himself had been trained, practically from birth, to kill, but as a soldier, not an assassin. And while he rarely ever drew steel these days, he continued to carry three swords wherever he went. He and Royce were a pair of fish thrown up on land to gasp and flop, stranded in a desert and seeking a body of water to call home. But at least Hadrian hadn't been a party to the murder of a woman for money. That was a low he had managed to avoid, at least for now, which meant this was a good day.

It's the little victories that provide men the strength to keep moving.

The weather was warmer but still cold, as it was apt to be that time of year. The displeasure was made worse due to the rumor that spring was close. That was the popular gossip, at least. Only the farmers and priests seemed to know. And despite the wet snow that fell as they rode, the days were longer than they had been, and the roads were clear of drifts.

The hazy white ball of light was nearly overhead as the two arrived back on Wayward Street in the Lower Quarter of Medford. Sun-afflicted icicles along the eaves of The Rose and Thorn Tavern dripped a soft rhythm on the roof of a coach parked out front. Coaches and carriages were not unheard of in the Lower Quarter. These days they weren't even unusual. The popularity of Medford House, home for professional comfort and congeniality, drew wealthy merchants and nobles to the otherwise destitute little alley. What a delight it must be for the prim and proper; how thrilling to adventure into the dangerous dark streets where secrets lacked the legs to exit into the light of day. What Hadrian found odd was that this particular conveyance did not appear to be a merchant's coach or a noble's carriage. It lacked the frills that made the fancy buggies look like debutantes desperate for approval. This was a no-nonsense, eight-seater, two-toned coach-and-four. The top half was lacquered black with sparingly implemented gold-painted filigree accents. The lower portion and spoked wheels were constructed from a heavily varnished and buffed-to-shiny red hardwood. On the door in elegant script was a bronze plate proclaiming HANSON AND SON.

Despite the snow, two men worked the coach. The elder, who was in the process of blanketing the four horses, had gray in his beard and years on his face. He wore a thick wool wrap like those worn by carriage drivers in the Gentry Quarter. A younger man with a darker, shorter beard inspected the wheels and displayed his youthful indifference to the weather by making do with but a thin tunic and leather vest. The two could be portraits of the same person painted thirty years apart, making Hadrian suspect they might comprise the titular Hanson and Son, though neither appeared wealthy enough to own their own coach.

Royce delivered Hadrian a puzzled look as the two dismounted. Hadrian shrugged in return. After pulling their gear and returning their animals to the stable, the two entered The Rose and Thorn, which at midday had few customers. The usuals were there — those between jobs, without jobs, or incapable of work. These were the sort who drank their meals. Dixon kept track of their tabs on a slate behind the bar. The present leader of the blackboard tally was a newcomer, a grizzled blacksmith named Mason Grumon who had recently opened a shop on Artisan Row but never seemed to work there.

"The boys are back!" Dixon shouted in his deep baritone as the two entered. Those at the bar clapped or hammered the wood with their mugs, as if Royce and Hadrian were walking onto a stage.

Royce scowled, then sighed as the two crossed to the hearth.

"I think it's nice," Hadrian said, pulling off his cloak and shaking the wet out before hanging it on a wall peg near the fire. "Sort of like having a family."

"If this were your family, you ought to sympathy-kill your parents."

"Okay, so it's not like I would brag about my siblings." He glanced around the common room, then approached the bar.

"Drink?" Dixon asked. "I just loaded a new keg of Imperial Gold."

"No!" Royce shouted sternly from the back of the room, where he was still shaking out his cloak. "Do *not* give that man a drink."

Hadrian nodded. "He's right. I emptied the barrel last night down in Roe. Doubt I'll be invited back anytime soon. But hey, I'm curious . . . whose coach is that out front?"

Dixon stuck out his lower lip and shrugged his big shoulders. "No idea. Been a topic of some interest for a couple of hours now."

"No one saw who got out?"

"That's just it," Mason Grumon said. "No one did."

"Someone had to, Mason. You just didn't see 'em," Kenyon the Clean argued. Kenyon was the owner of the soapmaking shop that most days defined the hallmark smell of Wayward Street. He was a welcome customer because everyone in the Lower Quarter could breathe easily so long as he was in The Rose and Thorn rather than stoking his vats.

"I'm telling ya that thar coach rolled up empty, or I ain't no blacksmith."

"Not sure whose side of this argument you're on now, Grumon," Roy the Sewer said and laughed in a maniacal manner that displayed his famously hideous set of twisted yellow teeth. There wasn't any part of Roy that didn't teeter on that side of macabre. He had one eye larger than the other — different colors, too. Both were doleful, but one was milky. His thin, greasy hair lay plastered to his skull, like he'd just gotten out of a bath. But if he had ever bathed, it was in the foul muck that ran in the stream behind the shops, which provided him with his unique smell and his well-earned title. After the sudden and disturbing outburst, everyone stared, causing Roy the Sewer to return to his occupation of swirling what was left of his stale beer as if trying to raise it from the dead. Each day he came in for a drink, but only one, and his name never appeared on the slate. Hadrian was certain that Dixon paid for his refreshment.

"Lucky me, sandwiched between these two," Grumon said, glancing at Roy, then Kenyon. "Put 'em together, and I don't know if they'd make good bug repellent or if they'd attract every fly in the city."

"Is Albert here?" Royce asked.

"Diamond Room," Dixon replied.

"Diamond? Not the Dark?"

"He and Gwen are chatting with some old fellow. Really nice sort, very friendly, but odd. Actually, I think he came looking for you two."

"Odd how?"

"Dresses in fancy robes. Talks a lot — uses big words. And he has these little round circles of glass perched on his nose."

Royce and Hadrian exchanged looks as they quickly headed for the archway that divided the bar area from the larger, diamond-shaped room. This was an addition that the owner, Gwen DeLancy, had built to join The Rose and Thorn to her other business — Medford House. The extension doubled the size of the tavern, but because it lacked a fireplace, it was chilly in winter, and patrons shunned it. There were, in fact, only three people in the Diamond Room: Gwen, Albert Winslow, and . . .

"Professor Arcadius?" Hadrian said the moment they entered.

The thin, elderly man, white-bearded and dressed in a blue robe, sat in the middle of a bench seat at the table tucked into the acute back corner of the room. At the sound of his name, he lifted his spectacles and peered up at them. "Riyria, I presume."

"What are *you* doing here?" Royce asked in a sharp tone as he approached the group. Royce looked at Gwen. "What's he been telling you?"

"Mostly how wonderful the two of you are." Gwen smiled at him, and instantly Royce stopped as if he'd hit an invisible wall.

His shoulders lowered, his eyes relaxed, and he stood staring at her as if he'd forgotten what he was doing. Hadrian guessed it was more the smile than the words. Such a look from Gwen had the power to incapacitate the thief better than a blow to the head.

"What brings you here?" Hadrian asked the professor.

"You two, of course. Had to come, didn't I? It's been four years, and neither of you so much as bothered to ride the few miles to Sheridan to let me know you're alive." He leaned toward Gwen as if speaking to her in confidence, despite talking just as loudly as before. "When I extolled that long list of virtues about these two, I left out their astounding thoughtlessness. We parted under less than perfect circumstances, you understand. I asked them to visit on occasion. Told them how I'd appreciate it if they eventually told me how things worked out, but they never did."

"The professor has been telling us how he brought you two together," Albert said. The landless viscount was dressed in his *work clothes:* a silk shirt covered by a lavish doublet, beneath a robe, and under a dress jacket. But like any common off-duty millworker, the collar of his doublet and shirt were unhooked and thrown wide. His legs stretched out into the room, shoes off, toes flexing within dark woolen hose. "Quite the interesting tale, actually."

"Was it?" Royce found his voice once more, and it retained that unhappy edge. "And what *exactly* did you tell them . . . professor?"

"Why, the truth, of course. How I persuaded the two of you to help me borrow a rare book, and how much you hated each other. It was just as likely that Royce would slit Hadrian's throat as it was for Hadrian to stab Royce through the heart. Was a dangerous gamble on my part, but I knew if they stuck together — if they were forced to stay united — they'd make a remarkable team. And I'm pleased to see I was right. Even a bit flattered that you adopted Riyria as your working name."

"Anything else?" Royce pressed.

Arcadius shook his head, wagging his white beard so that it brushed the table. "Like what? I mean, there really isn't much else to tell unless you want me to get into your ill-treatment of horses." He looked to Albert, then Gwen. "They left theirs tethered in the wilderness for days. Poor things nearly died."

"So did we," Royce pointed out in a brutal tone.

"*You* found Dancer?" Hadrian asked.

"I did indeed," Arcadius said. "Got worried about you and sent some of the older boys up north on a field trip. They failed to find you but brought your horses back to the university, and once I heard where you were, I had them delivered."

"Really?" Hadrian said.

"How did you think they ended up out front of The Rose and Thorn?"

"I don't know. I guess I just thought Dancer found her way back to me like one of those faithful hounds who sniff out their beloved master."

"And the note that was left in your saddlebag?"

"There was a note?"

Royce stood up against the front of the table directly across from the professor. The only light in the room came from the winter-brilliant windows behind him, and his shadow ran across the table and over the old man. He leaned in. "So, you did know we were alive. Then tell me, why are you here now?"

"Well, after you left, I heard rumors that two men narrowly escaped the ecclesiastical tyranny of Ghent. Seret knights seeking the fugitives followed their trail to Medford. And I later heard that a man covered in blood was seen on Wayward Street begging for help for his dying friend. Granted, that didn't sound at all like you. But it was remarkable that both of these men vanished without a trace. Then, a year later, there was this unpleasant business with Lord Exeter and a spree of public executions that reminded me of someone — murders that were in retribution for harm done to the ladies of Medford House." He dipped his head toward Gwen. "When I finally heard about a nefarious pair of evildoers calling themselves Riyria, well, you don't obtain the position of professor at a university by being stupid. Still, suspicions are not the same as knowing. The fact that neither of you had visited or sent word in four years had me worried. So, I came down to see for myself what had become of the two seeds I'd planted so long ago."

"Sorry we didn't visit," Hadrian said. "We just —"

"Don't apologize to him," Royce snapped. "He nearly got us killed. If it hadn't been for his idiotic demands —"

"You probably would have gone your separate ways," Arcadius said. "And both of you would likely be dead. The men I knew were mere shadows of the two that stand before me now. You've done well for yourselves here. And this lady beside me is quite a gem to have in your pocket."

"*This* is Gwen DeLancy, and she's not in *anyone's* pocket," Royce said.

"Of course not. I only meant she's a wonderful friend to have on your side. She's both intelligent and loyal. And if you doubt anything I've said, take a moment and try to recall that other Royce Melborn, the one of four years past. That vicious little thief couldn't name a single soul he trusted, but this fellow before me — *this* Royce Melborn of The Rose and Thorn — he has two friends, and a fine pair they are. Real wealth is not measured in the weight of useless yellow metal, but by the hearts of those that love you." The professor straightened up. "But don't worry, Royce. Your debt has been paid. I only stopped by to see how my handiwork turned out and possibly have a meal. I'll be heading back to Sheridan in the morning."

"Fine," Royce said. There was still a hint of suspicion in his eyes, but the trail of recrimination had gone cold with nothing deceitful to show for it.

"How did the job go?" Albert asked, his voice gloomy and weighted with apprehension, as if inquiring about a beloved horse who had broken her leg. Albert personally knew Lillian Traval, and Hadrian guessed he liked her.

"Quite well." Royce drew out his purse and dropped it on the table, where it hit with a considerable thud. "Got paid double."

Albert looked lost. "*You* got paid? I don't understand. That's *my* job. Was Hurbert there? Did he pay you?"

"Nope, and when you go to collect, tell Lord Traval his wife was alone when I found her."

"And was she?"

Royce smirked.

Albert's mouth opened and hung there. He looked at the bag on the table then back up at Royce. "Then where did the money come from?"

"Lady Traval."

"She's alive? . . . But you were supposed to —"

"She offered more."

"She offered — oh. Oh! That's wonderful!" A wide smile broadened Albert's face, his eyes suddenly bright.

"You took a job to murder a woman?" Arcadius asked.

"A known adulteress," Royce replied. "The job came from her husband."

"And you didn't kill her because she paid you more money?"

"Sometimes, even I get lucky."

"And you were fine with this?" Arcadius asked Hadrian.

The tone of disapproval was obvious, and Hadrian knew what the professor was getting at. Arcadius had coerced Royce and Hadrian to work as a team so that Hadrian might prove to have a positive moral influence on the unprincipled thief.

Before Hadrian could offer an apology, Royce answered for him. "He stayed in Roe and got drunk. And just like the job you sent us on, I knew that this one didn't require the both of us. And once more, I was proven correct."

"I see." The professor glanced at Gwen, then out the windows, as if pondering something profound. But then, Hadrian imagined everything the professor thought was deep.

Royce and Hadrian pulled up seats across from the professor, the viscount, and Gwen.

"Why are you all on one side?" Hadrian asked.

"For warmth," Arcadius answered.

Gwen sat up. "I was telling the professor how costly it would be to build a hearth and chimney in this room, and he suggested I might heat it by simply getting an iron box large enough to hold a few split logs. I could light a fire in it and use a big metal pipe to vent the smoke out through the roof. He thinks it would heat this whole room."

"It would indeed," the professor said. "And we wouldn't need to huddle like newborn pups to keep from shivering."

"I was thinking of asking Mason Grumon how much he'd charge to make it."

"By the looks of the board behind the bar, he ought to do it in return for a clean slate," Hadrian said.

Gwen gave him a wink and a nod. "My thoughts exactly."

"Royce, Hadrian," Albert said as he counted the coins on the table, forming four piles that would be their individual shares. Royce and Hadrian's were the largest; Albert's was half their size and Gwen's the smallest, "I know you just got back, but I have another job lined up and ready to go."

"Something's wrong," Royce said, watching Albert count the coins.

This caused the viscount to look up, concerned.

"You're actually doing your job. I don't know whether to be impressed or suspicious. What sort of assignment is this new one?"

Albert gave a hesitant glance at Arcadius.

"He's fine," Royce said. "I know where he lives."

"Though he doesn't appear to know how to get there," Arcadius lamented.

Albert shrugged. "I think you're going to like this one — the both of you. There's a Lord Byron down in Delgos who's interested in hiring the two of you to prevent a dwarf from sabotaging Drumindor."

"What's Drumindor?" Hadrian asked.

"Drumindor is an ancient dwarven fortress that guards the entrance to Terlando Bay and the city of Tur Del Fur," Arcadius explained. "It was built many thousands of years ago over the top of Mount Druma, a very active volcano that made settling Terlando Bay impossible until the dwarfs tamed it with the construction of Drumindor. It's quite an ingenious engineering achievement. Not only do the two towers safely vent the volcano's destructive gases, thus preventing eruption, they also can use that same buildup of geological pressure to spew molten rock hundreds of feet and sink any unfortunate wooden vessel that might seek to invade the bay."

"That's right." Albert looked impressed.

"He's the lore master at Sheridan University," Hadrian explained.

"Oh." Albert nodded. "The way Lord Byron describes it, Drumindor is a city utility, part of the Port Authority. Lord Byron administrates the Port Authority and is responsible for Drumindor. There's been some trouble down there with the dwarfs recently, and Lord Byron had to fire a great many that used to work at the fortress. One disgruntled fellow named Gravis Berling appears to have been particularly upset, and Lord Byron believes he may be plotting revenge."

"If this Lord Byron is the head of the Port Authority, doesn't he command a small army?" Royce asked. "Why does he need us?"

"The real power down there is a trio of merchants known as the Triumvirate; they appointed Lord Byron to his position. Apparently, Lord Byron reported his concerns, and the Unholy Trio — as some call them — have refused to do anything about it. Lord Byron isn't a fool. He knows that he'll be held responsible if anything happens, so he's interested in purchasing an insurance policy through Riyria."

"Why won't this Triumvirate do anything?" Hadrian asked.

Albert pushed up his lower lip in disregard. "It's just one dwarf, and an old one at that. The poor fellow lost his job, so he's vowing revenge over cups at the local pubs. But what can one dwarf do to a several-thousand-year-old fortress?"

"All right," Royce said, "but what exactly does Lord Byron want us to do?"

"I suppose he wants you to find and watch this Gravis fellow, and make sure he's not planning anything."

"And if he is?"

"Well . . ." Albert gave sheepish looks at Gwen and Arcadius. "We all know how you feel about dwarfs, Royce. That's why I thought you'd like the job. And seeing as how it's a public service sanctioned by the administrator of the Delgos Port Authority, it's not even against the law, which I thought Hadrian would like as well. Also, you can't beat the location. Tur Del Fur is one of the most delightful cities in the world. People of means travel there from all over. So many make a habit of it that they have a name for them — *turists.*"

"What makes it so popular?" Gwen asked.

"For one, it doesn't snow down there. Because Tur Del Fur is situated on the southernmost tip of Delgos and warmed by the balmy Calian currents that bathe its coast, it enjoys an eternal summer. It's all tropical plants and cool ocean breezes. And, being in the republic, it has some of the finest eateries, public houses, and entertainment anywhere."

"But it's a job," Royce said. "Not a vacation."

"Depends on how you look at it."

"That would depend on how much this Lord Byron is willing to pay."

"That's the interesting part." Albert pulled himself up before his little stack of gold coins and leaned forward. "He'll only cough up sixty gold, but —"

"Sixty?" Royce balked. "Tur Del Fur is a long way from Medford. And travel is not cheap. The price of horse feed is up this time of year. And how long does he want us to hang around and watch this guy? We could be there for months. That's a lot of expense, and it sounds like Tur Del Fur is pricey."

"It is, which is why I demanded he pay for all expenses."

"You did?"

Albert smiled. "How do you think I survived all these years as a landless noble?"

"You sold your clothes for liquor," Hadrian pointed out.

"Well, yes, but that was during a particularly low point. For years before that, I lived off the generosity of the wealthy. To be honest, the few gold coins they toss at Riyria is nothing compared to what can be had with an expense account. For whatever reason, it is a well-known fact that a miserly baron or prince, who would laugh at the idea of paying a fair wage to an employee, will happily expend a fortune to demonstrate his generosity in accommodations for those in his service."

"Why is that?"

"Honor." Albert said the word like it was a joke. "If you're in a noble's pay, that makes you the noble's man. What you do and how you do it reflects on them. The likes of Lord Byron would be ashamed to have *his men* walking about in filthy rags and staying in a hovel. It would suggest he's poor, or cheap. And there's this old tradition of hospitality and generosity that—while it doesn't extend to fair pay—demands that guests, even contracted ones, be treated like royalty. In the world of the gentry, reputation is their currency. To be seen as generous and true to your word is everything. And Lord Byron, while now a resident of the Republic of Delgos, is an old-fashioned noble, a transplant from Maranon. Like myself, he lost his family fief, but unlike me, he's a skilled and hard worker. Lord Byron realized he could make a fortune serving the merchant cartels of Delgos if he just swallowed a bit of pride. And he was right. Still, I can tell the man laments the loss of his noble heritage. He still attaches the title of *Lord* to his name in a place where that's more of a detriment. As a result, while we might not return with a dragon's hoard to squirrel away for our old age, we can look forward to an absolutely wonderful free holiday."

"*We?*" Royce asked.

Again, Albert looked abashed. "I took the liberty of explaining that it would be more than merely the two of you. That an operation of this sort would require additional support."

"Which includes you," Hadrian said.

"Of course. You'll need your liaison to meet with Lord Byron, secure lodging, make reports, provide updates, and collect the fee when the task is complete. And have you seen it outside?" Albert pointed toward the windows where the snow was coming down harder. "My frail constitution born of blue blood was not meant for such harsh conditions."

"That's brilliant," Arcadius said. "In fact, I think we should all go. Tell me, Gwendolyn, how long has it been since you've set foot outside of Medford?"

Gwen looked surprised by the question, shocked that she was being included in the conversation. "I haven't left since I first came here, years ago."

"Exactly. And I can say from personal experience that Tur Del Fur *is,* in fact, the most beautiful and enjoyable place on the face of Elan. The waters of the palm-tree-lined harbor are sapphire blue. The sunsets and sunrises are wonders to behold, and the music is so enchanting that a person could lose themselves in it. The food and drinks aren't merely sustenance but rather works of art crafted by master artisans. And there are dozens of theaters performing a variety of acts: everything from original dramas and comedies to acrobats, animal acts, and displays of magic. And this is in addition to the uncountable smaller shows in every danthum."

"What's a danthum?" Gwen asked, her face bright with the imagery that the professor painted.

"Oh, it's sort of like an upscale tavern, except they have entertainment every night and serve exquisite meals to order. They're very popular. You see, being a free city of the Republic of Delgos with a very liberal sense of itself, Tur Del Fur has attracted many great artists, poets, writers, dancers, and philosophers. With so much talent and so few restrictions, the city is a wellspring of creativity and an intellectual lodestone. A truly marvelous place that everyone ought to see at least once in their life. Besides"—he leaned toward her and winked—"have you seen it outside?"

Arcadius then faced Royce. "Having Gwen along sounds like an excellent idea. Or do you think that after all she's done for you, she doesn't deserve a few weeks' break from her toil and drudgery? Certainly this wonderful lady deserves a holiday."

"I'm more interested in how *you* fit into all this," Royce said.

"Chaperone, my boy. Really can't allow a gentle fawn such as Gwendolyn DeLancy to be traveling abroad with three wolves such as yourselves. This is what old men such as I were made for—one of the few things we're still capable of."

"How thoughtful," Royce said. "But I doubt Albert secured an allowance for five."

"Actually"—Albert rocked his head side to side—"I never said how many would be needed. An argument could easily be made that Gwen is your domestic help, and you have a particular fetish about never allowing anyone else to touch your things. That's actually quite a common eccentricity—some might say *affliction*—among the pampered gentry, something they'll understand and accept even if it seems absurd to you. And given that the professor is a teacher of lore at Sheridan, it's an easy argument that he's indispensable for his contributions of historical and cultural information that will allow you to unravel the complex nature of the dwarven culture and the history of the fortress."

"Albert," Hadrian said with a dash of awe, "you're amazing."

"That's nothing. I once lived for five years in a palace with an eight-person staff, my own personal carriage and driver, and three separate concubines, one of whom was the niece of the high chamberlain."

"What happened?"

"The chamberlain found out. Barely escaped with my life."

"What do you say, Royce?" Hadrian asked. "Job sounds easy enough. We go, check out this guy for a week or so, maybe even warn him off, and spend the rest of the time pretending we're wealthy merchants. Worst case scenario, you might have to kill a dwarf."

Royce picked up and slipped away his stack of coins, his expression taut with irritation, as if struggling with a puzzle he couldn't solve. "Seems a bit too good to be true."

"And what do you think, Gwendolyn?" Arcadius asked.

She took a deep breath and looked at Royce, that magical smile filling her face and making her dark eyes shine. "It does sound wonderful. I haven't ever been any place people would call nice. I couldn't afford it. And . . ." She looked around. "I certainly couldn't ask for better company. But I understand if taking me would bother you, Royce. I'm certain I would get in the way, and I don't want to be a burden. You all go. I have work to do here. The bathtub needs a good scrubbing."

Royce sighed. "We only have the two horses."

Once more, Albert grinned and drew himself up like a child at the adult's table. "Don't even need those, not when you're in the service of the nobility. I took the liberty of chartering a coach for the trip. That's it outside. Hanson and Son Stagecoach Service."

"*Stage* coach?"

"Oh, yes, the Hansons have been very successful with their innovative idea. They drive the coach, splitting the time on the reins and only stopping to switch horses at *stages* along the route. They claim they can get us from here to Tur Del Fur in only two to four days — depending on weather."

"Two days?" Hadrian said.

"I know! Normally it can take ten days to two weeks."

"And we're going to do it in two days?"

"Well, that's what they claim. There's a scheduled overnight stay in the small town of Kruger," Albert said. "But that's optional, so I told them we'd prefer to get there as quickly as possible." Looking at Gwen he added, "But I could change that if you prefer."

"I can handle sleeping in a luxurious coach. And it can take all of us?" Gwen asked, excited.

"Yes, it seats eight with luggage. Four inside, four out, so one of us will need to brave the elements."

"I'm certain Hadrian won't mind," Arcadius offered.

Hadrian didn't, so he nodded. He was used to poor-weather travel, and he certainly wouldn't expect the professor or Gwen to take a high seat in the cold and wet. As Albert had arranged for the coach, he also ought to have an inside seat, and Hadrian knew that Royce, while he would never say it, might literally kill to ride beside Gwen.

"Oh — but we can switch along the way," Gwen told him. "I don't mind a little snow in my face."

"It's settled then," Arcadius declared with a clap of his hands. "And if those poor men have been out in the cold minding their coach, we shouldn't keep them waiting much longer."

"I'll need to grab some things from the House and let the girls know I'm leaving," Gwen told everyone as she stood up, her eyes wide, her voice absolutely effervescent. She was all smiles. "This is so exciting."

"You sure?" Hadrian asked, "You seemed to be looking forward to scrubbing soap scum from that tub."

Gwen slapped him playfully on the shoulder. "This is going to be wonderful."

Gwen, Albert, and Arcadius moved off to pack, leaving Royce and Hadrian alone in the room. They watched the others exit, then stood there for a full minute in silence until Hadrian finally said, "You're terrified, aren't you?"

Royce continued to stare at the door. "I'm honestly considering drinking a beer."

CHAPTER FOUR

The Stagecoach

Hadrian rode with the luggage on the coach's flat roof. The combined belongings of Arcadius, Royce, and himself could have fit on his lap. But Gwen's bags and Albert's sea-captain-style trunks covered so much of the roof that Hadrian wondered about two things: what could they have possibly brought, and had he terribly underestimated his own needs? Ahead of Hadrian was the driver's bench, where father and son sat side by side.

The father, whose name was Shelby, rode on the left and drove the coach. His son, Heath, took the guard's seat to his right. The young man wore a short Grafton blade — a cheap but functional weapon that looked brand new. A light, olive-wood crossbow was strapped to the footrest between them — out of sight, but within reach.

"You know how to use that blade?" Hadrian asked.

Heath looked up and smiled. "Ya scared, sir? No reason to be. We run this route all the time. Never once seen a highwayman. Most travelers are on foot, you see, and the *Flying Lady* here, she doesn't stop."

"Then why the sword and crossbow?"

"Because you can never be too careful," Shelby replied. He possessed the deep, no-nonsense voice of a hardworking father who'd seen enough of the world to be more cautious than curious. He reminded Hadrian of his own father, who'd died close to six years ago while Hadrian was far away. That had been the cherry on the top of his stack of regrets, which began with fighting his best friend and ended with the tiger. There had been other mistakes since then, but all those had been honest errors. The ones before had been intentional.

"It's our job to see you safe to your destination, sir," Shelby said, holding the reins in one hand, a long whip in the other. Never once had Hadrian seen him use the whip on the animals. He only cracked it in the air. That was enough. "And we take our responsibilities seriously."

Shelby kept the horses at a trot, occasionally granting them a breather in the form of a walk, which usually followed climbing a hill. Hadrian marveled at the speed. It was still morning, and they were already past the village of Windham in the kingdom of Warric. Hadrian would never drive Dancer at such a pace for so long. An easy twenty miles was plenty for one day's travel. He knew from experience that—in an emergency—a horse could cover a hundred miles in a day, but the animal would be exhausted and need a long rest. Trading out the horses solved that problem. This wasn't a new idea. It had been utilized for military dispatches for ages, but Hadrian didn't think it had ever been applied to civilian land travel before.

He thought it was genius.

Not only was the travel fast, but it was also stunningly comfortable. Despite the frozen ground, numerous ruts, and the occasional rock or root, the ride was remarkably smooth. The coach rocked and bounced like a ship on a stormy sea, but it lacked the hard jarring he was used to.

"Whose carriage is this?" Hadrian asked.

"Mine," Shelby replied.

"Looks expensive."

"She is that."

Apparently dissatisfied with Shelby's refusal to say more, Heath spoke up. "My father and grandfather worked as groomsmen for King Fredrick of Galeannon. It was my grandfather's dream to move to Vernes and start his own river barge service on the Bernum. He died before he could, but he left his savings and the dream to my father, only—"

"Only I don't know a ruddy thing about barges," Shelby said.

"You tried, at least," Heath pointed out. "And you learned a lot."

"I learned I don't know nothing about rivers or barges. I also became just educated enough to realize I couldn't hope to compete with the companies already working the Bernum."

"You also learned about post stops," Heath said, appearing unwilling to allow his father to sell himself short. He turned a bit to face Hadrian. "Are you familiar with river barges?"

"I am. I traveled from Vernes to Colnora on one. Not a great experience."

"So then you already know how they change out the horses. Doing so lets them travel all day and night. That's what gave my father the idea of creating a *post* or *stage* coach. He kept the horses and sold the barge. Then instead of trying to compete with the river companies, he offered fast, reliable service over land, taking passengers to the off-river cities of Kilnar, Swanwick, Ratibor, Aquesta, and Colnora. No other public service goes there. We get a lot of business when the Bernum reaches flood stage or when there's a drought. And because we trade out the horses at coach houses along the route, we can keep moving at a nonstop rate. No barge, not even your royal carriages, go as fast."

"Yeah, I noticed that." Hadrian actually thought it was a bit too quick. Perhaps on a warm summer's day it would be nice, but the near constant trotting had left him suffering a cold wind and a face full of wet snow that made it hard to see.

"She rides smooth, though, doesn't she?"

"She does. Usually, a wagon rattles the teeth out of a man's head."

"That's my son's genius," Shelby said. "A cart is just a box on a pair of axles. Don't matter how pretty you make the box; it's still bolted to four solid wheels. Heath separated the box from the axles by putting it on . . . what do you call it?"

"Suspension springs," Heath said. "They're these long flat straps of bowed metal that are hinged on either end, and the chassis — the box — rides, and sort of bounces, on them. Some of the noble carriages make *sways,* hanging the chassis from leather straps, but that doesn't do much for the hammer sensation that occurs when you hit a rut, and the leather isn't as durable. When it comes to building a coach, usually there's a body-maker who fashions the chassis — he's more like a skilled cabinetmaker — and another guy, a carriage smith who makes the axles, wheels, and such. But there's this guy in Tarin Vale by name of Bartholomew — he's a master coach craftsman, and he does it all."

"Not the fastest of workers," Shelby put in.

"True, but after an accident broke one of our axles, I worked with him —"

"Heath here has long had an interest in smithing. A good head for it, too," Shelby said with undeniable pride. "He's always building stuff. Invented them springs you're bouncing on."

"I had the idea," Heath clarified. "Bartholomew made it work."

"You *both* did. Boy's a lot smarter than he looks. A sight brighter than his father, that's for certain. Ought to be an advisor to a king or merchant lord, but this is all I can give him."

"I'd rather be driving coaches," Heath told his father with sincerity. "I wouldn't like all the bowing, and I grin every time I see *our* name on the door." He turned to Hadrian again. "We've got Bartholomew working on another coach, one I call the *Hanson Hurricane*. The springs will be much better — we're using four separate stacks of thin leaf-style sheets — but the real difference will be the pivoting front axle that will change the base from a rectangle to a triangle because the wheel on the inside of the turn is able to rotate more sharply than the outside front wheel. It will make it easier to pull and less likely to turn over, which will really help in the mountains. With the *Hurricane*, I think we might be able to cut our travel time by a third."

"Horses might have an opinion on that," Hadrian said.

"Just need more teams. One day I hope to have a fleet of coaches running daily from all the major cities from Tur Del Fur to Lanksteer. Can you imagine that? Anyone who wants to can walk to a coach station, pay a small fee, travel to Colnora, spend a few hours getting what they need, then return home to Medford the next day — maybe all in the same day."

"Boy's a genius, but also a dreamer," Shelby said. "Gets it from his grandfather, I suppose. I'd be happy with a warm hearth, a full belly, a soft chair, and a softer woman. But not him. I'd like to remind you, Heath, that you owe me a grandson."

"I'll get to it."

"I didn't build this business for it to crumble because you're too busy changing the world."

"I just haven't found anyone yet."

"You're too picky. If she's got four limbs, two eyes, and most of her fingers, you shouldn't complain."

"As you can tell, my father's standards are high."

Hadrian chuckled.

"You're married, aren't you, Mister Blackwater?" Shelby asked. "A successful man like you. You must have a nation of children by now."

"Actually, no. I . . . ah . . . I was in the military for several years, and since then, well, you'd be surprised how hard it is to find a woman with most of her fingers."

This made Heath laugh.

"How old are you, Mister Blackwater," Shelby inquired, "if you don't mind me asking?"

"Twenty-four."

Shelby shook his head and sighed. "I don't know what to make of you young folk these days. I had a wife and child by Heath's age, three more by yours."

"How many children do you have?"

Shelby didn't answer.

"It's just me now," Heath said.

This provided an abrupt end to the conversation, leaving Hadrian thinking he'd gone somewhere he shouldn't have. He was disappointed, as the conversation had helped take his mind off the cold wind that managed to not only push through his wool shirt and cloak but also the blanket the Hansons had provided.

"I'm sorry if I said something wrong," Hadrian offered.

"Nothing to be sorry for," Shelby said.

Heath looked back at Hadrian. "About ten years ago, our family had a small place in Fallon Mire," Heath said softly as he pointed south and a bit west. "It's a little village down that way. I was eight years old and kept asking to go with my father on his route. I saw it as this grand adventure. He finally let me go that summer. The trip was terrible. Nothing went right. Weather was bad, and we got stuck in mud for two days. Then we busted a wheel in the middle of nowhere. My father had to take a job as a farmhand to raise the money to have it repaired. For over two months, we lived in this very coach — me guarding her and taking care of the horses while my father worked the fields, coming back late each night with only a small round of bread and some cheese. I kept thinking how unfortunate we were — how Mum and the rest were enjoying the summer while I was trapped alone in a hot coach all day. As it turned out, I was wrong. That was the summer the plague came to Fallon Mire. It's been just my father and me ever since."

"Sorry to hear that," Hadrian said.

"All the more reason to find a nice girl and start a family," Shelby advised. "You never know what will happen. Waiting is for fools."

Hadrian looked up at the falling snow that slapped his face and weighed down his eyelashes.

Shelby Hanson makes a good argument.

Royce hadn't known whether he ought to sit beside or across from Gwen. Both were good and bad, but for different reasons. When it came down to it, his choice had been random and based on no logic at all. He had sat beside her and regretted it from the start. She was so close. The tufted leather seat being narrow, their arms and legs touched. And when the coach got up to speed, the bouncing often threw them together, clapping them like a pair of applauding hands.

In the four years he'd known her, Royce had touched Gwen on so few occasions that he recalled each and every one. This intimate jostling, forced upon him under the watchful gaze of Arcadius and Albert, made him long for his days in the salt mines. He considered switching places with Hadrian. Sitting up in the cold and wet would be a joy compared to this torture, but two things stopped him. The first was the impression it might give. Royce didn't want Gwen to think he couldn't tolerate sitting beside her. Nothing could be further from the truth. Yet even if it had just been the two of them, he'd still have suffered. The pressure — the tension — was painful. Everyone else appeared happy and content. Albert and Arcadius even dozed on occasion. Royce sat with every muscle taut, as every second was one more chance for him to make a mistake, to say or do something stupid.

When did this become a problem?

Royce had always enjoyed Gwen's company. From those first few weeks when she'd nursed him back to health, he'd felt comfortable around her in a way he'd never known before. And yet, lately Royce had discovered a growing anxiety whenever she was near. He felt as if he'd found a fragile bit of exquisite pottery that had become essential to him, and he was terrified of breaking it. Gwen had become precious to the point of anguish. Certain that the humiliation of any misstep would be amplified by his spectators, Royce suffered unbearably.

He might be able to sell the idea of switching places with Hadrian as a self-sacrificing thoughtfulness for his friend's comfort, but while Hadrian could pull that sort of thing off, Royce lacked the precedent. And then there was the other thing. Despite the anguish born of exceptional humiliation and awkwardness, he found that sitting beside Gwen DeLancy, feeling the press and warmth of her body and inhaling the fragrance of her hair, was both insanely pleasing and horribly addictive. The experience was like getting drunk on Montemorcey wine. The aroma and taste were exquisite, and the more he drank, the more intoxicated he became. Soon he lost all reason and indulged far too much. His sober self would warn him away, but his alcohol-muddled mind lacked the capacity for good judgment. Before long, the wine would erase whatever sense he was born with and leave him exposed and vulnerable. Disaster would invariably follow. And yet whenever offered a glass, his sober mind, more often than not, accepted. He didn't understand how that happened any more than he knew why he was sweating.

"You're a remarkable woman, Gwendolyn," Arcadius said, after concluding his interrogation of Gwen's past and using the front of his robe to once more clean his spectacles. He'd done it four times since they had left Wayward Street, and Royce began to speculate that the dirt might be on the man's eyes.

Arcadius went on, "You've quite the head for business, and I can't help wondering what you might accomplish with a more formal education. There are programs at Sheridan for the scions of merchant families: courses in general and regional economics, business law, general accounting, and the best methods for organizing books and ledgers. Armed with such information and skills, a person such as yourself might soon be living in the Gentry Quarter, administrating a dozen legitimate endeavors and attending the Medford Autumn Gala by invitation from the king himself."

Gwen laughed awkwardly. "I'd have nothing to wear."

"Oh, I think by then you'd have money for a grand wardrobe."

"I wouldn't know what to buy."

"I'd be happy to help with that," Albert said. The viscount sat with his head against the padded wall near the window, where he had spent much of the trip trying to nap after claiming he hadn't gotten much sleep the night before. "I spent my formative years with my aunt at Huffington Manor surrounded by noble ladies; each saw me as a cross between a loyal servant and an adopted son. I know nothing about the sword, but I'm an expert when it comes to fine ladies' fashion."

Gwen shook her head. "I also wouldn't understand any of the conversations or know what to say. The nicest gown in the world couldn't help me debate gentlemen and ladies who judge a person by the whiteness of their skin. It all seems wonderful, but I don't think it would be. I'd just sit there feeling awkward and out of place, sweating and wishing I was anywhere else."

Given her profession, Royce didn't think Gwen was capable of shyness or embarrassment. She'd always been just as comfortable and commanding dealing with the many barons and knights that visited Medford House as she had with Roy the Sewer. Looking over at her, he realized he was wrong. She sat with hands clasped on the blanket laid across her lap, knees tight together, elbows held in close to her waist. She appeared stiff to the point of rigid. Maybe she was cold, but it wasn't chilly anymore. When they had first entered the coach, they could see their breaths, and the leather seats made a cracking sound when they sat down. But now, the combined body heat had warmed the space and fogged the windows.

They had made one exchange of horses already, a very brief affair that did not require, nor allow, time for them to stretch their legs before they resumed travel. Through the windows, trees and hillsides flashed past in a blur. Their progress was amazing. The wooden floor was still damp from the snow they originally tracked in from Wayward Street, but they were already approaching Colnora.

Colnora.

This raised another issue that worried Royce. The only way south by land was across one of the city's four bridges. Most likely they would take the Bernum or Langdon. Because they were the widest, these spans were the best for wagon travel. That meant the coach would pass right through the middle of the city. This wasn't good. Royce wasn't welcome in Colnora. If they didn't stop, and if he kept his hood up and the window drapes closed, it might be okay. He looked once more at Gwen, then at the door to the coach. No lock.

"Learning more about ledgers would be good," Gwen said. "So many of Medford House's customers want to pay on credit — the nobles especially — that it makes keeping track difficult."

"Oh, there's much more to be learned than just keeping track of credit," the professor said. "I'm certain you'll discover that the mercantile laws of Melengar, worked out between the king and his trade guilds, can aid you just as much as it does for big businesses and industries."

"Medford House isn't part of any guild."

"Perhaps that's something you'll seek to change once you know how. Could you imagine that?" Arcadius looked at all of them. "A day when the entire comfort industry has its own guild and can regulate prices and conditions for its workers all over Avryn, and have it protected by the might of the king's soldiers?"

Another big bump bounced them all and clapped Gwen and Royce together.

"Oh! That was a fine one, wasn't it?" Arcadius howled in delight. "Nearly hit my head on the roof that time."

Gwen looked apologetically at Royce. "Sorry."

"Not your fault. The road is filled with holes, and the Hansons are bent on breaking the land speed record. I didn't hurt you, did I?"

Gwen shook her head. "I just . . . I know this is awful for you."

"Awful?"

"To be trapped in here — with all of us — with me. If it were just you, Albert, and the professor, I'm sure you'd have your feet up, taking a nap. But because I'm here . . . well, you've barely moved since we've started. I just feel so bad about that. I don't think I should have come. I'm ruining such a nice trip for all of you."

"I, for one, can say that you are not ruining anything," Albert declared. "Honestly, you're a delight. Traveling with Royce and Hadrian is . . ."

Royce glared.

"Less than joyful."

"I concur," Arcadius said. "Having you along is like walking hand in hand with summer sunshine."

Gwen looked at Royce. Her eyes bored into him expectantly with a nervous mix of hope and fear.

Just then the coach came to such a sharp halt that he and Gwen were nearly thrown into Albert and Arcadius.

***

Hadrian didn't like the look of it the moment the roadblock came into view. Hidden around a narrow bend such that Shelby was forced to use the brake to stop the coach in time, two big, spiked barricades blocked the route.

Not highwaymen, at least.

A pair of wagons were off to either side, making the barricade impossible to drive around. Three men, dressed in uniforms and chainmail, mounted their horses and rode forward. Noticing the red-and-white combatant-lion tabards of Warric and the way all three wore only one gauntlet, Hadrian recognized them as scout soldiers of Lanis Ethelred.

"Did you go through this on the way up?" Hadrian asked the Hansons.

"No," Shelby said, his voice tinged with worry.

"Whose coach is this?" the lead rider asked as the other two men dismounted and took hold of the coach horses.

"Mine," Shelby replied.

"*Yours?*" the soldier asked skeptically.

Hadrian didn't know him, but he knew his rank was that of a low sergeant.

"Name is Shelby Hanson; this here is my son. And if you can read, you'll see that name on the side."

"That don't mean anything," the sergeant said without looking, which made Hadrian guess he couldn't read. "No matter who your master is, you'll need to pay the fee to travel the king's road."

"What fee?" Heath asked. "We've traveled this route hundreds of times. There's never been a fee."

"New king, new rules," the sergeant said.

"New king?"

"Old Clovis died. Lanis now rules. Let's see . . . I'll be a nice guy and only charge you"—he hesitated a moment as his eyes looked over the handsome coach—"three gold tenents."

"That's insane!" Heath shouted.

"Is it?" the sergeant said, and Hadrian didn't like the abruptly aggressive change in his tone. "Let's think about this for a moment. Why isn't a fine young lad like yourself serving in the new king's army?"

"We aren't subjects of Warric," Shelby explained. "We're just passing through. We run a coach service." He hooked a thumb back at Hadrian. "We're hauling customers to Delgos."

The sergeant's sight tracked to Hadrian. He looked at his face only briefly, then his eyes were drawn to the swords. "And what do we have here?" The sergeant urged his horse closer. "What are you, a mercenary? Deserter? Criminal?"

"Name's Hadrian Blackwater. Pleased to meet you."

"I doubt that. Why don't you strip off those blades and climb down here?"

"Because he's a customer," Shelby said. "And until we deliver him to his destination, he's under my protection. Now, I'll pay your fee, which means he can stay where he is."

The sergeant's eyes narrowed. "How many are inside?"

"None of your business," Heath answered.

The sergeant's jaw tightened. "I'm afraid it is, lad. Because the fee is three gold *per head*. And I'll be collecting that now."

The sergeant dismounted. As he did, Hadrian watched Shelby release the crossbow from the strap, but he kept it out of sight.

"Everyone out of the coach!" the sergeant ordered, heading toward the door.

Hadrian stood up. "Excuse me, sergeant. How far are we from Colnora?"

"What?"

Everyone, including Heath and Shelby, looked at him, all appearing more than a little puzzled.

"I asked how far we are from the city of Colnora."

The soldier studied him. "Just over the next rise."

"That's what I thought." Hadrian unbuckled his belt and laid his swords aside.

"Sir," Shelby said to him, "you don't need to be doing anything. Let me take care of this." He let his hand slide to the stock of the crossbow.

"I'd love to, Shelby, but I'd rather the world didn't end this morning." Hadrian slowly climbed down to face the soldier. "I'm afraid I can't let you open that door."

The sergeant's eyes narrowed, his shoulders tensed, and his hand moved to rest on the pommel of his sword. "Something in there you don't want me to see, eh?"

"It's more along the lines of something *you* don't want to see. Truth is — and I'm not exaggerating in the slightest — if you open that door, you'll die."

"And why is that?"

"Because there's a demon inside this coach. And if you open that door, it will come out and kill you." Hadrian frowned at the soldier. "Although, considering how you're disgracing that uniform, I'm inclined to open it for you. I used to be in Ethelred's service. I know there are enterprising field sergeants stationed at dull posts who sometimes make a few tenents by using the uniform to intimidate the local folk. But that sort of thing fosters distrust and a hatred not just of the soldiery but of the king himself. In that way, this abuse of power isn't merely corruption. It's a form of treason against the king and his subjects — those you're supposed to protect. Many a good man fought and died bravely wearing those colors you've got on. And now here you are . . ." He shook his head in disgust. "Honestly, I shouldn't care. I should help you with the door handle, but I know that it won't end here." He let his eyes rise in the direction of Colnora. "I don't want to see a whole city burned to the ground because of you three."

Silence followed. Even the horses seemed to hold their breath.

The sergeant stared at Hadrian, one eye squinting, his mouth open, tongue running along his teeth like a gambler deciding on his bet. "Is that so?"

After a short while, his decision was made. The soldier began to chuckle and relaxed his shoulders. "I appreciate the concern, but, believe me, I can take care of myself."

"That's just it. I *don't* believe you. So, before opening the door, how about you prove it?" Hadrian stepped clear of the coach and horses. He found a nice level patch of road where the snow was flattened from travel. He stripped off his cloak, tossed it aside, and raised his hands. "I'm unarmed — just one man. You have a sword. If you can truly take care of yourself in combat, go ahead and kill me. If you can manage that, then maybe you'll survive the demon."

The sergeant's brow creased, and his mouth wrenched up on one side in utter disbelief. "You want me to kill you?"

"Of course not. I want to humiliate you in front of everyone. I know that sounds awful, but in the process, I hope to save your life, those of your men, and maybe even teach you an important lesson. There's also a good chance I'll be preventing a war. So, there's a lot of upsides to this."

Hadrian stepped forward to within arm's reach of the sergeant and rested his hands on his hips. "Well, c'mon, we have a schedule to keep, and you're making us late."

The sergeant glanced at his men, who continued to hold the horses, watching with interest. They all smiled at each other as if this was great fun.

"I'll do it, you know?" The sergeant faced Hadrian with a sinister grin as he slowly drew his sword.

"Yes, I do, which is why I'm not too upset. And to any demons that might be listening, please stay inside."

The sergeant looked at the coach. A hint of suspicion appeared in his eyes, then vanished.

Hadrian couldn't have asked for a better adversary. The sergeant was a trained soldier who had learned the basic sword-and-buckler combo used in the standard Warric rank and file. His grip, stance, shoulder tilt, and even the way his off hand — despite lacking the buckler — was extended out alongside his sword hand, demonstrated classic Mid-Avryn military training. A complete novice would have been more dangerous because the untrained were also unpredictable. Warric sergeants were not.

Intent on making a quick end of the conflict, the man attacked with a vicious thrust designed to shove most of his short, standard-issue blade into Hadrian's stomach. If he'd succeeded, Hadrian would have died a slow and painful death. This was something Hadrian was certain the soldier knew, which became just one more reason not to be gentle.

One of the sergeant's many mistakes, and likely the most critical, was his grip. He held the weapon like it were a hammer. Not so much his fault. That was how all buckler-and-sword soldiers were taught. There was no need for finesse in the ranks. In the lines, it was all pound and slash. Except the sergeant wasn't in a line on a field, he didn't have his shield, and he wasn't trying to bludgeon Hadrian. As a result, when he thrust forward — as he extended his arm — his wrist rolled, presenting both the flat of his blade and the back of his hand to the sky. This wouldn't have been altogether bad if he'd skewered Hadrian, but given that the sergeant couldn't have announced his intentions any clearer, Hadrian easily stepped aside. Then with the sergeant at full extension, Hadrian slammed his fist downward on the flat of the blade, close to the man's hand. The sergeant's grip broke. The sword fell — but never hit the ground.

Before the blade touched the snow, Hadrian caught the sword with his foot and flipped the weapon up into his own hand. Then he placed the tip against the astonished man's throat.

The two other soldiers let go of the horses, and drawing their swords, they rushed forward to defend their leader.

"Do you really hate your sergeant *that much?*" Hadrian asked as he literally pressed his point against the man's throat. The sergeant gasped and stepped backward as Hadrian allowed the edge to cut. As a fine example of the Warric military, the sergeant had kept his weapon sharp, and it took little effort to draw blood.

"Stop!" Shelby shouted at the sprinting soldiers. He was standing with one foot on the driver's box, one on the rest, the crossbow cocked and aimed.

The men stopped so quickly that they slid on the snow. One comically fell, which caused the sergeant to close his eyes in disgust.

"Toss your blades aside, then lie down!" Shelby ordered. "Fetch 'em, son."

Heath jumped down from the coach and gathered the weapons.

Then nothing happened for a long moment.

"What are you going to do now, *Hadrian?*" the sergeant asked. "Kill us, and you're wanted for murdering the king's men. Let us go, and we'll hunt you down."

Hadrian rolled his eyes. "Careful, or you might scare me." He took away the sergeant's dagger and tossed it onto the pile Heath had made near the coach's front wheel. "You're more ambitious than your fellow soldiers, but that's like saying you're the fastest starfish on the beach. This buggy is pretty quick, and chasing us would be a lot of work. I wasn't kidding about the demon in this coach. Your reward for catching us would be an early grave — for you and a lot of innocent people. So, look . . . there'll be more travelers on this road who won't hesitate to pay the *Road Tax*. Stay here, enjoy the clearing skies, and consider yourself lucky you aren't dead or being hauled in on charges of racketeering in the name of the king. Being a *new* king with *new* rules, His Majesty might want to also make some *new* examples. We'll leave your horses tethered at the hitch inside the front gate." He gestured at Heath, who gathered up their mounts and walked them around to the rear of the coach.

Hadrian addressed all three of them. "You know, you could try to be . . . well, better. I know standing a post is boring and thankless, but honestly you can always be proud of a job well done. And money is good to have, but it comes and goes. Once traded, you'll never get your integrity back. Pride in yourself and what you do is —"

"Can we get going now?" Royce asked from inside the coach. "The demon is getting hungry."

Hadrian sighed.

CHAPTER FIVE

Trouble with Bubbles

Gravis Berling watched the bubbles rising in his glass of ale. Like all Berlings, he was born and bred for genius and knew that the gas was created during the fermentation process. Humans didn't understand that, but then humans didn't know much. They left brewing to their wives. These women, these *alewives*, had the audacity to add hops to their family gruit recipes and then call what they created bier, or beer, as if they had invented it. They had no idea what turned wort into the effervescent amber drink. For them that brewed it, the magic was believed to be in the family stick that their mothers and grandmothers handed down. Daughters were told to only stir the wort using the *magic stick*. What they didn't know — what they still don't — is that the *stick* was caked with yeast from all the other previous batches, and it was that unseen fungi that provided the magic to get the fermentation process rolling.

Fermentation was an old word, a Dromeian word. Gravis was certain of that, and also that the term described how yeast consumes sugar to produce gas and alcohol. The gas appeared in any fermentation process and was equally responsible for the holes in spongy bread and the bubbles in Gravis's ale.

When first brewed, there were a lot of bubbles, and many people liked it that way, but in a few days, all the bubbles were gone, and the drink went as flat as stale water. Sealing ale in barrels never worked. The gas always escaped.

"Master Berling." Baric Brock interrupted Gravis's study of his drink. He hadn't seen Baric approach, but he knew the voice. He was one of the in-betweens, a dwarf whose beard was tending toward gray but not yet committed to the cause. He was a middle-aged, middling meddler, who surely intended what else but . . . mischief.

Gravis didn't reply or so much as look up.

Baric persisted. "Terrible age we live in, isn't it?"

Gravis didn't care for Baric, but then he didn't care for most people. Not that Baric classified as *people*. He was a Brock. The whole family was a bunch of silversmiths who always made a sumptuous living while others starved. Worse yet, the Brocks were one of the *northern families*—those who left the peninsula and then came back. In Gravis's book, that made him one toe short of a traitor—a wealthy and insensitive toe-short traitor.

Baric leaned in, resting a meaty hand decorated with a silver ring on the counter of the bar inches from Gravis's ale—the drink with too few bubbles. "Heard Ena died. I'm sorry for your loss. I truly am."

"Leave me be, Baric." Gravis growled the words, thinking Baric ought to at least understand what any dog would.

"I'm just offering me condolences, Berling. Just trying to be decent."

"And I'm just letting you know to sod off. Now awa' an' bile yer heid."

"You don't need to be that way. There's no call for it."

"No call for it? No call for it, you say?" Gravis's head came up, his eyes torn from the too few bubbles to lock on Baric and his too few brains, who was also freakishly tall for a Dromeian.

Not just a traitor. The Brocks must have human blood in their past.

"They've banished me from her!" Gravis shouted and slammed his hand on the bar, turning every head in the alehouse.

"No one banished you, Berling. Ena just died. It happens."

"Not from Ena, you hampot! From Drumindor!"

"Drumindor?" Baric looked as dim as a dying candle. Then those eyes narrowed. "Are you hearing yourself, Berling? Your wife just passed away, and you're still going on about the blasted towers?"

Everyone was listening to them now. Scram Scallie wasn't a big place, and their raised voices echoed off the walls, killing any other talk. Gravis didn't like all the attention. Aside from Sloan behind the bar, only four additional patrons filled the room, but for Gravis, who lived a small life, it was a multitude. And while he'd like nothing more than to take the twists out of Baric's crooked thinking and set him straight, Gravis wasn't a public speaker. He didn't do well in arguments in front of an audience. He'd never been popular. Maybe there was prejudice against his family's name, which Baric had been using like a stick to beat him with. Or perhaps people shunned Gravis because he wasn't just a *little* smarter than everyone else, but a *lot,* and people couldn't begin to comprehend his thinking. Either way — and he felt it likely to be both — he knew he wasn't about to win minds and hearts by debating Baric. Feeling eyes on him, Gravis made a tactical retreat. "You're a Doritheian, Baric. You don't understand, and ya never will."

"Bah!" Baric waved a dismissive hand, signaling that the encounter was over, then he turned around to walk away.

While Gravis had been cognizant of the attention they had drawn, it was no surprise that Baric was slow in the awareness department. Why he didn't realize that everyone would be watching only sharpened the point of the argument that Gravis wasn't bothering to make. Instead, he watched it happen, knew it would. When Baric turned and saw all the faces, the miserable sod couldn't let it go — not with people watching, not in this sacred place.

Scram Scallie wasn't merely a dwarven bar — it was a historic site, and every Dromeian knew it. A literal crack in the wall, nothing more than a mousehole in the side of the grand Turian Cliffs, the little alehouse was invisible to the rest of the city, but to Gravis and his fellow Belgriclungreians, Scram Scallie was famous. The little shelter predated Drumindor. Legend held that Andvari Berling himself carved it out as a base while surveying the bay. Trapped inside by a storm that raged for days, he had used glow stones for light and invented the quintessential invisible rolling door. When the war with the elves turned dire, and the Orinfar was discovered, Scram Scallie became the model for all the rols built as safe houses throughout the north. Now, several thousand years later, it served as a place where Dromeians could get away from the *big people*—hence the name.

Not wanting to look weak on even that tiny stage, Baric pivoted, whirling around with theatrical drama. "Aye, you're right! I'm a Doritheian, and proud to be the descendant of the eldest son of Drome, one of the first thanes that founded Neith and ruled our people for nearly nine thousand years. *Nine thousand*, Berling. How long were the Brundenlins in charge? How long before your clan, and their *kings*, nearly wiped us off the face of Elan? Was it even an entire century, Berling? Was it?"

Feeling vindicated and victorious, Baric once more tried to walk away, but again, he failed. He turned back, and with a newly drawn breath, he added, "Until Linden of the Brundenlins declared himself *king*, that word was an unspeakable profanity. His wonderful grandson, Mideon, demonstrated exactly why that is. You want to bandy about lineage, Gravis? Keep in mind that you Berlings were right there by Mideon's side, supporting his war, his greed, and his bloated ego. And finally, that insanity with the golem! Who did that, *Berling?* Mideon had lost but refused to accept that fact, so he had Andvari use the forbidden arts to summon the thing that destroyed Linden Lott!"

"That's a lie!" Gravis erupted.

"It's an unproven truth—there's a difference. But I wouldn't expect a Brundenlin to understand that . . . *and ya never will.*" Baric whirled around and began to swagger out.

This time it was Gravis who couldn't back down. "There're too few bubbles, Baric!"

Baric didn't stop—not immediately—he was on a triumphal march, but he slowed. Because Scram Scallie was possibly the smallest alehouse in the world, he almost reached the door when curiosity finally tackled him. The others were silent and every face expectant as Baric asked the question that they all hoped he would. "What are you babbling about, you old fool? What do you mean by *too few bubbles?*"

Gravis lifted his drink. "In the ale. When first fermented, there's a fizz to it. It bubbles and froths with power, energy, and life. Drink it fresh, and it tingles the tongue. But let it sit in a barrel and the bubbles disappear, leaving the ale flat—leaving it dead, a mere ghost of its former self. You can still drink it, acourse, but the life is gone."

Baric waited as Gravis indulged in a bit of his own theatrics and took a swallow from his bubble-deficient glass. He made a revolted sour face as he glared at the ale. Then he pointed at the drink. "We Dromeians . . . we were once a great people, but we have sat too long in the barrel. We're out of bubbles, Baric. We aren't alive anymore. We just exist. Not that long ago, Dromeians were great, and the humans were small. Now we look up to them like a pet to its master and wag our tails when they throw scraps. We stand and watch as they defile our temples and great buildings, turning them into alehouses and brothels. We've forgotten who we are, Baric. We need to ferment again. We need our bubbles to rise once more."

"You're talking mince. Our days of glory are gone. We aren't a great people anymore. And who are *you* to criticize? You worked for them like everyone else."

"I worked for my forefathers. I labored at maintaining a legacy!"

"And look where it got ya." Baric grinned and searched the room for the agreement he knew would be waiting.

Gravis pointed a finger at him as if casting a curse. "You're why we will never be great again. It's people like you, who accept mediocrity and see nothing wrong with *good enough*, that are dragging us down. You're why the ale has no bubbles."

"Oh, I see." Baric nodded. "You have all the answers, don't ya? Of course you do. You're a Berling. So, tell us, Gravis, what would the celebrated *Berling* have us do?"

"Teach them a lesson they won't ever forget," Gravis said. "Give them a reminder of who we were and, Drome willing, may be again."

"And how do you expect to do that?"

"They don't deserve Drumindor," Gravis replied. "I'll take it back."

"You're daft." Baric snickered. "Ya going ta trot up there and ask them to hand it over, are you? Tell them it's *your* name on the deed? Or will you battle them for it?" Baric put up his fists like a prize fighter. "Gonna smite 'em all, and kick 'em out. I don't see how else you can do it, Berling. The towers are a bit too big to steal, don't ya think?"

"I have my ways."

"You're full of yourself, is what you mean."

From behind the bar, Sloan clapped a pair of mugs on the counter loud enough to catch the room's attention. "Leave him be, Baric."

Scram Scallie was Sloan's place — at least as much as it could belong to any one person. Sloan was a Bel. Her clan originally hailed from West Echo. But her family had come to Tur in the Silver Age of King Rain, back when the Bels were so important that their name came first. Some of them left when the Belgric Kingdom was accepted into the Novronian Empire and citizenship was granted to all. But out of commitment to a tradition older than any of her family, she and hers stayed to run the tiny heritage site. Then, when her father died, she took over. Now, some forty years later, it was just her. She wasn't all that old, but Sloan was as respected as an elder and one of the few dwarfs Gravis could stomach.

While Baric was an idiot, he wasn't stupid, and the dwarf wisely refused to lock antlers with Sloan the Bel — not in her own place. He yielded the field with a cowed look.

Sloan proceeded to serve Kiln the Miner his ale, sliding the drink down the bar and leaving a trail of wet that she wiped away with her towel. In all the years he'd known her, Gravis never once saw Sloan without the towel, either in her hand or over a shoulder. He often wondered if she slept with it.

She certainly isn't sleeping with anyone else.

Many had tried to woo The Lady Bel of Tur, but to his knowledge, that was one peak that had yet to be conquered.

"The big folk aren't all bad, Gravis," she said in a soft, calming voice. "They invited us ta Delgos, didn't they? No ghettos, no pogroms, no restrictions on where we can go, or what businesses we can open. They welcomed us as equals."

"And why did they do that? Not out of the goodness of their hearts, I don't think."

"Yer so smart ya can plumb the depths of human hearts, can ya?"

"They needed water." This bit of genius came from Trig the Younger, who because Scram Scallie was too small for tables or chairs, stood elbow to elbow with Kiln at the bar. The words were less proclaimed to the room than pronounced into his drink. Because he was the son of the water system administrator, however, no one was likely to doubt him no matter how he said it. "They have no idea how to turn a crank. Couldn't even if we drew them a picture. They're too big to fit in the access tunnels."

This made a few people chuckle, Baric being the loudest. But children and the simpleminded were easy to amuse. The laughter quickly faded, killed by the lingering tension.

"They also need the roads repaired," Kiln spoke up, "but none of them have a clue how to lay the stone properly. And they don't know how to work our quarries to get the required resources."

Covered with powdered-stone dust from a hard day's work, Heigal and Loc, who stood at the other end of the little polished counter, raised their drinks toward him and nodded.

"They've been replacing dwarfs in tier two positions for years," Kiln went on. "Now, they've done it to Berling and the rest of them at the towers." He shook his head over his mug. "Never thought they would. Since Drumindor was created, there has never been a time when a Berling wasn't in it. Isn't that right?"

Gravis was pleased to see that this wasn't a disputed fact.

"Those towers are everything to this place," Kiln went on. "The scallie have to know that, don't they, Sloan? They must realize that if something goes wrong, it's over — for them, for us, for everyone here. So, if they think they can get by without a Berling in Drumindor — a maze of a million levers — no one is safe, are they?"

"It will all happen here like it has every place else," Trig said. He spoke like a loved one delivering a eulogy. "The ghettos and the pogroms, the laws and restrictions — if we don't fight back now, all of it will follow."

"Fighting isn't the answer," Sloan was quick to say. "If ya don't believe me, come here on Doritheian Day. Auberon always visits fer a drink around sunset. Ask him what he thinks about fighting for our rights. Listen ta him for five minutes, and I guarantee ya will change yer mind."

"Not the answer? We're up against the sea here. Are you saying . . . do you think we ought to just give up?"

"It won't happen here," she said.

"You're being naïve," Trig said sharply. "Why would here be any different?"

"Because this is Tur Del Fur, the Jewel of the Belgric Peninsula."

"Not anymore," Gravis said. "This is Delgos now, Land of Trade and the Unholy Trio."

She shook her head. "This is Belgric, home of the old kingdom. That's in stone and can't be changed, and that's why here is different. I know what's happening. I'm not blind. This is our last stand. If we lose Tur . . . there's nothing left fer us . . . not here, not anywhere. I don't understand the curse that's been laid on our people, but don't think fer a moment that I don't know about it."

Sloan wrung out her towel, squeezing it hard. She hesitated, bowing her head so that her nose nearly touched the bar top. She took a breath and straightened up and gave the room a stare. "Look, I don't talk about it, but a few of ya know that not long ago, me sister and her husband were killed up in Vernes. Lovely couple. Kind, generous, and the sort ta always see the best in everyone. They were walking home from the market when they were beaten ta death in the street. The murderers called them *gronbachs,* and when it was done, bystanders applauded." Sloan shook her head slowly, pinching her lips together. "People actually stood by and clapped while me sister's blood pooled before them. It's hard ta keep breathing after something like that, hard not ta hate, and just about impossible ta hope."

"So why—" Gravis started, but Sloan held up a palm.

"Because when I walk outside"—she gestured at the invisible Andvari Berling door—"when I go ta the end of the tier, ta the turnout—ya all know the one I mean—and I look down at the bay, guess what I see? Those two beautiful towers still standing in all their glory. But I don't just see Drumindor. I see how all of it once was. Drumindor, the rolkins, the domes, the tiers, and the bay. They are all reminders etched in stone that we aren't cockroaches ta be stepped on. We aren't vermin ta be driven out fer the greater good. Here we stand, drowning in evidence that we deserve respect. And that's why here is different."

"I get that, Sloan," Kiln said. "I do. But we still see it happening, and if we do nothing, then nothing will change."

"So we'll do something, but fighting has never worked fer us. It only destroys, and we aren't good at breaking things—but we are exceptional at building. The proof is all around us. Our greatest legacy has always been what we create. So that's what we'll do. We must build, but not fortresses or weapons. We need bridges and respect."

"And how do we do that?" Baric asked. "Complain to the Unholy Trio?"

Several laughed at this, but there was no mirth in it, just a sad desperation.

"We could remind them why they welcomed us in the first place." Sloan looked at the towel in her hand. "They've fired the whole lot from Drumindor, haven't they? And yer right; they have been replacing all the supervisors in every position of importance all over the city. And doing that hasn't gone well, has it? They're trying ta figure out how ta survive without us. So, what if we give them what they want — but all at once with no time ta prepare. Why don't we let them see what it would be like, and in the process announce loud and clear that it's all or nothing? Either we are full citizens with equal rights, equally deserving of respect and appreciation or" — she held the hand holding the towel out over the edge of the bar and dropped it to the floor — "we all quit."

This is the problem, Gravis thought. *In the days of Mideon, the world quaked at the sound of dwarven boots. Now, we have leaders like Sloan, females, who tell everyone that being good little dwarfs is the best way.*

"Doing that won't work," Gravis said. "That sort of thing has been tried over and over."

"But this isn't Vernes, or Rochelle, or Dithmar," she replied. "This is Tur Del Fur, our ancestral home." She walked over to the wall and laid a hand on it. "Our people built this place, and they did so fer Dromeians. These are our tunnels, halls, and mines. Here, unlike everywhere else, we have the advantage."

Gravis didn't agree, but he said nothing more on the subject. They could do as they liked. He had his own plan, and he didn't need anyone's help.

Gravis Berling had lived in a wooden shack down by the docks. Four weathered walls with a shingled, sloped roof. He had made it himself years ago. It wasn't the first. He'd built dozens — all in the same place, more or less. He constructed the first one when he was a mere child of twenty-two. Still an apprentice working the cog room in Drumindor, always under his father's critical eye, he longed to be free. The shack was his answer.

He'd constructed the first one from what he'd found along the coast, driftwood mostly, and scrap from the shipyards: planks, mast poles, and canvas. He'd even scored a discarded cabin door that served as his entrance and made the whole thing look grand. The shack listed to one side and leaked when it rained, but it was his, and he was proud of it.

Then the first big storm came.

Gravis was working at the time, and down in the bowels of Drumindor, he hadn't the slightest clue that the gods of wind, rain, and ocean were having a tempestuous tussle. When he went home, it wasn't there. The whole thing, door and all, had been wiped clean off the face of Elan.

He remembered standing on the depression left behind. A light rain continued to fall from an indifferent sky as he looked at the dark and angry sea. He didn't ask why. He was a Dromeian. His people had stopped asking questions hundreds of years ago. Instead, he went looking for his missing door. Gravis never found it, but he'd discovered a host of other treasures. The storm, it seemed, hadn't just targeted him. The gods had attacked everyone. Strewn along the coast were the shattered remains of dozens of poorly sheltered ships. He found four new doors—two in nearly perfect condition. He snagged a full-sized window frame out of the sandy surf. Two of the four glass panes were cracked, the third shattered, but one was perfect. With these and more, he started rebuilding his seaside castle. This time he chose a more sheltered spot—a place where the storm seemed to have had difficulty reaching. Oddly, it was farther out on the arm of the headland, a stone's throw from the North Tower. That one lasted nearly a decade before the ocean took it.

By then, he had advanced out of the cog room and was courting a lass named Ena Schist. Ena always wanted him to buy a rolkin. Nothing big or grand, just a little hole in the wall with turquoise shutters and a flower bed. Gravis could have gotten one farther up the tiers, but he wanted to be close to Drumindor, and real estate near the water was priced out of reach. Years later, after his father had passed and he was appointed chief supervisor, Gravis still stayed in the shack. By then, it was home for both of them.

He spent his honeymoon within those walls. Nearly died of fever there, too. He and Ena had wept rivers of tears and laughed themselves sick on that little square of rock and shoal that shook with even a light breeze. But it had only been a few days ago that Ena had taken her last breath beneath that slanted roof. Gravis had spent most of his life inside Drumindor, but the best times — few as they were — had been lived inside that shack.

Standing in the dark and looking at the old place, Gravis couldn't even go inside — not anymore. In two hundred and forty-six years, Gravis had never been required to pay rent. They told him that was because he had been an employee, and it was one of the privileges they chose to grant him. He'd never told Ena, but he was sure if he had, she would have laughed herself even sicker to hear that someone thought their shack on a rock was a privilege. He was grateful she died before the eviction notice came.

Gravis stood in a light rain, staring at his home. The place was empty. He knew it would be — it would always be. No one else would ever want to live there. The Port Authority had driven him out for no reason other than spite.

Gravis couldn't stay. Lord Byron would have someone watching the place. If he lingered too long, men with blades would come and say he was on PA land and he must move. If he put up a fuss, they would drag him away. And if the commotion was too unruly, they'd likely drag him to the ocean.

Gravis wiped his eyes and looked up at Drumindor.

Unlike Sloan, he didn't see hope in those two towers. All he saw was pain. And if he could figure out a way to get back inside, he would whistle a merry tune as he waited on the full moon and the end of everything.

CHAPTER SIX

Kruger

Rocked gently in the snug little coach for hours on end, Royce had watched as each of the others succumbed to sleep. Their eyes closed, opened, then closed again. Heads drooped, only to pop back up. A hand might wipe lips, then the process would begin again. Finally, breathing would grow deep and regular. When that happened, limp heads stayed down, swaying from side to side and looking like their necks had been broken. At this point, even the biggest bumps and sways couldn't wake them.

Royce disliked the notion of sleep on principle. He saw no reason for it. Eating and breathing both made sense. Like a fire, fuel and air were necessary to keep the blaze going. But what purpose did sleep serve except to make a person helpless and vulnerable for several hours every day? If he needed the rest, that might make some sense, but most often he grew sleepy when doing nothing. He ought to be able to sit motionless indefinitely — for a month, at least. The arbitrary compulsion to sleep, whether he liked it or not, was a forced constraint and another reminder that he was a pawn in a game he didn't want to play. The whole thing was stupid.

At least he thought so until Gwen fell asleep with her head on his shoulder.

Resting like a feather near Royce's neck, her hair brushed the lobe of his ear, and her cheek rocked with the motion of the coach. He was fearful that her head might slide off its perch. This concerned him far more than he was comfortable with. He mentally argued that his anxiety was entirely due to his desire for her to rest and it was unrelated to how it made him feel. He twisted and contorted his body, leaning into her to form a safer resting place. The position was awkward and untenable. His muscles would soon cramp, his neck ache, but no power on Elan could make him move.

It's only because she deserves a good sleep. I owe her that much, don't I? A little discomfort is nothing compared to what she's given me.

For Royce the amount was measured and made greater by contrast with how little others had done.

The coach continued to roll and sway. The windows were hopelessly fogged. All Royce could determine by then was that the sunlight was weaker, the day slowly fading. This soft illumination filled the warm interior, made warmer still by Gwen's body pressing against his. With everyone asleep, Royce no longer felt exposed or watched, and for that blessed moment, he experienced a strange sense of peace. Unable to shift, straighten, nor even willing to cough, Royce resigned himself to just sitting. He tried to look at her but couldn't risk turning his head that far. Instead, he stared at the one exposed hand that rested on her lap near her knee. It wasn't much, but oh so better than looking at Arcadius, who was starting to drool, his head cocked against the seat padding.

Royce had never studied a hand before, never examined or appreciated one. He judged hers to be perfect and wondered what it might be like to place his upon it, to intertwine his fingers with hers.

His eyelids drooped.

Gah!

At that moment, more than any other, he didn't want to sleep. He gritted his teeth and silently cursed the name of every god he knew.

His head dipped. He pulled it back up in defiance, forced his eyes to remain open.

It makes no sense. No sense at all. And being so illogical makes me . . .

Royce awoke when the coach stopped.

The jostling caused Gwen's head to slide off his shoulder. She caught herself and jerked back. Sleepy eyes looked at him, then widened. "Sorry."

"It's fine," he replied.

Royce wiped away the moisture on the window with the heel of his hand. Outside, it was dark, but there was a light. In the center of the yard, a pole rose where a bull's-eye-style lantern hung, drawing a swarm of swirling insects. Its lonely gleam revealed the common clearing between buildings.

"Wake up, folks," the driver called, lightly clapping the roof. "Stretch your legs. Get something to eat."

Albert scrubbed his face with both hands and made smacking noises with his lips. Arcadius continued to sleep until Gwen reached out and shook his knee.

In response, the old professor lifted his head. "I wasn't sleeping, dear, just resting my eyes."

Gwen leaned forward and peered out the window. "Where are we?"

Albert yawned and stretched his arms out as wide as the coach allowed. "Another stage stop I suspect."

Royce opened the door and climbed out, feeling unpleasantly stiff. He was instantly greeted by the damp night air. While chilly, it wasn't cold, and there was no snow on the ground. Crickets and frogs chirped, and the air smelled of grass, dirt, and the distant suggestion of a dead skunk. Royce's feet landed on the rut-scarred lawn. A darkened stable stood to the right, a workshop of sorts to his left, and straight ahead lay a modest, single-story, wood-framed house.

Hadrian climbed down, looking haggard.

Royce yawned and wiped his eyes.

"You slept?" Hadrian sounded surprised.

"Nothing else to do. How about you?"

"Once the snow stopped, I got some sleep. I think. Hard to tell, really."

Gwen climbed down. She squinted, her hair mussed up on one side, her face still stiff from sleeping. "It's a lot warmer here."

"How lovely," Arcadius declared, exiting the carriage with all the nimbleness of a man trying out stilts for the first time. "It's like we've jumped ahead three months, skipped the rest of winter, and missed the worst parts of spring."

"Leave your stuff and go on up to the house, folks," Shelby told them as he unhooked the coach from the team. "We'll be a short while. Briar and Gus will feed you. They're a nice couple, and Briar is a fine enough cook."

The door to the house flew open, and Heath came running out.

"They awake?" Shelby asked.

"Are now," he said as behind him a light appeared beyond the curtains.

The first two things Hadrian noticed upon entering the coach house were the bright fire in the hearth and the smell of bacon. Before the fireplace was a large, sturdy table surrounded by chairs. Additional seating was stacked against the back wall. Above it all and hanging side by side from the roof beams was a strange duo: a wagon wheel and a ferryboat captain's wheel. The two were nearly the same size. Just below them, burned into a rough board that served as the mantle to the hearth, were the words Wheels of Dreams.

Already there were plates and spoons set out. A man, who was so tall and thin that he appeared stretched, was busy lighting the candles on the table. "Hullo, ladies and gentlemen!" he said brightly. "I'm Gus. Come in, have a seat, my wife will be —"

A short, ragged woman burst into the room backward, holding a blackened pot with towels on each hand. "Hot dish!" she announced, bustling her way to the table and slamming the pot down in the center. She straightened up and took several short breaths while wiping her face with one of the towels. "Sit down and eat. There's more coming." With that, she ran back out through the same door where she'd entered.

"That's my wife," the man said. "Briar Rose. You might not have caught it, but she's very pleased to meet you."

"Pleased to meet you as well," Gwen said, then yawned as they all spread out around the table.

"Indeed," Arcadius agreed. "It's a lovely place you have here."

"Oh, this house isn't ours," Gus said as he moved to the next candle. "Shelby built this place. He's got two coach stations, along with a string of little stables running from Tur Del Fur to Ervanon."

"*Had* two!" Briar shouted from the kitchen.

"That's right, he *had* two. The other one was up in Chadwick, in Fallon Mire. That used to be the main one. He got rid of it. And we're hoping to take this one over one day — make it into a proper inn. Heath thinks they'll have a dozen or more coaches working this route. That's a guaranteed revenue stream."

"I want to be a coachman," a young girl announced as she entered, carrying a basket of steaming rolls that she placed on the table. She displayed round cheeks decorated with freckles and a big smile.

"This is my daughter, Copper," Gus said.

"Her real name is Dorothy," Briar explained as she burst back in, this time with a sizzling skillet of bacon, the contents of which she scraped into the previously delivered pot. "But we've always just called her Copper. Don't have a clue why." Briar paused, looking at all of them, bewildered. "Sit and eat. Won't take the Hansons more than a hoot and a giggle to get rolling again. Those two are as dogged as hounds on a trail, and you won't be stopping again for hours." Then once more she was gone, her daughter chasing after.

They all took seats.

"Go ahead and dig in. Eggs are in the pot, too, I think." Gus shrugged. "Being out on the edge of Avryn as we are, we don't adhere to formality here, and regrettably we've slipped into heathen ways that the rest of our Maranon neighbors would shame us for. But honestly, we just don't have the time, and most of our customers don't, either." He smiled as if he'd made a joke. "Acourse, if you want, I could say a blessing?"

"Oh, I doubt that will be necessary," Arcadius said as he reached for the bacon dish. "We are a barbaric lot ourselves, I'm afraid. And given that we're headed across the border to the land of the godless, I think it's best we don't start practicing now."

Gus nodded, not the least bit surprised.

"Milk!" Copper shouted, returning with a pitcher. "Still warm!"

"Goat or cow?" Arcadius asked.

"We have three goats," Copper replied.

"Lovely! Cow's milk gives me indigestion. Bring it around here, my dear."

Royce remained standing near the door to the courtyard. When Hadrian looked over, Royce walked out.

"Excuse me," Hadrian said and got up. "I'll be right back . . . I hope."

Outside, Royce was walking without any urgency toward the lantern pole. Despite the chill, his hood was down.

"What's up?" Hadrian asked.

Royce turned. "A demon?"

Hadrian smiled awkwardly. "Would you rather I used your name?"

"Technically, that is my name — at least one of the ones they gave me."

"So . . . you're mad at me?" Hadrian normally didn't need to ask. When angry, Royce had two demeanors: quiet and brooding or bloodlettingly violent. At the moment, he was neither.

"Huh? No." Royce shook his head. Then he looked up at the lantern on the pole, where a small cloud of insects swarmed. He continued to stare as if fascinated by the concept of illumination.

Hadrian thought he knew most of his partner's moods and what they meant. This wasn't a hard thing to learn, for there weren't that many. What made it challenging was how Royce's attitudes indicated the opposite of normal people. Quiet, to the point of cold hostility, was actually his normal state and no cause for alarm. If he did speak, his words were curt and to the point, suggesting he'd already run through the conversation in advance and was only suffering the necessary obligation of letting the other person know how it turned out. Chattiness, however, was an indication of a problem. His need to talk, but failure to do so, was like seeing a fish floating upside down. "What's going on, Royce?"

"I wish I knew."

"Can I have a hint?"

Royce pointed at the light on the pole. "Look at all those moths."

Hadrian gave it a glance. "Can I have a better hint?"

"The moths just keep butting the glass of the lantern," Royce said.

"It's late, Royce. I don't even know the time, but after midnight, at least. I'm groggy, and just standing here I feel like I'm still riding the coach. And it's not like I've ever been good at puzzles, even when wide awake. So could you . . ."

"If there wasn't glass on the lantern, the moths would kill themselves."

"Uh-huh, they do that. We see it all the time with campfires. I actually think we've discussed this before. Can't recall why. Likely you were explaining something to do with the stupidity of people. Yeah, that seems right."

"The thing is, they can't help themselves, and it's not the light's fault, either. It's just there. Bright and irresistible. You'd think the moths would know better or should know better. Look at them hitting that glass over and over again, so intent on seeking their own death."

"You're starting to scare me now. What's going on?"

"I think there's a chance Gwen likes me."

"Of course she likes you. We've had *this* conversation before, too."

"Yeah, now I think she . . ."

"She what?"

Royce took a deep breath and swallowed. His face tensed. "She slept with her head on my shoulder."

"Okay. And . . . ?"

"*And?* What do you mean *and?* Did you hear what I said?"

"Did she say anything?"

"Of course not. I just said she was sleeping. You're not listening to me at all, are you?"

"I am. It's just that — never mind. That's — that's great, Royce."

"No, it's not!" he snapped and began to walk again, this time in a circle around Hadrian.

"It's not?"

"No!"

"Don't you like her?"

"Of course I do — that's the problem!"

Hadrian looked up at the lantern. "Can we go back to the moths again? I think I missed something."

Royce stopped moving, took a breath, and let it out. "I don't know what to do."

"You don't?" Hadrian finally understood why he had struggled to grasp the meaning of his friend's awkward rambling; this was a mood he'd never encountered before. Royce was seeking advice. "Okay, I get it. Not a problem. I actually have a decent amount of experience with women. It's easy. Not complicated at all. You really only have two options. You can express yourself—you know, tell her how you feel, and ask her how she feels."

Royce cringed.

"Or not." Hadrian rubbed his hands together and regrouped. "You're right. Words are not your strong suit. Sure. So, go the other way."

"What's the other way?" There was no hope in that question. Royce looked at him with a face full of dread.

"Kiss her."

The thief's eyes widened.

"You do *want* to, don't you?"

Royce's face hardened, and he gritted his teeth as if Hadrian were performing field surgery on him. "Yes, but that's . . . it's so . . ."

"You *have* kissed a woman before, haven't you, Royce?"

His answer was a violent glare.

"Oh? Oh. *Really?*" Hadrian stared, off balance for a moment. "I suppose I should have guessed that, shouldn't I?"

"I'm . . ." Royce began, then floundered into a series of short breaths. He turned away, once more being drawn toward the light on the pole. "I have no idea what to do. It's like I'm trying to pick up a soap bubble, and I'm terrified that if I touch it, the whole thing will burst." His hands clenched into fists. "I'd really love to slit Arcadius's throat for this."

"The professor? What's he got to do with it?"

"It's all his fault. 'I think we should all go,' he said. 'Certainly this wonderful lady deserves a holiday,' he babbled. Since I've known him, that old man has been nothing but trouble. I've killed whole families that were guilty of less."

"Royce, you're not going to kill Arcadius."

"Of course not—Gwen would hate me if I did."

"Ah . . ." Hadrian decided to let that go and take the win. "Okay."

"Which brings me to the point."

"It does?" Hadrian thought they'd already reached and plowed through that field, so discovering they still hadn't was surprising—and more than a bit scary. "I mean, what is the point, Royce?"

"That whole demon thing you did. Your handling of those three *tax collectors.* That was smart. With Gwen inside, if they had opened that door . . ."

"I know. I know."

Royce brushed the grass with the toe of his boot. "And Gwen would have had a front row seat for it all. She would have seen *the demon* at work. And if she had? After that . . . I don't think she would have slept with her head on my shoulder."

"Royce," Hadrian presented him with a sympathetic look. "After that, I don't think she would have slept at all."

"Exactly, you get my point. Good."

"So, are you thanking me?"

"No!" He looked aghast. "I'm merely pointing out that you did a good thing. I'm extending a compliment, but let's not get carried away." Once more, Royce looked up at the lantern and the moths. "I know exactly how they feel. They hate that glass, but it's all that stands between them and the abyss."

"You are *such* a romantic, Royce. I would definitely avoid talking to her. Go with the kiss. Even if you miss, slam teeth, slide off, and fall on your face, that will be better than comparing Gwen to a bottomless pit." He turned. "I'm going to eat now before Albert consumes everything Briar Rose cooked." Hadrian took a step. "Oh, and for your information, Gwen *doesn't* like you."

Royce spun in a panic. "You said she did."

"The woman is *in love* with you, Royce. I have no idea why. I'm not sure anyone does. I don't even think Professor Arcadius with all his knowledge can crack that one. But yeah, she loves you. So, relax. Talk to her, kiss her, murder a bunch of puppies in front of her—you can't lose this one. I only wish I could be so lucky."

"Dwarfs dwell in hollow mountains and underground—often in caves hidden behind waterfalls," Arcadius was saying when Royce returned to the meal. The professor sat at the head of the table, his long sleeves rolled up to the elbows. With his slick-with-grease fingers, he held a strip of bacon like a baton, which he used to conduct his lecture to the rest of the table.

"I've heard that lady dwarfs are ugly," Copper said as she cleared the empty serving plates. The little girl had a poorly assembled stack and struggled with the unruly tower that threatened to topple.

The professor shook his head, and while once more wielding his bacon baton, he explained, "While often suspected to be stocky and bearded, female dwarfs are actually remarkably beautiful, made all the more so by their petite size. And despite their reduced place in the world today, the dwarfs have a long and proud history and once fought with the elves for dominance of the world. That was back when their king ruled the entire peninsula of Delgos, and they mined gems and gold by the wagonload. But those days are long past. Still, each and every dwarf hides a treasure beyond imagination, but"—he paused to wink at Copper—"dwarven hoards are always cursed. So nothing good ever comes from stealing from them."

"Are dwarfs really made from stone? Do they live forever?" the girl asked, still hugging her shifting spire of plates.

The professor of problems is at it again, Royce thought. *He doesn't care whose life he ruins.*

Arcadius had used a child's curiosity to put the little girl in this jam. The kid had lingered too long at the table, enchanted by the stories of a senile old man, and now she would break a fortune's worth of pottery and obtain a beating for doing so. Her parents would pay as well, and maybe the family would go to bed hungry. They might even be removed from this cushy post and left homeless and destitute, all because the old man didn't know when to shut up.

"Nothing lives forever except love and hate," Arcadius said. "But dwarfs live as much as thrice as long as a man. And while they aren't made of stone and stand only between twenty-seven and forty-four inches in height, the dwarf possesses the strength of twenty men. Although, scholars believe the dwarf's vigor is due mostly to magical objects, which they manufacture at their grand underground forges and workshops."

"I thought the wee folk shunned magic, even more than the church," Gus said, coming to the aid of his daughter. Seeing what Royce saw, he promptly took command of the teetering stack.

"That is indeed a strange paradox with them. Dwarfs are disdainful of magic but wield their own. Each and every one knows full well how to make themselves invisible. They are rumored to be capable of traveling great distances instantly, and are known to have wrought enchanted rings, cloaks, and belts that multiply their strength and protect the wearer from hunger, cold, and so forth. They know where to find stones that when placed beneath the tongue grant the ability to understand and speak previously unknown languages."

"And they are universally hated," Royce said, taking a seat across from Gwen, who looked to be halfway through her meal of some sort of egg casserole and a slice of bread.

Royce hadn't eaten all day, but looking at her, he had no appetite.

I imagine moths don't eat much, either.

Arcadius put his bacon baton in his mouth and nodded while chewing. "They do suffer a good deal in the popularity department, that's true. What with the mass circulation of such bedtime stories as "The Dwarf and the Dairy Maid" and "Little Wren and the Big Forest," they face an uphill battle when trying to change the attitudes of adults who grew up with such gruesome fables. True or not, why parents wish to send their babies off to dreamland filled with tales of terror, I can't begin to fathom. But it is interesting to know that once upon a time, children used to leave broken toys outside their front doors at night in the hope that a dwarf might pass by and repair them before dawn. And an optimistic tot would also leave a sacrificed bit of food on a plate and perhaps a hat or pair of socks as a thank-you in advance. Such were the bright and happy days before literature murdered innocence in the cradle."

"You want some of this?" Hadrian asked Royce, scooping the last of the egg dish onto his plate.

Royce shook his head.

"It's good," Gwen said.

"Sure is," Copper agreed. "Mum is a great cook."

"But you don't want to follow in her footsteps," Gwen said. "You want to be a coachman. Isn't that right?"

The girl nodded. Freed of her monument of crockery, she stood between Gwen and Albert, leaning on the table with both hands and swaying with excess energy. "I'm gonna be like Heath and have my own coach. Only mine will be a coach-and-*six,* and I'll beat his time. Heath says ladies don't drive coaches, but I don't see why not. I'm good with horses, isn't that right, Pa?"

"Certainly better than you are with clearing a table," Gus replied.

"See!" The little girl glowed.

"Well, don't you listen to Heath," Gwen said. "Don't listen to anyone. You can do whatever you want. You just need to be smart and work hard."

"That's what I think." The girl looked around. "What is it that you do, ma'am?"

Gwen hesitated and bit her lip.

"She's the most successful businesswoman in the entire kingdom of Melengar," Royce answered for her. "And I think it's fair to say that she started from even humbler beginnings and faced greater challenges than you can possibly imagine."

Copper's eyes went wide.

Gwen looked stunned.

The girl stared at Gwen in awe. "What's your name, ma'am?"

"Gwendolyn DeLancy," she replied, "but you can call me Gwen."

Shelby entered, carrying the driver's box, and Gus quickly rushed over to help.

"Have Briar restock this," Shelby told him. "We've still got a long way to go. And remind her that we're going into warm weather. So she shouldn't include anything that'll spoil. Have her check the cellar for nuts and raisins. Those are good on the road. We can eat them as we drive."

"I think she's already got snacks made, but I'll tell her." Gus took the box into the kitchen.

"Everyone having a nice meal?" Shelby asked. His face was red and weathered from the wind and wet.

"Wonderful," Hadrian replied with a full mouth.

"Indeed," Arcadius said. "This has been an extraordinary delight."

"Good. Good." Shelby nodded. "Heath is nearly done switching out the team and refitting the wheels for the next stage of our trip."

"The wheels?" Albert asked.

Shelby nodded. "We'll be crossing into Delgos in just a few miles and dealing with less agreeable mountain roads for this next part, and there won't be any more snow. Heath is putting on smaller front wheels to grant the coach a tighter turn radius to get through the narrow passes. He should be done in just a few minutes, then we'll get rolling again. If anyone needs more blankets, just ask Gus or Briar. But honestly, from this point on, keeping cool will be more of a challenge than staying warm."

Outside the little front window of the coach house, Royce saw something big enough to be a man move. He guessed it was Heath, but as Shelby exited, he spotted Shelby's son near the stable.

"How many people are here?" Royce asked Gus when he returned. "Besides the passengers."

"It's just Briar, Copper, and me. Is there something I can get you?"

"No. I'm fine." Royce got up.

Hadrian was busy shoveling the remaining food into his mouth as Gus hovered, ready to take his plate. Albert sat back, breathing deeply and unbuttoning his doublet. Gwen was once more talking to Copper, and Arcadius busied himself by cleaning his teeth. No one said anything as Royce left.

Outside, he was once more greeted with the cool night air and that lingering scent of skunk that wafted in from the surrounding forests. This time Royce avoided looking at the lantern and moved into the shadows at the side of the house.

In the stable, the horses were acting up, whinnying, snorting, and stomping.

"What's with Jack and Rabbit?" Shelby asked from somewhere unseen, his voice carrying on the cool night air.

"Dunno," Heath replied. "Seems spooked."

But why? Royce thought.

He'd always had an intuition for trouble, a sense for when something was wrong. Long ago, he'd guessed it was his imagination, but decades of evidence had eroded logic. He'd come to accept it as a gift — at times he counted on it. At that moment, he fully agreed with the horses. Something wasn't right.

But what?

The courtyard was small. Just the house, the stable, and a workshop. There was one other building not readily visible, and Royce spotted the little trail that led into the scrub toward the obligatory outhouse.

It's over there. Whatever spooked me and the horses. It's hiding in the cover of the bushes and trees.

Drawing Alverstone, Royce started to hunt.

He followed the trail, then inched around the outhouse to where the thickets blocked the view from the stable and house. There, in the radiance of the moon, Royce spotted a man seated on the body of a rotting tree within a ring of young pines. Royce realized, with no small amount of concern, that he knew this man. He was certain he'd killed him just the night before.

The man remained attired in his tattered gray cloak, hood up; his sickly, pale face shone chalk-white in the moonlight. His long red hair and beard peeked out, providing the only color. He looked comfortable and relaxed as he watched Royce approach.

"We need our codex," he said in that familiar, raspy voice.

Royce peered at the man's neck. A dark mark proclaimed the place where Royce had sunk his knife.

Definitely the same guy.

This time, Royce maintained his distance, studying the man and trying to solve the bizarre puzzle.

He should be dead. And how did he find me? And how did he manage to keep up with the Flying Lady?

The man's presence was impossible, but here he was. Royce could think of only one answer.

He followed me back to The Rose and Thorn, saw us enter the coach, and when Hadrian and the drivers were looking forward, he jumped on the back.

This was the only plausible possibility, but *plausible* might not be quite the right word, and it only solved one of the haystacks of problems.

"Dost thou have our book?" the man asked, and Royce once again noted the odd accent, joined now with archaic language. But even buried under all that rasp, he had clearly said *book*.

He thinks I'm someone else.

"I don't have any books," Royce replied. "I'm not a big reader."

"Either thou possesseth it or thou knowest the place it now lies."

The man waited.

So did Royce.

"Thou need not be frightened of us, Royce."

So much for a case of mistaken identity.

"We cherish thee. Thou art . . ." He thought a moment, then nodded. "In truth, thou art our only friend. Thou hast freed us from our eternal prison, a kindness for which we are evermore obliged. And we trust that thy efforts in restoring unto us the vessel of our tragic youth shall be an effort worth rewards beyond mere silver or gold."

"Diamonds?"

"Eternal life." The man smiled.

"I'd prefer diamonds."

The man laughed at this — more cackle than laugh.

Royce advanced slowly. "Are you genuinely offering me a job? If so, I'll need to know exactly what you want and the price you're willing to pay."

"We must have our book, that which thou stolest from Lady Martel of Hemley Manor. In return, we shall grant everlasting life."

"You're after the diary?" At least one piece in this puzzle made sense. Nearly two years before, Royce had stolen the diary of Lady Martel. The contract had been arranged by Albert through Lady Constance. Neither Royce nor Hadrian nor Albert knew the identity of the employer, and it was presumed the employer didn't know the identity of the thieves.

"The codex of our writing belongs to us."

"And who are *we?*"

The ghost-white creature seated on the decaying log grinned, revealing a full set of gleaming teeth set in black gums. "We are Falkirk de Roche."

Royce knew the name. While not a history buff, he was aware that Falkirk de Roche had died a very long time ago. This meant the man before him was lying. The impostor also knew far too much about too many things, and he had made the mortal error of spying on Royce. The red-headed-wannabe ghost was also peerless among people walking the surface of Elan in that Royce had tried, but failed, to kill him. Any one of these would have been sufficient, but when combined, they made Royce's response less of a decision and more of a forgone conclusion.

Once more, Royce went for the throat, but this time, he made certain to go the extra mile and decapitate his unfinished business. Alverstone was no common blade, capable of cutting iron and stone. Slicing flesh and severing bone was a breeze. The self-proclaimed Falkirk fell again, but this time in two parts.

CHAPTER SEVEN

Tur Del Fur

When Hadrian came out of the coach house, rubbing his hands on his pants to get the last of the bacon grease off, he found that Royce had taken the spot on top of the coach. He sat up there like a crow on the peak of a roof, hood up, his cloak fluttering in the rising wind. As Hadrian approached, the thief glanced over but didn't say a word, and Hadrian didn't need to ask. The answer was obvious. If it had been anyone else, Hadrian might have suspected the underlying reason to be compassion, decency, or even straight-up friendship. Since Hadrian had suffered the cold wind and wet snow for hours, it was only fair that he be granted time inside the coach. But this wasn't anyone else — this was Royce — and Hadrian's welfare had nothing to do with the crow being on the roof. He was up there because of Gwen.

Being near Gwen DeLancy had always confused Royce. Watching him was as entertaining as witnessing a drunk trying to navigate a familiar room. There were times when the man seemed to forget his own name. Hadrian knew all too well what that was like. At the age of fifteen, he'd fallen for Arbor, the shoemaker's daughter, and he had been so smitten that he'd nearly killed his best friend. Such feelings were bewildering for anyone. But for Royce, who was already as twisted as a corkscrew, it must be a nightmare. The man rarely drank, for fear it would impair his ability to fend off the multitude of hazards — some real, others imagined — that he believed life constantly thrust at him. This trip must be frustrating beyond reason, so Royce wanted to be alone.

Despite his friend's distress, Hadrian appreciated the chance to ride inside. He hadn't slept much. His clothes were still damp from the snow, and a chill resided deep in his bones. He'd previously determined that if he sat in the cold long enough, the cold felt welcomed to stay. The lack of food contributed. The Hansons had provided eat-as-we-go provisions in the way of nuts, raisins, and such, but that was like wearing a hat in a rainstorm — it helped, but not much, and after a while, not at all. Briar Rose's eggs and bacon had provided the foundation for recovery, but what he really needed was a warm place to sleep. He took the seat vacated by Royce, next to Gwen and across from Albert.

"Well, isn't this nice," Arcadius said. "Royce is heroically giving up his coveted spot to poor Hadrian. What a fine act of gallantry — wouldn't you say so, Gwendolyn?"

She nodded. "If he hadn't, I would have."

Hadrian smiled at her.

"Here, take my blanket." Gwen draped her woolen cover around his shoulders.

Hadrian thanked her, and as the coach rolled out, he slouched down and laid his head against the soft, tufted leather padding that ran all the way up the walls of the interior. The coach resumed its rocking rhythm, which he found soothing. The others talked about the food, the family, and the true chances of Copper becoming a coachman — which started an amiable dispute between the practical-but-inexperienced Albert and an idealistic-but-veteran Gwen. Hadrian never heard how it turned out. He fell sound asleep and remained so, even through the rest of the horse exchanges.

When he awoke, the world had changed.

The interior of the carriage had shifted from not so cold to a little too warm. Hadrian had been damp from snowmelt, but now, buried beneath his layers of wool, he was wet from sweat. Opening his eyes, he saw the coach's windows were open, the drapes thrown wide. Bright sunshine flooded the interior, along with a pleasant breeze that carried the rumor of flowers and a salty ocean.

"But what *exactly* is a republic?" Gwen was asking as the coach continued to rattle and roll along. She spoke in a soft voice as if not to wake him.

"Simply put, it is a political system in which the supreme power lies in a body of citizens who elect — that is, choose by the greatest number of votes — the people to represent them," Arcadius replied just as quietly. The rocking of the coach caused his long beard to sway.

"So, there's no king?" Gwen asked.

The professor shook his head. "Nope — no nobility at all. In the case of Delgos, the government is a bit of a mix. They started as a democracy — that's a type of regime where all the people have an equal say in the rules and laws. But over time, it slipped into a mix of democracy and oligarchy, as most republics tend to do."

Gwen looked out the window as if trying to see this remarkable *republic* firsthand.

"Having everyone vote on everything was a bit of a nightmare, as you might imagine," Arcadius went on. The professor was one of those lucky people who loved his job. His was teaching, and it didn't take much encouragement to get him started. Getting him to stop was the challenge. "Everything was accomplished about as fast as a group of men trying to decide which of them was the smartest. As it turned out, those were the most successful business owners who, by virtue of their wealth and ability to provide others with jobs, convinced the citizenry that the tycoons ought to shoulder the *awful burden* of making decisions on their behalf. In theory, the people still get to vote on who makes the decisions, but in reality, it's always the same three. Not surprisingly, they are the most powerful business owners in the region."

"You make it sound bad," she said. "But I think there's a bit of sense in that approach. More, certainly, than getting to run everything just because you're born to the right family."

Arcadius nodded. "That's true, and I agree that it's a step in the right direction, but as wealth is passed on from father to son, it's not all that terribly different, either."

Gwen thought about this a moment, then asked, "Who are the three?"

Arcadius held up a hand and counted off on his fingers. "The shipping magnate, Ernesta Bray; metal manufacturer, Oscar Tiliner; and of course, the biggest of them all, both figuratively and literally"—and for this he used his thumb—"financier and banker, Cornelius DeLur. Together they are more commonly known as The Triumvirate."

"Ernesta? Is that a woman?"

Arcadius smiled. "Indeed, and she holds an iron grip on just about everything that enters or leaves the country."

Gwen scowled at Albert. "And you thought Copper couldn't be a coachman!"

"Where are we?" Hadrian asked, sitting up to discover his neck ached from the awkward position in which he'd been sleeping.

"The dead has risen!" Albert exclaimed. The viscount's dress coat was off, as was his robe, and his doublet was fully unbuttoned to reveal a white shirt. He was eating nuts from a cloth bag on his lap. "We're in West Echo. We passed the Tiliner Crossroad some time ago. Best estimate, I'd say we're less than five miles out of Tur Del Fur."

Hadrian yawned as he looked out the window at a changed landscape. Almost everything was buff-colored rock and scrub. Behind the coach, a cloud of yellow dust rose. In the distance were jagged mountains of inhospitable stone.

"I thought Tur Del Fur was supposed to be a tropical paradise."

"It is," Albert said.

"Looks more like a desert."

"Most of Delgos is a rocky highland." The professor couldn't help himself. "While there are green valleys and fertile fields, down here near the southern tip things get a bit bleak. But along the coast, where springs irrigate the terraces with hundreds of tiny waterfalls, a marvelous transformation takes place. You'll see."

"I'm sorry if I woke you," Gwen said. While cloak and hood lay stuffed on the seat beside her, Gwen remained trapped in a long-sleeved wool dress. She pumped her collar, trying to stay cool.

"Sorry?" Albert chuckled. "It's about time he opened his eyes. If it wasn't for the snoring, I'd have thought him dead. You slumbered your way through the morning like a real nobleman, my friend." Albert offered up a bag. "Nuts?"

Hadrian shook his head. "Don't suppose there's water?" His mouth felt like how the landscape looked. "Got a bit warmer, it seems."

The coach abruptly slowed to a walk, then without warning, it tilted sharply downward such that the bag of nuts slid off Albert's lap and clapped on the floor.

"Here we go!" the viscount announced, excitedly.

Apparently alarmed, Gwen put one hand on the seat and another on the ceiling. "Here we go where?"

"It's okay," Albert assured her. "It's just that Tur Del Fur is built into the side of sea cliffs. The road snakes through a bunch of switchbacks, and the angle is more suited to pack mules than a coach-and-four. But we'll be fine."

"You've been here?" Gwen asked, still not sounding convinced. "You've done this before?"

"A couple of times . . . in a carriage, as a guest of friends." The words appeared to conjure a memory as Albert then put his chin on the windowsill, took a deep breath, and sighed. "Honestly, I'd live here if I could afford it."

The coach continued at a slower pace than at any previous point in the last two days. Then they came to a complete stop.

"Are we there?" Hadrian asked.

Albert shook his head. Before he could answer, the coach began moving again, making a sharp right turn that caused the wagon to rock, tilting out to one side. Once around the bend, the *Flying Lady* proceeded down the first switchback.

As it did, Hadrian was granted his first clear view of Tur Del Fur. They were high on the side of a cliff descending into a sheltered cove, beyond which was the vast blue of the ocean that ran to the horizon. The cliff was stepped in tiers of lush green vegetation on which were built hundreds of colorfully painted stone and stucco buildings. Palm trees and flowers grew in courtyards, small gardens, and along roads. Far below and at the bottom was the bay that appeared as a pool of aqua blue bordered by white sand beaches, where ships of all shapes and sizes bobbed. The bay was sheltered by two rock promontories, stony arms that reached out and formed a natural breakwater, with a gap that served as a gateway. And upon the two headlands stood a pair of unbelievably tall towers.

The massive pillars looked to be a thousand feet tall. Waves crashed white at their feet, and on top were glittering gold domes. Carved from solid rock, the sides were deeply grooved, forming fins that caused the towers to resemble two massive gears set on their ends. From ports in these fins, smoke spewed as if from teapot spouts that pointed toward the ocean.

"One of those has to be Drumindor," Hadrian said.

"They both are," Albert replied. "It's hard to see at this distance, but there's a thin bridge that extends over the entrance to the bay that connects the two."

Hadrian recalled the Crown Tower. These were taller by no small amount.

"I thought you said the Crown Tower was the tallest structure ever built," Hadrian said to Arcadius.

"I believe I said it's the tallest surviving structure *built by man*," Arcadius replied. "Drumindor is arguably the singularly greatest achievement of the *dwarven* race. Those two columns are all that is left after the whole of an entire mountain was carved away, and with its passing, paradise was born."

More of the ocean breeze blew through the coach, and with it now came music: drums, horns, and strings that created an appealing rhythmic sound that Hadrian had never heard before. The lively, joyful melodies were so very different from the stiff chamber concertos performed in the Gentry Quarter or the jigs and reels played in the northern taverns. This was bright, airy, and emanating from multiple sources at once: different songs but the same sound.

Back and forth the coach meandered toward the bay. They passed shops that sold seashells and items crafted from them. Exquisite carvings of fish and other animals were offered in the window of another. A third appeared to sell nothing but polished stones. There was a shop offering fish teeth, where a set of massive shark jaws framed the entry so that patrons were forced to walk through them to enter the store. The carriage rolled by net shops and sweet-smelling confectionery kitchens selling taffy in the shape of fish. A variety of tailor and seamstress shops went by with clothes on display.

"They have ladies' underwear in the window!" Gwen exclaimed, shocked.

"That's not underwear," Albert said and laughed a little.

"It certainly is. Look at it."

"Believe it or not, that's a dress."

Gwen glanced at him in disbelief. "It's too short and thin, and it's all white—*bright* white."

"Bleached cotton, I believe. They grow it down here. It's very light, very soft. As you can already tell, it gets warm in these parts. Only pathetic visitors like us will be found wearing wool."

Gwen's head tracked as they passed the shop, unable to look away. "It's a dress? It doesn't even have sleeves. A woman in Medford wearing that would be arrested."

"Without a monarchy or much in the way of a formalized church, I think you'll find behavioral conventions to be a great deal more relaxed down here. Just about anything is acceptable, so long as it doesn't interfere with the making of money. This isn't considered a paradise simply because of the weather."

Hadrian was distracted by what looked to be a pair of Ba Ran Ghazel talking to a dwarf and a Calian outside a shop that sold tulan leaves. He leaned out the window, but the coach rolled past. "Are there ghazel here?"

Albert looked in the direction Hadrian had been. "I think those are Urgvarians. That's what I heard people call them in the past."

"I'm pretty sure Urgvarians are a tribe of Ba Ran Ghazel."

Albert shrugged. "Then maybe, I guess. You'll see a few around. Never heard of them causing any trouble. Usually, you can spot them down by the harbor. Most are sailors."

From that point on, Hadrian and Gwen sat like children at the windows, wide-eyed and open-mouthed as a circus of marvels paraded before them.

"That's a brothel!" Gwen announced, pointing at what appeared to be a little palace complete with a stone fountain out front. "It's lovely."

"Is that a tavern?" Hadrian asked as a two-toned, three-story stone building with a terrace and a copper-colored dome rolled by.

"That, my dear sir, is The Blue Parrot," Albert replied. "The best danthum in the city."

"Looks like a cathedral."

"If it were," Albert said dreamily, "I'd be a clergyman."

A group of dark men in white cotton roasted a pig, basting it with what looked to be cups of beer. A roadside pot stirred by a man wielding a huge wooden spoon emitted a strong lemony, garlicky, oniony scent that lingered long after they passed. A barefoot, shirtless blond man played a tin whistle beside a basket into which people dropped coins. Colorful fruit stands were everywhere along with donkeys and chickens that roamed wild through the streets and shops.

At long last, the coach came to a stop, and Hadrian heard the sound of waves.

"We're here, folks!" Shelby declared.

Feeling stiff and drowsy, Hadrian climbed out of the coach and into the hot sun. They were greeted by salt-sea air as they stood at the harbor in the shadow of a great stone sculpture of an old dwarf holding a hammer valiantly aloft. Overhead, seagulls circled and cried, their shadows swirling on the paver stones. On one side of the plaza, colorful boats were tied up to piers. On the other were rows of two- and three-story buildings with brilliant awnings where people sat at tables eating and drinking, laughing and singing.

"This is delightful!" Gwen had both hands crossed over her chest as if to restrain her heart as she looked about.

With Hadrian's help, Heath unloaded the luggage.

"I suppose I ought to check in with Lord Byron," Albert said. "We need to find out where we're staying. That's his office over there." He pointed at some stately buildings near where the larger vessels were docked. "I won't be long, I hope." He took a few steps, then turned back, looking a bit giddy. "Welcome to Tur Del Fur, everyone!"

Hadrian stared, fascinated by the ridiculously blue ocean. He'd seen one before, even ridden on it more than once. Twice, in fact, unless a different one bordered Calis, which it might. He had suffered terrible storms both on its back and along its shore and seen waves the size of mountains and heard them roar. Those were moments he could believe in a god — any god. Yet in all his experience with the ocean, it had never been this blue. And this ocean wasn't all the same shade of blue. Near the stone steps that ran down into the bay from the paved stone plaza where the *Flying Lady* continued to wait for Albert to return, the water was a bit greener. And where the waves lapped between the tied boats, the surface wasn't even that; it reflected the color of the nearby vessels. But the majority of Terlando Bay remained a stunning aqua, especially near the white sand beach, where a great many people sat beneath garishly decorated umbrellas, waded into the surf, or bobbed like fishnet buoys amid the rolling waves. But beyond the breakwater marked by the Drumindor towers, the sea became a cobalt blue so rich in color it didn't seem real. And finally, near the horizon, where the ocean got deep and serious, it turned the more familiar and decidedly angrier slate gray. But that ocean was part of a different world, a cold and colorless one. In that world, the streets smelled of piss and horse manure, and the air was filled with the angry voices of men realizing they had made one too many bad decisions. For now at least, Hadrian was here in this perfect land of music, color, hot sun, and cool breezes. Here, the succulent scents of roasting pork and baking bread wafted out of the many open-air cafés that were close enough that the travelers could hear the clatter of plates and at least one group ordering another bottle of wine.

"I can see why Albert likes it here," Hadrian said, only to discover he was standing alone behind the coach.

Having finished unloading the luggage onto the street, the Hansons were back to work, checking the horses and wheels. Gwen, lured by the lapping water, had slipped off her shoes, hiked the hem of her gown, and was testing the water. Arcadius, who had followed her to the bottom step, watched her progress.

"It's not cold," Gwen reported.

"But not bathwater either, I take it?" the professor suggested.

"It would be . . . refreshing to jump into," she replied with a mischievous grin.

"That's a most judicious answer, my dear, the sort designed to coerce an old man into making a terrible mistake."

Hadrian had lost track of Royce, who had been oddly aloof — even for him. Suffering a bout of uncharacteristic shyness, nervousness, or whatever it was that Gwen had caused was one thing, but disappearing altogether pushed the boundaries even for Royce. After failing to see him anywhere, Hadrian concluded he must have gone off with Albert.

As wonderful as it was to be standing at the tropical waterfront on a gorgeous afternoon just days after leaving the frozen north, being forced to linger under a hot sun in heavy wool was less so. Smelling the food, hearing the laughter and the clink of glasses quickly became a torment. Like a child presented with an unexpected birthday cake but told to wait until the candles were blown out, Hadrian was impatient. He, who might have lived his whole life never dreaming such a place existed, now couldn't tolerate another moment that divided him from the temptations that teased from all directions. He also felt conspicuous when standing beside the coach surrounded by a mountain of luggage. Worse still was that he knew Albert was not known for his haste or reliability.

We might be here for hours while Albert gets fitted for a new suit. Maybe that's why Royce went with him?

"We're all done here, sir," Shelby said. The man looked up and down the street. "Your friends are still not back?"

"They should be soon," Hadrian replied, as he peered down the street. "They've gone to find our host."

Shelby nodded, then looked up at the levels of carved stone buildings that formed the seemingly endless tiers of terraces that defined the bay's cliffs. "I know that seems like a lot of doors and windows up there. Sorta looks like a colony of cliff swallow nests, but there are only so many holes and lots of swallows. Tur fills up this time of year. People come down from up north — those who can afford it and some who can't but expect to find work and make their dreams come true. Are you sure you have a place to stay?"

I certainly hope so, for Albert's sake.

"I'm sure we do. Our host is Lord Byron; he runs the —"

"Delgos Port Authority," Shelby finished for him, nodding knowingly. "I had to deal with him when setting up this route. Turns out, people are considered just as much an import as oil or apples."

"Don't like him?"

"Didn't say that. He's good at what he does. Hard worker, smart fellow. Not certain he has a soul, but no one's perfect."

Hadrian smiled. He liked Shelby and regretted that he and Heath would soon be on their way.

"But you're right. I'm sure Lord Byron will find you a place." He opened the door to the coach, inspected the inside, then closed it. "We have another group we're taking back north, so we can't linger too long. I hope you understand."

"When do you sleep?"

Shelby smiled. "I sleep on the bench when Heath drives."

"I tried that. Didn't work so well."

"I have more practice. Besides, I'll sleep well enough when I'm dead."

"If you keep going non-stop, that might be sooner than you think."

"Now you sound like my son."

Hadrian nearly admitted that Shelby sounded like his father, but that might lead to questions he didn't want to answer right then, not in the dazzling fantasyland of Tur Del Fur. Thoughts like those were best left to the cold gray depths that lay far off on the horizon.

"I did want to thank you for the help back there near Colnora," Shelby said, his voice made a subtle shift to profound sincerity. "In Delgos, they squeeze us. The Port Authority demands a cut of our business in exchange for the privilege of driving over terrible roads they do nothing to maintain. But as irritating as it is to be extorted by Lord Byron, at least the process is orderly and consistent. I know what to do, and if I follow the rules, no one bothers me. Up north, it's different. We only passed through four kingdoms, but we must deal with dozens of petty rulers. Each one is a little tyrant like that sergeant." He shook his head. "Up there we never know what they'll do. I own the staging stables here in Delgos, but up north I can only rent because you can't buy sovereign land. That means they can take it all back whenever they like, along with all my improvements, and without so much as a *sorry, mister.*" Shelby looked at his son as Heath approached. "And they could have made good on that threat of forcing Heath to join their army. Might have, if not for you."

"How did you do that, anyway?" Heath asked, holding the nearly empty feed bag over one shoulder. "I've never seen such a thing before. The sergeant was — well, at least, he *looked* like a professional soldier — and you just took his sword away like he was a toddler. You made it seem so easy."

"He *was* a professional," Hadrian said. Having been taught to not take pride in such things and never boast, Hadrian would normally understate his actions, but he saw the look in Heath's eyes and noticed how the young man rested one hand on the pommel of the new blade at his hip. "That sergeant had every intention of killing me, and not in a nice way."

"There's a nice way?"

Hadrian nodded. "Oh, yeah. There's good and bad to everything, I suspect. In the sergeant's case, he planned on shoving about three feet of sharpened metal through my stomach, or thereabouts. If the point missed my spine, it would come out my back, probably after punching through my kidney. Being an experienced soldier and an absolute bastard, he would twist the blade as he pulled it back out, further carving me up and widening the holes through my muscles, organs, and skin. The bleeding inside and out would be significant, and shock would set in. I'd have immediately collapsed due to a complete loss of muscle control. Breathing would become incredibly painful. Thinking would also be difficult, not just because of the panic caused by knowing I was going to die, but because that sort of trauma messes with your head, causing anxiety, dizziness, and confusion. I'd lose control of my bladder and bowels. But there's a good chance I wouldn't lose consciousness. You see, that's the *not nice* part. I'd lie there, struggling to breathe and suffering the anguish of every inhale, hoping that I'd pass out — or even die — sooner rather than later. But I wouldn't — not for a long while. It varies on how big the puncture is and where exactly the blade went in and what it damaged. Often, it's not as bad as it seems. Odd as it might sound, the intestines will often slide out of the way of a blade, like a bowl of buttered noodles makes way for a finger. So, while I might die in less than a minute if properly skewered, in this case, I'd linger for a lot more than that, probably as much as a whole day. That's a long time to spend in excruciating anguish. And even if a physician managed to sew me up, I'd still die from a horrible fever. That would just take even more time."

Heath stared at him with a grimace.

"I know I told you I was twenty-four, and maybe that seems young, but not all years are equal. I've trained in combat since I was a small child and fought in multiple wars, dozens of battles, and countless conflicts across Avryn and Calis. You learn a few things doing that — a few million things, really. So, sure, just like your father knows exactly how far he can push a horse, I can beat most men in a fight. But even I've been wounded more times than I can recall. Came close to dying more than once. So yes, I made it look easy — it isn't."

Heath took his hand off the sword.

"Aw, crap," Shelby muttered, shaking his head as he drew their attention to four men in bright yellow uniforms striding with purpose toward them. The uniforms appeared militaristic, but the choice of canary yellow with white piping was the opposite of intimidating. They also bore no weapons. If not for Shelby's reaction, Hadrian might have thought they were street entertainers: musicians, jugglers, or acrobats. "And here I was just saying how much better it is in Delgos."

The lead man addressed them while still a few steps away. "I'm Officer Hildebrandt of the Port Authority Security. How are you today, gentlemen?"

"We're fine," Shelby said. "At least we were."

"Relax, Mister Hanson, I'm not here to bother you. I just saw the coach and thought it would be considerate to provide you with some news that will be affecting your exit from our fine city." The other men spread out behind Hildebrandt. They did not circle, merely formed an impressive line to either side, each standing with precision — straight and dignified.

"And what might that be?"

"There was a murder up in West Echo about a week ago, near the Tiliner cutoff. A courier was killed, his pouch taken. We have strong evidence that the killer took refuge in Tur Del Fur. It is our job to bring the murderer to justice and recover the lost package. As a result, we are inspecting every vehicle and vessel leaving this city to make certain the fugitive is not aboard. Your coach will, therefore, be stopped and searched before being allowed to leave. I am familiar with your business, and you and your son are held in high regard by the DPAA. We regret this inconvenience and hope you understand the need. I am informing you up front so that you can explain to your passengers in advance and avoid misunderstandings."

"And also to ensure we don't pick up any last-minute strangers?"

"That, too." He nodded politely to each of them. "Good day to you and yours," he said, then the four marched on.

"Who was that?" Hadrian asked as he watched them go.

"The Delgos Port Authority Association has a small security force that patrols the city. They are sort of like the king's guard up north, but their primary job is to oversee customs, enforce duties on goods going in or out, and stop the importing of contraband. It's a game they play with the pirates. Most people around here call them *Yellow Jackets.*"

Hadrian nodded. "I can see why."

"Never had them talk to me before. It's a little disturbing that they know my name."

"We're all set!" Albert called out as he strode triumphantly across the plaza, sending a gathering of seabirds into flight. He had his jacket slung over one arm and a little paper held aloft in the other. It caught the sun and shone bright white.

The viscount was alone. Once more, Hadrian scanned the plaza, terraces, and the street for signs of Royce, but found none.

"You met with Lord Byron?" Hadrian asked.

"No, one of his secretaries. A man named Tolly, but he was expecting us. He set up a meeting for me with Byron the day after tomorrow. But the important thing is that we have a place to stay. Sounds nice, too. He reserved a traditional rolkin for us."

"What's that?"

Albert pointed up at the multitude of whitewashed, blue-domed stone buildings that dominated the cliffside. "Rolkins are traditional dwarven homes carved right out of the natural volcanic rock of the cliff. They're very fun and quirky — loads of character. Everyone who comes here tries to get one. You'll love it."

Albert tapped the little paper to his lips and stared up at the labyrinth of buildings that appeared to be built one atop the other. He frowned. "Hmm. Tolly said the place was called the Turquoise Turtle and was located on Pebble Way just off the Fourth South Sea View Terrace, only . . ."

"You have no idea where that is, do you?"

Albert pursed his lips and shook his head. "I've only been here twice, and while I have done my fair share of wandering the streets, I was almost always drunk at the time, so my memory is a little fuzzy."

"These in front of you are the South Sea View Terraces," Shelby said. "Just need to count up four levels." He pointed at a set of bright-blue-framed windows and a bit of greenery.

"Wonderful!" Albert grinned.

"You folks have a nice time. We'll be back this way every two weeks, I suspect. If you need us, keep an eye out. We always stop here at the statue of Andvari Berling, usually around midday." He pointed at the stone statue of the dwarf.

Then Shelby and Heath said their goodbyes before climbing back aboard the *Flying Lady*, and they all waved as the coach-and-four moved off at an uncharacteristically slow plod.

Albert once more raised the little paper high and declared, "Let us sally forth in pursuit of the Turquoise Turtle!"

Hadrian grabbed up his pack and slipped it over his shoulder. "Didn't Royce go with you?"

"No." Albert looked around. "Isn't he here?"

Hadrian shook his head.

"You two go on and find this palace," Arcadius said. His shoes were off, and he was standing on the first water-covered step, the swells riding up to his ankles. "I'm too old to be wandering about in the hot sun. Gwen and I will stay here. We'll wait for Royce and keep a watch on the luggage while we continue to swim in these lovely waters."

"Swim?"

Arcadius frowned and shook his head. "This is as close to swimming as I get."

"Careful you don't drown," Hadrian said.

Gwen, who had given up on saving her gown, was waist deep. "Where's Royce?"

"Oh, I'm sure he's about somewhere," Hadrian said. "He tends to like to explore a bit. He can't relax until he gets a solid feel for a place."

She nodded but looked worried.

"If he's not back before I am, I'll find him," Hadrian said.

Gwen looked up, appearing thankful but a bit embarrassed. "I just don't want — I mean, how else will he know where we're staying?"

"Trust me, Royce can find us. But don't worry. I'll be sure to drag him out of the arms of whatever woman he's seducing."

Gwen scowled at him. "I wasn't thinking that."

"Not even a little?"

Gwen splashed water at him.

As Hadrian and Albert approached a switchback, they looked inside the Drunken Sailor, a public house composed of only three walls and designed to look like an old ship. The bar had a killer view — at least for the bartenders. All the patrons sat with their backs to the bay. Above their heads was a rough painted sign that read JOIN THE CREW! Hadrian most certainly wanted to do so as he stared at the drinks on the tables and the men lounging in hammocks strung between mini-masts. Albert looked to be of a similar mind as he licked his lips, staring as if a striptease were being performed.

Despite the temptation, they both weathered the turn and followed a small street that sloped steeply uphill. This dead-ended at a set of narrow steps that continued to zigzag upward. The stairs were bordered on both sides by white walls that had rounded edges, making them appear more like bleached-white, hand-formed clay than stone. Along the way, they passed vividly painted gates of lemon yellow and tangerine orange, but the most common color was cobalt blue, which matched the little domes that crowned many of the rolkins.

Albert paused to breathe. "I'm starting to think I have overpacked." He wiped sweat from his face with a grimace. "I am absolutely paying someone to carry my trunks up here."

They reached a modest terrace that overlooked the bay and sported two olive trees growing in planters. Between the trees, an unusually small man slouched with his legs extended on a stone bench. He wore a wide-brimmed straw hat with a blue feather in the band, a loose white cotton shirt over sunbaked skin, and sandals on surprisingly large feet. He had a snow-white beard even longer than the professor's. On his lap, and spilling down the bench onto the pavement, was a rope net that he worked on.

"Morning," he said.

"Is it still morning?" Albert managed to sigh in between gasps of air. He looked about miserably. There was another gate, two more down a new street, and more stairs. He frowned at Hadrian. "This may be hopeless. There are no signs. I haven't a clue which way to go."

"Looking for something?" the little man asked.

"Yes," Albert replied. "At the risk of sounding insane, we're searching for a turquoise turtle."

With a minimal amount of effort, as if moving too much was unwise, the man pointed across the terrace at the little road. "That's Pebble Way. You'll find your turtle up there."

Albert brightened. "Thank you! Thank you very much!"

"Lord Byron send you?" The small man in the straw hat had abandoned his net and followed them.

"He did indeed," Albert replied.

"Can I see the card?"

Albert looked confused despite still holding the bit of paper in his fist. "Do you work for Lord Byron?"

Though Hadrian found it was difficult to see under the beard, he was certain the man smiled. "He's a customer." Seeing a lack of understanding, the man added, "I own the Turtle, as well as a few others. I rent them to visitors like yourselves — at least I presume you're turists. Lord Byron reserved the Turtle for some folks coming down from up north on the Hanson Coach. Since it just left, I suspect you might be part of that group. Now, I won't know that for sure until I see Lord Byron's seal on that card you're waving around."

"Oh! Of course. Excuse me." Albert handed over the paper.

The man studied it for a moment. As he did, Hadrian concluded the fellow in the straw hat was not a short man at all, but a member of the dwarven race.

The dwarf handed the letter back to Albert. "Welcome to the Turtle, gentlemen. My name is Auberon. Allow me to show you around."

After searching the streets and alleyways of Tur Del Fur, Royce had found nothing.

Riding on the roof of the coach, he had been able to make certain no stowaways clung to it. The moment they stopped, he began a quick survey of the plaza, then a fast sweep of the streets. No one appeared to be watching — at least no pale, red-haired fellows.

Maybe I should have kept the head.

The idea had crossed his mind more than once on the trip down. On each occasion, he scolded himself for paranoia that exceeded even his own exorbitant standards.

I removed the man's head. I left it a foot and a half away from his body. The man is dead.

Royce understood this. Facts were easy to accept — most of them, at least.

But where was the blood?

He *had* severed the head, but it hadn't produced a single drop. This, too, was a fact — one not so easily dismissed.

Shouldn't matter. We covered many miles at high speed, and if Mister de Roche missed his ride — even if he isn't dead, which is impossible — it will take him days to reach Tur Del Fur, even if he knew that's where we were headed. And how hard is it for a headless man to travel?

Pretty hard, I suspect.

He's dead.

Right.

Satisfied — or as best Royce could ever be — he returned to where he'd left the coach to find it gone and a problem brewing.

Hadrian and Albert were missing, but Gwen, Arcadius, and the luggage were still there. So were two men. Big, brutish thugs with necks equal to the width of their heads. They were laughing at Gwen, who looked to have been thrown into the bay. She stood before them, struggling to wring the water out of her dress, which clung embarrassingly to her body. As he approached, Royce noted that neither man wore visible weapons. He also took into consideration the number of witnesses on the waterfront — *hundreds*. People of all sorts walked by or sat at tables with nothing to do but sip drinks and watch what happened in the street.

If it had only been one man, Royce might be able to make it look like the guy fell, maybe passed out from drinking and then . . . just happened to . . . roll into the bay . . . and drown. It would be a hard sell, but with two, he didn't have a chance. Whichever one he didn't knife would start hollering to the audience. While it was possible the crowd might applaud, Royce doubted it. Some art was too sophisticated for the common spectator. The smart thing would be to wait, follow the bastards, and when they made the mistake of walking somewhere reasonably isolated, Royce would bury them. Except . . .

Gwen had her head down, hair a tangled mess. She was dripping wet, her slight frame shook, shoulders rocking as she cried. The situation was obvious. The two brutes had been drinking at one of the cafés, saw the chests and bags and no one guarding them except an old man and a woman. They came over to take what they wanted, but they didn't expect Gwen. She fought back — of course she did. Most likely the scene of two big ogres robbing a beautiful woman didn't play well before the crowd, either. So, one or both turned it into a comedy by throwing her in the water. This would have set the crowd at ease.

"Oh, see that, they're just playing, and it's funny. She's a Calian — so that's okay."

Now the ogres were laughing at her; maybe the crowd had done so as well — all of them guffawing at Gwen's embarrassment, at her humiliation.

Royce's fingers squeezed Alverstone's handle so tightly they hurt. Maybe the crowd should be exposed to a higher form of entertainment.

This is going to be very bad.

"Are you her father?" one asked Arcadius. "Or a customer?" Which made the two thugs laugh even harder.

It's always the same two. Why is that?

The idea flashed through Royce's mind as he closed the remaining distance between him and his prey, moving on the pads of his feet.

Royce had repeatedly encountered these two guys his whole life. Big, lumbering idiots who, for no reason Royce could account for, felt they owned the world. Never kings or princes, these trolls always walked around with the idea rattling in their otherwise empty heads that other people needed to do whatever they — the trolls — wanted. Somehow it seemed that these oversized brutes failed to grasp the absurdity of the idea because they felt the need to prove it over and over. Not once did the rabid dogs appear surprised to learn that the rest of the world's population hadn't heard of their dominion. They showed an eagerness — no, a joy — in explaining their Right to Rule. It didn't matter if it was a small child, an old man, or a woman, they loved enlightening the universe.

Royce came up from behind the largest and whispered, "He's neither."

Future Corpse Number One jumped and spun. "Who are you?"

"Local exterminator," Royce replied. He held Alverstone just inside the fall of his cloak.

The man noticed Royce's hidden hand, and his face changed from jovial to concerned.

Concerned but not terrified — not yet. Still thinks he owns the world.

"Royce!" Gwen shouted.

He didn't waiver, didn't take his eyes off the two trolls.

Neck or heart? Ah yes, the age-old question. I could pretend to give him a big old hug like we were long-lost friends and then plant Alverstone in his back. It would have to be the back of his neck; anywhere lower and all I'd likely get is the lungs. He'd live way too long. And the bastard's too big, and it's too much to ask that he bends down. If they really were old friends that might work, but Mister Talking Cadaver and I — we just don't have the time.

"Royce, don't!"

He frowned. *She's giving away the punchline, ruining the surprise. The audience won't like it — they love sudden unexpected twists, and I've got a great one.*

Maybe it was the sound of her voice, or what Royce imagined was the look on her face — he couldn't tell because he kept his sight locked on his target, but The Talking Dead finally caught wind of the danger. Might also have been that eerie intuition people often exhibited.

If you stare at the back of someone's head, they always seem to turn around.

Most people, even the trolls of the world, had a special sense that alerted them to the presence of impending death. They felt it and responded in the same way. The ogre pulled back, eyes widening.

"Royce! They just asked to help with the luggage. This is Pete and Jake. They're nice people."

"Yeahthat'sright," the brute spewed so fast that it came out as a single word.

Royce still refused to take his eyes off the pair. He took a step closer and carefully enunciated his next words, slowly and precisely. "Explain . . . *help with the luggage.*" Royce did this not only to lower the chance of a misunderstanding but also to reveal how high the stakes were.

"I, ah . . . I mean, we were offering to —" Troll Number One pointed. "She was just standing here with all this stuff and looked like she could use some help. That's all. Jake and I — we just thought we'd — you know — lend a hand carrying this to wherever she was going." His eyes glanced back at where Royce's hand was still hidden. "That's all."

Royce allowed himself a glance toward Gwen. She looked terrified, but not of them. And there was no evidence of tears. No red or puffy eyes, no glistening tracks on her cheeks. "Why are you all wet?"

"I was hot. I went wading," She gestured at the stairs behind her. "The steps below the water are slippery." She made a regretful grimace and held up her dripping hair. "I fell."

"She made a lovely splash, she did," Arcadius declared.

"I thought you were crying."

"No! No, I wasn't." She shook her head, slinging water. "I was laughing." She pointed at Potentially Pardoned Pete. "He asked if I was married or if I had a man in my life. I told him I had *too many.*"

"So that's why he called you a whore?"

"I did not! I would never say such a thing." Prematurely Pardoned Pete was quick to say. "I *explained* how that sort of statement *might* be misunderstood. And that someone — not me — might *accidentally* take her meaning to be that she was a . . . you know . . . a . . ."

"A whore," Royce said, his eyes hard.

"And then . . ." Gwen smiled. "That's when I said . . . Not this week!" She waited, watching him. Then she shrugged. "I thought it was funny."

Jake laid a hand on Pete's shoulder. "I think maybe it would be best if we go have another drink, eh, Pete?" His voice was a work of labor as he tried to make it all sound casual.

Pete appeared to think this was a wonderful idea. He backed away and offered an infinitely polite wave to Gwen and Arcadius. Then the two retreated toward the cafés at not quite a run.

Gwen lowered her head and looked at the pavement. "I guess it wasn't that funny." She sounded hurt.

"I thought it was a delightful joke," Arcadius told her with a happy tone, as if oblivious to existence itself.

Royce stared at her and felt the sudden need to explain. "I just thought that, well . . ."

"I know what you thought." Gwen looked incredibly sad, and she turned away as if now she really might cry.

Royce didn't know what to do. He felt both helpless and confused — two things he desperately hated. Not understanding what was happening was bad enough, but he sensed things were moving too fast in a direction he didn't want them to.

"Hey, everyone!" Hadrian came bounding up with a brilliant smile. "Wait until you see where we're staying."

Royce glared at him. He wasn't in the mood for Mister Happy Sunshine. Then he spotted the nasty-looking red welt above Hadrian's eyes. "Has someone attacked you, too?"

"No one attacked me!" Gwen stated firmly, then followed the declaration with an exasperated huff.

Hadrian put a hand to his forehead. "Oh — no." He laughed. "We're staying in a rolkin — that's the name of a dwarven-style house — and the ceilings, beams, and tops of doorways are . . . well, low."

No one said anything for an awkward moment.

Hadrian looked at Royce then at Gwen, and his eyes grew concerned. He opened his mouth to speak, but Gwen replied in advance with a stern shake of her head that caused more droplets of bay water to fly.

"Ohh-kay," Hadrian said, then turned to ponder Gwen's bags and Albert's ship's-captain-style chests, one with brass handles and the other with iron. Each was covered in overstuffed sacks. Then he looked toward the cafés. "You think if I ask real nicely, I might persuade a couple of guys to help us carry these up?"

In unison, Gwen, Arcadius, and Royce answered, "No!"

CHAPTER EIGHT

The Blue Parrot

"This is stunning." Gwen walked through the rooms of the rolkin with her mouth open, her head turning from side to side, taking it all in. Her face was filled with an expression Hadrian could only describe as glee. They all looked that way to one degree or another, like kids discovering a secret place that would be used as their new hangout. "Because it's a hole in a cliff, I expected . . . well, I didn't expect this."

With walls of pure white, no sharp corners, and few straight lines, the place looked to have been formed from pristine snow crafted by gloved hands. Ceilings were arched into mini-domes, walls curved into circles, each edge smoothed. Light poured in through large, glassless windows, illuminating every corner. Cut deep into the cliff, the rolkin's ancient stone and ocean breeze kept the interior cool and smelling fresh. Built-in seats and shelves were carved out of the cliff. Tables rose out of the floor, with bowls built into them. Oil sconces, planters, coat hooks, and stools were all chiseled from the native stone. Additional furnishings were not simply placed within rooms — they decorated the spaces. Calian carpets of exquisite design accentuated polished floors. Petrified wood stumps supported green and black onyx sculptures of fish and dolphins. A tree planted in the common room grew up through the ceiling, its trunk appearing like a wooden chimney. A broad-leafed jungo plant spread out from a massive hand-beaten copper urn. And a huge clay pot that appeared to serve no purpose, except to look beautiful, stood to one side. In an obvious contrast to the stone was an overabundance of softness. Thick cushions and numerous brightly dyed pillows formed delightful sitting spaces.

And all of it was in miniature.

Royce and Gwen had no problem at all, but Hadrian ducked when passing through any doorway and often felt his hair brush the ceiling when he stood up straight.

"For once, I'm grateful for my age-imposed hunched back," Arcadius said as he moved about the rolkin. "Hadrian has clearly learned, but you need to be wary, Albert. This place is a death trap for the tall."

"I think it's cozy," Albert replied. He had already changed into a loose-fitting cotton tunic and was swimming barefoot in the fluffy cushions of the main room's oversized bench that was practically a bed. "And these big chairs are so nice." He hugged a bright yellow pillow to his face. "Why is it that up north we insist on hard wood, and the closest we ever get to comfort is lining a chair's seat with cane?"

"Because of the church, lad," Arcadius said, eyeing a stone chair laden with cushions. "Too much comfort means a closer relation to the body and a more distant one from the spirit. Misery makes all of mankind better people." He took the plunge and collapsed into the all-consuming pillow-chair that hissed as air escaped the cushions. Joining with the pillow's song, Arcadius sighed contentedly. "I fear that I'm doomed to wickedness."

Hadrian stood in the middle of the central common room, running through a mental checklist of things he wanted to tell everyone. Auberon had taken him on a lengthy tour of the home, pointing out all the amenities, quirks, and features. The dwarf had also made a point of touching a small recurring symbol painted in turquoise on the wall of every room: three thick vertical lines, the center one taller than those on either side, each topped with a little circle. It didn't look at all like a turtle, and though Hadrian inquired about many things he saw, he never asked about that. Something in the way the dwarf looked when he touched the lines suggested a profound and personal reverence that Hadrian didn't feel right inserting himself into.

"There's a well in the courtyard," Hadrian explained as he stood in the center of the common room while Gwen explored. "Also, that courtyard is our private garden and includes four trees: a mango, an avocado, a lemon, and a papaya. We can help ourselves to the fruit, but the mango isn't producing right now."

"You can see the ocean from the balcony up here," Gwen announced, her voice bouncing down to them from the upper story. "It's a great view of the bay. All the ships look so small."

"There are pots, pans, a big kettle, and plenty of wood," Hadrian continued. "A merchant keeps the woodpile stocked, but we have to pay for what we use."

"I'll just add that to Lord Byron's bill," Albert said.

"There's a hearth and stone oven inside and another set in the courtyard. But Auberon suggests we use the outside one unless it's raining or gets windy because otherwise the fire will make the house too hot. Also"— he looked at Royce — "there are no locks on any of the doors."

Royce nodded. "With no glass and simple shutters on windows that are big enough to ride a horse through, I can't see why there would be."

"There's an amazing fish mounted on the wall in one of the bedrooms!" Gwen called down.

"Auberon is a fisherman," Hadrian explained. "You'll see lots of that kind of stuff."

"Who is this Auberon you keep talking about?" Royce asked.

"The owner and, I think, possibly the builder of this place. He's a dwarf and will be coming by to take care of the plants and trees, and answer any questions, so don't be alarmed if you see him in the courtyard."

Royce, who had looked miserable since arriving, closed his eyes and shook his head.

"He's a nice guy. Owns one of those fishing boats docked in the bay. Very easygoing. Just being around him, you feel more relaxed. Talking to him is like gazing out at the ocean. You'll see."

Royce stared at Hadrian as if he were insane. "And you're sure his name is Auberon and not Gravis?"

"Yes, Royce, I might be making a massive assumption here, but I think there may be more than one dwarf in all of Tur Del Fur."

"You didn't tell him why we're here, did you?"

Hadrian frowned.

"What?" Royce said. "There was a time when you would."

"And there was a time when *you* would have already killed half a dozen people."

Royce looked abruptly stern and made a sudden slashing motion across his neck as Gwen reappeared, descending the curving steps.

"There are four bedrooms upstairs," Gwen said. "May I have one, or I suppose I could sleep down here if—"

"Yes, take whichever you like," Royce said louder than necessary. "Take that one with the balcony view. You seem to like it."

"I don't need the—"

Royce walked out.

The others watched him move with that disturbing quickness that caused his cloak to fly behind him, as if struggling to keep up. Everyone stared at the empty doorway for a moment, then they looked at each other, mystified.

"What was that?" Albert asked, rolling to his side and peering out the door.

No one answered for a short time. Then, still engulfed in the chair, Arcadius said, "There was a minor incident at the shore."

"Minor?" Albert asked. He looked back out at the courtyard, then rotated, placed his feet on the floor, and stood up. "How many are dead?"

"Please excuse me," Gwen said. "I think I'll settle into my room. I need to change my dress. This one is wet." Then she, too, disappeared.

Hadrian found Royce still in the courtyard, seated at the small table in the shade of the mango tree. "What's going on?"

"What do you mean?" Royce was drawing invisible pictures on the surface of the table with his fingertips.

"Well . . ." Hadrian pulled a chair out and sat down. "It's warm enough to go swimming, and you're sitting here wrapped in thick wool with your hood up. Add to that the fact you just walked out on Gwen in mid-sentence. These things make me think something's not right. Is it because . . . you know — did you talk to her? Did you tell her how you feel?"

Royce shook his head. "Haven't gotten a chance. I think she hates me."

"Hates you? What happened to that whole sleeping-with-her-head-on-your-shoulder incident?"

Royce slapped his palms on the table. "How should I know?"

"Arcadius said there was an *incident* down at the shore. Care to share?"

"There wasn't. Nothing happened." Royce sat back far enough that Hadrian could see under the hood. His friend looked angry, which wasn't all that unusual, but there was a hint of frustration in his eyes.

Staring at him and thinking it over, Hadrian realized that wasn't altogether strange, either. Still . . . "Something must have."

Royce's fascination with the little stone table continued as he rubbed the top with his thumb. It left a damp mark on the polished surface.

Royce is sweating? That's new.

"You remember Bull Neck and Orange Tunic?" Royce asked.

"You mean Brook and Clem from Dulgath?"

"They had names?"

"Think so. Their mother would have to be awfully careless to forget that."

Royce nodded. "They were just down at the shore. Only it turned out it wasn't them."

Hadrian was puzzled, but only for a moment. Not so long ago, Hadrian would have had no idea what Royce was talking about, and it both fascinated and slightly bothered him to discover he was able to work out exactly what his friend was saying. The sensation reminded Hadrian of when he first started to pick up the Tenkin language. He'd learned a word here, a phrase there, and then one day he found himself *thinking* in Tenkin. He felt the same excitement now — the realization that he had achieved a new level of understanding — but also, he had to wonder if he had had to sacrifice something in the process.

Royce pulled back his hood a bit and looked at the door to the rolkin. Arcadius and Albert were discussing something Hadrian couldn't hear, but he assumed Royce could. "I did absolutely nothing — nothing at all, but she got so upset." He sighed. "She was scared — scared of . . . me." Royce raised his hands in exasperation. "I don't know what I'm doing. This whole thing . . . it's . . . it's not going to work. She's"— at a loss for the right words, Royce opted to fold his arms in a violent manner — "well, you know." He took a breath and let it out slowly. "And I'm . . . well . . . *me*. Aren't I?"

"Yeah." Hadrian nodded again, this time wetting his lower lip. "I can't think of much worse than being you. That's tough, pal."

"It's worse than that," Royce said, completely ignoring Hadrian's joke. Or maybe he hadn't heard, or perhaps Royce didn't understand Hadrian was joking. "Gwen and I . . ." He shook his head and let out another loathing sigh. "It's not possible. I can see that now. Don't know what I was thinking. Clearly, I wasn't — I was listening to you, which should have been a huge warning right there." Royce pointed to an engraving of a marlin cut into the stone of the wall near the fountain. "We're from different worlds. She's like that beautiful fish there, and I'm a bird."

Hadrian nodded. "A vulture, I suppose."

Royce glared.

"Sorry."

"My point is, I don't belong with her."

"Really?"

The hood nodded.

"Well, maybe you're right." Hadrian pushed back in his chair. Somewhere overhead a bird was singing — several, in fact. Tur was filled with songbirds. The sun was shining. He and Royce were gathered in the shade of a fruit-laden tree as a cool breeze blew by, and Royce was as happy as a man forced to witness paradise without being able to enter. "But, let me ask you something . . . who does?"

"Who does what?"

"Who belongs with *her?* Do you think Brook or Clem ought to marry her?"

Royce stared at him like a tiger trapped in a cage while Hadrian used a metal pole to ring the bars.

Hadrian continued, "How about one of the nobles back in Medford? Maybe Baron Rendon or Sir Sinclair? They'd be a good choice, right? They have nice homes and lots of money. They could take her to fancy galas and such."

"She doesn't like them. They're clients. That's it." His voice was low and dangerous.

Hadrian was sliding on river ice but hoped his newfound fluency in Royce-speak would help him safely reach the far bank. "Okay, but how about Dixon? She likes him, right? What if he asked her to marry him? What if she said yes because the one she really wanted never said anything."

"Are you trying to tell me something?"

Hadrian rolled his eyes. "Obviously!"

"Did Dixon ask Gwen to —"

"Oh, for Maribor's sake! Honestly!" Hadrian ran both hands through his hair. While he might have made great strides in understanding his partner, Royce had regressed. "How can you be so perceptive and intelligent about most things, but so dim-witted about this? You're like a man unable to find the sun because that bright light in the sky is blinding him. My point is, you're being an idiot. Gwen's in love with you, and you're in love with her, and the only thing in the way is that neither of you feels worthy of the other. It would be hilarious if it wasn't so tragic. Worst part is how much the two of you truly need each —"

The hood jerked up as Gwen came out into the yard. "Don't mean to interrupt, but I was thinking that if we could get some food, I could cook it. I'm no chef, but after hearing the tales of Hadrian's campfire cookouts, I'm going to assume —"

"Absolutely not!" Albert shouted from inside. "No cooking! Tonight, we eat out. My treat — that is to say, I'll charge Lord Byron. This is our first evening in Tur, and we deserve the best. So, it is The Blue Parrot for us. I will spare no expense."

"Fine." Gwen lingered a moment. She looked at Royce as if on the verge of tears, then she turned around and went back inside.

"I think she might have heard us," Royce said.

Hadrian clapped the table between them. "Tell her, Royce! This stopped being funny a long time ago."

The Blue Parrot was the two-toned, three-story, stone building with the terrace and shiny copper-colored dome that they had passed on their way in. It actually had five domes, as there were four little towers, each capped with their own mini-domes, but those were tiled, not metal.

"*This* is a tavern?" Hadrian asked as the five of them rolled up in a pair of little donkey-drawn carriages that frequented the streets. The Parrot wasn't more than a mile and a half away, but Albert had arranged transportation as if they were royalty.

"Technically, it's a danthum," Albert said.

"But that's like a tavern, right?"

"I would consider them distant cousins. One could make the argument that Roy the Sewer and I are both human beings — and there are more than a few passing similarities to support this — but I would hope you wouldn't think we are the same."

The carriages only comfortably seated two. Gwen and Arcadius rode in one, but Hadrian, Royce, and Albert squeezed into the other. The fact that Royce chose to wedge himself into *the boys'* carriage rather than sit with Gwen was noticed by all.

The Blue Parrot's popularity was made obvious by the crowd waiting to get in and the line of carriages dropping off passengers. The gathering was a remarkably varied group, and Hadrian saw just as many ladies as men. There were plenty of fops, peacocks, and popinjays: men and women in huge hats, finely embroidered robes, and shiny leather boots, all too heavy to be comfortable. Others wore more relaxed attire, making do with simple, light tunics and sandals. Some brought their dogs; there were also a few cats, and Hadrian even spotted a pig on a leash, sporting a blue bonnet. But the most peculiar surprise was the variety of nations. Refined Avryn nobles stood shoulder to shoulder with rustic Calians, and men dressed in the frocks of the clergy waited alongside a group of Urgvarian sailors.

"What's everyone waiting for?" Gwen asked as the carriages abandoned them and promptly *clip-clopped* away. So many carriages, carts, and wagons created a nonstop clatter in the background.

"It's not open," Albert explained as he adjusted his doublet and checked the alignment of the buttons. That evening, Albert had insisted they all dress up. After washing at the courtyard fountain, he had changed into his *viscount* clothes, donning his black-velvet and silver-brocade doublet. He chose not to wear the usual overtunic, and in a breezy, carefree manner, he left the top buttons of the doublet and white shirt undone.

Arcadius had complied by throwing on a different but identical robe, the only difference being that the new one was made of linen instead of wool. Hadrian didn't have anything else to wear except a second shirt, which he changed into, leaving his leather jerkin behind. Albert explained that long blades were not allowed in the Parrot, so he left those, too.

Gwen put them all to shame. She disappeared upstairs and reemerged in a stunning off-the-shoulder white linen gown that wrapped her body with the intimacy of a silk cocoon. Her hair was brushed back with its normal luster, and she had rings dangling from her ears and bracelets on her wrists. Her lips were colored a pale red and her eyes painted dark, like smoke from a smoldering fire.

Royce, not surprisingly, ignored Albert's demands, remaining in his usual funeral-colored wool.

"Not open?" Gwen stared up at the marvelous edifice, disappointed. "Well, I can still cook. I'm sure not all of the markets are closed."

"Not to worry," Albert assured her. "Unlike the taverns and brothels in Avryn, many of the finer establishments are open for only a set number of hours each evening. This allows workers to rest, clean up, restock, and generally prepare for the next night's festivities."

Gwen looked up at the sky. The sun was well on its way to setting, creating a stunning spectacle of orange, pink, and gold over the bay. "Evening is almost over."

"Not down here it's not. In truth, it's just about to start."

The doors opened and the crowd cheered.

"We need to hurry if we're going to get a good seat." Albert pushed them forward into the fray.

The interior of the Parrot was as remarkable as the patrons. The place was the size of a small cathedral. The central room — with its three-story domed ceiling, fresco-decorated walls, twinkling lantern chandeliers, and towering stone pillars — only *housed* the extravagance. Within this grand chamber, a massive sculpture of an elephant, which was three times the size of those Hadrian was familiar with, stood to one side of a grand wooden stage. On the other end was an equally large gorilla, its arms raised as if holding up the ceiling. Part of the left wall had living fish swimming behind glass, and everywhere there were potted plants and full-sized trees, giving the interior a *jungle* feel.

"Parrots!" Gwen exclaimed, pointing up at a dozen beautiful green birds flying under the dome from tree to tree, startled at the flood of people pouring in.

"Over here!" Albert waved them toward a round wooden table. All the tables closer to the stage had already filled up, but the one the viscount had selected was only two rows back. "Five chairs. Perfect!"

The room roared with the conversations of hundreds as it rapidly filled.

"This is so exciting!" Gwen said, a great smile on her face, her eyes darting from one delight to the next.

"It's insane." Royce glowered. He, too, looked around but showed none of Gwen's amusement. Instead, he glared at every face that came nearby and even scowled at the parrots. "This is a madhouse."

"Trust me," Albert told him. "It only gets worse."

"Then why are we here?"

"Because in Tur Del Fur, *worse* is *wonderful*."

A small army of blue-jacketed servants dispersed from side doors into the sea of patrons. They moved from table to table, taking drink orders while somewhere unseen a band began to play. Strings, drums, and pipes joined to create a wave of sound richer and more powerful than anything Hadrian had ever heard. And it was lively to the point of decadence with a booming rhythm.

Albert leaned over to Hadrian. "So, yes — to answer your question, it's *like* a tavern."

"Good evening, gentlemen and lady," a blue-jacketed servant greeted them, shouting over the music. "My name is Atyn. I'll be your waiter. Allow me to welcome you to The Blue Parrot."

It took Hadrian a moment to realize that their waiter wasn't a man. His tapering ears, high cheekbones, and angled eyebrows proclaimed his heritage from afar, but Hadrian was so unaccustomed to seeing an elf in any establishment — much less employed by one — made his mind second-guessed his eyes.

"Is this your first time with us?" Atyn asked. He was looking right at Hadrian, who realized he had been staring.

"These three are novices to the city," Albert gestured to Hadrian, Royce, and Gwen, then he looked at Arcadius.

The professor shook his head. "Not my first time within these walls, but when I was last here . . ." He thought a moment. "I believe this was a municipal building."

The waiter looked stunned. "That would have been even before *my* time, and I have been here a good long while."

Arcadius smiled. "Sorry to admit that I'm just about as old as I look."

"A few things have changed," Atyn said with a perfectly expressionless face that made the professor smile. "Now, for those who have never been here, or haven't visited *this* century, please allow me to explain that The Blue Parrot is the finest danthum in the city, and tonight you will have the experience of a lifetime. The shows will begin soon, and when they do, it will get loud, so if you plan to eat — which I strongly advise, as we have delicacies unmatched anywhere in the world — you might consider deciding what you want to order while I can still hear you."

Hadrian, who had determined that the musicians were hidden in a pit just before the stage, was already forced to lean across the table to hear, and he wondered how much louder it could possibly get.

"Tonight," Atyn proclaimed with a flourish of his hand, "we are offering our *spectacular* flaming peacock."

"Oh, by Mar!" Albert reacted with physical delight. "We *must* have at least one of those!" He looked as if the very idea had sent him into a fit of ecstasy. "You have no idea."

"Also this evening," Atyn continued, "we offer roasted swan, complete with head and neck — tucked under the *left* wing, of course. We also have our popular Treasures of the Ocean, and for dessert, frozen blueberry and custard magpies."

"Magpies?" Gwen wrinkled her nose.

"That's just what we call them because they're served in a bowl that's been carved and painted to resemble the bird."

"Frozen?" Hadrian asked.

"Indeed!" the waiter said. "Barges of winter lake ice are packed in straw and sailed down the coast to fill our storehouse and provide you with such unmatched delicacies. We also have a special tonight, our legendary Flame Broiled Sea Monster."

"What, may I ask, is that?" Arcadius inquired.

"Grilled octopus," Atyn explained with a grin. "The tentacled beast is caught fresh daily, hung out to dry in the sun, and then grilled on charcoal. The outside is blackened to a wonderfully crunchy texture, but the inside is succulent and just as chewy as you'd hope. It's served with a wedge of lemon." Atyn took a needed breath. "I can imagine this is a great deal to consider, so in the meantime, may I bring the table a bottle of wine?"

"Oh, Royce," Albert said. "They have Montemorcey here."

Royce shook his head. "I'm not in —"

"Such a rare treat," Arcadius interrupted. "Bring two bottles to start."

"Excellent choice. I'll get that right away. And please enjoy the show."

Atyn bowed with an otherworldly grace and moved on to the next table, where the Calians were seated. *"Good evening gentlemen, my name is Atyn. I'll be your waiter. Allow me to welcome you to The Blue Parrot,"* he said in perfect Calian.

Hadrian continued to watch the waiter. The only elves he had ever seen were wretched creatures living lives of impoverished misery on the streets of the larger cities. Always filthy, they cowered in the shadows, eating from trash piles while hiding in fear of being attacked. Seeing Atyn dressed smartly and speaking eloquently in multiple languages was like seeing a polished gem that used to be a rock. "He's an elf."

"Delgos is a very tolerant nation," Albert said. "And Tur Del Fur is about as forward-thinking and free as you can get. Their creed down here is simple: do what you like, just don't bother others, and above all, don't interfere with commerce. I suppose I should have warned you."

"Nothing to be warned about," the professor declared. "The unjustified mistreatment of such individuals in Avryn is one of the great embarrassments of our civilization. They are people, plain and simple, and it is refreshing to find them granted the common courtesy that all deserve."

"But it does take a bit of getting used to," Albert said. "Last time I was here, the Earl of Tremore made quite a scene. It began with Tremore demanding that the elves — not just the staff, mind you, but patrons as well — be removed from the premises. The tension escalated when he stabbed one."

"Oh dear! What happened?" Gwen asked.

"They locked the earl up in the city prison."

"They did that to an earl?"

"He's not an earl down here. Happens all the time. Almost every night there is a noble fresh from the north who hasn't acclimated to the culture and thinks he's still in Avryn. Most of the time, it's just part of the entertainment. You'll see, this place gets quite boisterous as the night goes on, but sometimes it goes too far. This being Delgos, that's a long walk to be sure, but stabbing a waiter or waitress in The Blue Parrot is absolutely too far. And they have a professional crew to deal with that. As I said, interfering with commerce isn't allowed."

All around them, people flowed past, finding seats and settling in. The group of Calians at the neighboring table were dressed in the typical white linen thawb and loose trousers that Hadrian found himself envying. They wore tall festive hats, spoke loudly, and laughed a great deal.

Directly in front was a group of sailors, easily distinguished by their long, greased hair and the sail-canvas tar flap that protected the shoulders of their blouses. They were louder than the Calians but didn't laugh as much.

In this turmoil, Royce looked about as comfortable as a cat riding a sinking board during a flood. His hood was up, his eyes scanning the crowd.

"Let's have a toast," Arcadius said when the wine arrived along with the shocking luxury of crystal stemware. He'd poured everyone a glass, including Royce, who had pushed his away. "To Gwen DeLancy," the professor announced, raising his glass. "What might have been merely a pleasant trip has been elevated to the height of rapture by her presence."

Gwen looked embarrassed as everyone except Royce drank to her. He refused to touch his glass.

"What is it, Royce?" Arcadius asked. "Do you disagree?"

He looked over to see Gwen watching him with agony in her eyes.

"It's okay," she offered a sad smile. "He doesn't—"

Royce got to his feet.

Hadrian feared another abrupt exit, but Royce surprised everyone. He took up his glass and lifted it toward her. "To Gwen," he said, then he drank and sat back down.

Gwen continued to stare at him with dark, puzzled eyes.

CHAPTER NINE

Flaming Peacocks

The first act of the evening's show was a snake charmer who coaxed a huge cobra out of a basket, controlling it with nothing but a flute-like instrument made from a gourd. Almost everyone in the crowd was equally transfixed such that the room quieted to hushed whispers. But Hadrian wasn't impressed. He knew the act. Charmers in the East had once been healers who specialized in handling dangerous animals and treating snake bites. Over time, they learned to make more money by catching cobras, pulling out their fangs, imprisoning them in baskets, and making them lethargic and easy to handle by depriving them of water. Then they pretended to bewitch the poor animals with poorly played music. Some even went so far as to sew the snake's mouth shut, making a bite impossible and ensuring that the serpent would die of starvation. The crowd applauded. Hadrian did not.

Acrobats came next and were far more thrilling as they flipped, tumbled, and bounced across the stage. Most of them were elves, and their feats of balance and death-defying leaps from one high rope within the dome to another were gasp-producing.

"Hadrian?" Gwen said, standing up after the acrobats were finished and the crowd was clapping their appreciation. "Could I trouble you for a moment?" she said uncomfortably while placing a hand on her stomach and biting her lower lip. Then she gestured in a general sweep of the packed and boisterous room. "The wine. I think it would be best if I had an escort."

Hadrian looked at Royce, who sat between them. The thief didn't move or say a word, as if he hadn't heard.

"Of course," Hadrian said and followed Gwen as she excused herself and navigated away from their little wooden island, swimming into the sea of revelers toward the wall of fish. Gwen moved through the chaos with clear purpose. She knew the way to where she was going, and he imagined that at some point she'd seen others or had gotten directions from Atyn.

Every chair in The Blue Parrot was occupied, and more patrons stood in the spaces left between. Men made up the bulk of those Hadrian and Gwen skirted around, the ones who stood in the aisles or leaned against pillars or walls. Everyone had a drink in hand. Most were engaged in conversations. Some waved, trying to gain the attention of someone else. And a few appeared lost. Several men, and more than a few women, noticed Gwen, and they tracked her movements. Each also inevitably spotted Hadrian. It was then that he realized the wisdom of her choice of escort.

Gwen led him through an archway into a small corridor and up to a podium where a girl operated the cloakroom booth.

"May I help you?" the girl asked.

"Not at all, I'm afraid," Gwen replied, then turned to Hadrian. "I shouldn't have come." Her words were serious, intent, and desperate. She clutched her hands to her chest as her face flooded with anxiety.

Gwen looked past Hadrian at the main room they'd just left. Neither the stage nor, more importantly, their table and everyone sitting at it were visible. "This is a disaster, and it's all my fault. I just . . ." She struggled not to cry, but it was a losing battle. "I just wanted to go somewhere so I could enjoy myself for once. And I thought—I don't know—I thought Royce might *want* me along." She shook her head, dark hair rippling, earrings swinging. "He doesn't, and I'm just causing problems. He nearly killed those men at the waterfront. I could see it in his eyes. He thought they were going to hurt me, and he planned to make certain they didn't—not then, not ever. They almost died. Everything would have . . ." She did cry then.

Hadrian hugged her and was happy that the vestibule corridor hid them from the table. He knew if they were in line of sight, Royce would be watching, and then how would he explain? Holding her felt strange. Gwen's presence and the impact she had on the lives of those around her had always been so large that he was shocked at how small she felt.

"Are you certain I can't help?" the cloakroom clerk asked. She wore one of the Parrot's trademark blue jackets, but only the last two buttons were hooked, and one shoulder had slid free, revealing a bare shoulder and a butterfly tattoo. "I can do more than guard coats."

Gwen sniffled, drew back.

"We're fine," Hadrian said. "Thank you."

"And in the coach," Gwen went on, "if it hadn't been for you — if those men had opened the door — the same thing would have happened. All because of me. I'm a terrible liability, and I'm frightened that by being here someone is going to get killed, not to mention I'm putting Royce's life in danger. I should just go home. I thought this was going to be wonderful, but I was *so* wrong. There's got to be another coach, or maybe a ship I can take. I brought some money, so I'll be able to pay."

"Gwen," he said, "I don't think that's a good idea."

"Oh, Hadrian!" She sobbed. "Why doesn't he like me?"

"He does. Believe me, he does."

"No, he doesn't. He's always quiet and polite, but . . . it has been *four years*. I waited almost my entire life for him to show up, and when he did, I always thought — I mean, I knew there was no guarantee, but I hoped. I hoped so badly. And . . . there are times when he acts like he cares, moments when I'd swear he loves me, but then it's like a door slams shut, and he's on one side and I'm on the other. Except his side opens out, and mine is a prison. Oh, Hadrian, I think I was wrong — wrong about this trip, about Royce, maybe about everything."

"You're not." Hadrian gritted his teeth. "Except maybe about Royce being in danger because right now I'm strongly considering beating the man senseless for being such an idiot."

"Oh, no!" Gwen grabbed him by the front of his shirt. "You can't! I mean, I don't want to be — oh, I'm making such a mess of everything. I *can't* get between the two of you. I can't be a wedge like that!"

He took her by the shoulders and pried her off. "You aren't. I was making a joke . . . sort of. Look, Royce is in love with you. Trust me on that. He just doesn't know what that means or even how it works. This is a foreign language to him, and he's having translation problems. At the moment, he thinks you hate him."

"*Me?* Hate *him?*" She looked both devastated and lost. Her mouth dangled open as her glassy eyes searched the darkened corners of the corridor for words. Gwen appeared exasperated. "How could he ever think *I* could hate him? What have I done or said to —"

"Listen, I've been pushing him to talk to you, to explain how he feels, but that's like expecting a rabbit to have a heart-to-heart with a wolf."

"What do you mean by wolf? Am I the wolf?"

Hadrian rocked his head from side to side. "Sort of, yes. Royce is *terrified* of you."

Gwen straightened up, looking bewildered. She sniffled and raised her hands, palms out. "Okay, maybe we aren't talking about the same Royce Melborn. The one I'm speaking about has never feared anything, least of all me."

Gwen delicately touched the lower lids of her eyes with her thumbs.

"Here, honey." The cloakroom clerk reached out and handed Gwen a small white cloth.

"Thank you," Gwen said. Then she looked at the delicately embroidered cloth. "Oh no. This is too nice. I'll ruin it."

"Oh, don't worry. It's not mine." The girl planted her elbows on the podium, leaning over and allowing her jacket to slip farther down her arm as she watched the two of them.

"Whose is it?"

The clerk fluttered her hand vaguely behind her at the hanging garments. "Don't know, don't care. You need it more than whoever it belongs to."

"You're not very good at your job, are you?" Hadrian asked.

The girl shrugged.

Gwen smiled at the clerk and dabbed her eyes. "Now I'm ruining a perfect stranger's linen handkerchief. I can't do anything without making a mess of things."

"Are you sure you want to be involved with that guy, honey?" the girl asked. "He sounds a bit unhinged." The clerk peered up at Hadrian, her eyes running the length of his body. "What's wrong with *this* fella? He seems the pleasant type, nice shoulders, beautiful eyes, got all his teeth and a killer smile to prove it. Pardon me for saying, but I, for one, wouldn't mind being bounced around by him."

"Hadrian is just a good friend."

The clerk sighed and offered Hadrian a sympathetic look. "Oh, that's gotta hurt."

"Thank you for the handkerchief," Gwen began, "but—"

"I know, I know." The clerk stood straight, pulled her jacket up, and used her fingers to drum the surface of the podium with nervous tension. "I should mind my own business. The staff needs to be invisible. I get it. But it's pretty obvious you don't know a good thing when it's literally standing right in front of you." She appraised Hadrian once more and sighed. "I'm guessing this *other* guy is also fine looking, and maybe of the dark brooding variety—the sort who lives life on the edge? Oh, I've been there, honey. But let me tell you, that sort of thing—it never ends well."

Gwen looked past Hadrian. Her eyes went suddenly wide. "He's coming!"

"Who?" The clerk rose up on her toes to peer past them. "The brooding bad boy?"

"Please don't say anything to him!" Gwen begged.

"Me or Hadrian?" the clerk asked.

"Either of you!" Gwen threw the handkerchief back at the clerk. "Tell him I've gone looking for a chamber pot."

"It's called the *Throne Room* down here," the girl called after her as Gwen darted back into the crowd. "And it's up at the elephant. Elephant for ladies, gorilla for men."

Hadrian let her go, knowing he needed to intercept Royce to buy Gwen time to gather herself. He just hoped enough of the room's crowd of drunken men had already seen him with her and knew not to cause trouble. In that white dress, she was bait thrown on a still pond stocked with fish—a pond that included a black-hooded shark.

"So, are *you* married?" the girl asked Hadrian. Once more, she leaned across the podium, the little jacket slipping down again. "I finish my shift in three hours. If you'd—"

"What's going on?" Royce asked Hadrian as he entered the cloakroom vestibule, his sight fixed on Gwen's brilliant white figure as she navigated her way through the crowd toward the elephant side of the stage.

"Gwen's looking for a chamber pot. Apparently, they call it the Throne Room down here."

"That's a lot of heavy wool, sir." The clerk spoke to Royce. "Care for me to hold onto that cloak for you? Don't cost nothing."

"I'm fine," he replied.

"That's what I've heard."

Royce narrowed his eyes. "What?"

"Thank you, unusually friendly cloakroom lady," Hadrian said, waving at her as he led Royce back into the main room. "We should follow Gwen, make sure she's okay. Lots of strange people in this place."

"I heard that!" the cloakroom clerk called after them.

When they returned to the main hall, the naked din was as bracing as jumping into a cold lake. Everyone was clapping in unison to the band's beat, as onstage a group of women danced, kicking up their hems such that the audience could almost see their knees. Hadrian circled around a table of men wearing matching yellow hats and banging beer steins in unison. Feeling the growing need for a drink, he wondered what sort of beer a place like this offered. He considered looking for a bar or waiter, but that would need to wait. He had a job to do. His responsibility — as he saw it — was to stall Royce to grant Gwen time. Inspiration struck when he spotted one of the many palm trees. Close to twenty feet tall, it was planted in a six-foot ocher urn decorated with a splatter of parrot droppings. The tree's placement was no accident. Real estate was at a premium in the danthum, and because the tree wasn't a paying customer, it had been situated in a spot that lacked a view of the stage. This made the domesticated palm and the area surrounding it a veritable island oasis of privacy.

Hadrian reached the urn, took a breath, then turned toward Royce to play his best card. "Where were you?"

"What?" Royce asked.

"When we first arrived, you disappeared. Where'd you go?"

Royce looked irritated. "What about Gwen?"

"She's right there." Hadrian pointed to the stark-white-attired figure who waited in the line of women that ran left of the stage toward the elephant. By luck or by design, she had her back to them, chatting with the woman ahead of her. This was fortunate, because Royce's eyesight was probably good enough to see her smeared makeup. "So, what was with the vanishing act?"

Hadrian expected Royce to explain he had been checking things out as usual, but with Gwen along, he was just being extra careful. It was also possible that he might have needed to visit his own elephant. They had been on the road without a stop for some time. Either way, Royce's reply would put an end to the inquiry and force Hadrian to think up another subject to distract his partner. This was bad because he couldn't come up with anything — nothing important enough to demand they speak privately.

Hadrian was frantically searching for another topic when he realized Royce hadn't replied. The thief wasn't even looking at him or at Gwen. His partner stared at the urn, then the floor, then his sight fluttered aimlessly across the crowd.

"Royce?"

The thief frowned and then sighed. "You saw him, didn't you? Is that what you meant by there being *lots of strange people in this place?*"

"Saw who, Royce?" Hadrian asked over the band's growing crescendo and the hammering of ladies' heels.

Royce leaned in close to Hadrian's ear. "Falkirk de Roche."

"Falkirk de . . . what?" Hadrian was baffled. The name was only vaguely familiar.

"You know, pale guy, so white he looks three days dead. Has flaming red hair and a matching beard. Wears a cloak and hood and may or may not have an ugly scar running across his neck as if someone cut his head off."

Hadrian stared at him. "Can't say I've ever seen anyone like that. And if I had, I don't think I'd forget. What's this all about?"

Again, Royce frowned and looked away. "When I told you that I didn't kill Lady Lillian, that didn't mean I didn't kill *anyone* that night. There was a witness. He was outside the Traval Estate."

"A witness?" Hadrian asked. "To what? You said you didn't do anything."

"That's what he witnessed." Again, Royce spoke just loud enough for Hadrian to hear as the thief's eyes watched the crowd. "I couldn't allow him to return to Hurbert Traval and report that his wife *was* in bed with another man. So, I eliminated the threat."

"Eliminated the *threat."* Hadrian nodded. "You killed an innocent man?"

"He was trying to extort money from me, or so I thought."

"Is this pale redhead an associate of the guy you killed?"

"No, the pale redhead *is* the guy I killed."

Hadrian tried to puzzle out the riddle but couldn't.

"Given that I saw *him* again in Kruger just last night, I think we can safely rule out both *innocent* and *dead.*"

"Wait. You saw the man you killed in Melengar, two days later in Kruger? How's that—"

Royce folded his arms. "Obviously, I saw the man I *thought* I killed. Figured there was something wrong when I stabbed him in the throat and Alverstone came away without any blood on the blade. I have no idea how he managed that, but you can't argue with facts. The man is alive and spoke to me behind the outhouse while the rest of you were eating. Said he's after Lady Martel's diary. Offered me eternal life if I got it for him. So, when we arrived, I wanted to make sure he hadn't followed us again."

Hadrian smiled, almost laughed. "Okay, let's get this straight. The guy you killed—sorry, *thought* you killed—who saw you *not* kill Lillian Traval has chased us all the way here to hire you to find the Martel diary, and he's offering to pay you with *eternal life?*"

"Yeah."

Hadrian nodded knowingly. "Royce, you fell asleep on the roof of the coach. It's all a dream."

Royce frowned. "It's not."

"Really? You stab someone in the neck, and there's no blood? You kill a man, and he doesn't stay dead? Then he magically appears in the middle of nowhere? And what does he want? The diary that has bothered you ever since you stole it. And what does he offer in return? Well, the very sensible sum of eternal life! Of course, it's a dream, Royce. That was a long ride. You were alone up there. You got groggy. You fell asleep and had a nightmare."

"I didn't have a nightmare."

"How do you know?"

"My nightmares are never so pleasant." Royce looked across the room at Gwen, who was now at the front of the line. The little door between the elephant's legs opened, and the woman who had been ahead of Gwen stepped out. They spoke and laughed for a second, then Gwen went in. "And neither is my waking life." Royce looked miserable. "She regrets coming, right? Thought this was going to be a wonderful trip but has come to realize it's not."

"That's . . ." Hadrian began with the intent to argue but couldn't. "Honestly, that's stunningly accurate."

Royce nodded. "Told you it wasn't going to work. It's easy to fantasize when you see a person only occasionally and when they're on their best behavior, but if you see them nonstop for a long period of time, faults emerge."

"Really? What are the faults you found in Gwen?"

Royce looked at him with his familiar I-can't-believe-you-are-that-stupid expression. "Not her — me. She's finally seeing me as I really am."

"She's always known who you are. By Mar, Royce, she lives in the Lower Quarter, a place that you decorated with the blood of Raynor Grue! Believe me, she knows. And Gwen is an intelligent and realistic lady, not some pampered shut-in."

"Knowing and seeing are different. Everyone knows that a cute little kitty catches mice, but until you see the little tabby bite each leg off a mouse and then play with the still-living torso for hours, you don't truly understand."

"Have you ever owned a cat, Royce?"

"My point is, no self-respecting woman like Gwen could ever want anything to do with a man like me. And honestly" — he dipped his head, shading his face with the hood — "even if she did, I couldn't allow her to make that mistake. She deserves better. She actually deserves . . . well, someone like you."

Hadrian's brows went up.

"You're both *good* people," Royce said the word like it was an embarrassing deficiency. "I'm not and never will be. Fish and birds, there's no place for both."

"Are you saying it would be okay with you if I were to . . ." He gestured at the elephant. "You know?"

"Try it, and this cat will be playing with your dismembered torso."

Hadrian nodded. "So, that's a *no,* then."

Gwen emerged from the elephant and began heading back.

"Don't tell Gwen about Falkirk," Royce said. "It will just worry her."

"It was a bad dream, Royce. What should worry her is that you're so paranoid you think the monsters in your sleep are after you."

Royce ignored the comment. "Maybe if nothing else goes wrong, and if I stay away from her, she can still have a pleasant time."

Gwen headed for the table.

Royce made no attempt to leave the palm oasis. "Does drinking help?" he asked. "That's how *you* deal with these things, isn't it?"

"Sometimes. Never solves the problem, doesn't even let you forget, but it's good at numbing pain, even if it's only for a little while. And if you drink enough, you sleep. And sleep is a wonderful place where pain can't follow."

Royce watched Gwen reach the table, pull out a chair, and take her seat. "I think I might try a glass of wine." Then, like his very life was escaping his body, he sighed. "It's like being on the bank of a river and watching the greatest treasure in the world float right by, but there's nothing I can do — I never learned how to swim."

The flaming peacocks were exactly that. Several came out at once as waiters ran with them overhead on silver trays like barbarians with torches. Atyn brought their dish, setting the platter down in the center of their table. His face had a sheen of perspiration that glistened in the bird-born firelight. Hadrian could feel the heat. Just when it started to become uncomfortable, Atyn pulled the cork from a small bottle and poured a dark, thick liquid over the body of the peacock. As he did, the flames popped, sparked, and threw off a rainbow of colors. Then he smothered the fire with a silver lid, killing the flames altogether. Upon lifting it, a bird whose meat was already sliced was revealed.

Albert clapped, causing the rest to join in as Atyn bowed. "Enjoy," he said.

"Another bottle of Montemorcey, if you please," Arcadius said.

"Absolutely," Atyn replied, then he darted away as Albert passed around portions of the bird.

The peacock tasted much like pheasant or turkey. At least Hadrian thought so. He couldn't tell much because the sauce overpowered everything else, igniting a violent explosion of spicy heat in his mouth. The peacock wasn't *flaming* merely because it had arrived on fire. Hadrian was forced to sip his wine for medicinal purposes. And he wasn't the only one drinking. While Royce hadn't touched the peacock Albert set before him, he had drained his wineglass and refilled it, leaving the remainder of the bottle squarely in front of him. This was the most Royce had done since rejoining the table. The thief sat with his hood still up, slightly hunched, and hadn't eaten a thing or said a word.

Hadrian took another sip, swishing the wine around his tongue, trying to lessen the inferno. Despite Royce's years of praise, Montemorcey didn't taste much different from any other wine. It did have a strange way of vanishing off his tongue, taking with it any lingering flavor, which seemed like a cheat. It certainly wasn't thirst quenching.

Hadrian tried a new strategy and began sucking in air aimed at his tongue. This worked, but only while he was doing it. While busy firefighting, Hadrian noticed the other side of the room, the portion of the hall to the right of the stage. He quickly came to think of it as the *men's* or the *gorilla's* side. Where the elephant half had the lady's room, cloakroom, and the aquarium, the gorilla side had the men's privy, the bar, and . . .

"What's back there?" Hadrian asked Albert, pointing at a grand archway on the gorilla side, where two powerful-looking men stood guard. Both were shirtless, advertising an impressive display of muscles.

"That's the casino."

"Small house?" Gwen asked.

Albert looked at her, puzzled. "Did you say *small house?*"

She nodded. "Small house or gathering place; that's what *casino* means in Calian," she explained.

"Didn't know that," Albert said as he plucked up another skewer of still-sizzling peacock. Apparently, the viscount was immune to its effects or had already adequately killed his tastebuds. "But what I do know is that's the gambling room. They have all sorts of games of chance in there: dice, cards, wheels, just about anything you can think of and a few you can't. People lose a lot of money in there."

"Doesn't anyone win?" Gwen asked, adding her own morsel of peacock to her plate.

"They have to," Arcadius said, "or why would anyone do it?"

Albert shrugged. "I suppose it must happen, but I've never seen it." He raised a hand. "No, wait, I take that back; people do win . . . but only for a while. Thing is, they keep playing. You see, when they win there's nothing to stop them from continuing, but when they lose, they eventually run out of funds and are forced to stop. Doesn't seem fair in that respect, and no one ever seems to leave with more money than they entered with."

"Why do I think you know about this firsthand, Albert?" Hadrian only partially joked. Albert had nothing to show for his rank but the desire to live the life of the gentry, which included plenty of leisure time and all manner of vice to fill it.

The viscount used one of the peacock's drumsticks to point at him. "I can see where you'd think that, but no, I don't gamble. It may be the only degeneracy I *don't* indulge in."

"Interesting," Arcadius said. The professor was having an awful time eating the greasy, sauce-slicked bird, as it made a mess of his fingers *and* his beard. Hadrian imagined that having a white beard like Arcadius's must be like wearing a fluffy white shirt. Keeping it clean through any meal had to be impossible. "Why make an exception for gambling, I wonder?"

"Well, it was mostly by way of gambling that dear old Dad lost everything that his father before him had failed to squander. This led to the wonderful result of my vagabond existence." Albert made a sour face while shaking his head. "After watching him throw it all away . . ." He paused, the sour look changing to misery. "It was all so stupid." Albert licked the lava sauce from his fingers. "My father blew stacks of money on pricey liquors and expensive women — spent even more on the sort he couldn't buy — but none of that ever bothered me. I suppose I could understand *those* vices. Drinking provides a wonderful bliss. And who can argue with a beautiful woman on your arm or in your bed? But gambling . . . I don't know. It never made any sense to me. Always felt like he was just throwing the money away and getting nothing in return. So, no, I've never had a desire to indulge." He pointed at the casino. "At least not in *that sort* of gambling."

"What are the guards for?" Hadrian asked.

"Sore losers," Albert replied. "Always get a few each night." Something caught his eye, and Albert smiled and stood up. "Excuse me, I think I see someone I know."

Since they'd ordered one of everything, it wasn't long before the swan arrived. It came just as advertised, with its head tucked demurely beneath its left wing. The bird appeared to be sleeping, until, like a magician, Atyn pulled on its neck and wing and the whole feathered portion of the swan lifted off to reveal a finely roasted, pre-sliced body beneath.

"Amazing," Gwen muttered.

"They do put on a fine show here," Arcadius said. "Both on stage and at the table."

On the stage, a juggler was risking his life with swords, cleavers, and axes, accompanied by dramatic drumrolls, but few in the audience could be bothered to look now that food had arrived.

"Another bottle of wine, good sir," Arcadius told Atyn.

Hadrian looked at the full glass in front of the professor. He was certain Arcadius had only touched it once, when he took the tiniest sip during his toast to Gwen. How he had survived the infernal peacock, Hadrian had no idea. Gwen only had one glass also, but she was nearly done with it. The real drinkers at the table were Royce and Albert. The viscount started off the evening with a tentative sip while watching Royce the way a dog glances at its master before snatching a fallen morsel. Albert had once tried drinking himself to death, and Royce had established the edict that Albert must work sober to be part of Riyria. Either Royce recognized this night wasn't considered work, or he was too miserable to care.

Onstage, a man and woman began singing a duet, and Hadrian was surprised to notice they sang in the Tenkin language. His deep baritone and her high soprano filled the hall, and even though most of the audience had no understanding of the words, the crowd quieted a bit as several listened. Hadrian wasn't fluent in Tenkin but had a working grasp of the language and wasn't surprised at all when Gwen started crying.

"What's wrong?" Royce asked. This was the first thing he'd said in more than an hour, and he delivered the question with his usual harsh tone as if he expected her to say the wine was poisoned.

Gwen shook her head and pointed at the stage. "The song. It's sad."

Royce looked back and forth between her and the stage. He seemed confused. Then in a gentler voice he asked, "What's it about?"

She shook her head. With tears still in her eyes and her mouth pinched tight, she seemed in pain.

Once more, Royce looked — no, glared — at the singers as if he might pay them a visit later that night.

Hadrian intervened. "Tell him, Gwen."

She wiped her eyes, gave him a long look, then sniffled and nodded. "It's about a Tenkin named Lyco who was shamefully attacked by an awful man. Lyco defended himself and killed his attacker. In doing so, he won the man's wife, Dala, as his slave, as is the law. But afterward, he never touched her. Nor did he sell her, even though she would have fetched a great price. All he ever did was treat Dala with kindness. They lived together for years this way. Him caring for her in sickness, bringing Dala flowers and other gifts. Together they struggled against famines, wars, and droughts. But in all that time, he never touched her. She wished he had because Dala had fallen in love with him. It was only when they were both old and gray and when Lyco lay dying that he confessed how he had always loved her, even before the fight, but he knew that she could never love him because he'd killed her husband."

Gwen lowered her head as she cried. "I'm sorry, it's . . . it's just so sad."

Royce touched her arm.

Gwen froze. She seemed to stop breathing.

Royce noticed and let go. He promptly raised his glass and drained it.

"Hadrian?" Arcadius said. "I'm afraid I've had a bit too much wine, and this food is far too rich for an old man such as myself. I must say, I'm not feeling especially well. Could I trouble you to see me safely back to the Turtle?"

Hadrian looked at the professor's still-full glass of Montemorcey but nodded.

CHAPTER TEN

Fish and Birds

Royce was finding it hard to breathe.

Probably because all those blasted peacocks have filled the place with smoke.

Hadrian had left with the professor, and Albert was off doing who knows what, leaving him trapped alone with Gwen.

This is so, so bad.

All he wanted was for Gwen to enjoy herself, but he knew she wouldn't be able to if she thought he — or anyone — was unhappy. The woman was odd that way, but it was a nice odd. Thinking about it, if he had to pick a freakishly peculiar character flaw, this was about the best he could hope for.

At least she wasn't making the mistake Hadrian always did by trying to cheer him up. Gwen was respectful. She knew enough to leave him be.

Or is she just frightened of me? Is she sitting there right now absolutely terrified because she's alone with a murderer?

It seemed logical, but as Hadrian had reminded him, *"She's always known who you are. By Mar, Royce, she lives in the Lower Quarter, a place that you decorated with the blood of Raynor Grue! Believe me, she knows."*

Royce's plan had been a simple one. He would stay, so as not to give the impression he was angry or upset with Gwen, but he'd remain silent and still, so he couldn't say or do anything to upset her.

No abrupt moves, no misunderstood comments.

His plan should have worked, except everyone else had abandoned him. Now, it was impossible to go; he couldn't leave her unprotected. And because there was just the two of them, he couldn't sit in silence any longer. He had to say something, but he'd had too much wine. His silence wasn't a problem earlier because chatterbox Hadrian Blackwater could fill any void with an endless stream of useless babble. Royce could hide behind all that blathering. But now . . . he was alone, exposed, and he had to hold a delicate conversation where each word must be vetted and cross-checked, and of course, the wine hobbled him. He needed something to break the ice, something pleasant, fascinating, and perhaps even witty.

"Like your meal?" he asked.

She nodded. "It's very different. Have you tried the Flame Broiled Sea Monster?"

"No, and I'm not going to." His tone was harsh.

That wasn't good. I sound angry, but that's because I am. That's reasonable, isn't it? Most people resent being trapped. And that's exactly what happened. Arcadius isn't sick — not physically. The bastard left me on purpose. They all did.

Royce glared at the empty seats.

Atyn returned with a wide smile. He clapped his hands and rubbed them together with relish. "Are you ready for your frozen magpies, or shall we wait for the others to return?"

"Get away from us while you still can," Royce snapped.

Gwen gasped. "Royce!"

"Ah . . . I'll hold off on the pies then," Atyn said and promptly moved away.

Royce saw the shocked look on Gwen's face. He was only vaguely aware that the band was loudly playing, and a hundred different conversations were roaring all around them. As far as he was concerned, the room was utterly quiet. And in the empty space created by that choked silence, stress and tension flooded in.

"I'll leave in the morning," Gwen said, her voice the whisper of a butterfly. "I know you don't want me here. And I'm sorry I ruined this trip for you."

Gwen stood up.

So did Royce.

She was crying. Her face was away from him, but her body hitched, and he could hear the muffled sobs.

So much for making her happy.

Gwen started to dart away but halted abruptly as if something had grabbed her. It took a wine-soaked second for Royce to realize that something was him. He had a hold of her wrist. "I'm not going to hurt you, if that's what you think," he told her. "I would never do that, Gwen."

When she turned back, he saw the tears running freely down her cheeks, leaving ugly dark lines. "I know that, but—"

"I'd kill anyone who did, I swear it."

"I know, but—"

"Hundreds if necessary."

"Yes, but—"

"A whole city if—"

"I understand, Royce."

Remembering he was still holding on, he let go of her wrist.

I shouldn't have grabbed her. Doing so is frightening. What could be worse than being grabbed and held by a ruthless killer? What was I thinking? She'll run now.

Royce would have to let her go.

Fish and birds. She knows it; I do, too.

He would never see Gwen again. Or worse, he would, but she would be married to Dixon. They would have children. Of course they would; why wouldn't they? When Royce visited, she would smile and welcome him as always, as if nothing had changed, but he wouldn't talk to her—not really. He couldn't. It would be too awkward, too painful, and Dixon wouldn't like it. He'd never see her again, never hear her voice, never . . .

"I don't want you to leave," he told her.

A heartbeat passed, and then another. Gwen didn't run. She continued to look at him, stared at his face as if this was the first time she'd ever seen it.

"Royce?" Gwen took a step toward him. Slowly, gently, she reached up and drew back his hood. "Royce . . . you're crying."

"You don't actually need to walk me all the way back to the rolkin, Hadrian," Arcadius told him.

"No?" The two stood outside on the steps of the Parrot, the sound of the music dulled behind the closed doors. It felt nice to be out of the turmoil, like coming to the surface and taking a breath. "Feeling better already, are you?"

The professor winked. "I just wanted Royce to have some time alone with Miss DeLancy."

"I had a feeling," Hadrian said.

Night had arrived, and with it came a different world. Cooler by far, it was pleasant to stand on the warm stones, feeling the breeze and breathing the salt air that blew up from the harbor and smelled vaguely of fish. Shouts and laughter came out of the dark, and the donkey wagons and carriages continued to *clip-clop* along the streets. Far more people wandered the city than in daylight. The hordes of turists moved in small groups the way foreigners do when exploring a new place. The northern well-to-do, dressed in their heavy finery, no longer seemed foolish now that the sun had stopped its baking for the day. Some, those speaking louder than necessary, were inexperienced drinkers. One dignified fellow in a long coat and broad-brimmed hat who was momentarily lost in a fit of laughter walked right into a lamppost. He fell on his backside, nearly taking down the elegantly gowned woman beside him.

"She's a nice girl, isn't she?" Arcadius said.

For an instant, Hadrian thought the professor meant the woman on the arm of the collapsed drunk, whom he suspected might very well have been a duchess from the cold and colorless realm.

Seeing the confusion, Arcadius added, "Gwen, I mean."

"Oh. Yes. Very."

"And she likes him."

"It certainly seems so."

"And he likes her." This wasn't a question, but a statement of unbelievable fact that Arcadius followed with a shake of his head. "While I certainly had my hopes,

I harbored doubts that Royce Melborn could ever manage to muster enough sentiment to show affection for so much as a floppy-eared puppy."

"He hates dogs."

"Does he now?" Arcadius arched his brows while shifting his lips. "Doesn't surprise me a bit. That Royce has developed a fondness for a human being, however, that's a shocker. And yet it seems he has." Arcadius moved down the street and off to the side to avoid door traffic, and there, he took a seat on the step. "I must admit that I wasn't pleased when I heard about the goings-on in Medford a few years ago — with the fire and all."

"We had nothing to do with that," Hadrian was quick to assert as he took a seat beside the professor. The two, shoulder to shoulder, looked out on the lights that trimmed the tiers rising behind the nearby buildings.

Arcadius stared at him for a moment with judgmental eyes. "And Lord Exeter?"

Hadrian frowned. Wasn't much he could say in defense of that.

"*You* didn't play a part, did you?" Arcadius continued.

Hadrian shook his head.

"Good. But it still shows Royce hasn't changed."

"He has. Royce hasn't murdered anyone in the last two years."

"I suspect that's only because you stood in the way. Prevention isn't the same as real change."

"But I think he has, a little, at least."

Arcadius sighed. "Just recently, he took a job to murder an innocent woman."

"She wasn't innocent, and he didn't do it."

"Only because she paid him more." The professor took off his glasses and began wiping. "I had so hoped that just being around you would help Royce find his moral compass, but it has been four years, and he still appears as lost as ever." He looked back at the entrance to the Parrot. "But . . . perhaps *she* can help. A woman can do wonders for a wayward man. Should have thought of it sooner, but given the trouble I had putting the two of you together, I could never take that chance with something as delicate as a young lady."

"I think you'll find Gwen is far from fragile," Hadrian said. "The woman has faced more than her fair share of hardships and demons."

"You know, I'm getting that impression, which is good, considering who we're talking about. Wouldn't you say?"

Hadrian recalled the first year he'd worked with Royce, which he'd often described as similar to trying to tame a feral, knife-wielding wolverine, and nodded. "You were right about us, though. We make a pretty good team."

"I know," Arcadius said, and he looked back at the Parrot. "And I'm right about them, too. So, you go back inside and enjoy yourself but do me—and them—a favor. Take your time returning to the table. The furnace is just about the right temperature for the forming of another bond. They merely need a bit of time." He looked up at the front of the danthum. "And I couldn't have asked for a better forge."

Returning inside the Parrot, Hadrian was greeted by the spirited and rollicking sound of blaring trumpets, which had been included with the other instruments. He'd only ever heard trumpets on the field of battle or used as fanfares for dignitaries. This was not that. These horns were blasting out a bouncy rhythm along with the big kettle drums as a heavyset man in a vibrant yellow shirt sang on stage and somehow managed to still be heard. The song was intentionally silly, claiming that the singer was sad and lonely while the music was nothing of the sort.

Waiters were still weaving between tables, delivering plates, but several of the seats were now empty as people danced in front of the stage. Among the gentry of Avryn, dancing was a formal affair where men and women faced off in lines and performed strict pass-through maneuvers designed to maintain distance, decorum, and decency. It took training and practice, and partners—who switched often—rarely touched more than hands. Smiling was considered lewd, and if they had any fun at all, they didn't show it.

In the small country villages like the one Hadrian grew up in, they danced carols or rounds where men, women, and children held hands in a circle and did simple side steps and sweeps with their legs. In the taverns, they danced jigs and reels, in a sort of informal hopping stomp where folks kicked up their heels in brazen and shameless ways. Most often men danced alone, but if women joined in, they kept their distance.

What transpired in the Parrot was the sort of wild capering and close-quarter cavorting only seen in the east, where cultures and customs were distinctly different. Few, if any, northern turists were on the floor. They remained aghast in their seats, pointing and gawking wide-eyed and open-mouthed. Most of those stomping and twirling were locals or Calians, though Hadrian noticed that the entire table of sailors were out there. Those fortunate enough to find women danced with them; the rest made do with each other.

Royce and Gwen were still at the table. The two were sitting close and talking, which Hadrian took as a good sign. Royce's hood was down, which was even better. Something was clearly transpiring between the two, and Hadrian followed the professor's suggestion. Instead of returning, he wandered toward the gorilla side, where every stool was taken.

"Hadrian!" Albert waved at him. The viscount had a seat just left of center. Next to him was a beautiful woman in a bare-shouldered, front-plunging green evening dress who sat primly stiff. "Estelle, this is my good friend Hadrian; Hadrian, this is the Countess Ridell of Warric."

"Pleased to make your acquaintance, good sir." She spoke with the formal disregard common to noble ladies, a tone that let you know they were better than you. "From which house do you hail?"

"Excuse me?" Hadrian asked.

"He's not noble, dear," Albert told her.

"No?" she asked, then took a second look at Hadrian and relief filled her face. "Oh, thank the gods!" The countess slouched in her seat and crossed her knees, exposing an elegant calf as she grabbed up her drink and took a mouthful of something clear garnished with a slice of orange. "I come down here to get away from all that ego-bloated, politically infused bosh, and all those titled men with their lances jammed up their blue-blooded buttocks. I certainly didn't feel like putting the cloak of decency on again. I'm on holiday, by Mar!" She said this last bit as if the god of man could hear her.

"No worries here," Albert assured her. "Neither Hadrian nor I amount to anything at all. We're a couple of absolute louts."

"Wonderful!" Estelle grinned and raised her glass. "A toast to louts and knuckleheaded hooligans!"

"Hold on, my dear!" Albert stopped her.

"Why? You have something against degenerate ne'er-do-wells?"

"Of course not. I'm president of the Medford chapter where I serve with distinction. But poor Hadrian here is unarmed."

She looked him over again, then gasped. "Where in Elan is your drink, you poor fellow?"

Hadrian shrugged. "Don't have one."

"That's taking the whole ne'er-do-well thing a bit too far, don't you think? Get a weapon, my good man. This is war! We must band together to slay the foul wretch that threatens the world or die trying."

"Which wretch is that, Estelle?" Albert asked.

"Respectability, of course. He and his henchmen: Priggishness and Gentility and their sidekicks: Manner and Decorum. I particularly hate Decorum — such a bore." She swept her naked arm at the array of exotic-looking bottles behind the bar where shelves were lined with various liquors. In addition to the typical whiskeys and rums, they also offered the Calian spirit, Hohura: a Ba Ran Ghazel liquor that came in a dark wooden jug held fast by iron straps and a chain-linked cork.

"Have any beer?" Hadrian asked the man behind the counter who sported a thin mustache, slicked-back hair, and a damp towel over one shoulder of his blue jacket.

"Jareb, give the man a Regal Ale," an older gentleman on the other side of Albert told the bartender.

"Hadrian, this is Calvary Graxton, otherwise known as Mister Parrot." Albert swirled a finger in the air. "He owns the place."

"Pleased to meet you, sir."

Graxton was a plump man with a graying beard and long hair that he tied in a ponytail. He wore the same blue as the help, but his was a long formal coat with large gold buttons that he wore over a gold-colored waistcoat that made him look a bit like a macaw.

Mister Parrot, Hadrian mused.

"Nice manners for a roughneck," Mister Parrot said with a smile. "Jareb, put it on the house."

"Not necessary, Cal," Albert told him. "I'm on retainer this trip. All expenses paid."

"By whom?"

"Lord Byron."

Mister Parrot grinned. "Outstanding! In that case, Jareb, bring us all double shots of Terrible Typhons and put it on Winslow's tab." He leaned over toward Albert. "I get it from the pirates of Vandon. Who knows where they get it from. It's a ridiculously expensive liquor — but smooth as dwarf-polished stone and rich as Cornelius DeLur. Besides, old Byron will explode after discovering he subsidized the very contraband he's tasked with prohibiting." He clapped Albert on the back hard enough to rock him.

"Is that three glasses or four, sir?" Jareb asked, deftly holding up three cordial glasses and motioning at the countess with a fourth.

Estelle glared at Mister Parrot so viciously that if they had both been men, Hadrian would have expected a brawl to break out. "Careful how you answer, Calvary." She clacked her nails on the counter of the bar. "You wouldn't want to shatter a girl's innocence by saying something awful. You see, I've always liked parrots."

"Most pit vipers do," he replied. "But fortunately for both of us, I'm not the one paying." Mister Parrot grabbed Albert by the back of the neck and shook him. "What say you, Lord Winslow? Are you the sort to contribute to the delinquency of a countess? Does the wench get a sip?"

"Is this illegal liquor strong?" Albert asked.

"Very."

"Then by all means, serve the lady. I'll need all the help I can get tonight."

"Thank you, your lordship." Estelle batted her eyes. "Though you should be aware that absolutely no assistance will be necessary. Although . . ." She looked at Hadrian, and not so much at his face. "Hopefully, this one isn't *very* happily married or if he is, he doesn't have the morals of a paladin. If so, you may have competition." Then she smiled most wickedly. "Or better yet — company."

"And this is the lady you're concerned I might corrupt," Albert told Calvary.

The typhons were handed out. The cordial glasses were like tiny wineglasses and filled so high that the dark amber liquid spilled and drizzled down the sides like thin syrup.

"To our benefactor, Lord Byron," Estelle declared, holding her glass aloft with two delicate fingers. "May he one day learn that smiling is not a sin, and that laughter is actually good for the soul."

They all drank, swallowing the contents of the glasses in one go.

Having once sampled authentic Hohura boiled fresh in the jungle by a pair of Ba Ran Ghazel and served in bleached-white human skulls, Hadrian braced himself for the impact of this mysterious drink. The liquor warmed all the way down with a nutty, smoky, creamy flavor and left a sort of cherry aftertaste. Unlike Hohura, which made him seriously consider cutting his tongue out, the Terrible Typhon was a palate pleaser and didn't burn any more than a dessert wine.

The blaring, horn-led music stopped, and most of the dancers left the stage. This caught Mister Parrot's attention. "Jesse! Dex!" he called to his workers. "She's up next. Blow out the chandeliers and turn down the lanterns. Just leave the one big bull's-eye on the stage."

The word was passed, and all around the hall, men in blue jackets raced to lower the big chandeliers and extinguish their candles. Others turned down the wicks in the various lanterns around the hall.

"What's this all about?" Albert asked.

"A new girl. A singer. Andre sent her over." Mister Parrot explained.

The room darkened until the only lights were the little candles on each table that flickered like tiny stars. The stage itself was black. Conversations hushed in anticipation, then everyone heard footsteps on the stage and a man in a scarlet robe and royal blue cape stepped into the single beam of light thrown by a huge bull's-eye lantern.

"Ladies and gentlemen!" he addressed the crowd in a loud voice.

"That's Andre," Mister Parrot whispered to Albert. "Her handler."

"Tonight, I introduce to you a new talent. She's a bit shy, so extend the courtesy of your attention, and please welcome the magnificent Millificent LeDeye."

A few clapped, but not many, as Andre disappeared into the shadows. A moment or two later, a young woman emerged into the light. Dark hair, pale skin, red lips, wearing a long, tight-fitting black gown, she was breathtaking.

She began to sing, and her voice was clear as rainwater, but quiet as a whisper. So soft and delicate, that Hadrian had no idea how it carried across the room. All the previous acts were loud, bombastic performances with singers that shouted more than sang. They had to in order to be heard over the raucous din. Even the Calian duo had belted out their lyrics. But Millificent LeDeye whispered to the audience in a wickedly seductive voice that, by its intimacy, demanded attention. The hall gave it, and the room was silent. She sang,

> *"Here we sit together in the dark, just you and I.*
> *Two lonely people out for a lark, but too afraid to try."*

Hadrian thought she looked directly at him. Soft strings began to play, filling the gaps, flooding the shadows with an emotional, heart-swelling buoyancy.

> *"I want you; I do.*
> *And you know it, too."*

Soft drums slid in under the strings as Millificent LeDeye's voice rose in octaves and volume to a sustained heartfelt cry.

> *"Please lie if you must, but don't let me go.*
> *Hold me tonight, after the show.*
> *I'll be there. I will.*
> *If you want me still.*
> *Together, we two in the dark."*

The music grew and the song went on until Hadrian could genuinely believe that he and she were the only two in the room, and her words were a message specifically for him. Then he saw shadows. Patrons were on the floor again, only this time they did not stomp, or twirl, or hop. Embracing couples were swaying, barely visible in the candlelight.

Just then, Hadrian noticed his table was empty. Royce and Gwen were missing. The thought that followed was so absurd, it made him laugh.

※

In the confidential security of the dark, Gwen had drawn Royce to the dance floor.

"My mother taught me," she explained in a whisper. "It's easy. You'll like it. Just put your arms around my waist."

Royce didn't even hesitate. The thought never crossed his mind, but then most of his mind had been left back at the table in the bottom of an empty bottle of Montemorcey. There were people all around, but in the dark, they were easily ignored — just a bunch of shadows. And the music was so — personal.

"Two lonely people out for a lark, but too afraid to try."

The voice fluttered down from the stage, but it seemed to Royce that he heard Gwen: her words or perhaps her very thoughts whispered in his ears. It couldn't be. Not because it was impossible to hear thoughts or that Gwen's lips weren't moving, but on account of the world had never been so wonderful — not to him.

He considered that it must be a dream, but once more this explanation suffered from flaws, not the least of which was that — as he had so recently pointed out to Hadrian — he never had nice ones.

Unbelievably, his arms were around Gwen's waist, one hand on the small of her back, the other on a hip. Beneath his palms, these two parts shifted independently, rocking in time with the slow seductive rhythm of the song. She pulled him close. His body and cheek brushed against hers. She was warm and soft. Royce could smell tamarisk in her hair, and roses on her skin, and he felt each breath swelling her chest, and every exhale wafted warmly across his neck. He had no idea what to do, how to move, where to place his hands, what to say or even if he should speak at all. Oddly, he didn't care. Thinking was a product of the mind, and Royce no longer had his. He was drunk and knew it. Royce was also vaguely aware that he shouldn't be, not with Gwen. In all the world, she was the only person whose opinion mattered.

He ought to leave before making a fool of himself. He should play it safe and slink away. In the dark, it would be easy. He could apologize tomorrow. But the way her body moved beneath his hands, the feel of her hot breath on his neck, and the fact that his mind was *waaaay* back at the table trapped by a cork, made it easy, even sensible, to be reckless.

He pulled her closer, pressing their bodies tight until he could feel her heartbeat. His cheek pressed firmly against hers. He waited for a response, held his breath until her arms mimicked his, locking tighter around his neck.

Neither said a word. They didn't need to; the song spoke for them.

> *"I want you; I do.*
> *And you know it, too."*

All of it was so unreal, like loving families, promises kept, happy endings, tranquility, and contentment — myths and fairy tales all. That's how he knew it to be a hallucination. He'd never had one from drinking, but that night he'd had quite a bit and on an empty stomach.

> *"Please lie if you must, but don't let me go."*

If this wasn't real, then nothing he did mattered. And if nothing he did mattered . . .

"It's easy," Hadrian had said. *"Not complicated at all. You really only have two options. You can express yourself — you know, tell her how you feel."*

Royce tried to think of what to say, but that was impossible because, again, his mind was trapped in a bottle.

"So, go the other way."

Royce turned his head, pulled back slowly and felt the incredible softness of Gwen's cheek against his. As he did, he moved his hand, which had been on her back, up to the nape of her neck. His splayed fingers slipped into her hair. He tilted Gwen's head gently to one side.

*"I'll be there. I will.
If you want me still."*

His lips found hers and were welcomed with a trembling that ended as the two moved as one, rocking slowly among the shadows, intertwined within the music.

"Together, we two in the dark."

CHAPTER ELEVEN

Millificent LeDeye

"Never heard anyone sing like that before," Hadrian said. He was staring at the empty stage where the bull's-eye lantern continued to illuminate a small patch of floor.

"Spellbinding, isn't it?" Mister Parrot said, leaning back and resting his elbows on the bar.

"Who is she?"

"Some unknown ingénue Andre found. He's been grooming her — putting the girl in front of small audiences at the little clubs. Tonight is her official major debut."

"Who is Andre?"

Mister Parrot exchanged looks with Albert and Estelle, who offered no help at all. "I suppose you could say he's a talent promoter, an aspiring entrepreneur, and part-time danthum manager. He runs a little place called The Cave up on the Eighth Tier. Used to be a salt mine back when the dwarfs ruled, then a warehouse, and now it's this quirky little danthum. Not very nice, but it's popular in summer because the old mine stays cool. Mostly though, Andre is an officer in the DeLur Corporation."

"DeLur?" Hadrian asked. "He's a banker, right?"

Estelle, who was drinking, fell into a fit of coughing. Albert applied a not-too-helpful series of pats on her back while Mister Parrot sat up, and after looking briefly around the room, he said, "Yes, he's a banker."

Hadrian was disappointed when the lights came back up and the band once more played a happy tune. He looked at the empty stage. "That's it? She's not going to perform anymore?"

"Honestly," Mister Parrot said, "I don't think she knows more than the one song."

"I daresay our boy here seems smitten by the lady in black," Estelle declared with a pout. She plucked at the hem of her dress and frowned. "Knew I should have gone with a darker color tonight. I just didn't want people to think I was in mourning." She looked at Albert. "He's not married at all, is he?"

"Only to ideals, my dear."

"Argh!" She threw her head back dramatically. "An idealist! They're the rare faithful sort, and I've lost him to a torch singer! That's like finding the Heir of Novron and a moment later watching him trip and break his neck."

"I'll be certain to console you later this evening."

"You'd better!"

"Is there a way to get backstage?" Hadrian asked.

"There's a little door behind the gorilla," Mister Parrot said.

"Excuse me."

"And just like that, he's gone," Estelle lamented as Hadrian set down his beer and waded into the ocean of tables and currents of people. He stuck to the outside of the room, where he passed the casino guards. Up close they were even more impressive. Their powerful arms were accentuated by the way they crossed them over their chests. Each stood a head taller than Hadrian. The left one had a red mark on his forehead.

"Lousy dwarven doorways, am I right?" Hadrian said as he walked by.

The guard broke his professional scowl and smiled.

The gorilla statue was three stories tall, with a monstrous face that displayed bared fangs and wild eyes. Either the sculptor had never seen a real gorilla, or he had been forced by his patron to be creative. The entrance to the men's privy was appropriately found directly between the gorilla's legs. But around the side, a short set of stairs led to a nondescript door. Unlike the casino, the stage was unguarded, and Hadrian ducked under the low lintel and walked through.

Inside was a very different and dilapidated world. The ancient, traffic-worn wooden flooring was in a terrible state of neglect. The walls were rough with cracks in the stone. Marred posts and beams were wrapped in coils of thick rope. Ladders led up into the rafters, and sandbags hung like men on gallows. A number of people moved about, not so much with purpose as in a panic. A group of dancers, all in matching clothes, were lined up, preparing to perform. One man was in tears, and the rest showed signs of hysteria because — at least as far as Hadrian could tell — the sobbing man was lacking a kerchief that all the others wore.

"How could you have lost it?"

"Where did you last see it?"

"You're always doing things like this, Ludwink! This is why we hate you!"

"We don't hate you."

"I do!"

Hadrian skirted the dance troupe, carefully stepping over a coil of rope and around a wine barrel that was topped by a stack of parchment held in place by an old boot. Across from him and behind the dancers, Millificent LeDeye stood with hands on hips, talking to Andre.

"May I help you?" a man all in black asked as he appeared out of nowhere.

"Huh? Oh," Hadrian replied, "I was hoping to speak to Miss LeDeye."

"And who are you?"

"Hadrian Blackwater." He extended his hand. "And your name?"

The man ignored the gesture. "I'm sorry, but Miss LeDeye already left."

Hadrian looked over and pointed. "She's right there."

"You're mistaken. She's gone. Now, if you'll please return to the hall — guests are not allowed backstage."

"I just wanted to get a drink, Andre." Miss LeDeye had raised her voice. She sounded angry, and her arms were folded with as much conviction as the casino guards.

"I'll buy you one," Hadrian called to her.

Both LeDeye and Andre looked over in surprise.

The man in black stepped directly into Hadrian's line of sight. "I told you, she's not here."

Hadrian tilted his head around the colorless obstacle. "And yet my eyes are telling me otherwise."

"Your eyes are misleading you, and on their way to getting you into serious trouble. If you don't want them to be fixed, I would advise that you leave — now."

Hadrian would have left, except he saw Miss LeDeye smiling at him. "What do you like to drink?" he shouted to her. The smile grew.

"Alessandro," Andre snapped, "get rid of him."

The man in black grabbed Hadrian by the arm.

Hadrian twisted free. "Careful, I bruise easily."

Alessandro's hand went to his dagger.

"Relax, Alessandro. I'm leaving." Hadrian raised his voice once more. "Another time then, when you aren't so busy, perhaps?"

Miss LeDeye covered her lips with a hand, but her eyes were delighted.

He turned to leave, and Alessandro shoved him out. Hadrian didn't have time to duck and clipped the lintel with his forehead. The door slammed shut, and he stood there, dazed.

Behind him, Hadrian heard the voices through the door. "Who in the name of Novron was that?"

"Nobody. See his clothes? Just some serf from up north. The lady merely made an impression."

"If he turns up again, I want you to be the one to make the impression. Understand?"

"You don't pay me, Andre. Couldn't afford it. I'm here as a courtesy — *understand?*"

The voices continued but moved too far away to be heard.

Hadrian sighed, and climbing back down the stairs, he returned to the main hall, the music, and the noise.

"Lousy dwarven doorways, am I right?" the big casino guard said as Hadrian walked back past him.

Hadrian smirked. "This one had help."

When Albert and Hadrian returned to the table, Royce and Gwen were there, sharing a bowl of frozen magpie like a couple of teenagers at a summer fair. In unison, Hadrian and Albert looked at Royce, then at each other, and shrugged, as if they had practiced the routine.

"I trust you can all find your way back," Albert said. "There's a good chance I won't be returning to the Turquoise Turtle at all tonight. So don't bother waiting up. Estelle is the sort who finds it rude for men to run off before sunrise. Besides, she serves a wonderful breakfast."

"You found a lady already?" Gwen asked, impressed.

"An old acquaintance. She was married at the age of ten to a wealthy Warric earl, who at the time was in his sixties."

"She married at ten?"

"That's when she went to live with the earl. Arranged pairing, obviously, political in nature. One does hope that the marriage wasn't consummated for a few years, at least. To hear her tell the tale, they never did. Now she's twenty-eight and he's eighty-one, and they both spend a good deal of their time in bed—just not the same one."

Albert pulled a letter from inside his doublet. "Just grab a carriage and tell them to bill Lord Byron, and then show them this." He handed Hadrian a parchment with a seal at the bottom. Then he began to wade back into the depths of the hall, waving farewell as he went. "See you tomorrow—afternoon most likely. Ta-ta."

"Ta-ta?" Gwen said and smiled at Hadrian.

"He's had a bit to drink," Hadrian explained, taking Arcadius's old seat at the table, which was littered with empty bottles of wine, abandoned glasses, and plates. Onstage, the dancers were continuing their number, which was something of a complicated folk-style arrangement similar to a round but with lifts and twirls.

"How are you doing?" Hadrian asked Gwen. "Things seemed to have improved since I left, yes?"

Gwen didn't answer. Instead, she smiled at the melting magpie between them like a little girl with a secret. Something had happened—an event massive enough to reduce the-fearless-former-prostitute-turned-madam-and-successful-businesswoman into a bashful child. If this were Medford House *on the morning after,* Hadrian would have a good guess about the nature of the event, but given that the pair had never left The Blue Parrot, he was stumped.

Is the magpie that good?

He looked at Royce, who dragged a finger over the sauce remains in the bowl, then sucked on it in an uncharacteristically casual manner. His hood was not merely down, his entire cloak was off, slung across the back of an empty chair.

"Hadrian, I've been thinking," Royce began in a deeply serious tone that was worrisome.

Having advised Royce to admit his feelings to Gwen, and seeing the suppressed glee on her face, Hadrian assumed that's exactly what had happened. But now he had to wonder if Royce had traveled farther down that road than expected.

Did he ask her to marry him? Did she accept? Is Royce about to declare his days of banditry and lawlessness to be over? Is this goodbye?

Hadrian had never been comfortable with their line of work. He found it better than outright murder, which — if he was honest — was a fair assessment of what he'd been doing before teaming up. Others called it war or combat. Some even suggested that arena fights were a sport — especially the ones who wagered money. For them, he imagined, it was also a business. But just as beating a child to death could hardly be mistaken for discipline, what he'd done for the four years before meeting Royce had been murder — lots of it. Stealing, spying, and bounty hunting were better than that, and far superior to starving. Hadrian knew there was a whole spectrum between those two options. He could get a job on a farm, fishing boat, or in a warehouse. As redemptive as atonement through sweat and humility seemed, he knew it wouldn't be much different from crawling into a bottle. He wouldn't be living, just hiding.

"One doesn't use a sixteen-folded, single-edged Tiliner blade to dig a ditch," his father used to say. *"There are shovels for that."*

So while Royce steered their enterprise, Hadrian was able to keep it on the road. At least he tried. All too often a wheel, or even two, ran off into the weeds. Lately, Royce had been pulling harder than usual for the open field, and Hadrian had been feeling concerned that a division was coming. Their partnership had been good while it lasted, but Royce was one sort of person and Hadrian another. A breakup was inevitable, and Hadrian had come to terms with it — or thought he had. Faced with the reality of severing ties and going back into the world alone, he was surprised to discover that it depressed him. Nevertheless, he was happy for Royce and Gwen. Arcadius certainly would be pleased.

Bracing himself for the words he knew would follow, Hadrian asked, "Thinking about what?"

Royce took a deep breath, sucked on his finger again, then pointed the glistening digit at Hadrian. "Mister Hipple."

Those were *not* the words Hadrian expected. He glanced at Gwen, who showed no insight whatsoever. "What?"

"Mister Hipple — you know?"

"The dog?"

Royce nodded gravely. "We shouldn't have left him. Those winters in Alburn — it gets cold there. The dog might die."

Hadrian remained lost as he studied them both, wondering if this was a joke. Neither smiled, and Royce was as grim and pensive as ever. "That was a year ago, Royce."

"We should go back and get him." He said this while looking off into the distance as if seeing the mutt shivering in the cold.

"Go back? To Alburn? Are you insane?"

Gwen shook her head and smiled apologetically. "He's had a bit to drink, as well."

Hadrian nodded dramatically. "I would say so."

Gwen rubbed Royce's back. "Maybe we should call it a night."

"No — no." Royce waved a hand at them both. "I'm just starting to enjoy myself. Anyone notice the dancers? They look ridiculous. That one is missing a kerchief." He reached out and began picking up empty bottles, presumably searching for more wine. He grabbed up an empty one with its cork jammed back into it. He stared at the bottle for a moment and began to nod. "This is the one." He looked at Hadrian to make sure he noticed. "Whatever you do, don't pull the stopper out of this bottle. I have something trapped inside, and I need to keep it safe."

Hadrian studied the empty bottle. "What?"

Royce looked at it, then at Hadrian. He did this three more times, then narrowed his eyes and shook his head. "Don't worry about it. You don't need to know. I've said too much already."

Hadrian stared at the thief, dumbfounded. "Yes, I do believe it is absolutely time to call it a night. Royce, can you walk?"

The thief smirked at him as if Hadrian had made a bad joke.

"Can he?" Hadrian asked Gwen.

She shrugged.

Great. Both are about as useful as an ax with a missing handle.

The trip back to the Turtle wasn't nearly as bad as Hadrian had expected. Royce could walk just fine, causing Hadrian to wonder exactly how drunk his friend was or wasn't. The thief had certainly emptied his fair share of the wine bottles — must have because Hadrian had only ever seen Albert helping him. Gwen had had a glass or two, but she wasn't drunk, although not entirely sober, either. He could tell by the way she was quiet. Some people got loud when they drank, others withdrew, as if suddenly shy. If asked, Gwen might say she was tired, but the truth, he guessed, was more likely that she was still sober enough to know she couldn't trust herself and that talking would be dangerous.

Hadrian managed to flag a carriage right away, and the three piled in. The driver knew exactly where to find the Turquoise Turtle, which was good as Hadrian wasn't certain he could find the rolkin in the tiered maze of whitewashed grottos. The ride back was a tranquil *clip-clop*. Neither of his two companions spoke. Gwen curled up and laid her head on Royce's shoulder, and if the thief had anything more to say on the subject of empty, corked bottles, he appeared content to let it wait. As far as herding the happy went, Hadrian had an easy go of it.

It felt late. The air was clammy and cool. The moon cast long shadows, stripping the world of color, leaving the domes and awnings to appear like many shades of silver. Far fewer people walked the streets at that hour, and the sound of music was restricted to the open doors of various-sized establishments where light and people continued to spill out. Under it all, the sound of the sea rolled its constant rhythm.

The Lord Byron letter Albert had given Hadrian worked like a magic talisman, and after only glancing at its tattered face, the driver smiled warmly and waved as they walked away without so much as paying a copper or giving a name. The whole night was turning out to have been a wonderful experience, right up until the moment they reached the gate to the Turtle and found it open.

A lack of locks was one thing, but the latch was unhooked, and the gate thrown wide. Hadrian remembered being the last one through, and he knew he'd closed it.

Arcadius must have done it.

The old professor had returned early. He must have been tired and was just the sort to absentmindedly fail to hook the latch. Hadrian was feeling pretty good about that bit of deduction, clever even. Then he noticed the courtyard with all the urns and pots lying on their sides. The table was turned over, along with the chairs, and the door to the rolkin stood wide as well.

"Arcadius?" he called, more hopeful than earnest. His mind had dismissed the idea of the absent-minded professor and jumped forward to simply hoping Arcadius was alive. The lack of reply chilled him.

Hadrian reached for the grips of his swords, only to remember he didn't have them. They were inside, all the way upstairs, hanging on the wall pegs of his chosen room — or at least they had been.

"Why is it so dark?" Gwen asked as she stared at the open door and black windows.

"Wait here." Hadrian grabbed one of the courtyard lights. They were common handheld lanterns that hung from the top ring, but they still had the bail handle just in case. None of them were lit.

Hadrian took the candle and lit it off the streetlamp.

Royce had his knife out, but he hadn't gone in. "Best that I stay with her," he explained.

Hadrian nodded. Raising the lantern before him, he stepped inside.

The interior of the Turtle was silent and an absolute mess. As if a hurricane had blown through, everything that could have been dislodged, toppled, or rolled had been. Looking like a hatched dragon's egg, the big clay pot lay shattered.

The jungo plant had been ripped from the copper urn and all the dirt dumped out. Even the carpets were flipped, though some were neatly rolled as if prepped for stealing, but none were missing. The black onyx dolphin was on the ground, its tail broken. Cushions were flung everywhere, and extra bedding had been pulled out of cupboards and thrown across the floor.

Hadrian moved through the wreckage and up the stairs, heading for his room and his swords, despite believing the act was futile. Their time together may have tempered Royce's more violent habits, but those same years had also changed Hadrian. This was driven home as he moved through the ransacked rolkin, all but convinced of two things: his blades were taken, and the professor was dead.

Like the rest of the rolkin, his bedchamber had been torn apart. Blankets, sheets, and pillows were thrown about, the mattress ripped apart, feathers everywhere. His bag had been emptied, the contents scattered. To his amazement, all three swords remained untouched. Taking up his short blade in one hand while still wielding the lantern in the other, he searched the rest of the rolkin. He entered Arcadius's room last and was shocked to find it empty.

Hadrian returned to the common room, where he found Gwen busy lighting lamps.

"Where's Royce?"

"He went out."

"Out?"

"Looking for whoever did this, I suppose."

"That can't be good. Stay here. Close the door after I leave. There's no lock, so prop something against it. I doubt whoever did this will be back, but better to be safe."

Hadrian left the courtyard and had only moved down the street a short distance when he found Royce: uncloaked, his dagger out and gleaming in the moonlight. "What are you doing? I thought you were guarding Gwen?"

"I heard something," Royce said, then he stumbled into a rain barrel, bounced off, and nearly fell.

"You're in no condition to be doing this. Come back to the Turtle."

"I'm fine."

"You're drunk."

"I just had a little wine. I've seen you drink *waaay* more. I've watched you fight after running the taps out. You did fine." Royce stumbled against the rain barrel again. He stopped and stared at it, confused.

"Yeah, Royce," Hadrian said. "It's the same barrel."

"Really?"

"Yep. And you might want to put that dagger away before you accidentally cut off your own fingers. Whoever ransacked the Turtle is long gone."

"And Arcadius?"

"No sign of him."

Royce leaned on the rain barrel and struggled to put Alverstone into the sheath that hung on his belt. He tried three times and failed. "I hate being drunk."

"I can see why. You're lousy at it."

"You make it look so easy."

"Years of practice, my friend." Hadrian took the dagger away. "Let's get you back to Gwen."

Hadrian put his arm around Royce, and the two began walking in sync. At least they tried. Royce was like a dancing partner who wanted to lead but didn't know how to dance.

"I kissed her," Royce said.

It took Hadrian a second to catch up to the drunken side trip his friend had unexpectedly embarked on. Not only was it off topic, but also shocking both in subject and message. That Royce could kiss anyone was a hard image to conjure; that he had opted to speak of it was unthinkable. Hadrian suspected this blurted confession was the tail end of an extensive internal monologue Royce had just run through in his head. To the thief, it likely made perfect sense.

Those three words explained a lot.

No wonder Gwen had that giddy but coy look. She was bursting to share but knew better than to boast — certainly not in front of Royce.

"How'd that go? I take it she didn't slap you or anything."

"It was nice."

"I would have expected as much."

"No, you don't understand. It was *really* nice. I mean, *really, really* nice."

"It'll be even better when you're sober."

"Now what in the name of Maribor are the two of you doing stumbling about like a couple of drunken sailors just in from a five-year voyage?" Arcadius asked as he walked toward them. "Are you two just getting back now?"

"There you are!" Hadrian exclaimed. "Where have you been?"

"Yeah, Grampa," Royce said. "Better not have been at the brothel again or Gramma is gonna poison your dinner."

The professor paused to cast a sidelong stare at Royce. "I take it he's suffering from a few too many bottles of wine?"

"The ones you put in front of him, by the way," Hadrian replied.

"They were for everyone, Hadrian, and yet you don't seem nearly as fermented."

"I don't like wine. You know that. And Montemorcey is the only thing Royce drinks. You know that, too."

"True, but I didn't force it down his throat. And it was only wine. A case could be made that the man needed a bit of encouragement to shake off the shackles of the north and embrace the warmth of those around him."

If Hadrian needed any further confirmation that the professor had done it on purpose, that was it. Arcadius had manipulated the events from the start. Very likely his intentions were benevolent. The professor had long sought to banish Royce's demons, teaming the two of them in the hope that Water could convince Oil to be more social. It hadn't worked, or at least it hadn't worked well enough. Now, Arcadius was calling in reinforcements.

"Let's shave Grampa's beard off." Royce grinned at Arcadius and began searching for his dagger, which Hadrian still had, but now kept out of sight.

"What about you?" Hadrian asked the professor as he once more resumed guiding Royce back toward the Turtle. "What happened? You were coming back here. Did you get lost?"

"I was just out for a late-night stroll. I really wasn't feeling altogether well. Too many years of eating the horrible stuff they call food at the university have left me incapable of digesting the real thing. The cool night air did just the trick."

"So, you haven't been back to the Turtle yet?"

"Just returning now . . . Why?"

Royce frantically patted down his tunic. "I think someone stole Alverstone."

CHAPTER TWELVE

The Search Begins

Royce remained in his room until after midday.
Hadrian and Gwen had spent the early morning hours cleaning up the Turtle. The biggest hurdle, by far, was re-stuffing the mattresses. Just collecting all the feathers had been a big job. Gwen, being the expert on restoring order to desecrated bedrooms, barked orders at Hadrian, who responded like a dutiful foot soldier. Working together, Hadrian's, Gwen's, and Albert's beds had been pretty much restored. Then their attention had been turned to the common area. In a surprisingly short time, the Turtle was set as close to right as possible.

They were just finishing up when Albert returned, appearing surprisingly chipper. Gwen had insisted on going to the market, and the two had gone out shopping — she for something to cook, he for a new hat. As far as Hadrian could tell, Arcadius — like Royce — was sleeping late.

When Hadrian's partner finally came down, the thief looked about as happy as a cat dragged through a storm drain. Royce spoke no more than a dozen words — most of them variations of *no*. The thief skipped breakfast, which at the time could only have meant fruit from the courtyard because Gwen hadn't yet returned.

Donning his cloak and growling something about *getting the lousy job over with,* Royce led the way out and Hadrian followed.

The first step in satisfying their contract would be finding Gravis Berling. According to Albert, Lord Byron had no idea where Gravis lived. Tur Del Fur wasn't like Rochelle, where all the dwarfs were forced to cluster in a designated portion of the city. Still, Hadrian found it odd, and more than sad, that a person could work at a place for nearly a hundred years without his employer having a clue where he lived or might be found. Apparently, all the other dwarfs had also been *let go* — a nice way of saying *kicked out* — and with them went all knowledge of Gravis Berling. This forced Royce and Hadrian to begin their assignment by wandering the streets, looking for short people.

Hadrian discovered that Tur Del Fur wasn't as complicated as it had first appeared. It had one main road, which ran from the heights down to the harbor. All the other streets branched off it, creating loops at various levels — or *tiers.* The lower the number, the closer to the water, and of course, the more desirable the neighborhood. The Turquoise Turtle was on Tier Four, while The Blue Parrot was on Tier Two. Hadrian and Royce spent several hours searching the city from the harbor to the heights, finding absolutely nothing useful regarding Gravis Berling. For a city founded by dwarfs, precious few of them walked its streets.

By late afternoon, they stood in the shade of the green-and-white-striped canopy of a food vender named Angelius. The balding, middle-aged man sat cross-legged just off the road in a wrap of white cotton. Beside him, a stone-ringed cook fire heated a blackened iron pot. Hadrian had purchased a stuffed flatbread from him and lingered in the awning's shade to eat. Royce continued his silence, watching him and grimacing with each bite.

"You really should have something, too." Hadrian told Royce between mouthfuls.

"I should cut my own throat is what I should do," Royce replied. He had his hood up, his head drawn deep into shadow.

"Hangover *that* bad? Have you been drinking water? Trust me, that helps — especially after wine."

Royce shook the hood, which was sort of an answer, just not a very clear one.

With no place to sit, they stood a step off the main street just outside the cloud of smoke that wafted from Angelius's cook fire. A wagon filled with carpets and hauled by a team of goats rolled past, followed by another filled with urns of oil. One of the containers was cracked and, in the wagon's wake, a dripping dark line was created in the dust-covered pavement. No dwarfs in sight.

Hadrian took another bite of his meal. Like everything else he'd eaten in Tur Del Fur, it was a bit too spicy, but flavorful. He swallowed, then voiced the conclusion to an idea he'd been pondering all morning. "I don't think it was a robbery," he said, shifting his grip on the flatbread, which was starting to come apart. "Nothing was taken. Not that we had much to steal, but my swords would have been worth the trip, and I'm sure Albert's clothes are valuable. So, I think someone was looking for something."

Royce nodded.

"Do you think it might have something to do with your new nightmare client, the Gingerdead Man?"

Royce lifted his head enough that Hadrian spotted a smile.

"Ah-hah! I knew you were in there somewhere."

Angelius looked over, "Sounds like you were the victim of someone looking for the courier's package. You would not be the first."

"What courier package?" Royce asked, peering at Angelius as if the man had just appeared before them.

Hadrian wiped his mouth clean with the sleeve of his shirt. "A courier was murdered along the road that leads here. His pouch taken."

"How do you know about this?"

"How do I . . . Oh, that's right, you weren't there. When we first arrived, a bunch of Yellow Jackets — that's what they call Port Authority soldiers — they talked to Shelby about it."

"It is not merely the DPAA," Angelius said. *"Everyone* is looking for that package."

"Why?" Royce asked. He was back to staring at Angelius.

"A reward has been offered . . . by Cornelius DeLur himself."

Royce took a step toward him, a slow careful one that made Hadrian stop chewing. "And why would *you* think someone would search *us?*"

Angelius shrugged. "Because you were robbed, but you don't know what they were looking for. The city has gone all crazy searching for this package."

The thief continued to stare. Hadrian imagined Royce's hungover brain was struggling to determine the odds that he and Hadrian had randomly stopped to eat at the stand of someone connected to those who ransacked the Turtle. It took longer than usual, but Royce sighed in resignation. "Hadrian, just swallow the rest of your boiled rat so we can move on."

"It's fried, and it's fish." Angelius corrected with a bright smile.

"Sure it is."

"Really tasty, too." Hadrian unfolded the brown-spotted bread to reveal the contents. "There's peppers and onions, goat cheese, and a spread that I think is made from chickpeas, garlic, and—"

"Shut up," Royce said through gritted teeth.

Hadrian knew exactly how Royce felt, and he sympathized. But he also remembered the dozens of mornings their roles had been reversed. At those times, Royce had been demeaning, self-righteous, and failed to express even a grain of sympathy. A frequently used phrase was, *"You did it to yourself, remember?"* As a result, Hadrian found it difficult not to acknowledge when Providence decided to return the favor by spreading the love.

Hadrian felt a drip running down his wrist. He closed up his meal and licked his arm.

Witnessing this, Royce shook his head. "You really are quite disgusting sometimes."

Hadrian grinned as if this were a compliment and took a big bite, moaning with ecstasy.

"It is good, yes?" Angelius grinned up at Hadrian from where he sat beside the fire, his back rested against the stone wall of a lamp shop.

Hadrian nodded and struggled to speak around the food in his mouth. "*Under*-ful."

"It is fresh hakune," Angelius explained, "A fierce whitefish with a great fin on its back that my brother caught just this morning out in the deep sea. I cooked it using an ancient recipe my grandmother taught me that *does not* include any *rat*."

"Oh, don't mind him." Hadrian waved a dismissive hand. "He's suffering from drinking too much wine last night."

"Ah!" Angelius brightened. "I have just the thing!" He dug into one of the many sacks beside him and pulled out a jar. "This is a perfect remedy." Removing the lid, he revealed a viscous goo. He scooped some out with his finger and held it up. "I will stuff this up your nose as far as it will go, then swirl it around. I will do this for both nostrils and be generous with my scoops."

Royce recoiled. "Hard to do after I cut off your hands."

Angelius clearly didn't take the comment seriously and said, "Oh no, it is fine, trust me. I have a brother who drinks too much all the time, and he swears by this remedy."

"The one who caught the fish?" Hadrian asked.

"Different one," Angelius said. "I have several."

"What's it called, this hangover cure?" Hadrian picked up the jar with his free hand to study it.

"Doesn't have a name, but trust me, it works."

"I *don't* trust you," Royce said. "And as for your anonymous goop in a jar, I suspect it contains what's left of at least one brother." He looked at Hadrian. "You can walk and eat at the same time, can't you?"

"To be completely honest," Hadrian told Angelius as he handed back the jar, "I don't think his foul mood is entirely due to drinking. I mean, first of all, he's usually like this anyway, to one degree or another. But the real reason I think he's so grumpy is because he kissed a woman last night."

Royce huffed. "Just stuff what's left into your big mouth and let's go."

Angelius looked confused. "Is this woman horribly grotesque? Or maybe she's suffering from a contagious sickness."

"Neither. She's actually incredibly beautiful, and he's in love with her."

Angelius narrowed his eyes as he put away the jar. "Then I'm not understanding."

"That's just it, no one does. No one can. Anyone else would be dancing their way through the streets and singing sappy songs since morning."

"Why are you still talking to him?" Royce asked. "He's busy. Now that he's sold you his rat, he'll need to hunt another."

"Because I want a second opinion," Hadrian replied. "Actually, that's not true. I want *you* to hear reason and realize how dumb you're being."

"And I don't want to discuss my personal life in the middle of a busy street with a destitute vagrant who sells boiled rats to naïve strangers and gets happy sniffing the remains of his dead brothers from a jar. So, while we still have some light left, let's try finding Gravis Berling."

"What do you want with Gravis?" Angelius asked, wiping his finger off on a towel.

Hadrian and Royce faced him with sudden interest.

"You know him?" Hadrian asked.

"That is like asking if I know the name of this street, which if you aren't aware, is Berling's Way — it's named after Gravis's family."

"Do you know where we can find him?" Royce asked.

Angelius pulled the top from his kettle, releasing a steam cloud. He stirred the contents of the pot with a large wooden spoon. "I suppose that depends on what business you have with him."

"We owe him money and are looking to repay the debt, but we're only here for a short time."

Angelius laughed, then looked at Hadrian. "Your friend is not a good liar."

"Actually, he is, but as we've established, he's off his game today."

"Ah yes, he drunkenly kissed the beautiful woman he loves. I can see how that would ruin anyone's week." Angelius stopped stirring and looked up sharply, pointing at Royce with the dripping wooden spoon. "Did she — did this love of your life — did she refuse you? Push you away? Slap you?"

"Why does everyone ask that?" Royce muttered.

"Because a rejection can be understood," Angelius clapped the spoon on the rim of the pot, then replaced the lid. "Humiliation such as that would certainly make a man miserable. I remember when I first fell in love with my sweet Velencia. She was —"

"Can we get back to Gravis?"

"She didn't slap him," Hadrian said, gathering up the last of his flatbread wrap into a final bite-size bundle. "From what I can tell, she was quite pleased with the kiss."

"Do you or do you not know where he can be found?" Royce pressed.

"The one you owe money?" Angelius grinned at Royce. "Since you are in a hurry, leave the coin with me, and I will get it to him."

Royce clapped slowly. "How nice. The destitute rat seller can afford a sense of humor."

"Honestly, Royce, why *are* you depressed?" Hadrian asked. "Would you have been happier if she *had* slapped you?" He stuffed the last of his meal into his mouth. It was bigger than he'd expected, and Hadrian struggled to chew it into submission.

Royce stared at him for a moment with an expression of astonished disgust. "I would have preferred not to have made a fool of myself."

"Oh, I see," Angelius nodded gravely. "Are you that bad at kissing?"

"'Ertainly 'asn't 'ad much 'actice," Hadrian managed to say.

Angelius nodded. "But then how does anyone *really* know? Women tend to be kind about such things. They never tell the truth because they know how much it would hurt. My Velencia, she —"

"That's not what I meant," Royce said.

"What do you mean?" Hadrian asked, having swallowed the last of his food.

Royce's face tightened, then he glared down at Angelius. "How about this. Tell me where I can find Gravis Berling, or I'll kill you and all your surviving brothers and provide the world with true justice by letting the rats feast on your remains out of an unmarked jar. And *trust me* I'm serious this time."

Angelius shook his head. "Threatening me will not help. I have no idea where to find the last Berling. I doubt anyone does now."

"Why's that?"

"Have you not heard the rumors? Gravis was stripped of his position at the Great Towers. He vowed to take revenge at nearly every alehouse in the city, saying that if he couldn't have Drumindor, then no one would. Most thought it was bluster — bitter ravings against a cruel world, but then . . ." Angelius lowered his tone and in an ominous voice said, "Then his wife died, and now he has nothing to live for. Many say there's nothing to stop him; he's got nothing to lose."

"What can a single dwarf do against a fortress?" Hadrian asked.

"He's no ordinary Dromeian. Gravis is a Berling. His family created Drumindor. All of them are geniuses, and he knows more about those towers than anyone alive. If he wants to, I believe Gravis could destroy this whole city. And I heard from Hiseron the Baker, who heard it from Danis the Butcher up on the sixth terrace, that Gravis has disappeared, gone underground as he prepares his abominable plans."

"If that's so," Royce asked. "Why aren't you leaving town?"

"I don't know if it is true. You hear all sorts of things on this street. Most of it is the talk of people trying to be noticed. And I can't just walk away. I have an excellent spot. And the fish is good, yes?"

"Absolutely," Hadrian said.

Angelius smiled. "See?" Then the smile faded.

"What?" Royce asked.

The Calian shook his head and shrugged as he looked up and down the street. "I haven't seen a Dromeian in days."

"Dwarfs, you mean?"

"Yes, but actually they're Belgriclungreians."

"They're what now?"

"The Bels, Grics, Lungs, Doritheians, Nye, Derins, and the Brundenlins — the seven clans of the Dromeians. But whatever you call them, I haven't seen many. Some are good customers, but for the last week or so, I've not seen them. It makes a person wonder."

"Wonder what?"

"What they know that we do not."

When they got back, Royce and Hadrian discovered at least one dwarf that hadn't vanished. Gwen was in the courtyard speaking to Auberon.

The dwarf was once again in his billowy white cotton shirt, matching baggy trousers, and worn-out sandals. He wore the same straw hat with the blue feather, but this time he'd pushed the front brim up in a friendly manner as he faced Gwen.

"We are so terribly sorry," Gwen said, as if she were personally responsible for a death in Auberon's family. "She's such a beautiful jungo plant, but I'm worried. Some of her roots were torn. I wetted them and set her back in the pot as best, and as soon, as I could, but — I don't know."

"There's no need to apologize," Auberon said. He spoke with a well-worn accent only noticeable in some words and phrases, his tone gentle, almost tired, like the voice of an ancient tree. "This isn't your fault. I'm just pleased no one was hurt."

Gwen would not be so easily consoled. "Last night one of us should have stayed behind — no, *I* should have watched over the house. I had no business going out like that. I was being selfish."

Auberon shook his head. "Not at all. This is my place, not yours. You're my guests and not responsible for protecting my property. It's my duty to safeguard you while you're under my roof. And usually that's not a problem. Tur has very little crime. This is . . ." He spotted Royce and Hadrian entering the courtyard.

Gwen saw them, too, and her dour expression transformed into an excited smile. Hadrian read her body. She took a step and was about to run to Royce, then caught herself and stopped. "How are you feeling, Royce?"

"Better," he said, his eyes on the dwarf.

"Auberon, this is my partner, Royce," Hadrian said. "Royce, meet our host."

"Welcome to Tur," the dwarf said and tipped the brim of his hat. Then he moved to the front door to study the frame. "Sorry for the incident last night. Such a thing is . . . well, it's very strange."

"Why strange?" Royce asked. "In my experience, people are robbed all the time. Especially when they don't put locks on their doors or windows."

Auberon continued to study the door. "We're a small community. Most know the Turtle and me, so they leave us both alone. Besides, as I was just telling the lassie here, we don't normally see this sort of thing in Tur. Folks in these parts come in two flavors: the content and the lazy." He turned and looked around the courtyard that, as far as Hadrian could tell, had been returned to perfect order. "By the look of things, a lot of discontented ambition visited my house last night, and that is a very curious thing."

"Have you eaten?" Gwen asked Royce, then looked at Hadrian. "Has he?"

Hadrian shook his head. "I tried. He refused."

"Albert and I found a wonderful market just down the road. I got some grapes and crackers." Gwen faced Royce with a smile as bright as the sun. "We can wake up your stomach with that before trying anything more adventurous." She grinned wider, then darted inside before Royce could protest.

Royce watched her leave, then once she was safely inside, he approached Auberon to speak more quietly. "You're a dwarf?"

Auberon looked up and winked. "You noticed that, did you? Was it the way I buckled my sandals that gave me away?"

"Ever heard of Gravis Berling?"

Auberon smiled, then chuckled. "Normally, at this point, I'd make a smart comment, like 'No, but have you heard of Herbert Cantrell?'"

"Who's that?"

"He's a farmer in Rhenydd."

"What makes you think I've heard of him?"

"Exactly. It's stupid to assume that everyone who lives in a certain place, or happens to be of the same race, knows each other."

"But?"

"As it turns out, I do know him, but that's not a fair example given that he's sort of famous, or *infamous*, depending on which side of the fence you sit on." Auberon ran his hand along the door frame, studying it, assessing damage.

"Do you know where he can be found?"

"These days — usually in a bottle."

"Can you tell us where he lives?" Hadrian asked.

"Nope. He used to sleep in a shack on the North Arm beach — him and his wife Ena. When the Port Authority took his job, his rent was no longer covered by the DPAA. No job. No money for rent. No home."

"We heard she died," Hadrian said.

Auberon gave up on the door frame and sighed. "Aye, she did that."

"What about family? Brothers and sisters? Kids? Anything like that?" Hadrian asked.

"Gravis and Ena never had any children. And he was an only child. Gravis was the last — the last of the Berlings."

Hadrian frowned at Royce. "Fellow works his whole life, but only makes enough to live in a shack; they fire him for what seems like no good reason, and he's kicked out and his wife dies. I'm starting to not like Lord Byron."

"Oh, don't blame him, Hadrian," Auberon said, now moving toward the once-toppled furniture that Gwen had set right during their absence. "Berling could have had a nicer place, but he chose to live in that hovel. Couldn't get him to move. And Ena's death had nothing to do with Byron firing Gravis. Let's see, she died the night of the full moon, and he was driven from that shack about a week after Ena's death. And yes, things grew bad for him then, but Berling never so much as looked for another job."

"I get the impression you don't like Gravis," Royce said.

"Never cared for any of the Berlings. They're all too full of themselves, always have been. Andvari and Alberich may have been geniuses, but that well went dry thousands of years ago. And it was the hubris of Andvari and Mideon that ruined us. Their combined arrogance destroyed our ancient capital of Neith and set the rest of us on a doomed course. We Dromeians — we weren't defeated by anyone but ourselves. And now, its gonna happen again."

"What do you mean?" Royce asked.

"Since the Republic of Delgos was established, there's been a huge wave of dwarven immigration returning home. Most come back looking for a better life, but a few — the loud ones — chatter on about the Belgric Kingdom, and the good ole days of dwarven rule. That sort of talk doesn't fly so well in a republic. Gravis is one of those with a big mouth and a small brain. He's always spouting off about fighting to reestablish a long-dead and, quite frankly, pretty awful sovereignty. Gravis lost his livelihood, and poor Ena could have died in the street because Gravis was too proud to take a conventional job. He's a Berling, you see, and Berlings can't stoop to doing laundry, watering plants, or sweeping a floor. I have no patience for that kind of thinking. You do what you must to take care of you and yours."

Hadrian saw the way Auberon looked around the courtyard as he spoke, and an idea clicked. "*You* were one of those who offered him a job, weren't you?"

"I did. Not so much for his sake, but for hers. Even so, Ena wasn't innocent. The lass shoulda known better than to marry a Berling. Nothing good could have come from that."

"So, you don't know where to find him?"

Auberon shrugged. "I'd look for any place willing to give away strong drink. But barring that, I suspect any vacant patch of gutter would be a good bet." Auberon lifted his straw hat, revealing a balding head. He wiped the sweat from his brow then set the hat back, adjusting it level this time. "Why do you ask?"

"We're supposed to have a talk with him," Royce said.

"There's a rumor he might be planning something that could destroy the whole city," Hadrian added.

The dwarf took a hard look at Hadrian then Royce, then slowly nodded. "Uh-huh, I see. So, you're the muscle Byron hired?"

They didn't answer.

Auberon pointed at Hadrian. "You're a swordsman, a good one, maybe a bit more than good. And you"— he gestured at Royce — "you'd be the cutthroat. The one who says *talk* when he means *kill*." He moved to the table and adjusted the placement of one of the chairs. "Listen, I'm old. I've seen a lot — too much, really. On the other hand, the both of you are still young. So let me give a bit of advice that I wish I'd had when I was your age: find a new line of work. Doesn't have to be fancy. You don't need to make a lot of money — just enough to live a simple life. Do something you like, more than one thing even, so you don't get bored, but be sure whatever you do is something you can be happy to tell your children and grandchildren about." He looked at the open doorway to the Turtle. "And as my people are fond of saying, *yer aff yer heid* if you don't take good care of that fine lassie you've got in there. She's a keeper, she is, and it would be worth making a change for her."

Auberon moved to where they had stacked up the remains of the broken pottery and sighed.

"I'm sure Lord Byron will be willing to pay for any damages," Hadrian said.

"Not his fault." Auberon bent down and lifted two shattered pieces of clay. "But someone certainly made a mistake. I'll find out who that was, then he and I . . . well . . ." Auberon winked at Royce. "Maybe we'll have a wee *talk*."

CHAPTER THIRTEEN

Auberon

Gwen invited Auberon to stay for supper. With Albert's help, she had purchased something she'd never seen before: a dark-skinned fish the size of a small calf with a blade-like snout about the length of a good hand-and-a-half sword. The thing was so heavy it had to be carted to the Turtle on a wagon and lifted out by three men.

"Please stay," she had begged Auberon. "We have *a lot* of fish. Not sure what I was thinking."

After admitting she had no experience cooking such a beast, Auberon agreed to stay, if only to make certain the fish was well prepared, and the leftovers properly stored. "You take an animal's life, then you have an obligation to make its death worth something. And I have some experience with fish."

He butchered the monster out in the courtyard, put the numerous thick pieces on a saltwater-soaked, five-foot cedar board that could have had a previous life as the bottom of a sea chest. Then, as he got coals ready in the courtyard's open-air hearth, he had them gather lemons from the tree and dill from plants near the door. He added that to the fish, then he put the whole thing over the smoldering coals and covered it with a metal lid. In about an hour, the fish was done.

The day was fading when they all sat at the supper table. The dazzling lightshow that was sunset sliced through the Turtle's massive windows, turning the whole place golden. Albert pulled the cork on a single bottle of wine, which was more than needed, as no one was in much of a drinking mood. Royce looked like he might kill Albert when the viscount poured him a glass.

"This is incredible, Gwen," Arcadius said, smacking his lips in delight. "Better than The Blue Parrot."

"Don't look at me. Auberon is the chef. I invited him to supper, and he went ahead and made the whole meal. And thank Maribor he did. I'm certain I would have desecrated this poor fish." She looked at the dwarf. "I'm not a great cook, you see. I just know I'm better than them."

Albert nodded at Auberon as he swallowed. "I wasn't aware your people were such wonderful chefs."

Auberon smiled politely, and Gwen closed her eyes and shook her head.

"What?" The viscount looked surprised. "It's true, isn't it? Dwarfs are known for metal crafting and stonework, but no one ever speaks about their talent for food."

"And all women are great at cooking, and Calians are known for fortune telling and haggling, right?"

Albert stared back at her, flummoxed. "But you just said you're better at cooking than we are, and you're a *very good* businesswoman, and you've been known to tell fortunes."

Gwen rolled her eyes while Albert continued to look lost.

"I believe that what the lady is saying," Auberon ventured, "is that it might be wise to withhold judgment on a whole nation of people and instead stick with evaluating the person in front of you based on their own merits and not the track record of hearsay."

"Exactly," Gwen said. "And the only reason I can cook better than the rest of you is because you're all too lazy to learn."

"When we camp on a job, I cook," Hadrian declared. "I think I do pretty well."

Royce coughed like he might choke.

The dwarf took a sip from his wine and wiped his mustache and beard. "As for me, I couldn't smith a doorknob or build so much as a stone step. Never had the talent."

"I thought you . . ." Hadrian looked around. "Didn't you build this?"

"The Turtle?" Auberon shook his head. "No. This place was carved out of these cliffs thousands of years ago by the Brundenlins." He pointed at Royce. "That's the clan your Gravis Berling hails from. While the rest of the Dromeians were content to live up north in Neith, sleeping over the grave of Thane Dorith, the Brundenlins were never known to be content. They also didn't like bowing to the Doritheians. They came down here, and once Mount Druma was tamed, they built these. That was the start of the Golden Age, as they call it. The time of Andvari Berling and King Mideon, who did away with the old thanes and created the First Kingdom." The dwarf took another bite and sat back, his eyes looking out the front windows at the sunset over the harbor. White boats bobbed in gilded water, and the twin towers of Drumindor stood black, casting huge shadows on the city.

"Have you always been a fisherman?" Hadrian asked.

"Me? Oh, no. I'm certain you're a better cook than I am a fisherman. I rarely catch anything and hardly ever keep the fish when I do. I just like being out in my little boat all alone, rocking on the ocean, rolling over the waves, and listening to the wind and the gulls. It's peaceful out there."

"So, what did you used to do?"

Auberon sucked in his lower lip and looked back out the window. "That's a long story."

"I love stories," Gwen said.

"But this one involves a lot of sad, dwarven history. No one likes that—not even dwarfs. I think it's sufficient to say I'm not from here. I was born up north, near Lanksteer in the Dithmar Range. That's where a lot of dwarven families relocated after the Old Empire annexed Belgric back in 1912."

They all stared in shock, which caused Auberon to chuckle. He stroked his white beard, lifted his straw hat, and scratched his balding head. "I know I look ancient, but I'm not *that* old. Despite what you may have heard, Dromeians don't have the lifespan of a mountain. Twas my grandparents who moved us. And I've done a great many things; I just never had a use or talent for the pick or hammer."

And Hadrian couldn't say he had much talent for numbers, but given that 1912 was well over a thousand years ago, he didn't think *grandparents* solved the riddle. "So, then, the little symbols on the walls in each room. They were already here?"

Auberon lowered his head and looked at the table. "No, I painted those." He lifted his sleeve to reveal the same markings tattooed on his arm. "As you can see, I'm not much of an artist, either."

"What's it mean?" Albert asked.

Auberon hesitated.

"Has it ever crossed your mind, Albert," Gwen said, "that people don't generally put permanent marks on their bodies as a lark? Usually what they *mean* is personal. You might as well ask Auberon if he dresses to the left or the right."

Albert's eyes grew in comprehension. "Oh. Sorry."

While this appeared to clear up the matter as far as the viscount and Gwen were concerned, Hadrian, Royce, Arcadius, and even Auberon looked mystified.

"Do you mean which leg he puts in his trousers first?" Hadrian asked.

Gwen closed her eyes and lowered her head. "No," she said, "just let it go. We have a guest."

Everyone looked at Albert, who smiled back. "It's something a tailor would ask before taking the inseam measurement for trousers, preferring to do his work on the, ah"—he glanced at Gwen—"unoccupied side."

Gwen groaned.

"It's all right," Auberon said. "The tattoo—it's a simple symbol because I'm a lousy artist. It's my family. The tall line with the circle above is my dear wife, and the two shorter ones on either side are my sons. They died many years ago."

"I'm sorry," Gwen told him.

Auberon nodded. "Aye, so am I."

Royce never felt he knew a place until he saw it from above. The slopes, walls, primary arteries, choke points, and vulnerabilities of a city were best viewed from rooftops and only at night. A man standing on a high point during the day was a thing of curiosity. People pointed, gawked, and shouted, but at night, no one could see him. Paired against the black sky, he was invisible and free to study the playing field below. That's how he saw it, because someone was definitely playing a game with him.

This was no great feat of awareness. His opponent wasn't being subtle, which meant his adversary had no worries about repercussions. This either meant his enemy had no idea who Royce was, or knew but didn't care. The former would be his challenger's mistake, the latter, his. This left Royce with the age-old puzzle: who, what, and why. These sorts of riddles were best wrestled with on rooftops, where he could be alone with his thoughts.

That evening, after they said goodnight to Auberon, and as the others slept, Royce had slipped out and perched himself on the dome of a building that shared a wall with the Turtle; all the buildings in Tur Del Fur were connected in some fashion. From this vantage point, Royce could see how the rolkins had been carved from the same cliff. Each were individual residences but contiguous parts of one sculpture. Walls and stairs formed connecting tissue, and the multitude of narrow streets below looked like the tracks on a single worm-eaten board.

Trekking around the city in his cloak all day had sweated out the remainder of the wine and cleared Royce's head. Supper had replenished his strength. Now, the night air was breathing life back into his spirit. He knew he needed to think, but his mind continued to slip back to the same topic, which didn't help at all.

Royce had woken to regret, knowing he'd made a fool of himself with Gwen.

I think I danced with her!

Blessedly, that part wasn't so clear. All he remembered were lots of shadows, soft whispering music, and holding Gwen obscenely close as they swayed together. He recalled the press of her body, the contours, the softness. Royce had no idea how long they'd danced, who may have seen them, or what else he may have done. But one thing was undeniable.

I kissed her.

He was certain of that. The kiss stood out bright as the sun — too intense to look at straight on or think about directly. His pickled brain had formed its own blurred tribute of an instant too beautiful to ruin by study. Better that he remembered the myth — a singular moment of purity and passion that transcended every other experience in his life. And as Hadrian pointed out, Gwen didn't appear to mind. As hard as it was to fathom, if he was honest with himself, he had to admit she actually seemed to like it. This was revelatory, and like everything connected with Gwen, wholly unexpected.

But kissing her had crossed a line, a dangerous one.

Over the years and despite all efforts to restrain himself, his feelings for Gwen had grown. The two of them got along well. She was comfortable, and he enjoyed her company, which was rare since he hated most people. They shared a kinship of sorts. Gwen hadn't talked much about her past, just enough for Royce to know the woman's life wasn't a parade of candies, cakes, and compliments. Her mother had fled Calis when Gwen was just eleven, never giving an explanation. Alone, the two had traveled hundreds of miles down dangerous roads into an unknown region where *their kind* weren't received with welcome arms. Then, somewhere around Vernes, her mother had died. Royce didn't know how old Gwen was when she joined the bursting ranks of the officially orphaned, only that she was too young to be on her own. While Royce had always been alone, his youth must have been easier. A poor, attractive, foreign girl abandoned in the wilderness of ruthless men made his days of competing with gutter rats for meals seem rosy.

Royce had known multitudes of men and women forced to face terrible hardships, but few had done so with the grace, wit, and intelligence that Gwen exhibited. And none of them had ever come through the sewer smelling sweet, their dignity and humanity still intact. Gwen had. He admired that in her. She was a better person than he, better than anyone he'd ever met.

How it was that such a lady as Gwendolyn DeLancy could see him as anything but disgusting was right up there with why the sky is blue. And it wasn't simply that she thought he was a few shades lighter than deplorable. Gwen genuinely respected him in much the same way he esteemed her. This incomprehensible, wide-eyed admiration granted Royce an invitation into the land of dignity and self-respect that had always been locked behind garden gates. When he was with her, he felt important, smart, and as ridiculous as it seemed—*good.* In her eyes at least, he was a hero of sorts, and through that colored glass he saw a future that wasn't dark and tragic; he spied a reflection of himself that was more than a mistake. But with this treasured gift came the desperate fear of ruining everything. Royce was terrified of falling from his pedestal and seeing that look of respect fade forever from her eyes.

Of course, there was an outside chance that while inebriated, he had been suave, and eloquent, dashing, attractive, and . . . *and with enough yarn, cows might learn to knit sweaters.*

He sighed till his shoulders slumped, then took a deep breath.

I need to stop this. I have to think.

Too much was happening. Royce was a man in a forest, single-mindedly gathering wood for a fire while ignoring the ceaseless snapping and rustling all around. He had stabbed a man in the throat, but not only had this not ended a life, the ought-to-be-dead man followed him halfway across the world to offer him a job. The sheer number of inexplicable issues arising from that one set of events was mind-boggling enough to make him wonder if Hadrian wasn't right about it being a dream. Now, they had only just arrived, and someone had invaded and searched the house they rented, and he hadn't a clue who it might be or why they had done it. Nothing was taken, so it wasn't a petty robbery. No one was hurt and no threat made, which meant it wasn't intimidation. No effort had been made to hide the act, so secrecy wasn't a concern.

Who were they? What did they want? And did they get it?

Since Royce and the others had only just arrived, and they hadn't done anything unusual it seemed unlikely that any of them were the target.

Perhaps the search has nothing to do with us. Auberon is a shady character with an unexplained past, and after all, it's his rolkin. We might be the unlucky bystanders in a local clan war. Or maybe Angelius is right, and someone is just looking for the courier's missing package.

These were bizarrely optimistic ideas, and Royce shooed them away, attributing the thoughts to the lingering effects of poisoning his mind with wine. Instead, he concluded he knew two things. First, the incursion had been timed for when the Turtle was empty, which meant someone had been watching their movements. Second, Royce had insufficient information to reach a reasonable conclusion on anything else. This total ignorance led to his roosting on the rooftop that night. He hoped that whoever had been watching was still at it. There was a chance Royce might obtain the answers needed by polite inquiry. But if he were lucky, it would take more than merely asking.

Overhead, in the star-filled sky, half a moon had reached its high point, casting a cold silvery radiance in a line across the ocean and illuminating the whitewashed roofs and walls of the city. Beneath Royce, some lanterns still burned, casting a warm yellow glow. He found an unexpected beauty in the contrast, a statement shouted at the night—an echo lingering from centuries before when dwarfs first made a campfire on those shores and declared they would stay.

Royce had never cared for the diminutive, devious crafters. Like barking dogs and track-revealing fallen snow, they served as awful obstacles to his trade by creating doors and boxes impossible to open. And yet he had to admire the work done here: the cliff dwellings and of course, the massive towers—a pair of dark, giant legs straddling the headlands—shadows too big to be real.

How long had it taken? How much labor went into such a feat? How had this warren of roads, stairs, and buildings managed to fit together so perfectly? And most of all . . . How did they carve two towers from one volcano and tame the beast in the process?

Tur Del Fur, however, wasn't all starlight and ocean breezes. There was also ugliness. In the streets below, he witnessed the dark side of life in paradise. Two rolkins down, a couple were fighting in their courtyard. She complained he drank too much.

Just like home, Royce thought.

A while later, a trio of barefoot young men in shorts—two topless, one in a cheap vest—walked through the city, toppling rain barrels and ripping down awnings. Then they broke a window with a potted palm. The noise was almost as loud as the woman's scream, and the perpetrators raced off, laughing maniacally.

After that, another couple who was taking a late stroll paused beneath the single lantern at the four-way intersection. The man knelt and held up a small object. The woman whispered something and nodded. Then in that pool of light, they embraced, kissed, and hadn't stopped for over an hour. At last check, the man's shirt was off, and the straps of the woman's dress were heading that way. This left Royce wondering how wise a decision the woman had made if the wretch couldn't afford so much as a room.

Then, of course, there were the two quiet watchers—both reflections of himself. One sat on the public terrace bench outside the Turtle's gate. He wore a night uniform: clothes that were dark but not quite black and loose enough to provide ease of movement but cinched at the cuffs. He rarely moved.

The other watcher remained farther out. He was down the zigzagging stairs, so far away that he appeared little more than a shadow even to Royce's eyes. The first watched the Turtle, the second watched the first. Both had been there nearly as long as Royce, showing up just after moonrise. Neither appeared to notice him.

Dropping down off the dome on the far side, Royce circled around, staying low. He moved to the back of the terrace, judging his position by way of the swaying palm that grew next to the bench. Then, silent as a mute cat, he crept over directly behind Watcher-number-one and placed Alverstone to the man's neck.

"Why are you watching the Turtle?" Royce didn't need to say more. Explanations wouldn't be necessary. The man on the bench was a professional.

"What do you mean?" the watcher replied, unperturbed. "I'm just out for some air."

"Answer the question."

"Why?" the watcher asked.

Royce didn't like the man's attitude. He was far too relaxed, too confident.

I'm missing something.

He glanced down the street, but Watcher-number-two hadn't moved. Royce could now also see he didn't look to be in the same league. Watcher-number-two was dressed more like the three kids who had broken the window, except for the hooded cape he used to hide in.

Not a professional.

Didn't matter. Realizing Royce was looking at him, Watcher-number-two fled.

It's not him. There's something else.

"You don't want to kill me," the man on the bench said. "Do that, and you'll have to drag my body *all the way* down to the harbor to dump it. That's a lot of work, and you're here on holiday."

From the arched doorway of the neighbor's gate, Royce noticed movement. A third player in that evening's theater appeared. He stepped into the moonlight like an actor making an ominous entrance on stage. Dressed like his compatriot, he had added to that ensemble by accessorizing it with a standard-issue crossbow aimed at Royce.

"Now," Watcher-number-one said, "how about you take that dagger away from my throat? I have some questions for you."

Thwack!

Royce instinctively pulled back, dodging at the sound but knowing he was too late. At that range, he didn't stand a chance. His final thought was one of utter bewilderment.

Why'd you kill me if you wanted answers?

But it wasn't Royce's last thought.

Instead, the crossbowman collapsed. He hit the stone with a grunt. That's when his still-loaded weapon fired. The bolt cracked against the terrace wall two feet to Royce's left. Behind the dead crossbowman stood another, much shorter, person.

Auberon emerged from the same shadowed doorway. Without taking his eyes off them, he reloaded his weapon with the same degree of expertise as a grandmother of ten who sewed socks. In seconds, he was lethal again.

"You don't have to haul bodies from here," Auberon explained. "I usually just throw them over the wall behind you. They tumble right into the water near pier five. A fishhook and drag line will take them out to deep water. Sharks love 'em."

The dwarf pointed his bow at Watcher-number-one.

"Wait!" Royce said. He was feeling like a waiter holding too many plates and having more thrust at him. For a sleepy harbor town, Tur Del Fur was turning out to be absolutely hectic, and Royce still wasn't one hundred percent.

Auberon lowered the bow, surprised. "Friend of yours, is he?"

"No."

"Good." Up came the bow again.

"Wait, I said!"

"For what?"

"I'm trying to get some information here."

"Really?" Auberon narrowed his eyes. "What do you want to know?"

"To start with, who he is and who he works for."

"His name is Ellis Pratt, and he works for Cornelius DeLur. Need to know his shoe size, too? No? Then we're done here."

"Stop!" Royce growled.

"This fella invaded me house, broke me pot, the dolphin's tail, and tore up me jungo plant."

"Do you also know why?"

"Don't care. I live here in Tur. My houses and boat are off limits. Everyone knows that. Now, I have a reputation to uphold. If I don't, worse might happen."

"If he kills me," Pratt said, "The Company will assume it was Royce Melborn who did it, and they'll come for you. If I live, I can report that it was the crazy old dwarf who murdered Vigus."

"Murdered?" Royce said. "The man had a crossbow aimed at me."

"And you had a dagger at my throat."

"So, there aren't any innocent murder victims here, now are there?"

"Did I mention the sharks?" Auberon said. "These two trespassers weren't murdered. They just disappeared. Maybe they joined the pirates and had a wonderful career in the unorthodox maritime acquisition trade. No bodies, nothing to blame on you."

"Look," Royce said, "efficacy and expediency are all fine and good, but there is an art to this. I have a list of questions that I need addressed."

Auberon frowned and rolled his eyes, then he turned to Pratt. "Go on then. Tell the man your shoe size so we can get you rolling down the terraces."

"Why should I answer any questions if the dwarf is going to kill me anyway?"

"We'll all make a deal," Royce explained.

"I don't like deals," the dwarf said. "People go back on promises all the time, but no one cheats death."

I used to believe that, too, Royce thought with a wistful nostalgia for simpler days.

"A lack of information can be as deadly as a weakened reputation. Now consider this. We let Pratt live, in exchange for him telling us what they were after, *and* for assurance that neither you, nor I, nor anyone staying with us will regret letting him go."

"That'd be fine," Pratt said. "If I trusted *your* word."

"Trust *my* word?" Royce asked. "Where'd you get that from, some old poem? You're either going to be a late-night meal for a family of sharks, or you'll tell me something no one cares about that might save your life. Tough choice, I know."

"I still don't like deals," Auberon said. "This bastard tried to kill Daisy. Poor thing still might die."

"Who's Daisy?" Royce asked.

"The jungo plant."

Royce tilted his head in disbelief. "You have a tropical plant named *Daisy?*"

"Is that a problem?"

"Probably, but thankfully, not mine." Royce turned to Pratt. "Well?"

"Fine. We were sent to find a book."

"What book?"

"Don't look at me," Pratt said. "I can't even read."

"How were you going to identify this prize, then?"

"I'm illiterate, not stupid. I know what a book is."

"I don't have a book."

"Figured you'd say that, which is why we didn't knock and ask politely."

Royce frowned, then faced Auberon. "I want him to go back and report to DeLur that I said I don't have this book."

"And I'd rather he didn't go back and report that I killed the other one."

"Why not? Thought you had a reputation to uphold. How does that work if Pratt and Vigus have a wonderful career in the unorthodox maritime acquisition trade? Besides, Mister Pratt here is going to do his very best to convince Cornelius to let this killing go."

"Why is that?" Auberon asked. "Once he's gone, he's gone."

"I'm a bit curious about that myself," Pratt said.

Royce moved around in front of Pratt. "Cornelius warned you about me. Did he happen to mention why?"

Pratt shook his head. "Just told us not to underestimate a fella named Royce. Which I assume is you."

Royce grinned, feeling considerably better about everything. If Pratt and Vigus were kept in the dark, then Cornelius DeLur considered them expendable. The *Big Guy* wouldn't risk a war over the likes of them.

"And I'm guessing the name Royce Melborn means nothing to you?"

Pratt nodded.

"Then let me offer another name that you might be more familiar with, a name that will provide you with a better understanding of the situation and why you might want to assure your boss that Vigus wasn't murdered after all." Royce leaned in close. "Up north, they call me . . . *Duster.*"

It took a second, then Pratt's eyes widened. "How do I know you're him?"

Royce threw back the shoulder of his cloak, loosened the ties at his shirt collar, and exposed his shoulder. "Because there is only one living person with this brand that isn't in Manzant."

Pratt stared at the scarred flesh in the shape of a stylized letter M and nodded.

"Now, if Cornelius tries to punish Auberon, or causes harm to me or anyone in my party, I'll respond in kind, but rest assured you'll be at the top of the list. Now tell me, Pratt, when you get back, what will you tell the Big Guy?"

"That Vigus decided he'd rather try a career in the maritime acquisition trade."

They didn't need to bother with the crossbowman's body. Pratt took care of it with the sort of professionalism that made Royce wonder if he had underestimated the man. Royce certainly overestimated his ties to his partner, whose remains he treated like a sack of refuse.

Ultimately, Royce concluded that his night had been well spent. The *what* remained a little vague, and the *why* was just as much a mystery as it had always been. But the *who,* at least, was answered, which also explained the lack of subtlety. His adversary, it turned out, wasn't a fool. They knew each other's reputations well, but as Cornelius DeLur was as powerful as any king, fear of Royce Melborn didn't rank high on the Big Man's list.

Although, now Royce had another puzzle to work on.

"Who are you?" he asked Auberon once the two were back in the Turtle's courtyard, which now felt like a fortress.

"You're a bit young to be going senile," Auberon replied. "We've already met. Maybe you should keep a notebook."

"And you're not nearly senile enough to not know what I'm talking about. What is your occupation? Your trade? You're not a fisherman, and you crossed out all the other traditional dwarven occupations."

"I'm old. I don't *do anything* anymore."

"So, what did you used to do?"

Auberon looked at the house and sighed. "I *used* to be stupid. And I was *very* good at it, too."

"Where'd you get the crossbow?"

"This?" Auberon lifted it into the moonlight. "Got it off my boat. This here is my *fishing rod*." He smiled at Royce. "Got some real nasty fish down here." He winked.

"Not going to tell me, are you?"

"How I wasted nearly four hundred years of my life? No. I'd rather not. It's a miserable story anyway, starring an idiot who lost everything while chasing an impossible dream. The sort of tale that old people bore young people to tears with, and I'm done making mistakes like that. Point of fact, I'm just about done with *everything*. I'll be four hundred and sixty later this year, and while my ancestors were rumored to have lived past five hundred, these days I'm considered ancient for a dwarf. I don't have much time left, and I plan to use it wisely. But if you'd like to thank me for the help, I'm all ears."

"I wasn't in any danger."

"They had a crossbow on you."

"They wanted information just as much as I did. No need to kill me for that."

Auberon stroked his beard while he eyed Royce. "You part of that crowd? Is that how you're so sure?"

Royce nodded. "I was. I used to work for Cornelius's son, Cosmos, up in Colnora. They have a different crew down here — not a thieves' guild because Cornelius owns this place. So they're more like his personal constabulary."

"You were in Cosmos's Black Diamond?"

Royce nodded.

"But not anymore?"

Royce shook his head.

"Didn't know you could quit."

"Neither did they."

"Well, if it helps you sleep," Auberon said, "I used to do something sort of like that, only bloodier, uglier, and ultimately way less profitable. But just like you, it's behind me. Now if you don't mind, I'm going to go and water Daisy. Poor girl has been through a lot."

CHAPTER FOURTEEN

The Missing

Scram Scallie was packed. This was no great feat since a capacity crowd numbered only a dozen warm bodies, but that night, two dozen and more squeezed in through the ancient stone door. A larger venue ought to have been chosen, but the little alehouse was the only place near the center of town that every Dromeian knew but the big folk didn't.

Everyone but Gravis was there for the meeting; he came for a drink.

"All the drain lines are nearly blocked from Tier Seven to Tier Five," Copper Pot said. His real name was Niblangree Optimverganon, but only his mother ever called him that, and it was suggested, by more than a few, that she had only gone to the trouble on his first birthday and regretted doing so ever since. "While I can't say, because I haven't looked at 'em me self, it would be my assumption that most of the drains are in dire need of a washout."

"The freshwater lines are even worse than the sewers." Trig the Elder leaned in at this point. "The Alabaster Chute portion of duct-line seven had a cave-in. Nothing devastating, mind you. Happens all the time. Roots push through the soil and rock, and then runoff gets in there and erodes the ceiling. The Chute is a special problem because it draws from the hot springs, and with that, you also get steam, which can be mischievous. Normally, I'd have sent a team in to reinforce the section and clear the debris, but acourse we're not doing that. And while the Alabaster Chute isn't the only blocked or clogged feed, that chute services the baths, and problems there . . . well, that's something the scallie notice. They go in to soak and find the basins barely deep enough to cover their knees."

"What about drinking water?" Sloan asked.

Trig cleared his throat. "Tur's not likely to ever run out of that. The ancient runs are nearly foolproof, but the end lines, the ones that go from the big channels to the homes, those might be impacted. I know that cutting off fresh water was what you were hoping for most. An inability to drink would put the fear of Drome in the scallie, but it's not likely to happen, and that's probably for the best. You don't want to be losing the primes. A lack of potable water out here, with all these people, would be more than dangerous. Whether you're Dromeian or human, no one can last long without potable water."

"It's not working, not having enough of an impact." Sloan leaned hard on the bar. "I thought they would come around, ask for help, but they haven't."

"And didn't I tell you it wouldn't work?" Gravis said. He was on his fourth pint and had never been a big drinker, though he was getting plenty of practice lately. Bubbles or no, the ale went to his head and loosened his tongue. The normally taciturn descendant of Andvari and Alberich Berling was becoming more opinionated every day.

"You also said you were going to steal Drumindor, now didn't you, Berling?" Baric shouted at him. "Well, what happened with that plan? Towers are still there, aren't they? Sloan here is trying to actually *do something*. You, on the other hand, just talk and talk. Big words always coming out of your little mouth, but you never *do* anything."

"Leave him be, Baric," Sloan said. "He's right. He did tell me it wouldn't work. And it hasn't. It's as if they've forgotten we exist."

"That's your fault, not theirs," Auberon said. He was near the door. Either the ancient one had slipped in late or just liked to be near the exit. At the sound of his voice, the room went silent.

"Auberon," Sloan said, surprised. "I wondered if ya would come."

"You invited me, didn't you?"

"I did." She nodded and gathered herself. "And what do ya mean by, *it's my fault?*"

The old dwarf with the sunbaked skin and pure white beard took another step into the room. He was what the word ancient was invented for, and yet he managed to stand straighter than any other in the room. "Everyone's underground," he said. "That was your plan, yes?"

Sloan nodded.

"Smart idea. You never know how things will turn out, so it's best not to leave families vulnerable to revenge or to be used as bargaining chips. But the problem is, you didn't leave anyone topside for them to negotiate with. With the complete absence of Dromeians, they think we've left."

"Left?" Sloan stared, confused. "Where would we go? This is our home."

"They don't see it that way. All they know is the dwarfs are gone, which is what they wanted all along."

Sloan studied the bar counter for answers. "Maybe I should go and talk ta them," Sloan said. "Perhaps I should . . ."

She looked up to see what everyone else saw: Auberon shaking his head.

"No?"

"You go down there as spokesperson and they'll target you as a leader or, more accurately, an agitator. Appear before the Triumvirate and lay out an ultimatum, and they will see an insurrectionist intent on starting a revolution — an enemy. You want to start a war, that's a good way to go about it."

"I don't want a war."

"I know you don't, and that's good. Wars never achieve the goals that start them, but they do make living with the prior problems more palatable by comparison."

"What should we do?"

Auberon shook his head. "I'm the last person to ask. More than anyone here, I've proven I'm an idiot. And only a fool would ever take my advice."

"Yer the wisest person I've ever known," Sloan said with a sincerity that no one hearing those words could doubt.

Auberon nodded. "You should get out more."

She continued to stare at him with desperation in her eyes.

"That's what I came to say. Listen or not. Good luck to you," Auberon said. "To all of you." And with that, he made use of his proximity to the exit and walked out the door.

Sloan continued to stare at the place where the ancient one had stood.

"We need to let them know we're still here," Kiln said.

Sloan nodded. "But how do we do that? How do we stand up for ourselves — how do we demand fairness without appearing to threaten them?"

"Everything frightens the scallie," Trig the Elder said.

Sloan had her towel over her shoulder, and she walked out from behind the bar. The place was packed tight, but they made room for her to pass. She wasn't going anywhere, just walking and thinking. Then some of those thoughts spilled out of her mouth. "We need ta show them we're still here . . . we need ta show them . . ." She stopped, her eyes shifting left and right. "But we also need ta show them *who we are.*"

"I think they know that," Baric said.

"No, they don't." Sloan's eyes widened. "All they know are the stories — the bad ones. The tales of Gronbach. All they ever see are dwarfs scurrying about like rats — fixing this, tinkering with that. We've become fairy tales ta them — and cautionary ones. We need ta show them we're more than that. We need to show them our true history in all its glory."

"Got a crystal ball, do you?" Gravis asked. "Even if you have, how would that help?"

Sloan looked at the floor. "I don't know."

"Bah!" Gravis waved a dismissive hand.

"Aw, go and be on your way, Berling!" Baric shouted at him. "Be off — you and your mouth. Don't you have a pair of towers to steal?"

"Baric, please." Sloan said gently, trying to make him heel.

"He's no right to denounce anyone," Baric went right on. "The dwarf is a bag of air. He blows out all manner of grand talk, but he hasn't the courage to act. I pity you, Berling, I truly do. You've only ever been good at being a cog in a machine, and now here you are without any teeth."

Gravis wanted to remove a few of Baric's teeth, but he saw no allies in the place — not that this was new. During his entire life, he'd been alone except for

Ena. She had been his friend. She had loved him, but he had only realized that fact on the night she died. Gravis saw no more point in being there. So, not quite as dignified as Auberon, he walked out.

"Don't be pushing him, ya fool!" Sloan's shout whispered through the stone. "Do ya also jump on thin ice? The poor fellow is suffering. Can't ya see that?"

"Where do you think he goes?" someone asked. "They forced him out of his shack, you know."

"He's a Berling," Trig said. "Lived here his whole life. He knows places the rest of us have never discovered."

"Likely has a secret palace somewhere deep in the cliffs."

"Aye, he's probably in a room of gold, sleeping on King Linden's bed."

Their voices faded as he walked away into the dark.

CHAPTER FIFTEEN

Lady Constance

"Feeling better this morning?" Hadrian asked when Royce emerged from his bedroom, boots in one hand, his cloak in the other. Once more the thief was the last one up, but at least it was still morning.

"Much," Royce replied as he came down the stairs, then stopped mid-step the way cats do when startled. He squinted painfully at the early sunlight blazing through the windows, brilliantly beaming off the white ceiling, walls, and floor.

Does he keep it dark in his room? Hadrian thought, then immediately chided himself. *Of course he does. Royce likely has the shutters closed and nailed shut.*

"Doesn't it ever rain here?" Royce grimaced, then continued down the last few steps.

Hadrian sat with his legs out on the long, cushion-covered bench, the same way Albert had on the day they first arrived. His bare feet clapped against one another to a beat and rhythm all their own. On his chest was a small burlap bag filled with peanuts that he was eating, skins and all. Gwen had bought them the day before, eager to express her trials in getting them. Apparently, the grower took issue with Gwen and Albert calling them pea-*nuts* because they weren't. While they resembled and tasted like walnuts, almonds, and cashews that grew as hard-coated fruit, peanuts were actually legumes that grew underground. The proper term, the seller had explained, was *ground pea*.

Hadrian glanced out at the blue sky. "It *is* sort of like Dulgath, isn't it? Did you want it to rain?"

"Be cooler if it did." Royce set down his boots, then swirled his cloak in an elegant circle as he pulled it over his head.

"Be cooler if you didn't wrap yourself in five sheeps' worth of wool."

Royce peered out of the hole. "We both know that's not going to happen." He tugged his head through and adjusted the shoulders. "Where is everyone?"

"Arcadius and Gwen went to the beach, and Albert is reporting to Lord Byron. Apparently, he's expected to make daily reports on our progress."

Royce sat at the table to slip on his boots. "What's he going to say?"

Strange that Royce puts on the cloak first, then the boots. Who puts on a coat before shoes? Of course, to Royce, his cloak isn't an outdoor garment.

Hadrian looked down at himself: loose and untied shirt, bare feet, and cloth trousers — his self-styled *holiday uniform*. The two men were night and day, but Hadrian couldn't decide which was better. He was undoubtedly more comfortable, but he admired Royce's dedication, which made Hadrian look like a ne'er-do-well layabout.

And I haven't the slightest idea where my boots are.

He thought they might be in his room or behind the stairs. He doubted he'd left them outside but couldn't rule it out.

"He's going to explain that we are working very hard, but that progress is slow because we only just arrived and are still getting a feel for the place."

"Really?"

"It sounds much better when he says it."

"I figured that, but I was just . . . I mean, that's actually the truth."

"Right." Hadrian nodded. "But there's no need to lie. This is a legitimate job."

Royce paused in hauling on his left boot and simply stared into the distance for a long moment. "I suppose you're right. Strange."

Royce finished outfitting his feet and stood up, clapping them on the floor to test his work. "Any of that fish left?"

Hadrian grinned. He set the *ground pea* bag on the table, then coaxed Royce to a pair of nearly invisible doors in the wall with all the intrigue of a thief during a heist. When he pressed a bit of stone, it turned to reveal a handle that, when pulled, opened a cabinet. Inside was a huge piece of ice, half melted.

"What—" Royce started to say, but Hadrian held up a finger to stop him.

Closing the ice door, Hadrian revealed a second handle below the first and opened another cabinet. This one was stocked with perishable food.

"Auberon calls it an *ice box*." Hadrian explained. "Says the ice lasts several days, and he gets new ice regularly. Comes off boats from up north. A wagon brings it. Everyone on the street gets deliveries like they do milk in Gentry Square. The fish is at the bottom because cold travels down. Arcadius explained the whole thing as if it was common sense, but I think it only made sense to him."

Royce grabbed up the fish that had been wrapped in paper and nodded. "It's cold, but not frozen. Is that good? Why do I want cold fish?"

"Arcadius insists that the cold preserves it—you know, like salt or smoke, but without changing the taste."

"Huh," Royce mused, looking back at the cabinet. Slowly he began shaking his head. Then, like a curse, he muttered, "Dwarfs."

"Where are we off to today?" Hadrian asked as he brushed the remnants of peanut shells from his chest.

"Tell you on the way, but we're going to need water, too. Any idea where the well is? You said it was in the courtyard, but I never saw it. Or does Auberon have a special device for that, too?"

"Actually . . . you're not going to believe this." Hadrian went on to spend the better part of an hour showing Royce how the indoor well worked.

"Arcadius says the idea isn't new. Apparently, the Old Empire had them, too."

"And it's fresh water?" Royce kept saying as he stared at the spigot that ran into a stone cistern with a stopper at the bottom.

"Both. This is fresh, but there's another for seawater that flushes that bucket under the chair in the privy."

"There's a privy? I was using a pot in the bedroom."

"You aren't the only one. That's how this whole thing started—with Auberon calling us barbarians. It's behind that little door in the archway beneath the stairs. Anyway, when you pull the lever in the privy, all of it runs out into tunnels that flow under the city and back out to the sea."

"Sewers." Royce nodded. "Ratibor has them. Like a man-made river beneath the city. Very convenient. Got rid of a lot of bodies that way."

"Gwen calls the flush bucket the best thing since shoes."

"This is why dwarfs scare me." Royce pointed at the tap as if it insulted him. "If they can do stuff like this, what else are they capable of?"

Royce led Hadrian down to the harbor, then around to the seawall of the quay, and past the numerous piers and jetties to one of the two arms of land that together made a circle that created the bay. Royce still hadn't said where they were going. This wasn't unusual. Royce, never talkative, was especially taciturn when others were within earshot. When he and Hadrian reached the far northern end of the harbor, Royce led Hadrian over a one-story retaining wall. On the far side, they dropped down into what looked to be wilderness. This portion of the coast hadn't been developed and gave a glimpse as to what Tur Del Fur had once been — a jungle. Mangroves, palms, eske trees, spikers, abra berry plants, and massive jungos were familiar to Hadrian from his days in Calis, but many others were new to him. As he and Royce plunged into the canopy of green, the screened sun made it instantly cooler, but they also lost much of the wonderful sea breeze.

Walking beneath the canopy of leaves was like being indoors. The air was still, the sounds of the world shut out and replaced by new ones: the drone of insects, rustle of leaves, whooping of gibbons, and the too-numerous-to-count bird songs. Hadrian suffered from flashbacks of his years in the Gur Em rainforest of Calis. This was nothing like that. The scale was wrong. Everything in the Gur Em was mammoth; even the raindrops seemed bigger. The animals and insects certainly were. But the biggest difference was that Delgos had no ghazel — at least no aggressive Ankor goblins. Hadrian knew this. His rational mind took the time to patiently explain it over and over, but it was like being introduced to a pet dog after having been nearly torn apart by wolves. He had to keep reminding himself that this was a tame forest.

Royce trekked through the dense foliage, heading seaward out along the northern arm. When they were about halfway, he finally spoke. "I was thinking about Gravis last night while I was on the roof." Royce pushed aside a five-foot jungo leaf—not nearly the biggest that Hadrian had seen. In the deep Gur Em, they grew so large that Tenkins were able to make rafts out of them.

"How long were you up there?"

"Most of the night." Royce stepped deftly over a moss-covered log and around a series of hanging prop roots. "Anyway, I was thinking about what the rat seller said."

"Angelius?"

"Whatever. He mentioned that no one would find Gravis because he's hiding. So, I reasoned that if I were planning on sabotaging Drumindor and people knew what I was up to, I'd hide in the one place I wouldn't need to move from in order to complete my plan."

They climbed out of the dense vegetation and onto a stony scrubland that steadily rose in elevation until it became a plateau of solid rock that formed the foundation for the northern tower of Drumindor. "I think he's in there."

Both of them tilted their heads back to look up at the tower's full height. Together they just stared at it for a while. Clouds shrouded the top and sea birds circled at the midpoint. Big sailing vessels passing beneath the bridge appeared like toys. Amazing as it was, Drumindor wasn't at all beautiful. There was a terrible austerity to it—all straight lines with no embellishment. The two towers were like pillars with fins instead of flutes that jutted out at precise intervals and looked like huge teeth on gigantic gears. These extruded ribs displayed sharp spouts that protruded in an ugly manner resembling thorns on a stalk except that these spikes smoked. From the tips of each and from the very top of the tower, black smoke leaked like the memory of a fire or the promise of one to come.

"It's not all that incredible," Royce said, "when you realize they didn't build it. They only cut away what was here."

"Yeah." Hadrian chuckled. "Erasing an entire mountain is no feat at all. I was thinking of turning Mount Mador into a multi-story tavern next week. Wanna help?"

Royce peered at him. "Busy."

Having escaped the trees, they climbed the foothills, following goat paths through the scrub until they reached the bare rock of the headland, which Hadrian guessed to be the last natural remnants of Mount Druma. He tried to imagine what it might have looked like — this massive mountain that was probably flat on top, similar to Mount Dag off the coast of Calis. That, too, was a volcano, but a quiet one. Legend held that centuries ago, Mount Dag had blown its top, and the resulting wave had nearly erased Dagastan. Judging from the span between the Drumindor towers, Hadrian estimated Mount Druma's base and guessed the mountain hadn't been very large, at least not by comparison to other mountains, but as an inhabitable structure it was ridiculous.

Yeah, not incredible at all.

As they climbed higher and farther out into the sea, the wind picked up once more, and they heard the crash and boom of waves. The wind returned more powerful than before, throwing Hadrian's hair back. Circling overhead and perched in crevices, gulls and shore birds clustered en masse. The rocks of the promontory appeared splattered with gallons of white paint as centuries of built-up bird droppings teared the stone faces. Soon they spotted evidence of chisels, and the rock became squared-off stone. Another few hundred feet and they reached the official base of the northern tower. There was no entrance visible, no window, porch, or steps.

They paused in the comfort of a constant breeze to drink and eat what was left of the fish.

"So, what's the plan?" Hadrian asked, sitting on a ledge of rock where some thousands of years ago a dwarf looked to have chiseled his initials, or his mark, or something undecipherable into the stone step.

Royce was staring up at Drumindor, shaking his head. "Huh? Oh, we'll just tell Byron to conduct a thorough search of the towers. My guess is they'll find him hidden away in some broom closet in there. They'll have him for trespassing and attempted sabotage, which will give them the excuse to keep Gravis locked up until he dies."

"Really? Then why are we here?"

"Because Byron will probably catch Gravis tomorrow, which means we'll be leaving the day after, and I wanted to see this up close."

Royce finished his meal, wiped his hands, and leaped up to where the surface of the tower began. He laid a hand on the rough stone, then craned his neck back. "It's taller than the Crown Tower. I'd estimate something like eighty stories — eight hundred feet or so, maybe a bit more. Entrance must be through the other tower. Impressive." He turned and dropped back down. "This might be the easiest job we've ever had."

Hadrian nodded. "I am a little disappointed we'll be leaving so soon. We should go out to the Parrot one more time. Everyone seemed to like that."

Royce glared at him.

Hadrian laughed. "You'll be fine. Just remember: less wine, more food."

"Easy for you to say. What if she wants to dance again?"

"Then dance. What is with you and Gwen, anyway? It's like you're terrified of her, which is insane."

Royce shook his head. "I'm wearing two layers of black wool in the tropics. Where did you get the idea I was sane?"

Albert was still not back when The Blue Parrot opened, leaving Arcadius, Gwen, Royce, and Hadrian to go without the viscount. They got a table identical to the last, only this one was a row back. Nevertheless, they were greeted once more by Atyn. The waiter arrived in his pressed-and-perfect blue uniform, bright-eyed and smiling wide enough to show teeth, as if this was the first real day of his life, and he was determined to make the most of it.

"Welcome back," the waiter said with such joy Hadrian thought he might genuinely mean it. "We missed you last night."

"I believe several of us needed a day of rest after that first culinary encounter," Arcadius said, slowly settling into his seat between Royce and Hadrian — his back to the stage.

"I understand," Atyn smiled, or rather, he continued to do so.

The man's face muscles must be capable of lifting an anvil.

Atyn ran through the menu, which consisted of fresh-charred hakune on a bed of sea breeze foam; deep-fried aquatic cave bat garnished with a lemon-lime relish and peas; beach buzzard, which was explained as a long-legged, white shore bird and not an actual vulture; and of course, their staple dish, Flame Broiled Sea

Monster. He took the liberty of bringing a bottle of Montemorcey and set it on the table in front of Royce. Then he left them to ponder their choices.

"So, Royce," Arcadius began, his elbows on the table, hands folded together, peering over his spectacles, "rumor has it that you and Gwendolyn had an interesting night when last we were here."

"Rumor also *has it* — whatever that means — that you insist cold goes down. What do you mean by, it *goes down?* Cold isn't a living thing; it can't choose a direction. Nor has it weight like a raindrop or snowflake. It's a temperature, it can't *move.*"

"You're purposely changing the subject." Arcadius gave Royce that knowing look that made everyone receiving it feel stupid.

"I know," Royce replied with his own signature grin, which made others feel stupid for being in the same territory. "Only seems fair since you're *purposely* bringing up *that* subject. This is Delgos, after all. There's no hereditary authority, so we all get a say on topics of conversation. You want to chat about me and Gwen, and I prefer to discuss your theory on temperature. In fact, I'd like to propose an experiment where I drop you in the ocean and you find out if it is indeed colder at the bottom. What do you say?"

"Personally, I think I will have the hakune." Hadrian spoke up and rapped the wood of the table with his knuckles as if pronouncing some judgment. "I had some already, and it was wonderful. How about you, Gwen?"

"I was actually thinking about the buzzard," she said, tapping a finger to her chin in a dramatic expression of deliberation. "I saw them at the beach when Arcadius and I went swimming. They're these cute little white birds with long yellow legs and beaks. They scamper up and down across the wet sand, chasing the waves in and out in the most adorable manner you could imagine. And you know, upon seeing them, my very first thought was that I need to eat one of those."

This made Hadrian laugh and drew smiles from both Arcadius and Royce.

"Thank you, Gwen," Hadrian said. Then he reached out for the bottle of Montemorcey. "For that, you deserve another toast."

Atyn returned and took their orders and apologized in advance for a possible delay. "Like everyone else around here, we are having trouble. Our ovens are suffering from ventilation issues. Don't ask me what that means. I don't know.

That's just the problem; no one does. And of course, we can't get anyone to repair it."

"And why is that?" Arcadius inquired.

"Like most everything in this city, the ovens are of dwarven design. Only *they* know how to fix them."

"I'm still not seeing the problem. This is Tur Del Fur; I suspect there are quite a few dwarfs to be found who could help."

Atyn nodded. "Normally, you'd be right, but all the dwarfs have disappeared."

"How's that now?" Arcadius asked, taking his glasses off as if that might help him hear better. "Did you say *disappeared?*"

"They're all gone. No one has seen a long-beard in over a week."

Royce gave Hadrian a concerned look.

"And it's becoming a problem," Atyn continued. "There's a shortage of salt, the baths are closed because of issues with their plumbing, and now I heard there's something wrong with the sewers."

"In just a week?" Hadrian asked.

"Hellooo, everyone!" Albert announced himself from two tables over as he waded through the growing host of arriving patrons searching for seats. With him came a beautiful woman in a lavish gold gown. She was tall, with a pronounced hourglass shape and a tower of hair piled high. The neck of her dress went deep and wide, revealing a panorama of shoulders and the tops of prominently displayed breasts. These were embellished with a slender silver chain that dangled a massive diamond in the valley between the hills, which precisely matched her earrings.

That she was noble was as obvious as a hailstorm to the hatless. Everything about her screamed *elegance*. The way she walked bowstring straight, chin up, eyes peering down on everyone as if they were revolting bugs she feared stepping on, defined the lady long before she opened her mouth. The moment she did, however, the woman annihilated all doubt.

"Please forgive my extemporaneous and presumably tiresome extension of what I assure you is a most sincere salutation to gentleman and lady alike." She said this in the most perfect and precise manner Hadrian had ever heard. She spoke as if her tongue and lips were a troop of militantly disciplined acrobats who would surely be put to death if they stumbled.

Albert presented her like a prize item at an auction. "This is Baroness Constance Constantine of Warric, Consort of the Courts, Queen of the Balls, Grande Dame of the Galas, and professional social butterfly." Then he pointed at each of them in order. "Constance, I give you Professor Arcadius of Sheridan University, and Gwendolyn DeLancy, Royce Melborn, and Hadrian Blackwater each from Medford — my dearest friends."

"How lovely, Albert," the lady said. Then she formally faced the table, being certain to make eye contact with each. "I am delighted to make the acquaintance of you all."

Albert looked at Atyn. "Can we get two more chairs?"

"Right away, sir."

Arcadius presented the lady his usual whimsical expression, which could best be described as mildly mischievous. Royce scowled at her, which was his reaction to meeting anyone new. Gwen was the surprise. She stared open-mouthed and wide-eyed at the lady. Then as they took their seats between Arcadius and Royce, Gwen looked a little sick.

"How did the meeting go?" Hadrian asked.

Albert shrugged. "Fine. Lord Byron is understandably anxious to resolve the matter but accepted my assurances. But that's mainly because he hasn't any alternative. No one else seems to care."

"These are the two, then?" Constance asked Albert while gesturing toward Royce and Hadrian. "This is the infamous Riyria?"

Everyone at the table straightened up, except for Constance, who couldn't improve her posture any more if she were hung by her wrists.

"Oh please. There is no need for apprehension." The lady spoke in a soothing, reassuring tone. "Riyria holds the prestigious rank of my most favored company. Never would I betray your confidence, as I am a verifiably trustworthy person, but more importantly and to the point"— she gave Royce a flattering glance — "I have also commissioned the two of you on enough occasions to be acutely aware of how deliriously fatal such an indiscretion would be."

Albert nervously drummed the flat of his hands on the table as he watched Royce. "She's actually the one who suggested you to Byron, so technically she and

I are sharing the percentage on this one. And given that the bulk of this job is the perks, she deserved a night at the Parrot. I didn't know all of you were coming."

Royce stared at Albert; Constance stared at Royce; Gwen stared at Constance; and Albert stared hard at the open bottle of wine.

"Forgive me if my presence is an imposition." Lady Constance stood up.

"Do you drink wine?" Royce asked. "Because we've got a bottle here that's bound to be wasted otherwise."

"I have been known to indulge, if it is good. I see no point in granting space in my life for the mundane."

"It's the best there is, which is why I don't like the idea of wasting it." Royce looked to Hadrian.

"A toast to Lord Byron then?" Hadrian lifted the bottle.

Constance sat back down.

"Oh, by Mar, yes," Albert said, and held out his glass, shaking it with impatience. "Stress is a terrible thing, and a day dealing with nobles wears a man out."

Lady Constance tilted her head back and raised her elegant eyebrows at him. "Really?"

"Not you, dear," he assured her. "You are a raft to a drowning soul."

"A raft? Is that how you see me? A handful of rough-hewn logs lashed together?"

"It's the stress from dealing with Lord Byron, my lady. Give me time to down a few glasses of this, and I will compose a sonnet to your beauty."

Albert drained half his glass in one go, then sat back with a sigh. Lady Constance swirled the contents of her glass, sniffed the wine, then took the tiniest sip before placing the stemware before her on the precise center of the decorative napkin.

"So, how are things going?" Albert asked Royce. "Have you found him?"

"I have an idea, but it's mostly speculation. This city lacks witnesses. Have either of you heard anything about dwarfs vanishing from this city?"

"Vanishing?" Albert asked. "Getting abducted, you mean?"

Royce turned his stemmed glass upside down as Hadrian made his rounds. "No idea. The waiter just mentioned that all the dwarfs in the city were missing. No one has seen them in over a week."

"Over the last few years, there has been a great deal of trouble with the native Dromeians, and recently it has reached a new level," Lady Constance said.

"What did they do?" Hadrian asked.

"Oh, they haven't done anything." Her hands were on her lap, and she spoke like an eager classroom student excited to answer her first question. "Aside from growing too numerous. The problem lies with the non-Dromeians. They are concerned that having so much of the city's crucial infrastructure controlled by such a small and insular community isn't wise. Especially when there are many dwarfs who are growing more adamant about the restoration of the old Belgric kingdom — by force, if necessary. The Triumvirate has taken measures to limit their involvement."

"Which is to say, they forced the city administrators to dismiss hundreds of dwarfs from excellent-paying jobs out of an *abundance of caution*," Arcadius said disapprovingly and followed the comment with an uncharacteristically large swallow of his own wine.

"That is one way of putting it." Constance nodded politely. "This has caused some hardships." She nodded toward the professor. "Both for the native Dromeians *and* for the city as a whole."

Arcadius frowned. "The prevailing wisdom of the addlebrained geniuses in power is that not only are the dwarfs unnecessary, but that the city would fare better in the hands of humans. It never occurred to the captains of commerce that this city — all of Delgos, in fact — was built by dwarfs, for dwarfs, with nary a thought to men."

"Why is that a problem?" Hadrian asked.

"Your forehead has already noticed what you and the Triumvirate haven't. If you think the doors are a problem, they are luxuriously large in comparison to the access tunnels, vents, shafts, sewers, and valve rooms that lie beneath Tur Del Fur."

Lady Constance nodded. "They resorted to using children, only —"

"Only your average child isn't as strong as a man, and your average man isn't as strong as a dwarf. An eight-year-old boy can't turn a valve that two big men would struggle with."

"As a result," Constance went on as Arcadius took another drink of wine, "the last decade has seen a marked reduction in proper maintenance. The sewers have been backing up, the plumbing is a mess, and the mines have all but stopped producing. As a result, there is a scarcity of salt, rock, and ore, leaving the roads and buildings in disrepair."

"But this has been going on for years," Royce said. "So, what happened recently?"

"If allowing the native Dromeians to maintain the mines, sewers, and plumbing was considered irresponsible, then allowing them to operate Drumindor was believed to be criminally negligent. The Triumvirate finally took action, and Lord Byron was ordered to dismiss all the Dromeians working in the towers."

"So, their disappearance could be a protest of some sort?" Hadrian asked.

"Or maybe," Royce said, "they might be fleeing a house they know is about to be burned."

CHAPTER SIXTEEN

The Admirer

While they waited for the food to arrive, Lady Constance continued to captivate everyone at the table. Especially Gwen. She stared at the woman with equal parts admiration and animosity and wasn't pleased about either. Just because a woman was beautiful, educated, refined, confident, and rich enough to dress in diamonds and gold didn't make her worthy of respect.

And just because she smiles at Royce with more than her lips doesn't mean she's evil. It just feels that way.

Constance was a lady, intelligent and educated. She spoke eloquently, discussing complicated topics with ease and used words Gwen had never heard. Confidence radiated from the woman as if she were the sun. She was poised and graceful. Her clothes fit as if tailored to her that very evening, and her makeup was perfect — not too much, not too little. And for a man who spoke infrequently, Royce talked to her a great deal.

Since setting out on this trip, Gwen had been nothing but a lump. She was out of her element and had nothing to do. Back in Medford, she hardly had a minute to herself. Everyone depended on her to deal with a constant flow of emergencies.

Up north, she was useful, capable, and valued, but here . . . it was easy to see why Royce would be attracted to Lady Constance.

Gwen didn't stand a chance.

Food arrived. The beach buzzard was far better than its name, but Gwen found she lacked much of an appetite. She had even less once Lady Constance spoke to her.

"Lady DeLancy, is it?" Constance asked over her plate of cave bat. She was the only one at the table brave enough to order it. Constance claimed it was delightful, but Gwen thought she was lying.

Okay, perhaps not lying, but exaggerating, certainly.

"Just Gwen."

This response appeared to puzzle Constance for a moment, but she quickly recovered. "What landholding is DeLancy? I've not heard of it before. Is it in Calis?"

"I don't have any land," she replied, feeling uncomfortably warm. To be grilled by Constance in front of everyone — in front of Royce — felt like she was taking a test she hadn't prepared for. But Gwen didn't like giving up the field without a fight. She wasn't without merit. She had pulled herself up out of the gutter to become a successful and respected businesswoman. She had nothing to be ashamed of and a great deal to boast about. "Well, I do own Medford House and The Rose and Thorn Tavern. Although, it's true I don't actually *own* them. The king owns them. I rent from him. But it's *like* I own them. They're very successful. I'm successful. I think so, anyway." She took a breath. That hadn't come out nearly as good as she'd hoped. Seeing the pitying expression on Lady Constance's face, Gwen felt like crawling under the table.

"What is Medford House?" the lady asked.

Gwen didn't answer; she couldn't. Instead, she lowered her eyes and thought, *I want to die right now. Why can't I just drop over, plant my face in the beach buzzard, and just be dead.*

"Has anyone heard anything new about the murdered courier?" Hadrian asked, his voice loud and booming over that of the woman.

"What's this?" Albert asked. Like everyone, he had been listening to Gwen and Lady Constance when Hadrian rudely blindsided the lot. "Who was murdered?"

"A courier. Everyone's been talking about it."

"Yes," Constance said, turning away from Gwen and drawn by the more interesting subject — although Gwen imagined that the mating habits of dung beetles would have been more fascinating.

"Why was he killed?" Albert asked. He had finished his fish and was using a bit of bread to clean up the remainder of sea foam on his plate.

"For whatever he was carrying, I would think," Royce replied.

"And what was that?"

Everyone looked at everyone else. And Gwen took the opportunity to stare at Hadrian. When he looked back, she mouthed the words, *thank you.*

Then Albert turned to Lady Constance. "You must have some idea. You're the Gossip Queen of the North, and you visit here every year. You have contacts. What do you know?"

"Well" — the lady smiled and played with her peas in a coy fashion — "there are many rumors, but what makes this so intriguing is that literally everyone is looking into it: the Port Authority, the Chamber of Commerce, and a whole host of shady figures including pirates. Anyone with an ounce of ambition, really. Even the Triumvirate is actively searching. Of course, no one cares a thistle about the courier. It is the package that has captured everyone's attention. With so much interest, general speculation has concluded — and I think rightly so — that the courier's pouch contained something of immense value."

"And does anyone know what that might be?" Royce asked.

Constance shook her head. "Sadly, there is no conclusive determination on that hard nut, but as always, there are a host of ideas. The leading one is that the courier was carrying a treasure map."

"To what?" Royce asked, pushing his empty plate away.

"King Mideon's gold." Lady Constance set her own dish aside to better wield her hands in service to her words. She wasn't a *big-hand* talker; Gwen had known a few of those who had made her duck. Lady Constance was more of a hand whisperer: her gestures dainty and always graceful.

"You see," Lady Constance continued, "The Church of Novron has been digging into the ancient city of Neith. *Literally digging.* I know this for a fact because to get here I take the barge down from Colnora and then a little boat across the channel to the port of Caric, which is well within sight of Neith. We always have to wait there for the carriages—sometimes overnight. Two years ago, I saw seret knights' tents appear on the slopes of Mount Dome, and a massive excavation project had started. The seret had an army of diggers—mostly Dromeians. The whole thing is absolutely eerie. It is difficult to explain unless you are there. Unless you are standing on that windblown rock, peering through the haze of dust clouds and watching all those bearded Dromeians wielding picks and shovels in the light of a hundred lanterns and the glow of a blood-red sunset. All you hear is the wind and the clink of picks and hammers. I swear, it is like being transported to another place and time—a time before Man."

"What is Neith?" Royce asked.

"It's the ancient capital of the dwarfs and was once the seat of King Mideon, their greatest and wealthiest king," Arcadius explained. "He ruled over both their cultural apex and their fatal fall. The dwarven city was lost in a great war, then destroyed—collapsed by magic. There have long been rumors of the riches of that golden age still buried deep beneath the rubble."

"Precisely." Lady Constance nodded.

"But what does that have to do with the courier?" Royce asked.

"Well . . . eleven months after the digging started," Constance went on, her hands working once more like a magician casting a beautiful spell, "the whole operation stopped. And it was a huge endeavor. As I mentioned, there were hundreds of workers but also roads, cranes, and scaffolding. I even think they set up an irrigation system to supply water to the site. But one day the entire thing just halted. This was in the spring, right about six months after Essendon Castle burned—if you recall that. Inquisitive by nature and curious by career, I queried the locals. The sentinel who led the project was none other than Garrick Gervaise, and witness accounts all concur he was never seen without two books in hand. One was said to be the ancient works of King Rain—who was a digger himself. That dwarf had spent time in Neith before its collapse. The nature of the other book, however, remains a source of great speculation, but one thing is indisputable: the day the excavation was shut down, Sentinel Gervaise arrived at the worksite carrying only *one* book: the works of Rain. The other one, the tome of great mystery, was gone."

"A *book* went missing?" Royce said skeptically.

"Not merely *any* book. The Dromeians I talked to said the sentinel was using its contents as a guide. So, what is the obvious conclusion? The missing book must have contained a treasure map of some sort, and without it, Gervaise had to give up his search." The lady paused to drink.

"And you think the courier was killed because he had it?"

"Sounds like something a lot of people would be interested in, doesn't it?"

"Sounds like a lot of wishful speculation," Royce said. "And if that happened only a few months after the burning of Essendon Castle, where has this map been for almost two years? And why is it popping up now? And who stole it from a church sentinel? And where was the courier taking it?"

Lady Constance smiled at him. "Welcome to the world of Tur Del Furian speculation and gossip. You are now properly equipped to enter any bathhouse and engage in the idle chit-chat of the city — well, if any bathhouses were still open, which due to the inexplicable vanishing of the entire dwarven community they are not."

"Oh, by the name of Our Lord Maribor!" a man exclaimed as he walked past their table. He came to a full stop and stared at Gwen.

He was a young man with dark hair and a handsome face who had the bearing of a noble and was dressed in a sky blue doublet to prove it.

"Gwen DeLancy?" he said with enough awe in his voice to tempt her to look around for another by that name.

"Who is asking?" Royce replied, his voice low, soft, and heart-stopping to those who knew him, which this gentleman clearly did not.

"You don't remember me?" the man said, ignoring Royce. "Of course you don't. We didn't actually meet, did we? You are always so very busy. Just sort of passed each other. And who would remember me anyway? I'm Everbryant, ah — Baron Everbryant, if you must put a point on it. But of course, you'd know me as Tim."

"Tim?" That did trigger Gwen's memory. "Tim Blue!" she exclaimed, smiling at him.

"Yes, that's me." He pulled at the chest of his doublet. "Tim Blue. It's so wonderful to see you again." He looked at the rest of the table. "Pardon my intrusion. It's just, I mean, this woman is a legend. But you're having your meal with her, so of course, you already know that."

"Some of us are still in the dark about *Miss DeLancy*," Lady Constance said. "Please illuminate us. Why is this woman a legend?"

Tim appeared overjoyed to have the opportunity to explain. "This lady, this goddess, is an inspiration to us all. She started with nothing, you know. Scratch that—she started with *less* than nothing. I mean, really, to have begun as a destitute scarlet woman at the Hideous Head, and to have clawed her way out! By Mar." He smiled at the very thought. "Then to go on to build Medford House out of nothing, making it the premier brothel in all of Medford—scratch that—all of Melengar! I daresay, Gwen DeLancy is a hero among entrepreneurs. She is what someone such as I aspire to emulate. She is the dream incarnate, the undisputed proof it can be done. If I could only be half the person you are, dear lady . . . and . . ." He gave a nervous laugh. "And you're sitting right here. You're right in front of me. It's such a thrill to speak to you. You have no idea."

Gwen sighed. She glanced at Lady Constance, whose gaping mouth looked like a door left ajar after the homeowner spotted a tornado.

No matter what Gwen said or did, the likes of Lady Constance would never approve of her. This had been obvious from the start, but Gwen had hidden from it and pretended that the rules were different down here—that somehow, in the shade of palm trees, a Calian woman of ill repute could be accepted as a real person. She wouldn't have bothered if Royce hadn't seemed so interested in the noblewoman. But Tim Blue . . . Gwen smiled at him. The man was an utter delight. He, too, was northern nobility, but he didn't see a dark-skinned brothel madam; he saw his hero.

So if I offend Lady Constance, she can just take back her 'most sincere salutations' and her 'Lady DeLancys.' I don't care anymore.

"It's so very nice to see you again, Tim," Gwen said in welcome.

Hadrian thought Tim Blue's timing couldn't have been better. Whoever the man was, his arrival had turned the tide. In that instant, Gwen returned to herself. Gone was the timid child playing dress-up, and back was the formidable woman in comfortable shoes kicking up her feet. Royce couldn't see it, likely because the man had a blind spot when it came to how Gwen saw him, but his attention to Lady Constance had been torturing her. Gwen had her own blind spot, of course. She failed to grasp that Royce would murder everyone at that table, including Lady Constance, Hadrian, and even himself to spare Gwen the pain of a paper cut. In reality, Royce was only captivated with Constance in the same way a boy is fascinated with a millipede. He had no interest in the woman, just the information she could provide. With the arrival of Tim Blue, everything changed, and Hadrian saw it in the smile on Gwen's face.

Hadrian was enjoying the praise the man poured on Gwen and was equally delighted by the stunned wonderment of Lady Constance. The woman sat round-eyed and speechless. Then Hadrian saw something else. Through the crowd of endless shifting bodies, he caught a glimpse of a figure standing just inside the door to The Blue Parrot. Hadrian wasn't inclined to have his attention pulled away, but something about the person across the room demanded it.

The figure stood awkwardly, close to the exit, not coming in or going out. This, in itself, was strange. That anyone would linger at the door suggested a purpose beyond the norm. The person was a young man dressed in poor clothes. That, too, was odd for the Parrot, as all workers wore blue uniforms and the patrons either dressed in casual elegance or wore finery. Riyria was the distinct exception. But the most remarkable thing about the figure was that Hadrian thought he seemed familiar.

The young man was stretching up, tilting from side to side, struggling to peer over the heads of the crowd, searching for someone. Failing this, he turned and left the Parrot. Only then did Hadrian realize who it was.

That's impossible.

Hadrian stood up and stared at the entrance, not knowing what he hoped to see. He turned to speak to Arcadius, but the professor's chair was empty.

Hadrian looked back at the doors. *Can't be.*

"Something wrong?" Lady Constance asked as Hadrian remained standing and staring, which in turned caused everyone else at the table to look at him.

"Hmm? Oh, no I—I'll be right back." He threw down his napkin and set off into the crowd. After he dodged his way to the exit, a blue-jacketed usher opened the door for him.

"Did you see a poor-looking kid just leave here?"

"Yes, sir. He seemed to be looking for someone. Was it you?"

"I don't know. Maybe. Do you know who he is?"

"Never seen him before, sir. Sorry."

"Thank you." Hadrian stepped out into the night, once more jolted by the difference between Tur Del Fur by day and how it was after the sun went down. Standing in the dark, he peered up and down the street at the gleaming lights, feeling more foolish every second.

It just looked like him, that's all. I'm being stupid. He's dead — has been for years.

This wasn't the first time. Whenever there was a crowd, he always imagined seeing that silly face somewhere in it.

Because that's how I first saw him — in a crowd.

Depression filled Hadrian as he remembered the scene on the dock and that unforgettable voice shouting at him. *"Here! Over here! This way. Yes, you, come. Come!"*

Hadrian sighed, feeling the hollow pang of loss and regret. The idea of returning to the Parrot, to the crowd, to the table, felt suddenly a chore. When the Ghost of Pickles haunted, he could only be exorcised with strong drink. Luckily, in Tur Del Fur there were plenty of places for that.

Hadrian was just about to head for the Parrot's bar when, instead of Pickles, he spotted a consolation prize standing near the curb. A dark-haired woman in a black dress stared down the street expectantly. She was alone.

He walked toward her. "Still thirsty?"

The lady peered at him. Her eyes narrowed.

"You wanted a drink, but Andre wasn't interested. I promised you one, remember? I hate breaking promises." He motioned to the Parrot. "Shall we?"

She smiled at him. "I think not."

"Is it the shirt?" Hadrian looked down at himself. "I knew I should have worn my gold doublet and chartreuse tights this evening, but it's just so hot down here, you know?"

"I don't think you have a doublet, and I'm positive you don't own chartreuse tights, but it's not the clothes. I just came out of there." She looked at the open doors through which spilled music, light, and laughter. Her expression darkened. "I'd rather not go back."

"Is Andre inside?"

"No, but Alessandro is — which is about the same thing. I'm tired of them. I was heading back to The Cave. Ever heard of it?"

Hadrian shook his head.

"Yeah, that's the problem. The Cave is Andre's excuse for a danthum. It's way up on the Eighth Tier. I sing there most nights. Live there too — now. No one goes there."

She looked down the street again. Her shoulders slumped, her eyes weary.

"Shall I flag down a carriage for you, then?"

She hesitated and then smiled. "You're nice."

"I like to think so."

She gave up on the street and sauntered the remaining distance between them. "How about you walk me back to The Cave?"

He glanced up at the steep rows of lights that defined the cliff at night. "To the Eighth Tier?"

"It's a nice night." She gestured toward the stars. "We can get to know each other better. And that's not going to happen anywhere around Andre or Alessandro. What do you say?"

"I say, it's a nice night for a walk."

A group of men came in. They spoke to the girl who operated the cloakroom, and she pointed in Royce's direction. There were five, all dressed well. Not quite the wardrobe of nobility, but they could have been well-to-do merchants. And who knew? Maybe they were. Things worked differently down here in Delgos where the inmates ran the prison.

Royce had expected something. He didn't know what, but after the shenanigans of the night before, he knew there would be an immediate response, a judgment, a recompense. His suspicion had been confirmed when he noticed Pratt among them.

I probably should have told Hadrian.

It hadn't seemed important at the time — still wasn't, really. Royce knew these people — not the individuals, but their type. He'd grown up among them. In a sick and twisted way, they were his family — the sort you hid from new friends and loathed to introduce to your fiancée.

Hadrian would just get in the way. He'd make it harder, but it might be good if he at least knew what was going on — just in case.

Royce wasn't terribly concerned. Knowing the list of possible scenarios, this was a pretty good one. They were approaching him in public, which was a positive sign. In the realm of the underworld, a meeting in public was about as close to a white flag as it got. They fanned out in a wide circle around the table. Two more appeared, taking positions at the exit doors. None held, or appeared to hold, a weapon. All of them smiled as the line of dancing girls was once more slamming their heels to a boisterous tune, making it possible for a person to scream and not be heard, or at least taken seriously. Crowds were funny like that.

"Good evening, Mister Pratt," Royce shouted over the noise.

"Good evening, Mister Melborn." Pratt wore a fine doublet with a smart cape. He stood straight, hands clasped before him. "A certain someone of importance would like to have a word with you."

"He wants to talk?" Royce asked.

"Yes."

"Where?"

"At his estate. It's not far: Tier One."

"I'm in the middle of a meal here."

"You've finished," Pratt said, motioning at the empty plate. "He knows how expensive meals are at The Blue Parrot. He appreciates good food, too, and he insisted that we wait until you were done. But you can't expect him to stand by all night. Please, if you will join us?"

Royce glanced over and saw Hadrian still wasn't back. Arcadius was also missing, and Royce had to wonder if the professor's and Hadrian's absence were linked with Pratt and Company. The dandy, Tim Blue, was sitting in Hadrian's seat. The boy-baron had been talking to Gwen, but their conversation — all conversation at the table — had halted with the arrival of Pratt and his quartet.

Royce acknowledged that Pratt might be there to kill him in retaliation for the death of his crossbow-wielding partner, but that seemed unlikely. It was also possible they planned to kill him for some other reason or just on principle for past deeds. But all of this rested in the low-probability category. Whatever issues Royce had had with Cosmos had been laid to rest, and there had never been any with his daddy. The risk of going with Pratt was low, the potential for information high, and refusal dangerous.

Gwen was the problem. He didn't like leaving her alone. Of course, she wasn't. They were in The Blue Parrot, surrounded by more than a hundred revelers. And Albert and Lady Constance were there, as was Tim Blue, who seemed harmless enough. A landless, powerless noble of low rank, he was someone Gwen knew and apparently liked. The woman was about as safe as she could be without Hadrian and himself flanking her. And given that there was a good possibility that Hadrian and even Arcadius were, at that moment, being held as hostages, the decision wasn't very difficult.

"Albert, Gwen," Royce said, "when Hadrian gets back, tell him I went to have a friendly chat with Cornelius DeLur."

Neither Hadrian, Royce, nor Arcadius had returned by the time the meal was cleared and the dance floor opened up. Albert and Lady Constance made use of it. This left Gwen alone with the stained tablecloth, the never-quite-empty glasses of wine, the discarded napkins, and Tim Blue. The young man had poured himself a drink from the still half-full bottle of Montemorcey and remained in Hadrian's chair, sitting straight and proper, facing Gwen as if she were his lodestar.

"Would you like to dance?" Tim asked with an effervescent energy.

Gwen's eyes widened, and she bit her lip. Just imagining Royce coming back and finding them on the floor with Tim's arms around her, made her . . . "I think that might be dangerous."

Tim looked at the dance floor, then back at her, concerned. "I give you my word I would never—"

"Oh no, I didn't mean—never mind. It's complicated."

Tim stared at her for a moment, then nodded. Gwen imagined she could admit to being the Heir of Novron, and he'd believe her.

She turned in her chair to view the entrance, hoping to spot Royce. The big doors remained open, letting in the cool night air. A few people, those just off the dance floor mostly, stood in the breeze with drinks in hand, breathing hard and fluttering their collars. She saw no sign of Royce or those he'd left with. The entire pack of sinister men with the pasted-on smiles and cold eyes had followed Royce out.

Royce knows what he's doing. He does this sort of thing all the time. I just never see it.

Gwen realized there were benefits to ignorance. She knew the work he did was dangerous. That was the case for many men. Sailors, loggers, soldiers — they all went out, and some never returned. The women they left behind imagined all manner of dangers but could always tell themselves they were being silly because the threats were vague things, nothing more than hazy dreads, monsters without faces. They didn't see the gargantuan storm-born waves, the deadwood poised to fall, or the ranks of the enemy with paint on their faces.

How much harder it is to hide from terror once you've met it face to face, once you've seen those cold eyes and pasted-on smiles.

Royce hadn't seemed worried, so maybe she didn't need to be, either. But was he just pretending for her sake?

"Can I say something to you?" Tim asked Gwen, as he pulled his chair closer, scraping it across the stone tile. He looked distressed and began wringing his hands. "I haven't been entirely honest tonight. I have an ulterior motive for approaching you. You see — let me put it bluntly — I need money. *Need* is really too gentle a word for it. I'm absolutely desperate." His words appeared to contradict his smiling expression until she looked closer and saw the lines around his eyes and brow. Then she understood he was not bursting with joy, but manic with fear.

"You see, I was recently married to a wonderful lady, but of no great fortune, and my family isn't in a position to give me anything. It was my task then to find an income. So to make a living, I tried to emulate you. I decided to become a businessman. This was an embarrassment to my family, but a man must do what he must for the security of his family, right?"

He looked at her with pleading eyes. For what, Gwen didn't know.

"Delgos is known by everyone to be the ideal place to run a commercial enterprise, so we moved here a year ago. Only, starting a business — as I'm sure you know — takes a lot of money. Money I didn't have. So, I borrowed it."

"Oh dear," Gwen said, already guessing where the conversation was headed.

Tim's lips trembled, and he took a moment to gather himself. "Yes, I know, but I wanted so much to be like you, only it's not as easy as you make it look."

"It wasn't easy, Tim. Believe me when I say that."

Tim forced a hard swallow, and for the first time, he looked away from her. "I lost everything, and now the men have asked me to repay it, and I can't. Time has run out. I have to . . ." Tim's voice cracked, and his eyes began to well up. "I have to pay them first thing in the morning."

Tim's hand cupped his mouth as if he might be sick.

"Or what? Prison?"

He shook his head, his hand still pressed to his lips.

"They're going to kill you?"

"Oh, if only that were true!" Tim exploded as tears filled his eyes. "They have my wife."

"Oh no," Gwen muttered.

Tim nodded. "This is Delgos, you understand. Commerce is king. They don't care if you're a threat to your fellow man. Everything is money. If you have it or make it, you're forgiven any transgression. But if you lose it, then the debt must be paid — any way possible."

Gwen stared at him, terrified of his next words.

"In order to recoup their loss, if I don't repay what I owe, they will *sell* my wife." Tim began to shudder, his whole body shaking. "Did you hear what I said? Sell her! I'm not even sure what that means. I'm . . . I'm . . ."

Gwen watched him rock forward and back, tears on his cheeks.

"How much?" she asked. "How much money do you need?"

"A hundred gold tenents."

Gwen was astounded. She had started her business with only four gold coins. "By Mar, Tim, what did you do with a hundred gold?"

"Things are expensive here. It's not like getting a writ to do business the way it is up north. Here you have to buy everything. The building alone was nearly fifty. Then it had to be refurbished, and goods needed to be purchased and, and it just . . . oh, it all just fell apart."

Tim reached for the glass he'd poured himself and nearly toppled it. He had to use two hands to bring it to his lips. Then he drained the whole thing.

"But you can sell the building, right? You can get back most of it, yes?"

He wiped his mouth and shook his head. "As things got worse, I grew desperate and mortgaged against the property. It's already been seized. I have nothing."

"I don't have a hundred gold, Tim. Even if I did, I wouldn't have traveled all the way down here with it. I only have a few coins."

"How many?"

"Just four."

"That could be enough. Anything you can spare, really."

"Why, what good would that do?"

Tim took a breath. He looked up at the ceiling, pressing his lips together so tightly they lost color. Then he sighed and shook his head. "I'd like to lie to you, I really would, but I can't." He drew himself up to confess. "I want the money to gamble with." He tilted his head toward the casino. "It's all I have left to try."

Gwen blinked. "That's not a good incentive to make a loan. But I'm starting to see why your business failed. Is this why you're here at The Blue Parrot tonight? To gamble?"

He nodded. "My Edie, she's the love of my life. They took her because of me. I heard her screaming as she was dragged away. They are going to *sell her!*"

He broke down weeping again.

Gwen sat back in her chair feeling awful for him, worse for his wife, and at least to a degree, guilty for it all. She had inspired Tim to take the risks he had. Unintended and accidental as it was, Gwen had been his guide, and she had led him to ruin. "Have you tried speaking to the people in charge of the city? There must be a law against kidnapping and slavery."

He shook his head. "The people who took her — they *are* the ones who run this city. I borrowed the money from the Bank of DeLur."

"*When Hadrian gets back, tell him I went to have a friendly chat with Cornelius DeLur.*"

Gwen felt herself becoming a little queasy as all around her carefree, wealthy people laughed, sang, ate, and drank to excess. The plight of poor Tim Blue was as invisible as an ongoing war of ants.

"It's all so hopeless," Tim blubbered into his palms. "I'm such an idiot. A miserable, wretched, asinine fool. I offered myself, of course. Asked them to take me — to sell me. You know what they said? They told me she was worth more . . . as if I didn't already know that!"

Gwen reached out and took hold of Tim's hand. "I'll give you my coins, Tim."

"Really? You're such a wonderful person." Tim frowned and ran a hand roughly through his hair. He looked angry. Then he shook and lowered his head. "No. Thank you, but . . . no."

"If it can save your wife —"

"That's just it. I don't know if it can. In fact, I'm certain it won't. No one wins in the casino, not the sort of money I need. The odds . . . never mind. I'm sorry I bothered you."

"But if you knew for certain that it would save her, you'd take them, right?" Gwen asked.

"If I knew for certain, I'd offer to be *your* slave for those four coins."

"I don't need a slave," Gwen said, then looked at the casino. "Just let me look at your hand."

CHAPTER SEVENTEEN

The Casino

Hadrian concluded that he liked the nights even more than the days in Tur Del Fur. In the daytime, the sun was just a bit too bright and the weather too hot, but at night amid all the twinkling lights, the city took on a romantic atmosphere that the days lacked. At least it seemed that way to him as he and Millificent LeDeye walked up Berling's Way. There was little traffic, so they traveled side by side up the middle of the road that was built of flat, interlocking stone. She walked beside him, placing one foot in front of the other, her hips swaying side to side, which in turn made the gown swing. Hadrian didn't want to stare, but at the same time, he did.

"So, tell me, Hadrian Blackwater, if that is your real name, what are your dreams? What are the goals for a man such as yourself?"

The two had reached Tier Four, where traffic was less congested and the city quieter. In the dark and muffled hush, the world became a more intimate and personal place where delicate starlight made the ordinary byways magical.

"Can't say I have any," Hadrian replied.

"You have no dreams at all?"

He shook his head.

"Oh, that's so sad. Everyone should have something to hope for and work toward. Otherwise, why are any of us here?" Her speaking voice was similar to how she sang: sultry, enticing, playful. She whispered more than talked, just as she sashayed more than walked.

"So, what are *your* dreams, Millificent LeDeye — if that is your real name."

"It isn't." She spun and fixed him with a pair of wicked eyes and an incorrigible grin. "That's my stage name."

"Then what is the real one?"

She looked him up and down, then turned and sashayed off once more. "No, no, I don't think I will tell you. Don't know if I can trust a man without dreams. There's something disreputable about that, practically dishonest — if you're not lying to me, then you are to yourself."

They reached Pebble Way, where if it were daylight, Hadrian could have seen the bright blue dome of the Turtle. With everyone at the Parrot, the house would be empty and remain so for at least another hour. He considered inviting her in and wondered if she would agree.

"All right then, at least tell me your dream," he said as they crossed Pebble Way and left the Turtle behind.

"I want to be the greatest performer who has ever lived. I want people to come from all over the world just to see me — to hear me sing." She did a pirouette in the middle of the street, her arms and dress flying out gaily. "And I want to be rich enough to buy my own venue — not a lousy eat-and-listen place, but a real theater with velvet curtains, one designed so that the sound of my voice would carry even to the cheap seats. And I want my own band who plays what I say, and how I tell them to play it. I suppose what I really want, Hadrian Blackwater, is liberty and freedom. Freedom to be whoever I want and the liberty to change my mind if I so choose."

Millificent was absolutely not a typical woman, but as it turned out, Miss LeDeye wasn't all that much older than a girl. She had seemed mature and worldly on stage, but up close he guessed she was no more than seventeen. The dress, the makeup, that voice, and the dark all conspired to hide the child behind sophisticated curtains. But when she moved those hips and rolled her shoulders, Hadrian conceded that no — Miss LeDeye was *not* a child.

"Are you and Andre . . . you know?"

"I don't see how that is any of your business." She scowled at him.

"So, that's a yes?"

"I suppose *he* certainly thinks so."

"But you don't?"

"Andre sees me as a tool to achieve his goals; as such, he views me as property. It's never occurred to him that I see him in much the same way. Not that I view him as property, but more a step on my staircase, an unpleasant puddle to wade through. I wasn't always the glamorous lady you see before you." She grabbed the sides of her gown with both hands and swished it. "This, dear sir, was all earned. You see, I'm not from here; I wonder sometimes if anyone truly is. The entire population of Tur Del Fur has been transplanted from afar, you know. Lunatics and stargazers all come hoping to be reborn as geniuses and visionaries. We're all dreamers looking for acceptance among our kind in this magical place where — if you are dedicated enough — fantasies come true."

"Where are you from?"

She dipped her shoulders and peered at him as if he were up to something devious. "I suppose there's no harm in telling you that. I was one of eight children living in a small, disgusting flat above my father's tailor shop in a frozen, dirty northern town called Eckford; that's in the province of Asper, way up in the kingdom of Melengar."

"Melengar? Really?"

"You've heard of it? I know, it's hard to believe anything good could come from there. And I would have suffered a miserable life as the wife of some ignorant dirt farmer or brutish tradesman. Then I'd have died, becoming just one more wooden marker stuck in a field until that, too, would one day rot and take away all evidence I had ever lived. If anyone did remember me, it would be as that poor daydreaming girl with the lovely voice."

"How'd you get here?"

"One of my father's customers, Lord Daref, put the bug in my ear."

"He what? Did you say he put a *bug* in your *ear?*"

She laughed. "Yes. Never heard of that? I guess it means he gave me the idea in such a way that I couldn't ignore it any more than you can ignore an insect buzzing in your ear."

"I — ah, yes, suppose that's true."

"Anyway, while Lord Daref was getting measured, or waited for his new suit, I would complain about how cold it was, and he would tell me tales of Tur Del Fur in the far south. A place where it was always warm and there were palm trees and aqua waters, and where they had stages where people sang and danced before an audience — and got paid for it! So, at the age of sixteen, I ran away from home. I went to Roe — that's a little harbor town. There I stowed away on a southbound ship called the *Ellis Far*. I realize now it was a little crazy. All I had was a note of introduction written by Lord Daref to a lady named Zira Osaria here in Tur Del Fur, someone Lord Daref said could help me."

"You made it all the way from Roe to Tur Del Fur hiding on a ship? That must have taken several days, at least. What did you do for food? What did you drink? How did you avoid being seen?"

"Actually, I was discovered on the first day out! I was brought before the captain, who was inclined to drop me in Aquesta until I showed him the note. I pretended that Lord Daref had hired me to be a maid at his winter home, but I lacked the funds to travel. I told him that if I didn't make it on time, I would lose the job. Captain Callaghan showed pity and saw me safely to Tur Del Fur. Of course, the crew assumed I was sleeping with him. And to be honest, to get here I would have, but the captain was a strict and religious man. He kept his word. Then, when I stepped off the *Ellis Far* onto the docks of Tur Del Fur on that glorious morning . . ." She closed her eyes and sighed. "I knew I had found paradise." She opened her eyes and frowned. "I thought so, anyway. Turns out paradise is a bit of a fixer-upper."

"What happened?"

"I found Zira Osaria easily enough. She's a small innkeeper who lets out rooms for cheap. I thought the note would grant me free accommodations, but that was the dreamer in me walking into the first imperfect wall of my fixer-upper paradise. I had to pay rent, but I had so little money and no means of getting more. But again, the kindness of strangers stepped in. Zira helped me get a job in a scullery at a local danthum — the Hoot Owl — which was a terrible attempt to imitate The Blue Parrot. Employees had to wear hideous masks that made them look like birds, but they only served to make it hard to see straight. I worked myself to death. My hands shriveled up and turned red, my feet blistered, my back ached. After only a few months, I felt like an old woman who ought to be quick about picking out that wooden grave stick. And all the money went to rent."

She displayed an overacted pout and followed it with a drawn-out sigh. "I was edging dangerously close to giving up my dream when one of the girls who worked the cabaret heard me singing in the kitchen. Her name was Vida Rider—well, that was *her* stage name. I never knew Vida's real one. All performers, I discovered, have professional names. Then one day when an act didn't show up, the master of ceremonies—that's the guy who hires the performers and organizes the show—was desperate. So, Vida told him to put me on. She gave me one of her crazy outfits, shoved me out, and told me to sing. I nearly died—no actually, I did die, sort of, because I was someone else afterward. You see, the crowd loved me, and when the master of ceremonies asked my name, and not knowing better, I told him my name was . . ."

Hadrian waited as she peered at him, and then she shrugged.

"Millie Mulch. Yes, that was me. Millie Mulch of backwater, backwoods, backward Eckford Gulch. Millie Mulch, the poor tailor's daughter with the big voice and matching dreams." She waited a heartbeat or two for Hadrian to react. He didn't, so she went on. "The poor man probably thought I was making it up to mess with him or something. But anyway, he just rolled his eyes and when he turned back to the audience, he introduced me as Millificent LeDeye. No idea where he pulled that from. Some prostitute he frequents up on one of the high tiers, I suppose. Regardless, good old Millie Mulch the tailor's daughter died on that stage at the Hoot Owl. She perished in the roar of applause that followed. I've been Millificent LeDeye ever since."

A donkey-drawn, open-air wagon, whose facing bench seats hauled eight very drunk revelers, *clip-clopped* slowly toward them. The wagon riders were all swaying in unison, more or less, and singing the old northern folk song, *Calide Portmore*. Millie didn't hesitate. She joined in; but she didn't so much *join* as take *command.* Hadrian knew the song. He'd heard it since childhood and had sung it himself in taverns all over Avryn as it was a grand drinking song. Only that wasn't how Millie sang it. She didn't perform the piece as a rollicking ditty. Instead, she raised it up with sincerity and heartfelt passion. Millie Mulch didn't merely sing the words, she *believed* them. And through her, everyone else did, too. She let loose on the impossibly high notes, adding an emotional range to the lyrics and hanging on to the words beyond what a single breath should allow. And just when it seemed she could rise no higher and would need to breathe, she pushed up another octave, reaching a soaring, quavering beauty that staggered all who heard. The drunks went silent. The wagon driver pulled his donkey to a halt. They all stopped to listen as Millie Mulch of Eckford took them all to another place and time, a land known as Paradise — a world of broken-down dreams that a young girl had fixed up.

The DeLur Estate was just as opulent as Royce had expected, which was to say beyond *anyone's* expectation. Cornelius owned what had to be the best property in Tur Del Fur, and very likely all of Delgos, and possibly in the entire world. His home was off by itself on the southern side of the harbor, where he had his own private docks that were nearly as large as the commercial ones. Tied up to his piers were a pair of massive pleasure ships as well as several smaller craft. Pratt had been truthful but modest when he stated the estate was on Tier One. The sprawling villa was also on Tiers Two and Three. In truth, the blond stone structure stretched out over a wide plateau and extended several stories up the facing cliff. Far from ostentatious, the DeLur Estate was almost austere, even simple, with its sleek lines of unadorned horizontal buff-colored stone that blended into the rock wall but not quite so much that it disappeared. Instead of forcing itself on the scenery, the architecture exemplified and promoted the landscape around it. In some ways, it completed it, showing nature where it went wrong.

That said, this was true dwarven design. Unlike the humble rolkins, the DeLur Estate exemplified the more familiar excesses of the diminutive race to build unnecessarily massive things. Passing through the three-story stone doors carved with stunning geometric patterns that suggested a mountain near the sea, Royce felt small. He also felt crowded as he was now surrounded by a group of escorts — two on each side and in back, and one out front. Most were new acquaintances, and they were armed: two with swords, two with pikes, and two with crossbows. The one out front was Pratt; he guided them up wide, shallow

Sketch of the DeLur Estate from the notebook of Michael J. Sullivan

steps into a massive reception room with a near-panoramic view of the city and the bay. Cornelius DeLur waited for him, sitting on what could only be described as a giant stone throne.

While never having met or even seen Cornelius, Royce identified him immediately. The man was huge, dwarfing even his son, Cosmos, in his quest for physical size. It was said that Cosmos believed in four things: that a man's wealth and power is demonstrated by his amassed bulk; a poor man could never have enough funds for food to put on any substantial weight; fearful of being assailed, a despot couldn't allow himself to bloat; and most importantly, that only a truly wealthy and powerful individual had the luxury to wallow in his achievement. It was easy to see where he got the philosophy, and Royce knew Cosmos would forever be playing catch-up to daddy.

Cornelius DeLur didn't so much sit on the chair as puddle in it. Thigh-sized arms extended out to either side, lying on wide rests. His head, a massively jowled pumpkin of a thing, appeared tiny in comparison to the rest of him, and he appeared as a man on a bed peering down over his massive stomach at Royce.

"Mister Melborn, how kind of you to visit." Cornelius sounded exactly like a talking kettle drum: deep, loud, but with a little tinny ring.

Royce took a moment to glance at his escorts. "How could I refuse?"

"How indeed." Cornelius smiled. "Tell me, are you enjoying my city?"

"Yours?" Royce didn't bother to look. "I've heard you described as just a humble banker."

This made the big man chuckle. Royce expected to see his mounded belly jiggle, but it didn't move. The man's head barely stirred. Seeing him speak and laugh was like watching a ventriloquist without a dummy.

"Yes, yes indeed I am. A simple coin collector who, because of the size of my accumulated collection, requires an entire country to store it."

"I was also under the impression you weren't alone in running this place. You have a couple others who share the burden. Isn't that right?"

"You refer to Oscar and Ernesta? They are my right and left hands, certainly, but I am the head."

"I see," Royce said.

Cornelius lifted a finger, and immediately a pair of servant girls — two of the many who waited in the shadows of the massive chamber — brought forth a gold cup and a silver pitcher. The two were dressed identically in lavish robes of shimmering cloth with elaborate headdresses imitating tropical birds. One put the cup in the big man's meaty hand, then the other poured what appeared to be wine, although it was best not to jump to any conclusion. Knowing Cornelius by reputation and now seeing him in person, Royce thought the scarlet liquid might just as well have been the fresh-squeezed blood of puppies or unicorns. Cornelius had that sort of reputation.

"So, to what do I owe this honor?" Royce asked.

Cornelius managed to carry the cup to his mouth and drink. "Oh, come now. Must you pretend innocence? I didn't ask you here to play games."

"That's good. I'm not a fan, either. But that doesn't change the reality that I don't know why I'm here. Although if I were to guess, it has something to do with what a certain dead courier was carrying — a book, I believe. I suspect this because it can't be anything else, and because Pratt busted up the Turtle looking for it. Sorry for the mishap, and the loss of your boy. That wasn't me, by the way. Auberon dropped him. Things would have gone better if you had just politely asked."

"Not to worry, not to worry. I'll deal with the old freedom fighter in due time. He's an annoying sliver that needs to be pulled."

"Well, in Auberon's defense," Royce said as another peacock-dressed servant arrived with a tray of fruit, "you did trash his home, then showed up the next night and pointed a bow at his guest. How would you feel if *I* ran through *your* cupboards?"

Cornelius lost his smile and handed off the cup. "Enough of the prattle. You stole the book — my book — and I want it back."

"What makes you think I took it?"

Cornelius frowned and made a *harrumph* sound. Around the room, all those present — the small army of servants as well as the small army — responded with expressions of dread.

"Let me rephrase," Royce said. "Do you know *for a fact* that I took it? If you do, someone is lying."

"My son was the one who hired you to pilfer it from the Hemley Estate."

"The Hemley . . . *Lady Martel's book?* Is that what we're talking about?"

"What else?"

"I don't know. Up until now I always figured there was more than one book in the world."

"So, you admit to having stolen it?"

"Not if you're going to arrest me for it or plan some other more inappropriate entertainment. Besides, I can tell you that Lady Martel's diary was delivered to the client. I don't have it."

"Yes, I know. You delivered it to Lady Constance of Warric. Cosmos hired her, and she in turn approached Albert Winslow with the job. You and the Black Diamond have some sort of territory truce going on. My son didn't want to send his own agents, so he hired Riyria."

"Interesting," Royce said. "Then you ought to know that we don't have the book in question. Now, if it didn't get back to Cosmos, you might want to talk to Lady Constance. I hear she's in town."

"My son received the book just fine, had it for two years, kept it in his vault."

Royce paused, looking around him at the many faces. In such an assembly, he'd expect some glassy eyes, even a few yawns — not here. Every last one watched the proceedings like cats with a dog in the room. The only question was, who were they more concerned with? Regardless, Royce searched their expressions — not so much for sympathy exactly — but for acknowledgment that what the fat man just said was evidence of Royce's innocence and Cornelius's insanity. "So, if you have the book, what's all this about?"

"While in captivity, the merchandise got *hot*. The church came sniffing. Since I don't allow the church in Delgos, Cosmos sent the book to me."

"And the courier never arrived."

"That's correct. And now I find Riyria on my doorstep — a pair of accomplished thieves and one of a handful of people who know of the book's existence. I don't think that's a coincidence. Now, if you have it, I want it. If you delivered the package to a client, I want the name and location so I can collect my belongings. Mind you, I understand you are a businessman, so am I. This doesn't need to get personal. It doesn't have to become messy. All I want is the book."

"Wish I had it or knew where it was."

The big man frowned again. He made another *harrumph,* and this time one of the girls took a barely noticeable step back. Royce couldn't imagine why. Cornelius might be the most powerful person in the room, but he wasn't about to leap off his chair and attack anyone. Royce doubted he could stand, much less walk, and wondered if he slept in that chair or had a special detail of handlers who carried him from place to place like worker ants with their queen. Cornelius couldn't have always been like this. He had a son after all, and there was no doubt Cosmos was a blood descendant, as the two looked like bookends on the same shelf of massive volumes. But the recoil did answer one question . . . the dog in the room wasn't Royce.

"Look, we're down here to do a job for Lord Byron. He works for you, so you can verify that easily enough. As for the diary, we haven't seen it since it was delivered to Albert Winslow, but . . ." Royce hesitated to say more. He was trying to make a believable case to a skeptical man.

Cornelius's eyes narrowed. "But what?"

He won't let me leave without something.

Royce made his own *harrumph* sound, which no one noticed. *I'm definitely not the big dog here.* "There's another interested party who knows about the book. A fellow who made the same mistake you did in thinking I had it."

This brightened the pumpkin face a bit. "Who?"

"I don't know, exactly. I bumped into him up in Melengar, and by *bumped*, I mean I stabbed him in the throat. Figured I killed him. Most people would make that assumption, I suppose, at least until he showed up again in Kruger. He also thought I had Lady Martel's diary. I found it a little disturbing since, as I said, I was fairly certain I'd killed him."

"What happened?"

"That's the strange part. He said he wanted to hire me to bring him the diary."

"And did you take the job? Is that—"

"No."

"No?" Cornelius showed his disbelieving, disappointed, frown face again. "Why not?"

"Three reasons. First, I was already working on a job—the one for Lord Byron. Second, I thought it risky to work for a guy so eager to hire me after I tried to kill him. And third, he didn't have any money."

"Did he expect you to work for free?"

"Oh, he was going to pay me. Promised to grant me eternal life."

Cornelius stared at Royce, shifting his comparatively tiny lips. They were normal, perhaps even big, but anything sensible looked much too small on that bloated face.

The big man stared, clearly perplexed, and Royce knew why. Despite both professing a distaste for playing games, they were engaged in a very high-stakes one. Cornelius was a shrewd man experienced in dealing with dishonest characters, and he knew Royce was deceitful. He also knew the thief would do or say whatever was necessary to escape. Making up a story about a vague *someone else* was as old a ploy as a child saying, "I didn't do it; it was some other kid." The problem sprouted from the bizarre nature of the tale Royce spun.

He's not surprised that I made up a story. He's baffled as to why I would create something so unbelievable. He knows I'm not an idiot, and I wouldn't try to lie. So, there is only one explanation for why I would tell such a bizarre tale.

"I don't suppose this persistent potential client gave a name?"

"Actually, he did. And it might be a name you know."

Again, Cornelius's eyes brightened, and Royce imagined he might have sat forward if such a thing were possible. "And what is that?"

"He called himself Falkirk de Roche."

As Gwen led Tim toward the casino, Albert and Constance were still on the floor, lost in the crowd, and the band had shifted to another rollicking tune, this one featuring the horns and drums. Gwen had Tim by the hand; he was pulling back a bit. "I'll never turn this into a hundred gold. Like I said, I'd have to win too many times. If you gave me fifty gold, I'd only need to win once."

"I don't have that much, Tim."

"But this won't work."

"It will if you do as I say. You need help, and I'm giving it."

The casino was reached through a wide, peaked archway made to look like a Calian palace, or perhaps more accurately, what the local northerners thought a Calian palace looked like. To either side, short, fat-trunked potted palms grew out of huge urns, and in between them stood the guards like a pair of ancient giants in blue vests and loose pants.

"Men only," the wall of muscle told them.

Gwen stopped and rolled her eyes. "Are you serious?"

"Do I look serious?" The guard on the left glared down at her as if she were an unruly toddler.

In the sleeveless vest, the man's folded arms displayed biceps bigger than her head. His face was misshapen and misaligned, one eye higher and bigger than the other, and his nose appeared flat and blunted, as if having once been crushed. She imagined whatever cruel event mangled his nose also took out his front teeth, causing him to speak deeper in his throat and making his voice more cavernous. This was neither a happy nor a pretty face but rather a weapon of intimidation, a visage of violence, and it was aimed at her.

Most people would have fled in terror, or at least backed away. Tim tried, but she held tightly to his hand and refused to let him go or to budge from her spot. Tim's only chance to save his wife was for the two of them to get into the casino. If poor old Tim Blue tried without her, he would lose. Gwen had seen that in Tim's palm. The read had been short, taking only a few seconds because there wasn't much future to see. Tim's life was scheduled to conclude in only a few hours. The next morning Tim would watch as they sold Edie, manacled her wrists and ankles, and put her on a ship. Then, as the slave trader set sail, consumed in grief and guilt, Tim would leap to his death from the coastal cliff. While quite the romantic ending for Tim, his wife would go on to suffer for the rest of her life.

Gwen couldn't allow that, not if she could do something.

The real question is, can I?

Her mother had the gift of foresight, a talent that passed to her daughter, and before Illia died, she had trained Gwen to read palms. But there were two ways to see a person's life. The palm was the safe and easy method because it could be read like a book, whereas peering deeply into a person's eyes, with intent to seek answers, also revealed the past, present, and future. However, the viewer, unlike the reader, had no control. They saw, even if they didn't want to. When Gwen looked into a person's eyes, she didn't just learn events in a person's life, she experienced them. Gwen knew there was a story within the eyes of the casino guard, just as there was a story behind every face. The preview to this particular tale, however, advertised a tragedy, perhaps even a horror story, that she'd rather not experience.

And Gwen had no idea if it was worth the trauma.

While she had the gift, as far as she knew that was all she had. She could see the past, present, and future of a person — other than herself — but didn't know if the future could be changed. If what she saw could be altered such that it didn't happen, then wouldn't that mean she couldn't see the future at all? Everyone made guesses about what would happen if someone did or didn't do something, and sometimes they were right and sometimes they were wrong. If what Gwen saw could also be undone so that sometimes what she saw *didn't* happen, would her gift be any different? Would she have a gift at all, or just be a good guesser? Since her readings and visions *always* occurred, Gwen had believed she saw what would happen after all the events played out — including attempts to alter the prophecy. As such, nothing could change the future as she saw it.

Except there was one possibility.

What if the actions of a seer are different from the actions of anyone else? What if my ability to know the future also grants me the power to change its course? And perhaps that is why I can't see my own future.

The idea was both exciting and terrible. If it worked, the power she wielded would be incredible. But then, ideas of spending the rest of her life wandering the world reading palms and fixing fates ran into reality's wall.

What would happen if I did something to alter destiny and that action caused a million other unforeseen changes to occur? What if there is a balance that needs to be maintained between good and bad? There is so much that is awful in the world, but at least I know it isn't my doing. But if I take hold of the reins and pull providence off course, if I start upending the natural direction, then it could be possible that the next time a sparrow drops dead it might be my fault.

But is there such a thing as fate? Is there a 'supposed to,' and aren't I part of this world, too? Why do I have this gift if not to use it? If a man dams a river, it's an unnatural change that by hubris could have horrible and unseen consequences. But if a beaver does it, it's fine. A flat-tailed rodent doesn't act out of pride, so the big lake it makes isn't a disaster. It's what's supposed to be — as natural as rain. So what am I, a conceited trespasser throwing the natural order into chaos, or a blameless beaver?

The larger philosophical question would need to wait for another day. First, she had to prove it was possible, and this was as good a place as any to find out. Guessing that the casino guard wouldn't let her read his palm, Gwen took that opportunity to look into the man's eyes.

When the visions came, she was surprised and disappointed in herself. She, of all people, should have known better than to judge a face by its scars. Afterward, it took a moment to recover. Deep dives into another's soul were as emotionally taxing as an all-night fight with a loved one. Gwen took a breath and wiped the tears from her eyes. "Salen is alive," she said softly, her voice almost drowned out by the horns and drums.

The casino guard unfolded his arms. They came apart like the bolt of a lock whose key had been turned. His face lost its hard edge, and he gaped.

"You think she's dead because they showed you a mangled body dressed in her clothes, only that wasn't her. It was Habba. Salen will tell you what happened.

I don't know when, but it can't be too far in the future; your hair is still dark, and you look pretty much the same. Salen explains how scared she was when the men abducted her. How she cried and told her captors that they would be sorry when you found them. She calls you *Baba,* but that's not your name — it's something she's called you since she was very young. Later, Salen will explain what the men did to her, and she will want to know why you never came, why you let it happen, and why you never tried to save her. No matter how many times you tell her, it isn't enough. It will never be enough. She was going to marry Amster. They had plans to leave the city and start a new life in Collier, but that never happened because they told you she was dead, and you believed them. When Amster discovers the truth, they will kill him, telling you he killed himself out of grief. You'll believe that, too."

The other guard stared at Gwen, then at Baba, looking frightened.

"How do you know this?" Baba asked.

"I'm Tenkin." She pointed to the swirling tattoo on her shoulder. "And I know that you know what that symbol means."

He stared at the mark.

"I also know how your face got like that. I'm sorry." Tears welled up again. She brushed them away. "The same people who told you your sister is dead are also the ones who told you women weren't allowed in the casino. And I have to assume they *really* wouldn't want a Tenkin seer to go into a place where money is won or lost by chance."

Baba looked at his partner. As scary as that face had looked before, it was a true terror now. "Maybe she's just a crazy woman. If so, someone might complain that we didn't stop her. But if she wins, it will prove she's telling the truth. I'm going to let her in. What are you going to do, Amster?"

Amster smiled and nodded. "Welcome to The Blue Parrot Casino, miss."

CHAPTER EIGHTEEN

As Rain Falls

When Hadrian and Millie reached the Sixth Tier, it started to rain. Hadrian felt a drop, then saw a pair of wet dots on the street. Soon he heard rain on rooftops and the soft patter on cloth awnings. By the Seventh Tier, it was really coming down.

"My dress! My hair!" Millie shouted and sprinted for the shelter of a nearby arched doorway. It wasn't much but had the benefit of being illuminated by a nearby lantern.

Millie climbed the three shallow steps and put her back to the closed door as if the rain would kill her. Hadrian joined her in the small space, and seconds later, the patter became a pour. A foot away, a curtain of water appeared like a solid thing, and the world was lost to a violent roar as if they stood beneath a waterfall.

Millie's hand fluttered about, checking her hair and dress for dampness and damage.

"So, it *does* rain here," Hadrian said, peering out, fascinated by the volume of the noise.

"It rains everywhere," Millie declared.

Hadrian almost replied but thought better of it. Some things had to be experienced to be believed.

"I hate rain," Millie said, wiping the wet from her forearms as if it were something vile.

"How can you hate rain?"

"It's a killer." She pointed toward the street but didn't extend her arm for fear of getting wet. "In another few seconds, I would have melted away." She waved a hand up and down her body. "This takes hours of hard work, a labor the rain can destroy in seconds. Do you know what rain can do to curled hair or makeup? It doesn't just wash off, *it bleeds.* Long ugly streaks of black and red tear down my face, turning me into some grotesque melted-wax freak. And then, with enough water, it's all gone, all of it. Millificent LeDeye dies an ugly death and all that remains is Millie Mulch."

"Is that so bad?"

She stared at him as if he were insane. "I don't want to be Millie Mulch. I don't ever want to be her again. If I could cut her throat, burn her to ash, and then scatter those ashes to the four winds, I'd do it. Millificent LeDeye is so much better. She's beautiful and not afraid of anything, or anyone."

She stopped wiping her arms and turned sharply to face him. The frustration, fear, and anger at the *near-death* experience faded, and Millificent LeDeye stared at him with predatory eyes. She moved closer, pressed against him, and laid her head on his chest. "I'm cold; keep me warm."

He put his arms around her bare shoulders. She didn't feel cold. Her skin was almost hot, like something was burning inside. She sighed into him. The lantern on the street went out, killed by the rain, leaving the two in darkness. Everything else was consumed by the deluge that drowned out the rest of the world.

This was the stuff of dreams, the sort men never share — not because they're lurid, but because the experience can't be summed up in words any more than a flavorful dish can be described by its ingredients. Any attempt to express sensation, atmosphere, anticipation, or excitement always fell short. But at that moment in an exotic foreign city while sheltering from the storm and tenderly embracing a strange and beautiful woman, Hadrian knew this was one of those times. They didn't come often, and he was determined to cherish it.

"Thing is," she said, and he could feel her voice against his chest, "I'm so close to my dream. I can see it. My future is right there, but I can't quite grab it. I have talent, but that's not enough. It's the money. Whoever has it holds the power, and those with power are misers. I get the dregs, and I always will because they know if the tides turn, I'd flip the table. I would make my own decisions and cut them off. But I can't do anything without money. If only there was a way to make a small fortune on my own."

Hadrian caressed her back. The dress was cut low, the material nonexistent. His fingers glided over smooth, damp skin.

Her head turned. She rested her cheek on his chest and looked up into his eyes. He thought she might be inviting a kiss, so he squeezed her tighter as he —

"Have you heard about the courier who was killed?" she asked.

Hadrian hesitated, wondering if he had somehow misread the cues or if Millificent LeDeye was more peculiar than he thought. Flighty was one thing, scatterbrained another. "Actually, I have."

"Cornelius DeLur has offered a handsome sum to get his hands on what the courier carried, and I know what it is: a book," she went on, still resting her chin on him so that her head bobbed as she talked.

Then Millie sighed, and he felt her body mold to his.

Beyond the shelter of the archway, the rain continued to pour. And as mini cataracts spewed off the roofs of neighboring buildings, a small river washed down Berling's Way. Hadrian continued to caress Millie's back, feeling the contours of her body. He lowered his hands to her waist and felt the damp fabric.

"Mmm," she purred, rubbing her cheek against his shirt as her hands began their own exploration of his body. She found the open V of his loose shirt, pushed aside his medallion chain, and kissed his chest. "Unlike Millie Mulch, Millificent LeDeye is a brave adventurer."

"Brave is good," Hadrian whispered. "And I like adventures."

"If Millie had the book, she'd sell it and use the money to go independent, but if Millificent LeDeye had it, she would never sell it."

"We're back to that, are we?" Hadrian said, more than a little disappointed.

"It's a treasure map, you know?"

"I've heard that."

"It shows the way to a dwarf king's gold. Can you imagine? The accumulated wealth of an entire nation, a dwarven kingdom! You know what they say about them: they hoard treasure like a dragon. There are probably rooms upon rooms of gold bars, bags of coins, goblets, statues, and who knows what else? That's what everyone with a brain really wants — not the book." She pulled back a bit to look into his eyes again. "You have it, don't you?"

"What?" he asked, suddenly lost.

Hadrian was still trying to understand how this conversation about a book and treasure had anything to do with the two of them. He assumed it didn't. She was making small talk the way some people hummed while working or taking a bath. He'd also thought it might be some sort of fancy metaphor where he was the book and she the treasure. Millificent LeDeye seemed the sort to think in abstract romantic terms. He liked that. It made her seem more intriguing, like a person who could see more colors or knew multiple languages. But now . . .

"Andre told me you do."

"Andre?"

Clearly not abstract at all.

"How could he know anything about me?"

"Oh, he works for Cornelius DeLur. A lot of people do, but Andre is high up the ladder. He hears lots of things. He knows you and your friend are the ones who killed the courier and took the book. You don't look like the sort to kill anyone, so maybe it was your friend that did it. Unfortunately, you don't have the book on you at the moment." She sighed. Her exploring hands fell away, and she straightened up. "Cornelius's men searched your place the other night, but Andre said they didn't find anything." She drew farther away. "I'm guessing this other guy, this friend, has the book, right? He's the brains. Carries it wherever he goes. That would be smart in this town."

"Is that why . . ." Hadrian stared at her. "Did Andre send you to search me?"

She nodded. "His exact words: do *anything necessary* to get the book."

Hadrian was disappointed but impressed by her honesty, at least. "Oh."

Seeing the look on his face, she followed up with, "I wasn't going to give it to him. That's what Millie Mulch would do, and I'm Millificent LeDeye, remember?" She smiled. "So, here's the deal. While I don't have a fortune, I do have money, enough to pay for supplies: a wagon and a donkey. You get the book from your friend, and the two of us can slip out of town real quiet. If we meet anyone, like the Port Authority, we can pretend to be newlyweds off to start a new life. We'll travel up to Neith — two days, tops — and hire a few dwarf diggers. They have a lot of them up there. We won't be able to afford too many. I don't have *that* kind of money, and this might take a while, so we need to pace ourselves. The important thing is that we must do this on the sly. No one can know what we're up to, which means we can't let the dwarfs leave once they take the job. Can you handle a sword?"

Hadrian stared at her, watching the atmosphere wash away like so much makeup in a rainstorm.

She's right. The result is ugly.

"I've used one before."

She looked him over. "But you don't have one." She sighed. "Something else to spend my money on. Given that I'm investing my life's savings in this, I hope you'll understand that I will be making the decisions. You're cute but don't impress me as all that bright. If things work out the way I see them, you and I will have a wonderful adventure secretly digging up ancient dwarven treasure by day and, sharing a tent at night." She gave him a wicked wink. "After all, we'll need to keep up the newlywed ruse. And I figure, since the church worked on this for almost a year, all the really hard work is probably done. So, in a couple weeks, a month tops, you and I will be the richest lovers in the world. Then I can build my own theater and realize my dream. And because you're handsome and don't have a dream of your own, you can be part of mine. What do you say?"

Neither Royce nor Hadrian had returned, and Gwen had no idea where Albert had disappeared to. Tim Blue had also left. She was alone and didn't feel like sitting at the big table by herself, so she took a seat at the pretty bar, which was made to look like a festive jungle hut. The countertop was made of dark teak, the front face adorned with vertical bars of bamboo and completed with a brass footrest. Overhead, thatch made an unnecessary awning while equally uncalled-for wooden posts were wrapped in maritime rope as if to moor a ship. All the stools were painted bright green.

Several seats were open, so she claimed one and sat. The man behind the bar had his back to her as he fiddled with a troublesome tap. Holding tight to her purse, she waited.

Jollin had given her the little bag as a birthday gift a year ago. Nothing more than a cinch-sack, but it held the four gold coins. Jollin, Mae, Etta, Abby, and Christy had saved the money and presented it to her as a thank-you and repayment for the four coins Gwen had spent to save them all from Grue. Just like the original four, Gwen refused to spend these. While not sacred talismans anymore, these coins were sentimental keepsakes. At least they were until Gwen informed the girls she was going on a trip to Tur Del Fur.

"Take the coins," Jollin had told her. "Take them and buy something wonderful for yourself."

"Oh no!" Gwen protested. "Those are —"

"They're money, Gwen. You're supposed to spend money. Look, you buy *us* stuff all the time. This is a chance to get something for yourself; that's why we gave them to you. We're doing good now — great even. You don't need to worry anymore. Enjoy your life. Use the coins. Get something nice, something fun to remember the adventure. Then *that* can be your keepsake. You might even get a nightgown that could appeal to a certain someone who moves with the speed of a legless turtle."

They *were* doing well, but Gwen still worried. The ladies of Medford House had become her responsibility the moment she convinced them to stand up and leave Grue. But Jollin was right. What good was money if you never spent it, and she already had plenty set aside for a storm. But how do you spend symbolic gold? No trinket would ever do.

She'd given the coins to Tim.

It was fitting, even necessary. In doing so, Gwen was paying off a debt, one she owed to a man whose name she never knew. This was the fitting fate of symbolic gold, and the only way the coins could honestly be spent. The question of whether she'd done the right thing, however, lingered, and she still didn't know if her plan would work. Fate might find a way to correct her well-intentioned meddling. Tomorrow morning, someone might still find a dead body wearing a sky blue doublet on the coastal rocks. There was even a chance that because she broke some cosmic law, the sun itself might never rise again. Wondering if she'd just caused the end of the world came with no small degree of stress.

I could really use a drink.

As Gwen waited for the bartender, someone took the seat beside her. Turning, she saw a well-dressed man she guessed to be in his late fifties. His intense black hair looked to have been slicked back with tar. Gwen knew some women who dyed their hair, but she'd never heard of a man doing it — and so badly. His vanity didn't stop there. He was dressed in a doublet and a pair of hose. The doublet was of the new short style — tight to the waist and splitting strategically just above the codpiece that was prominently displayed and decorated in jewels.

He smiled at her. "I've not seen you here before. You're from Calis, yes?"

If his voice were legs, the man's swagger might be crippling.

"Melengar," she replied.

The man looked puzzled, then laughed as if she'd made a joke. "You're very beautiful, no matter where you hail from. Absolutely gorgeous eyes." The comment was odd as he wasn't looking at her face.

"I'm with someone," she explained.

"Is he a duke? Because I am." The man squared his shoulders and lifted his chin. "You know what a duke is? Only a king or prince outrank me."

Gwen knew all too well what a duke was, although at Medford House they called them something else, something similar, but which better described the two dukes who had visited. Both were terrible: conceited and demeaning. The fact that this duke wore an overly large codpiece strongly suggested he was a licensed member of that same club.

He put a hand on her shoulder and leaned in. He might have intended to whisper something to her, but she suspected a kiss was on its way. Dukes were busy people and couldn't afford to waste time. She knew this because they so often reminded everyone of this terrible hardship along with having to suffer living with a hag-wife who they were forced to marry. The ladies of Medford House described the haste of dukes in less flattering terms, but followed it by pointing out, *"the faster the better, really."* They considered it proof that Novron was a benevolent god.

"Good evening, Your Grace," Lady Constance said, coming up from behind the duke. She looked a little less perfect after her stint on the dance floor. Her skin glistened, and a few strands of hair were out of place.

After their initial introduction, Gwen never wanted to see Lady Constance again, but now, when trapped with the Duke of Dark Hair who was visually molesting her and no doubt plotting to advance to the real thing, Gwen welcomed the lady's company.

"Ah, Lady Constance, how nice to see you again." The duke greeted her with the level of contempt in his voice usually reserved for hated mothers-in-law and despicable ex-wives. Then he frowned and expelled a disappointed sigh.

"I'm sure," Constance said with an iron smile. "Now, allow me to save your life by informing you that this woman is already taken."

"So she has told me," he replied, this time using a tone that declared he didn't care in the least, and eyes that, despite the presence of Lady Constance, continued to roam Gwen's figure as if it were a banquet and he a starving wretch. Gwen was certain about the wretch part.

"And she is not joking."

"Lady Constance, I have to say I don't appreciate your interruption or your advice. I'm a busy man, and I don't have time to . . ." He hesitated. "Wait . . ." The duke narrowed his eyes at Constance. "What are you saying?"

"Just this. When I tell you I am trying to save your life, I'm not joking, either."

The duke looked back at Gwen. His eyes did another lap over her body, only this time apprehension filled his face, and he leaned back as if she bore a plague. "Who? It's not Frederick, is it?" The duke raised his head like a bird in high grass as he surveyed the room.

"Forgive me, Your Grace, but I honestly think it best not to say."

The duke stood and looked around once more. He gave Gwen a nasty glare as if she had been plotting against him all along. He took Constance's hand. "Thank you, my lady." Then in a quieter voice he added, "I owe you for this."

Lady Constance whispered back, "Yes, you do — more than you know."

The duke quickly strode off, bumping a table and nearly toppling a drink. Both women watched his struggles to get clear of them. Then Lady Constance took the seat the duke had vacated. She looked at the empty counter before her, and then at the little purse Gwen clutched. "You are not attempting to purchase a drink for yourself, are you?"

"Actually, yes, I was."

Constance shook her head. "Oh, no. That is not allowed."

Gwen let her shoulders fall as her head shook. "Which is it? A woman can't drink at the bar, or are we not allowed to purchase alcohol?"

"What? No," Lady Constance said, shaking her head, then she clapped her palm on the bar. "Hello? Jareb?" The bartender turned, revealing a thin mustache. "The lady here would appreciate a drink."

"And what does the lady want?"

"I am not certain, but whatever it is, charge it to me, and anything else she cares for. Her coin is no good here. To be blunt, Jareb, if she manages to pay for *anything*, I will be *most disappointed*—do we understand each other?"

"We do indeed, ma'am."

Gwen stared, baffled.

"Do you want a list?" Jareb asked, coming over. "Wine perhaps?"

"Ah . . . no, had too much of that before," Gwen replied. "Do you serve good old-fashioned beer?"

"Is ale acceptable?"

"What kind?"

"Regal is our house tap."

"Never heard of it."

Jareb shrugged. "It's what I drink after closing the bar."

"Then pour away, good sir."

"Coming up," Jareb said smartly and reached for a metal mug with the engraving of a parrot on it.

"Make that two," Lady Constance said.

Gwen stared at her, knowing such a thing wasn't proper and that the lady would most likely see it that way. She would be offended *and* affirmed in her belief that Gwen was an uncouth tramp—a common woman of the streets.

Gwen wanted to hate her, and yet . . .

That duke was definitely going to kiss me. And a Calian madam can't slap someone of that rank and expect to keep her hand.

"Ah . . . thank you for stepping in," Gwen told her. "Nobles are . . . " She hesitated, knowing full well who she spoke to, but she was done walking on eggshells. Gwen had just challenged Fate to an arm wrestling match for the lives of Tim Blue and his wife, worrying about insulting Lady Constance was no longer in her. *"Difficult."* She finally settled on, but quickly added, "The higher the rank the more challenging. Dukes in particular are unpleasant. I can't insult them, but I also can't stand them."

Constance suppressed an unexpected laugh. "I could not agree more. And if Royce were to walk in and see him mauling you—"

"Oh! You know, I didn't even think of that."

Lady Constance's brows rose. "That was *all* I could think of. Your boyfriend doesn't respect rank. He'd murder the Lord Our God Novron if he tried to do what Duke Ibsen was contemplating."

"Why do you say that?" Gwen asked as Jareb delivered the pair of mugs. The liquid was a deep amber color. Both had foam spilling down their sides, and each was garnished with a slice of orange.

"I have hired Riyria, remember?" Lady Constance said. "On numerous occasions. As such, I very much know their reputation, which I can assure you is considerable."

"I know all that. I meant the *boyfriend* part."

The lady laughed once more and put a hand to her face as if ashamed of herself. "Well, I have eyes—two in fact—and they both work. The man is in love with you, and about as jealous as a squirrel with one acorn facing an endless winter."

This made Gwen laugh. She made no attempt to hide it.

"I didn't mean that as a joke," the lady said.

"Oh, sorry. I just had this image pop into my head of a squirrel wrapped in a dark hood and cape."

Lady Constance put her hand back over her mouth, but Gwen could see the snicker in her eyes. "Oh, wonderful. Now the same picture is in my head." She stared off for a second. "All you can see is his little snout poking out of the hood, right?"

They both laughed together, loudly enough to make Jareb stare.

"What's so funny?"

They both waved him off, shaking their heads.

Constance looked at Gwen fondly. "Since I can see we are having a moment . . ." She raised her mug. "To Tim Blue and his good luck charm."

Gwen froze and stared at her.

"I saw what you did," the lady said.

Gwen looked down at the teak counter with the two puddles of dead foam. "I thought women weren't allowed in the casino?"

"You are correct." Constance took a sip, then set down her drink. "But you caused enough of a ruckus that no one cared — least of all the casino guards, who abandoned their posts to watch."

"Am I in trouble?"

Lady Constance made a most unladylike face and spewed a *pfft* sound through her lips. "Not with me, certainly. You know, it is rare to witness a truly genuine act of kindness. I am guessing you barely know him. Tim Blue is what? A customer at Medford House who uses a false name while there, I suppose?"

"He *used* to be a patron. Tim got married, and we never saw him after that. Usually, that isn't the case. I guess that's one of the reasons why I like him. Most of the girls do, too."

"They say you walked in with four gold and walked out with over a hundred. But I know that's not true. *You* didn't walk out with anything. Baron Everbryant, as everyone else knows him, collected *all* the money."

Gwen held up her purse. "I got my four coins back."

"Wait — that was *your* money he wagered? And you let him keep all the winnings?"

"I didn't *let him* keep anything. He did all the gambling. I just watched."

"Of course you did." Lady Constance grabbed one of the green cloth napkins that perfectly matched the hue of the stools and set her drink on it. Just as before, she set it in the precise center, as if to do otherwise would be a sin. "And were you *simply watching* when he wanted to keep playing, but you told him . . . what was it now? How did you put it? 'We're not doing this to get rich, Tim. You have what you need to save Edie. It stops here.'"

Gwen didn't reply. That Lady Constance had heard was awkward, that she recalled it word for word was concerning. Gwen lifted her drink to take a sip, then made it a gulp.

"Baron Everbryant has been struggling," Constance said. "Everyone knows that. He and his wife haven't been doing well, but I suspect few knew the depth of his situation until tonight."

"He's paying his debt now," Gwen said. "Left as soon as the casino paid out."

Constance took another sip, this one bigger than the first, and the two sat for a moment, watching Jareb fill the order of a trio of men at the far end of the bar, all three of whom smiled in their direction. Then Constance swung her knees around on the stool and faced Gwen straight on. "I am sorry if I made you feel awkward earlier. That was not my intention, but well, my vocation is courtly politics. I flirt with the men and eviscerate the competition — which is usually women. At this point, it is a reflex. You see, I was unaware that —" She paused and thought a moment. "I did not know that I was in the presence of a *real* lady." Constance took a breath. "I must say with regard to your profession, my dear, you are as pure as starlight." Constance wiped her mouth, then stood up.

"Are you leaving?" Gwen asked. "You haven't finished your drink."

"My intention was to apologize, not intrude."

"I would have sat at the table if I wanted to be alone." She looked at her drink. "Weren't we going to toast Tim's good fortune?"

Lady Constance smiled. "Generous, kind, and now gracious. Careful, you are likely to ruin my cynical worldview of women, which I daresay, might hinder my livelihood because most of my clients and clients' victims are of the fairer gender."

"Sorry . . . I guess?"

Constance sat back down, and they toasted Tim, then watched as the last open dance was played out.

"Are you and Albert a couple?" Gwen asked.

Constance smiled thoughtfully. "Albert is one of the few people who understands me. We get along because we are alike — both blatant pursuers of self-interest. We love wealth, gossip, fine liquor, wild parties, and lives of reckless debauchery, all while making everyone else believe we are a pair of chaste virgins. And both of us adore the politics of power — and we're good at it. I often wonder how good. It is easy to overestimate oneself, especially when you must play the game properly, but I have often wondered if he and I were to join forces for more than a profit or a laugh, what it is we might be capable of accomplishing. After seeing you in the casino, you must feel the same way about Royce."

She shook her head. "We're not that far along. I've been in love with him for over three years—longer than that, if I'm honest. And while I'm certain now that he loves me, too—and that there's never been any other woman . . . he . . . ah . . . well . . . it was only two nights ago that he finally kissed me. And he was so drunk that I'm not sure he remembers. We're an odd couple. Both broken, I guess, and it's hard for two shattered hands to mend one another."

"Another round, ladies?" Jareb asked.

The two looked at each other. "Oh, absolutely."

The dancers left the floor, and the band adjusted for the late-night set of acts, leaving The Blue Parrot in unaccustomed silence, at least of the musical variety. Plenty of plates and glasses clinked and fists pounded on tables, and a hundred conversations continued to rumble like a loud wind or rushing river.

Jareb delivered the new drinks, placing them on the puddles left by the prior ones. Lady Constance promptly cleaned up the mess with her napkin. Then she procured a new one and reset her mug in proper order.

"So, how did you do it?" she asked Gwen. "How did you beat the casino?"

Gwen took a sip of her drink. "You wouldn't believe me if I told you."

"Try me."

Gwen, who was just starting to feel the ale, spoke into her cup. "I can see the future."

Lady Constance smiled and shook her head, dislodging another wayward strand of hair. "Very well, keep your secret. I suppose I would be reticent to reveal such a thing, too. And not to me of all people. Secrets are my stock-in-trade, and I would sell you out in a minute."

Gwen stared at Constance again, but this time she really looked, not at the imposing noble lady, but at the person. Constance had a small rebellion taking place with her hair, as a host of locks had escaped the tower, causing her to brush them aside. Her face was a bit flushed. Her forehead and neck glistened because The Blue Parrot had heated up, so much, in fact, that the main doors were now propped open. She sat with her elbows on the bar. Her lips lost their neutrality, choosing more often to smile. Gwen saw an actual woman behind the façade of the perfect lady.

"I don't think you would," Gwen said.

"No?"

Gwen shook her head. "You aren't a cold-hearted, selfish mercenary. That's a mask you wear. You're hiding a lot and have your own secrets that you can't tell anyone. Makes me sad, really. Maybe it isn't just me and Royce. Maybe, deep down, everyone is a little broken. Some are just better at hiding it than others."

Lady Constance reached for her ale and toppled the cup. "Oh dear, look at that. I am clumsier than I thought."

✥

Royce returned to the Parrot and felt an awful sinking in his stomach when he didn't see anyone at their table.

"Where are they?" he asked.

The man who had entered with him remained silent, and very well could have been mute.

"You realize that if your boss harms any of them, you'll be the first to die. Nothing personal. You're just the closest."

The man smirked. Royce didn't know his name and didn't care. He still had Alverstone. Cornelius's men hadn't searched him. Royce didn't know how to interpret that.

Incompetence? A show of trust? Or a demonstration of how little they fear me? Maybe a bit of all three.

"Royce!" Gwen shouted and waved from the little jungle bar where she sat beside Lady Constance.

Relief washed through him. He made quick work of the crowd, slicing across the room to where the two women sat. Gwen was on her feet, a great grin on her face. Royce fought a terrible desire to hug her. If they were alone, he would have, but not with Lady Constance there, and absolutely not in front of the ghost. "Are you all right?"

"I'm great," she said, smiling more than usual. "How are you? I thought you'd be back sooner. Is everything okay?"

"Yes, everything is fine. Where is Hadrian?"

"He hasn't come back yet."

He had expected her to say he went to the gorilla or was off with Albert and Arcadius. Royce was already picking the words to berate him for leaving Gwen alone. Now, he had another worry.

Two steps forward, one step back.

"Do you remember him saying anything about where he was going?"

She shook her head. "Just said he'd be right back."

"Are you going to introduce us to your new companion?" Lady Constance asked, her eyes gesturing at the ghost.

"No."

"It is most rude to ignore a person, Mister Melborn."

"He's not a person. He's a ghost."

"Seems pretty real, Royce," Gwen said, as she now also stared at him.

"I don't mean a *real* ghost. He's . . ."

In the Black Diamond, everyone understood the term *ghost* just as they did *bucketman,* or *sweeper,* but the terms never fully translated to the outside world. You could say a bucketman was an *assassin* and a sweeper a *pickpocket* to convey the essentials. But still this failed to explain the totality of the details, and *ghost* was even harder to define. Royce struggled to think of a word that came close. "Well, he's . . . I don't know . . . like a *chaperone,* I guess. His job is to watch me — that's all. So, he's just a ghost, understand. Ignore him."

Gwen and Lady Constance looked at each other, appearing a bit amused and a little too chummy for Royce's liking. "Have you been drinking?"

Gwen nodded, then proudly stated, "We both have. Regal Ales." She looked at Constance. "Isn't that right?"

Constance nodded. "Indeed, two cups each."

"Yes!" Gwen agreed, and she grinned at the Lady. "Are you good with numbers? You are, aren't you? I should have you do my accounting. Better yet, I should accept Arcadius's invitation to study at his school."

A drumbeat that began outside grew dramatically louder. A few shouts of surprise and curiosity erupted near the entrance, and the crowd pulled back as through the open door a procession of dwarfs entered The Blue Parrot.

Royce counted twenty, all dressed in fine clothes, their beards braided and adorned with metal clips and rings. With a long beard and dressed in silver and gold, the lead dwarf wore pieces of old-fashioned battle armor and carried a blue-and-black flag with a mountain crest. Behind him, a drummer beat a marching rhythm. Each dwarf wore an empty scabbard. They all filed down the middle of the hall and walked right up to the stage, where they turned and faced the crowd. The drum went silent, as did the room.

Royce noted the congestion near the exit and calculated exactly how best to get Gwen out before trouble started. He reached to take her by the wrist, but then the dwarfs started to sing. The song began softly and all together as a choir. Their voices were deep, and united as they were, the sound shook the room. Then another, much higher set of voices joined in, floating above the rest, as a second group entered the Parrot. These were female dwarfs dressed in lavish gowns of vibrant colors. They entered in a slow procession, stepping with the beat of the drum.

Royce didn't understand the words. Yet, ignorant as he was of the dwarven language, he felt the impact as the voices dropped low, rumbled, then burst into a soaring chorus. Tears glistened on the faces of the singers as they held the notes until their breaths gave out.

Silence followed as everyone stared, stunned.

Then, just as they entered, they left.

"What was that?" Albert found them at the bar as the last of the dwarfs passed out of the Parrot.

Lady Constance replied, "The Belgric Royal Anthem."

CHAPTER NINETEEN

Footsteps in the Dark

The rain had ended, but the streets were filled with puddles, and with so many open lamps extinguished, Hadrian struggled to keep his feet dry. Once again, the city had changed its disposition. Dark, slick, and silent, except for the dripping that was everywhere at once, this new temperament felt not at all wholesome.

He had delivered Millie to The Cave, which was pretty much just that, a hole in the side of the cliff where long ago salt had been mined. Because the miners had been dwarven, however, they embellished it with columns and engraved designs that Hadrian was certain meant nothing to anyone now, but once had. Hadrian had declined Millie's offer to take the book from Royce and run off with her to excavate dwarven gold. First, he explained that stealing from Royce was about as intelligent as slapping a rattlesnake, and second, that Royce didn't have a book to steal. He didn't bother mentioning that even if the first two weren't true, he still wouldn't do it because he and Royce were more than partners, they were friends. For some reason, Hadrian got the impression she wouldn't understand that part.

Millie refused to believe he didn't have access to the book, and that had dampened the mood far more than the rain. For his own good, she'd refused to let him into The Cave, because Andre would be inside, and she thought it best that fire and grease should be kept a safe distance apart. She wasn't the sort to take no for an answer, so she asked him to think about it. If he changed his mind, Hadrian was told to tie a white cloth to the hammer of Andvari Berling's statue, the one down at the harbor, and she would meet him at the Parrot at sundown. Later, as he made his way back along Berling's Way, heading back to the selfsame danthum, Hadrian wondered if she had chosen a white flag because it was easy to come by, easy to see, a symbol of a truce, or the flag of surrender. He wanted to think it was one of the first three but suspected it might be the last.

He walked all the way back down to Tier Six without seeing another living soul, although he did hear the distant bark of a dog, which only made the night more dismal. Something about a lonesome animal howling in the dark always set him on edge. In the military, sentries often had dogs. They were trained to be quiet but to bark and growl when the enemy was nearby. As it was difficult to train a dog to know who the enemy was, the mutts barked at anything unusual. Strangers mostly, and generally they were right. He spotted the lamp shop where Angelius had his stand. The roadside chef, the awning, cooking pot, and campfire were all gone. In their place was a dark puddle where the rain had mixed with the ashes of the old fire.

It's the emptiness and solitude.

Hadrian had been trying to pinpoint why he felt so anxious. There was a sense that he was somewhere he shouldn't be, except he'd been there before and had felt fine. Hadrian remembered talking with Angelius and enjoying the hakune and the conversation. Now, the same place felt forbidden, even a tad sinister.

It's the lack of people. He looked up. *And the lack of stars.*

Invisible clouds hid everything overhead. Without the sky, he felt as if he were walking through a cave — one that belonged to someone who might not like him being there.

No, he reconsidered, *not some*one, *some*thing.

And what bothered him was wondering if they — or it — was still there.

Once more, Hadrian lamented his lack of weapons. Albert had said The Blue Parrot prohibited swords, but he wondered if the city itself had an ordinance. Since arriving, he'd not seen a single one; not even the Port Authority officers had worn any. The lack of long blades had made the city feel friendly, inviting, and safe. People wore weapons for a reason. If they didn't—that was for a reason, too. He liked that about Tur Del Fur. The whole place felt polite, respectful, and civil, which was where he supposed the term *civilized* came from. Hadrian had also enjoyed how light and unencumbered he felt in just his cloth shirt. He didn't need to be paranoid about turning and knocking over an expensive vase. But that was all beneath the sun and the moon, when the streets teemed with people. In this dark world of shiny streets and inky pools, Hadrian felt naked and vulnerable.

He was just passing the puddle where Angelius had sold him the hakune his brother had caught when Hadrian heard the first sounds other than dripping water and the barking dog. The noises were exactly what he expected to hear in that place under a black sky: scuffling, grunting, and a cry. Hadrian also anticipated the sound of ripping, snapping, tearing, and eating.

The memory of a voice from the past sprang to Hadrian's mind. *"The murders happen at night or around dusk in a heavy fog, and in every case, the victims are eaten."*

It had been in Rochelle, almost a year ago, and Seton had been the one to say those words to him. He'd thought she was a young girl, but it turned out she was probably close to a hundred years old with next to no human blood in her veins. Yet that wasn't the point, but rather, how on particularly dark nights something hunted people and ate their faces. Hadrian had once stumbled onto such a victim on just such a night. This night was a lot like that: different city, different country, same state of affairs.

And me without my swords, or even my blue scarf.

The sounds came from just off Berling's Way. They bounced around a little, but Hadrian guessed the *something happening* took place behind the cabinetmaker's shop across the street. Like most every building, the shop had been carved from the original stone. But up on the higher tiers, where the land began to flatten a bit, there were more connecting streets, turning the place into a complicated maze of stone islands hewn into buildings. In any other place, a passerby would likely guess that the shop carved in such a lofty fashion from solid rock might be a small church, but in Tur Del Fur *all* the buildings were made of stone. This one had a signboard in the shape of a cabinet, and on its porch—safe under awnings swollen heavy with pooled rainwater—were a half dozen examples of the woodworker's craft.

The dog barked again, this time louder and closer and from the same direction. The shadows behind the cabinet shop appeared to be a popular place. But that prompted the question: popular with who, or . . . what?

Just keep walking, he told himself. *Nothing good ever happens behind a cabinet shop in the dead of night.*

"Nowhere else to run. I'm gonna kill you, boy." A man's voice so filled with hate that to Hadrian it sounded inhuman. It came from — where else — behind the cabinet shop.

Why Hadrian began circling around the building was still being debated in his head. The word *boy* was an obvious trigger. An actual child wouldn't be out that late. Given the sounds that accompanied the words, he deduced that an angry man was about to kill the dog for barking. Starting with this premise, Hadrian filled in the rest of the picture. He surmised that the man was a light sleeper and that the dog had woken him. Now the frustrated man was going to silence the animal forever. Hadrian also imagined that under the light of day, the would-be killer of over-excited mutts would never dream of harming a cute little pooch.

I'll be doing the guy a favor and saving him the guilt and grief he'll feel in the morning.

Hadrian believed this was the case, but his gut weighed in with an opposing and convincing argument: *Nothing good ever happens in the dead of night behind a cabinet shop. Walk on.*

Hadrian ignored his gut and moved around the building.

The rear of the cabinet shop was a fenced yard that housed sawhorses and numerous piles of lumber. Some were out in the rain, some covered in tarps, but most were stacked high beneath the shelter of roof-and-post sheds. An elderly man dressed in a knee-length nightshirt was out in the yard brandishing a long-handled broom. He was barefoot, his thinning white hair a tousled mess. The dog, a fair-sized mongrel, was well within broom distance, barking incessantly. All of this was expected, but from that point on, the scene diverged from Hadrian's imagined narrative. The animal wasn't barking at the old man, and he wasn't yelling at the dog. He wasn't even looking at the mutt. Both of them were focused on something perched on the roof of one of the sheds. Treed like a fox, a person, wrapped in a cloak and hood, clung to the steep roof.

"Help!" the figure cried.

The man swung and just missed a foot that dangled.

"Hold it! What's going on?" Hadrian demanded, trotting into the yard.

The man, who didn't seem surprised to see Hadrian, pointed and said, "He's up there."

"I can see that, but why?"

The man appeared confused by the question. "There's plenty of lumber. Get yourself a good stick. We'll drag him down by the ankles and beat him to death."

Hadrian shook his head. "Again, I must ask why?"

The man stared, puzzled. "Look at him!" he shouted, and what followed was more of a scream. "HE'S PURE EVIL!"

At the outburst, Hadrian took a surprised step back. The elderly fellow in the wrinkled nightshirt began panting, breathing violently through his mouth as he wrung the broom handle with bony hands. The dog alternated between snarls and growls. The animal's hair was up, and long strands of saliva dripped from its jowls as hiked lips exposed fangs.

"Oh, please help me!" the guy on the roof cried.

"Call off your dog," Hadrian ordered the man with the broom.

"Not my dog," the man said.

"This isn't your dog?"

"Not my rats, either." The man pointed with the broom at several dark rodents that leaked out of the woodpiles and climbed the shed posts. Two made it to the roof and bit at the legs of the cloaked figure. Dirty feet kicked them off the edge. The rats' bodies thumped hard on the dirt, but the fall didn't kill them, nor did it change their minds. A moment later, they were climbing again. The dog didn't interfere.

What's going on?

Hadrian looked at the old man, the dog, and the rats all unified in their hatred of the person on the roof.

"Oh dear! Please help! I can't keep holding on." The voice was that of a young man who spoke with a southeastern accent that reminded him of—"Master Hadrian, please, help me!"

"*Pickles?*" Hadrian didn't say it loudly. He said it mostly to himself in the way a person might use profanity to express shock. "You're alive?"

"Yes! Yes! And so are you. We are both so very much alive . . . but for not so very long, I think. Please help. This roof is steep, and I am losing my grip."

Stunned, overwhelmed, and baffled beyond knowing where to start, Hadrian didn't bother. He set the whole thing aside while he dealt with the issue at hand. Grabbing the broom handle, he wrenched it away from the elderly man. Hadrian expected a fight, but once more the man just seemed confused. Using it, Hadrian struck the rats climbing the post. They scattered. Then he charged the dog. The mongrel startled, retreated, then halted. Looking back, it growled. Hadrian advanced again, swinging the broom and shouting. The dog gave up and trotted into the shadows.

"Okay, come down, Pick—"

The boy fell and thumped onto the dirt, letting out a yelp of pain.

With no more than his bare hands, the old man advanced. Hadrian stepped between them.

"You need to kill him," the man declared with religious passion.

"Why?"

"Because he's evil!"

"He's not. He's Pickles."

Hadrian heard the flutter of wings as a seagull swooped down and clawed at Pickles, who lay on the dirt, fending off the feathered attack with one hand. He got in a good swipe, and the bird flew off into the dark.

"See!" the man said. "When have you ever seen a gull attack a person? A gull—at night! This thing is a demon and must be destroyed!"

Hadrian stared after the bird.

That is *really strange.*

"Ah-ah!!" Pickles shouted in pain. Turning, Hadrian saw the kid slapping himself on his arms and legs as he quickly scrambled to his feet.

"What now?" Hadrian asked.

"Spiders and ants! They keep biting me!"

Hadrian looked at the broomless man, then back at Pickles.

He appeared like the kid Hadrian used to know, sort of. His hood had fallen back, revealing that familiar face, only now a bit thinner — older. The features, as Hadrian had predicted, were different, too. Not so carefree or innocent as before. The boy had become a man.

"But you were dead, and now you're here, and everything is trying to kill you. Taken altogether, that's . . . disturbing."

"Oh yes, Master Hadrian, you must believe, it is me. You must help me."

That he was older, Hadrian took as a good sign. Hadrian thought that if he were a ghost or a demon posing as Pickles, he would appear exactly the way he had at his death. Seeing this mature version suggested it really could be the genuine article.

"I am as much of flesh and blood as you," Pickles said. "But . . ."

Hadrian's eyes widened. "But? How is there a *but* to that?"

Pickles looked down, ashamed. "I'm not a demon, or a ghost, or anything like that. But I am cursed."

The man whose broom Hadrian held had wandered away, muttering to himself about how late it was and how his lumber was likely to warp because of the rain. The rats, too, had vanished back into the countless holes under the woodpiles, and the dog, wherever it was, had stopped barking.

The clouds thinned in just the right place, and the three-quarters moon cast the yard in a pale light that gave Hadrian a better look at his old friend. Pickles wasn't doing so well. His eyes looked weary: dark, with puffy circles beneath them. The cloak he wore was tattered and frayed along the edges. Beneath it, he wore only a stained vest and short trousers, but in his right hand, he held a . . .

"Pickles? What is that you're holding?"

The boy — turned young man — glanced down at the book he clutched to his chest and performed his old familiar embarrassed grin while rocking his head.

"Is that what I think it is?"

Pickles bit his lip, then said, "That all depends on what you are thinking it is being."

"A book."

Pickles looked down again as if to verify. "Then yes, your thinking is most correct."

"And what do you mean by being cursed?"

Pickles lifted his shoulders. "Forgive me, Master Hadrian, but I do not know any other way to say it. It has been a bad week."

Hadrian continued to stare, dumbfounded. He planted the end of the broom on the ground and shook his head. "Arcadius told me that they executed you. He said Angdon accused you of attempted murder. He said they . . ." Hadrian shook his head. "But you're alive."

"I am, but once more I am thinking perhaps not for so very long." Pickles was staring past Hadrian with a look of dread on his face.

Hadrian turned and, in the moonlight, saw another figure enter the lumber yard. A man with cadaver-white skin and hair the color of a robin's breast approached. He wore an old-fashioned gray cloak that looked to have seen more miles than the rag Pickles was wearing. His hair was long, his mustache thin, and his beard pointed. Across his neck was a thin red line.

Behind Hadrian was a friend he thought was dead, and in front, a man who looked every bit alive, but whom Hadrian suspected might be dead.

This is a nightmare — but it's not mine. Hadrian took that moment to apologize to his gut: *This wasn't good. What happened to my irritable old man angry at a mangy mutt for keeping him up at night?*

Maybe the redhead is just really sick.

But Royce said he cut off his head, and that looks like the sort of mark such a thing might leave.

But dead people don't walk around. So, maybe . . .

What? Head severing isn't what it used to be?

I'm dreaming. That has to be it.

But what if I'm not?

Facing a walking corpse while wearing only a light shirt and no weapons in the empty ink of an eerily dark night was enough for Hadrian to give up the field. He would have fled in the hope that the walking dead were not the best of runners, except . . .

Pickles has his book.

The man wasn't there for Hadrian; he was after Pickles. If everything from ants to seagulls to old men were drawn to murder the kid, why not the dead as well? Just as when they first met on the docks at Vernes, Pickles forced his decision to stay and fight.

Hadrian braced himself for the attack, but the man surprised them both. He approached just short of arm's reach, then stopped. Giving only a momentary glance at Pickles, he turned to Hadrian.

"Thou dost not wish his death?" the corpse asked, his voice a horrible rasp. At least there was nothing especially demonic about it.

Hadrian shook his head. "He's a friend of mine."

"Such shouldn't matter." The corpse continued to study Hadrian, looking puzzled. Then he looked at Pickles. "If thou returns our book, the curse shall be lifted. Heed not, and each day thou shall endure ever greater suffering."

"The book is cursed?" Hadrian asked.

"Only if read," Falkirk replied. "He hast read the words."

Hadrian looked at the man and guessed he wasn't the sort to haggle. "Pickles, I think maybe you ought to give the nice man his book."

"But you don't understand, Master Hadrian. I have gone through so very much in the obtaining of it. You are a great warrior. Can you not defend me?"

Hadrian continued to watch the redhead, who stood before them with the patience of the perished. Concern was nowhere in his posture. "I don't have my swords, and I don't think it's that kind of fight. For one thing, I think he's already dead. Give him the book."

"But Master Hadrian, this book holds the secrets to ancient treasures in the lost dwarven city of Neith!"

"Pickles," Hadrian began, "We already have all the dwarven troubles we can handle at the moment. We don't need any more. There's a good chance a dwarf named Gravis Berling is going to use Drumindor to destroy the whole city. I really don't care about dwarven treasures."

"But Master Hadrian, this thing I carry is important; my life is not."

Hadrian finally turned. "It is to me."

CHAPTER TWENTY

Under the Fancy Fin

In the light of a three-quarter moon, the sand was bright when Gravis reached the beach. He was well north of the towers, away from the city and its lights, where the world was normally as dark as it had been at the beginning. While he'd lived in Tur Del Fur all his long life, Gravis knew that the city — this sparkling gem at the tip of the world — was not a big place. He was no more than a mile, maybe two, outside its influence and already he walked a virgin coast — a world untouched by anyone since time began. But tonight Drome had left three-quarters of a light on for him.

With few exceptions, Delgos was all rock and saltwater. Rich farmland she was not. The whole peninsula was an arid plateau, especially around the southern edge where cliffs kissed the sea. Only Dromeians would look at a landscape of stone and think *paradise!* Few others had ever tried to hack out an existence in the rough beyond the city, and fewer still managed to do it. Of those, none succeeded for long. As a result, the rocky coast ran desolate and empty for hundreds of miles in either direction. Barren beaches were dotted by massive sea stacks — great rocks that had been eaten away from the headlands until they stood alone as massive monuments to a forgotten past. Driftwood and seaweed littered the sand that was home to howlers, seabirds, and turtles, but nothing that walked on two legs.

Gravis couldn't imagine a less inviting place. The sea was too vast and unpredictable; it rendered the same anxiety he felt standing too near a sheer drop. The stone was harsh, jagged, and sunbaked such that touching it burned bare skin. Everything else was worthless sand. Little wonder the majority of Delgos was never settled, and this particular tract of beach never built upon. And yet for the two hundred and sixty-eight years Gravis had called it home, he'd never once noticed the desolation. Strange how the view through the shack's cracked windowpane had always seemed so beautiful — as long as Ena was looking with him.

The wet sand was easier to walk on, and not wanting to risk soaking his boots, Gravis traveled barefoot, leaving perfect toe-topped prints in a waddling line. The damp beach glowed with moonlight, and the sea had a bright line stretching across it, but to either side of the moon's reflection, it was black — nothing more than a void. Only it wasn't nothing. Even the abyss was something, and hearing the waves crash, Gravis imagined a tail flicking back and forth as the void watched him with far more interest than it should.

Thinking he had missed his new home, Gravis began to worry. More than once, in bright daylight, he had walked right by. He might overshoot and never realize his mistake.

How far is too far?

If he did miss it, if he walked into oblivion, what might be waiting in the dark? This was a real concern because Gravis was haunted. Since Ena died, he had felt untethered, adrift in a storm. His dreams were bad but not the sort he expected. Any sane widower would face nightmares centered on the loss of his wife. Gravis dreamed of Drumindor.

The towers had been his home for well over two centuries. The ancient fortress had always been a playground. He knew and loved every lever and gear. Gravis had worked day and night within those walls, often sleeping on the floor before the great furnace. In no other place had he spent more time, nor would he have wished to, but since Ena's death, Drumindor frightened him.

The dreams began the night Ena died. He hadn't fallen asleep — he had fainted. Gravis was down on his knees, bent over their bed with Ena's hand in his, and her last words in his ears. He cried until his body and mind just gave out — then the dreams came. Drumindor called to him with a muffled voice.

Gravis didn't understand the words, but he grasped their meaning. Someone was trapped inside and wanted to get out. He heard the pounding, felt the vibration of the struggle. Gravis went to the South Tower but couldn't get in. Lord Byron had sealed it against him. Still the voice begged for help. There was nothing Gravis could do, and even if there was, he didn't know if he should. Something about that voice and the pounding disturbed him. The tone of both was too deep, and so strong that he felt it. And there was something else. With each successive dream, Gravis became certain that the sounds did not come from within Drumindor, but from underneath.

All but certain he must have missed his new home, Gravis was lost in a mental debate, wondering if he ought to turn around or not. That's when he spotted the bone-white body of a tree lying on the beach. The wooden cadaver appeared oddly whole, except for a lack of leaves. The tree wasn't ravaged, not shattered or broken after the fashion of all other driftwood, but it lay preserved as if having died of fright. The pallid remains, though sad and even a tad morbid, were a welcome discovery. He knew the tree was a landmark that declared his new home was just ahead.

"Likely has a secret palace somewhere deep in the cliffs."

"Aye, he's probably in a room of gold, sleeping on King Linden's bed."

Gravis smirked. *If they only knew how grand my new abode really is!*

Veering up the beach into dry sand, Gravis soon spotted the shattered hull of an upside-down fishing boat. Mostly buried, the stern looked to have been bitten off by a giant sea monster. Gravis had found the old skiff shortly after the Port Authority had thrown him out of his shack. On that day, he had wandered in a daze down the beach, trying to decide what to do with his life. His choices had bounced between walking north until he died of thirst or swimming past the breakwater until he drowned. As he argued with himself, he found the old boat.

The skiff was one of the dory types, or so he figured because it had flared sides and a flat bottom. But Gravis wasn't a shipwright. All he knew for certain was that he'd seen similar boats on the decks of schooners and also spotted fishermen using them to haul nets in from beyond the bay. This one was a sad thing; a once-useful tool that carried the lives of men through storms and high seas, now rotted on the beach. Looking at it, Gravis forgot about swimming. He wiped the sand away from the prow and revealed the name painted there — letters that were nearly weathered off — *Fancy Fin.*

For no reason he could determine, kneeling in the sand with his hands on the hull, Gravis had cried until he was weak. By then, it was late, and he was tired of walking and didn't feel like getting wet. So, like a groundhog, he had dug an entrance on one side, crawled under and slept with the upturned prow acting as his roof. Like lying in his grave, he found it suited him. Each day afterward, he told himself he'd find some better place. Each night he returned to the boat — to *Fancy Fin,* to his grave.

He had improved it — sort of. Gravis now had a blanket, and he had spread out a sheet of canvas over the sand, making a more civilized floor and limiting the nocturnal sand fleas' access to his space. He had built a tiny fireplace out of smooth beach stones with a chimney that ran through a broken plank. He had made it out of boredom but guessed it would work. Still, he had never tried to light it for fear the draft would fail and he'd smoke himself out, or the flames might even catch the hull on fire. He also had the ends of several loaves of bread that had been pulled from garbage bins. They were all stale but had very little mold. He had accumulated as many as eight pieces but guessed some would be stolen by crabs, rats, gulls, or who knew what. He took little precaution to protect his treasures since he didn't have much of an appetite anymore. These days he drank his meals, just as he had done that night at Scram Scallie.

Gravis crawled under the hull, careful not to get too much sand on the canvas. He considered checking his bread supply to see what was left, but it was so dark. The hull blocked the light the moon allowed, and all he could see was a line of silver edging the side where his hole was dug. He abandoned the idea and lay back. There wasn't room to do much else. The sand was soft but lumpy. He squirmed a bit to smooth a trench for his body, then laid his head down, taking inventory of all the aches and pains that plagued him. Tonight, it was the pinched ache at the base of his neck that took the top prize. He tilted his head, first left then right, and after finding no relief, he sighed and gave up on that as well. He shook out his blanket and spread it across his body, tucking in the sides. He would check for the bread in the morning. Light made everything better, whereas the dark was an awful realm increasingly ruled by fear. This was something else he'd never noticed before. Age had a lot to do with it. As the birthdays piled up, the world — which in his youth had been so big and full of opportunities — had been shrunk to little more than a hollow husk that in his old age he filled with the two primary consequences of passion: guilt and regret. This, too, had only been a faint hint on the edges of his mind while Ena lived. She had somehow kept all the wolves at bay, shielded him with such great skill he never even noticed. He had rarely seen his wife, spoke with her even less, but just knowing she was there kept all the demons chained in their holes. With her last breath, she'd unleashed them all. And as he lay looking up at the black underside of the *Fancy Fin,* those demons came knocking to remind Gravis that nothing mattered anymore — that previously perceived important practices such as eating and breathing were pointless. For him, life was over.

Wind blew across the hull, brushing sand and making that now-familiar but never-pleasing mournful wail. Outside, the crash and retreat of waves, the swish of beach grass, and . . .

Gravis held his breath as he heard something else, something new. Faint but not too far away, he picked up the disturbing, regular pattern of *thumps.*

That almost sounds like footsteps.

The idea was absurd. He was in the middle of nowhere in the dead of night.

Still, the sound came closer.

The muffled slap spoke of feet on wet sand that soon shifted to the soft padding on dry. Then Gravis saw something block the light that entered around the edge of the hull. He held his breath.

What might be out there in the dark?

"Gravis Berling?" a voice whispered — not a wholesome sound at all. Even if he'd heard it in the full light of midday in a crowded market, such a voice was certain to raise every hair on Gravis's beard; whispered in the dark of a forsaken beach, it was heart-stopping. Clutching his blanket to his neck, Gravis no longer tried to hold his breath. He couldn't have breathed if he'd wanted to.

He didn't answer, didn't dare speak, and couldn't move except to shiver.

What is out there?

The idea it might be a *who* never crossed his mind.

Something thumped the hull, making Gravis flinch and forcing sand from the underside to fall on his face. He sputtered and wiped his mouth.

"Gravis Berling? Dost thou cower beneath this shell?"

In terror, he blurted out, "Who wants to know?"

A brief pause followed, during which Gravis was certain the *Fancy Fin* would be thrown aside to reveal a demon of smoke and red eyes bearing down on him. Instead, the voice replied with quiet resolve, "We are a friend."

"Gravis Berling has no friends," he declared truthfully. Over the course of his long life, Ena had been the only person who could have honestly worn that mantle, but even she was always more his wife. If he was honest with himself, Ena *had* been his friend; he just hadn't been hers.

"'Tis not true, for we are he," the voice from beyond the hull said.

"And who might you be?"

"We who shall grant Gravis Berling his heart's desire."

Nothing about this sounded good. In the plentiful catalog of dwarven epic sagas, bets were most often won by wagering against optimism. Dromeian history was full with the debris of promises made but never kept. Still, a talking demon was better than one that bit. "And what might that be?"

"Drumindor."

Gravis debated whether this was a person or an evil spirit he chatted with. Someone might have followed him to the *Fancy Fin*. He had taken no precautions to avoid pursuit. But no sane and mortal person could make such a promise. "No one can do that."

"We can," the voice said once more in a whisper. "At least such power shall be ours most soon."

Gravis, still on the fence about mortal versus demon, didn't want to ask the next question, but he was still a Berling: solving puzzles and a need to know defined them all.

And that's what's led to our undoing.

Unable to help himself, he asked, "Why?"

Once more, the voice whispered in reply, but this time so low the waves nearly took the words away. "For reasons equal to thine. Just as thou wishest entry, the masters desire to escape."

CHAPTER TWENTY-ONE

Raising the Dead

With Pickles in tow, Hadrian didn't bother returning all the way to The Blue Parrot. He had too many questions but decided to wait until they were safely behind walls before pausing to talk. After getting the book, the redheaded corpse had just walked away. No fight, no threat, no comment at all. The whole transaction went as smoothly as one could expect between two ghosts in a lumberyard. Falkirk wandered off deeper into the tier. He didn't appear to be intent on getting anywhere. His eyes remained locked on the book, which he caressed like a lost love, and his feet, left to their own discretion, meandered. No dogs barked, no rats chased, and not a single bird attacked. The night lost much of its tension, but Hadrian didn't care. He wanted his weapons. Paradise had taken a sharp turn away from tranquil.

The lamps of the Turtle burned brightly as they came up Pebble Way. Light spilled out of the front windows, revealing a slice of the mango tree's trunk and one of the courtyard chairs. Because it had been *that sort of night*, Hadrian pondered what the odds were that thieves had returned and ransacked the place again. He concluded burglars wouldn't light the lamps, but it wasn't until they got closer, and he heard Albert's voice, that he relaxed.

Hadrian opened the door just as Royce was on his way out with his hood up and determination in his eyes. The two nearly collided. Shocked, the thief stopped and stared. Then he frowned as if Hadrian had taken the last sausage from the pan.

"Where are you going?" Hadrian asked. "It's the middle of the night."

"I *was* going to search for you."

Looking past Royce, Hadrian saw that everyone was still awake and gathered in the main room around the big oil lamp. Gwen and Arcadius shared the soft cushioned bench that had become the professor's favorite perch, while Albert stood mid-stride as if he'd been pacing. Heads turned toward the door, each telling the same tale of surprise abolished by relief.

"There he is!" Arcadius announced with a smile as he clapped his hands, applauding Hadrian's arrival as if walking through a door were a great feat.

Gwen jumped up, rushed forward, and hugged him. "Thank Maribor you're safe."

"You were all waiting for me?" Hadrian asked. "Why?"

"You were out past curfew," Royce grumbled as he closed the door.

"There's a curfew?"

Gwen slapped his shoulder. "You said you'd be *right back!* What were you thinking? Didn't you know we'd be worried?"

Hadrian looked at each of them and saw the truth of it as Albert's shoulders relaxed, Arcadius took a deep breath, and Gwen continued to hold him as if terrified to let go.

"Sorry." He showed a guilty grimace. "Kinda nice, though. It's like I have a family again."

"You do have a family!" Gwen declared. "And you scared us to death." She slapped him a second time, then hugged him once more.

Looking over her head, Hadrian noticed that his family had grown by one. A white-haired, well-dressed gent with folded arms leaned against the wall. Standing with one leg up and a cape draped off his shoulders, he looked a bit like a great blue heron one-legging it in a stream.

"Who are *you?*" Hadrian asked.

"Ignore him," Royce replied on the newcomer's behalf. He sounded oddly irritated. "He's a ghost."

"Really? Another one?" Hadrian stared hard at the man, noting the expensive white doublet, matching shirt, and how the casually slung cape was edged in gold thread. "At least this one dresses better."

"Better than who? What are you talking about?"

"Well, tonight we —" Hadrian turned, expecting to see Pickles standing behind him, only he wasn't. Hadrian took a step back, opened the door, and scanned the courtyard. None of the outdoor lamps were lit, and everything was lost to darkness except for that slice of mango tree trunk caught in the moonlight. Royce watched him, puzzled, then concern filled the thief's eyes. He moved to the doorway and peered out.

"Is he still out there?" Hadrian asked.

"If you mean the sinister figure in the hooded cloak loitering in the shadows near the lemon tree, yes," Royce replied. "Was he following you?"

"More me dragging than him following. Apparently, the kid's suffering a bout of shyness." Hadrian raised his voice. "Come on in, Pickles."

"Pickles?" Royce asked.

The lad came slowly forward. He shuffled rather than stepped through the doorway. Once inside the rolkin, Pickles pulled back his hood and stood before them with shoulders high and head low. His mouth was tight, teeth clenched, and his eyes squinted as if he expected to be beaten.

"Everyone . . . this is an old friend who we thought was dead. His name is — believe it or not — *Pickles*."

Albert and Gwen, who hadn't a clue, politely introduced themselves. The ghost said nothing. Pickles ignored all of them as he stared at Arcadius. The young man appeared frightened of the professor to the point of being sick. Seeing anyone fearful of Arcadius was about as odd as Royce dancing a jig. For his part, Arcadius remained his same old self, except that he looked a bit disappointed.

The professor sighed, took a slow breath, then nodded and said, "It's good to see you're safe, although you do look a bit like something Royce might have dragged in."

"It's been a bad week, sir," Pickles replied.

"Safe? He's supposed to be dead," Royce said. "Weren't you —" Royce turned to Hadrian. "You said he was executed — killed in response to my saving your life."

"You mean in response for your knifing an innocent child," Hadrian replied.

"Angdon was neither a child nor innocent."

"Perhaps, but you didn't save my life. Still, you're right. I was told Pickles was charged with conspiracy to kill a noble and executed on some anonymous hill and that his body was carted off." He turned to Arcadius. *"You* told me that."

The professor smiled. "Yes, I believe I did."

"And you don't seem at all surprised to see Pickles alive."

"He's not even surprised to find him here," Royce added. "Sort of like he knew all along. He just didn't want us to know."

Hadrian stared at the professor. "You lied to me?"

The old man rocked his head side to side. "For the most part . . . yes."

Hadrian glared. "I nearly killed Royce because of you!"

"That's right. Hadrian nearly died because of you," Royce said.

The professor sighed.

"I am sorry, sir," Pickles told Arcadius. "I did my best to stay hidden, but—"

"It's fine," the professor said in a resigned voice, then he leaned back into the cushions. "I'm just glad you're alive. I was starting to have doubts."

Pickles nodded. "We kept missing each other, I think. I'd go to the Parrot, you'd come here. I'd come here, you'd be gone. I couldn't—"

"It might be best if you let me explain things to the rest of them first," the professor said, smiling at the lad. "We don't want Royce and Hadrian getting the wrong impression."

"There's a *right* one?" Royce closed the door once more, but more deliberately this time. If it had been Hadrian, he might have slammed the thing to demonstrate his growing anger. Royce made the same point by the slow care he took.

They both scowled at the old man.

"To begin with . . ." Arcadius began, then caught himself. He looked at the ghost. "I'm not entirely certain he ought to hear this."

"Can't ask him to leave," Royce replied. "It's part of the deal."

"Who is he?" Hadrian asked.

"We'll get to that. Right now, I want to see if this old wizard can perform a magic trick and save his own life."

Without his glasses, which rested on the table beside him, Arcadius tilted his head down to peer at the thief. "I can see you're not pleased with me, Royce."

"He's not alone," Hadrian said.

"Then I have no choice. The truth is I did lie to the both of you, but it was for a good and noble purpose."

"You admit to lying," Royce said, "then expect me to trust your word that it was for a good cause? How does that work?"

Arcadius frowned. "Give me a minute, Royce. Some explanations take more than a dozen words. And some words are important. For example, this young man's name isn't *Pickles*, it's Rehn Purim." The professor waited for a response. It took a second, but it finally came . . . from Albert.

"Purim?" Albert said. "You don't mean — he's not one of *those* Purims, is he?" Arcadius nodded.

"But . . . there aren't any more Purims. They were all killed."

Arcadius nodded again. "Lord Raster Purim of Hornwell was indeed arrested by the seret knights and tried by The Church of Nyphron. He was found guilty of heresy at Blycourt in the winter of 2983. Then Lord Raster and his entire family were executed outside Blythin Castle — all save one. Rehn Purim was away at the time. The youngest son of Lord Raster and Estee Purim was attending Sheridan University."

"Estee?" Gwen said. "That's a Vintu name."

"It is indeed." Arcadius nodded. "The Galeannon noble had taken a Vintu wife, which is what started the whole issue. You see, the church believed that Estee, by virtue of being Vintu, worshipped Uberlin and had poisoned Raster's soul. And for that, they murdered him, her, and all their offspring, as a way of ridding the world of evil."

"You hid him?" Hadrian asked.

"He was innocent of any wrongdoing . . . and he was my student," Arcadius said simply. "I smuggled the boy out of Ghent. Moved him south to live with a friend in Ratibor, who imperiled her own life keeping him safe. Then, when Rehn was sixteen, he was no longer content to hide. It's hard to blame him. Who among us would be satisfied spending such formative years languishing in obscurity?" The old man fixed Hadrian with a keen eye. "Rehn wanted to pay me back and asked what he could do. It just so happened I was expecting an important visitor from the far east who was arriving in Vernes by ship. I thought this fellow might need assistance reaching the university. Because four years had passed, the church was no longer searching for Rehn Purim. He hadn't been that big of a fish to begin with, and the trail they followed had gone cold. Given that a boy with Vintu heritage is nearly invisible in Vernes, I felt it was safe to send Rehn to bring Hadrian to Sheridan. I expected it would be an easy assignment."

"You sent him *and* me?" Royce asked.

"Believe it or not, Royce, I didn't exactly trust you. For you, that trip was more of a test. As such, I needed a reliable set of eyes and ears to tell me how it all went. Of course, none of it went according to any known plan. Rehn was detained in Vernes, and when he eventually reached Sheridan, it didn't really matter anymore. The job was done. So, I told Rehn to stay out of sight until I could determine what to do with him next, and he did. Then came the Angdon Incident." Arcadius peered at Royce. "Seret were bound to come after that catastrophe, so once more Rehn had to disappear."

Arcadius found his glasses on the little table and began cleaning the lenses with his sleeve. He never did put them on.

"I had a problem with this — two, in fact. I needed Hadrian to do the Crown Tower job, but he had grown fond of Pickles. This meant the boy couldn't just leave. If Hadrian thought Pickles was in danger, Hadrian would refuse to leave the boy's side. The second concern was that the seret would be looking for a boy by the name of Pickles, and the Knights of Nyphron are nothing if not tenacious. There was only one solution. Pickles had to die. So, shortly after the two of you left — the first time — Pickles disappeared. And when you came back, I told you the tale of how Pickles was killed by the church for the assault on Angdon. If I had told you Pickles had been adopted by a wealthy landowner, or his long-lost parents had reunited with their son, or he'd fallen in love and run off in a state of blissful happiness, neither of you would have believed me. But the equally outrageous story of the church blaming a boy for a crime he didn't commit, instantly executing him, and burning the body, was just the sort of thing Royce would never think to question. I'll admit that Hadrian was the surprise. It seems his years in Calis have left him with more calluses and scars than I anticipated."

"And what did you tell the church?" Royce asked. His tone carried a rise and fall as if he already knew the answer and sought not information but confirmation.

Arcadius developed a guilty look. "I told them an equally interesting story. The tale of a mysterious man in a dark cloak who had been seen on campus recently and had left earlier that day in great haste in the company of a young man who was not a student, but who appeared to come from Vernes. Angdon and his allies unwittingly supported this misleading account about a mysterious hooded assassin, and he made the assumption that the dark cloaked man had left with Pickles. I wasn't privy to the interrogations, so it's also possible Angdon and company believed the hooded attacker *was, in fact,* Pickles and that he left with Hadrian. The boys had been traumatized by the assault in the stables, and their stories were a bit of a jumbled mess, which is why the seret placed more credence on my account."

"And you told them we were riding north, didn't you?"

"I did. Better that they chased the two of you than Rehn."

Royce looked at Hadrian. "That's how the seret found us in Iberton. If I had known —"

"You would have been very unhappy with me. I understand that, Royce," the professor said. "Which is why I didn't tell you."

"What about Pickles — ah — Rehn?" Hadrian asked.

"He went back to Ratibor at first, but as I said, the seret are nothing if not tenacious. Too many questions were asked. So, I relocated him to a safer place."

"You sent him here," Royce said. "There's no church in Delgos."

"There is not." Arcadius smiled. Then he looked at Pickles and frowned. "Of course, a young man is even harder to contain than a boy. And how could anyone expect Rehn to be content by hiding in a hovel in such a place as this?"

"I'm sorry, sir," Pickles said, but now without the accent. What came out of his mouth were the words of a southern noble: refined but with a faint tang of eastern tonality. "When I heard about the church digging at Neith, when I learned they were using books, I suspected it was something the professor would be interested in. I saw it as a way to help repay you."

Hadrian stared, dumbfounded, as much by what was said as by how he said it. "You really aren't Pickles, are you? You never were."

Rehn shook his head.

"All these years I . . ." Hadrian continued to stare. His skin felt hot, his throat tight. Anger, disillusionment, and a terrible feeling of betrayal welled up in him. He didn't see the point of talking or listening anymore. Giving up, he turned and walked out.

In the courtyard, Hadrian sat in the chair that wasn't touched by the light. Low-slung, with a seat that was higher in front than in back, the chairs were especially odd because, unlike most things in Tur Del Fur, they were built of wood. Wood didn't survive long against salty air. It appeared that few things did.

Hadrian sat in the deep seat, his arms on the wide rests, staring into the dark. He didn't look at the stars or the white wall that managed to catch enough starlight to appear like a ghostly veil. He focused on a patch of blackness across from him that no light reached. He saw nothing but emptiness, a void where something ought to be but wasn't — not anymore. As he peered into the dark, he imagined the dark staring back. While it had no face, Hadrian pictured a sinister grin. There was laughter, too.

How could I have been so blind? First, Millificent LeDeye; now, Arcadius and Pickles. I travel with a professional thief, assassin, and liar, who in this quartet — by comparison — is a paragon of virtue.

Of the three, Arcadius was the least offensive. His actions were based on well-intended kindness and a desire to keep Pickles — Rehn — safe. Hadrian could forgive him for a little deception. His only wish was that the old man had said that Pickles had run off with a homely girl with a good personality. It was possible — probable even — that Hadrian would see through that, but it was better than the lie about the boy's death.

Millie, on the other hand, bothered him the most. She was beautiful, and her voice was the sort of gift that gods only bestowed on the righteous. He wanted so much to like her, but she wasn't what she appeared. At least she wasn't what he thought she ought to be — a virtuous and perfect being of divine light. Falling so far below that mark was like seeing a falcon hit the ground. It was more than disappointing. It was tragic.

Pickles, however, was a whole different story. Hadrian already liked him—loved him, even. In such a short time, the kid had become something of a younger brother or perhaps even a son. Over the years, Hadrian had cried at his loss and in his memory. Pickles had lost all his faults and gained only merits, making him less a person and more a sacrosanct ideal. The boy was no longer a cute but often irritating street urchin. Through Hadrian's tortured mental tributes, Pickles had become the grand sum of all things innocent and pure—and Hadrian had let him die. But the boy *had* existed, and the mere memory of Pickles remained and formed a single pinprick of light that illuminated Hadrian's darkening world, declaring hope was not gone, not in a world where Pickles had once walked. But now . . .

Now Hadrian stared into the all-consuming dark, and the dark laughed.

"Perhaps we should start over?" The kid had crept out of the house and stood, arms slung at his sides, with his head bowed. "Hello, my name is Rehn Purim. My family was murdered because my father loved my mother. I grew up mostly alone and isolated. Then I made a wonderful friend and was forced to lie to him to stay alive. Now, he hates me."

"I don't hate you," Hadrian said, shifting in the chair so that it creaked. "How could I? I don't even know you."

"Rehn isn't all that different from Pickles. Not really."

"See, the Pickles I knew would know that's not true. That Pickles would never lie to me—that Pickles would never lie to anyone. He wasn't well educated, but he knew right from wrong. And he had an accent that was endearing and honest."

"I still have an accent. My mother talked just like Pickles. I did, too, when I was a child. I've worked very hard to suppress it. I wanted to be more like my father. I failed. In truth, I've failed at everything I've ever tried, including being a friend to the one truly good person who gave me the chance."

Rehn stood half in shadow and half in the light. His chest rose and fell in labored breaths. "I came back to Sheridan about a week after you left. Arcadius hadn't learned much about your trip to the tower except that it hadn't gone according to plan. What we knew was that all of Ghent was out searching for two thieves. There were all sorts of rumors. I was worried. I was scared for my friend.

I wanted to search for you. That's when Arcadius told me I couldn't — I couldn't because I was dead — executed by the church, just like the rest of my family."

Hadrian looked up. "You didn't know?"

"I was just told to leave. And I knew why, so I didn't argue, but I didn't know what the professor was going to tell you. I wish he had found another way."

Silence fell between them.

The ocean breeze blew through the mango and lemon tree leaves that rustled overhead.

Salt air destroys everything.

"You know," Rehn said quietly, "it is strange, but ever since then, whenever I was in a crowd, I couldn't stop looking for you. Especially when I came here. I would go down to the docks. Big ships filled with turists came in from the north. I'd stand on the pier and watch and . . ." He sighed, shaking his head. "I would look for you just as I had that night in Vernes. When I did, I wondered — if I saw you, what would I say?"

"And what did you decide?"

Rehn shrugged, then he looked at his feet, and a frown filled a face that had once eternally beamed. "That I was sorry for not doing a better job with the watching and the warning, and that I was no longer brave because I had lost my great friend who was better than all others combined."

Rehn lowered his head and walked away.

Hadrian let him go.

Watching Rehn step back inside the Turtle looking worn and weary, Hadrian felt sorry for the kid. It wasn't all his fault. He had just been doing a job. And to do it, he played a role because he couldn't be himself anymore. But Hadrian couldn't forgive him for lying because he had no proof it wasn't still happening. That was the problem with trust: shattering it was easy, reassembling it wasn't. It would take a lot of time and work, and there would always be missing pieces that could never be replaced.

"What did you mean by *another one?*" Royce asked, causing Hadrian to start.

The thief stood, barely visible, leaning against the trunk of the lemon tree, arms folded, eyes on the door to the rolkin as Rehn entered and closed it.

"I need to tie a bell around your neck," Hadrian said, relaxing again.

"Not my fault you suffer from night blindness, and your ears are only ornamental."

"How long have you been here?"

"Long enough to witness the kid's attempt to revive his acting career."

"You think that was all fake?"

Royce tilted his head. "I'm still trying to work out the *real* reason you didn't leave me on the Crown Tower. Stupidity continues to pop up, but it's just so obvious; I feel there has to be more." Royce pushed off the tree and swung around to the empty chair, where the light slashed him across the chest. "You didn't buy it, either. If you had, I would have been forced to suffer an embarrassing display that would certainly have included hugs and possibly even tears." He grimaced.

Hadrian shrugged. "Their story does make sense."

"Are you joking now, or do you honestly believe in the myth of *sense?* In all the world, nothing makes sense, be it common or rare." He raised his hands to the fruit trees. "Why do trees appear to die each autumn, just to come back in spring? Not these, of course, but the ones we know. Does that make sense? And why do people have to sleep? For that matter, why do we eat and drink? And when we do, why don't we consume everything? You drink a mouthful of water and most of that comes right back out. So, why bother consuming it in the first place? The world is nonsensical. Given this, do you really expect our companions, the Father of Falsehoods and the Heretic's Son, to provide a truthful explanation for the kid's death and resurrection?"

Hadrian frowned. Royce wasn't helping. Just as with Millie, Hadrian wanted to believe.

"And while we are speaking on the topic of impossibilities, what did you mean about there being another *ghost?*"

"Another . . . oh." Hadrian shook his head. "Hard to believe I actually forgot. It's just this thing with Pickles — I mean Rehn, it —"

"Forgot about what?"

"I ran into your nightmare man."

Royce slid forward in his chair, which for some reason didn't creak. "He's here? You, you saw him?"

Hadrian nodded. "Pickles and—I mean, Rehn and I—both did. Sorry for not believing you."

"What happened?"

"Good news is that he won't be bothering us anymore. He got the book he was after."

"And the bad news?"

Hadrian frowned. "You cut his head off. I could see the mark, and yet I had a perfectly civil conversation with him."

"Yeah, I get that, but how is that bad news?"

Hadrian shrugged. "Just more evidence that you're right. Nothing makes sense."

CHAPTER TWENTY-TWO

The Locked Door

The next morning it was Hadrian's turn to be the last one awake. He hadn't slept well—not much at all, really. Dreams plagued him. In all of them, Pickles had died. But it was Rehn Purim they hanged from a lonely leafless tree on a desolate hill outside of Sheridan University. Hadrian stood and watched, unable to do anything except hear his last words: *Sorry for not doing a better job with the watching and the warning.* Hadrian would jolt awake and find himself once more staring into the endless dark. It wasn't until the morning's light pierced the windows that he was able to close his eyes and sleep. When at last he rolled out of bed, the sun explained that morning had come and gone. He didn't much care. What else was there to do that day?

He was just pulling on his shirt when he heard the raised voices from below.

"They can't," Albert said. "It's locked!"

The viscount wasn't the sort to shout. Something was wrong. Hadrian grabbed his blades and headed downstairs.

"But I was right, wasn't I?" Royce was saying as Hadrian descended into the common room.

Rehn, Arcadius, and Gwen sat together on the cushioned bench while Albert stood center stage playing the part of the teacher. Royce paced near the door. His hood was down, which was good, but he looked angry, which was bad. This wasn't his take-the-family-and-leave-town rage, but more a back-away-slowly irritation. Still, after seeing him, Hadrian felt he was watching Albert set a glass on the edge of a table. Someone would inevitably bump the furniture, the glass would shatter, and then everyone would lament about how such a thing could happen.

"It's quite likely you were right," Albert replied. "But since no one can get in, it's impossible to say for certain. However, Lord Byron certainly thinks so, which is why he's so upset."

"How can he be angry? I found Gravis and explained how to solve his problem."

"Yes, but you don't seem to hear me when I keep saying, *it's locked.*"

"What's locked?" Hadrian asked. He'd just finished buckling his sword belt, and only then noticed Royce's *ghost* standing in the archway, watching the proceedings with an amused smile.

"Drumindor!" the viscount practically screamed.

"I'm sorry, Albert," Hadrian said. "I didn't hear that part—just rolled out of bed, okay?"

Albert frowned, huffed, then nodded. "I'm just . . ." He turned away in frustration.

"What's wrong?" Hadrian asked the rest of the room for help.

"Lord Byron fired us," Royce replied. "Apparently, that's his solution to all problems."

Having composed himself, Albert turned back. He took a breath, then in a calm tone, he explained things to Hadrian like an exasperated mother speaking to a tribe of temper tantrums. "As per instructions, I told Lord Byron that Gravis was hiding in Drumindor, and he ought to search the place. Well, this morning he tried. *Drumindor is locked.*" He shot a glare at Royce. "No one can get in. Not even Lord Byron. And yes"—Albert looked again at Royce—"it *is* entirely likely, and widely suspected, that Gravis Berling *is* inside and that he *is* the one who locked it. But that doesn't help the situation. Lord Byron is complaining that we failed to achieve the goals for which we were hired—namely, preventing Gravis from sabotaging Drumindor."

"Locking the door is far from *sabotage*," Royce grumbled.

"I would agree," Albert said. "But Lord Byron—let's just say he was quite agitated. The man is famous for being as unflappable as a wingless bird, and yet—and I kid you not—he threw a vase at me. Not a cheap one, either. My guess is that the Unholy Trio is blaming him for this situation."

"What *situation?*" Royce asked.

Albert rolled his eyes. "You're not *listening*, Royce. I told you Drumindor is—"

"Locked, yes, I understand, but a locked door is not the end of the world. Locks are nothing more than a nuisance. They don't prevent invasion. They are employed in the hope that by being so troublesome, any would-be invader will skip it and move to an easier one. I open locks all the time, and I do it in the dark of night while avoiding guards, dogs, and often while dangling upside down. Or are you telling me Lord Byron has misplaced the key? If so, that seems more like *his* problem. But even if he did, his lordship can break down the door. It's *his* door—or the Trio's, at least."

"I don't think it's that easy, Royce," Arcadius said. "Drumindor is a dwarven fortress. It is, in fact, *the* dwarven fortress. If any place can be defined as impregnable, it would be those two towers."

"Nothing is unassailable," Royce said. "And I'm familiar with dwarfs, which is why—if it were me—I wouldn't bother with the lock or even the door. Lord Byron has the resources to make a new one. Rumor has it that there used to be a mountain here, and the dwarfs chiseled it all away. Surely, the combined might of Delgos can bore a hole in the side of one tower that's big enough to get through. Besides, he doesn't even need to do that. The Trio can just ignore Gravis. The dwarf can't stay inside forever. He'll eventually come out or die from lack of food and water. Who really cares? The towers serve as a defensive feature. So, unless an armada is on its way, the towers are nothing more than pretty ornaments. But if a quick solution is desired, Byron only needs to go down there and talk to Berling." Royce dropped himself into the seat near the door, stretched out his feet, and then crossed his ankles and his arms. "Gravis is just trying to bring Lord Byron and the Trio to the bargaining table—an attempt by him to get his old job back or something like that. Has to be. What other reason is there for locking himself in a prison?" Royce thought a moment. "Unless . . ." He glared hard at Arcadius. "You said the towers spew molten stone — that it's used to defend the bay. But can it also attack the city?"

"I don't believe so," Arcadius said, then he looked at Albert for confirmation.

The viscount shrugged.

Neither response satisfied Royce, and the room fell silent.

It was Rehn who spoke next. Squished between Gwen and the professor, the young man looked uncomfortable. "Every month since I've been here, the towers put on a show. The dwarfs celebrate the occasion like a festival, and it is — sort of. I go to the dock to watch. A lot of people do. There is a massive party, and crowds fill the bay area. Those with boats anchor them in the harbor, giving them the best seats. Then, after sundown, there is a growl. The ground shakes and the towers erupt. They become fountains, spraying brilliant plumes of yellow flame far out into the sea. It is dazzling: both fabulous and terrifying all at once. But none of the spouts point toward the shore, so it can't harm Tur Del Fur."

Satisfied, Royce nodded and settled deeper into his chair. "Then yeah, there's no cause for concern."

"Is Lord Byron asking for his money back?" Gwen inquired. She sounded concerned.

"Oh, no" — Albert shook his head rapidly — "he would never do that. It would be . . . *impolite*. He was paying for the *attempt*, knowing we couldn't guarantee *success*. But that doesn't stop him from being upset. So no, we don't have to pay for the expenses, *but* . . . he is cutting us off. We'll need to leave here right away, and unfortunately, our trip home will be coming out of our own pockets."

"We should take a ship then," Arcadius said. "It will be slower and less pleasant but a good deal cheaper."

Albert grimaced at the thought, no doubt imagining a week living in the airless, unsavory underbelly afforded by a steerage ticket.

Royce, on the other hand, glared in open contempt. "I'm going to take a look at this so-called locked tower." He got up, headed to the door, then stopped to look at Hadrian. "Coming?"

"Why?"

"For protection."

"You expect to be attacked?"

"Not for me — for whoever might get in my way."

By the time Royce and Hadrian arrived at the harbor, a crowd had formed that stretched from the statue of Andvari Berling to the South Tower. No one seemed to care about the north one. Hadrian figured this was because Terlando Bay bulged way out on the north side, and reaching it required a long trip through undeveloped coastal forests and windswept beaches, while the southern tower was so close that it formed part of the harbor and the western end of Cornelius DeLur's estate. More than that, the North Tower didn't have a door — at least not one that he and Royce had seen. Being a defensive structure, the towers likely didn't have a bunch of entrances. One door was enough, and since it wasn't in the North Tower, it had to be in the South. Looking up at the pair of soaring pillars linked by a bridge, Hadrian thought they looked like two giants holding hands. He didn't envy the daily trip of anyone who worked at the top of the North Tower.

How many steps is that? The workers must have legs of steel.

So, while Hadrian had a firm grip on why Royce headed for the South Tower, he was hazy as to why they were visiting either. The job was over. Lord Byron had canceled their contract. Maybe Royce didn't like being pulled off mid-job, or perhaps he was concerned news of a failure would harm Riyria's reputation. But Hadrian's best guess was that Royce didn't want to fail in front of Gwen.

While still on the port's boardwalk, they passed through open gates that, when closed, would seal off DeLur's private portion of the harbor from the public. No one seemed surprised to find them open. Hadrian surmised this was a regular occurrence during daylight hours to grant access for deliveries and visitors. This was understandable considering that circumventing the gates was as easy as jumping into the bay, swimming twenty feet, then climbing back out on the other side of the partition. The gate would only protect the boats at dock from casual mischief; the estate itself was in no danger of being invaded. The rambling palace that rose up the tiers was partitioned off by a far more formidable wall, closed gates, and grim guards. The gathering crowd flowed by them like a stream past jagged rocks.

Intent on keeping his eyes on Royce, who plowed through the sea of humanity, Hadrian noticed movement in the sky. He caught only the vague rumor on the edge of his vision. Something was dangling from Drumindor's bridge. For a half-second, he thought it might be a person kicking their legs, then he realized that given the distance, they'd have to be huge. "What's that up there?"

Royce slowed and tilted his head. "Looks like a flag, maybe. Has symbols on it."

"Was it there before?"

"I don't think so," Royce replied.

"What kind of symbols?"

"Dwarven, I guess."

"Is it writing?"

Royce turned. "How should I know?"

Hadrian smiled with self-conscious guilt. "I'm irritating you, aren't I?"

"You think?"

"Why are you so upset, Royce? We had fun, and the job was never going to pay all that much."

Royce continued walking.

The crowd was mostly composed of gawkers; some had drinks in hand as they apparently saw the gathering as an impromptu party. Passing conversations centered around a general ignorance of — and inquiry into — what was going on.

"Why is everyone here?" was the common refrain.

This was often followed by, "Well, why are *you* here?"

Invariably, this would be concluded with the predictable, "Because everyone else is."

People stagnated in groups like debris caught in shallows, forcing the flow to part around them. Some wandered slowly, looking around with bewildered faces, searching for familiarity. Others stretched up on toes and waved arms, calling to someone to join their particular dam project. Royce guided Hadrian unerringly around these obstacles until they hit the jam at the end of the boardwalk. A few hundred feet from the base of the tower, a barricade of sawhorses had been set up. A dozen Yellow Jackets formed a line on the far side, armed now with shields and clubs.

Royce didn't even slow down. He dodged past the remaining spectators, dipped beneath the barricade, and slipped through the Yellow Jackets like wind-driven smoke.

"Hey!" a guard shouted and reached out to grab Royce but caught only air. Two more made similar attempts with the same result.

Royce didn't run; he kept on walking as if oblivious.

Several more guards joined the endeavor. The rest turned to watch, allowing Hadrian to step through unnoticed. Two guards finally caught up to Royce. Both cried out in pain.

A couple of years ago, Hadrian would have panicked, assuming the thief had stabbed them. Now, he knew that if Royce had drawn Alverstone, the men wouldn't have cried out. Three more closed in from the sides, and a half dozen from the base of the tower ran in their direction.

"Get these idiots off me before I —" Royce began but didn't need to finish.

Hadrian, who was shocked by his partner's extraordinary and atypical frontal assault, prepared for an old-fashioned brawl. Given the numbers, the confrontation would not go well unless Hadrian drew a sword. The whole affair was bizarre. This was more like the actions of a drunk Royce. The silver lining of this particular storm cloud was that no one else carried steel, which meant he and Royce would just take a beating; death — even severe injury — was not likely.

Hadrian scanned the battlefield. He had two Jackets nearby — neither were looking at him. First, he would take the club away from the nearest, and then pummel the next closest. After that —

"Leave them alone!" The shout came from directly behind Hadrian, who spun, ready to fight. What he saw was Royce's ghost.

The Port Authority guards froze, looking unsure.

"They're with me," the caped observer declared with authority, and as he did, the man held up a small gold key on a chain.

The Yellow Jackets stared for a moment, then looked briefly at each other. Finally, with an annoyed frown, they gave up and walked away.

Hadrian watched what looked like a magic trick, then stared at the ghost. "Thanks," he offered. "That might have gotten messy."

The ghost offered only a patronizing smirk.

Searching once more for Royce, Hadrian discovered he was already far ahead and closing in on a circle of people gathered just outside the entrance of the South Tower. Hadrian ran to catch up.

Half a dozen men and one woman composed the discussion ring that gathered just short of where the sea spray wet the rock. Most were dressed like workers: worn trousers and stained tunics pulled tight by thick leather belts. The woman and the man next to her were not like the others, and they stood out from this group like blood on snow.

At Royce and Hadrian's approach, heads turned.

"Baxter?" the woman said. She looked confused.

"What are you doing here?" the man beside her added. He was tall and a bit gangly, with ivory hair that was slicked back. His attire — a long white-on-white embroidered coat, stockings, and shoes — was the best illustration of casual wealth Hadrian had ever seen. Elegant in appearance, the ensemble nevertheless appeared comfortable, and the profusion of immaculate white declared not only a lack of labor but also a man who never walked where dirt could be found.

"He's my ghost," Royce answered.

"And who might you be?"

"I'm keeping an eye on these two," the ghost explained. "They are of special interest to the Big Guy."

"Special interest?" the woman said. "That doesn't explain why any of you are here." She, too, was the picture of opulence but displayed her wealth through jewelry. She wore her gray hair up like a sculpted work of art — not, it seemed, as a fashion statement, but to accentuate the display of her diamond earrings and matching choker. Discontented with showcasing enough shiny stones to buy Medford Castle, she augmented this exhibition with what appeared to be her entire collection of pearl necklaces. She had five looped in ever-longer strings around her neck.

"He's here because I'm here," Royce said. "And I'm here because I really don't like sailing."

"Are you all drunk?" the lady asked.

Baxter the Ghost sighed. "This is Royce Melborn, and that is Hadrian Blackwater, they're the two men Lord Byron hired to stop Gravis Berling. Royce is here, I suspect, out of wounded pride and the conceit that he thinks he can provide aid and help Byron regain control of the tower."

"Tsk, tsk, tsk," Royce muttered, shaking his head slowly. "Very bad form, Baxter. Ghosts aren't supposed to talk, much less offer up names and details about the haunted."

Baxter replied with a nonchalant shrug.

"So, you're the ones responsible for that bloody dwarf taking control of Drumindor?" The woman shrouded her accusation in the form of a question.

"Only if the word *responsible* has a different meaning here than it does everywhere else," Royce replied. "The Triumvirate fired Gravis Berling from a job he's held without incident for more than a century. And for what? Out of an *abundance of caution?* Which is otherwise known as stupidity and fear. That's why this happened. But you already know that because you're Ernesta Bray, and the tropical snowman here is Oscar Tiliner. Don't worry. I don't blame either of you. Everyone knows you're just window dressing. Cornelius is the one *responsible*. Where is *the Big Guy?* I assume he's aware of the situation, and as we're on his front lawn, he could have walked over. Can he walk?"

"Get them out of here!" Oscar ordered Baxter.

"He can't," Royce said. "He's a ghost. Not even supposed to talk." Royce glared at Baxter. "Only allowed to listen, which is what I need all of you to do, too. I'm going to open your door for you. In return, you're going to explain to Lord Byron why he should keep our deal, so I don't have to resort to sailing on the open sea."

Without waiting for a reply, Royce walked past the dumbstruck group.

"Beautiful pearls," Hadrian said, smiling at Ernesta as he followed Royce.

This snapped her out of shock. Her hands went to her hips.

"This isn't some ordinary farmhouse with a rusty latch, you fool!" Ernesta shouted after them. "It's Drumindor — a dwarven masterpiece in the form of a fortress."

Without looking back, Royce replied, "And I'm no ordinary lock picker."

The problem with the door was immediately apparent — it didn't exist. The walkway ended at a sheer stone face, not a mark on it. Royce stared at the shiny surface silently for several minutes, then he began to make disagreeable grunting sounds. Eventually he walked around the base — at least as far as he could without getting wet. The sides and the rear of the tower were cut sheer to the ocean. This left Royce in front pacing back and forth. The grunting grew louder.

He ran his fingers across the surface of the stone and investigated where the walkway met the wall. "There's no seam, no gap, no edge anywhere. If it wasn't for the eroded walkway, I'd swear this was just a wall of stone." He looked up. "No windows — just those spouts and that bridge."

"What about your idea of cutting a new door?"

Royce shook his head. "The stone is . . . well, I'm not an expert, but it looks really hard . . . fine-grained and . . . I think it might be granite. Maybe it could be cut, but it'd probably take years." He looked around. "The whole mountain couldn't have been made this way." He ran his fingers over the smooth stone that looked to Hadrian like the surface of glass. "They polished it," Royce said, amazed. "All the way up, it looks like. Who polishes eight hundred feet of stone?"

"I'm getting the impression you're not going to be picking the lock," Baxter said with thinly veiled satisfaction. As always, he stood just behind Hadrian, watching.

Royce ignored him and began examining the paving stones. "How is this normally opened?"

"No one knows," Baxter replied.

"What do you mean, *no one?* Someone has to. People work in there, right?"

"This has always been open. I'm fairly certain no one had a clue it was a door — certainly not one that could be closed, or locked, much less disappear altogether."

"The entrance to Drumindor was left open to anyone?" Royce asked.

"You have to understand that the base of this tower is the headquarters of the Port Authority Security. Behind what used to be a door is where an army of Yellow Jackets is based. As such, locking this door was never seen as a problem. In fact, if Gravis was found, this is where they would have brought him."

"So why is it sealed? Why isn't Gravis in chains?"

"Unknown." The evident pleasure Baxter got from watching Royce fail was the familiar face of competition. "But what I do know is that this was the only entrance and now there is no way in."

"Why do you say that?" Royce replied.

"Because I've lived here for several years. These dwarfs . . ." He scowled and shook his head. "Honestly, I stopped bothering with them long ago. It's easier to squeeze money out of Cornelius DeLur than it is to open a dwarven lock."

Royce got to his feet and studied the tower again. "Well, we could bypass the door entirely. It wouldn't make much sense to lock the entrances on either side of that bridge up there."

"You're right, and there's a reason for that," Baxter said. "People don't have wings."

"Don't need any. Just have to climb."

Baxter sniggered. "Climb? Do you see how high that is?"

"Don't need to go to the top; that bridge is just a bit more than halfway."

"That's still too far. The wind would blow you off even before your strength gives out."

"Not really," Hadrian said. "It will toss you around some, and granted it's scary, but the ropes help a lot. Besides, the wind is warm here — imagine making a climb like that where it's cold."

Baxter stared at Hadrian as if he'd just revealed himself to be a warthog. "Do you see cracks, seams? Finger or toe holds? Assuming you *could* find something to grip, how would you anchor the ropes? Try hammering a piton into that rock. The spike will give before the granite does."

Royce continued to rub the surface and sighed. "I've disliked dwarfs for some time now, but at this point, I'm really starting to despise them."

CHAPTER TWENTY-THREE

The New Deal

Royce didn't say anything the whole way back. Hadrian knew better than to ask questions. While it had taken years, he had finally realized words weren't so important between them. Hadrian saw conversation as a way to fill gaps — to breach the chasm of ideas, ethics, and experiences that divided people. Words were rope bridges that made crossing divisions possible. But Royce didn't like words, didn't need them. In retrospect, it shouldn't have taken so long to understand. Hadrian had worked with horses. He'd fought on their backs in battles where teamwork and communication were the difference between life and death, and horses never talked at all. Like horses, dogs, or cats, Royce had a language all his own. The thief's hood was up, and that was all Hadrian needed to know for now. If it was important, Royce would fill him in. At least he hoped so — no, not hoped — *trusted.*

Such an odd word to bandy about in relation to Royce Melborn, and yet . . .

Back at the Turtle, everyone was outside, enjoying the sunshine. Arcadius and Albert sat at the table while Gwen ferried out supplies, and Pickles — Rehn — cut fruit. Something savory was smoking in the courtyard hearth. The lid was down, and blue smoke escaped the gaps. Auberon was back and tending the coals, tinkering with them, using a built-in foot bellows and an assortment of iron tools he pulled from a metal barrel alongside the grill.

"I can understand that," Auberon said over his shoulder to Arcadius, who lounged on one of the reclining chairs, drinking something in a fancy bit of blown glass that tinkled when he moved it. "Dwarven numerics is a nightmare even for dwarfs. You have a nice tidy system inherited from the Novronian Empire, what with your zero and all. Dromeian numerical tradition goes back before such innovations. *We* have a separate symbol for every number up to ninety-nine and names for each."

"So do we," Arcadius said.

Auberon eyed him wryly. "Sure, you do, but you call them sane things, like sixty and three. Dromeian numerics were born in a more innocent and ignorant age. Our numbers are called things like *Hildebreeth,* which as far as anyone can tell is just a name, like *Albert,* except it means sixty and three. Sixty-four is called *Jedline.* No rhyme or reason, they're just names. Engineers say it's more accurate—less chance of mistaking *Jedline* for *Hildebreeth.* But I think they're in cultural denial. Do something long enough, and it's too comfortable to change. Do something your parents and their parents did before you, and that's just the way it is. Your folk often say we Dromeians are like unto stone. Acourse, they mean we're heartless and unfeeling, which I can tell that *you,* at least, know is nothing more than institutionalized propaganda." He shrugged. "And your folk aren't the only ones to play in that cesspool. You should hear some of the jokes we have about the scallie. But the truth is, we Dromeians are like stone when it comes to traditions. Anything we used to do is better than anything new. *How it is,* is written in stone, and change takes eons of erosion."

Arcadius was the first to spot Royce, Hadrian, and Baxter entering the gate. "Ah! They're back. How did it go?"

Royce ignored him and everyone else. He walked inside, followed by Baxter. This left expectant eyes to focus on Hadrian.

"Well," he began, "not good. There's not even a door. Just a sheer, polished wall. Hard to pick a lock when there isn't one."

Gwen was making her next trip out from the rolkin, carrying ceramic bowls of fruit and a stack of plates.

"What's going on here?" Hadrian asked. "Aren't we leaving? Lord Byron isn't paying anymore, right? We can't afford to stay."

"Auberon has graciously offered to treat us to a farewell supper and one last night on the house," Albert replied as Gwen shoved a bowl of mangos at him, instructing the viscount to take a knife and begin cutting. Then she checked on Pickles's — Rehn's — progress. She smiled and nodded.

Hadrian turned to the dwarf. "That's awfully nice."

Auberon shrugged. "Don't have anyone else knocking on the door to stay here." He stepped on the foot bellows, bolstering the fire. "And I caught a big fish this morning. Way too much for just me. Everything worked out for all interested parties; I don't waste a noble animal, and you don't need to rush out the door."

Hadrian stood staring at him, flummoxed. At times like this, he was stunned at how the world appeared enthusiastic about proving itself wrong. Before him stood a kind and generous dwarf—which, according to general wisdom, was as possible as *slave wages.*

Auberon shifted the coals with an iron rake. "I know what you're thinking."

"I hope not," Hadrian replied, and meant it. The thought wasn't flattering. That such ideas wandered loose in his mind was not a point of pride. He took solace only in the belief that thoughts were not as bad as words: if not spoken, at least they couldn't spread.

Auberon smiled. "Not entirely your fault, you know. It's all those stories, isn't it? You're raised on them. Got nursery rhymes about Gronbach, the evil bastard who — if he was a real person and even half of what he is painted to be — was a real arse. But imagine if all humans were stamped evil on account of one hampot — and I bet you know more than just one."

"That depends. What's a hampot?"

"A dafty, a dobber. You know, an idiot."

"Oh yeah, we have quite a few of them."

"Don't beat yourself up. Instead, learn not to judge a beach by its slope or color, but by each grain of sand. Do that, and you might start to realize how it's not just the beach you're learning to see more clearly."

"What are the Powers That Be planning to do about the tower?" Arcadius asked, rattling his little glass, which Hadrian now saw had a piece of chipped ice in it.

"No idea. Might just have to wait Gravis out. As Royce said, he can't stay in there forever." Hadrian looked out over the wall and roofs of the nearby buildings and looked at Drumindor's towers. "Is there such a thing as a dwarven flag?"

"A what?" Auberon asked. "A flag?"

"Yeah. You know, a symbol of the dwarven people, or the standard of a king — something like that?"

"There're many various banners . . . why do you ask?"

"It's just . . . there's a big piece of fabric hanging off the bridge between the two towers that I don't think was there before. Has symbols on it. I was thinking it might be a flag. Something Gravis hung to declare he has taken the fortress. That kinda thing."

Auberon set the rake down and walked out to the terrace to get a clear view. He peered down and grunted. "My eyes aren't so good anymore. What do the symbols look like?"

Hadrian started to say that he couldn't make them out either, but then Royce came out of the rolkin with Baxter following in tow.

"A half circle," Royce said, "followed by a full circle above a chevron." He walked to where Auberon stood, and peering down, he added, "followed by three wavy lines, then a man with a pickax."

"Is the *man*"— Auberon said the word with a strange emphasis, as if he didn't think it was a man at all — "walking or standing still?"

"There's a leg out. So, walking, I guess."

Auberon nodded with a decidedly grim expression. "It's not a flag."

Royce looked at the dwarf intently. "It's a message, isn't it? What does it say?"

"It's a warning. Gravis Berling is telling the Dromeians to leave Tur Del Fur before the rising of the next full moon."

"Now, why would he be doing that, do you think?" Arcadius asked, with an ominous tone to his voice.

Auberon continued to stare down at the harbor. "Because, unfortunately, Gronbach isn't the only hampot we dwarfs have, either."

"I'm not your servant," Baxter the Ghost said as the three of them walked back down Berling's Way, retracing the path Royce, Hadrian, and their unwanted shadow had just climbed.

Royce had accepted Baxter as his personal shadow because he had to. Never in his wildest dreams did Royce expect the dapper dandy to prove useful — certainly not twice in one day. As expected, Cornelius hadn't assigned a novice to the post. The key Baxter showed to the Port Authority officers, and the fact that Ernesta and Oscar knew him by sight, revealed a lot.

"No," Royce agreed. "But you are Cornelius's servant — so act like it."

"I'm not his servant. I only work for him."

"I'm not interested in what helps you sleep at night. I need to speak to the Big Guy, and you're going to make it happen. Whether you are a servant or an employee, it's part of your job."

"My assignment is to watch and report anything of interest. Specifically concerning the diary of Lady Martel."

"Trust me, this is of interest."

"I don't believe you."

"Good. You might have a future in this career choice of yours."

"My *career* is already renowned."

"Uh-huh. And you don't see the problem with you needing to explain this?"

They hit the boardwalk and found that while the crowd had diminished, no success had been achieved at the tower. There were now wagons filled with supplies and several groups of what looked to be tradesmen: masons, carpenters, even some men with pickaxes whom Royce assumed were miners. Others filled in the crowd. Perhaps they were foremen or engineers or architects. All he knew was they dressed better than the workmen, but not as well as the commerce kings.

The harbor gates were still open, and Royce led the way through, but he made a left and headed for the big wall that guarded DeLur's estate. As expected, the guards stepped in their way. Royce heard his shadow give out a loud sigh.

"Let them in," Baxter said.

The guards, four men the size of weapon-endowed, armor-clad mountains, hesitated.

The ghost once more displayed the key, dangling it before them like some magic talisman. "Now," he said.

They stepped aside.

Having been there before, Royce knew the way and quickly strode up the walk and into the palace, where more guards decided not to challenge their visit. Royce had to admit it was nice. Seeing it in daylight, he approved of the sleek, unadorned lines and minimalistic decor. Its multiple stories had a way of appearing like stratum in the rock wall.

Royce also noted how Hadrian's three swords clapped as he walked. Neither the guards nor Baxter had forbidden them. Not patting Royce down was one thing, but openly granting access to a stranger toting a whole arsenal was something else. Royce wondered how far that courtesy would extend. How much fear did the Big Guy have of them?

As it turned out, not much.

Royce and Hadrian walked right up to the *throne* room. Guards — the fancy-dressed version — made another attempt to stop them, but Baxter shooed them away. This time he didn't need the key. The ghost had more clout than Royce expected. Once inside the room, they were stopped, not by an army of brutes, but by a beautiful woman who Royce hadn't seen on his last visit — dark hair and eyes, and dressed in a long, unadorned gown. She brought their little procession to a halt with but a raising of her palm.

"They want to speak to him," Baxter said in a respectful tone.

She studied each carefully without expression, then nodded. "Wait here."

The woman advanced to where Cornelius sat. As far as Royce could tell, the Big Guy hadn't moved an inch since the day before.

Does he take baths here? Does he bathe at all?

The woman whispered into Cornelius's ear, "Royce Melborn and Hadrian Blackwater are here to see you."

DeLur peered at them for a moment. "Send them up."

She descended the dais. "He will see you."

"You have information for me, Baxter?" Cornelius asked.

"Not much," the ghost said. "Only that a kid in their association, a Rehn Purim, was after the diary. No evidence yet, but I think he might have been the one to kill the courier and take the book. Doesn't have it with him now, though."

"You're certain of this?"

"I searched thoroughly."

"You searched Rehn's room?" Hadrian asked. He sounded angry.

Royce would have been dumbfounded if Baxter hadn't rummaged through Rehn's stuff. "The kid had it," Royce declared, taking a step forward, and putting himself first in line. This was a conscious act, an announcement to both Baxter and Hadrian that he would be handling the rest of this meeting. He wasn't sure if Hadrian would understand, but he thought he might. The man — who had for years proved oblivious to the most obvious of gestures — had recently started to catch on. "But the book was taken last night by Falkirk de Roche."

"The boogeyman who can't die?" Cornelius frowned.

Royce nodded.

Around the throne were similar retainers as before, holding silver trays of food, sweets, and drinks. Either Royce and his companions were intruding on an early evening meal, or Cornelius always surrounded himself with food to be had at the lift of a finger.

"And where is this walking dead man now?"

"No idea," Royce replied. "Can't say I care much, either."

"And I can't say I am pleased with this report."

"That's fine, because we aren't here about that. You have bigger problems than finding a noblewoman's memoirs. I need to know exactly what happened this morning regarding Drumindor."

"That is no longer your concern. Lord Byron dismissed you for your failure to accomplish a single goal in your contract."

"You're right, which seems a bit strange. Why hire us on the hint of a threat, only to dismiss us when the threat becomes real? I bet you had something to do with that decision. Maybe you're thinking that I'm using the job as a cover, and perhaps if you press us to leave, the book will fall out of our luggage on the way out. Or maybe you're just frustrated and want to punish me in a way that won't start a war. Best guess is all of the above. Honestly, I ought to be busy booking passage on the first sailing ship out of here, but so far, you've proven yourself reasonable, so I thought we could help each other."

Cornelius squinted his little eyes at them. "Help with what?"

This was what Royce appreciated about the DeLurs. If Cornelius were a noble, a king, a duke, or an earl, the conversation would already be over. Those born to their station found all others so far beneath them that the mere act of listening was considered not merely a waste of time, but demeaning. The DeLurs had clawed their way up, and that ascent had been achieved by any means possible, which meant nothing was beneath them — and listening cost nothing.

"As you pointed out, we failed to fulfill our contract with Lord Byron. If it gets around — and it will — that sort of thing can hurt our business. So, I want another crack at it."

"You want the contract reinstated?"

"To start with, yes. But I'll need sufficient funds and resources, and Lord Byron doesn't have the kind of budget I'm talking about."

"So you want the contract to be with me, is that it?"

"Precisely. But I also need information. For instance, how did Gravis get into Drumindor? From what I've been told, there is a small army inside, which should have stopped him. So, I am naturally curious."

"I see. And what do I get out of this? The book?"

Royce shook his head.

"I want it."

"I don't have it."

"Then I don't see —"

"If I'm right, and I think I am, I'm going to give you something you value far more than Lady Martel's diary."

"And what would that be?"

"Your life."

Cornelius leaned forward. For most people, it would be an unconscious act. For Cornelius DeLur, it had to be a monumental undertaking. In any case, the shift was as disturbing as a rockslide, and his flock of servants took a step back. "I can't imagine you are threatening me. You're not *that* foolish, and being a professional, you would never warn me in advance. I also didn't summon you, so there is no reason for this visit."

"You're curious why I would come and rattle the lion's cage when I can just walk away."

"Exactly. So, please explain yourself." If Cornelius had been a real lion, that last part would have been said with bared teeth.

"You haven't been outside, have you?"

Cornelius's eyes narrowed.

Realizing he was pushing it, Royce was quick to add, "What I mean is that you haven't seen the little banner hanging from Drumindor's bridge."

"You're speaking of Gravis's homemade flag of victory?"

"I thought the same thing. Except it's not a flag. It's a message. Gravis is warning the dwarfs to leave Tur Del Fur before the next full moon."

"Why would he do that?"

"That's a question I've been asking myself from the start. Why would Gravis Berling announce his plans for revenge? Why would he disappear? And why would he lock himself in Drumindor? At first, I assumed he was merely angry and irrational, like some pouty child making a scene. You likely thought the same or Gravis would have suffered a fatal accident weeks ago. But then I learned the guy is some sort of genius. That made a temper tantrum harder to believe. So, I figured he was looking for leverage to get his job back. What else could it be? But as it turns out, I was wrong again."

"So far you are not impressing me with your intelligence."

Royce smiled. "Tell me, why does Drumindor put on a light show every full moon?"

Cornelius shrugged, which for him looked more like his head and neck were sucked down and then popped back up. "Just a standard operation, a regular drill to make certain the machinery works."

"Everyone thinks that . . . except the dwarfs, who know the real reason. But I'm guessing you don't rub elbows with the native population much."

"And what is this reason?"

"In order to understand, you need to realize what Drumindor actually is. Everyone here keeps calling the twin towers a fortress, but only because everything the dwarfs build is militaristic. Given even the little I know about their history, it makes sense. You and I are prudently cautious because of our line of work, but dwarfs have been persecuted for centuries. They've acquired a sort of generational paranoia. Their homes, shops, warehouses, and temples are citadels because they need to be. It's how they build everything. For example, this palace of yours was once a dwarven building. A temple, or something, right? And with very few defenders, this place could hold off a small army."

"So, what is Drumindor if not a fortress?"

"For one thing, it's the largest and most advanced forge in the world. You want to make something out of metal — anything — Drumindor is the place to do it."

"So, what is Gravis making?"

"Nothing. He's not a smith or metal worker — turns out not all dwarfs are handy with a hammer. His skill, his specialty, is Drumindor itself, which apparently, he knows inside and out. But Drumindor wasn't built to be a forge any more than it was built to be a fortress. You see, there's another thing dwarfs are renowned for — securing treasures. It's hard for us to imagine, but those two massive towers are not much more than a pair of pins in a tumbler lock."

Royce felt like a fisherman trying to land the legendary *big one*, and he was pleased that Cornelius hadn't snapped the line and gotten away, but now it was time to set the hook. Royce harbored his doubts that the grand master of all thieves' guilds, who went by the underworld moniker The Diamond, would believe what he was about to say. Royce was working on unfamiliar ground and at a terrible disadvantage because in this case he was telling the truth.

"Everyone knows Tur Del Fur was once a volcano named Mount Druma, which was whittled down and tamed by Gravis's ancestors, but I suspect few understand what that means. I certainly didn't, not until I had a talk with a very old dwarf."

"Auberon," Cornelius said. "You've been chatting with the freedom fighter."

"You called him that before . . . why?"

"Because he is. Auberon was born in the Barak Ghetto of Trent. Attempting to help his people, he waged a two-century-long war against the Lords of Lanksteer. In the process, he became a hero to the helpless but lost everything. Now he owns a handful of rolkins that he rents out but lives on his little fishing boat, the *Lorelei*."

Royce nodded. It explained why the old man used a crossbow as a fishing rod.

"And what did the old freedom fighter tell you about Drumindor?" Cornelius asked.

"That no one can *cap* a volcano. There are forces deep underground that want to get out, forces so powerful that nothing can stop them."

"And yet I live in a paradise where no volcano bothers me."

"And that's because Drumindor is a cap with a vent. If you put a lid on a boiling pot, the lid will blow off and make an awful mess. But if you frequently lift it, just a little, you can avoid disaster by letting some of the steam escape. That's what Drumindor is: a locked cap with a vent. Whenever the dwarfs want, Drumindor has the power to spew molten lava in defense of the city, but every full moon the volcano *must* vent its excess pressure, or the lid will blow."

Cornelius sat back and stared at the ceiling. "You are suggesting that Gravis is going to blow this lid?"

"I'm telling you that he has likely already locked the cap, and in two weeks and three days, if someone doesn't get in there and pick that lock and vent the pressure, there will no longer be a Tur Del Fur. Your wonderful paradise will be a memory."

"I can't say that I like your prophecy."

"I'm not too thrilled about it either, which is why I should be booking passage on the first ship north before the general population gets wind of this and takes all the best seats."

"Why aren't you?"

"Funny, I keep asking myself the same thing." Royce paused, and not at all for effect. He wasn't acting. Doing an honest job had also forced him to be awkwardly sincere, something he was neither good at nor comfortable with. "Look, I don't like failing, and as I said, it's bad for business. Not to mention, I really do hate sailing." Royce looked around them. "You've got a nice place here that you've spent a long time building. You're going to want to save it, but you can't unless you get into that tower. If there is one thing everyone seems to agree on it's that Drumindor is impregnable. You're going to need all the help you can get, and at the risk of sounding modest, I'm better at breaking into locked buildings than anyone you've ever known. You want me here working on this project. But, seeing how pricey everything in Tur Del Fur is, I can't afford to stay. So, here's the deal.

You continue to pay my expenses and provide me with the resources I need, and I'll get you in."

"What will you require?"

"First, tell me exactly what happened this morning."

CHAPTER TWENTY-FOUR

The Diary of Falkirk

By the time Hadrian and Royce returned to the Turquoise Turtle, it was getting dark. Everyone else had eaten, the fire was out, and Auberon was gone. Gwen had saved plates for the two of them, which they ate outside at the little table beneath the lemon tree. Gwen had set aside a dish for Baxter, too. Constantly shadowing Royce, the man was always present, but Hadrian had never seen him eat or sleep. Hadrian wasn't certain how he did it. To Royce, Baxter was an annoyance; to most of the others, he was an intruder. Only Gwen saw a man forced to do an unpleasant job, and she took pity on him. When she handed him the plate, Baxter looked surprised but took it and ate by himself on the other side of the yard.

The fish was once again amazing, and Royce and Hadrian ate by Gwen's side as the tranquility of night gathered around them.

"Albert says he can get us on a ship leaving tomorrow." Gwen told them. "Nothing fancy, of course. We won't have a room, or even beds. To hear him talk, we'll be stuffed like sacks of grain into a darkened hold and trapped there for a week. Personally, I can't wait. I've never been on a ship before."

She smiled with such bright eyes and contagious cheerfulness that for a moment Hadrian believed her.

She's a great liar, he thought, and he wondered if this ability to make a person feel good about any situation was a skill of her trade.

"We're not leaving," Royce said without looking up.

"We aren't?"

"Not yet."

"Did you find a way in?"

Royce shook his head. "Not yet."

Gwen stared at him, puzzled. "But I — we — can't afford to stay. I've been to the market. The prices here are insane. That bag of ground peas I got for Hadrian cost a whole silver. A silver for a bag of nuts is nuts. I won't tell you what the fish cost. I wouldn't have bought a thing if Albert hadn't been with me. He said the reason the prices are so high is because of all the rich tourists — people who don't care about the price or even bother to look. He explained that the money goes to people who need it more than the likes of Lord Byron, and that buying things help the local residents."

Hadrian already knew Albert was an excellent liar because it *was* the primary skill of *his* trade, but the viscount's talents never failed to impress him.

"I do have a few coins," Gwen told them. "But —"

"Money is not a problem," Royce said.

"Is Lord Byron hiring you back?"

"I doubt Lord Byron will even talk to us — or Albert, for that matter," Hadrian said.

"Then how —"

"I negotiated a new contract with his boss." Royce wiped up the last of the sauce with his index finger.

"So, we have money again?"

Hadrian chuckled, leaving Gwen confused.

Having sucked the last of his meal off his finger, Royce produced a small gold key with a diamond in the grip and held it out to her.

"What's this?" she asked as he placed it in her palm.

"That is a key to the city." Royce pointed at the ghost. "He has one, too. Possessing it means you're working directly for Cornelius DeLur. Show this to any shopkeeper, produce vendor, Yellow Jacket, city administrator — anyone in Tur Del Fur, really — and you'll get what you want. All doors will open for you."

Gwen stared at the thing, looking half amazed, half terrified. "And he gave this to *you?*"

"Scary, isn't it?" Hadrian said, cleaning his own plate.

Gwen nodded. "I don't think I want to hold this anymore."

"Sorry, but you're the official key bearer," Royce told her.

"Why me?"

"Because there's no one I trust more with unlimited money and power."

"What if I lose it?"

"Don't do that," Royce said. "In fact, tomorrow, first thing, go out and buy a nice necklace to put this on, wear it on the outside of your clothes, and never take it off."

"On the outside? Won't someone try to steal it? There's a diamond in it. And this looks like real gold."

"Oh, it is real gold and a real diamond, believe me, but no one will steal it." Royce said this as if the very idea was absurd. Then, seeing the confusion on her face, he added, "Anyone carrying one of these in this city is as untouchable as an Imperial princess. Harming a key holder is tantamount to suicide." Royce pointed at Baxter. "In fact, I would have slit his throat days ago, if not for that."

"You're trying to keep me safe, then?" Gwen asked.

"You also do most of the shopping."

"I'm not sure Auberon will honor the key," Hadrian pointed out.

Royce considered this, then nodded. "You're probably right. We may still have to find a new place, after all."

"I'll talk to him in the morning," Gwen offered. "He can't have anyone else scheduled to stay here, and if this key works the way you say, I could pay him in trade. Maybe he needs paint for his boat or a net for fishing. Do you think I could buy those things with this?"

Again, Hadrian laughed. "You could buy The Blue Parrot with that."

Gwen looked down at the key, once more appearing terrified.

"Good," Royce said. "Now, where is Arcadius?"

They found the professor inside. The old man was on the main floor but tucked within the infrequently used niche near the stairs. He sat on a big yellow cushion directly across from Albert. Between the two was the little table, the one with the strange design on the surface. Like much of the furniture, it was part of the house, carved right out of the floor, standing on a single pedestal leg. Hadrian always wondered what the thing was meant to be used for. The table was too small for a desk and too tucked away for meals. The complexity of the design on the surface was the real mystery. It didn't look like a decoration, as it didn't extend across the surface but took up a small area in the center. The image was composed of twenty squares in an irregular pattern, and within the squares were smaller, more decorative designs. Both men stared at the table intently while Rehn, who sat cross-legged on the floor, had no trouble seeing the action on the dwarf-high table, and he watched with great anticipation.

"What's going on?" Royce asked.

"We're playing a game," Arcadius explained as he stroked his beard thoughtfully.

Hadrian noticed there were four little black pyramids on the table along with fourteen stones—seven of one color and seven of another. Albert moved one of the dark stones three spaces along the rectangular design. He grinned at the professor, who appeared displeased.

"Oh, that's a problem," Rehn said in a decidedly Pickles-like voice, and Hadrian wondered if excitement caused his mother's accent to escape.

Arcadius provided commentary to the newcomers as he scooped up the four little pyramids. "Despite being the youngest one here, Rehn is the reigning champion. Of course, it helps that he grew up playing this."

"It is a very old game," Rehn said. "I think perhaps it is the oldest. My mother taught me how to play when I was just a child. She brought it with her from the Old Country, and she said it was ancient."

The professor dropped the pyramids on the table, which rattled with a small sound.

"Two!" Rehn shouted with delight.

Arcadius moved one of the light-colored stones up two squares onto one with a flower design. "I toss again, correct?"

"You do," Rehn confirmed, his voice serious.

The professor gathered up and dropped the pyramids once more. Both Rehn and Arcadius shouted in delight, then Arcadius removed one of Albert's dark stones from the play area, replacing it with his own.

Albert slumped down on his cushion, and looking up at them said, "I think he cheats."

"Actually, cheating is allowed," Rehn said, "if you can get away with it. But in truth, the professor is not in need of cheating."

"I need to speak to the two of you," Royce said, indicating the professor and Rehn.

"That's fine," Albert declared. "All I do is lose."

Arcadius struggled to climb off the big yellow cushion, which was no easy feat for an old man. He returned to the more conventional bench, where Rehn took a seat beside him. "What can we do for you, Royce?"

"I need to know who Falkirk de Roche is, or was, and what's so important about his diary."

Arcadius nodded, puckering his lips as he did. "I see, and may I ask why?"

"Because when Gravis Berling locked himself inside Drumindor, he wasn't alone. Cornelius said it's been reported that a pale, red-haired man in a hooded cloak went with him."

"The one who took the book?" Rehn asked and looked at Hadrian.

He nodded. "That's what we suspect."

"And this same guy claims to be Falkirk de Roche," Royce added. "He's teamed up with Gravis, who according to Auberon, intends to use the volcano to erase this entire city in a pretty spectacular act of revenge."

"That sounds almost like praise," Arcadius said disapprovingly.

"If it wasn't also suicide, I'd consider it genius. Point is, to stop Gravis, I need to know what I'm up against. So why are the two of them together?"

Arcadius spread his hands in a show of surrender. "I honestly have no idea."

Royce looked at Rehn, who also shook his head.

"All right then." Royce dragged over a little stool and sat down facing Rehn. "At least explain why you stole the book from the courier."

Rehn looked uneasy seated so close to Royce, who was making no attempt to appear friendly.

Rehn shrugged. "Because I thought the professor would like to see it."

"Why?"

"I'm the lore master at Sheridan University, Royce," Arcadius said. "I'm always interested in old books, particularly when they are surrounded by mystery. The book you fetched for me from the Crown Tower was just such a tome. This one is equally interesting."

"Why?"

"Its age for one, but mostly due to the turmoil and interest that surrounds it. As far as I have been able to discover, the book was stolen from a seret sentinel named Garrick Gervaise by a thief posing as a monk."

"Why'd he take it?"

"He was working with another fellow who made a living out of digging up and selling old artifacts. I believe his name is Bernie DeFoe."

Royce tapped his chin. "There was a Bernie DeFoe in the Black Diamond. He was what we call a *digger*—a tomb raider. He had his own team, but he worked mostly out east in Vilan Hills. Got some good stuff, I heard. The Jewel, that's Cornelius's son Cosmos, never thought highly of the endeavor. Results took too much time, cost too much money, and rarely turned a profit. Cosmos was going to shut Bernie's operation down, but the digger was obsessed, and he wouldn't stop. That drove a wedge between him and the BD. So he broke ranks. I never heard what happened to him. I always thought he was dead, but it looks like he's still digging and thieving."

Royce stood up but continued to peer down at Arcadius. "So that's it? You wanted this book because it was old and because a digger wanted it?"

"There's more," Arcadius said. "Bernie's partner, the one who actually took the book from Gervaise, was a fellow by the name of Virgil Puck."

"Really?" Hadrian said. "Royce and I knew a poet named Virgil Puck. Well, that's a bit of an overstatement. We were hired to haul him in on charges of unlawful carnal knowledge of Bliss Hildebrandt. He was murdered before we could." He turned to look up at his partner. "You think it could be the same guy?"

"Given he told us he knew Lady Martel and had read her diary — yes."

"If he read the book, wouldn't he have been cursed too?"

"He certainly wasn't having the time of his life when he was with us, and then he was killed by the king's men for reasons that were never clear. If he wasn't cursed, he certainly wasn't blessed."

"When I found Rehn, it seemed everything was trying to kill him. So, if Puck was cursed, I'm just surprised we didn't want to kill him, too."

"Technically, I did," Royce said. "You were the one against it."

"True." Hadrian nodded. "Okay, so Gervaise's book was stolen by Virgil, who was working with Bernie. But how did Lady Martel get it?"

"My guess is that Bernie and Virgil were using her," Royce said. "You steal from a sentinel and it's like hitting a beehive with a short stick. They'll come after you, and you don't want to get caught with the goods. So, you hand it off to an unsuspecting innocent and pick it up later."

"But before Virgil could retrieve it," Hadrian ran with the thought, "we stole it from her and gave it to Lady Constance. So how did Rehn get it?"

Royce began to pace. "Cornelius told me that the Black Diamond had the diary for the last two years. I suspect Cosmos DeLur was angry about Bernie and Virgil stirring up trouble without permission. When he found out the stolen merchandise was in Medford, he decided to teach the pair a lesson — a fatal one in Puck's case. But seeing it was in Medford, Cosmos didn't want to start a turf war with the Crimson Hand, so instead of sending one of his men to get it, he hired Lady Constance, who contracted us. According to Cornelius, the church began to suspect Cosmos had the diary and that's when he decided to move it down here, out of their reach. That's when Rehn intercepted the courier." Royce stopped pacing and turned to face the young man. "I'm guessing you killed him?"

Rehn didn't answer, but looked sick, causing Arcadius to lower and shake his head.

"It wasn't like that," Rehn said.

"Not like what?" Royce asked.

"Not like I laid a trap and murdered the man." Rehn clutched his elbows and bit his lip, then he began to rock his head. "Okay, so . . . I did lay a trap, but I didn't murder him." He looked at the floor. "I only killed the man."

Royce looked perplexed. He turned to Hadrian. "You speak Bothered Conscience, don't you? What's he saying?"

"I think he means he never intended to kill the courier, but something happened?"

Rehn nodded enthusiastically. "I only meant to rob him. My plan was simple. I was going to bang him on the head and take the book. But the courier was traveling on horseback, and I had no horse. I knew he was riding down the West Echo Road and would go right by the Tiliner cutoff. There is a signpost there — two, in fact. They stand opposite one another. I got a length of rope, and I tied it across the road between the two posts. I knew he would be on top of a horse, so I shimmied up and tied it high on the poles as I didn't want to catch the horse. I would be so very upset if I hurt an innocent animal, you understand. Then he came. I didn't expect him to be in such a hurry. He was riding very fast, and as it turned out, the rope was a little too high." Rehn grimaced. "The man's head was almost entirely severed by the rope. Would have been if the rope hadn't snapped." Rehn put his face in his hands. "I never meant to kill him."

"But you got the book?"

Rehn nodded, his face still covered by his hands.

"You're lucky he died. Had you tried to *bang him on the head*, there's a very good chance he would have killed you."

Rehn didn't seem to hear Royce. He was still shaking his head in remorse. "Then everyone began looking for the book and for me. I sent word to the professor, begging for help."

Royce narrowed his eyes and turned to Arcadius. "I *thought* your random visit to The Rose and Thorn was a bit too well-timed. We don't see or hear from you for years, and then you pop up just as this holiday-of-a-job arrives."

Royce then focused on Albert, who was still at the little table, fussing over the tiny stones. "For your own sake, tell me you didn't receive this job from the old man here and then pretend he had nothing to do with it."

Albert held up his hands. "I was approached by Lady Constance. Or rather, she sent me the job proposal because she was already down here."

Royce turned back and peered at Arcadius.

"As you so frequently point out, I'm an old man," the professor said. "Rehn needed help, and I needed a ride. I also was concerned that there might be violence. I have no sons to call on. All I had was the two of you." Arcadius sighed. "I'm sorry for the deception, but I had hoped to preserve the lie I told you about Pickles, and spare Hadrian the pain of a reopened wound. But as it happened, none of my plans worked."

"Oh no, professor," Rehn objected, "you saved my life. If Master Hadrian hadn't found me when he did, I would have certainly died."

Hadrian said, "But at least now that we gave the book back, no one else should suffer."

Arcadius sighed, "And whatever information the book contained is forever lost. I so wanted to read it. It would have been fascinating."

"Right up until the nightmares make it impossible to sleep," Rehn said. "And everything you do fails, and each day your life gets worse and worse."

"I thought you told me you couldn't read," Hadrian said.

Rehn shrugged. "That was Pickles."

"Right." Hadrian frowned. "Did you read the whole thing?"

Rehn nodded. "It was taking the professor a long time to arrive, and I was bored."

"What was in the book?" Royce asked. "Was it a diary?"

"It certainly started that way. All of it was handwritten with beautiful penmanship, but from what I could tell, it was the diary of a man named Falkirk who was leaving on a trip with two other men. So it was sort of a travel journal, I suppose. The other two men who went on the journey were significant, at least Falkirk thought so. One was a great artist named Dibben, the other a fellow named Bran, who Falkirk held in very high esteem. At least at first."

"What happened?" Arcadius asked, now just as interested as everyone else.

"They traveled together to a tower called Avempartha — an elven tower. Bran was looking for something — a book, I think. They didn't find it, and the general conclusion was that the book went over a waterfall. They had lingered too long at the tower and winter was upon them. On the way home, however, the three were beset by a terrible snowstorm. Dibben kept them alive, somehow, but the situation was dire. They were out of food, and Dibben was getting tired of whatever he was doing. Then they came to an old fortress on the sea. In the dark of night, as the storm grew into a blizzard, they sought refuge.

"Falkirk described the castle as dark and unsettling. The whole of the place, he said, was ancient beyond belief, but their host was a young woman so beautiful Falkirk lacked the words to describe her. Whenever he wrote about Lady Mileva, he sounded like a lovesick boy. Also, there were two other visitors from afar. One was a young but despondent fellow who Falkirk described as a *Fhrey*."

"A what?" Royce asked.

"That's an ancient term for an elf," Arcadius explained.

Rehn paused a moment to make certain they were done, then went on. "This young Fhrey fellow had a companion named Trilos, who was described as most mysterious. All that was said about him was how he disagreed with Bran about the fate of the book they all searched for, which spoke of such things as the Great Cauldron, the Dark Fork, the Five Thousand Stairs, the Great Gate at Rol Berg, the Hall of Glass, and something called Death by Steps."

"The Great Gate at Rol Berg is the entrance to the ancient city of Neith." Arcadius said this more to himself than to them.

"See, you know about these things," Rehn said. "This diary was important, wasn't it?"

"I don't know," Arcadius said. "The church certainly appeared to think so. They were clearly using those directions in their dig."

"So, the diary *is* a treasure map?" Hadrian asked.

"In some sense, yes, but not one leading to gold and silver, I don't think. Was there anything more about this book the three sought, the one said to be in Neith?"

Rehn shook his head. "Not that I remember. Falkirk wrote about it casually, as if anyone reading his journal would already know."

"I see. Well, that's a disappointment," the professor said. "Go on."

"Falkirk described how the three were trapped by deep snows and bitter winds for weeks, and how in that time Falkirk fell in love with their hostess. She appeared equally smitten by him. That's when the diary begins to change."

"Change how?" the professor asked.

"The penmanship got worse, the entries shorter and more infrequent, and the topics grew strange. Falkirk wrote about secrets that Mileva was showing him, and how she was older than she looked. His obsession with her grew, and there were hints that he and she had entered into a bargain of some sort. Then the diary lost most of its *what I did today* format. He began writing strange gibberish like: *she has shown me the way, and I will live forever now*, and *these pages will be my pile of bones*, and *I can't do it . . . he is my friend*. At times, it seemed like he was arguing with himself.

"Then there were several pages of symbols and gibberish, and then a series of names that were written in a different color ink. On these pages were strange symbols that were not drawn but seared into the page. After that, there was a final horrible passage that has been burned into my mind word for word. It said: *If you read this, you will be cursed with ever-increasing and unrelenting misfortune until you return this book to me at the temple. That is where I am trapped, and you must move my body outside the ring of the horrible prison where Dibben ensnared me. Do this and not only will the curse end, but I will bestow upon you the gift of eternal life.*"

Rehn shuddered. "It might seem silly to you now, but in that little hovel all alone in the dead of night, those words terrified me." He took a breath and wrung his hands. "I can't explain it, but I knew it was true, as if the words reached out from that page and grabbed me by the throat."

"I think they terrified Lady Martel, too," Hadrian said.

Royce looked up and nodded. "That's what she and her dog, Mister Hipple, were doing in Rochelle. She must have been looking for Falkirk's tomb. Somehow, she knew he'd been buried there. But his temple wasn't very easy to find."

"What happened to this woman?" Rehn asked.

"Not sure," Hadrian said. "We found her dog curled up on a fresh grave in a pauper's cemetery. We kind of thought it might be Lady Martel's because we couldn't think of any way her little dog could have ended up there."

"Lady Martel went missing a little over a year ago," Albert confirmed. "No one knows what happened to her. One of the great noble mysteries, really, and a popular topic of speculation."

"So all the pieces have fallen into place except the one we need the most." Royce resumed pacing. "What does any of this have to do with Gravis? He and Falkirk are in this together now, literally. They are both inside Drumindor, but why?" Royce's sight settled on Arcadius. "Is there anything from your study in lore that can help?"

Arcadius sat back and stroked his beard once more. Apparently, he'd given up on trying to clean his glasses in favor of this new obsession. "All I know is that Dibben was the founder of the chief monastery for the Monks of Maribor, which is still located north of Vernes, and that Bran is a nearly mythical religious figure."

Hadrian raised his hand. "I actually know about him. Learned all about the guy in Dulgath. Bran was the protégé of Brin, some legendary hero who did all kinds of crazy stuff that Bran later wrote about. He was also the founder of the Brotherhood of Maribor."

"That's right." Arcadius pointed a finger at him. "I am impressed. Very good, Hadrian. Now where was I? Oh yes — Falkirk. Let's see, Falkirk de Roche was an early, first-century member of the Monks of Maribor. We know this because of inscriptions on the first-century temple in Alburn."

"I know that place, too," Hadrian said. "Royce and I both do."

The professor peered at him. "Indeed. From what I heard, the two of you burned the place to the ground."

"Had to," Royce said. "Villar was . . ." Royce stopped and stared at the wall.

Hadrian looked at the same space and saw nothing.

They all waited while Royce blinked a few times.

"When he does this," Hadrian filled the silence, "I can never tell if he's thinking or hearing something."

"Thinking," Royce replied. "Remembering to be exact. The duchess said they pulled *two* bodies out of the temple. One was Villar, the other Falkirk de Roche." Royce lifted his hand and shook a finger in the air. "And in Kruger, Falkirk thanked me for *freeing him from his eternal prison.*"

"You *spoke* to Falkirk de Roche?" Arcadius asked.

"Spoke to him once, killed him twice; didn't take either time. But if that wasn't his tomb, if he wasn't even dead, and if cutting his head off didn't kill him, I suppose the man could survive several centuries and a fire, right?"

"I will live forever now," Rehn quoted eerily from the diary.

"The temple was on sacred ground, remember?" Hadrian said. "Maybe that has something to do with it?"

"That's right. What do we know about immortal beings who can be trapped on sacred ground and have a thing for books?"

Arcadius frowned. "There are a lot of legends, Royce. The Manes are the dead that eschew the afterlife in order to return and haunt the living. And there is the story about Kile and the White Feather: a god who supposedly wanders Elan in the guise of a man, but nothing like . . . well, now that I think about it . . ." The professor tapped his lips. "There is the legend of Rowfinn."

"What's that?"

"An old wives' tale about a witch named Rowfinn, who lived in a forbidden forest and killed anyone who entered. She is said to have slept on a pile of human bones out in front of her cave. The pile supposedly granted this witch eternal life, but she had to add to its pile once a month and couldn't sleep again until she did so. But there's nothing in the story about a book. Indeed, the most notable thing about that story is that Rowfinn ate all her victims, and for no reason ever explained, she began her feasts by eating the victims' faces."

"Sounds like the Morgan," Hadrian said.

"The Morgan? You mean the ghost of Glenmorgan the Third?"

Hadrian nodded. "Heard about him in Rochelle."

"That is what we in the trade call the *Myth of Guilt*. The man was murdered by greedy, power-hungry cowards, and their guilt created this irrational fear that their crime would come back to haunt them."

"It's just strange because they say the Morgan also eats its victims' face first."

"And the Morgan legend comes from Rochelle," Royce said. "Where Falkirk was trapped."

"So, maybe there is a kernel of truth in all of this?" Arcadius pondered.

"Fun as all this is, it doesn't help stop Gravis," Royce said. "And we no longer have the luxury of time. This job has a deadline, and right now I don't have the slightest idea how to go about getting inside Drumindor, and if I did, I wouldn't know how to stop the volcano from blowing up."

Gwen entered carrying their cleaned plates. "You'll figure it out, Royce," she said. "I know you will."

CHAPTER TWENTY-FIVE

Exodus

Just as in all the previous attempts, the wind was the culprit.

Gwen watched as a gust off the ocean pushed the scaffolding's exposed corner — the one everyone was worried about, and for good reason. This slight kiss from a gentle sea breeze sent the whole structure twisting. It didn't fall — not right away. The massive framework bowed out then back, almost like it was doing that swaying dance she and Royce had enjoyed at The Blue Parrot. Each time it rocked, however, it twisted farther and farther.

Men raced down the steps; others slid like raindrops down the anchor ropes. At the bottom, everyone scattered. This was the third and final attempt to build a structure that would grant them access to Drumindor's bridge. The first scaffold had collapsed before reaching halfway. The second made it to the three-quarter mark before it blew down. This last one had come so very close, but there was a growing movement to the framing. No matter how much they anchored it, it continued to wobble. Seeing something that tall move at all was frightening.

Now, with a terrible tilt, lean, and snap, the scaffolding splintered, shattered, and fell. The majority of it came down upon itself, imploding like a tower made of straw, except it had been built of the biggest logs that could be found. Some toppled over onto the dock, punching holes through the boardwalk, but the very top had fallen into the bay, where it caused a huge splash. A series of waves burst white against the dock and sprayed the plaza, wetting the backside of the statue of Andvari Berling who, Gwen noticed, had a white cloth on his hammer that morning. Boats that had been moved to what was believed to be a safe distance bobbed at anchor as wildly as children's toys in a violent bath. Once the worst was finished and the last of the cracks and groans quit, workers jumped to the task of searching the wreckage for the dead and injured.

"That's it, then," Royce said miserably as he sat beside her at the little table on the plaza. "There's not enough time to try again."

It had been two weeks since Gravis had taken control of Drumindor. Full moonrise was only four nights away, and in all that time, no one had solved the problem that one dwarf had caused.

The two sat on the plaza at the tiny café that went by the plucky name Table by the Tea. The dainty little storefront with the happy red-and-white-striped awning serviced a handful of wrought iron tables placed out front. The café was squeezed in between the Hammer & Anvil and the Drunken Sailor, a pair of boisterous open-air bars that, given the early hour, were presently vacant and therefore quiet. Yet even the café suffered unoccupied tables.

The city was emptying.

Gwen and Royce had made a habit of eating breakfast at the café each morning. Along with coffee, tea, and fresh-baked pastries, the shop provided the best view of the South Tower. The Table by the Tea was also one of the few places still open. Word had circulated, and ships departed from the harbor each day. What had been a forest of towering masts was now a deserted cove.

The turists were the first to leave, and with them went most of the business. At first, shops opened for only a few hours each day, and then, not at all. A greatly pared-down food market continued to serve those who remained. The price of the produce was slashed as farmers sought to turn their commodities into coin as fast as possible. Those who couldn't afford to book passage on a ship left the city by mule-drawn wagons. Some departed on foot.

With little else to do, the remaining inhabitants of Tur Del Fur came down to witness the battle to save the city. Royce had directed engineers to attempt to bore into the face of the tower, but after two weeks, they had hardly made a shallow depression, and they had spent more time sharpening tools than working.

Not content to rely on any single plan, Royce — who had determined that the stone surrounding the South Tower was more pliable than the tower itself — had also ordered the digging of a tunnel aimed at burrowing underneath, but the excavators discovered the tower's granite base just kept going down.

Unhappy with Royce's progress, and also not satisfied with relying solely on him, Cornelius called in locksmiths from all corners of Delgos to no avail. As Royce had repeatedly explained, there was no lock to work on.

One fellow, a mason who had moved to Delgos to learn stonework from the dwarfs, proposed building a sister tower but admitted it would take longer than a month.

Even Arcadius studied the issue. He suggested creating a balloon that would be inflated with hot air that would rise. He explained that an empty wine barrel could be attached, and a passenger could be lifted to the level of the bridge. This was believed to be ridiculous by everyone, and the idea was flatly ignored, frustrating the professor to no end.

Finally, Royce recruited an army of carpenters and directed the engineers to erect the scaffolds.

Each day the crowds witnessed failure after failure, and as the days passed, the audiences grew smaller and smaller. The collapse of the scaffolding that morning heralded the end. This slapdash pile of scavenged wood had been their last hope.

"Don't bother paying me," the owner of the Table by the Tea announced to everyone. Her name was Olivia Montague, at least that's what she told everyone. Gwen had come to realize that transplants to the city assumed a "Tur name" that was always more flamboyant than the one they left behind — the first step of a fresh start. Even some turists adopted temporary names, wearing them like masks at a disreputable ball. In Tur Del Fur, everyone was free to be someone else, and no one yearned to be called Bertha or Walter Frump. In this way, Gwendolyn DeLancy felt at home. Her mother, it turned out, was ahead of her time.

Olivia Montague was a woman deep in middle age who made everyone feel noticed and welcome. Like the black tea and the morning sun, the smiling face of

Olivia always made the days brighter. "Everything is free. In fact, you can take the cups and plates with you. I'll be leaving tomorrow, and I can't carry it all."

There was a sympathetic and disappointed groan from the patrons, and Gwen joined in. "I'm going to miss her," she told Royce, who didn't seem to hear, as he was staring at the towers like he wanted to kill them. Gwen never joined in his ritual morning glare. She had taken to sitting with her back to the bay. The towers frightened her.

Since the first night after Gravis sealed Drumindor, she had suffered horrible dreams. They always began with the pounding. The beating was so loud the world itself could have been the anvil and the hammer the fist of a god. The sound came from deep underground. In her dreams, she walked down Berling's Way toward the towers, and as she did, Gwen felt the vibration in her feet and legs. So powerful were the blows that she staggered. Fruit and some leaves fell from trees, buildings collapsed, paving stones buckled, and the water of the bay boiled. Something — no — some *things* very far below were trying to get out. She didn't know how she knew this, any more than she knew how she could see people's lives through the windows of their eyes — she just did. Gwen also knew the source of the banging was not at all good. *Bad* didn't describe what she felt, even *evil* was too weak a word. All Gwen knew was that she was horrified by the thought they might succeed. In her dreams, whenever she looked at the towers, Gwen thought she caught glimpses of them. There were three, huge and horrible, and whenever she saw them, she knew they saw her.

"Is that it?" Gwen asked, pointing out at the third pier where the last big three-masted schooner was tied. Men were rolling barrels up the planking onto the deck.

"Yes," he replied. "That's the *Ellis Far*. She'll be leaving tomorrow, bound for Roe."

"Looks like a nice ship."

Royce scowled.

"You don't like ships, do you?"

He shook his head. "I'm okay with short trips, or boats on rivers where there isn't too much rocking, but oceans and I don't get along."

"So, what are you going to do? The Hansons won't be back in time, and there aren't any more horses for sale."

"Suppose I could walk."

"Most of Delgos is an arid plain surrounded by desolate mountains."

"You noticed that, too, did you?" He frowned.

"The *Ellis Far* is the last ship, isn't she?"

"The last public one." He pointed at the massive vessel docked at the DeLur private pier that was also in the process of taking on supplies. *"That's* the last ship — Cornelius's luxury yacht. He'll wait another few days before leaving. The guest list, I hear, is a mark of distinction. I suspect that, in the future, the world will be divided between those who were on it and those who weren't." Royce looked over at her. "You booked passage on the *Ellis Far,* right?"

"I made reservations for six." She touched the key around her neck. "And we won't be jammed in with the barley bags and the mice. I insisted on a stateroom. Of course, the ship isn't very big, and I didn't want to be greedy. The room normally accommodates only two. So, it's going to be tight, but much better than bedding down alongside the bilge water pumps in the hold."

"I thought you'd never been on a ship?"

"I have a talent for learning things quickly."

He nodded. "Yes, you do." Then he looked back at the towers and frowned. "I'm sorry this didn't turn out better."

"Better?" She sounded astounded. "How can it be better? I can quite honestly tell you, Mister Melborn, that I never once dreamed I might one day laugh under the light of different stars, swim in the Sharon Sea, drink ridiculously expensive wine, and sit in a bayside café sipping tea, much less dance with you on the polished floor of The Blue Parrot. This was the time of my life, Royce. Thank you."

She touched his hand.

He let her.

"I still wish it had been better."

She shook her head and pointed toward the empty chairs beside them. "Just a week ago, we — you and I — sat right there and spent an evening talking with Sir Adwhite."

"The old guy?"

"Yes, the *old guy.*"

"He didn't seem very impressive for a knight."

"He wasn't knighted for his prowess with a blade. He wrote *The Song of Beringer*. The man is a famous author, philosopher, and world-class thinker. And do you recall the man who was with him?"

Seeing he didn't, she rolled her eyes. "His name was Alfonzo Duran. He's a painter. A good one. I visited his shop; his work is amazing." Then she gestured at herself. "And I, insignificant little Gwen DeLancy of Wayward Street, spent a night discussing literature and fine art with two masters, while sipping spiced rum on a moonlit bay where both a monkey and a leopard wandered by. I think the reason you're disappointed in this trip is because you haven't been paying attention."

"I pay attention. For example, the monkey and the cat didn't just happen past. They were pets."

Gwen grinned and nodded. "Yes! Exactly! People walked by us with a monkey and a leopard as *pets*. Royce, this has been . . ." She looked up at the sky shaking her head. "I wish Sir Adwhite were here because I can't begin to put into words how incredible this has all been."

"I still wish it could have been better."

"How, Royce? How could this have been better?"

He never replied, but once more he looked back at the towers, which was answer enough. In his mind, he had failed, and she had been there to see it.

Royce and Hadrian surveyed the wreckage around the South Tower. Not much had been done to clean up after the scaffolding came down. With its collapse, the laborers, foremen, carpenters, and engineers abandoned the site because now, all thoughts focused on escape.

As always, Baxter was following Riyria. He appeared continually amused by Royce's frustrations. "Looking for a crack you missed the first twelve times?" the ghost asked.

"Shouldn't you be packing?" Royce asked. "The *Ellis Far* is leaving in the morning, and you strike me as the sort that has a lot of things."

"Don't need to. My bags have already been stowed in my private stateroom on the *Crown Jewel*." He pointed to DeLur's yacht, which at that moment was taking delivery of a wagonful of straw-packed ice. Baxter grinned. The iceman apparently thought the expression was for him and he waved back. "The chef from The Blue Parrot will be on board and needs the extra ice for his frozen magpies." He looked toward the boat at the public docks. "But I'm sure the accommodations on the *Ellis Far* are just as good."

Baxter was goading Royce, or trying to. The ghost had no idea that needling a stone only resulted in a dull point. Royce wasn't impressed by opulence. Jewelry was a hindrance; clothes that didn't serve a practical purpose were pointless, and anything else was generally a nuisance—a chore to protect. And all ships bound for sea were equally unpleasant.

Royce continued to walk around the base of the tower. As he did, he ran his hand along the smooth polished surface. Then Royce stopped and looked out across the ocean. "Which way is the wind blowing?"

Hadrian peered up at the numerous banners and flying advertisements hanging before the shops. "North to south, I think."

"That's what I think, too. It was blowing the same direction yesterday and the day before. I get the impression it usually blows that way."

"Worried about your trip north?" Baxter asked. "I'm no sailor, but I believe they have ways of sailing into a wind. It will be slower, of course. So, it is a good thing you're setting out tomorrow. I believe the *Crown Jewel* will be heading south, then east along the warm southern coast before heading north and landing at Vandon."

"Good to know," Royce said.

"You've become awfully talkative," Hadrian said to Baxter. "I thought ghosts were supposed to be quiet and invisible."

Baxter shrugged. "You don't have the diary, and you're not likely to get it now. So, there isn't much point of ghosting. This job is winding down, and I'm excited to see Vandon. Never been before, but I've heard it's supposed to be a wild pirate town, a real open port. No laws, no money. Everything is barter, and the only rules are what you can back up with a blade. Should be fun. Why I'm still on this assignment is beyond me. Everyone should have known when the dwarfs abandoned the city it was time to set sail. I mean, if you see rats running for it, you *know* it's time to go."

Hadrian scowled at the comment. "I'm really starting to see how you found my constant talking so annoying, Royce. I hope I wasn't this bad. Was I?"

Royce didn't reply.

"Seriously? You think I was —"

Royce held up a hand. He was trying to listen.

It sounded like the low rumble of thunder or the roll of big waves, but it came from the city. There was a rhythm to the noise, and soon Royce could make out a regular and repeated *thump!* pounding like a drumbeat. It didn't take long for him to break out the separate sounds: an army of feet marching in unison on stone and the deep chant performed by a chorus of voices. The whole of it presenting a decidedly militaristic cadence.

A moment later Baxter turned toward the city. "What's that?"

"I think it's your rats," Royce told him. "They're coming back."

Down the center of Berling's Way, marching in perfect rows of five abreast, came a host of dwarfs. This time they were dressed in work clothes, carrying tools and wearing belts adorned with hammers, and over their shoulders were coils of rope. They sang together as they approached the harbor. Once more the words were in the dwarven tongue, which echoed of another age, another time. When they reached the wharf, they turned and marched past the shops and bars as they made their way around toward the southern tower.

Along their route, doors opened, shutters were thrown back, and people came out to see what was happening. No one tried to stop them. Even when the column reached DeLur's harbor there were no guards, and the gate was still open. No one was on the docks except the three of them and the longshoremen busy preparing the ships. All of whom paused to watch the procession pass by.

"What do you think they're up to?" Baxter asked.

From out of the DeLur Estate, dignitaries issued. Ernesta Bray and Oscar Tiliner were at the forefront of the opulent mob. Both held drinks in cut-crystal glasses. If Royce had to guess, he'd say the passengers of the *Crown Jewel* were all holding a multi-day celebration to commemorate the death of the city, a sort of advance wake. The lady was there, too, the one with dark hair and eyes who had granted Royce and Hadrian an audience with Cornelius DeLur. This time she wore the appropriate black mourning gown, complete with elbow-length gloves.

The dwarfs ignored all of them and continued across the battered boardwalk, advancing relentlessly toward the three. For a moment, Royce wondered if they were coming for him. Trapped against the sea and seeing what looked to be several hundred dwarfs bearing down on him was alarming — a sort of nightmare scenario. Then they stopped, and the strict lines dissolved. Without a word, the dwarfs set to work clearing the debris of the old scaffold.

Bray, Tiliner, and the woman in black spotted Royce and Baxter.

"What are you doing?" the woman asked with more authority and anger in her voice than would be expected from a receptionist.

"Standing here, much like yourself," Royce replied.

The woman showed little patience and gripped Baxter with her eyes. "Explain. Now."

"Actually, he's right, Cassandra," Baxter said. "We have no more to do with this than you."

The woman whirled to view the small army who had already cleared a narrow path. "Where did they come from? Why are they here?"

One of the dwarfs, a female who had a towel draped around her neck, heard her and looked up. "We live here," she said, seemingly dumbfounded by the nature of the question. "We have fer more than five thousand years. And as fer why"— she extended her arms, then clapped them on her sides — "it's because this is our home. Always has been. We made this place, built it with our hands, poured our blood into it. We buried our dead beneath its rock. That's why we're here. Why are you?"

"Are you here to stop it?" Ernesta blurted out, pushing past Cassandra and spilling her drink. She most certainly had heard the conversation that took place directly in front of her, but Ernesta was angry. After all, she, Oscar, and Cornelius had a pretty good thing going. Watching it all erased by something as ludicrous as a disgruntled ex-employee had to be aggravating. But buried beneath the slurred frustration and bombastic arrogance, Royce thought he caught a tone of hope as if she believed this parade of dwarfs was the happy ending she'd been looking for. "Are you here to open Drumindor and get that lunatic out?"

Perhaps imagining himself to be the voice of reason but still sounding like a drunk parent scolding disobedient children, Oscar threw in, "If you're here to put a stop to this nonsense, you're arriving awfully late! We could have certainly used your help building the scaffolding or cutting into the stone!"

The female dwarf stared at them with the not-unexpected expression of disgust and bewilderment. Then she shook her head. "We can't open the towers any more than you."

"What?" Oscar gestured at the workers stacking aside the logs. Two had already set up a station and were sawing the timber into more manageable lengths. "Then what are you doing here?"

"They're begging Gravis to stop," Hadrian said.

Everyone looked at him, including the lady dwarf. She didn't say anything, which said a great deal.

"What are you talking about?" Oscar bellowed. "That crazy saboteur is almost a thousand feet up. How is he going to hear them beg?"

Hadrian pointed at the banner on the bridge. "That's a warning to get out of the city. It's written in the dwarven language. I've never met Gravis, but I suspect he could have written it in Apelanese so everyone could read it. He didn't because the warning wasn't for us. He was telling them." Hadrian gestured at the dwarfs — several of those close enough to hear him stopped working to listen. "He let his people know so they could save themselves. And he gave them plenty of time to pack up and get away. Only they didn't. Just by being here — by showing themselves — they're letting Gravis know they haven't left and they're not leaving, and that if he goes through with it, he'll be killing all of them. You're right, he can't hear them beg, but I suspect it's hard not to notice a thousand dwarfs, even from that height."

"He'll still do it," Royce said, but not to Oscar, Ernesta, Cassandra, or even Hadrian. He was addressing the little lady dwarf with the towel around her neck. "This isn't entirely his decision. He's not alone up there."

Enough concern crossed her face and those of the other dwarfs to prove they knew nothing about Falkirk.

"Doesn't matter," the dwarf said. "It changes nothing. This is still our home . . . our only home. We have no place left ta go."

CHAPTER TWENTY-SIX

The Last Night

That evening as the sun kissed the ocean, painting the bay in a dazzling gold, Hadrian thought the city appeared abandoned. He didn't see a single person on the street, and because no donkey carts were operating on Berling's Way, he and the others were forced to walk down to The Blue Parrot. Hadrian didn't mind. Despite the blinding glare coming off the bay, a sunset walk in the growing cool of the evening was pleasant. Albert lamented this dismal state of affairs as if the sun itself, once down, would never return. Hadrian had to admit it did sort of feel that way. Matters only got worse when they arrived and found no one waiting out front.

"Is it really closed this time?" Gwen asked, disappointed.

Albert bore the weight of a worried face as he climbed the steps and tried the handle. The door swung open. He ducked his head in, pulled it back out, and flashed them a smile. "Lights are burning, and people are at tables."

"Oh, good," Gwen said, relieved. "I wanted—I mean, it only seemed right to say goodbye." As she entered, Gwen let her hand trail across the doorframe, a melancholy expression on her face. "It's such a beautiful place. The first time we were here, I kept thinking it was just a wonderful dream, that it couldn't be real, that places such as this can't actually exist." She looked at Royce. "What do you think will happen to it?"

Royce paused with her but didn't reply. She nodded as if he had, and together the two walked in.

They had no trouble finding a table. The big room beneath the great dome was less than half full. Still, all the lanterns and chandeliers were lit, and musicians tuned up in the pit, making plinks and plunks and gritty whining sounds.

"Welcome, my friends!" Atyn rushed to them, his fingers laced with the stems of wineglasses, his arms wide as if to hug all of them. "So wonderful to see you here on our . . . our last night." He squeezed his lips tight and breathed deeply through his nose. "I am sorry, this is just so . . . never mind. Tonight is a celebration! This will be an evening that people will remember when they recall the glory that was Tur Del Fur."

"Are you traveling on the *Ellis Far* tomorrow as well?" Gwen asked.

Atyn shook his head, looking a bit embarrassed. "No, fine lady. I . . . I would not be welcome on such a ship."

"Oh," Gwen said. "But you *are* leaving?"

He rolled his shoulders and shook his head. "This is my home. In all the world, there has never been such a place for someone like me." He gestured with his wineglass-endowed hands at the dome. "I am allowed to work here in this palace, to make money, to have a place of my own. I can walk the street like anyone else. I talk to wonderful people like you—who pretend, or perhaps don't care, that I am different. In Tur Del Fur, this isn't an uncommon experience—but everywhere else such behavior would be as rare as snow in summer and rain falling up because the world is upside down."

"You're just going to stay, then?" Royce asked. "You are aware what's going to happen, right?"

Atyn nodded. "I know it seems strange, but I'm not the only one. There are others like me who feel the same way. Being here gave us the chance to see what was possible but also how impossible it is to go back. Life beyond this little bay is simply not worth the effort anymore."

He set out the wineglasses on their table. "So now, for this evening, there are no specials, for everything served tonight is exceptional, and there won't

The Last Night • 319

be any selections because everyone will receive everything the kitchen has to offer. Enjoy."

Music began playing. The tune was lively as ever, but Hadrian couldn't help but think it sounded sad, like the brave greeting of a widow at her husband's funeral. Albert must have had a similar thought because he got up and peeked into the orchestra pit. Then he looked around before returning. "More than half of the orchestra is missing," he reported. "A lot of the wait staff, too. And yet the casino is still open. Can you believe it?"

"Oh, yes," Arcadius said. "Makes a sort of sense now, don't you think? Those who have chosen to remain are all gamblers after a fashion. All of us are taking a terrible risk. What if a storm wrecked the last few ships? What if Gravis did something to cause Drumindor to erupt early? No, the ones who play it safe, those who don't care for gambling, they left at least a week ago. Those of us still here who could have left are risk-takers. You might even say that some of us are irresistibly attracted to the thrill of coming within a breath of disaster but manage to escape its clutches at the last second. Such a heart-pounding experience makes ordinary life nearly unbearable."

"You never impressed me as a daredevil," Royce said.

"In my youth, I was a great adventurer, but even in my old age, well . . . I kept you in a paper cage for three years, Royce. You must admit that's a fair bit of risky behavior."

"Why was that?" Royce asked. "People gamble for profit. What gain was there in what you did?"

Arcadius fiddled with his napkin, folding and unfolding it. His old fingers never seemed to stop. "Men waste fortunes to climb a single mountain, Royce. It may be hard to understand, but sometimes the act itself is the reward. I would even go so far as to say that it is the best compensation. For after spending whatever money your work provides, you have nothing to show. But the man who finds satisfaction in the achievement, he will keep his treasure forever. No one can take it away—no thief can steal a memory or erase an accomplishment. And the dividends are more than the means to procure food. They are the building blocks of self-confidence, courage, respect, even admiration. I'd be wary of that last one, though, as it is a bit too much like wine." He winked at Royce who didn't appear satisfied but didn't press.

"I never actually sat in here," Rehn said, his eyes as round as his head, turning left and right. "They always stopped me at the door. I suppose I didn't look like I could afford a meal or a drink."

"In that case," Royce said, "you might want to watch out for the wine as well. It's dangerous."

"Dangerous?"

"As are the lady singers," Gwen added, but looked at Hadrian as she did. "They are beautiful but also hazardous."

"What does that mean?" Hadrian asked.

Gwen offered him a pitying frown. "It means she's not the one."

"The one? Who's not? And the one what?"

"She's not the one." Gwen repeated, this time adding a sympathetic pat on his hand.

"Good evening, everyone!" Calvary Graxton addressed the audience from the stage. As usual, Mister Parrot was dressed in his long blue coat and yellow vest. "First, I would like to extend my sincere apologies for being incapable of providing you with our signature peerless service this evening. Our staff is a bit thin tonight. There's some rumor going around that the world is on the verge of ending. I tried to explain this was no reason not to report to work, but you'd be surprised how many disagree."

The audience responded with guarded laughter. It sounded like a joke, but maybe it wasn't, and they were still sober enough to care.

"Even the parrots quit." He twirled a finger toward the dome, pointing out the absence of the birds. "Truth is, of course, I set them free. Not that they were complaining, mind you. I took better care of them than I do you. At least they didn't have to pay."

The lanterns around the hall were dimmed, and the room grew dark, making the lights on the stage appear more intense.

"For those who are joining us for the first time, my name is Calvary Graxton—Mister Parrot to those who know me. I own this place. Twenty-five years ago, I came down here and survived by capturing and selling parrots. Problem was, I grew to like the birds too much to sell—too much to even capture them. So, I shifted to cooking and selling food on the street. I bought an old cart that I painted blue with yellow wheels, and I called it The Blue Parrot. Would you believe I managed to turn a little profit?" He held up his hands, inviting them all to notice the grand hall and the magnificent dome. "Who knew? Truth is, this has been a lifelong labor of love." He paused and took a breath. "But also, it has been a wonderful privilege to have served and been a part of this community. I've come to know — became friends with — so many. Most of you will be leaving tomorrow, never to return. But for my part, I'm going to stay. I'm just too damn old to start over again. That, and I still have a cellar full of Hohura that I just can't waste." He smiled, showing this *was* a joke, but no one laughed.

"Tonight, however, we are pulling all the corks, banging all the drums, and ringing all the bells as a tribute to what once was and will likely never come again."

While their host was speaking, Atyn had poured wine into everyone's glasses. Then, shockingly, he poured one for himself as onstage a young boy carried a drink to Mister Parrot. Calvary Graxton raised the glass to the room. "Go forth, all of you, and tell the tale of Tur and fishermen, the Unholy Trio and the Yellow Jackets, the dwarven towers and of the place where dreams came true"— he wiped a tear from his eye — "and most of all, of parrots of blue and a way that was new, that hopefully one day might be again. A toast to Tur Del Fur!"

"To Tur Del Fur!" the audience responded, and the sound was deep and loud.

Turning away from the stage, Hadrian saw that more patrons had come in behind them. And by the glow of the stage lights, he saw many of them were dwarfs.

Everyone including the staff drank. Even Royce took a sip from his glass but appeared neither proud nor sad. If anything, he looked oddly thoughtful.

"Now for your entertainment," Mister Parrot said. "Once more, please welcome Miss Millificent LeDeye."

Hadrian had expected she would be there and applauded as Millie walked on stage. He had tied a bit of sailcloth to the hammer of Andvari Berling's statue that morning, indicating he wanted to speak with her. Hadrian had no idea she would perform but was pleased that she did. Her singing was nothing short of magical. She wore the same dress and, not surprisingly, performed the same song. This time around, the rendition was less spellbinding than the first, but she was still radiant in the glow of a half dozen bull's-eye lanterns, and this time he was certain she really was looking at him. He stared back, lost in the moment and trapped in a spell. That enchantment ended when he made the mistake of glancing at Gwen, who glared and slowly shook her head.

Hadrian couldn't understand what she had against Millie. He hadn't said a word about her to anyone. He supposed Gwen was making an assumption based on the way Millicent looked and maybe how he stared, but he felt there was more to it.

The song ended, and Millie went off stage. He faced Gwen. "Why do you keep—"

"Miss DeLancy!" Tim Blue shouted for joy as he charged the table, an attractive woman in tow.

"Tim!" Gwen shouted right back, and jumping up, she embraced the lapis lad as if the two were lifelong friends who hadn't seen each other in years.

"Oh! I'm so happy we found you," Tim exclaimed. "I had no idea where to look, no clue where you might be, and this was our last chance." Tim appeared close to tears as he introduced the woman he was with. "This is my Meredith."

"Meredith?" Gwen asked, concerned. "What happened to Edie?"

Tim nodded. "Edie is short for Meredith. It's what I've called her for forever."

"How is Edie short for Meredith?" Royce asked.

"It doesn't matter," Gwen said and moved to Edie.

Tim's wife was a tiny thing with braided hair. She wore a cheap dress. The woman stared at Gwen with tears in her eyes and whispered, "I want to hug you, but I don't know if that's appro—"

Gwen pulled her tight.

"Thank you. Thank you. Thank you," Edie cried into Gwen's shoulder.

Bewildered, Hadrian looked at Royce, who shook his head, equally at a loss.

Gwen invited Tim and Edie to join them. More chairs were found, and they all squeezed tighter.

"Are you leaving tomorrow?" Gwen began. "Do you have passage on the *Ellis Far?*"

Tim nodded. "We do." He took his wife's hand. "I had just enough money left over. We will return to Avryn poor as mice in a monk's monastery, but we'll be safe. I've heard back from my family, and they will meet us at Roe. Things will be difficult for a while, but nothing so bad as they were."

"We owe you our lives," Edie said.

"I can't help feeling that we're missing something," Royce told Hadrian.

"There does seem to be a story worth telling here," Arcadius said.

Atyn came over to the table. "Sir," he addressed Hadrian, "there is a lady who wishes to speak with you."

"Millificent LeDeye?"

"One and the same, sir. She's waiting out front for you."

Hadrian stood up. "Fill me in when I get back."

Gwen took his hand. "Remember, Hadrian. She's not the one."

"And don't be out too late," Royce said. Then he grimaced and added, "We have to be on a ship in the morning."

To Hadrian, stepping outside The Blue Parrot after having gone in was always a strange occurrence. As if by some bizarre feat of magic, one world was exchanged for another. As usual, the sun was down, the evening cool, but this time the resulting world was different. The enchanting sparkle of a hundred shining windows was missing. Shops and homes were dark. Streets were quiet. No music spilled out of doorways, no rattle of wagon wheels or boisterous laughter cut the night. Tur Del Fur was an empty house after a party, and its silence was deafening.

Millie stood alone near the curb on a street devoid of life, waiting for him. "I saw the flag," she said. "You certainly took your time." She sashayed toward him. "But leaving now has its advantages. All the shops will be empty tomorrow. We can take whatever supplies we need."

"That's not why I asked to see you."

Millie stopped and stared at him, appearing confused. "What do you mean?" She tilted her head and looked him over. "And where's the book?"

"That's just it. That's what I wanted to tell you. The book—it's the diary of Falkirk de Roche. It's not a treasure map at all."

"Where is it?"

"Right now? Best guess?" He pointed at the bay. "It's inside Drumindor."

"What?" Her whole face scrunched up into a ball of befuddlement. Not her best look, but he didn't think Millie was capable of ugly.

"But like I said, it doesn't matter because the diary wasn't a map, and it wasn't treasure the church searched for in Neith — just a different book."

She continued to stare as if working out a translation. "So, I don't get it. Why are you here, then? Why did you hang the white flag?"

"Because I wanted to make sure you knew to get out. I didn't want you sticking around and thinking the book was still a possibility. Everyone seems to be aware of what's going to happen, but I don't know your particular situation. Perhaps Andre and Alessandro don't tell you everything. Maybe they keep you isolated."

"What? So, you think I'm an idiot or something?"

"No! Of course not."

She folded her arms and glared.

"Look, I just wanted to tell you that . . . well, if you don't have a way to get out, I could arrange to get you on the *Ellis Far* tomorrow."

"The *Ellis Far?*" Her eyes threatened to fall out of her head. "Are you serious?"

He nodded. "We have a stateroom, and I think maybe —"

"That's the ship I took to come here. You know that, right? That's the ship Millie Mulch stowed away on. Millificent LeDeye will not be getting on the *Ellis Far!* She will not be going back!"

"Fine, but you can't stay here. This whole city is going to explode, catch fire, sink, or whatever happens when a volcano blows its top."

"You don't know that," she scoffed, her arms still folded, elbows high.

Hadrian waved at the empty street. "And all of these people agree with you."

Millie frowned.

"Everyone is either gone or leaving," Hadrian said.

"Yes, I know. Fools are easily frightened."

Hadrian had known many willful women. Usually, it was a trait he admired, but there was a difference between stubborn and oblivious. "Millie, Cornelius DeLur has loaded his ship with everything he wasn't willing to send out by wagon. His entire household is preparing to leave. Do you think he's a fool, too?"

"My name is Millificent, and everything DeLur is doing is just for show. He's likely behind this whole thing. For him, this could be a version of spring cleaning. He gets everyone out, then slinks through the city—"

"What are you talking about? Millie, you need to leave."

She locked her jaw, her body rigid, as she glared at him with ice-cold eyes.

"Sorry, *Millificent*."

She thawed a drop. "If it really is a problem, Andre will get me out."

"That's the other thing I wanted to talk to you about. You need to get away from them."

"Them?"

"Andre and Alessandro."

"Are you suggesting I should—oh, I see." She unfolded her arms and began swinging them at her sides as she walked in a small circle around him. "You don't just want me to leave, you want me to leave with you."

He showed a dumb grin. "Would that be so terrible?"

She pondered this. He could tell because of how her tongue played along the front of her teeth. Arcadius cleaned his glasses or stroked his beard; Royce stared at nothing; Albert blinked several times while smiling, and Millie Mulch stroked her front teeth with the tip of her tongue as if pondering whether or not she ought to bite.

"Look, all I'm asking is that you get on the *Ellis Far* with me. We don't have to go back to Melengar. We can go to Aquesta. They have a new king there now; it could be exciting. We could also go to Mehan. Maranon is very pretty—extremely green. If things don't work out between us, I'll at least see that you're taken care of—that you're safe."

"So noble of you." Her face pretended seriousness. "Are you certain you aren't a knight?"

"Definitely not a knight."

Millie looked back at the doors to the Parrot. "I couldn't even if I wanted to. Andre's in there. Alessandro is with him. They think I'm visiting the elephant. In a few more minutes, they'll begin searching. And they won't like finding us together."

"Fine, come with me now. I'll see you have a safe place to spend the night, and in the morning, we can leave."

"All my things are at The Cave."

"Is there anything you really need?"

"Well . . . I have thirty gold I'm awfully fond of."

"Thirty!"

She straightened her back and folded her arms once more. "Yes, thirty. I've worked very hard and saved every copper. And I'm not leaving it all behind."

"Okay, but you say they're both in the Parrot at this moment, right?"

She nodded.

"Fine, so we can just go to The Cave right now and get it. And then you can spend the night with me, and tomorrow we'll board the *Ellis Far* and start a new life."

She thought about this. As she did, her eyes continued to creep fearfully toward the door.

What did they do to her?

"And if they catch us? You're unarmed, and Alessandro is especially good with a blade."

"Best not to let them catch us, then."

Gwen couldn't take her eyes off Tim.

He's alive! And Edie is safe!

When she had heard nothing for so long after helping him, Gwen had suffered doubts. So many things could have gone wrong; so many things *should* have. She had changed the direction of fate; otherwise, Tim would have been dead for two weeks, and at that moment, Edie would likely be learning her literal worth at some seedy auction house. But no, they were here. And like a child who had broken a plate, Gwen worried about the consequences. Would she even know what they were? Obviously, she knew Tim and Edie were having dinner with them at the Parrot. That was something that wouldn't have happened. But could it affect anything important? Gwen was also forced to suffer through Tim's telling of her heroics. How she faced down the "evil casino guard," then risked her own money at the tables, telling him what to bet on and when to pull his money.

She expected questions or concerned looks. Gwen had never hidden her gifts, but no one took them seriously. That was the way in the west. In the east, future-telling was as common and accepted as being a seller of rugs or sandals. And just like any weaver or leather worker, those who were talented were respected.

In the west, things were different. Illia always warned Gwen to watch out for people — especially the ones who don't believe. *"They take a seat, thrust out their palms, and laugh with their friends, as if it is some grand joke,"* her mother had told her. *"Then you tell them what you see, and they stop laughing. Some recoil and call you a witch. Others . . . well, some become violent, especially if it's bad news."* Gwen watched Albert, Arcadius, and most especially Royce to see their reactions.

All three listened carefully to a mostly factual report. Albert continued to smile. Arcadius nodded and played with his napkin, and Royce . . . showed no reaction at all.

Tim said, "When we had made a bit more than what was necessary, Gwen told me to stop, gather my winnings, and leave. And that's exactly what I did."

"Did you get your coins back?" Royce asked Gwen.

She nodded. "Tim insisted."

"Good."

"I have to admit," Albert said, "that is the only gambling recount I've heard where anyone walked away a winner."

Gwen was at a loss. She had expected more. No one had called her a witch, or kicked over their chair and stormed out, or suggested that she help them take over the world.

They just think it was luck.

She took it as a win, but two wins in a row made her nervous.

Gwen thought of ripples in a still lake after tossing a stone. A single splash was followed by ring after ring of spreading waves. By asking Tim and Edie to sit with them, two chairs were pulled over — chairs that someone else could have sat in. The couple ate food that wouldn't have been eaten before, at least not by them. And where did they stay? Who did they speak to? How many other things could these two have done that wouldn't have been done before? *Does any of that matter?* Not knowing how fate was supposed to turn out, Gwen had no idea. There was only one thing that . . .

Gwen stopped breathing as the thought coalesced in her mind.

What if I changed that? She looked at Royce's hands that lay flat on the table. *What if I look at his palms again and see something different now?*

Then another awful thought struck her.

What if the awful thing has already happened?

More than anything, it was the timing that chilled Gwen to the bone. *Could it really be merely coincidence that instead of finding Tim's body, they found Drumindor locked? What if Tur Del Fur will be destroyed because I saved Tim?*

The first course arrived, but seeing Atyn smiling at her, Gwen had lost her appetite.

What have I done?

Feeling a wave of fear and guilt, Gwen sat back, biting her lip, and it was then she noticed that Rehn was missing.

CHAPTER TWENTY-SEVEN

The Cave

The hike to the Eighth Tier emphasized Hadrian's point. They passed no one. The entire trip up Berling's Way had been as silent as if they were walking through a forgotten graveyard. Not so much as a dog barked. The journey had also been dark. No candles flickered behind windows; no one had lit the streetlamps. They had traveled only by the shine of the moon, which in its frightening brilliance and cold light was just another reminder of the danger and the speed at which sand ran out of the glass.

The Cave hadn't changed from Hadrian's last visit. It was still the overly ornate salt mine it had been. Despite the stunning bas-relief sculptures of dwarfs digging and hauling salt, the entrance was still a hole in the side of the cliff with an entrance that was disturbingly small. Hadrian could see how the place struggled to turn a profit. There wasn't much around it. The Eighth Tier was high on the cliff, not far from the top of the plateau. Less vegetation grew here where the tropical terraces met the high desert. The businesses at this height were the ones no one wished to have at the bottom. Just as Kenyon the Clean's soapmaking shop was relegated to the Lower Quarter of Medford, the Eighth Tier was home to the equally smelly tannery and some livestock yards. The loud and messy stone quarry was also up there, which only made sense as hauling stone down was so much easier than dragging it up. The same went for water, and Hadrian spotted huge and numerous cisterns carved into the tops of the sheer cliff walls. They were designed to catch rainwater and then send it down into the lower levels. While all of this revealed the technological marvel that had been the ancient dwarven city, it didn't scream, *Come visit!* This was the Wayward Street of Tur Del Fur, and The Cave was its Rose and Thorn.

Hadrian had tried to follow Millie inside, but once again, she asked him to wait out front. There would be others, she said. Not as bad as Andre or Alessandro, but those who could cause trouble if they saw her with a strange man. So, Hadrian waited. He stood for a time, studying the carvings to either side of the entrance. Then he paced the length of what appeared to have once been raised wagon rails. They looked to have been made of wood that had long ago rotted away, leaving ruts where wagons must have been rolled. Pondering the pile of wheels and rotting wood, he imagined they had once been carts. He heard a clap like a window shutter not far to his right and concluded that a cat was hunting in the centuries of debris. The dark clutter looked perfect for a multitude of rodents.

Another likely reason people don't wait in line to get into The Cave.

Hadrian wondered what was taking Millie so long and was weighing the pros and cons of going in to check on her when he heard footsteps. Two men came up the road. Hadrian could hear the telltale clap announcing that they each wore blades. Given the location and the time of day, Hadrian didn't need to see their faces to know who they were.

"Hadrian Blackwater, I presume," Andre said as he and Alessandro approached.

The two appeared similar. Both had tailored beards — Andre's was longer and came to a point, while Alessandro's was short, but his mustache curled up elegantly. Both had dark hair; Andre just had more, which lent him a conceited arrogance that Alessandro lacked. Hadrian didn't think they were related by blood, but people of similar circles tended to have a uniform look. Theirs was refined-and-well-to-do thug.

"How nice of you to visit." Andre stopped short of arm's reach. "But alas, The Cave isn't open tonight."

"I can see that. Too bad. I figured you must have great ground peas."

Andre squinted. "What's a ground pea?"

"You know, peanuts? They're best covered in salt, and salty foods make people thirsty, so I figured, being a taproom in an old salt mine, you'd have lots of great salted peanuts on hand. I have a weakness for them. Always find them in taverns, and I've spent many a night where my only meal was a free bowl of nuts. Walnuts and almonds are good, too. But almonds are harder to get up north. Plenty of them down here, though."

"Does he have the book?" Andre asked, looking past Hadrian.

Millie appeared just inside the entrance of The Cave. She shook her head.

"Why the white cloth, then?" Andre asked.

"He was concerned for my safety," Millie replied, sounding as if it was the most absurd thing she'd ever heard. "Wanted to make sure I got out of the city before it blew. He'd be irresistible if he weren't so stupid."

"So, you're not taking my advice, are you?" Hadrian asked her.

She laughed at him. "Poor boy thinks I should abandon you, Andre, and run away with him to Warric or Maranon." Millie laughed again. "I imagine he sees me as his dutiful housewife who must be reminded which of his possessions he saddles and which ones he just rides."

Maybe Millie is capable of being ugly after all.

"Where's the book?" Andre took a step closer and put his off-hand to the neck of his scabbard.

Hadrian read the man's fingers. They told the tale of a brute who didn't draw his sword often. "As I explained to Millie —" Hadrian started.

"Millificent!" she nearly screamed, still at her perch in the doorway.

"Yes, that's her, the very talented but also very misguided woman in the doorway. I explained to her that the book is not a treasure map. The church was using it to find another, older book."

Andre made a show of dangling his right arm in a loose and threatening manner as if he was on the verge of drawing his sword. "No one spends a fortune to unearth just a book. This other tome is likely part of the treasure, or the book is exceedingly valuable. Either way, I want it. So, where is it?"

"It's in Drumindor."

This didn't make Andre at all happy. His already trademark frown took a sharp downward turn. "I don't think you're being entirely honest."

"And I don't think you're a good judge of the truth. Look, I came here to see if Millie—"

"Millificent!"

"— if she needed help getting out of this city before it disappeared so that she wouldn't vanish along with it. I can see now that her answer is no. Apparently, she has you two fine gentlemen to watch over her. So, I no longer have any reason to remain. Goodnight to you all."

As expected, it wasn't Andre who drew steel; it was Alessandro. Andre stepped to the side, granting his associate access.

Alessandro turned sideways and swept a slightly curved cutlass side to side, letting it sing. The blade didn't have an appealing song. As a weapon, the cutlass was as elegant as an ax, and often used in the same manner. Sailors loved it because it was just as ideal for hacking a trail and cutting ropes as dismembering people. And those who used it were about as skilled as a lumberjack. Still, Hadrian appreciated the demonstration. Alessandro must have thought he was executing the age-old practice of pre-fight intimidation. Instead, the man was providing Hadrian with a table of contents to Alessandro's level of skill and the extent of his training, which was just slightly above the average highwayman and not quite as good as a typical man-at-arms. Hadrian wasn't worried about fighting either Andre or Alessandro but . . . something wasn't right.

Alessandro's bravado was labored. The show he put on was too much, too excessive for an experienced swordsman facing an unarmed man.

Why work so hard at frightening me?

Could be anything, he reasoned. Alessandro might be the showy sort or the kind who liked to play with his victims — scare them. Could also be he wasn't feeling well, or perhaps Alessandro might just be the cautious type, but still, Hadrian started to worry that—

"Look out! Behind you, Master Hadrian!" Pickles's voice shouted.

With no idea about the nature of the threat, Hadrian both ducked and sidestepped. He heard a *thwack!* The sound was as familiar to him as the moo of a cow to a dairy farmer, and an instant after, he felt the breeze of the crossbow bolt pass by his head.

"Look out! Look out! There are more! Two are behind the big water barrel. One is running out of The Cave, and there is another one with a crossbow who is —"

Thwack!

Pickles's voice was cut off.

Turning, Hadrian saw it all. Three swordsmen who had lain in wait among the rotting carts left their shelter and charged. Behind him, two others bent to the task of reloading their bows. Millie was gone — back inside, Hadrian guessed. Seven men had come to capture him. Millie had been the bait. But he didn't have the book. With no reason to keep him alive, it was crossbow time. The quick and easy answer to anyone's murdering needs. Andre drew his blade now but backed away. The refined thugs would leave the dirty work to the real ones.

In an instant, the scene explained itself, except for . . .

Where did the other bolt go?

The thought blew through Hadrian's mind as he went through the motions of disarming the first swordsman to step within arm's reach.

What is Rehn doing here?

Hadrian threw the man to the ground, stole his opponent's weapon, and surprised his next attacker, who had been ill-informed by his own eyes that his victim was a helpless unarmed man. This mistake cost him his life.

Why did Rehn stop talking?

Hadrian used his stolen sword to kill its owner before the man had a chance to stand up.

Rehn can't be —

Hadrian used the cleaving power of the cutlass to nearly decapitate the first of the two bowmen.

Pickles can't be —

With two quick steps, Hadrian used both hands beneath the knuckle guard and a growing anger to send the other bowman's head rolling with speed down Berling's Way.

Not again!

Hadrian spotted the third swordsman running back into The Cave. Maybe he went for help, or perhaps he just didn't want to be outside anymore. Pivoting to face Andre and Alessandro, he saw that they weren't there, either. Hearing rapid footsteps, Hadrian saw the pair running down the slope. He was alone in the street except for a small figure lying on the ground.

At the foot of a stone wall that was decorated in a moonlit spray of blood that ran broad tears down its length, Hadrian found the prone body of Rehn Purim. The kid was on his back, the feathered end of the bolt just visible as it pinned his tunic. There was no blood on the front of him. Nothing came out of Rehn's mouth or nose, just that sunburst of red on the wall behind him.

"Master Hadrian . . ." Rehn said. His eyes were wide, staring up at the night sky.

"What are you doing here?" Hadrian asked, his voice angrier than intended.

"I saw you leave. I was worried. So, I followed — just in case. And it was good I did . . . yes?"

Hadrian put his arms under Rehn's knees and his back and lifted him. "I'm taking you back. You stay with me, you understand! You stay alive, Pickles! You hear me?"

"I did better this time," Rehn said. "So much better with the watching and the warning, didn't I, Master Hadri . . ."

Rehn went limp in his arms.

Albert returned with a dwarven physician who didn't bother with so much as a wave before entering the Turtle where Rehn Purim lay in Arcadius's bed. Gwen, the professor, and Auberon had already been working on the kid for nearly an hour.

Hadrian had been told by Gwen, in her most gentle voice, that he had done his part in getting Rehn back alive. Now Hadrian needed to let others work. In other words, he wasn't helping, and she needed him to wait outside. But waiting wasn't easy, and Hadrian began pacing back and forth from the courtyard to the bedroom door and back again.

"Wanna go kill them?" Royce asked as Hadrian passed him during the courtyard portion of his circuit. The thief and his ghost sat at the table beneath the lemon tree.

"Who?" Hadrian asked, then shook his head. "Oh . . . no. I already killed the crossbowmen."

"What about this Andre and the other one who was with him?" Royce asked. "They got away. We can kill them, right?" He looked at Baxter. "You don't care, do you?"

Baxter shrugged. "Andre is an ambitious idiot who imagines he's one move away from ruling the underworld, but he doesn't have a key or a stateroom on the *Crown Jewel.* Doubt anyone will notice he's missing."

"So, we can kill him?"

Baxter nodded. "I won't get in the way, if that's what you're asking."

"See," Royce said. "The ghost doesn't care. We can start by playing a game of Ten Fingers, and I can be clumsy."

Hadrian shook his head. "Killing them won't save Pickles."

"You mean Rehn."

"Yeah. Right."

"Okay, you want to go get drunk, then?" Royce asked.

Hadrian stopped and thought for a moment, which was difficult since his mind was a cluttered mess of stress and fear. "Since when are you interested in getting drunk?"

"I'm not, but I'll watch you. Make sure you get back."

"Nothing's open."

"Really? I hear there's a quiet danthum up on the eighth called The Cave. I'm certain they will open if we ask real nice. Then maybe after a few drinks to loosen you up, you might change your mind about Andre."

Like a cat that dropped a dead mouse on the bedroom floor of its owner, Royce had a unique style for comforting loss. He meant well, and that was the important thing.

"He's going ta be fine," the physician assured the three of them.

Doctor Koll Rudd was as classic a dwarf as Gwen could imagine. A full head shorter than herself, his eyes were old and deep and shaded by eyebrows long enough to be brushed. His nose — the centerpiece of his face — was large and full of character while the top of his head was mostly bare, exposing deep and weathered worry lines. He wore a mostly white beard whose length allowed it to be braided and decorated with bangles and beads. Gwen guessed that the ornamentations were not decorative. The objects, size, material, and shapes likely displayed religious, social, or professional significance. After her time spent with Auberon, Gwen had learned that dwarfs did little without meaning. They were long on history and tradition and light on popular trends. The doctor moved and spoke with confidence and appeared the sort to know what he was doing and felt comfortable doing it.

The question in Gwen's mind remained . . . *can he be bought?*

"I'm not even sure why I was called. The three of you did a fine job," Doctor Rudd said as he closed his old wooden toolbox and refastened the leather straps, buckling up his medical gear into an ingenious pack that he wore. "Doesn't hurt that Drome threaded a needle with that bolt. As far as I can tell, it slipped right between the liver and spleen and missed the spine by less than an inch. And I am pleased to see you refrained from packing the wound with animal dung, nor have you bled the poor boy dry. Humans have a tendency to do such things, which I believe is the real reason Dromeians tend to live longer."

Gwen, Arcadius, and Auberon clustered together around Rehn in the tiny bedroom. They had as many lamps and candles as they could find in the house, and all were burning around the bed. Likewise, a big pot of feverfew leaves steeped in apple cider vinegar boiled in the corner, filling the room with a bitter but fruity odor that Gwen always associated with sickness.

Rehn was all cleaned up, wrapped neatly in pristine white bandages, and draped in a linen sheet. He was unconscious and had been since Hadrian carried him in.

"The shock to his body and loss of blood will leave him on his back for a few days, but after that — barring a fever — he'll be able to walk a bit. If he wants to, let him, but don't let him overdo it. In a couple of weeks, he should be in decent shape, and after a month or two, he should make a full recovery."

"It certainly looked worse than it was," Arcadius said.

"Well then" — Doctor Rudd reached for his gear — "I'll be —"

Auberon put his hand on the toolbox, preventing Rudd from taking it. "You're right. We didn't send for you to save the lad."

The doctor stared at Auberon for a moment. "So, why *did* you bring me here?"

Auberon took a deep breath, and to Gwen it appeared as if she were watching two bighorn sheep preparing to ram. "It's very important that everyone in the world — aside from the four of us in this room — believe this boy died from his wounds."

"How's that, now?"

Auberon pointed at the closed door. "Outside, you may have noticed four other gentlemen. Two are dandies, and the other two consist of a big mercenary and a smaller, black-hooded fellow."

"I saw them." Doctor Rudd peered hard at Auberon. "The big fella pleaded with me to do my very best."

"Right, his name is Hadrian, and he's the one who needs to believe that young Rehn here is dead."

"And why is that?"

"Two reasons, and both come down to the survival of Tur Del Fur. You see, those two — the big and the little — are going to save us all."

Doctor Rudd, clearly unconvinced, focused on Arcadius. "You look like the smart one here. How do you feel about this foolishness?"

"To be honest, I'm not overly comfortable with it," the professor replied. He had moved outside the ring of lights and taken a seat on the little chair in what used to be his room. "But there is the matter of Tim Blue, an incident that lends enough doubt that I think it's best if I stay out of this. I have personally witnessed a great many things that have proved to me, more than once, that one and one don't always equal two. In addition, I would be quite the hypocrite to argue that faking that boy's death is unscrupulous."

"I see." Doctor Rudd turned to Gwen. "You appear to be a morally decent and principled lady. What are your feelings on the subject?"

"It's my idea," she said.

The doctor's expression turned sour.

"Do you see the mark on her shoulder?" Auberon asked.

Gwen adjusted her dress enough to reveal a small swirling tattoo.

"That's the mark of a Tenkin seer."

"A fortune teller?" Doctor Rudd said in a less than impressed tone.

"She's more than that. I'd ask her to prove it, but we neither have the time, nor do I think it will be necessary. Gwen here took the liberty to look at the lad's palm. We were concerned our combined medical knowledge might have missed something, so she checked to be sure his lifeline didn't end today or tomorrow."

"But she saw something else, didn't she?" Doctor Rudd stared at Gwen as if she were now something other than a morally decent and principled lady.

Gwen nodded, then she spoke in a whisper. "Recently, I helped a man who I know as Tim Blue. I saw his future, and then I interfered and changed it by saving his life and the life of his wife. I thought it was such a tiny thing that it wouldn't matter, but tiny things can have huge effects."

"I see. So, which one of you is going to lose money? No, I suppose it's all of you, isn't it? You wouldn't be in such agreement if it were just one. An old man, a Calian girl, and the great freedom fighter . . ." He shook his head, wagging his beard. "I am surprised and disappointed in you, Auberon, but I suppose reputations never equal the person, do they? So, what is it? What sort of effects are you speaking of?"

Doctor Rudd stared at her, still as stone. Only his eyes shifted as they darted to catch the reactions of the others, perhaps thinking this was a joke and he would see them smile or laugh.

No one did.

"In a little less than three days from now," Gwen went on, "Royce and Hadrian are supposed to climb up the North Tower of Drumindor and save the city."

Doctor Rudd glanced down at Rehn. "And they won't do this heroic act if they think this boy is fine?"

"Exactly." She nodded her head. "You see, Hadrian saved Rehn's life two weeks ago, but he wasn't supposed to. Hadrian shouldn't have even been there when Rehn was attacked. If I hadn't meddled, Hadrian would have become involved in a dispute at The Cave where Tim Blue would have gone because that is where he thought they were holding his wife. Then by the time Hadrian passed by the cabinet maker's shop, Rehn would have already been dead, and Hadrian wouldn't have known that the boy he knew as Pickles had survived the incident at Sheridan University. And if Hadrian hadn't been there, he wouldn't have mentioned Gravis

Berling's name in front of Falkirk de Roche, which — and this is speculation here — I think doing that caused Falkirk to seek out Gravis and provided Berling access to the tower. Do you understand?"

The doctor shook his head. "Not a word."

"Okay, let's try this, Hadrian is very protective of Rehn, and if he knows Rehn is injured, Hadrian won't leave his side. Because of that, tomorrow, when Royce suggests they stay and climb the tower, Hadrian won't agree, and Royce won't do it alone. As a result, the city will be destroyed, or worse."

"What could possibly be worse?"

"I've had dreams — terrible, terrible nightmares. There is a reason why those towers were built, and it had nothing to do with taming a volcano or defending a bay." She slowly shook her head. "They are a gate of some sort, a lock on a prison door. Something inside is clawing to get out — three things actually. They're ancient and horrible beyond understanding."

Doctor Rudd peered at Gwen, shifting his lips back and forth, bristling the short hairs near his mouth. Then he turned to Auberon. "What I find the most baffling is not that bewildering haze of an explanation, but the fact that you have thrown in with this"— he waved a hand at Gwen — "insanity. I never thought you to be the sort swayed by Calian prophecies. And I thought you'd learned your lesson. After all those years of trying to save the Dromeian race, you still can't shake it, can you? Lost your whole family out of sheer stubbornness with nothing to show for it, and here you are at the end of your life still grasping at wild ideas. You'll do anything to make their sacrifices worth it."

"Aye, you're right," the old dwarf replied. "But what Gwendolyn said reminded me of something else — which forms the second reason."

"And that is?" The doctor waited.

"You don't see it?"

"See what?"

"The lady here just said, two men — those two presently in the courtyard, the big and the little, the mercenary with three swords and the thief in the dark cloak and hood — are going to scale Drumindor's North Tower."

"I heard her, but I don't —" Doctor Rudd froze. Then his eyes narrowed, those dramatic brows folding down like cat's ears. After a second or two, his whole mouth dropped open. "You don't mean to say that . . ."

Auberon was nodding. "I didn't send for you because we needed a physician, but because everyone knows Doctor Koll Rudd has a fascination with Dromeian history. As such, you know The Wall as well as I—the same way that every Dromeian should, but too few do. You've memorized the images that are carved there."

"No," Doctor Rudd shook his head. "Can't be. The Wall shows the creation of the world, the First War, the Elven Conflict, and the foretelling of King Rain. But this . . . this is . . ." He waved his hand. "It's just not in the same category."

"The city is about to be destroyed by the eruption of Mount Druma," Auberon said. "I'd say that ranks as a cataclysmic event worthy of inclusion. And then there's what she said about the three monsters trying to get out."

The doctor scrubbed his beard in thought.

"So, if this Tenkin seer says we need to convince everyone that the boy here is dead to ensure these two fellas climb one of Drumindor's towers, I was thinking maybe we ought to call Doctor Rudd and see if he can help make that happen. What do you think, Doctor Rudd?"

CHAPTER TWENTY-EIGHT

The Last Ship Out

Hadrian refused to believe it. He shouted and hit the walls in what, to Royce, seemed like uncharacteristically excessive behavior. He might go so far as to label it irrational. After all, Hadrian had seen plenty of death. His alleged history suggested he had been present for hundreds of brutal killings, and Royce could personally attest to Hadrian taking dozens of lives. Never before had he seen his partner so violently distressed.

One thing that Royce did understand was the skepticism, especially considering Arcadius was in the room when the kid died. Anything that man had been involved in needed to be questioned. What made Royce shake his head was why the kid's death had mattered so much to Hadrian. Rehn Purim was a minor league operative working as a scout for Arcadius. He had posed as a Vernes street waif named Pickles for reasons Royce still wasn't clear about.

And then there is the odd name, probably a last-minute panic when the kid realized he couldn't use his real name.

Failing his assignment of traveling with Hadrian to Sheridan University, the kid showed up some time later to serve no purpose whatsoever. Shortly afterward, Pickles "died." As best Royce could calculate, Hadrian had known Pickles for only a few weeks. During that period, Royce had been working extensively to teach Hadrian to climb; as such, Royce estimated the time Hadrian had spent with Pickles to be best measured in hours rather than days. Why it was then that Hadrian broke down when they took him into the bedroom to view the body was baffling.

There are just some things I doubt I will ever understand about that man.

They left Hadrian alone with Rehn while the rest of them packed. No one slept. There would be plenty of time to do that on the ship.

What else is there to do?

Royce hoped he could sleep through most of the voyage as well but doubted it would be possible. He had only been on a ship once before. That had been enough. The rocking didn't agree with him, and he had been horribly sick for three days. Royce's friend and genius-in-residence, Merrick Marius, had explained that while some people were prone to the sickness, one incident didn't mean Royce was one of those. Even if he was, it didn't dictate that he would always become sick on a ship. Still, the memory of that agony had kept Royce from any further experiments beyond short river or coastal trips, which rarely bothered him.

So maybe Merrick was right. Perhaps it wasn't the ocean at all but something I ate. It's possible that this time I'll enjoy a lovely pleasure cruise holding hands with Gwen as we stand on deck and gawk at the sunsets . . . and I suppose I will also wake up and discover I am the Heir of Novron and she the Queen of Calis.

Royce had nothing to pack. Instead, he waited in the courtyard, listening to the birds begin to stir and watching the sunrise. Despite himself, he had to admit this had been a nice trip. The food was good, the work easy, and there was that one night in The Blue Parrot when . . .

Royce had refused to even think about that. He had been terrified that if he analyzed that evening too much, he would realize he had made a fool of himself. Over time, however, the terror faded. Gwen showed no signs of hating him. In fact, he noticed how she stood closer than before. And where in the past she never dared, she now touched him. Just a light press on his shoulder or a brief tap on his hand to get his attention, but a touch, nonetheless. And once, while at The Blue Parrot, when Royce was perfectly sober, he had swept a strand of hair from her face, and only afterward did he realize it had happened. As he watched the rising sun, Royce edited his earlier dream of waking up a prince to waking up beside Gwen.

Auberon, who had left during the night, returned that morning with a freshly made coffin and dragged it inside. Shortly afterward, Hadrian came out, carrying his swords and pack. He looked exhausted, his eyes red and underlined with shadows. Dropping his burdens near the table, Hadrian collapsed on the chair opposite Royce as if he weighed a thousand pounds.

"Doesn't affect you at all, does it?" Hadrian asked. There was anger in his words.

"I didn't know him the way you did."

Hadrian leaned forward, opened his mouth, then stopped; he looked puzzled and sat back.

"What?" Royce asked.

Hadrian shook his head. "Nothing, it's just that the last time we had this conversation, your answer was either *'uh-huh'* or *'nope.'* Something like that. I forget. I just remember it really made me mad."

"That was several years ago," Royce said. "You've matured since then."

"Hold on. You think that *I*—"

"Can I interrupt?" Gwen asked, coming out with Albert. "We need to carry Rehn to the *Ellis Far.*"

"Now?" Hadrian asked.

"I arranged permission from Captain Callaghan to bring the body onboard," Albert explained. "But we need to load the coffin early, as it will be going into the ship's hold, and things will get tight in there once passengers arrive."

"Auberon is closing the coffin now." Gwen looked at Hadrian with soft eyes. "I thought you would like to take Rehn back and give him a proper burial."

Hadrian nodded.

"Can you help carry him? Both of you? And, Albert, you go, too. Help make sure there's no confusion with the quartermaster or whatever. Arcadius and I will see that your things are packed while you're gone. Ship leaves at midday."

Baxter filled in as the fourth pallbearer. He had to go with Royce anyway, and it must have seemed stupid not to help out. The ghost had grown lax in his duties of aloof, silent sentinel. Royce had caught him playing that game with Albert and sleeping on the cushioned bench. Couldn't fault him; there never had been any point.

The lid of the coffin had been sealed tight, which Royce appreciated. Seeing Rehn tucked inside the box would likely as not have set Hadrian off again. Even so, the trip home was not going to be a happy-go-lucky party. Instead, Royce imagined it would be one of those lengthy journeys where Hadrian would be too quiet.

Strange, I never thought I could get used to something so annoying and yet have its absence become irritating.

Rehn was a thin kid and not terribly heavy. Between the four of them, they had no trouble hoisting and hauling him down to the harbor. People were already on the dock. Most stood in a patchwork of clustered luggage, waiting their turn at the gangplank, where a host of dock workers tossed up chests and sacks with all the care of manure shovelers clearing a stable. Pickles's coffin-bearers were forced to wait while Albert went up to speak to the longshoremen, or what he called the "wharfies."

As always, the seagulls *cawed* from overhead while the ocean waves, crippled by the breakwater, lapped against the quay. The sky was oddly overcast, growing dark with rain clouds, which added to the anxiety of those waiting in line. As the minutes rolled by, Royce contemplated sitting on the coffin but imagined that was just the sort of thing to set Hadrian off. As it turned out, Royce well remembered the conversation the two had shared after Pickles's previous death. It had ended with the two promising to kill each other.

Funny how life repeats itself.

If Royce were more optimistic — if he were Hadrian, for example — he might fancy that the world gave individuals repeated chances to get things right. Being Royce, however, he understood the proper philosophical takeaway: if a person will fall for it once, they will likely be deceived a second time. In the thieving world, this was known as the Rule of Threes. If you robbed someone who had no lock on their door, odds were that you'd be able to do it a second time, but not a third. After the first theft, the victim convinced themselves that if something awful happened once, there was almost no chance of the same thing happening again. The second burglary would change that, and they'd get a lock. Given that Royce tended to see life as a sadistic entity that reveled in causing misery, he also imagined life making use of the Rule of Threes. Royce hoped to avoid making the same mistake twice and refrained from sitting on the coffin. Instead, he wandered to the edge of the quay, which was white with bird droppings. Standing at the edge near the center of Terlando Bay, Royce had a perfect view of the two towers of Drumindor. They were indeed huge. Not quite mountain-sized, but bigger than anything he'd seen crafted by a hand. They were so big that the clouds were obscuring their tops. And yet, they were only about a third taller than the Crown Tower. *A third.* The thought repeated in his mind. *Only a third.* He found this significant because the bridge was just slightly higher than halfway. That meant . . .

The distance to that bridge is shorter than the height of the Crown Tower — and even Hadrian was able to climb that.

The problem, of course, was the dwarven craftsmanship. Unlike blocks of stone laid one upon another and stacked side by side, this was carved from living rock. No seams were available to exploit.

Everything is just too annoyingly smooth — polished even. Except for —

"Royce?" Gwen's voice drew him back.

She arrived with Arcadius, Auberon, and their luggage in a little wagon that the dwarf pulled.

"You going on the *Ellis Far,* too?" he asked the dwarf.

"No," Auberon replied solemnly. "I'm done traveling. This here is my home."

"Your home is going to disappear in a couple of days."

"And at my age, that still makes it a race as to which one of us will die first."

"How is Hadrian doing?" Gwen asked.

"He's in his quiet phase. It will last until he finds beer, then he'll shift into his loud phase. Not sure which I hate more."

Gwen took his hand and drew him aside. "A lot of people are going to die here, Royce."

He nodded. "Strange, isn't it? That people would choose to die? I suppose I can understand Auberon. What does he have to look forward to, really? A couple more years, then the misery and humiliation of his body breaking down will —"

"That's not my point," Gwen said. "What I'm saying is that a lot of people here are going to die that might not *need* to."

Royce looked at her, puzzled. "That is my point, too. No one here needs to die. They can leave. Even if they can't get on the *Ellis Far* or the *Crown Jewel,* they can walk. They have two days left. They could easily clear the cliff and get miles inland."

"Still not my point, Royce."

Again, he looked at her, puzzled.

"These people can't abandon this city. They love it too much. Most of them have already seen how the rest of the world is, how it treats people like them. They know they'll never find a better place. Tur Del Fur is special. It is one of a kind. Nothing like it has ever been before, nor do I imagine it will ever exist again. It breaks their hearts to see it destroyed—so much so that they can't imagine breathing another day if it's taken from them. Royce . . ." She took both of his hands in hers and looked into his eyes. "When they look at this city, it's like when I look at you. I could never feel the same way about someone else. It just wouldn't work. You are as unique as this city, and I can't imagine continuing to breathe if you were gone."

Royce didn't know what to say. He was still feeling the warmth of her hands in his as they squeezed. In her eyes was a desperation.

"Royce, I know you can stop it." She turned and looked at the towers. "You can climb it. I know you can. What's more, I know you know it, too." She looked back at him. "Don't you?"

Royce hesitated. Looking back at her, seeing those eyes so desperate and yet so certain, he said, "There is one thing I suspect everyone may have overlooked."

Gwen smiled at him. "Take Hadrian with you."

"I didn't say I was going to do it."

She simply smiled at him.

"Aren't you afraid I'll fall? That I'll not make it and be killed in the explosion?"

She shook her head. "You won't." Her hands squeezed his again. "The one thing that has ruined this trip for you is having me see you fail. You want to climb that tower as much for yourself as for anyone, but you'll do it for me. And because of that, you won't let yourself fall. You're going to do it, Royce. You and Hadrian will climb Drumindor and save this city from destruction. You will. I know it. I believe in you."

Tears welled in her eyes as she said this.

She was right. He had wanted to try climbing Drumindor ever since he first saw it, especially now given that his alternative was a risky ocean voyage where he would likely become disgustingly sick in front of Gwen. And it wasn't suicide — not really. He still had time to escape the city on foot if his idea proved unviable, but her request clinched the deal.

The tears sealed it in stone.

☙

Behind the curtain of rain, the *Ellis Far* cleared the shallows, then turned to face the big waves head-on as the ship headed north out into the Sharon Sea. Royce was surprised the ship was only now clearing the bay. They had said their goodbyes on the dock close to an hour ago.

The ship had been packed with escapees. Those with rooms or berths paid for the privilege, but after that, Captain Callahan waived passage fees and took on as many as he could. Royce recognized the nameless faces he'd passed time and again over the last month. Among them, he spotted Tim and Edie as well as Angelius, who stood with several other men whom Royce guessed to be his many-storied brothers. Apparently, whatever boat they used for fishing wasn't good enough to flee on.

Gwen returned the diamond key to him, then gave Hadrian a hug and Royce a kiss that no amount of ocean spray had the power to wash away.

"Get going!" Gwen had ordered them. "You don't need to stand here and wave. You've a lot to do and very little time left. I'll see you back in Medford. I believe in you, Royce. I believe in you both. Now go!"

About two hours later, Royce was standing at the base of the North Tower, hopelessly soaked. A wave exploded on the rock. Not only were the waves breaking on them, but it was raining. Overhead, clouds of gray churned and boiled, while below, the ocean mirrored the sky. Gone were the happy aqua waves crowned in white, now replaced by the colorless rearing fists of an angry sea. Looking out across the water at the *Ellis Far* rocking over those great, white-knuckled fists, Royce had but one thought.

Take care of her, little boat. See her safely home, or I'll track down every board, nail, rope, and sail and burn it all to ash.

"You're absolutely right," Auberon told Royce as he studied the stone of the tower.

"He's still insane," Baxter shouted over the roar of the ocean as he joined all of them in staring up at the heights of the North Tower. "You can't climb this. No one can. Go up there, and the wind will rip you off and toss your body into the sea."

"Maybe," the dwarf said, "but at least this one is climbable."

"You call *this* climbable?" Baxter shook the water off his face, his long hair whipping like a dog. "I used to be a second-story guy. My specialty was drainpipes and steep roofs, but this — this is vertical. And there are no grips."

"Yes, there are," Royce said, running his hands over the surface, reading it with his fingertips. "The face of the South Tower is smooth as polished glass, but this is pockmarked, coarse, gritty."

"The salt spray," Auberon said. "Eats everything. Chews up boats, rusts metal, even erodes granite. What made you think of this?"

"The way everyone always went to the South Tower," Royce said. "Each attempt to climb was made there. Not a single person thought to come out here."

"It's too far, too much trouble to hike through all that brush," Baxter said, like the husband of a cheating wife as he denounced marriage. The ghost was a city boy who seemed uncomfortable trudging through anything more challenging than a dark alley. "Carpenters aren't going to carry lumber all this way through that forest and scrub. I suppose they could have boated it out, but why bother when the South Tower is right on the paved square, and that's where the old entrance always was. Just made sense to try there."

Royce nodded. "Everyone thought that . . . even the dwarfs."

"Of course!" Auberon's eyes widened just before another wave burst behind them. The water wasn't cold, but accompanied by the wind and without the sun, it wasn't warm, either. "No one ever came out here. There was never any need. They kept the South Tower in pristine condition because that's where everyone went in and out, but they never bothered to do any maintenance out here where it was difficult to get to, hard to build scaffolding, hard to provide workers with food and water. And I guess *everyone* gets lazy."

"And . . ." Royce crawled around as best he could until he could see the ocean side. There was no place to stand over there as the tower went all the way down to the water, which was why he never bothered to inspect the northwest side before. Seeing it now, he smiled. "Just as I thought. The winds primarily blow in off the ocean and have been salt-blasting this unseen side of the North Tower for thousands of years." Royce peered up, studying the route he planned to take. "The stone isn't just roughed up; it has cracked in places. See it? There's even a little crevice that crosses the fins going right up toward the bridge."

"Your eyes are better than mine," Auberon said. "But then there's not much left of me that's any good."

"If I could climb up to that jog, I could catch hold of it. Problem is, I'll need anchors."

"Can't hammer a piton into solid rock," Baxter said.

"No. For that, I'd need to drill and set bolts, and we don't have that kind of time. I'll just climb to the crack and hammer anchors in."

Baxter pointed. "The crack is way up there; how you gonna reach it?"

Royce examined the wall. "I'll press into the corner here where the fin joins the cylinder. The stone is rough; there's plenty of friction."

"I don't know where you come from, but the laws of nature and man don't work that way."

"No?" Royce looked back and waited for the next set of waves. When they finished breaking, he leaped up, and using fingertips, elbows, knees, and toes, he pressed himself into the sharp V where the tooth of the gear met the tower's body. The stone was wet, which made holding himself by pressing out significantly harder, but as expected, he managed to locate — mostly by feel — tiny dimples in the stone that were just large enough to catch a hold and keep him in place. He found more and climbed up about ten feet, then dropped back down before the next set of waves arrived.

Royce smiled as he nodded to himself. Gwen was right. He could do it. Wouldn't be easy, but once he drove an anchor into the crack and hooked a line, the rest would be inevitable.

"It's like you're a fly or one of those little lizards they have here," Baxter said.

"Don't worry. I'll be doing that part. You can climb the rope behind me like Hadrian."

"Oh, no thank you," Baxter replied. "I'm not climbing anything. I said you're insane, and I'm standing by that."

Royce faced him. His hood was up but starting to sag under the weight of the wet. "I'm going up. As my ghost, you're obliged to follow."

"That's okay. I'll stay here and dodge your falling body instead."

"And you realize that the book is up there. Hadrian and I could find it and sneak out while you're twiddling your thumbs. The Big Guy wouldn't like that."

"Don't care." Baxter looked up at the dizzying height of the tower. "All the money in the world isn't going to convince me."

Now that the storm had arrived, the top was no longer visible. Even the bridge was mostly lost in clouds. "You're scared of that?" Royce asked. "I thought you were renowned."

"Renowned — not suicidal. A year ago, I led a team that assassinated a sitting magistrate — in his own home."

Royce shrugged. "I murdered my first judge all by myself when I was sixteen. Honestly, what passes for elite these days?"

Royce looked at Hadrian for agreement, but his partner was letting the rain drain down his face as he stared out at the waves. He wasn't looking good, and Royce was starting to suspect he might be doing this alone.

"You have another problem," Baxter said. "You have no gear, do you?"

Royce scowled. "This job was supposed to be an intimidation contract — a simple killing if that didn't work. Didn't expect to be rock climbing."

"What do you need?" Auberon asked.

"Several blade pitons of varying lengths — one to five inches, I suppose."

"What are those?" Auberon asked.

"Just thin bits of strong metal I can hammer into cracks and tie a rope to — having a flange on the end and a hole through it would be nice. And obviously I'll need a little hammer, and lots and lots of rope — good rope, light and strong. And we'll need harnesses, some clamps, and I could use hand claws, too. And a few light bags that are easy to open and close. Maybe some chalk powder. Don't usually need it, but it's warmer here. It's possible I'll sweat."

"*Possible* you'll sweat?" Baxter blurted out, then laughed. "You'll be pissing yourself before you get halfway."

"Can you make a drawing of these claws and other stuff?" Auberon asked.

"Why?"

"Easier to make them that way."

"I didn't think you knew anything about crafting metal."

"I don't, but you'd be surprised how many of my people do."

Royce stared at the dwarf for a long while as he finally faced the truth. He had been eager to give up his bed on the *Ellis Far* because he'd rather walk home than take that ship. Gwen's request had provided him a wonderful excuse, and he was going to take it. No one could fault him for failing to do what everyone knew was impossible. But then came those tears and that kiss, and with them a stupid desire to actually try.

It only took a fraction of a second to stamp out the spark, but in that instant, Royce caught a glimpse into the mind of Hadrian and felt sorry for him.

He likely feels this way all the time — upset at disappointing others.

Royce wanted to please Gwen. He'd steal her a pony if she showed the slightest interest because he knew he could do that. The odds were well in his favor, and the reward far outshone the risk. But climbing this tower was nearly impossible — at least it had been until he confirmed the poor upkeep of the North Tower. Still, Baxter was right. They didn't have the gear or the time to obtain it, and that had left scaling Drumindor a fantasy . . . until now.

This is really going to happen, he thought.

"She's not on it," Hadrian said, and Royce realized he was still looking at the *Ellis Far*.

"What?" Royce asked concerned. "Who? Gwen?"

"No. Millie."

"Millie? Who's Millie?"

Hadrian shook his head. "A woman who has a habit of not listening to me."

Royce didn't like his partner's despondent tone. He'd had no difficulty persuading Hadrian to stay, no problem convincing him to climb the tower. That right there was odd. This melancholy was worse. "Hadrian? How do *you* feel about climbing this tower?"

"Huh?" He looked up as if he'd been asleep, as if he'd forgotten why they had hiked out through the brush in a pouring rain. "Oh." He shrugged. "I don't care."

"You don't care?" Baxter mocked him. "You two are nuts. You try to climb that, and you're both going to die."

"If they don't try," Auberon said, "a lot more will."

CHAPTER TWENTY-NINE

Scram Scallie

With a touch of Auberon's hand, a solid stone wall in the bare-faced portion of the cliff rolled back to reveal a hidden room. As it did, and for the first time since Rehn's death, Hadrian bothered to notice his surroundings.

Auberon had led Hadrian, Royce, and Baxter up Berling's Way in the pouring rain. Hadrian didn't know where they were headed and didn't care. The flood of water rushing down the pavement served to remind him of that first night alone with Millie: the way the storm had trapped the two of them in that darkened doorway and how nice and warm she felt when pressing against him. Millie was different: ambitious, brave, playful, exciting, and incredibly talented. He felt she was just the sort of woman he could spend his life with. Someone who would challenge him, push them both to be more than either thought possible. He really suspected he might find happiness with her . . . right up until he realized she was only after the diary. Every time Hadrian thought of that book, his hands clenched into fists. That diary had caused the deaths of Lady Martel, Virgil Puck, and the courier. Then it had nearly killed Rehn Purim. Hadrian had told Rehn to give the diary to Falkirk to save the kid's life. He thought it had worked, but now Rehn was dead. If there was ever an evil book, the diary of Falkirk was it.

Hadrian was deep inside this moist and muddled world of hatred, regret, and pouring rain, when the sliding wall of stone drew his attention. Like an elephant balancing on a stool, it just wasn't something you saw every day. The power of this novelty would have worn off, leaving Hadrian to slip back into his comfortable depression, except for two additional things: one was the crowd of dwarfs inside who went abruptly silent at the sight of them; the other was the smell of ale.

Auberon led the way into what looked to be a well-to-do cave. An eerie green light illuminated the small space that was graced with a fine floor but rough-cut stone walls. Unlike the Turtle, this didn't appear to be a stylistic choice so much as laziness. In the same manner, the ceiling was low, and no effort had been made to smooth or finish the furrows and gouges left behind by a chisel, which endowed the ceiling with an interesting textured pattern. While all of this was intriguing, Hadrian's eyes were drawn to a stone counter laden with mugs, which looked enough like a bar to give him hope. Filling the place were more than a dozen dwarfs who stood shoulder to shoulder . . . motionless. Some held drinks nearly to their lips; others held mouths open as if about to speak; all heads were turned to face them; eyes stared in shock. But no one moved.

"Auberon!" The lady dwarf with the towel, who Hadrian remembered from the day before, broke the spell. She rushed out from behind the bar with that same towel slung over one shoulder. Her eyes were just as wide as the rest as she approached, holding her hands out as if to stop Auberon and his companions.

"Good day to you, Sloan," Auberon greeted her.

"Auberon! Are ya outta yer mind?"

"Relax, dear. Everything is fine," the old dwarf assured her.

"Fine? And how is it ya calculate that figure? I'd like ta know. By Drome's beard, nothing is anywhere near close ta being fine today." She pulled the towel off her shoulder, whipping it in the air. "Humans are abandoning the city like ants off a hot skillet. No one can get into Drumindor, and Gravis-bloody-Berling is gonna blow this whole place off the map. And now"—she whipped the end of her towel in their direction—"ya walk in here with them? The name of this place is Scram Scallie, and ya stroll in with three of them? Are ya daft, sir?"

Auberon smiled mischievously and gave her a wink. "Set the four of us up with a pint of your best ale, and I'll explain why it is you're going to kiss me as if I were a dashing young colt again."

The old dwarf shooed away those at the bar, and they scattered at his approach. When he reached the brass rail, he turned and faced the crowd. "First, allow me to introduce our friends. This is Royce Melborn, an assassin and thief of notorious reputation. And this is his partner, Hadrian Blackwater, a onetime soldier turned mercenary, and now he's a disillusioned seeker of truth. They were hired by Lord Byron to prevent Gravis from causing trouble."

"Not terribly good at their profession, are they?" Sloan accused as she walked back behind the bar and pulled mugs from the rack. She took her time doing it, as if she hoped serving them was a sentence that still had time to be repealed. "And who's the other one?"

"That's Karl Baxter, agent of Cornelius DeLur sent to keep an eye on them."

Sloan turned around with four empty mugs in her hands. "So, all three are worth about as much as a gold tenent made of wood. Is that what yer telling me? Maybe I ought ta wait before pouring these drinks until ya clean up this rainstorm puddle ya invited in."

Auberon leaned forward across the bar. "They're going to save us all, dear."

Sloan looked unconvinced. "Ya spent yer whole life trying ta free us from human tyranny. Even here, we knew of ya. Auberon the Avenger was a hero ta us all. Ya broke hearts when ya gave up. One of those was mine. Many a night I prayed ta Drome that ya would find passion again and rejoin the cause — that ya would do something, anything ta help us."

Auberon nodded. "I cursed Drome for that passion. It drove me to try to save our people from their indentured servitude, from the humiliation, and from forgetting who we once were. I spread hate like a plague. Hundreds died, the ones I killed and the ones who helped me do the killing. In the end, none of it helped, but it succeeded at making everything worse. After two hundred years of fighting, I only proved the rumors were true. That's why I quit, why I retired."

Sloan shook her head in disgust. "And today, of all days, ya come out of retirement . . . and what do ya do? Ya bring three humans into the Scallie."

"If what I just told you about them saving us isn't true, does it really matter if they know about the Scallie? And if it is the truth, don't you think they deserve a drink?"

This bit of logic left her trapped, and she filled the mugs.

Auberon handed the drinks out. Royce declined his, and it was left on the counter.

Sloan took note of this and glared at him. "It isn't poisoned, ya know. I'll admit I'm not pleased Auberon betrayed a thousand years of trust by showing ya the door ta our only safe haven — which is also a sacred shrine of sorts . . . or at least it was." She shot the old dwarf a stabbing look. "But if yer under this roof, and I'm serving ya, ya gonna get the best I've got. And it's served in a clean mug."

"No offense intended," Royce replied. "I've just never cared for any barley-based drinks. And it won't go to waste; Hadrian will drink it."

Sloan scrutinized them both as if trying to decide something. In doing so, she noticed Hadrian had already emptied his mug.

Sloan shrugged, then shook her head.

"How are they going to do it?" the tallest dwarf in the room asked.

Auberon took a sip from his mug, wiped a thin line of foam from his mustache, smiled, then once more winked. "They're going to climb the North Tower." He pointed at Royce and Hadrian. "I think Baxter will be on the *Crown Jewel* when it leaves tomorrow, yes?"

The ghost nodded.

"With everyone gone, who will make sure these two get the job done?" Sloan asked, her voice laced with cold cynicism.

"Ah." Auberon grinned at her, undaunted, and gestured at the room with his ale. "*We* will."

"We?"

"Aye, my dear. Starting right now, you and I and every Dromeian in Tur Del Fur will do whatever it takes to help these two."

Sloan shook her head. "I still don't understand what's going on in yer wee heid. The Unholy Trio, with an army of workers, a treasure house full of gold, and over two weeks ta work with, tried and failed ta do anything. What makes ya think these two have any chance at all?"

"I don't," Auberon admitted. "As I've often said, I'm an idiot. I spent centuries spilling blood only to realize I had become what I was trying to stop." Auberon put the mug down on the bar and looked hard at Sloan. "No one should ever take my advice or listen to my counsel. That much is clear. But that's not what I'm asking you to do because I'm not the one who's saying they're going to save us. I'm merely delivering the message."

"And who is that?" she asked with a sneer, her tone showing that she expected disappointment.

Auberon stood up straighter and in a clear voice declared to the room, "Beatrice Brundenlin, daughter of King Mideon."

The sneer vanished from Sloan's face. Confusion replaced it. Then her eyes shot to Royce and Hadrian, who she stared at as if they had just that moment materialized before her. "Yer not implying . . . these two, ya say?"

Auberon nodded. "Aye. These two."

Sloan moved out from behind the bar to gawk at them anew. "By Drome's beard, and ya say," she muttered, then asked, "it's them that's gonna *climb* the tower?"

"Day after tomorrow, I think. If we can get them equipped. They asked for rope and a few other things."

Royce nodded. "If we can start earlier, we will. No sense waiting until the last second. Just need the gear and for the rain to let up."

Sloan was walking in a circle around them, nodding her head. "Yes, yes"— she glanced at Auberon—"I can see it. Yes, and if we—they and us—manage this . . ." She looked at Auberon, her eyes bright. "If they all see what we do . . ."

"We might be saving a whole lot more than just a city."

Sloan and others began to nod. "What can we do ta help?"

"They're going to need an assortment of tools and things," Auberon said. "They can explain, even draw pictures if needed."

Royce nodded.

Sloan pulled over a crate and used it to climb on top of the bar, which brought her head close to the stone-chiseled ceiling. "Listen ta me, everyone!" she shouted. "Here we were up all night emptying the kegs, singing the old songs, toasting the end, and lamenting the burning of our world and our lives. And while we were preparing ta make our peace with Drome, wouldn't ya just know it, Auberon wasn't done fighting fer us. If ya want ta live, if ya want Tur Del Fur ta survive, ya will fetch yer tools, come back here, and do whatever these two men ask of ya." She slapped the ceiling with a palm. "By Drome's beard, we're not done yet!"

With that said, she jumped off the bar, grabbed hold of the old dwarf and kissed him.

※

"It's not a big deal," Hadrian said again. He was certain he'd repeated this at least once before, but he always had trouble with short-term memory and numbers when he drank. A perfect example was the empty mugs on the counter. He wasn't certain if they were his or someone else's because he had no idea how many he'd had. The number eluded him, but by the swing of his head, he could tell he'd had a pleasant number, yet far from enough. He also couldn't understand why the empties hadn't been cleared. Usually, the bartender did that to keep the counter tidy, but he reminded himself that this was no ordinary alehouse.

The lack of tables and chairs was a huge giveaway. This absence of seating left him standing, which was challenging given that the ceiling was a foot shorter than himself, forcing Hadrian to alternate between slouching and bowing his head. Luckily, everyone he talked to were dwarfs, and looking down was mandatory.

"Why are there no chairs?" he asked.

"Tradition," the thin dwarf with the short brown beard replied. Hadrian was all but certain his name was Trig the Younger. Hadrian had been introduced to so many and so quickly that, like the mugs, he'd lost track. "In ancient times, our people had a problem with drinking."

"Lack of beer?" Hadrian asked.

The dwarf chuckled. "Not too little, too much. Everyone drank all the time. People were passed out everywhere. Nothing got done 'cept the brewing of ale. So, the king — we had one then, that's how far back this goes — he ordered that no alehouses should have chairs. And he further proclaimed that anyone who couldn't stand couldn't remain in a public house. Most folks don't like to stand in one place for too long, and if you drink too much, standing at all becomes a challenge."

"I guess that makes sense."

"Yeah, and it's also too small in here for both people *and* furniture."

They both laughed, and Hadrian wondered if young Trig had made all that up or not.

"You're really gonna do it?" Kiln the Miner asked. He was a little fella with hands and arms that looked capable of choking a tree. "Climb Drumindor, I mean."

Hadrian nodded. "Like I said, it's not a big deal."

"Are ya sure about that? I'm asking because I don't think a scorpion could climb either one of them towers."

"You don't think so?" Trig asked. He had become Hadrian's drinking partner, and this honor came with a certain obligation: to match his colleague in mugs and to defend his side of any argument. "Scorpions can climb anything, I think."

Heigal heard this and felt the need to add his opinion. "Can't climb smooth surfaces. They got these pincers on their feet." He made a claw out of his hand, opening and closing it. "They grab hold, but they got nothing to grab if it's smooth."

"What about a squirrel?" Trig asked.

"Same thing. Still need something to grab."

"Okay, but how about a cockroach or—no—what about an ant? They go straight up anything. I bet an ant could climb it."

"Do you know how far the top of Drumindor would be to an ant, lad?" Heigal said. "It would take the thing a week. It'd die of starvation or thirst before reaching the top."

"That's assuming it didn't blow off." This important observation was added by Loc, who stood beside Heigal. He was equally bound by the rules of drinking to side with his brass-rail associate.

"A slug then," Trig said. "A slug won't blow off."

Heigal shook his head. "A slug would move slower than an ant."

"Oh, you're right. But how about a spider? That's a wall crawler for you. And they can make a web and catch food on the way. What do you think of that?"

Those close enough to have heard the debate all shrugged, leaving Trig with a proud smile.

"Hear that?" Kiln said to Hadrian. "The lad here thinks you'll have an easy time of it. Just don't forget your web."

"Royce is as good as any spider," Hadrian said and looked around for the thief before remembering that Royce had left with Auberon and a few others. They were going to get started on crafting their equipment. No one saw any reason for Hadrian to go—especially Hadrian. He was more than satisfied with his prowess at climbing into mugs and had all the necessary gear.

"I certainly hope ya can manage it. I surely do," Sloan said. "But I fear that getting ta the bridge is only gonna be the start."

The tall dwarf heard this and waved a dismissive hand. "Bah!" he said. "Gravis Berling is an old, insane fool. And look at this man. Look at his swords!" He spoke with a tone of awe. "Why, it will be like a ruddy pig slaughter, it will."

"Watch yer mouth, Baric!" Sloan snapped. "This is just as much yer fault as anyone's."

"Mine?"

"Ya pushed Gravis into it. Insulting him, making fun, daring him. The poor soul has nothing. Lost his life's work, his home, and then his wife, and ya go on spitting on him. He's a Berling! His reputation is all he has. But ya had ta show him, didn't ya? And now he's showing you — showing all of us." Sloan looked near to tears as she leaned hard on the bar. "We've all suffered. Suffered so much that we're turning on each other when we should be . . ." She looked down and sniffled.

"What did you mean about getting to the bridge is only the start?" Hadrian asked.

"I don't know exactly," Sloan wiped her face with the towel, then held it over her mouth so that her words were muffled. "I just have this feeling, ya know? This sense of dread. Up until now, I was convinced we were all certain ta die, so that's understandable, isn't it?" She lowered the towel and looked about the little room with far-seeing eyes. "But it's more than that, really. I guess a lot of it comes from the fact I haven't been sleeping well. Keep having awful dreams — nightmares about something beneath the towers, pounding, as it — or maybe them — tries ta break out. It terrifies me, and I wake up screaming and crying like a child."

Sloan stopped speaking as she noticed all around the Scallie random conversations had stopped, and the room had gone frighteningly silent. Everyone was looking at her, wide-eyed.

"I'm not the only one who has had that dream, am I?"

The Bristol Foundry and Metal Works was located on the upper west side of the city. Located behind a row of identical warehouses, each featuring unlovely yards of ugly rusted rubbish, the place appeared out of step with the rest of the cliffside oasis. No flowers, no palms. Only dust and stone defined this neighborhood known as the Seventh-and-a-Half Tier — for no reason that anyone bothered to tell Royce. They were, however, quick to point out that it wasn't Bristol's foundry at all. It had belonged to Diederik Dolin, who had built it and whose family ran it for seven hundred years. Dolin, as it turned out, had the misfortune of being a dwarf. Apparently, this Alan Bristol fellow from Swanwick did not suffer the same curse, making it possible for him to purchase the workshop — not from Dolin, mind you, but — from the Unholy Trio. This was presented with all the melodrama of someone naïve enough to believe that power was only cruel to short people.

Royce was as sympathetic as any man in the rain listening to another soaked person complain about the weather. The dwarfs with him might perceive the situation differently, but then everyone saw everything through their own eyes. It made neither of them right but did make for an interesting, albeit a generally disagreeable, world. Yet even that was up for debate because there was such a thing as a Hadrian.

None of that mattered, as the entire tier was deserted. They hadn't seen so much as a stray cat since leaving Scram Scallie. And the rain couldn't be blamed. The storm had passed, although what remained was a humid drizzle that left a person unsure if they were soaked with rain or sweat.

To everyone's surprise, the foundry's gate was locked. Alan Bristol was apparently a complex man: optimistic enough to believe anything of value would survive the cataclysm, but also a pessimist in his expectation of being robbed. By virtue of this magnificently twisted worldview, Royce thought he might very well find a kindred spirit in Mister Alan Bristol.

While the small army of dwarfs began pulling hammers and chisels from belts and satchels, intent, he imagined, on burrowing through a wall or something, Royce unlocked the gate. News of this circulated by way of elbow jabs. Then they all looked at him as if he'd defied the natural order of things. Perhaps they thought him a witch — or worse, in cahoots with Alan Bristol. Auberon, who was the undisputed leader of this fellowship, spoke a few words in their language, and everyone went back to smiles and nods.

If anyone — anyone — had told me two months ago that I would be a member of a dwarven gang raiding an abandoned metal workshop at the bottom of the world in order to stave off annihilation, I would have . . . The thought hit a wall. Royce didn't have a clue how he would have reacted, but belief would not have been within the realm of possibilities.

The foundry was large — not traditional dwarf huge-beyond-reason — just big. The ceiling was three or four stories above, with metal beams running between stone pillars. Chains hung from the beams, as did massive buckets. A large wheel was connected to a massive bellows, which was motionless for now. There were piles of coal, wood, and metal ingots. A hoard of soot-covered iron tools that could easily double for implements of torture were neatly arranged on the walls. Wooden tables and benches with buckets, pulleys, hammers, and countless other devices Royce couldn't begin to classify furnished the place.

A number of the dwarfs grumbled at the sight. A few shook their heads, and one cursed, *"Durim hiben!"* This was one of the very few dwarven terms Royce knew — not the exact translation, but well enough to use it correctly in conversation. The same fellow followed the profanity saying, "What a mess!" Then he shouted, "Get the lights on in here!"

The rest scattered.

Auberon directed Royce to one wall that looked to be made of black slate. A huge wooden box filled with chalks of various colors and sizes was mounted to the side of a moveable set of stairs, allowing access to the whole height of the board. "Draw what you need us to make."

Royce sketched the simple shapes of the pitons. In the past, he had made do with scraps of things he'd found over the years. Nails and iron door hinges worked, but gate latches were so ideal he used to steal them.

Beside him stood a bald dwarf with a wreath of bright hair and eyeglasses like those Arcadius played with. These were much bigger with thicker glass, and unlike the professor's, which lived on the end of his nose, the dwarf's pair covered and magnified his eyes, making him appear like a bearded owl. He tapped on the drawing of pitons, leaving dark dots on the blackboard. "And what are these thingamabobs used for?"

"I hammer them into cracks and hook a rope to them."

The dwarf studied the drawing. "That's what the hole is for? To run the rope through?"

Royce nodded.

"And you do this while dangling hundreds of feet up?"

Royce nodded again.

"Seems a bit fiddly." He scratched his ear. "You'll want something better. Something that will clip and snap, suitable for one-hand work."

"Aye," another dwarf agreed. He was shorter than the first and had a head of wild white hair that seemed to stand on end like a dandelion gone to seed. In his mouth, he chewed on an unlit pipe. "Snap and clip, that's the way for sure. Needs to be strong enough to hold the weight of a man but light enough to carry dozens of bundles up a wall."

"You'll also be wanting some V-shaped wedges of various widths and lengths to account for crack size," the fellow with the glasses said. "Need to get a good ping for maximum anchorage."

"How do you know all this?" Royce asked. "Have you climbed before?"

He shook his head. "No — I'm a dwarf."

Royce didn't know which question that answered — probably both.

More questions were asked about the harness.

"Gonna be in this a while?"

"Several hours, at least."

"Belt and leg loops will need to be adjustable to accommodate clothing depending on the weather. You'll want a thickly padded waist, as well as the leg loops, for comfort and support while you are hanging and waiting on your partner."

"Aye." Dandelion-head nodded. "Thick. Very thick and soft, like the breast of a dove."

Royce moved on to the hand claws and chalk bag. The dwarfs had improvements for everything, including how to carry rope, what sort of hammer to use, a better pack, the possibility of using a pick, and a lengthy discussion on footwear.

"What about the rope?" Royce asked. "I'm going to need a lot. Good quality is important, but it needs to be light."

"I'll talk to Elinbert," the bespectacled dwarf said. "He's the real genius when it comes to fibers."

"Oh, yes!" Cloud-head agreed with passion. "Elinbert is a wizard of wimbly-nimbly filament and fibril."

"Don't worry," Glasses said. "You'll get what you need."

"How long will all this take?" Royce asked.

"We'll work all night and through tomorrow. No one will sleep until this is done. You'll have everything no later than tomorrow night." He looked at the puffball beside him, who nodded — a thing that caused the cloud on his head to sway and shimmy.

"That will give us a night and a day to get up there and stop Gravis." Royce nodded. "Should work."

The dwarfs looked at each other. "No *should* about it. Three nights from now the Wolf Moon will be at its height, and Beatrice has never been wrong."

◈

"It's the pounding that's awful," Trig was saying. "It seems so loud. So frightening. Louder than thunder, and you can feel it with your feet."

"In my nightmares, there are three of them," Heigal said. "And they stink of rotten eggs."

The whole of the alehouse was clustered tightly around the bar as each of them gave reports of their dreams. Only they didn't act like they were dreams. To Hadrian, they were like a group of blind men fashioning a common image from the combined impressions of tiny hands.

"They're old," Sloan said. "Beyond ancient. That's what I got. And they're evil."

This last bit resonated universally with the group. They all nodded agreement.

"But it's a dream," Hadrian said as he stood at the miniature bar. For him, the counter was low enough to be a seat, and he'd have liked to swing his thigh up and use it as one but knew that wouldn't go over well. "Dreams aren't real."

"If it isn't real . . ." Sloan said. "How is it we're all having the same one?"

They all nodded again, and Hadrian felt more like Royce as he faced a group of believers armed only with reason. He thought to say that they really weren't sharing the same dream but were simply scared and feeding off each other's anxiety. He saw them all groping for an answer that was less horrible than the all-too-ordinary-and-meaningless reality that one person's blind hate and horrific selfishness could be so cruel. That anyone could do this was unthinkable, but that the culprit was one of their own was too much to accept. In its place, they would welcome any other answer. A trio of nameless, ancient, and evil monsters was so much better than an aging, brokenhearted dwarf.

And Hadrian understood grief. He suffered his own nightmares. His centered around the smiling face of a young man who had tried to mend a bridge that he'd never burned. Instead of open arms, Hadrian had turned his back, making a happily-ever-after into a tragedy. But there was no pounding, no rotten egg smell, no sense of ancient evil on the rise. That was just a way of blaming others for his own mistakes. Such a thing was oh-so easy to do when a blunder threatened embarrassment; how much more enticing when a mistake had cost an innocent life?

Hadrian grabbed his dwarf-sized mug and emptied it. The ale was good but weak, and the tiny tankards slowed his drinking. He wanted to get blazingly drunk and then pass out. But he could already tell that wasn't going to happen. He sighed.

Sloan picked up his mug and, apparently taking his sigh as a sign of fear, stress, or worry, she laid her little hand on his. "Don't worry, ya will do it." She said this with a mother's comfort, then turned to refill the mug from the barrel. "Beatrice said so, and if that isn't enough, three nights from now is the height of the Wolf Moon." Sloan turned back with an encouraging smile and set the brimming mug before him as the whole of the group murmured their affirmation.

"And that all means what?" he asked.

Sloan smiled self-consciously. "Oh, sorry. I'm not used ta talking ta the non-initiated. Scram Scallie is a haven from big folk, and I never did get out much. So, I'm guessing ya never heard of Beatrice?"

Hadrian shook his head. This brought some jeers and scoffing sounds, but Sloan waved them down, chiding them with, "And I'm guessing ya know the names of all of *their* princesses, do ya?"

"Only the one," Baric bellowed, using his height to speak above the crowd. "And we'd all just as well forget her."

This brought a round of hearty and like-minded mug clapping.

Hadrian watched them, baffled. He knew of very few princesses. The only one he could name was King Amrath of Medford's daughter, Arista. But he seriously doubted they meant her as she was just a girl.

"A sorry state of affairs indeed." Sloan frowned. "Beatrice was a Belgriclungreian princess and . . ." She paused and studied him a moment. "Do ya know what Belgriclungreian means, laddie?"

Hadrian sheepishly shook his head. "I think I recall a fish vendor mentioning it once, but I can't remember the details."

"Ya certainly ought ta learn the word, as yer surrounded by the buggers right now." She lifted her chin and raised her voice. "And an awful lot we are."

The room erupted with false outrage.

"Ya know us best as *dwarfs,*" Sloan went on, "which is a dash derogatory, but not nearly so bad as other names we've been called. Being the children of Drome, we're actually all Dromeians, but that was a long time ago. Drome had seven sons, ya see: Dorith, Bel, Brunden, Derin, Gric, Nye, and Lung. Each became a clan unto themselves with Dorith being the thane — that's the supreme chief of all the clans. Now, fer a long time we lived up north in the city of Neith, and Clan Dorith ruled, father ta son, with Clan Derin and Clan Nye supporting them. Eventually, the rest of us drifted south, spreading out across this peninsula. Then with the success of Drumindor, the Brundenlin clan took prominence. They forced the northern clans ta submit, and Linden of the Brundenlins became the first Dromeian king and started building a new, more central capital city that became known as Linden's Lot."

"You gonna bore the man with ten thousand years of history, are you?" Baric asked.

"Bah!" she replied. "He looks like the sort who appreciates a bit of knowledge. Unlike some folk."

This brought a wave of "oohs" from the gathering.

Sloan looked back at Hadrian, frowned, and sighed. "Anyway, ta make a long story short"— she gave a wicked glance at Baric —"Fer those of ya who have the attention span of a goldfish, there was a war with the elves, which made everyone kinda hate the Brundenlins. They were overthrown by the three other southern clans, namely the Bels, the Grics, and the Lungs. Fer a long time, folks called them by their clan names until the three names sort of merged into one and became the Belgriclungreians. Over the centuries the term extended itself and became the modern name fer all Dromeians — making Dromeian a rather archaic word usually used ta refer ta ancient times or when yer making a point ta include everyone. So, when I say that Beatrice was a Belgriclungreian princess, I mean she was a dwarf."

Trig shook his head. "Couldn't you have just said that?"

"Technically, Beatrice was a Brundenlin," Kiln said. "So, calling her a *Belgriclungreian* isn't even accurate."

"Sloan likes to call everyone *Belgriclungreian* because she's a Bel," Baric said.

"But Beatrice predates *Belgriclungreian* as a term, so it doesn't even come close to making sense," Kiln added.

"Oh, fer the love of Drome!" Sloan said. "It's close enough fer the likes of him, I think."

"*Dwarf* would have been close enough for the likes of him," Kiln said.

Sloan gave the miner a cross look, and Kiln made a show of closing his mouth and taking a step back.

Loc, who stood just to Hadrian's left, tugged on his sleeve. "It's not you," he whispered apologetically. "It's always like this."

"There now," Sloan said, disgusted. "Ya have made me go and forget the point of all this."

"Beatrice," Hadrian reminded her.

"Ah-ha!" Sloan tapped the end of her nose, then raised the same finger in triumph. "Beatrice! Yes! She was a prophet who lived over five thousand years ago, and she said ya would climb Drumindor. As all of her prophecies have proved accurate, we know this will happen."

"Five thousand years ago?" Hadrian said. "Is that even possible? The world is only — I mean — this is the year 2991, so how could—"

"That's the Novronian calendar yer using, deary," Sloan explained. "It doesn't even begin until the founding of the Novronian Empire. There's a whole lot of stuff that happened before that. The Belgriclungreian calendar goes back a mite farther. Fer us, this is the year 777,745."

"Really?" Hadrian glanced now at Loc as if he might be the only sane one in the room. "And when does *your* calendar start?"

"When Eton first shone on Elan," Sloan replied for him, "which I believe is a better place ta begin, don't you?" She thought a moment, then shrugged. "Granted, no one was actually there ta witness the event, so I'm not certain how accurate the counting is."

"A little late to start questioning it now, don't you think?" Baric asked.

"And the Wolf Moon?" Hadrian inquired. "What's that all about?"

"That's part of our calendar as well. The whole thing is based on the moon's phases, so there are twelve moons a year. We're halfway through the Wolf Moon. And everyone knows that if yer in trouble, there is no better friend shining on ya than that. Last month was the Snow Moon, and if ya were attempting yer climb then, I would've been concerned; that month always brings bad luck."

Hadrian felt he was going to regret the question, but . . . "What makes the Wolf Moon so good?"

Sloan pointed up at the ceiling as if it were the night sky. "The moon is Elan's sister." She said this as if he already ought to know.

Hadrian spread his hands, suggesting this didn't answer the question for him.

Sloan looked to the crowd with wide eyes and pointed at him as if to show off the novelty of what she'd just found. "The moon was once very powerful, but at the start of the universe, she sacrificed everything ta save Eton and Elan . . ." Sloan waited, watching him as if this comment would trigger some memory and he would exclaim, *Ah-hah!* or something. He didn't, and she shook her head. "Ah . . . well, afterward, the moon diminished ta a pale remnant of her former self, but she is still out there, watching and guarding. She's the savior goddess of martyrs and heroes, and at this time of the year, she is the closest she gets ta Elan. And it is on the full moon of this month when the wolves call ta her that she pays the most attention ta Elan and those of us who walk upon her."

"Okay, but what makes you think this moon goddess would help Royce and me? We're not Dromeians. We're *scallie*. Isn't that right?"

Sloan smiled at him. "I was starting ta think ya were a few trees short of a forest, but ya learn fast, at least." For the first time, Hadrian got the sense she was starting to warm up to him, and not just because he was destined to save the city. He also thought that if she did, then it was in spite of herself. "The moon is not a Belgriclungreian goddess; she is universal, like Eton and Elan."

"What is Eton?" Hadrian asked.

Sloan blinked and appeared — at least for a moment — to be stunned beyond the use of words.

"Before you answer," Kiln said, "might we get another round, lest we all die of thirst while you answer that one?"

"Yer treading on quicksand, laddie," Sloan said, but took their mugs just the same.

"Have you never been outside and looked up?" Baric asked Hadrian.

"Aye," Kiln said. "Never once noticed all that stuff up there? The sky, the sun, the stars. That's Eton. He's married to Elan, which is all that lies beneath Eton, and from them came everything else."

"And the moon is Elan's sister?" Hadrian asked.

"So maybe I was a bit premature with my assessment of yer mental prowess," Sloan said with her back to all of them as she worked the taps.

"Still don't see why the moon goddess would care about me and Royce." Hadrian drained his mug.

Sloan heard the hollow sound when he set the mug on the counter and snatched it up. "She's sort of the champion of lost causes, I suppose. They say she was very powerful once, but she lost everything, even the ability ta speak, when she sacrificed herself ta save her sister. Now she exists as a mute sentinel, forever guarding against that same evil." She set the full mug back on the counter and, sliding it to Hadrian, leaned over to whisper, "And that's something else I got from the dreams. That evil — part of it, at least — is what's pounding, trying ta get out. And that's why I think the moon will be on yer side."

Hadrian took the mug. "Here's to the moon, then."

"Ya don't believe a word I'm saying, do ya?"

She was absolutely right. It was hard enough for him to believe in the myths and fairy tales he was brought up with. Adopting foreign fables was asking too much. But he was enjoying the conversation. Her passion made it easier to momentarily throw off the blanket of guilt that threatened to smother him. Listening to her, there were whole seconds that went by in which he didn't think of Rehn.

Hadrian wiped the foam off his lips. "I'm not even convinced that you believe it yourself."

She grinned. "Okay, I retract me retraction concerning yer intelligence. Honestly, yer a hard person ta fathom. Being a bartender all me life, I pride myself on accurately evaluating a person at a glance. Pinning ya down is like trying ta grab a fish out of a clear pond. It looks simple at first, but once ya put a hand in, ya discover nothing about it is simple."

Hadrian shrugged. "What can I say? I'm a mystery."

Sloan wiped the counter in circular motions that slowed down as she went until she stopped altogether. Then she looked up. "There is one other thing."

"What's that?" Hadrian took another sip.

"Andvari Berling created Drumindor. Well, he and a few thousand Brundenlins. At the time, Linden—who went on ta become our first king—was chief of the Brundenlin clan. He funded and backed the project. Alberich Berling, Andvari's son, finished the two towers that made the city possible. And when it was finally done, Mideon, Linden's grandson, was king, and his father was named Math."

"So?" Hadrian asked, hoping he wouldn't be expected to remember all those names.

"So, why is it that where we are standing right now is called *Tur Del Fur,* which in case ya don't know is Dromeian fer the City of Tur?" She whipped the towel back over her shoulder. "Who, by the white of Drome's beard, was Tur? And what contribution did this person make that was more significant than either of the Berlings or the Brundenlin kings?"

"You have a theory?"

"She always has a theory," Baric said.

"Given that I just thought of it now, I wouldn't call it anything so grand as that. Just a strange idea."

"Which is?"

"What if Andvari Berling had help? What if it wasn't even his idea ta create Drumindor? What if he never even wanted ta come down here ta what, in his day, would have been a desolate and treacherous point? I say this because it is a well-known fact that Andvari was as much a world explorer as I am. So what made him come? What made him climb down in a raging storm and forced him ta seek shelter in this place that was nothing but a small crack in the face of the cliff? What if it was someone named Tur, someone who wasn't a Dromeian, and as such, he could have been expunged from our history in everything except the name of the city?"

She rocked her head as if the ideas inside had gotten stuck and needed jarring. "And since I am already this far out on the *what-if* branch, let's take one more precarious step and ask . . . what if the reason had nothing ta do with taming the volcano so as ta allow fer a city ta be built and an obscure clan ta rise ta prominence? What if it was an open passage that needed ta be closed? A doorway that needed ta be locked ta prevent something awful from climbing out — what if Drumindor is really, *Druma's Door?*"

"*It's hard for us to imagine,*" Hadrian recalled Royce saying, "*but those two massive towers are not much more than a pair of pins in a tumbler lock.*"

For the first time since Hadrian looked upon Rehn's lifeless body lying in that bed, he had something else to worry about.

CHAPTER THIRTY

The Crown Jewel

Royce and Hadrian had agreed to sleep late the following morning. They planned to start their climb just after sunset and knew they would need plenty of rest. Despite this, both were up with the sun.

"Was I making too much noise?" Hadrian asked from his seat at the little table in the courtyard, where he was eating the rice-and-lentil dish that either Gwen or Auberon had left in the icebox.

Royce shook his head as he sat down. "Just the opposite. It's way too quiet. The city is practically empty of people, but . . ." He looked up. "Do you hear that?"

Hadrian shook his head.

"Exactly," Royce said. "Every morning, I've come out to this courtyard and suffered the incessant chatter of birds."

"You hate birds now, too?" Hadrian asked in between mouthfuls that he was scooping up with his fingers. "I thought it was just dogs and dwarfs."

"Birds are new to the list. I added them the morning after dancing with Gwen."

"Oh." This Hadrian understood. "Yeah, loud noises, bright lights — I once cursed the sun for shining. As for the birds, we have been here for a month. It's spring. They fly north."

"All of them?"

Hadrian tilted his head back and listened. Royce was right. Not a sound. He looked to the sky. Nothing moved except clouds. "Strange."

Royce pointed at the bowl. "How is that?"

"Good. Want some?"

"Maybe. It looks light and easy to both carry and eat."

"You know," Hadrian said, "the last time we climbed a massive tower, you wanted to kill me. You had hoped I'd fall."

"Third time's the charm."

"Then you're out of luck. This will only be my second."

Hadrian scooped another mouthful and chewed as he watched Royce, who appeared perplexed.

"No, that's not right," Royce finally said. "We climbed the Crown Tower twice."

"*You* did, I only made the one trip. The first time you went up alone, remember? Left me in that little town in Ghent. I don't even recall its name anymore. Then you went off by yourself and stole the book. Arcadius wasn't happy, so the next night, I went with you, and together we put it back."

Royce shrugged. "Maybe, but we didn't put it back the next night . . . did we?"

Hadrian considered this. He remembered being mad that Royce had abandoned him. When he returned to Sheridan, Royce was already back with the book. Arcadius said Hadrian and Royce had to put it back, and also . . . "The professor told me Pickles had been killed while we were away, and I remember leaving right after that."

"That's right," Royce said. "You were too angry to make dinner. And now here we are doing the same sort of thing again. Funny how life can repeat itself."

"I wouldn't call it funny."

Baxter entered the courtyard, looking especially fresh and dapper and in a better mood than Hadrian had ever seen. "The *Crown Jewel* is leaving this morning," the ghost announced.

"You disappeared yesterday," Royce said. "I was worried."

Baxter rolled his eyes. "I'm officially done with you two, but Cornelius requires his key back. You can give it to me if you like."

Royce made a sound like laughter and flashed an expression similar to a smile. "You're cute."

Baxter frowned. "Just make sure you get it back to him before the ship sails."

"Or what?" Hadrian asked. "If we succeed in this, he'll owe us more than a lousy key. And if we don't, the key will be buried with us at the bottom of the sea under brand-new rock, I would suspect."

"Is Cornelius still in his palace?" Royce asked.

Baxter shook his head. "He's on the ship."

"We should see him off, then," Royce told Hadrian.

"Why?"

"Because you're right. If we pull this off, he will owe us. I just want to make sure *he* knows that."

The *Crown Jewel* was a ship in the same way Cornelius DeLur was a thief. The vessel was huge — twice the size of the *Ellis Far*. It had five masts with five sails each and three jibs. The hull was painted a pristine white with blue trim and gold hardware, which even included the anchor. Royce had made the early assumption that the massive, bifurcated hooks designed to be dropped into the ocean to keep the ship from drifting were wrought iron that was *painted* gold. In the month he'd spent in Tur Del Fur, he now had reason to doubt that bit of common sense. The extent of Cornelius DeLur's extravagance was not to be underestimated.

At the dock, two lines had formed, one at each of the dual gangways. One admitted last-minute supplies and luggage dragged up by shirtless men with glistening backs. The other accommodated passengers: travelers dressed as if they were on their way to a summer gala. Most wore white, but some stood out in brilliant oranges, reds, and dazzling yellows. Ladies sported immense, broad-brimmed hats and full-length gowns while holding aloft delicate parasols. The men wore doublets, hose, and capes.

Royce plowed ahead of Hadrian up the ramp, using the key to cow nobility of all ranks. No one wanted to be on Cornelius's bad side that day, leaving Royce to ponder how much the Big Guy had made each of them pay. Given the priceless opportunity, he guessed that for many of them, it was more than money. On the way up, Royce spotted Lady Constance — all in white — standing in line with another woman of equal extravagance — all in yellow.

"Why . . . Mister Hadrian, isn't it?" the woman in yellow addressed them. "How lovely to see you again." She held out a hand.

Hadrian looked awkward as he gave the woman's hand a firm shake.

"You're supposed to kiss the back, my dear," the lady explained.

"Oh, sorry." Hadrian gave her hand a quick peck, then turned to Royce. "This is, ah, the Countess Ridell of Warric."

"Oh, please." The woman frowned. "We're still in dock. Until we return to the misery of civilization, call me Estelle." She smiled wickedly. "And please do call me . . . any time . . . either of you . . . or both, if you wish. My stateroom is said to have a very large bed."

"We aren't staying on board," Hadrian said.

"No?" She appeared perplexed. "But this is the last—you aren't staying *here*, are you?"

Lady Constance then asserted herself as only she could. "Oh, my goodness gracious, are all of you still in the city? Do you require assistance? I will speak to Cornelius the moment we get aboard and—"

Royce held up the key, causing Lady Constance's brows to rise. She stared at the bit of jewelry, transfixed. "So then . . ." she stumbled. "Now I don't understand in the slightest."

"Gwen, Albert, and Arcadius left on the *Ellis Far*," Royce explained. "We're staying, and I am here to return this."

Constance looked back and forth between the two. "Are you insane?"

Both Royce and Hadrian hesitated, then rocked their heads side to side. Each noticed the other and smiled.

Constance's eyes went wide, and she brought both white-gloved hands to her cheeks. "Oh no, you can't be serious." She turned and looked up at the tower that loomed overhead. "You wouldn't. It's suicide."

"Care to let me in on the madness, dear?" Estelle asked.

"They're going to try to stop it by climbing the tower and killing Gravis."

Estelle looked at Hadrian. As she did, her shoulders drooped, her head tilted back, and her eyes took on a longing look of awe. "By Mar, where have you been all my life? If I had but known there were men like you walking the face of Elan, I'd have poisoned my husband years ago."

"If all goes according to plan, you'll be able to toast us next year at The Blue Parrot," Royce said.

"And if it doesn't?" Lady Constance asked.

"Then toast us in Medford. I don't see that it matters much to you."

Lady Constance looked as if he'd slapped her. "I . . ." She hesitated. "I wish you the very best of luck. I truly do."

"Please don't," Royce said. "Luck and I have never gotten along."

"Same here," Estelle said. She gestured at Hadrian. "Before me stands a god of a man whom I'd murder my husband for. Just this morning, I learned he is suddenly available once again, and here I am forced to flee. Luck hates me."

"Suddenly available?" Hadrian asked. "What do you mean?"

Estelle looked surprised.

Constance took hold of Estelle's wrist. "He doesn't know," she whispered, and Estelle stiffened.

"Know what?" Royce asked.

"I'm sorry," Estelle said.

"What do you mean by I'm available?" Hadrian asked again.

Estelle looked to Constance, as for once the countess appeared at a loss for words.

"Millificent LeDeye died last night," Constance said. "Her body was found up on the Eighth Tier."

Hadrian looked like he'd been stabbed but refused to fall. His teeth clenched. "Who did it?"

"One of Cornelius's men. Andre DeButte. He was the one who introduced her on stage at The Blue Parrot."

"Anyone know where he is?" Hadrian asked the ladies, then looked at Royce.

"We've got time," Royce said. "And I'll help or just watch if you like."

"He's also dead," Constance reported. "According to Alessandro Ugarte, the two had a fight. Miss LeDeye started it by stabbing Andre in the stomach. Apparently, he had the time and inclination to return the gift in kind."

"Sounds like this Alessandro Ugarte may have killed them both," Royce said.

Hadrian shook his head. "No, it doesn't. It sounds exactly like Millie." He put a hand to his stomach. "Gwen was right."

When Royce and Hadrian reached the rear of the vessel, they were stopped by armed guards who didn't step aside at the sight of the key. Instead, after hearing their request, one entered the doors they protected while the other stared at the two of them menacingly.

Hadrian wasn't looking good. His eyes held a faraway gaze that didn't bode well for their climb.

Maybe I should leave him behind. No, that won't work. If I had done that last time, I'd be dead. And there is Falkirk to consider. Besides, death isn't an unexplored frontier for Hadrian, and he is stronger than he looks.

The door opened, and the now-familiar woman with dark eyes and raven hair stepped out. "I'll deliver the key to Cornelius," Cassandra told Royce and held out her hand that was now devoid of baubles and bracelets.

"Everyone is so eager to play courier this morning," Royce replied. "But it's not in my nature to trust anyone. I'll hand deliver this to him or keep it as a souvenir. Your choice."

"Do you think Cornelius keeps these in his pocket? He's not even going to see it. He doesn't want to. He has courtiers and clerks who handle these trivialities. I will pass the key on to the treasurer and inform Master DeLur that you returned it."

Royce shook his head.

She frowned. "Do you have any idea who I am?"

Royce smiled. "Look up there," he told her and pointed at the North Tower. "Around sunset this evening, I'm going to free-climb that using finger grips half the size of the buttons on your gown, fighting winds that would threaten to capsize this ship, and I'll be doing it at night, so Gravis doesn't see me coming. If I make it, I'll need to get inside the fortress — a place I've never been — kill Gravis and figure out a way to undo whatever the dwarf did, which I am told is like untangling a ball of twine after a cat has played with it for an hour. There's also a good chance I'm going to encounter a guy who can't be killed but might want to stop me. And if I fail to do all this before moonrise tomorrow night, I will have a front row seat for the uncontrolled eruption of Mount Druma, which is expected to not so much vent as explode, taking the city, the bay, and most of the cliff with it. Do you really think I care who you are?"

In truth, Royce had a good idea. He'd gotten her name from Baxter; the rest came from simple observation. Cornelius was the founding father of the world's biggest and most successful thieves' guild. He had managed to transmute this illegal success into a legitimate career as a self-made king, but the business was in his blood. He'd spent most of his life navigating the shoals and jagged teeth of the shadowlands — the place where trust was nothing but a lever, and friendships had the lifespan of a mayfly. More than any monarch who murdered an uncle or older brother to claim the throne, Cornelius awaited treachery with the same confidence as the coming of winter. And with his money, he could afford to buy the best furs to guard against the cold.

In the substratum society of thieves and their associates, there were believed to be five assassins in the world who could claim the title of *Bucketman* with a capital B. Royce knew this because he and his onetime friends and fellow Black Diamonds, Merrick and Jade, were three of the five. The remaining two were a mystery, which meant they were not members of the BD. Royce had a strong belief that Cassandra only pretended to be DeLur's chancellor. Perhaps she, too, had grown tired of the blood and longed for a legitimate career in a place where such things seemed possible. For her, this might represent a second chance. For Cornelius, she was a guard dog like no other. To get to him, everyone had to go through her. Royce was confident none made that journey alive.

"Why do you want to *see* him?" she asked, and the singular tone of the word was unlike all her previous ones. Here now was not the exalted chief executive of DeLur Enterprises. This was the voice of a Bucketman.

"To talk," he replied. "Nothing more. I don't bite the hand that feeds me, and I'm here to inquire about a feast."

❧

Cornelius DeLur lay upon a luxurious divan the size of five beds. Plush aqua upholstery lined a whimsical golden frame made to mimic an ocean wave. The recliner rested inside a stunning room the size of the entire stern of the ship, made to appear all the larger by virtue of the rear wall being all glass. Royce had never seen windowpanes of such size and clarity. Altogether they provided a breathtaking view of the bay. The rest of the room was like a parlor in a mansion: with fancy rugs, potted plants, filled bookshelves, and paintings with elaborate frames. The whole space had a high ceiling and a sweeping staircase that led to . . . Royce had no idea other than *up*.

With Cornelius were the usual suspects: Ernesta Bray, Oscar Tiliner, and a handful of other unknown but equally wealthy faces. These were the merchant barons of Delgos, the men and women who pretended to have prestige equal to the northern nobles just as the northern nobles pretended to possess wealth equal to the merchant barons. In the relative wasteland of the room's dark side, Lord Byron stood, leaning on the opulent framework of a dark fireplace. Despite the insurance of the double-blind system that required Albert Winslow to proxy for Riyria with clients, Royce had followed the viscount, unannounced, to a couple of meetings. Royce had been bored, and he also wanted to see the face of the man who'd hired them, just in case the too-good-to-be-true assignment was just that. He found the man to be the human equivalent of the color gray. Neither tall nor short, nor fat nor thin, he nevertheless managed to stand out by being dull. In a room of shiny gemstones, he was a lackluster clod of dirt. Appearing to know this, he receded into the shadows, where he stood with as much dignity as he could manage.

Cassandra led the two of them in, and all conversation halted.

"My good friend, Royce," Cornelius greeted him without rising, or even sitting up. "How are you, my boy?"

"Thanks to *your* boy, Baxter, I'm sure you already know, along with the name of my barber's second wife."

"You don't have a barber."

"Exactly."

Cornelius grinned. "Indeed, but I still don't know where the diary is."

"You do; you're just not willing to believe what I say because if it's true, you can't get at it."

"I know only what you told me, and what you allowed Baxter to see. That's the trick for any good magician, isn't it?"

"Not being a magician, I wouldn't know. But as a professional liar, I can see that telling the truth has created an uncrackable riddle that I admit is entertaining."

Cornelius chuckled. A moment later, the rest joined in.

"All that is history now, as everything else will soon be," Cornelius said with a hint of melancholy. "So, tell me, what brings you to my vessel? Returning the key? It will be worthless after today."

If any statement illustrated Cornelius DeLur, that was it. He was the only man who could describe a solid gold key with a flawless diamond in the stem as *worthless*. And say so with sincerity.

Royce produced the bit of jewelry. "It clashes with every outfit I own." He handed it off to Cassandra, who stood disturbingly close. "But there was one other matter."

"How am I not at all surprised?"

"How much is Tur Del Fur worth to you?" Royce asked.

"Be more specific."

"At moonrise tomorrow night, this whole place will be erased. Everything you've worked for, everything you and your associates here have built for the last few decades will be gone. Everyone has had weeks to stop it. No one has. So, I'm asking, what would it be worth to you if I did?"

Cornelius smiled, which was a small thing on that massive face. His eyes, nose, and mouth were kept to a limited area of his head like a child drawing a face on a pumpkin and fearful that they may run out of space. "Not nearly so much as you might hope, dear boy," Cornelius said. "While this is the trophy city of my holdings, I still control all of Delgos. I am fully prepared to start over down the coast, making this but an inconvenience. I also don't understand this proposition. We already have a contract for that job, and just as when Lord Byron hired you, the results have been far from successful. So why come to me now asking for more?"

"That other contract failed to include extreme hazard pay. The requirements got a lot harder, so the price has gone up. And it isn't like you have nothing to show for your investment in me. I provided the information that turned your death sentence into — how did *you* say it — *an inconvenience?* That was worth more than the price of a room and a couple of dinners at The Blue Parrot. Now, I could leave with everyone else and let this place sink, or I could risk my life climbing

Drumindor in the hope I can get in, kill Gravis, and vent the pressure before the full moon tomorrow. I just want to know: if I go to that much trouble and succeed, what would you pay?"

Cornelius stared at Royce for a long moment, and the room went silent. The big man's little tongue licked his little lips. Watching this, Royce considered how the man's face wasn't small — his eyes, nose, and mouth were all normal-sized — everything else was just so big.

Finally, Cornelius put his fingertips together, and pumping them like a spider on a mirror, he took a deep breath and replied, "Nothing."

While Royce had hoped for a ridiculous fortune, he knew he wouldn't get it. Cornelius was too shrewd for that, but he expected something — certainly more than nothing. Shock turned to irritation that quickly shifted to anger. Royce looked to the floor to hide his expression.

Fine, I'll let it all sink. The city, the whole point, can blow up. I don't —

"But . . ." Cornelius said. "I would be willing to pay for the book."

Royce looked up.

"We have an existing contract with regard to Gravis Berling," Cornelius said. "But we've never made one concerning the book. If what you tell me is true, and given it's in the neighborhood, it should prove no great hardship to pick it up and give it to me. The way I see it, to fulfill your earlier contract, for which you have already been paid but haven't completed, you're forced to go up the tower. Failure to do so would leave you in willful breach. Being that I lack the courtesy of the noble-minded Lord Byron, I will require that you repay all the funds provided thus far. If need be, I have means of getting that money from you. And we both know that three week's rent on a Tier Four home in Tur Del Fur and *multiple* dinners at The Blue Parrot are not cheap. So, unless you plan to work for me for several years to pay off this debt, you will be going up the tower. Preventing the destruction of Drumindor will wipe out your debt. However, returning the book to me is something I'm willing to pay handsomely for."

"How attractive is *handsomely?*"

"What would you like?"

Royce was feeling oddly off balance, and it had little to do with the rocking of the ship, which was just another distraction. He'd gone from risking his life for nothing to an invitation to name his price. It made sense. Cornelius wasn't so much offering to pay a fortune for the diary as ensuring, without looking weak, that Royce had the necessary incentive to save the city. And like any good negotiator, Cornelius pushed for what he knew he could get. Even if the diary didn't lead to a treasure, it could be sold, and the profit would likely defray the cost of doing business with Riyria. While the offer was intoxicating, Royce knew such a thing was fraught with peril. This was like a nursery tale where a magical creature offers a wish that always turned out to be a trap. Royce was amazed at how realistic children's stories always were.

For a moment, he thought of asking for the world. This was Cornelius DeLur, the richest human being on Elan. Nothing would be too extreme, and Royce's mind imagined wonders beyond anything he'd ever thought possible. He could have a home, a real one. Not a cot in a room of many, not a stairwell, or a shed, or a wagon, but a place with its own door and maybe a window with glass, and a bed of feathers with sheets. He could keep things there, have possessions in a number greater than he could carry. His house could be a place with streets that smelled of flowers instead of urine. It could be somewhere that Gwen might like, and that they could one day share, a home where a wolf might not mind curling up before a fire.

When Royce failed to speak, Cornelius provided a suggestion. "How about this ship? It is four hundred and thirty-nine feet and has a fifty-four-foot beam and twenty-eight sails. And as you can see, it has every conceivable amenity. You could live on board free of all laws and explore the world at your leisure. You could be a pirate. Captain Melborn, scourge of the high seas."

Royce took this as a repulsive joke, but the others in the room gasped and whispered amazement at the offer. Some even suggested Cornelius had lost his mind, just not loud enough for the Big Guy to hear.

"This ship?" Royce said, knowing full well he was back in the realistic realm of a treacherous fairy tale where the magical mage offered horror in the guise of insane promises. "I appreciate the offer, but I hate ships. To run this . . ." He looked around at the little indoor garden and the crystal chandelier above it. "I'd need a crew of hundreds, I'm guessing, and that just seems like work."

Cornelius chuckled and nodded. "All right then, what about a nice little danthum? You seemed to enjoy The Blue Parrot. Perhaps you'd like your own. You could settle down to a life as a successful businessman, much like Calvary Graxton. It just so happens that a cozy little place called The Cave just became available."

"That's the one up on the Eighth Tier?" Royce asked Hadrian, who nodded absently as he stared out the stern windows. Royce peered at Cornelius. "Are you seriously offering to reward me with life in a *salt mine?*"

Cornelius frowned. "How callous of me. Yes, I can see how that would be out of the question. You tell me, then," Cornelius said. "What is it you want? A big chest of coins?"

Royce considered this. Gold was practical, or would be once he was back in Medford. The problem was transportation. Gold was heavy, cumbersome, and hard to hide. With all these witnesses, word would spread, and an army of thieves would descend on him like seagulls on a freshly caught fish. By the time he returned to Melengar, he'd have an empty box.

Once more, Royce returned to the beautiful idea of a little home. But what good was a house in a place he couldn't ply his trade? He'd carved out a territory in Melengar but didn't think the Trio would grant him a free hand here in sunny Delgos. He'd have no income. And how could he ask Gwen to leave Medford House? She was dug in. And if she didn't come, what value was there in an empty house?

"What do you want?" Royce whispered to Hadrian.

"I don't care," he replied with an oblivious shrug of his shoulders. "Whatever you decide is fine."

Royce stared at his partner for a moment, frowning. The biggest windfall they could imagine, accompanied by perhaps the most dangerous mission, and yet Hadrian was indifferent to the point of boredom.

What Royce needed was something of high value but low weight, hard to steal and easy to move, and it had to be practical to use. "How about you just make the privilege of the key permanent?"

Cornelius narrowed his eyes as he considered this. "The key opens doors and grants favors. People will give you things for free, true, but it doesn't buy everything.

It has limitations. And it only works here."

"That's fine. And as I'm not planning to stay, you'll be able to sleep at night, knowing I'm not going to bankrupt Delgos."

"What will you use it for, then?"

"Maybe I'll become a regular turist." He smiled. "Mostly, I'll keep it as insurance against disaster. Auberon advised us to find a new line of work. Doesn't have to be fancy, he says — don't need a lot of money to be happy. But I was thinking that one day we might need a place to disappear. A key to the city could make that happen."

"That's an oddly sensible request," Cornelius told him, which was something no children's story wish-granter had ever said to the likes of a greedy child on their way to an early doom. The big man drummed his fingers on the blue cushions as his eyes took in the room. It would be harder to go back on a deal brokered in such a public manner with such a well-appointed set of witnesses. On the other hand, given that it was a reasonable deal, it didn't surprise Royce when Cornelius answered, "Bring back the book to me, and you'll have your key."

When they came out, Royce and Hadrian found Baxter leaning on the ship's rail. His head was back, his eyes closed as he appeared to be sunning himself. Beside him was a young woman. She had short, boyish hair, wore a loose, sleeveless top, and on her arm was the tattoo of a butterfly.

"Well, if it ain't Hadrian the Handsome and the Brooding Bad Boy," the woman greeted the two.

"You're familiar," Royce said.

"She's the cloakroom girl from The Blue Parrot," Hadrian told him.

"Do you hear that, love? The *girl from the cloakroom.*" Baxter laughed. "You'll need to forgive them. They aren't very well connected. I suspect they normally live in a hole or under a bridge somewhere." The former ghost hooked his thumb at the girl. "This is the famous Whiskey Neat, also known, in certain local circles, as Paradise Patty. Up north you used to go by a Black Diamond name of some sort. What was it?"

"Opal," Royce said, surprising all of them. "I *thought* I knew you."

The woman stared at Royce, confused.

"Yes," he said. "You were part of that new group of kids who made the cut that summer. You were only what? Thirteen, maybe fourteen? I remember Jade liked you. She didn't think you had the killer instinct, but I suppose that's why she liked you."

As he spoke, the woman stiffened. "Oh, bugger me!" she sort of screamed, but the outburst was stifled into a quiet, desperate cry.

"Funny," Royce said to Hadrian. "Scarlett Dodge greeted me the same way when we met her in Dulgath." He leaned in toward Opal, who shuddered. "You'd have known her as Feldspar."

"Is she still alive?" Opal asked, her voice quavering.

Royce rolled his shoulders. "It's not like she sends me letters."

"What's going on?" Baxter asked. "Why are you acting so strange?"

"I'll tell you later," Opal said, then looked at Royce, terrified. "There *is* going to be a *later*, right?"

"Goodbye, ghost," Royce said as he walked away. "Happy hauntings."

CHAPTER THIRTY-ONE

Fate Lends a Hand

By midday, the last of the supplies and luggage had been stowed aboard the *Crown Jewel*, and the lines of passengers were gone. Royce and Hadrian, along with several hundred dwarfs who lined the harbor, watched as Auberon, Sloan, and a couple others were called up the ramp. They stood at the rail and spoke with Bray, Tiliner, and Cassandra. It wasn't a long meeting, and soon they returned. The gangway was thrown off as were the mooring lines. Some of the dwarfs helped with this and even waved goodbye.

Then the *Crown Jewel* set sail. The white canvases unfolded, dropping down, catching air, billowing out, and pushing the huge ship very slowly backward. Once away from the dock and into the clear bay, the sails turned, their rotation revealed as shadowed canvas shifted to sun-kissed brilliance. The ship pivoted with all the speed of a shadow on a sundial. Then the canvas fluttered loudly only to snap full again. Aiming for the gap between the two towers, the *Crown Jewel* unfurled all twenty-eight sails. The sight was stunning. So much unblemished cloth so brilliantly displayed in the midday sun made the ship appear top-heavy. As she picked up speed, the *Jewel* drew a white-water wake, making an arrow pointing toward the exit. At first, Royce wondered how such a behemoth would manage to sneak through so narrow an opening, but as she moved away, the ship appeared to shrink. Then, as she passed between the towers of Drumindor, the *Crown Jewel* appeared like a children's toy, just a bobbing bit of painted wood and some glued pieces of cloth.

She rounded the point and then was gone. The last ship, the last passengers, and perhaps the last survivors were away.

"What do you think that meeting with the dwarfs was all about?" Hadrian asked as the two walked back up Berling's Way.

"I don't know," Royce replied. "Maybe some last-minute insults."

"Or maybe the Trio is congratulating them."

"For what?"

"Well, this is the first time in like a thousand years that Tur Del Fur is back under the control of the dwarfs, isn't it?" Hadrian swept his hand in a half circle around him. "With only a few exceptions, they're the only ones still here. They own the place again."

This truth became abundantly obvious as they climbed up the four tiers back to Pebble Way and the Turquoise Turtle. Royce didn't think the city could feel any emptier, but it did. Nothing moved on the streets. They didn't see a single person of any height on the way back. What's more, the ever-present chickens and roosters that always clogged the streets were missing. Cats and dogs were absent as well, which made Royce wonder about the rats and their fame for leaving sinking ships. He suspected they, too, had left.

The little rolkin looked just as before. The same aqua blue door, shutters, banisters, and railings accented the white courtyard, where a garden of potted plants and four fruit trees continued to grow. But it wasn't the same. The place felt dead. The whole city was a graveyard and the Turtle just another corpse.

Inside, the cozy and cool place was unchanged: the big, cushioned bench where Albert had lounged, the icebox, and the jungo plant named Daisy. For the last three weeks this was where Royce could always expect to find Gwen — the longest he'd ever come to living with her. His memories struggled to remind him that it hadn't been all sunshine and jungo plants, but oddly, all he remembered was her face caught in the sunlight that beamed in patches through the branches of the lemon tree. How she smiled, and how beautiful and happy she appeared.

"When they look at this city, it's like when I look at you," Gwen had said, and now here he was, staring at a door and seeing her. *"You'll do it for me."*

Hadrian dropped himself into one of the courtyard chairs, the one that faced the lemon tree, then threw his head back and released a tortured sigh.

Royce stared at this puddle of a man who, with arms flung out, head hanging, and legs extended, appeared to lack bones. "If you don't care," Royce asked, "why did you stay? Why are you making this climb with me?"

"Honestly?" Hadrian replied. "I think I'm kinda hoping twice *will* be the charm."

Royce rolled his eyes. He hated when Hadrian got like this. He loathed it even more when it was hours before an important assignment. And this wasn't just a big job — climbing that tower would be a *dangerous* undertaking.

Royce hadn't said so, tried not to think about it, but this climb wasn't going to be as easy as he had let on. If he was honest, he'd admit to being a bit scared. This wasn't as high as the Crown Tower, but Royce had had months to prepare for that job. He'd studied the face of the tower, done partial practice runs — and that building was made of stone blocks. Unusually massive slabs to be sure, but still set in the traditional manner that left a regular pattern of seams. Climbing it was little more than repetition. And it got easier as he neared the top because the blocks grew smaller, granting him more options. Drumindor was smooth. All he could exploit were the fickle cracks that nature had generated at random. A lot could go wrong. How shallow might the cracks be? How much wind was up there?

And then there was the mystery of what might happen as they neared the bridge.

According to Cornelius, Gravis Berling and Falkirk de Roche had simply walked into Drumindor's South Tower. This was odd because the tower hadn't been empty. Drumindor never was. The base level acted as the headquarters for the Delgos Port Authority Association. There would have been more than a dozen Yellow Jackets just inside, all of whom knew not to let Gravis in. But somehow, this didn't act as a deterrent.

As much as Royce was worried about Falkirk, he was more concerned about Gravis. While Drumindor was a forge and a volcanic cap, it was also a fortress. Given the icebox and the flush bucket, what other clever tricks might a dwarf fortress possess? Were there secret passages, traps? Could Gravis release a trickle of lava that would flow down the tower's grooves? That would really ruin their day.

And then what would happen when they reached the bridge? Would they just be able to walk in? What if there was another hidden door? Royce hoped to reach the bridge before dawn tomorrow using the darkness to hide, but also if they couldn't get in, a whole day remained to rappel down the ropes and get out of the city before the place blew. But what if Gravis had a surprise planned? Could he destroy the bridge? From the ground, it looked as thin as parchment.

And if they got in, if they encountered Gravis *and* Falkirk — the man who refused to die — what, then? Royce might need Hadrian — a living, breathing Hadrian, with bones and everything.

"I might need you at the top," Royce said. "Hate to get all the way up there and not be able to save the city because it takes two men to turn a dwarf-sized crank."

"What are you talking about? I'm going with you."

"Are you? First, Pickles dies — again — and now, this Millificent woman checks out. I know how you get. You blame yourself for their deaths, get drunk, and are good for nothing for weeks."

"I'm sorry for having a conscience, for having feelings. If I were you, I suppose I wouldn't so much blame myself as *take credit* for their deaths."

"I need a partner up there, Hadrian. I need someone I can count on. Otherwise, you aren't just killing yourself, you're killing me, too."

Hadrian didn't say anything. Royce wished he would. A good fight might be the best thing. Hatred for Royce had motivated Hadrian up the Crown Tower. Maybe it could work a miracle again. But times had changed. He and Hadrian weren't flint and steel anymore.

An army of dwarfs led by Auberon arrived at the Turtle, driving a wheelbarrow full of climbing gear. They unloaded it and began making last-minute adjustments and explaining design features, none of which Hadrian cared about. After they sized his harness and measured his feet, Hadrian escaped and climbed the stairs to his room, where he threw off his swords and collapsed face-down on the bed.

Maybe this time Royce should climb alone. I've already killed two people, and they say deaths come in threes.

Hadrian lay with his face swallowed by the pillow, trying to understand how this time he'd killed two people without drawing a sword.

I haven't even worn them! I'm like a disease. Wherever I go, people die.

Royce killed for a living, but he had never been this good. Apparently when it came to causing suffering and death, Hadrian was a natural prodigy of misery.

He hadn't completely closed the door and heard it creak open. "Hadrian?" a dwarven voice asked.

"Not here," he replied into the pillow.

Footsteps entered and the door closed. "Trying to get some sleep, are ya?"

Hadrian rocked his head and, opening one eye, spotted Auberon sitting down in the stone chair beside the bed.

"If I was, I doubt I'd need company. Sleeping is usually a solitary effort."

Auberon nodded sagely. Certain people had that ability. Arcadius oozed wisdom. The professor could sneeze and make it appear all mystical and lesson-worthy. Auberon was the same way. Age had a lot to do with it, but Hadrian had seen a lot of old men who radiated a far more doddering-fool mystique.

Maybe it's the long white beard?

"Royce tells me the two of you are going to begin your climb tonight."

"If he says so, I'd listen to him." Hadrian punched up his pillow.

"He also suggested that you might not be up to the task."

"Nearly four years and nothing's changed," Hadrian told the pillow.

"He also says you blame yourself for Rehn's death."

Hadrian cocked his head clear of the feather-filled bag. "That's usually what I do when someone would still be alive except for my getting them killed. He sacrificed himself to save me."

"Did he now?" Auberon asked.

"There isn't much a man can do when someone fires a crossbow at their back. So, yeah. If not for him, I'd be the one sailing home in a coffin."

"Interesting." Auberon did that wise-old-soul nodding thing.

Knowing it was some sort of trap, Hadrian hated himself for asking but couldn't help it. "What's interesting?"

"It's just that . . . well, you might have noticed that my people are a bit on the cynical side. Over the last month, perhaps you've witnessed some of the reasons why. And out of this pessimistic attitude comes a certain sprout of fatalism — a belief that if someone's life is saved, then fate had a hand in it. Granted, if you're a Dromeian, the reason is almost always awful. But fate is fate, and the whole thing is made worse if the savior is killed in the act. If that happens, fate isn't just tapping you on the shoulder and saying big things are headed your way. No sir, if the person who saves your life pays for it with theirs, then fate is coming to settle a score, and you're already deep in debt. I suppose the part I find interesting is how curious a thing it is that here you are about to attempt the impossible — to save the homes and the lives of so many people. Coincidence struggles to explain such a thing away."

"You're trying to tell me that Rehn died so I could save Tur Del Fur?"

Auberon shook his head. "No. I'm not much of a believer in fate or destiny or any of that nonsense. That sort of thing is for priests and monks, and I am far removed from both. I just know that while you can't change what's past, you can alter the future. Sometimes when the world breaks your heart, it also gives you the needle and thread necessary to do a fair job of stitching it back together. Won't be the same, acourse, but it sure beats walking around without one. So maybe fate didn't kill Rehn to save this city, but if you do go up that tower and stop Gravis, then doesn't that mean Rehn didn't die for nothing? Young as he was, Rehn made the world a better place — or at least he tried to. Whether *he* succeeds or not . . . well, that depends a great deal on you, doesn't it? One selfless act leads to another until a chaos of kindness overwhelms the world." Auberon smiled at him. "It's just a thought, but I find sometimes young men need a reason to carry on. And besides, you're making a disaster out of my pillows."

Hadrian sat up and stared at Auberon. He really did look ancient, even for a dwarf, which was saying something. From those he'd seen so far, Hadrian imagined they all looked like little old men by the age of ten. Auberon had the appearance of an ancient oak tree, the sort with deeply grained and gnarled bark whose roots were exposed: twisted and bony. Mostly he looked tired.

"What happened to your family?" Hadrian asked.

The dwarf bowed his head and remained silent until Hadrian was certain he wouldn't speak, then the old head came up. "They were killed because of me. I fought for more than a century. I thought I could change things. All I did was murder some and get others killed. My eldest son joined me in the fight and died young. This broke my wife's heart. She begged me to stop, to walk away, to come here and live a quiet life with her and my last living son. But I was stubborn. I couldn't let it go. I was driven to do something. I had this calling, or maybe it was a sickness, but I believed I had been born to save my people — only I didn't. I just made everything worse. I'd say my wife and sons paid the price for my madness, but I dunno. You see, because my enemies couldn't catch me, they took my family. Maybe there is a Fate, because I can't think of any other reason I've lived this long, other than to suffer each morning by waking and remembering what I did and didn't do."

"And the calling — the sickness. Is it still there?"

The old dwarf stood up and nodded, then as he left, he paused to touch the three-mark symbol on the wall. "I miss you," he said. "And I'm sorry."

As the shadows grew long, Royce and Hadrian were back to hiking through the mini-rainforest and tidal scrublands that made up the northern arm of Terlando Bay. Concerned that Gravis would see a boat and might spot a parade, Royce insisted they go alone. This forced the two of them to carry on their backs everything they would need. To make this easier, the dwarfs had created special sacks with shoulder and waist straps that the dwarfs themselves packed with great care. Hadrian was amazed at how brilliant the bags were. Each was a good four feet tall and stuffed tight with food and gear, and yet Hadrian barely noticed he had it on. Most of what was inside was new to Hadrian, and he suspected the same was true for Royce.

"Seems like a lot of stuff," Hadrian said as Royce led them down the now-familiar trail.

"Most of it is rope," Royce replied.

Hadrian jostled the sack he wore. "I remember rope being a lot heavier."

"We won't need as much this time, and this rope is different."

"How so?"

Royce gave a sour glance back at him. "It's thin and light."

"You don't like it?"

Royce shrugged. "I tested it, and it works fine, but—I don't know it's... different."

"What do you care? You don't use it. The rope is for me, right?"

Royce was quiet for a moment then said, "The other stuff is different, too. You'll see what I mean when you put the harness on. And they made a lot of things—stuff I didn't even ask for. There're these metal hinges with a spring and teeth on them. You squeeze the ends together, stick them in a crevice, and let go and they open up, gripping the rock."

"And that holds you?"

"They say it will." He paused to look back at Hadrian. "You'll be the first to find out."

"Oh, joy. How wonderful. They are aware I weigh more than a dwarf, right? You told them that, yes?"

"What do you care? You're hoping the *second time's the charm.*"

"I may have changed my mind on that."

"Really? Was it Auberon or the threat of my using the spring hinge?"

"Auberon," Hadrian answered. "He's a smart guy." He thought about that, then changed his mind. "Maybe he's just wise."

"There's a difference?" Royce asked.

"I think so. Smart means you know lots of stuff; wise is understanding what to do with the stuff you know."

The light was fading fast as they reached the end of the thick brush and exited onto the open scruff of the rocky arm. Everything from this point was rock, sand, grass, mangroves, and the open sea—that and a whole lot of wind. At the far end stood the North Tower. The last rays of the dying sun threw its massive shadow across them and on into the forest. They both took a moment to look up. The height was dizzying.

"Auberon told us to find a new line of work. Do you remember?" Hadrian asked as they stood together and stared. "'Doesn't have to be fancy. You don't need to make a lot of money—just enough to live a simple life.' Do you remember him saying that?"

"What's your point?"

Hadrian nodded at the tower. "I think climbing that is what he'd classify as *fancy*."

"I think climbing that is what everyone else would classify as crazy."

"Thank Maribor that everyone else isn't here, then," Hadrian said.

CHAPTER THIRTY-TWO

Can You Hear Me

Gravis Berling sat near the center of the bridge that connected the two towers of Drumindor and watched the sun lowering itself into the sea. He'd seen the sight a thousand times before, but no two were the same. Even on days when no clouds were present, the colors were always a little different. And it was all about the colors. This evening the yellow ball was surrounded by a vast orange light, but the sea below was dark except for that diminishing line of fading gold. Gravis wanted to stare unblinking, to see the entirety of the sunset, but he couldn't. He was crying again.

He'd watched the last ship sail out earlier in the day. The big one that — when seen from Drumindor — didn't seem large at all. From his perch, Gravis saw only a tiny speck of white. The ship could just as easily have been a discarded handkerchief drifting out to sea. Next to Drumindor, nothing was big. Even Cornelius DeLur was small.

I suspect they're regretting how they treated me now.

About a month ago, he'd been nothing more than a speck of dust, a sad little joke, the lingering stench of a bygone age.

No, I wasn't a joke. That is the worst part. They thought me a liar.

No one could believe in a time where the Children of Drome ruled the world, when insulting a Dromeian was a dangerous thing. Watching that ship depart, he knew they had changed their minds.

Now they're sorry they messed with me.

He'd proven his point and could stop there. He had emptied the city. Gravis Berling had put the fear of Drome into everyone. Yes, he could stop it, vent the pressure, and walk away. The idea was welcoming. Bearing the responsibility for destroying Drumindor was a heavy burden that weighed on more than his mind. The towers were designed by his ancestor, the legendary Andvari, and built by the greatest Brundenlin engineers and crafters who'd ever lived. Drumindor was a wonder of the ancient world.

Who am I to destroy all that?

But of course, he couldn't simply walk away. Things had progressed beyond such naïve notions. After causing this much trouble, they would never let him get away with it. He'd chased Cornelius DeLur out of his own city. The Spider King would track him down no matter where he went. Gravis's life was over. One way or another, this was his end. And yet, fear of retribution didn't even rank in the top two reasons why he had to see the plan through.

One of those reasons was happily busying himself in the bowels of Drumindor. Thankfully, Falkirk spent all his time down near the forge and never came up this high. The two coexisted as estranged neighbors. Too lazy to build a fence, they simply knew not to breach each other's territory. Falkirk stayed in the basement whereas Gravis enjoyed the upper reaches of Drumindor. That was just fine with him. Gravis found Falkirk more than disturbing. He hadn't discussed the situation with him, but he was certain Falkirk would not be pleased if Gravis changed his mind.

Since the master gear was in the walking-corpse's territory, there was a sizable deterrent to changing his intent. Falkirk wanted him to blow up Drumindor and had no problem being ringside for the event. As the man was already dead, this likely accounted for his recklessness, but Gravis suspected something more.

The dreams had a lot to do with this.

Gravis still had them, and they had grown so much worse that he hardly slept anymore. When he did, the pounding was earsplitting and incessant. In his nightmares, he felt the vibration coming up through the stone. Despite wanting to escape, to run as far away as possible, he always descended the steps to the base of the North Tower. As Gravis grew closer, he could see the stone shake, crack, and begin to glow as below him pressure pushed magma up the main shaft. But there was something else. He heard voices. Deep, distorted utterances speaking in an ancient language. There were always three, shouting, crying for release, demanding their freedom. Gravis didn't understand a word, wasn't even certain he heard words, but still he understood their meaning. And down in the molten pool, Falkirk called to them, prostrating himself, reassuring those awful voices that the time was nigh, and in turn, they assured him of his eternal reward.

Those who patronized Scram Scallie often called the merchant barons who ran the city the Unholy Trio, but they had no idea what moved beneath their feet. If they had, the likes of Baric wouldn't be so flippant. The sounds Gravis heard, the sense of terror and dread conjured in his soul, became too great to bear, and he always woke up screaming in the tiny cell that had been his office. The dreams were horrible, but the worst part was that after he woke he thought he could still feel the pounding: fainter, more distant, but still there.

Gravis knew Falkirk would kill him if he changed his mind. And the dead man was more than capable. When they had first entered, the main floor security force greeted them. These were men who Gravis had seen every day for years, the old officers and the young recruits. Falkirk had killed them all. He hadn't acted in self-defense. None of the guards had threatened them in any way, but Falkirk had jumped to the task. At least two managed to stab him. Falkirk hadn't appeared to notice. Exactly how he killed the guards was still something of a mystery. The dead man had no weapons, just his bare hands and . . . teeth. Gravis thought he remembered Falkirk biting into a guard's face, but that had to be wrong. Not having seen the totality of events, Gravis had the luxury of denial. As it turned out, he hadn't seen much. Sickened by the bloodletting, he had turned away. In truth, he cowered beneath the reception desk for what felt like hours, but he couldn't escape the sounds. Shouts were followed by screams, screams faded to whimpers, and then there was only the sounds of tearing and . . . *chewing?* When at last he found the courage to crawl out, Falkirk had stood before Gravis, drenched red as if the man had bathed in a tub of blood.

"I'll collect their skins later." He told Gravis with a giddy glee. "Show me the furnace."

Terrified, more by the grisly sight than any sense of mortal danger, Gravis nodded. There was simply no sense in discussing anything with a blood-soaked, murderous corpse who looked as happy as a six-year-old sitting in a mud puddle. Gravis led the way up and across the bridge to the North Tower, and then he escorted Falkirk down to the bottom. Gravis set the chutes and locked the master gear. The two parted ways soon after, with Falkirk haunting Drumindor's base while Gravis stuck to the towers. To unlock the master gear, Gravis would need to go back down. Still, this was only a supporting argument to why Gravis couldn't walk away. The real reason remained that he had more than one ghost haunting him.

"I loved you," Gravis said softly as he sat on the edge of the stone bridge, his legs dangling, watching the sun die. Then he listened, waiting and hoping to hear a reply, but he knew it would never come.

Surprisingly, something else drifted to his ears. From far below, the sound of singing wafted toward him.

He pulled his legs up and stood. Turning away from the ocean side, he crossed the width of the bridge to where he'd hung his flag. He peered down at the harbor. The city should have been empty, but the sheltered port was filled with lights. Hundreds, maybe thousands of flickering dots moved down Berling's Way. They fanned out, filling up the dock, illuminating the wharf and piers like a swarm of fireflies.

Candles, Gravis thought. *Or perhaps lanterns, maybe a bit of both.*

He knew the song they sang. It was not the Belgric Royal Anthem, but it might as well have been. Dromeian voices lifted the words of the *Hagen Ere Brock.* The ancient song was so old that no one could say where it came from or who wrote it. Every Dromeian knew the tune and the lyrics by heart because the song was sung at every funeral. Not understanding this, other cultures who found the ballad beautiful played it at parties and weddings, butchering it in taverns near and far. For Dromeians, merely hearing the tune made them cry. Singing it was a challenge, as it choked their throats and broke their hearts. All of them had used those words, sung in that manner to say goodbye to someone they loved. *Hagen*

Ere Brock was a mourning song, and a thousand Dromeian voices sang it to him as the last light of day faded.

He knew why. They were begging him to stop, to have pity. But at that moment, all Gravis could think of was how he hadn't sung the song to Ena. He remembered her last minutes in their lonely shack on the night of her death. While the wind blew and whistled through the bleached planks, he was down on his knees at her bedside. He held Ena's hand as she lay soaked in sweat. She'd been that way for hours, and then she woke up.

Her eyes found him, and in a horribly lucid moment, she said, "It was always the towers you cared for." He was surprised to hear her speak and was still processing what she'd said when Ena took her final breath and used it to whisper her last words, "You never loved me."

Then she was gone.

He stared at her, shocked. In a moment of panic, he told her she was wrong. He shook her by the shoulders, begging her to listen, only to realize there was no one there. He was alone. Ena had left. She was gone forever, and he would never be able to explain.

Now, Gravis stood on the bridge, peering down. The builders hadn't bothered with a wall or rail, and his toes flirted with the edge. He whimpered and jerked as he cried. Tears blurred the many tiny lights into one swirling smear, and as their song came to an end, he shouted up at the appearing stars. "I do love you! Can you hear me? I've always loved you!"

But his words were beyond her reach.

That's why he had to destroy Drumindor. Gravis needed to prove to Ena — to her, and everyone else — he needed to show the world the truth.

Gravis wiped his eyes. Then he looked down once more at the lights. Over the course of the song, they had shifted position and now spelled out the word Please.

"I don't know what to do." He sobbed. "I don't know what to do."

CHAPTER THIRTY-THREE

The Climb

Just after full darkness, Royce and Hadrian reached the base of the tower and set down their packs. Royce had picked the north side, as it was opposite the bridge. The tower had no visible windows, which put them in Gravis's blind spot. They made their base on the big natural shelf that remained stubbornly resolute against the eternal crashing of waves. The wind sprayed saltwater and worked hard to shove the pair off the slick stone.

"Can you see?" Royce asked Hadrian as the wind whipped the thief's hood and tossed Hadrian's hair.

"Yeah," he replied. "Outlines and such, but don't ask me to read small handwriting."

Truth was, Hadrian could see a bit more than that. A surprising amount of warfare occurred at night, and he was always surprised how well a person could see in the dark. Standing on a narrow spit of land surrounded by a starlit ocean, he could make out Royce's eyes beneath his hood, discern the various plants, and see individual waves rolling in. He also found it disconcerting how the bushes and tall grass waved about, battered by the wind. Hadrian didn't remember any wind when they stood at the base of the Crown Tower, but by the time they reached the top, it had been intense. He looked up at the impossibly massive wall of stone that appeared to go on forever, silhouetted against the night sky.

What's it going to be like up there?

Hadrian had accused and found Rehn guilty of murdering Pickles. Maybe that was part of why he was so upset. Reality and his emotions didn't line up. Hadrian had loved the lad. When the boy died, it was like losing a son. Discovering Pickles had never existed was too much. Someone needed to be punished for that — at least, that's how Hadrian saw it. But . . . his view was blinded by pain. And so, through a grand cascade of absurdities, Hadrian took it out on Rehn. He blamed the victim for breaking his heart.

The conversation with Auberon had altered his view a bit. Hadrian still wasn't worth the air he breathed, but maybe something good could still come from his mistake. If he could help save the city, he had to try. He owed that much to Pickles, and now also to Rehn.

"Here's your harness," Royce said, pulling what looked to be a giant spider out of his pack.

When they had scaled the Crown Tower, they used a simple arrangement of leather straps that looped around Hadrian's thighs and waist and were held by rivets that dug into his skin. The new harness was all black and made from lightweight cloth. If there was stitching, Hadrian couldn't find it.

"Is this going to hold me?"

"Tested it with a one-ton block of stone. So I suppose it depends on what you had for supper."

Hadrian stepped into the loops, pulled the belt up and buckled it around his waist. "It's padded, and . . . wow, this is actually comfortable."

"Quiet, too," Royce added. "The rings won't clack. We won't even need to take them off."

"What are the big loops on the belt for?"

"For these." Royce showed him how dozens of clamp assemblies were hung from the loops on his harness's belt. Each clamp assembly was composed of two clamps connected by a short cord. "After I drive in an anchor, I'll hook one of these to it, and the other end to the rope." Royce pulled one off his belt and handed it to Hadrian. The clamps weren't a solid circle; they had a hinged mouth, and Hadrian played with the spring latch.

"As you come behind me, instead of pulling out the anchors, you'll only need to unhook your rope, unclip the clamp from the anchor, and attach it"—he took the clamp back from Hadrian—"to the loop on your belt." He snapped it back onto his own belt. "Like that."

"Well, isn't that something?" Hadrian said and meant it. "Are we going to have enough anchors?"

Royce replied by pulling out a massive string of linked pitons.

"How heavy is that?"

Royce gave it to him, and Hadrian was stunned. He could have been holding a necklace of feathers.

"Here's the rope." Royce handed over a massive coil.

"This is ridiculous." Hadrian hefted its weight. "This isn't rope, it's string. Was this tested, too?"

Royce nodded. "They test everything."

"And you believed them?"

Royce rolled his eyes.

"Stupid question, but how'd they manage all this in one day?"

Royce chuckled. "You're going to love this." He reached into the bag and hauled out a pair of shoes. They were tiny compared to Hadrian's big leather boots and looked like stripped-down slippers except the tops were canvas and the bottoms looked to be made of a thick tar.

"You asked them to make shoes?"

"I didn't ask them to do half this stuff. Apparently, they all wanted to help. Hundreds worked day and night. Try them on."

Hadrian sat down on the flat stone of the promontory. Royce did likewise, and together they traded big boots for strange slippers.

"This feels really odd," Hadrian said, standing up and bouncing on his toes. "It's like I'm barefoot."

"They're made of something called *rubber* that the dwarfs make from the sap of local trees."

"And you're going to climb in these?"

Royce nodded. "I had my doubts, too. Then I tried them." Royce stood up, moved to the base of the tower, and without using his hands, he began to climb. He went up two strides before dropping back down, but that was enough to make Hadrian's jaw drop. Royce had appeared to walk up invisible steps.

"How'd you do that?"

"Small imperfections in the stone combined with the gripping power of the rubber is an amazing combination. The shoes are better than bare skin. I'll have four hands instead of two."

"This isn't even going to be a challenge, is it?" Hadrian asked with mock disappointment.

Royce looked up, and a grimace overtook his usual frown. "Oh . . . it will be a challenge."

The two finished suiting up. Royce explained in detail the new system the dwarfs had devised. Instead of a pouch dangling from a drawstring, nearly all their gear hung individually from the big loops on the belts. The dwarfs had supplied everything from the chalk Royce would need to keep his fingertips dry, to their meals, and even a small healing kit, all in easily attached containers. In total, everything weighed less than Hadrian's three swords.

"Change your mind about dwarfs yet?" Hadrian asked.

"Are you kidding? This is exactly why I hate them. I'm a thief, and they make locks, doors, and boxes as cleverly crafted as that icebox and these shoes. If anything, this trip has revealed how absolutely awful they really are. Dwarfs are weeds to a farmer, chainmail to a blade, a deep body of water to an armored knight, or an antidote to a poison."

"So you're the poison?" Hadrian asked. "That's surprisingly self-aware."

Royce scowled. "If you're looking for accuracy, they are the pebble in my shoe — small, trivial, but irritating beyond belief."

"You realize you're about to risk your life to save thousands of those frustrating pebbles?"

"Every job has a downside."

They tied up their bags and used rocks to keep the wind from being a thief. Then Royce moved slowly around the tower to a point that faced the open ocean. He pointed at a section of the wall where the fin, or gear's tooth, made a sharp

V with the body of the tower. "I'll start going up along this wedge. You wait here until I reach that crack up there — see it? I'll pound in an anchor, then run a rope down to you. After that, it should be like old times . . . until we get up to there. See that big crevice?"

Hadrian spotted a section a bit more than halfway to the bridge where a massive chunk of the stone fin had fallen away, leaving a bare spot. "We'll need to cross that to get to the niches on the far side and to reach the bridge."

"You make that sound as if it will be a problem."

Royce didn't answer, which was answer enough.

The thief walked him through the steps of the climb, narrating the trip like they were embarking on a stroll about town. Royce wasn't really speaking to him, as Hadrian had nothing to do with the process; he only needed to do what he had done at the Crown Tower — pull himself up along the rope line that Royce secured. Royce was speaking to himself, verbally expressing the mental map he'd created. As he did, the whole of the world illuminated as the moon dawned.

In the span of only minutes, night receded before the advancing brilliance of moonlight, and it quickly became obvious why Royce chose the route he did. The moon was rising in the east; they would climb in the hidden shelter of the tower's dark side.

As Royce made one last check of his gear, Hadrian watched the slow creeping rise of the moon. "It's huge."

Royce looked up and stepped to one side to see. "Near perfect circle. It will be full tomorrow night." He looked at Hadrian. "We can watch it from the dock. I'll even steal a bottle of Montemorcey from The Blue Parrot to toast with."

"Steal? If we're alive to toast the full moon," Hadrian said, "Graxton will *give* you all the wine you can drink, and he'll likely cater our dockside picnic."

Royce frowned. "Killjoy."

Royce began the climb using the corner. He pressed out with his arms and legs, relying on counterbalancing, shifting opposing hands and feet and keeping a hip against the wall to avoid peeling off. He moved upward like a splayed-out water bug. This wasn't a new or difficult technique; it only looked tough. Most of his weight was on his legs, and since they pushed against each other, the effort was low. Balance was the struggle, and the solution was his hips. Leg swings and hip rotations controlled so much more than anyone ever realized — unless they were climbing a nearly vertical wall. With chin to stone and hovering hundreds of feet above the ground and sustained by three points while reaching for the fourth, one got to know the mechanics of their body really well. Even the expansion of his chest for air moved the center of balance outward, and outward was bad.

The truly disconcerting part was the rope. Royce had never used one except for their climb on the Crown Tower. Now, once more, he had this annoying tether like a long tail dangling from his waist. The weight was negligible, but he had to avoid stepping on, or tangling himself in, the line. The first crack was only a few stories up, and once he got a good toehold and set his hip, he was able to grab his hammer and drive his first piton. He connected the rope to the anchor using the handy-dandy double clips the dwarfs had fashioned, then he followed the crack upward. Always searching with his eyes and fingertips, Royce looked for holds or cracks to exploit and new points to anchor.

The line went briefly taut, a signal from Hadrian announcing that he had a hold of Royce — meaning that if his partner slipped, that single piton and Hadrian on the other end of the rope, would keep Royce from falling. At least that was the rumor. While climbing the Crown Tower, Royce found the rope and anchor system tedious, annoying, frustrating, and utterly stupid.

This time is different.

That single announcement-tug felt reassuring. The sensation was unexpected, and the more Royce thought about it, the more disturbing the thought became.

Different.

Royce had scaled hundreds of walls, terraces, and towers where a fall would have killed him. He'd leaped across the gaps between rooftops that he wasn't entirely certain he could clear. Never once had he worried. But now his heart raced, and not in a good way.

Stop thinking.

Climbing was as much in the head as in the limbs. Everything else needed to disappear, to be replaced by a simple operation: hold to hold, step to step, a pause to rest and breathe. Royce struggled to force out distractions and establish a calculated rhythm, his eyes constantly scanning the rock for the slightest imperfections that might be exploited.

For Royce, scaling a sheer wall was a meditative process that brought the world down to a single focus. There was a beauty to the motions, an art to the act. He found it again, and soon he was in a different place where the concerns of the world disappeared and time stopped. He knew there was wind, aware he was rising above a dark ocean, and he had a vague sense that Hadrian was with him, but these were mere ghosts, shadows cast from a different reality. The wall was his world now. The warmth of the rock made it a living thing. Texture gave it personality. Cracks and chips became the imperfections that lent character. The shifting grains suggested a certain attitude and values that could be plumbed by the firmness of edges. He didn't conquer walls; they were a team working together. Rock, Royce felt, was more reliable, more generous, than people. When his fingers went in search of a hold, the wall granted his wish. Often, this gift was not exactly what he had hoped. The wall had a mind of its own, but the way was there; he just needed to find it. The rock spoke in a different language. Learning to bridge that linguistic gap was key. With each reach, step, and pull, Royce learned more about his dance partner, and together they grew close.

The string of clamps and anchors jangled free as he methodically advanced, using mostly his toes while seeking to keep his arms straight to avoid fatigue. The wall was not nearly as perfect as he'd first imagined. Salt, wind, water, sun, and time had devastated the upper reaches where the party really got fun. Whole gashes revealed themselves. From the ground, they appeared as tiny pits or dimples. Up close, they were the yawning mouths of shallow caves where a giant slab of rock had sheared away. Reaching a broad, luxurious ledge that was nearly a whole six inches wide, Royce set a pair of pitons, double-anchored the rope, and tied it tight. Then he tugged three times on the rope. A couple of seconds later, the rope went taut and stayed that way as Hadrian began his climb.

Tethered and seated with knees up, Royce peered out for the first time, and all he saw was ocean and sky. Both were surprisingly bright as the nearly full moon was already high. It hadn't crossed to their side of the tower yet, but it wouldn't be long. While time didn't exist in the climbing mind, it ran through the real-world's hourglass at a shocking rate.

Trusting the anchored rope, Royce leaned out and looked up to check their progress. He was more than halfway to the bridge, which looked a lot larger now. The ledge he rested on was the start of the crevice they would need to cross. Looking down, Royce spotted Hadrian. He was using the pulley-clamp system the dwarfs had built where Hadrian lifted himself by a foot in a loop, then he slid a clamp up and pressed down again. The whole process made him look ridiculous as he jerked his way up, but it was fast, and sooner than expected, Hadrian was up to the ledge.

"This thing works great!" he said, grinning as his head appeared. "It's so much easier than last time."

"Glad you're enjoying yourself," Royce said as he studied the next step.

It hadn't looked like this from the ground. In fact, it had looked nothing like this.

"What's wrong?" Hadrian asked. "Something's wrong. You drop your knife? 'Cause if you did, you're never going to find it."

"I didn't drop my knife."

Royce pulled him up on the ledge. The combined pitons and clamps jingled like poorly tuned bells on a sleigh. Hadrian was puffing for air, his face glistening. Some hair was sticking to his forehead. He brushed away loose stones from the ledge. Royce watched them fall and noticed how they didn't go straight down. The currents of wind caught the pebbles and whirled them out away from the tower, then threw them back against it, where they slapped and bounced off. Eventually, they hit the sea, but at that distance, and in the angry surf, he never saw a splash.

Hadrian tilted his head out and looked up in the direction Royce had been staring. "Okay, so what is it that's spooked you? You didn't spot any soldiers dressed in clothes that would make a clown jealous waiting for us on the bridge, did you?"

"No."

Hadrian pulled two sticks of jerky out of his little pouch and offered one to Royce. "Then why the look?"

"What look?"

"The one you've got right now."

Royce sighed, then he shook his head. After a moment he said, "Different."

Hadrian peered at him and frowned. "That's not an answer, Royce. Not a question, or even a statement. That's just a word."

Royce glared. "This ledge, this gouged-out chunk, I thought it would be different from this."

"How is that a problem?"

"We need to get over that way." Royce pointed in the direction of the bridge.

"I know that."

"So, do you see a way to do it?"

Hadrian laughed and shook his head while chewing. "I didn't even see a way to get here."

"Yeah, well . . . take a look at that gap. We need to get across it. Can't climb on air. I thought this gash made a little bridge. It doesn't — just a nasty cliff."

"What if we go higher?"

"These gear teeth run the full height of the tower. We either have to go all the way to the top and then come back down, or we start over from the bottom, except on the other side of the fin. And if we do that, we run the very real risk of Gravis spotting us."

"And you can't, you know, crawl in and out of the trench?"

"I don't think so. I've been using the inside corner to get up, pushing out, using friction and pressure. To get over there, I'd have to go around the *outside* of the tooth. Pushing out is easier than squeezing, and I'd be more in the wind, and the stone looks pretty smooth. It would be like scaling ice."

"What about up there?" Hadrian asked, pointing to the top of the gash on the far side of the gap where a sizable rock protruded. "Looks like a good handhold there."

"And if I could fly, that would be great."

"So, we're gonna have to climb down?" Hadrian sighed, looking below them. "It will be dawn by the time we get back up to this point."

"Did it really take that long?"

Hadrian nodded. "We're running out of time, Royce. And if we have to pull out all these anchors to use again . . ."

Royce looked up at that single handhold of rock the size of a small lemon. It was up and over the gap. He'd need to run the length of their six-inch ledge, then literally jump through the air across the open gap and hope to catch it.

"What are you thinking?" Hadrian asked.

"I might be able to jump it."

"Jump?" Hadrian looked shocked, but only for a second. "Sure, of course. You'll have the rope. If you fall, it will catch you, and I'll reel you up."

Royce shook his head. "I won't make it with the rope."

"You're going to jump without a rope?" Hadrian looked down and then back up at the rock. "It's a long way down, Royce."

"I know, which makes this a big decision."

The moon was well up. It had to be getting close to midnight. If they went down now and then came back up, it might be daylight by the time they reached the bridge. Gravis would easily see them. If there was a door where the bridge joined the tower — and there had to be — the dwarf would lock it. And if that lock was anything like the one at the base — and Hadrian couldn't think of a single reason why that wouldn't be the case — it was over. Tur Del Fur would be destroyed, hundreds, probably thousands, of lives would be lost, and Rehn Purim would have died for nothing.

"You're thinking something," Royce said. "What is it?"

Hadrian pushed down the sickening sensation that always rose whenever he had to do something ugly. "Just wondering why it took so long to get up here."

"It's a long climb."

Hadrian shrugged. "You climbed the Crown Tower a lot faster."

"This is harder."

Hadrian stared at Royce, feeling sick. The climb hadn't done it. Even sitting on that six-inch ledge — so high up that if there were birds, they would be flying beneath his feet — hadn't done it. Hadrian was sick because of what he was about to do. He pursed his lips and made a dismissive sound. "Maybe. Could it also be that you're scared?"

This brought Royce's head around, eyes glaring.

"It's Gwen, isn't it?" Hadrian said. "You didn't know her when we climbed the Crown Tower. You didn't care if you died because you didn't have a life, nothing to lose. And don't bother denying it. I know it's the truth because I felt the same way. Still do, sort of. No friends, no family, no real future; neither one of us has anything we're upset at leaving behind. At least we didn't until now. I still don't, but you . . . you're afraid now because you've got something to live for. You danced with her, kissed her. You know for the first time you have a future that isn't all blood and death. You're terrified of losing that. It's easy to bluff when your pockets are empty; it's a lot harder to make a blind jump when you've got skin in the game, right?"

Royce stared at him for several seconds. "No," he said, but it lacked anger or even the usual dismissive tone Royce used when he thought Hadrian had said something stupid. Then Royce sighed. "I'm afraid of letting her down. She said she believed in me."

"Gwen's a big girl, Royce. She'll find someone else — someone better, I suspect. Just about anyone would do, really."

"Since when did you become a bastard?"

"Same time you became a coward."

Royce's eyes narrowed. His mouth leveled out into that straight thin line. "Careful, this is a thin ledge."

"Do it," Hadrian dared.

Confusion flooded Royce's face. "You really want to fight me . . . here?"

Hadrian rolled his eyes. "No! I want you to make that jump!"

"What? Why? What do you care, Mister I-have-nothing-to-live-for? What difference can it make to you? Don't tell me you're jealous."

The last statement hurt because deep down, Hadrian couldn't deny there was a little jealousy. Gwen was an incredible woman. To have someone like that love you? If the situation were reversed, Hadrian wouldn't risk that jump. He wouldn't even have started this climb. Only one thing could get him to do it. "Because I don't want to watch you tell Gwen that Tur Del Fur is gone and thousands of people died because of her."

"Because of . . ." Royce was bewildered. "It's not because of her; it's because of me."

"Yeah, sure." Hadrian took another bite of the jerky. Then he wagged the stick of meat at Royce as he chewed. "Really think she'll see it that way, do you?"

That did it. Hadrian saw it in Royce's eyes. They went wide. This was a new factor in his calculations—a big one. Royce was incapable of imagining how Gwen might blame herself. In his world, that notion was the same as considering the possibility that rocks might float or that time might start running backward. But Royce had gotten to know Gwen. He saw firsthand how a healthy normal conscience worked. He knew her well enough to realize that some rocks did float.

Royce gritted his teeth and looked again at that distant handhold. It made Hadrian want to vomit.

Hadrian had seen him make longer, more precarious, leaps. He wouldn't have pushed him otherwise, but there was a difference between making a jump you're confident about and attempting one you're not. In battle, doubt was often the point of failure, while confidence tipped the scales in a person's favor. The slightest mistake would see Royce falling hundreds of feet to his death. Doubt was deadly.

Royce didn't say a word, but he reached down and unhooked the rope from his harness, letting it dangle from the clamp. Then he stood up and moved to the end of the ledge and peered across the gap. The wind blew back his hair. His cloak had been stowed for the climb, and without it, Royce looked small and thin, like a long-haired cat soaked to the bone. He let go of the wall and stood like a tightrope walker. Then he backed up.

Hadrian got out of his way, granting him as much ledge as he could.

Please, Maribor, Novron, Drome, and anyone else who can hear a prayer—give him wings.

Royce crouched. He took several breaths, puffing his cheeks in the process. Then in a burst, he sprinted forward. His footfalls made no sound as he ran. Then reaching the end of the short track, with his last step, Royce leaped.

If it had been Hadrian, he would have flailed through the air, then slammed into the far wall, bounced off, and fallen to his death. Royce flew tight, elbows in, face forward. He landed across the gap and just stayed there. Hadrian had seen flies pull similar stunts on windowpanes. In an instant, Royce mantled up, climbed to another tiny ledge, and sat, legs dangling. "Throw me the next coil of rope," he shouted back. "Keep an end."

Hadrian took several breaths, letting his heart calm down before throwing the line over. Royce hauled it up, drove in a new anchor and tied it off. "You're going to have to swing across now."

"Royce," Hadrian said. "You know I did that on purpose, right? I didn't want to, but I knew you needed a little push. I was honestly terrified for you."

Royce grinned back. "Are you worried I might cut the rope as you swing?"

Hadrian looked down at a whole lot of nothing. He hadn't until that moment. "Maybe."

"If it makes you feel better, I knew what you were doing."

"You did?"

"I'm not an idiot."

"Wait . . . So you knew I was manipulating you, and you decided to make the jump anyway but didn't tell me? What if you'd fallen? What if you died? I'd be here thinking I killed you."

"I was okay with that."

Hadrian frowned. "Allow me to return the bastard crown to you."

"Careful, you have a dangerous swing to make," Royce shouted back to him over the roar of the wind. "We'll be using this new coil for the rest of the climb, but keep that other line attached to you so we can use it if we come back this way. Just make sure you leave enough slack to make the swing."

Hadrian kept the old line hooked to his belt and ran the new line through as well. Then he grabbed hold of the new rope, took up all the slack he could for his pendulum swing across the gap. When he stepped off the ledge, he fell.

There was a brief tug-and-give as Hadrian felt the anchor pop. He also thought he heard a faint *ping!* and felt like a child on a swing if the branch above had snapped. The rope went limp. Hadrian's stomach flew up into his mouth as he began the free fall. In a panic, he reached out, but just as Royce had explained . . . *"can't climb on air."*

So, this is how I die . . . Interesting.

CHAPTER THIRTY-FOUR

The Bridge

Hadrian woke with a bright light in his eyes. He suspected it might be morning, but it turned out to be the dazzling brilliance of the moon. He was facing up, dangling from a rope that was pulling him upward at the waist with short unpleasant jerks.

"You awake?" Royce called from somewhere above. His voice was strained and out of breath.

"I think so."

"What do you mean by you *think* so? You're talking."

"Maybe I'm dead."

"I wouldn't bother pulling you up if that were the case. Now, grab hold of that line and pull yourself the rest of the way. I'm tired."

Hadrian caught hold of the rope attached to his waist. As he did, he noticed a ringing in his ears, and his head was throbbing. Reaching up, he felt bandages.

"Can you climb?" Royce called.

Hadrian pulled and found nothing wrong with his arms, back, or legs. "I think so."

"Okay. See if you can get up. I'm gonna rest a bit."

Hadrian gritted his teeth against the pounding in his head that only increased as he exerted himself. Using feet wrapped around the rope and the old-fashioned hand-over-hand method, Hadrian scaled the twenty or thirty feet to where Royce waited on a broad ledge of rock.

"By Mar, you're heavy," Royce said.

"What happened?"

"I didn't cut the rope."

"I didn't say you did." Hadrian was rubbing the back of his head where a big bump had grown.

"If I had wanted you dead —"

"I'm not accusing you, Royce."

The thief scowled at him with angry eyes.

"I'm not," Hadrian insisted. "But what did happen?"

"The anchor on my side came free the moment you started your swing. You fell and the other rope caught you. Then you swung back and clapped your head on the wall. You've been out ever since."

"How did my head get wrapped?"

"I did it," Royce said, his voice still irritated. "You were bleeding. Skull wounds are nasty that way. What else was I going to do?"

"I'm not complaining."

"Sounds like it."

"I'm just confused. How did you wrap my head *before* pulling me up?"

"I didn't. I had to climb down, swing over to where you were dangling like a fish on a line. Then I had to stop the bleeding. I wrapped and cleaned you up — all while the two of us dangled in midair. I now know how a spider feels wrapping a fly. Then, because you were still breathing but not waking, and we have a schedule to keep, I used that dwarven pulley system to haul you."

"How far up did you . . ." Hadrian looked around.

His first thought was about the luxuriousness of the ledge they were sitting on. An instant later, he knew it couldn't be a ledge. *Too big, too broad.* Leaning back, Hadrian looked past Royce and saw a span of rock that ran all the way to the South Tower. "We're on the bridge?"

"Just so you know," Royce said. "I was using that same anchor for support when you pulled it. I fell, too. I was able to catch myself, so you weren't the only one to take a spill."

"It's okay, Royce. Really."

Royce glared. The man was angrier than Hadrian had seen him in years. Hadrian couldn't understand it.

"It's not okay." Then his eyes focused on the bandages around Hadrian's head. "It's not all right at all."

Hadrian found it a bit hard to believe that he was standing on the bridge. After three weeks of looking up at it and framing that seemingly thin span as an impossible goal — here they were. In less than two days, he and Royce had done what — after weeks of trying — a city full of some of the most capable people in the world were unable to achieve.

Tur Del Fur lay below them, dark and empty. Hadrian could finally see the entire story revealed. From the flat and barren tabletop of the West Echo plateau, the pale white of the cliffs appeared as a violent gash cutting down through the wall of rock. Zigzagging to and fro across the cliff, the greenery of the many tiers dressed the wound, giving it color and life on its journey to the sea. More than that, Hadrian could see the pattern left behind by the towers' creators. Circles, invisible from the ground, radiated out from Drumindor's base as if it were the center of a great quarry. Hadrian had assumed the cliffs were natural and the tiers added to them. Now he saw that the bluffs had been created when the whole of the point had been mined away, leaving the two towers at the bottom. The tiers were merely extensions of the road. Berling's Way was just that, the route Berling and his workers took to get to the bottom and back out. Tur Del Fur wasn't a natural paradise. The whole of Terlando Bay and the cliffs that surrounded it were the dressed-up remains of a construction site. The rolkins, temples, mansions, and shops were merely added afterthoughts.

They now had access to both towers but stayed with the north one, as they were already there and crossing the bridge was an unnecessary risk, not to mention

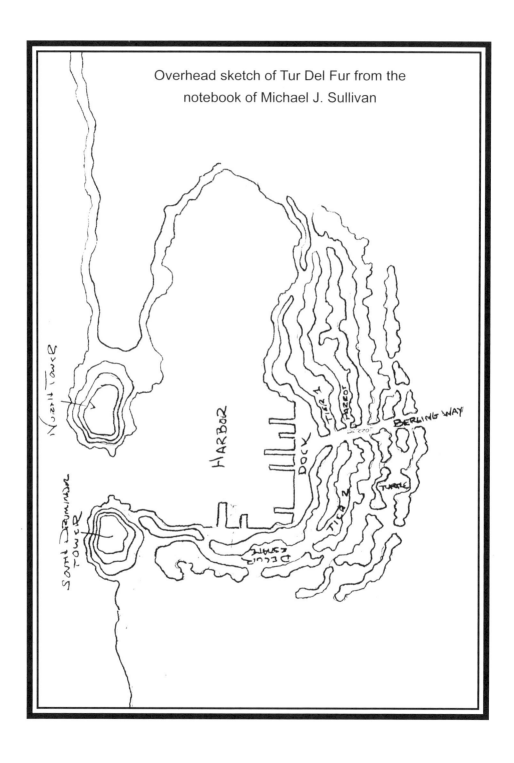

the distance between the two wasn't insignificant. With the moonrise, the open span felt as exposed to watching eyes as a barren field was to a pair of deer.

"Well, at least I can see it; that's something," Royce said as the two approached the place where the bridge met the tower. At the intersection was an elaborate sheltered porch created from three recessed openings that nested one within the next. Each was decorated with dwarven symbols etched inside squares. At the center of them was a thin grooved outline of a rectangle that indicated the presence of an entrance.

This was no ordinary door. The thing was made of stone, lacked hinges, and had no massive nails studding its face, and most terrifying of all: no keyhole, latch, knob, or handle.

Royce studied the threshold for a long moment, then placed his hand at the center and pushed. Then he pushed again. Then Royce did nothing for a long time, and Hadrian felt his heart sink.

Eleven hours later, they were still on the bridge.

By then, the sun was high, and Hadrian sat inside the porch. He opened his little pouch to search for more to eat. They hadn't brought much. Food and water were heavy, and they had needed to be light. The climb was only supposed to take a few hours. As the night had dragged on, the excitement and fear of discovery faded into boredom. Hadrian had walked the length of the bridge several times. When morning came, he slept in the meager shade of the multi-tiered entryway that the door allowed. Royce, who was back in his cloak and hood, had stood, sat, paced, and examined the door at the other end of the bridge. The two were identical, right down to their impenetrability.

"Want a jerky stick?" Hadrian asked, holding one up as if Royce were a dog.

Royce, who sat across from the door, glared at him.

"You know, a little nourishment might help. I personally can't think on an empty stomach. Can't do much of anything on an empty stomach, really. It's probably why you haven't gotten anywhere."

"I'm not hungry."

"Thirsty? We have a little water left."

"I'm not thirsty, either."

"You've got to drink, Royce. You're sitting in the sun in a black cloak. That's how they make game pies, you know. They cover a bunch of songbirds with a blanket of crust, toss in a few mushrooms, carrots, and onions, then bake. And up here, you do sort of look like a blackbird."

"That's not how they make game pies," Royce told him. "If you did it that way, there'd be feathers. The meat is pre-cooked into a stew, then added to the pie."

Hadrian nodded. "You might be right about that."

"Will you please shut up; I'm trying to think."

Hadrian took a bite of the pork jerky, which had been spiced with pineapple juice, brown sugar, and rum. It tasted wonderful, and he suspected it would have even if he hadn't been trapped with a limited amount of food. If push came to shove, however, he'd have traded it for a game pie. "You've been *thinking* for nearly half a day and haven't gotten anywhere. You realize we've only got about ten hours left to get away."

Royce faced him with a look that explained in painful detail that he knew all this and did not appreciate the recap.

Hadrian took another bite: a small one. He needed to make the meal last. He sat with his back to the door, his legs stretched out. His feet were now in the sun and getting hot. The never-ending wind helped, but the constant burning light was bothersome when he couldn't escape it. Also distressing was that he was able to eat in peace. Hadrian had never been to a coast where gulls did not fill the air with their constant *caws* and squeaky-door squeals. Normally, he'd be fighting them off in order to have his meal, but not today. And it wasn't like he was sitting too high. The birds used to be there — the face of the bridge had plenty of white splotches. Now there was only the constant howl of the wind. The silence was absolutely creepy.

What do the gulls know that I don't?

"And I *have* gotten somewhere," Royce said.

"You have?"

Royce waved an arm at the entirety of the nested porch. "Come out here and look."

Hadrian stood up, walked out from underneath the overhang, bending over until he was free of it. Then joined Royce's study of the doorway.

"This is a combination lock, and the symbols around the doorway are tumblers. Each one is carved into identically sized squares. I'm guessing if you press on them, they'll slide in. If you engage the right ones, the door will unlock. So, the question is which ones to push."

"You read dwarven runes?"

"I don't need to because the code is just a date. I only need to figure out which one, and how to indicate it."

"And what makes you think that?"

Royce looked over with the face of a card player who'd had his hand called but wasn't bluffing. "A date would be easy to remember. It could be the year of their first ruler's coronation, or something far more obscure, but still a date every dwarf would know but no one else would." He indicated the smallest threshold. "Drumindor is purged of pressure once every full moon, putting it on a lunar schedule. So the first two thresholds are easy. This frame has twelve symbols etched in it, and there are twelve lunar cycles in a year." He pointed at the middle one. "This one has twenty-eight, the number of *days* in a lunar cycle. And the big one has ninety-nine symbols. Which I am guessing somehow indicates the year, but last I checked, there are more than ninety-nine years of recorded history. So I don't know why there are —"

"Dwarfs have ninety-nine individual numbers. I remember Auberon saying something about that."

"Okay. Still doesn't solve the issue but good to know."

"So, we need to figure out the most significant date to the dwarfs or at least to the builders of Drumindor and —"

"No," Royce shook his hood. "The combination has been changed."

"How do you know? What makes you think that's even possible?"

"You can't build something that has a combination and expect it to stay the same for thousands of years. Someone is going to tell the wrong person, then it becomes useless. So the lock must have the ability to be changed from time to time — either when the current date is discovered, or on some regular basis. But it certainly isn't the same one as when the tower was first built. When Gravis entered, he closed the door, and since no one else knew how to open it, he must have also changed the locks."

"That means we need to figure out what date *Gravis* would have used."

"Exactly." Royce nodded. "And we also need to determine how to enter it. As for possible dates, I've limited it to three possibilities: Gravis's birthday, the date Drumindor was completed, or the day he was fired. Do you know when Drumindor was finished or Gravis's birth date?"

Hadrian shook his head.

"Neither do I, nor can we find out, so we might as well ignore those. As for when he was fired, we can take a stab at that. We got the job three weeks ago, so let's work backward from there. Given that Albert already had the coach waiting when we got to Medford, he must have commissioned it the day before, so let's add a day for that. Now, it would take time for a courier to deliver any message from Lady Constance to Albert. Assuming the messenger took the conventional route, that would add another eleven days. The difficult question remaining is, how much time was there between the day Lord Byron fired Gravis and when he hired Lady Constance? Albert mentioned the Triumvirate weren't going to do anything, which forced Lord Byron to hire us, so we can assume he met with them prior to speaking to her. That means he probably didn't hire Constance the day Gravis was let go. In fact, I suspect it took several days. Let's say, I don't know, about a week?"

"Sounds reasonable."

"So what does that add up to?"

"Forty."

"Okay, that's more than a month, which would put it in last month's lunar cycle."

"I still wish one of us could read dwarven runes."

Royce shook his head. "Not necessary, but we are missing some pieces to this puzzle, like whether a dwarven lunar cycle starts with the full moon or when there is no moon at all."

"I can answer that for you."

"You can?" Royce looked shocked.

"Do you remember Sloan? The bartender at that hidden dwarven pub? She said we were reaching the height of the Wolf Moon, so we're at the halfway mark, meaning it doesn't start with the full moon; it starts with the *new* moon."

Royce nodded and frowned. "That makes perfect sense."

"You're upset because you didn't think of it, aren't you?"

"Less upset and more surprised." Royce thought a moment. "Okay, since we're at a full moon now, the start of the last moon's cycle would be exactly six weeks ago. So forty-two minus forty is two. If we were trying to indicate the first day of the cycle, we would use the first symbol. If we add two to that, we'd use the third one."

Royce studied the symboled frames. "Assuming the numbers are presented in order from lowest to highest, we can just count starting at one side or the other. Do you know if they read left to right or right to left?"

"Does it even matter? You could try it from each direction, right? If you had started pressing random squares when we arrived, you probably would have it opened by now."

Royce shook his head. "There are millions upon millions of possible combinations, so probably not. Sure, a typical lock is forgiving in that it relies on frustration to make you give up before you get in. But this is a dwarven door, which means it's anything but ordinary. If you go through enough trouble to use a combination, it's a safe bet that there will only be a certain number of attempts before punishing the forgetful or the uninformed. And who knows what that might be."

Royce looked up at the tower as if it was watching them. "It could be a stone that falls and crushes us. Maybe there's a hidden trap door that looks like you're standing on solid stone until it opens and —"

"Or the whole bridge might collapse." Hadrian looked down at the stone beneath his feet. He imagined the entire span slipping free of the towers and falling as one piece, or maybe the whole thing would be rigged to shatter into tiny blocks.

Royce nodded. "In theory yes, but I doubt it. Destroying this bridge would punish more than the idiot at the door who didn't know they changed the lock. Most likely, too many failed attempts will disable the mechanism for a period of time — could be hours, could be days." He looked up again. "Or it could still be a block of stone to the head."

Royce returned his attention to the doorway and pointed at the first set of markings. "And there's another thing. It's not just whether you count from the left or right, but you have to know which month comes first."

"The first month follows Wintertide," Hadrian said. "The rebirth of the sun."

"For *us,* yeah, but dwarfs might have picked *their* first month based on the day one of their kings was born. When you think about it, there's no reason for us to mark our years starting at Wintertide. Why not Summersrule? It's a much better time to celebrate than a cold, dark day in winter."

Hadrian shrugged. "Hope, I suppose."

"Hope?"

"Be pretty pessimistic to start your calendar looking ahead to diminishing days and the cold bleak of winter."

Royce considered this, and as he did, Hadrian stepped closer and studied the twelve symbols. They weren't entirely abstract; each was a little stylized picture. He spotted a dog symbol third from the end and next to it was a snowflake. He grinned. "Dwarfs read right to left, and they do start their calendar on Wintertide just like us."

Royce stared at him skeptically. "Why do you say that?"

Hadrian pointed at the snowflake symbol. "Last month was the Snow Moon."

"Did Sloan teach you the entire dwarven calendar?"

"Only those two, but because the dog — or wolf — is to the left of the snowflake, they read right to left."

Royce smiled at Hadrian. "You're not nearly as useless as everyone says."

"You're welcome."

"Okay, now comes the hard part. The year. How can you specify a particular year — that runs into the thousands — with just ninety-nine symbols?"

Hadrian added, "And that number would always be increasing, I doubt they add symbols, and at some point you'd run out of room on the lintel."

Royce nodded. "They must have come up with another way to indicate years." Royce touched the door frame sliding his fingers up the stone. "Whoever designed this lock wasn't a poet. He was an engineer. To work, this thing needs to be simple and logical." Royce thought a moment, then turned to Hadrian. "Why didn't you bring a chair up here to sit on?"

"You need to sit to think?"

"Just answer the question."

"Because it would have been stupid."

"Be more specific."

"Why do you need a chair, Royce?"

Royce shook his head in irritation. "Just answer the question. Why didn't you haul a chair up here?"

"Because a chair is too big, heavy, and cumbersome to carry up this tower and we don't need it."

"Exactly," Royce grinned. "A practical mind abhors waste. If you don't need it and you're short on space, don't bother with it. Everyone knows this is the year 2991, and if I said remember back in '88 when Essendon's castle burned down, you wouldn't need me to explain it was 2988, would you? That makes the first two digits a bit unnecessary. So what if this outer frame is just for the last two digits in the year?"

Hadrian was unconvinced.

Royce waved at the doorway. "It's the only way it can work."

Hadrian shrugged. "Well, we have to try something. So why not?"

"Okay, this is the year 2991, so let's count back nine from the left."

"Wait!" Hadrian said.

"What?"

"It's not 2991."

"I'm pretty sure it is."

"No, that's the year in Imperial Reckoning. For dwarfs, it is the year 777,745."

Royce stared at him for a long moment as if unable to decide which question should come first. "Let me guess, Sloan again?"

Hadrian nodded. "Yeah, she told me the dwarven year differed from Imperial Reckoning. Theirs is based on the day Eton first shone on Elan."

"What is Eton?"

Hadrian waved a hand dismissively. "Doesn't matter."

"And you remembered the *exact* number?"

Hadrian thought about it and shrugged. "It's strange. I usually can't keep track of the number of drinks I've had, but well, you don't spend as much time in bars as I do. I've learned that knowing bits of otherwise useless information comes in handy. And dates are usually worth remembering. One day some fella is going to wager a round on that very number and be devastated when I know it. So, my mind stores stuff."

"You live in a completely different reality, don't you?"

"Compared to yours? I certainly hope so."

Royce looked back at the symbols. "Okay, let's do this. We'll start with the year then the month; if we can't get those, the city is doomed — unless Gravis pops his head out to see who is messing with the door and we manage to trap it open with a toe. Honestly, as far as I see it, that's our best chance. The choice of day is more than a bit of a guess, but we might get enough tries to vary that a couple times. Hopefully we'll get lucky."

Royce counted to forty-five starting from the right. Before he pressed it, Hadrian verified the spot with his own count. It did, indeed, push into the frame and stay. Hadrian hadn't a clue if the sliding block was good or bad. It was, however, something, which was oh-so better than nothing. Royce moved to the set of twelve and pressed the snow symbol. It, too, stayed in, and Hadrian thought it was a positive sign that the first one hadn't popped out.

"Okay, here we go," Royce said. He hesitated with his finger over the third symbol from the right, then pressed. The moment it slid in, all the symbols, including the last one, popped back out, and there was a noticeable *clap*.

Royce pushed on the door, but it remained immovable. "Okay, that wasn't right. And I didn't like the sound of that clap."

"Try a different day," Hadrian suggested.

This time Royce pressed on the second symbol. Again, the pieces of stone snapped back and once more came another *clap*.

"How many more guesses do you think we have?" Hadrian asked.

"Not sure."

"Considering all the estimates and speculation we used, I hope it's a lot."

Royce pondered his next choice. As he did, Hadrian began to have second thoughts.

"Then his wife died, and now he has nothing to live for. Many say there's nothing to stop him; he's got nothing to lose."

Royce was about to try again with the fourth symbol when Hadrian stopped him. "Wait, I think we have it wrong."

Royce almost chuckled, "I'm guessing we're wrong about a great many things, but what specifically are you referring to?"

"Think about it. Gravis is about to destroy Drumindor. But you don't destroy something you love."

"You do if you don't want anyone else to have it."

Hadrian rocked his head considering the thought. "Maybe, but let me ask you this: if Gwen ran off with Dixon, would you kill her?"

"No, but Dixon might want to watch his back."

"Exactly!" Hadrian said.

"Why are you always talking about Gwen and Dixon?"

"It doesn't matter. Just shut up and listen. This isn't about Gravis's job. He wants *revenge* for the *loss* of what he loved most. So the date that has become most important to him is the day he lost his wife!"

Royce looked at Hadrian, appearing perplexed. "You could be right. Strange."

"What is?"

"That you figured that out, and I didn't."

"Because you think I'm stupid?"

"No, I've never thought that. Intentionally naïve to a fault, sure, but not stupid. No, it's just that revenge is my language, not yours. Okay, so when did she die? Did Sloan mention that, too?"

"She died the night of the full moon, and he was driven from that shack about a week after Ena's death."

"No, Auberon did. He said Gravis's wife died on the night of the full moon."

Royce smiled. "That would have been last month's full moon, so no change there." He kept the year and the month the same. Finally, he held his finger over the fourteenth symbol. "Ready?"

Hadrian nodded. "Let's hope Gravis loved his wife."

Royce pressed the symbol.

Nothing happened.

They both waited for several seconds. There was no snapping back of symbols, no clap. Nothing.

"Did you miss one of them?" Hadrian asked. "Are they all in as deep as they should be?"

Royce looked. "Yes, they're all in." But he pressed each one again to no avail.

"Try the door."

Royce placed his hands in the middle of the outline cut in stone and pushed. Nothing.

"Now what?" Hadrian asked.

"Give me a minute," Royce said. "Let me think."

A minute turned into another seven hours.

Royce was certain they were close. In fact, he was positive the door was unlocked. The symbols he had used must have been correct or they would have popped out just like the other two tries. All he needed was to turn the knob, but he had no idea how to do that. The knowledge was beyond infuriating. The answer had to be a simple thing, and yet it left him utterly defeated.

"Royce," Hadrian said, "the sun is going down. We're almost out of time. If we go right now, and jog all the way, we might make it to the top of the cliff."

"I'm so close!"

"You tried your best."

"Bastard dwarfs! By Mar, I hate them!" He kicked the stone.

Click.

"You want to go down first or—"

"Quiet!" Royce said. He listened. "Did you hear it?"

"Hear what?"

Royce studied the entrance. "Look, you can see a seam now. This is a double door."

Hadrian stared. "You managed that by kicking it?"

"I'm too tall. I'm not a dwarf. I was pressing too high earlier."

Royce felt the surface of the stone at dwarf level, letting his fingers examine what his eyes couldn't see. He found two indentations, one on each of the double doors. He pressed one. It clicked but then popped out such that it was once again flush with the surface.

"Okay, I heard it that time," Hadrian said and joined him. "Door still doesn't open?"

"Not yet," Royce said.

Using both hands, Royce reached out, located the two triggers, then pressed them at the same time.

Click-clack.

"What does that mean?" Hadrian asked.

Royce grinned. "It means I have it."

He placed his palm on the center — of what had been, for the last eighteen hours, a solid stone wall — and pushed. A pair of double doors swung open.

CHAPTER THIRTY-FIVE

The Wall

Stepping through the small door, Royce and Hadrian entered into a strange new world of bewildering confusion. Everywhere they looked were stairs, platforms, axles, and gears. Thousands of interconnected cogs ran vertically, horizontally, and on varying angles. There were flat gears, round gears, solid and hollow gears. Some were diamond-shaped while others looked like grooved toy tops — the serrated heads of giant drills. Hadrian spotted some the size of thimbles and others as big as ships. A few were so massive that he couldn't tell if they were gears or parts of a wall. Some spun with a soft whir, others clicked with constant and perfect repetition, and the big ones didn't appear to move at all. There were levers, also of varying sizes and lengths, along with dials, switches, and cranks. The place was illuminated by yellow and green light. The green came from colored crystals similar to the ones used in Scram Scallie but far larger. The yellow, which was far too golden to be sunlight, shone out of massive glass-covered apertures, as if a great fire burned behind them. Some natural white light spilled from high overhead, but it was faint and hazy, as if showing signs of wear from having bumped and bounced its way down. The whole of the interior smelled of grease, oil, smoke, and cut metal.

The two stood just inside the door, overwhelmed. There had to be a dozen different directions to go, all of them leading into the jungle of cogs and the maze of stairs and catwalks.

"How long do we have?" Royce asked.

Hadrian looked back out at the sun. "Two—maybe three—hours until sundown. Then what? Another hour before moonrise? So, three to four hours, I guess."

Royce sighed. "Up or down?"

"Down, I think."

"Why?"

Hadrian shrugged. "Because up is harder."

"Works for me." Royce picked a path much the way he did in a forest, relying on a sort of gut instinct: this one feels better than that one, and he started down a set of narrow stone steps. "And remember, when we find Gravis—don't kill him. We'll need the little monster alive."

"Yeah, because between the two of us, I'm the one prone to mindless murder."

Everything appeared to be moving. All around them was the sound of machinery: clicks, claps, whirs, ticks, and even the occasional tolling of a bell. After a short while, Royce noticed it wasn't all noise. The sounds repeated. An ongoing rhythmic symphony composed of a million instruments played in the background. Without realizing, Royce began keeping pace, stepping down the stairs to match the common time subdivision of beats. To move out of sync annoyed him.

They came upon rooms large and small. Some were a mystery, like the tiny cubicles lined in sheets of hand-beaten copper, but most were easily identified. There were loads of storage rooms. One they found jammed full of broken cogs, while another was crammed with unbroken ones. They passed by meeting rooms, eating halls, dormitories, even baths, but most of the doors they passed led to workshops. These, too, presented a variety of tasks that could be deduced by the layout of furniture and tools. Stone blocks, hammers, and chisels, not to mention works in progress, defined the abode of a sculptor. Saws, planers, mallets, files, and drills, arrayed on a pegboard beside boxes full of various-shaped spindles, told the story of a woodworker whose main task had been to make handles for tools. There were glassblowing shops, rooms that made nothing but nails, and others that made only screws. All told, Royce and Hadrian found just about everything except the flesh and bone of a living dwarf or a walking dead man.

They were on what appeared to be a productive path that led down several flights of curving stairs only to find the route going back up. This frustrated Royce until he spotted a new passage hidden behind and beneath a complicated series of gears and pulleys. At another point on this insane trail of whirling sprockets, the solution to the baffling dead end was through a trapdoor in the floor, where the two descended by way of sliding down a brass pole.

Then, after a lengthy descent, the two passed through an ornate double door and entered the strangest chamber so far. Five stories tall, at least by dwarven standards, the room had six walls of smooth stone and a domed, vaulted ceiling. By some magic of stonework, sunlight penetrated the space, making it brighter than any other. The reason was obvious, for while there was not a scrap of furniture in the room, the walls were covered in murals.

Royce was reminded of the frescoes he'd seen in the Abbey of Brecken Moor. These had that same flat approach to art, lacking any sense of depth or perspective, but they were not frescoes. These images were painted directly on naked stone. They were also far simpler as they lacked backgrounds or any concept of shading. The colors were flat, making heavy use of outlines, often aided by chisel work that added a three-dimensional aspect to the image. And while each wall was composed of a different set of images, the palette was always limited to only three colors: ocher, turquoise, and charcoal black.

On the far side of the room was another door, which Royce made for straightaway with Hadrian close behind. The door was the typical sort that required ducking to get through, but the moment Royce touched it, the whole thing appeared to dissolve as if it too had only been painted on the wall. Royce gave it a solid shove just the same, receiving nothing in return.

"Dead end," he told Hadrian.

Turning around, Royce saw a gray-haired dwarf standing just outside the room, looking at them.

"Gravis!" Royce hissed and lunged forward.

Inside the shortest measure of the fastest tick of the gears, the other door, the one they had just entered, closed. Before Royce could reach it, the door dissolved.

"That can't be good," Hadrian said as Royce frantically searched the wall for any sign of what had once been. They both scanned the chamber for any means of escape and found none.

"Change your mind about dwarfs yet?" Royce asked, seething.

Hadrian continued to study the walls and floor while slowly pivoting but nodded. "I'm starting to see your side of the argument."

"Hello, gentlemen, and welcome to Drumindor." The voice came from high above, where a small portal opened inside a portion of the vaulted ceiling. Barely big enough to pass a hand through, it offered no hope of escape. On the far side, filling the entirety of the little peephole, was the face of Gravis Berling. "It is awfully nice of you to visit. Impressive, too. That was a long climb, wasn't it? The important thing is that you made it here just in time for the show. The curtain goes up in just a few hours, and granted, for you, the spectacle won't be a long one, but I guarantee you'll never forget it as long as you live."

Gravis slammed the little peephole door shut.

With the little door closed, Gravis's feigned bravado dissolved. He collapsed, shaking and breathing hard both from the sudden activity of running around and sealing the men in the mural room and from the stress that if his trap had failed the men would have killed him. Gravis lay in the little access loft that was used for cleaning the upper portions of the ancient murals, a tight narrow space even for a Dromeian. He felt trapped, and the close quarters had little to do with it.

Who, by Drome, are they?

Gravis lay on his back, his heart pounding as he stared up at the dark ceiling that was only two feet overhead.

Why would anyone come in here now? To stop me, acourse. But why now? Everyone else has left. All the tall folk, anyway. Who are these people?

Gravis knew the answer; he just didn't want to accept it. But there was no mistaking their equipment. The rope they used, the harnesses around their waists—those were not made by men. That they were able to open the bridge door said a lot. The fact they were here just hours before the rising of the full moon, making their quest a likely suicide, revealed even more.

"What do you want from me, Ena?" he whispered in the dark. "Why are you making this so hard?"

He waited, listening as he always did. And as always, he heard only silence.

"All right, all right, I admit it, I wanted revenge," he bellowed, and his voice rattled down the length of the horizontal duct, sounding small and sad. "I wanted to hurt them — kill them. Drumindor belonged to me. I have a greater claim on it than anyone, and it hurt to have it taken away . . . but it only hurt my pride. Acourse that's what they warned you about, isn't it, Ena? That in the end, the pride of the Berlings would break your heart. That's what they told you, and you died believing it — believing they were right."

"Gah!" Gravis punched the stone wall so hard he nearly broke his fingers.

"And yet, everything they did to me is nothing compared to what I did to you." His words became tiny whispers that barely cleared the hairs of his mustache. "I don't want to hurt them, Ena. I don't want to hurt anyone. I just want . . ." Gravis wiped tears with his beard. "All I want is for you to hear me. I want you to know that I do love you. Why did you have to die before I could say it, before I could prove it? I'd have done anything, if I had only known. And I still will. I'll set fire to the scraps of my pride and bury the legacy of my entire family if that's what it takes to convince you. But there are innocent people now. I thought they would all leave. Why didn't they go? I told them. I put out the sign. I warned them! They know what's coming. So why?"

Gravis cried. His beard was long, but not long enough, and soon it was as soaked as his face. Then he lay still until his breathing returned to normal. "What do I do with them? I'm not a murderer, Ena. You know that. I'm just a stupid, old dwarf, a lousy Dherg, who was too blind to see the treasure that slept beside me each night. I'll do anything for you, Ena. But is this what you really want? Can you hear me, Ena? Because I can't hear you. Please, love, please talk to me. Tell me what you want. And if it isn't too much trouble, could you make it quick? Because time is running out."

Royce made a frantic but detailed study of the tiny chamber, inspecting every corner, angle, and seam in the stone — cursing as he did. He knew there had to be a mechanism. Somewhere was a way out. No one decorated the interior of a prison cell with murals, and he doubted an imprisoned artist would have had access to paint.

"Royce," Hadrian said.

"What?" Royce growled. The thief was down on all fours, his head touching the floor as he made his way around the room, searching for a dent or seam.

"Up there."

Hadrian was sitting with his head tilted back as he stared at the wall opposite him.

Thinking his partner had spied a way out, Royce followed Hadrian's line of sight. It only took a second to see what prompted the comment, and while of no help, Royce was just as captivated by what he saw. In bewildered disbelief, Royce got off his hands and knees. Then he, too, sat down and stared at the art on the wall, dumbfounded.

Painted in the still crisp but ancient ocher, turquoise, and charcoal black was the image of two men scaling the side of the North Tower of Druminder. The figures were simple, mostly silhouettes, but shockingly descriptive. One figure was smaller than the other. He wore a cloak and hood and climbed ahead of his companion. The other one, the larger of the two, who relied more on ropes, carried three swords — the one on his back was huge.

"I wasn't wearing my cloak," Royce said.

"Seriously?" Hadrian scoffed. "You're quibbling about the accuracy of the wardrobe in the illustration? These must have been created a long time ago — thousands of years, maybe." Hadrian began to nod. "This is the prophecy of Beatrice. She was a dwarven princess who predicted things that always came true."

Royce peered at him. "Let me guess . . . more tavern trivia?"

Hadrian looked over and nodded. "At that little pub, Sloan went on about her for quite some time, saying how five thousand years ago she foretold that we would climb the tower. This must be what she was talking about. All these images are prophecies."

This caused both of them to look at the other walls, and armed with Hadrian's explanation, Royce saw how each told a different story in a series of panels that read from top to bottom.

On the one to the right of the door and starting at the top, a man and woman were shown trapped by a terrible monster that was ill-defined and drawn as a huge and vague black shape. Then the woman sacrificed herself: splitting in half. The man used the pieces to create the stars, the moon, and the world. Near the bottom of that wall, the last panel simply showed a beautiful landscape with the sun shining and a wolf howling at the moon.

The next wall depicted a great city and a wondrous tree beneath which were many children. Then that same dark monster appeared again, and the tree turned dark, as did all the fruit upon it. One was given to a man, who ate it. In the next panel, that same man had turned dark and was wearing a crown, robe, and cloak. He also held a spear. He stood on a pile of corpses. In the last panel on that wall, the tree was dead and the man who ate the fruit and led the battle wept.

On the third wall, the weeping man—who no longer wore a crown—was seen directing a dwarf to build two great towers over a volcano. Then a dwarf wearing a crown led a war against elves. A young dwarf girl was on her knees before him, arms up as if pleading, but the king had his back to her. In the next panel, the dwarven kingdom was in ruins, and elves surrounded the two towers. Nearby, the weeping man and the elven queen stood within a doorway, and they wept at the sight of the dead tree.

On the fourth wall was a dwarf who dug down into the underworld. There he received a great sword from the dwarven king from the previous wall. This dwarven digger returned with the sword and was himself crowned king. He married a dwarven girl, and together they sat on thrones in a great castle.

The fifth wall showed the two men climbing one of a pair of towers joined by a thin bridge on the night of a full moon. Beneath the towers, three terrible monsters clawed upward to get out. This part of the image was disturbing because the monsters were horrific and so huge that they made the two towers of Drumindor look like blades of grass. Royce took this as a stylized symbol of the power of the volcano — because what else could it be? In the next panel, the two men fought a tall, thin creature with claws, while a dwarf pulled on a lever connected to a massive gear. Aiding him was a dwarven woman with long hair. In the next panel, one of the men threw a book into the mouth of a great fire. In the last panel, four figures stood together embracing before the South Tower as a full moon shone and wolves howled.

The sixth wall portrayed a great door being opened, and a multitude of people rushed out. They divided themselves into two groups and fought. The three monsters from below the towers on the previous wall escaped and devastated the world. Great cities were destroyed, mountains torn down, oceans drained, and even the sky was darkened as a great war was fought. Then the same dark monster from the first two walls reappeared. It had grown so huge that it consumed the entirety of the world, taking with it the sun and the stars. The final image was of the weeping man down on his knees. He once more wore his crown, robe, and mantle, but instead of his spear, he held a fruit that gave off light. Kneeling beside him was a beautiful woman, and around them was a multitude, but beyond this . . . nothing but the darkness of a charcoal wash.

"Who are you?"

The little peephole had opened once more, and through it, Gravis Berling peered down.

"I'm Hadrian Blackwater, and this is Royce Melborn," Hadrian said in that infuriatingly cheerful and friendly greeting he always had handy.

The dwarf frowned.

"Who sent you?" Gravis asked.

Royce thought a moment as a list of names ran through his head: Lord Byron, Cornelius DeLur, even Pickles put in a showing. They all had a hand in it. Each contributed to their being in that room, but only one person sent them. "Gwen DeLancy."

"Who?" Gravis asked.

"Gwen DeLancy sent us."

"I don't even know who that is," Gravis replied.

"Your loss."

Gravis thought a moment, then asked, "My people are still in the city, aren't they?"

Royce nodded. "A lot of people are."

"Why?"

"They haven't any place else to go," Hadrian explained. "Tur Del Fur is their home. It's the only one they have, but more important, it's the only one they *want*."

Gravis frowned again and looked decidedly miserable. "I don't want to kill you. I didn't want to kill anyone. But . . ."

Royce didn't like the *but*.

"I can't do anything about it now. We're nearly out of time. All the spouts have been set and the master gear has been locked. Besides, it's *down there*." He said the words with revulsion. "Even if I was convinced to stop, even if we had time . . . I couldn't reach the master gear. Not now."

Auberon and the others had all admitted they didn't know how Gravis would accomplish the feat he threatened. Even the other Drumindor workers couldn't offer a guess as to what exactly Gravis had done. According to them, the towers had a fail-safe system that auto-vented when the pressure rose too high. With so much at stake, the overflow valve had been made idiot-proof. It couldn't be closed or locked. But given that Gravis's knowledge of Drumindor was unmatched, everyone agreed he could deliver on his threat.

Royce's plan had always depended on forcing the dwarf to undo what he'd done. Royce just assumed that if he began administering pain that Gravis would comply, but that no longer appeared likely. He couldn't reach the dwarf, and it seemed as if it wouldn't change anything even if he could.

Royce felt defeat like a kick in the stomach. He had no answer, and time was running out. Turning, he faced Hadrian, who had followed him blindly without even asking why, much less how. "Hadrian, I—"

"Why are we on your wall?" Hadrian asked Gravis and pointed.

"You're not," the dwarf replied without looking.

"Really? 'Cause it sure looks like us: him in his cloak and me with my three swords, and both of us scaling the tower just before the rise of a full moon. What's the order here? It starts with that one over there, right? The one where the couple escapes from the dark blobby thing? That's just to the right of the door we came in, and since you read right to left. It goes this way round, correct?" Hadrian swung his arm in a circle about the room. "So, that means that because Royce and I are here — this moment in time right now — is what was prophesied on . . . one, two, three, four — the fifth wall. Isn't that right?"

Gravis didn't answer.

"Which makes you . . ." Hadrian walked over, reached up, and tapped the dwarf pulling the lever. "This guy here. But who is this with you?"

Gravis looked down. He stared at the image, stunned. "By the beard of Drome!" Gravis shouted, then promptly slammed the little door shut once more. Royce heard a faint and muffled scurrying.

"What's going on?" Hadrian asked.

"I think he's coming down."

The door to the room appeared once more. It opened with a sudden jerk, and Gravis Berling entered. Ignoring both of them, he strode to the fifth wall and beheld it with an open mouth. Then he turned to face them. In his eyes were tears and a desperate longing.

"Lift me up," he said to Hadrian. "Please."

Hadrian glanced at Royce, who shrugged. He had no idea what was going on, but the door was open, and he took that as a good sign.

Hadrian reached down and hoisted Gravis up onto his shoulders.

"Move closer to the wall."

Hadrian did as he was told, and Royce watched as Gravis touched the image of the lady dwarf helping him pull the lever. Gravis ran his finger along her outline, then rising up on his toes, such that he balanced on Hadrian's shoulders, he put his lips to the wall and kissed the little image. "I hear you, Ena. I can hear you now."

CHAPTER THIRTY-SIX

The Big Room

The ground shuddered, and Hadrian nearly fell.

"Are you sure you want to come for this last bit?" Gravis asked as he led the way down the steps of the North Tower. "My, ah, *friend,* as he calls himself, is a dangerous person, to put it mildly. He knows I've already locked the master gear and that the fires below Drumindor will rupture the encasement all on their own unless I unlock it. When he sees me, he might suspect the truth. If he does, then that will be that. But you two — I'm pretty sure he'll kill both of you straightaway. And don't go thinking those swords will help." Gravis paused briefly and glanced back over his shoulder. "I can see you're a warrior. Hadrian, is it? And a good one perhaps, but *my friend* is far less a man and more — well, something you've never seen before."

"We've both already met him," Hadrian said.

"Oh, you have?"

"I've met him twice," Royce replied. "Cut his head off once."

This caused Gravis to stop and make a full turn to look at them, and Royce in particular. Given that the staircase they descended looked to go on forever, this was not an idle thing. The steps were shallow, perfect for little legs, but Hadrian couldn't help thinking that if a person fell, once they got rolling, they'd keep going. Gravis showed no sign of concern, at least about the stairs.

"So, I suppose you know he's not completely human?" Gravis asked. "Or alive, for that matter."

"His name is Falkirk de Roche," Royce replied. "He's a few thousand years old, was one of the early members of the Monks of Maribor, and appears to be a zombie of some sort, but he charmingly keeps a personal diary."

"He also slaughtered the entire Drumindor garrison of Yellow Jackets in the first few minutes after we walked in," Gravis said. "And then he ate them." The dwarf paused a moment to let that sink in. "After his meal, he skinned their bodies and carefully hung the pieces up to dry."

Since releasing them from the mural room, Gravis had led them to the top of the tower where they worked to clear the spouts and portals that the dwarf had previously sealed. The spouts were giant tunnels bored out of the rock through which molten lava would blast on its way to the sea. There were dozens, each one aiming in a different direction, their access to the mountain's core sealed off by gear-controlled portals. Once they finished this task, they climbed to the top of the South Tower and did the same. On their way across the bridge from the south to the north, Hadrian watched the sun vanish below the horizon. They were nearly out of time, but according to Gravis, all that remained was to unlock the master gear that overrode the fail-safe relief trigger.

"Falkirk will be at the bottom, I suspect," Gravis said. "At least that's where he has spent most of his time. If you want to know what a dead man who doesn't sleep in a coffin in a hole does, I can certainly tell you. They kneel, chant, and sing to the primordial fires in the bowels of a dwarven fortress. Never too close, though; Falkirk doesn't like fire.

"I've watched him, and if it was anyone else — like, say, a living person — I'd conclude he's either drunk or lost his mind. He crouches on the floor opposite the great fire and . . . well, it seems to me he's talking to someone or something, calling and inviting them up for a sit-an'-chat, so to speak. What I've heard him say is mostly gibberish, and I would guess he was mad, but it makes me wonder. How does a man keep walking around and talking when by all rights he ought to have been a maggot mansion centuries ago? Maybe all his worshipping is how.

Anyway, if he's at the bottom of the tower, at the base of the big gear, we'll have an easy time of it because we don't need to go down that far. The lock is on top of the master gear — three floors up from where Falkirk has been holding his parties. All we need to do is raise the stone wedge that is locking the gear's teeth by lifting the Armtarin — that's Dromeian for *grand fecking lever.*" Gravis gave a chuckle, which under the circumstances sounded a bit unhinged.

They passed the room with all the murals. This time there was another way to go, a separate staircase that hadn't been there before. Hadrian guessed they had to be getting fairly near the bottom.

"So, what's your plan?" Gravis asked.

"Seems pretty straightforward," Royce replied. "Hadrian and I distract Falkirk while you do your magic and purge the system of pressure, hopefully in time to save this portion of the world."

"You might find *distracting him* a bit of a challenge. He's stronger and faster than he looks."

"So am I."

"But you can die."

"Point taken."

"According to the Wall," Hadrian said, "one of us is supposed to throw Falkirk's diary into a fire. If someone who lived thousands of years ago went to all the trouble of painting that onto a wall, it seems sort of important."

"Not just any fire," Gravis said. "At the base of this tower is the hottest forge in the world. We call it the *Haldor Gigin* — the Dragon's Mouth. That's what was depicted in the prophecy painting. It's essentially the gaping maw of Druma, the throat of the volcano, and the altar at which Falkirk has been chanting."

"That brings up a question I have," Hadrian said. "How is it you've worked here so long and didn't connect us to the painting on the fifth wall? You've obviously seen it."

"Oh yes, many, many times, too many, I suspect. When someone says: 'How are ya?' every day for years, it stops being a question and becomes just an obligatory, meaningless greeting. I've seen those murals so often I became blind to them. Never imagined anything depicted on it would come to pass in my lifetime. I certainly never thought *I* was on the Wall. Even a Berling isn't that arrogant."

Another violent tremor shook the tower, and Hadrian put a hand out to steady himself. "Why is this place shaking?"

"Pressure," Gravis said casually. "She gets to jumpin' before we let her loose. These towers are like a cork in a bottle of fresh wine. If you seal it while there's still sugar inside, the fermentation process keeps going, and it builds up bubbles — the sort you'll find in ale. That creates a terrible pressure, and sooner or later, the bottle bursts. Elan has an unlimited amount of sugar, so to speak, and we've corked her good." Gravis looked up at the dark stone ceiling as if he could somehow see through it. "The sun has set," the dwarf said. "And the moon will be rising soon. This time of year, I'd already have my hands on the release valve. No sense taking chances. We wait until the last moment to blow the core because the greater the pressure, the cleaner the blow. It saves us from having to shimmy up the spouts and chisel out the residual crust — which is about as enjoyable as it sounds. Still, while the old girl is stout, Elan is stouter. If we wait too long, the safety would vent the pressure automatically, but since I locked the master gear, it can't. So now, when it reaches a certain point — pop goes the wine bottle."

"All right then," Royce said. "Gravis, you do whatever it takes to get to the master gear and crank that lever. In the meantime, Hadrian and I will do our best to entertain Falkirk. And while I have no idea what good it will do, if either of us gets the chance, we'll incinerate his cursed memoirs. Then we'll all gather for our victory huddle at the bottom of the tower just like in the picture. Apparently, Beatrice is never wrong in her prophecies, so this is a guaranteed win for us."

Hadrian thought about that. In the image, there had been four people in the final panel.

Who is the fourth? he wondered.

Then he realized that maybe what he should be asking himself was whether he and Royce were even part of the four.

Hadrian called it the Big Room, not so much because it was indeed a huge chamber, but because everything in it was so massive it made him feel — a bit ironically — like a dwarf in a giant's workshop. And yet despite the Big Room's size, it still couldn't house more than a quarter of the master gear, which rose up out of the floor like the back of a sea serpent. The thing was massive, reaching nearly to the ceiling. The teeth of the gear reminded Hadrian of crenellated parapets on a castle — if said castle belonged to said previously mentioned giant.

Hadrian was able to identify the lever only because he knew it had to be there. The great metal beam that rose out of the floor at a slight angle and ran near to the roof alongside the master gear was just too big to be a tool. Instead, it appeared like part of the room's support structure. Two things told Hadrian it wasn't. First, was its location; second, was the depiction of it in the painting. Hadrian had worked with siege engines and was familiar with the power of a lever to lift and move heavy things. He felt that this gigantic bar, and its unseen fulcrum, could allow a mouse to move a mountain. Large green glow stones in the floor and yellow hearth-fire windows above provided ample light and revealed plenty of other lesser gears, but it appeared as if this massive chamber was built entirely to house the master gear and the *"grand fecking lever."* As it turned out, there was one more thing of great significance in the room.

"Salutations, valiant heroes!" Falkirk de Roche said, his sandpaper voice magnified by the hard stone. He sat atop the highest tooth on the master gear. Wrapped deep in his cloak, Falkirk appeared to be little more than a dark mound with eyes. "Gravis Berling, Royce Melborn, and Hadrian"—he hesitated—"Blackwater," he pulled out. "Friends be you all, come to revel in glory on our day of jubilation. I welcome thee." He stood up slowly, like an old man after sitting too long, and as he did, his hood and cloak fell away. In the bright light, which was gold from above and green from below, Hadrian saw him clearly. Pale as the underbelly of a dead fish, he was tall, lanky, and thin — disturbingly so, like a starved man reduced to nothing but bone and muscle. His arms were longer than normal; so was his red hair. Thin strands hung to his ankles from a head that appeared soft as a rotting melon. On his fingers were sharp-pointed nails of ebony, and his teeth were a sickly yellow set in black gums. What clothes he had hung in rotted tatters except for what looked to be a new black leather belt that was cinched tightly around his tiny waist. Tucked into it, such that it appeared tied to him, was the diary.

"Fitting indeed we four stand present, as each hath performed equal in shares the toil necessary for this moment."

Gravis gave Royce a curious glance.

"Did they not tell thee, Gravis?" Falkirk asked. "Royce and Hadrian freed us from our prison."

Hadrian saw worry and a flash of fear run across the dwarf's face. He hesitated for only a moment, then began walking forward a bit like a condemned criminal with Royce and Hadrian flanking him in the role of guards.

"You say we've all contributed equally," Gravis said to Falkirk. "And it appears to me that you're expecting a reward of some sort. I was wondering if we'll all be sharing in that particular bounty? I only ask because I've spent too many years toiling while receiving practically nothing at all."

"Everyone will receive treasures beyond imagination."

"I see, but let me ask you this: once this grand old lady blows, how are any of us going to collect? The whole of the Horn of Delgos will be incinerated. This part of the world will be remade. If enough lava spews, then Mount Druma will make a bit of a comeback. The ash cloud will obliterate the coast, kill all the plants and animals, and poison the nearby seas — at least for a time. As for us, why, there won't be so much as a fingernail to remember the three of us by, so how might we be receiving this gift?"

"Such a little mind, but what a greedy heart," Falkirk said. "'Tis to be expected. We, too, remember doubt, fear, and confusion. Be not troubled, little one. Thou dost not need to believe in the Old Ones and their master, for they believe in thee."

"Well now, that is a wonderful thing to hear, very grand indeed," Gravis said as he reached the base of the gear. "Sadly, I haven't a clue what any of it means. Would you mind explaining it for us while I check my work? Don't want anything going wrong at the last minute, do we? Also, it would help to understand the situation better. After all, this is a mighty big sacrifice I'm making here."

"Sacrifice?" Falkirk said the word with disgust. "Shouldst thou but know what *we* suffered." Falkirk shook his soft melon head, making the greasy red cords sway. "Mileva convinced us to join her. She taught us how to extend our life. That is not a pleasant process."

Royce and Hadrian waited at the base of the master gear as Gravis began climbing. They watched him go. Hadrian looked to Royce, who made no move to follow. They really couldn't and still maintain the ruse that Gravis was merely going to *check his work* to make certain nothing went wrong. Once Gravis yanked the lever, however, Hadrian was certain Falkirk would guess the truth. By then, the dwarf would be beyond reach of his aid.

"We required a reliquary, a container for the souls we took." Falkirk tapped the diary. "A book made of skins, written in blood, and protected by a curse of great power — 'tis not as mighty as a pile of bones, but it has the benefit of portability. And this was utmost in her mind, for Mileva cared not for sharing. The Dark Lady was not willing to grant us space to set up shop in *her* house. Oh, no! Not the great Mileva Hitartheon! We were cast out, kicked as a baby bird from the nest and tasked with murdering our beloved friend. How wouldst thou like to do that, Gravis Berling?"

Gravis didn't answer. He was too busy, focused on climbing the teeth of the gear, which, given his size as compared to them, was a challenge.

"And 'twas not the end of the suffering. Far from it! Dibben sealed us in our own temple, the one we built along the ley line for Bran. We thought he and Bran fled, but they did not. Away they ran, but *to* the temple. We spent centuries trapped in that tomb, that prison, listening in mute anguish to the voices above and starving such that we longed for the peace of death, but death refused us. Our immortal life thus became our eternal torment. Until our saviors, Royce and Hadrian, arrived, and we were dragged out with the corpse of Villar. At long last, we were free but at the cost of years measuring in the thousands! So, do not moan and wail to us about sacrifice, Gravis Berling!"

With each tooth the dwarf conquered, he came closer to Falkirk, who went on, his voice growing in volume, sounding more and more like a preacher giving a sermon to a tiny flock.

"Yet immortality was only a means to an end, for life itself is not the problem. Chaos, you must understand, is the natural order. Non-existence — being the native land of all things — gives birth to homeward longing and the gnawing aspiration to return to that barren womb of oblivion. This is why everything decays, falls apart, crumbles, and cracks. All life, all existence, arose from nothing, and 'tis back to nothing that creation yearns to return. Here then is reasoned proof why nothing lasts. See it not, dost thou? There is no eternity whilst reality remains. The universe is a mistake, a false delirium wherein all suffer. The very act of being allows for pain, for fear, as all things trapped within existence pine for something. Men crave knowledge, love, power, dominion over animals and each other, even the freedom from these very wants. Animals desire food in the form of meat or vegetation. Plants fight over sunlight and water. Water must fall as rain, return to the sea, and be reborn only to fall again in an endless, tortuous cycle. Even a rock will covet other rocks, thus seeking to fall, and must suffer being ground to sand. Existence is conflict, and opposition renders pain. But in Chaos, there is nothing: no desire left unfulfilled. No hunger unsated, no fear nor dread. There is nothing . . . not even time. And without time, there is permanence, and eternity, and peace — the way it was meant to be, the way it had always been . . . before the rebellion."

Gravis came to Falkirk at the apex of the gear. The width of the teeth was such that he had ample room to walk past, which he proceeded to do, keeping as much distance as possible.

"But change 'tis always difficult," Falkirk continued. "The unknown, forever disturbing, invites fear, and doubt lurks in the shadows. We understand this, which is why we shall help thee, Gravis."

Hadrian read Falkirk's weight. His emaciated body made reading his muscles as easy as comprehending the nature of a scream. Falkirk had no intentions of letting Gravis get by. The dead man had known all along and had waited for them.

"Gravis! Look out!" Hadrian shouted.

He was too late. The ruse they hoped to exploit had failed, and Gravis paid the price.

Falkirk swiped at the dwarf with his claws, cutting him across the waist. The dwarf's light shirt sliced open. With a burst of blood and an anguished cry, Gravis went over the edge. The fall, while not guaranteed to be deadly, was bone breaking, and Gravis struck the floor like a stack of porcelain plates.

Stillness filled the chamber as all eyes fixed on the dwarf, prone on the floor. He wasn't dead. Hadrian saw his body draw breath.

Once again anticipating Falkirk's intent, Hadrian ran to Gravis. He arrived just as Falkirk leaped off the gear and landed beside the dwarf. The long fall did not appear to have hurt or even slowed Falkirk, and Hadrian charged him. Drawing both side swords and running at Falkirk's exposed back, Hadrian planned to remove the dead man's head.

To Hadrian's shock, his blades caught nothing but air.

Falkirk ducked and dodged at blinding speed, then countered with a swipe that left five gaping cuts across the leather of Hadrian's jerkin. Two more rapid attacks followed, and Hadrian used both swords to block a swipe to his face and another to his midsection.

What happened to the old man who'd had trouble getting to his feet?

The good news was that as Falkirk pressed his attack and Hadrian retreated, the dead man was nowhere near Gravis anymore. The bad news: he was closing on Hadrian, who rapidly concluded that Falkirk was far more dangerous than the ex-mercenary had ever dreamed. This was no man. This was something else, and it moved with superhuman speed and strength.

Beatrice was wrong. We're not going to win.

CHAPTER THIRTY-SEVEN

Chain Reaction

Seeing Hadrian miss with both swords was like seeing a drunk miss the floor. In that instant, Royce recalculated their odds of success to be less than half of what they had been a moment before. This was bad because, on a scale from *inevitable* to *doomed,* it pegged their chances at a solid *unlikely,* except for two things.

By the time Hadrian had performed his dodging dance of retreat, Royce had maneuvered behind Falkirk. He timed his advance as best he could. Falkirk had proven himself to be extremely dangerous — not quite as fast as lightning, but not much slower, either. He also didn't seem stupid, which really irked Royce. Most of his past adversaries had tended toward the skull-half-empty side since thuggery and brilliance were paired about as often as polka dots and plaid. Royce was about to play the part of a mouse slapping a cat on the back, but the risk was worth the reward — at least he hoped so.

Royce got as close as he dared and lashed out at Falkirk's midsection with Alverstone, catching only the black leather belt. He didn't wait, didn't look; he ducked. As expected, this saved him from having his face removed as Falkirk spun with claws out. Royce retreated as Falkirk launched a series of rapid attacks, but the thin black blades at the ends of those fingers caught only Royce's cloak.

Then the fight stopped.

Falkirk looked first to the floor, where his severed belt lay, then at Royce, who did his best to appear as innocent as possible. Finally, Falkirk spun to see Hadrian holding the diary, having picked it up off the floor while the dead man wasted time pursuing Royce. "Give it back!"

Royce sprinted toward the exit. He was halfway to the doorway by the time Falkirk rushed Hadrian. With an excellent wrist flip, Hadrian threw the book to Royce, who caught it without slowing down and made for the stairs.

There was a grunt and a clang. Then with a booming voice that echoed in the chamber, Falkirk shouted, "Leave and he dies!"

Royce stopped and looked back.

Hadrian lay on the floor, one sword spinning across the stone, the other trapped by a foot as the pale, ginger-headed corpse crouched over him, back hunched, mouth wide, teeth dripping. Black claws touched Hadrian's throat.

"Dost thou think we did not view the murals?" Falkirk said. "Bring my diary back to me or he dies."

The room was silent enough for Royce to hear the beat of his heart, Hadrian's panting breath, the hissing inhalations of Falkirk, and the faint, distant clicking of little gears. In that still moment, Royce felt as if the world teetered on some high ledge. He usually liked high places, but not this one. Only a few years ago, Royce wouldn't have stopped.

Is it possible the idiot couldn't find the rope?

"Why'd you do it?" *Royce had asked.*

"What?" *Hadrian had replied.*

"Come back. You were safe. You were at the rope. Why'd you come back?"

"Same reason I'm not leaving you here."

He remembered calling Hadrian an idiot for not abandoning him on the Crown Tower, and yet now . . .

The silence was broken by the unlikely sound of laughter. Royce could have expected as much from a maniacal demon-creature, who believed he'd won . . . but it wasn't Falkirk who laughed.

Hadrian had started with a snicker that quickly shifted into a giggle and then rolled right on into a full-blown guffaw. "Oh, did you *ever* pick the wrong guy."

Hadrian struggled to get out between breathing and laughing. "What are you offering him? To let me go so that Drumindor explodes and kills us all? Good plan. He's not an idiot. And he knows he can't kill you. So, what kind of choice is that? Go ahead and slit my throat, then you can see who runs the fastest. You're quick in a fight, but no antelope, I suspect. So, my money is on Royce."

Falkirk looked from Hadrian to Royce, then back.

Royce knew Falkirk would kill Hadrian. He had to. The Gingerdead Man couldn't afford to leave anyone alive in that room who could throw the lever. Royce couldn't get to Hadrian before Falkirk slit his throat, and even if he did, they would both likely die. Time was on the corpse's side. Any delay granted him the win. Whatever Falkirk was, he was more than a match for Riyria, and this would be the end of the game except for the *second* thing.

The diary had been the *first* thing. It gave Royce and Hadrian a chance at success. After all, it had been featured in the mural. Falkirk knew it, which was why Royce imagined he had strapped the book to his waist, thinking it was the safest place. As Royce had already cut Falkirk's head off to no effect, fighting the ancient corpse was pointless. But he could fulfill the prophecy and burn the book. This, he hoped, would somehow make Falkirk die, or become vulnerable, or do something to improve their odds. All of it was a full step and a half outside rational, but so was Falkirk's audacity at walking around after decapitation. So Royce was willing to play by new rules.

As it turned out, Royce appeared to be only half right. The diary did appear to be Falkirk's weakness, only the trip to burn the book would cost Hadrian's life, a cost Royce only then realized he was unwilling to pay. This was where the contest might have ended except that Falkirk had mentioned the name *Villar*. That one word had reminded Royce how he had once survived a similar confrontation with an equally impossible foe. The whole affair had been just as bizarre as this encounter, and in many ways, it seemed to be an extension of the events that had occurred in Rochelle. That was just shy of a year before. And if it had worked on the roof of a cathedral, why not here?

So, Royce employed the *second* thing.

He drove the white blade of Alverstone into the face of the book, piercing it straight through the cover, the pages, and out the back. Falkirk screamed in anguish. His body shuddered. He let go of his hold, and in that unexpected opportunity, Hadrian threw him off.

"Go, Royce!" Hadrian's words caught up to the thief only after he had already started down the stairs. The flat, shallow steps were easy to take four or five at a time. Royce was able to gauge the depth and the distance to the finish line by the circumference of the master gear that remained visible the whole way down. He clutched the diary to his chest, and left Alverstone spiked into the book.

Racing as he was, Royce reached the bottom in no time at all. Instead of a fiery pit as he was promised, he once more faced a massive—and of course locked—pair of dwarven doors.

"Little bastards!" he shouted. He pulled Alverstone from the book and spun, expecting to see Falkirk right behind him, but the steps were empty.

Royce was gone before Hadrian got back to his feet. He grabbed his lost sword, then turned to deal with the aftermath of Royce's genius, which turned out to be a carrot-topped corpse writhing on the floor. Falkirk lay on his side, jerking and shuddering so rapidly that the movements defied the eye's ability to follow and appeared as mere blurs. His distorted and disturbing twists of arms, legs, and head appeared to ignore the very concept of joints and muscles.

Maybe I should cut his head off while he's thrashing, but would that help?

The way Hadrian saw it, all he needed to do was buy Royce time to burn the book. If that killed Falkirk, Hadrian would then need to climb the gear and throw the lever. To this end, he backed up and positioned himself between Falkirk and the exit.

What happens when Royce burns the book? Will it kill him outright, or just make him vulnerable? How will I know? How much time do I have before the moon—

The floor beneath Hadrian's feet jumped as the whole tower shuddered so violently that he was thrown to the floor. The room suffered a shower of dust and pebbles. Slabs of fractured stone, previously part of the ceiling, fell and burst on the floor. Shards came off the walls and toppled like great trees. An axle holding one of the overhead gears, the size of a small house, snapped and let fall the cog. The big gap-toothed wheel hit the floor and rolled halfway across the chamber before slamming into the far wall, where it toppled with a terrible crash.

Hope we don't need that one.

Maybe waiting isn't such a good idea.

Hadrian started toward the master gear when he heard something; he felt it, too — the pounding. Something was hammering from down below. And for a moment, Hadrian thought he heard voices. Distant but deep, powerful, and not at all human.

Then Falkirk stopped his contorted thrashing and sat up, his eyes sharp, his mouth set to a vicious snarl. Without a word, Falkirk got to his feet and charged Hadrian. In a way, this was good. Better that he came at Hadrian than go after Royce. Hadrian held no illusions of winning the fight. If Royce was fast enough, and if burning the book killed Falkirk, Hadrian might still survive. Either way, Hadrian hoped Royce had enough time remaining to burn the book and then return and pull the lever before the big boom.

The dead man attacked with a fury. All Hadrian saw were claws and those yellow teeth flashing, but there was a change. The swings and jabs were not as fast as before.

He's wounded.

Hadrian couldn't see it. No blood dripped, no cut oozed, yet Falkirk was noticeably slower and weaker. However, not so much as to make Hadrian believe he could win. Falkirk was unlike any adversary Hadrian had ever fought. He couldn't anticipate Falkirk's motions because the dead man's body didn't move as expected. Forecasting him was like trying to read another language with only enough time to skim the pages. The storm of claws held Hadrian's blades on the defensive. The few attacks Hadrian attempted were dodged with such ease that Hadrian's confidence plummeted.

What is *this thing?*

Royce turned back to the huge, ornately cast, solid metal doors.

It took me eighteen hours to open the last one!

In frustration and rage, he slammed his palm against the metal and heard a rattle. Looking down, Royce noticed an ordinary chain and padlock partially hidden by a beautiful set of horizontal handles.

Are you kidding me?

In a flash, it all became clear. This door didn't lock. None of the doors *inside* Drumindor appeared to — although at least two had disappeared — but Falkirk had seen the mural. He kept the book in the safest place possible — on his person. Then he took sensible precautions to prevent anyone from accessing the forge. He just didn't know who was coming to visit. A chain and a lock would have stymied almost anyone else. As it turned out, the rotting redhead could have delayed Royce more by setting out a glass of milk and a plate of cookies. Royce popped the lock in record time. The chain fell free, and he kicked the doors wide. Inside was another world.

Heat blasted Royce the moment the doors opened and revealed a vast chamber brilliant with the orange-and-yellow glow of molten lava. From the entrance, more steps went down to a bridge that crossed a molten lake and churning pools that bubbled, spat, and popped. At the far end of the walkway, which terminated at the center of the chamber, was the great forge, the *Haldor Gigin,* which was carved to look like a dragon's open mouth. Overhead, blackened chains swayed, and massive crucibles hung on suspended tracks. More rails ran the length of the bridge, and several heavy-duty carts were set off to one side. The place looked as inviting as a cook fire to a rabbit.

The sheer breadth of the space was far larger than the tower could afford, and Royce guessed he was below sea level, where the magma bubbled up. This couldn't be the genuine mouth of the volcano. Nothing held pressure here. It must be some sort of overflow holding pond. Whatever it was, the lake reflected the volcano's irritated temperament by roiling and occasionally spitting plumes of liquid rock dozens of feet in the air. This was an angry and violent room — a wild animal furious at being chained. It wasn't the core, but as close as Royce would get, and that was fine with him.

Awe didn't quite encompass what he felt as he took his first few steps down the long, dark aisle that arched high over the burning lake of liquid stone, which frothed and splashed the walls like ocean waves crashing a rocky coast in a hurricane. The sensation was more a concoction of horror mixed with equal parts of this-cannot-be-real and why-would-I-expect-anything-less. Then the ground shimmied such that sections of the cliff walls sheared away and fell, throwing up a massive plume of burning rock. Seeing this, feeling the intense heat, Royce descended the steps to the bridge, moving at considerably less than a sprint.

He was halfway to the *Haldor Gigin* when he heard the voices. In the chamber, they sounded like screeching metal, the sort of noise that made people cringe. But in his head, Royce heard words or thought he did. But that made no sense because the voices spoke to him by name.

It took less than a minute for the inevitable. Hadrian finally guessed wrong, which left him late to block Falkirk's next blow. He managed to avoid the claws, but Hadrian lost his balance and fell. And he didn't just fall, he fell with his back to Falkirk, leaving him exposed and blind to the next attack.

It's over, he realized.

The claws would enter the back of his neck. Hadrian wasn't certain if they could decapitate him, but that was also a possibility.

Behind him, Falkirk made a muffled grunt, but Hadrian felt no pain. He didn't feel anything. Then Falkirk cried out.

Hadrian managed to twist around and saw the dead man lying on the floor halfway across the room. He howled in rage and struggled on his back as if pinned to the floor, but nothing was there. A moment later, Falkirk appeared to shake off his invisible restraints. He focused on Hadrian and once more charged. This time Falkirk raced at him on all fours, scraping the stone like a leopard.

Hadrian raised his swords and braced for the impact.

While still twenty feet away, the ruddy-haired remains were thrown sideways across the room as if hit by something. Falkirk rolled, then slid to a stop among the shattered debris created by the fallen cog.

Are you doing that, Royce?

Once more, Drumindor shook. More stones fell, and Hadrian smelled sulfur and felt tremendous heat. At first, he thought he was hot from exertion, but he realized he was mistaken when he noticed the walls glowing red.

Time was running out.

Hadrian ran for the master gear.

He climbed the first and second teeth, which he was surprised to learn were covered in fresh blood. Reaching out for the third, something caught his boot and yanked. Hadrian was pulled down, and he fell to the floor on his back, knocking the wind out of him. A weight landed on his chest as his arms and legs were pinned. Above him, Falkirk grinned. "It's too late. The spirits from the book annoy me, but they can't pull the lever. And the moon is up. It's over." The grin opened, once more revealing his yellow teeth in black gums. "Such a pretty face."

Over the hunched back of Falkirk, Hadrian saw movement on top of the master gear.

CHAPTER THIRTY-EIGHT

Full Moon Rising

"*Climb, you old fool!*" Ena shouted.

"When I said I wanted to hear you, lassie, I didn't mean I wanted to hear ya scream," Gravis replied as he pulled just as hard as he could to mount the final tooth. He was nearly out of strength. If he was honest with himself, he had actually passed that mark a while ago. Gravis was running on sheer determination now.

Falkirk had lacerated his abdomen, and the cuts had been deep. He didn't dare look down. He didn't want to see his innards trailing out. How he managed to scale the gear was beyond his comprehension, nor did it hold much interest. None of it mattered. Even the condition of his ripped-open belly was inconsequential. He knew this beyond any doubt because Ena told him so.

"*I don't care a fig if you don't like the tenor o' my voice, Gravis! You dig in, you bearded boil on the butt of a baboon! You only need to do one lousy thing. In your whole life, this is it! Don't you dare fail now! You say you love me — so prove it. Prove it to me now, you daffy old hampot! Stand up and pull that lever!*"

Gravis pushed to his knees.

The world was swirling around him. The walls had gone red and were smoking. As far as Gravis could tell, Drumindor ought to have already blown. The moon had to be up by now, should have risen a while ago. And when its full pale light had kissed the walls, the Grand Old Lady ought to have popped like a cork, ushering in a new year of death and destruction.

Perhaps I underestimated the stubbornness of the old gal.

Looking up, Gravis spotted the chain that dangled from the Armtarin. It swayed with the rocking of the tower. He raised his arm but couldn't reach it.

"You've got to stand, love!" Ena shrieked in his ear.

Gravis had absolutely no idea how she was there, and much like his astounding climb, he didn't much care. All that mattered was that she'd heard him, and he could see Ena on her knees by his side, cheering him on. She was a dainty thing in her white nightgown, young and beautiful, just as she had always been in his mind's eye.

"For you, my love, I'll do anything."

"Don't tell me — show me!"

"Aye, that I will."

With every fiber of his body, and the last droplets of strength that remained in him, Gravis pushed to his feet. He caught the swinging chain, gripped it tight, and then as darkness folded in around his vision, he proceeded to wrap, wind, and bind the chain around his wrists.

"I do love you, Ena," Gravis said. "I always have."

"Anything you desire!" the voices told Royce as he walked the long dark bridge toward the Dragon's Mouth.

"Riches beyond your imagination!"

Royce kept walking as the molten lake bubbled and burst. The temperature was bad, but not horrific. The stone bridge shielded him from the worst of it. He could see the blurry waves of intense heat to either side, and when a spout of lava blew up high enough to reach the level of the bridge, he felt a blast like a furnace on that side. Breathing was easier than he expected. The air smelled like rotten eggs but wasn't overpowering. There was a reason. The dwarfs had built in a ventilation system that pumped surface air, which circulated through the room, or at least along the bridge. Royce knew this because he felt a cool breeze that had no business being there. Entering that chamber had seemed to be certain suicide, but feeling the fresh air, Royce was reminded that this was a forge, and dwarfs had worked here. The conditions had to be bearable.

Iceboxes, doors, and now this — the little monsters will take over the world one day.

Through his ears, he heard what could best be described as teeth dragging across a sharp blade, but in his head, he heard, *"We'll give you everlasting life, Royce!"* They weren't words, not really, but it was difficult for him to separate words from thoughts.

Can anyone think without words?

It must be possible. People without sight and hearing who couldn't read still thought; he just didn't know how. What Royce experienced as he crossed that bridge did not impress him as words so much as a simple understanding, an idea that became clear in his head, which his mind translated into words.

"We will make you a god!"

This one made him smile. Maybe the idea that something was speaking to him was only a hallucination brought on by heightened anxiety, or perhaps he was experiencing a form of delirium stemming from the noxious fumes. He leaned toward the latter — but either way, he found the promises humorously off target.

"Let me guess," Royce said aloud. "To become a god, all I need to do is *not* destroy this book?"

The chamber roared with a positive affirming answer.

"I should just, what? Sit down, take a nap, and wait for this whole place to be obliterated?"

Again, the euphoric response.

Royce reached the *Haldor Gigin*. The mouth was the size of a giant's cave, and the doors were closed and sealed by a massive metal bar that he had no hope of removing.

"That's interesting. In order to become a god, all I must do is die. But let me ask you this: who are you to create gods of men?"

"We are greater than gods."

"Okay, prove it," Royce said. "You say that for me to receive my reward I need to die. Fine. I'll do what you want if you prove that you are greater than a god by opening this furnace door."

Nothing happened.

"Obey us, child of dirt! Or you will pay!"

Royce studied the door and realized that it made no sense for the forge to be so large. Did the dwarfs really open this whole thing and face exposing themselves to all that heat if all they wanted to do was melt enough metal to forge a bracelet?

Like most dwarven doors, these were ornate and subdivided. He spotted a small hook hanging off to the side of one of the smaller squares and saw the answer. The mouth of the dragon could be opened in a variety of ways: a tiny aperture, a set of multiple squares, and all the way up to the giant chasm of the full mouth. Whatever size was required was available. The bar was likely there as a safety precaution.

Royce grabbed up the metal hook, and after catching it on the side of a relief image depicting a dwarf hitting an anvil with a hammer, he swung a door open. Foolishly standing directly in front of it, he was singed, and only his quick reflexes saved him from a severe burn.

Royce raised the book.

"NO!"

The chamber shuddered and groaned, and the lava pool splashed and churned as Royce tossed the diary of Falkirk into the *Haldor Gigin*, trying his best to do it in the same fashion as had been depicted in the painting. He wasn't taking any chances.

"Turns out I have no interest in being a god or living forever, nor do I want riches, or even a key to the city of Tur Del Fur," he said, speaking either to himself or his delusion as he trotted back across the bridge. He didn't really think it mattered at this point. "There's only one thing I want." As soon as he said it, he knew that wasn't quite accurate. "Okay, so that's an understatement. There're *five* things, but I always had the first four, and now it looks as though I've got a good shot at the fifth."

Hadrian threw Falkirk off.

The dead man's body hit the floor and slid a few feet.

Hadrian rolled to his knees, awaiting the next attack, but Falkirk didn't move. He looked to be nothing more than a long-dead corpse. As he stared at it, Hadrian noticed it wasn't merely Falkirk who had stopped moving. The tower had grown still, and everything was quiet.

At least for a moment.

Royce appeared in the doorway just as the master gear rotated one tick, but that click resounded with authority, and once more the tower shook. Instantly, a hundred other gears whirred to life. The big ones that never moved crept forward. The medium-sized wheels beat a determined pace, and the little cogs spun so fast that they sounded like a hive of bees.

"You did it!" Royce shouted while looking up at the ceiling of gears that performed a show like a ballroom of couples putting on a grand dance.

"I didn't do anything," Hadrian said.

They both looked to the place where Gravis had fallen and found only a pool of blood. A scarlet trail smeared its way across the floor and up to the top teeth of the master gear. There, dangling from a chain attached to the retracted lever, the dwarf hung by a single wrist, limp and unmoving. They pulled him down, but Gravis Berling, the last of his bloodline, was dead. Still, his eyes were open, and on his face sat a smile.

Gwendolyn DeLancy and Rehn Purim sat beneath the stars outside Table by the Tea. Gwen leaned forward with her elbows resting next to the steaming cup of black leaf she had made for herself. She didn't think Olivia Montague would mind. Gwen had put everything back the way she found it and doubted Olivia would even notice. In doing so, she smiled to find all the silverware, cups, and plates hadn't been touched. Despite Olivia's offer, no one had taken a thing.

Rehn sat with his feet up in the chair across from Gwen. The white of his fresh bandages peeked out beneath his shirt.

"Where's the moon?" Rehn asked, concerned.

"I'm certain it will be along," Gwen replied and sipped the hot tea.

Rehn narrowed his eyes at her, his mouth turning up in amazement tempered with a dash of disbelief. "You're so . . . *relaxed.*"

"And you should be, too. Getting all worked up isn't good for your recovery. You need peace and quiet. You should have gone back with Arcadius and Albert like I told you to."

He shook his head. "I'd rather die — for real this time — than to do that to him again."

Gwen nodded. "Very brave of you."

He scowled in return. "You don't mean that."

"I do . . . sort of. For you, this is still a question. We could die at any moment, so your decision to stay is very courageous."

"But it's not heroic for you?"

Gwen smiled and shook her head.

"How can you be so sure?"

"Experience," Gwen replied. She set her cup back down, then smiled. "Look, there's your moon."

"What's wrong with it?" he asked, shocked, as in the sky hung a dark circle that appeared nearly invisible and a tinge red.

Gwen herself would have been equally aghast if she hadn't already seen the sight through Rehn's eyes and confirmed the story through a few others. She had left nothing to chance. Gwen had no idea what it meant but knew it was nothing bad. Still, witnessing that blood-red disk — seeing it with her own eyes — made her wonder what was happening. Something amazing, certainly, something in the realm of the divine, and it frightened her to think she was involved — possibly even the cause.

Will this make the gods notice me now?

The thought was terrifying.

The moon had already been well above the horizon revealing that she had risen unseen several minutes ago, draped in a dark and blood-colored cloak. Now as they watched, the moon began to peel off her covering, exposing the familiar white light beneath. The pale radiance displayed storefronts, tables, and chairs, and for the first time, Gwen discovered there were others at the dock — small groups standing silently around the boardwalk, watching.

And then it happened. The night exploded in a magnificent burst of yellow-illuminated brilliance as Drumindor vented.

Like a fountain of light, all forty-eight spouts fired, and dazzling streams of gold spewed in gorgeous arcs out into the ocean. The whole of the harbor lit up in its fantastic glow as gasps and screams turned to cheers that burst from the assembled crowd. Gwen watched all of them. What looked to be more than a thousand dwarfs, several dozen mir, many Calians, and even a few Ba Ran sailors mingled together, faces glowing with relief and delight. Fists were punched in the air; shouts of joy and leaps of exuberance were everywhere. Among the revelers, Gwen spotted Calvary Graxton, Jareb, Atyn, Baba, Salen, and Amster, and not far away, Auberon, who did not cheer — he cried.

Atyn embraced Jareb. Mister Parrot got down on his knees and kissed a lady dwarf. Hugging and kissing became something of an epidemic that spread through the crowd. Rehn slammed his palm on the table, upsetting Gwen's tea. Then he rose to his feet and proceeded to hop up and down.

"Stop that, you'll hurt yourself!"

Rehn ignored her. "They did it!"

Gwen righted her cup.

Hugs and kisses shifted to dancing, as the dwarfs began impromptu jigs with music provided by slaps, stomps, and voices that soon fell into rhythm. Incredibly, this strange assortment of people began to sing together. They started with the dwarven anthem, which the taller folk tried their best to lend voices to. Then the multitude rolled right into *Calide Portmore*, which everyone knew by heart. Then came the Calian folk song *Old RaMar* and finally *Ibyn Ryn*, a song Gwen had only heard sung by the mir in the alleys of Wayward once a year. Hearing the song brought Atyn to tears.

As the songs died down, the moon finally cast off the remainder of her dark cloak and climbed the sky in her full circle of silvery splendor. And off in the distance, spilling down the cliffside from the high ridge, Gwen heard the lonesome howls of wolves. She thought this strange as she wasn't aware they even had wolves in Delgos.

"There she is," Gwen told him. "There's the lady of the evening. She arrives making a delayed but dramatic entrance that no one will ever forget."

"Now I just have to hope that Hadrian doesn't hate me and want me dead," Rehn said. Then he looked at her. "He doesn't . . . does he?"

Gwen lifted her cup and sipped.

CHAPTER THIRTY-NINE

A Different Dawn

Hadrian and Royce stepped out of the South Tower into a throng of deliriously happy people—each of whom had expected to be dead. Everyone had gathered at the water's edge to die together. Instead, they witnessed the fiery venting of twin towers that made tear-soaked cheeks glisten. By dawn, those who had fled on foot would likely see the venting from the highland plains and turn back. The *Crown Jewel* would also spot the spray and return by sunrise. But that first night was special. Everyone who stood on that boardwalk at moonrise had faced and accepted death together. The truth of their differences had been revealed by the darkness of that penultimate pause as absurd foolishness, and this clarity of understanding formed everlasting bonds. Dwarfs, elves, Calians, subjects and the nobility of the seven kingdoms of Avryn, and even Ba Ran Ghazel were forever welded together by the great forge of Drumindor into a family—not of shared blood but of collective spirit. The returning residents would celebrate the survival of the city, but those who hadn't left experienced a transformative rebirth. Their lives, hearts, and minds forever changed. And every member of that unlikely tribe had witnessed Royce and Hadrian exit Drumindor.

Hadrian spotted Gwen and Rehn waiting just outside the door to the South Tower, as if they knew in advance where he and Royce would be. This mystery was crushed by the reality that Gwen was there at all, and her presence was obliterated by seeing Rehn alive.

Joy, relief, exhaustion, bewilderment—it all blended together the way it sometimes did when Hadrian drank too much. He remembered hugging Rehn and squeezing too hard, making the young man yelp. He recalled asking questions and not hearing the answers. And he remembered the full moon shining on them as somewhere in the distance a wolf howled.

Then the crowd came in. They formed a circle and began expressing gratitude with words and handshakes, then with hugs, kisses, and tears. Sloan pulled Hadrian down and kissed him on the mouth. Mister Parrot, who was openly sobbing, took Hadrian's hand as if to shake it, but just held on and never said a word. Everyone felt a need to approach, to thank, to touch them as if to prove their saviors were real, or perhaps that they were only men.

Auberon came last. His face was slick.

This is what it looks like to get tears out of a rock.

"Thank you," the old dwarf said. "I spent over a hundred years trying to do what you managed in a single day."

"Couldn't have done it without you."

Auberon nodded. "I know. Strange how life works. You can spend your whole life pushing on a door only to realize it needs to be pulled." He smiled. "Did the two of you have a *talk* with Gravis?"

Hadrian shook his head. "We only *spoke* with him." He gestured at the skyward streams of lava that continued to spray but whose arcs were shortening. "He did that, not us. Him . . . and his wife."

Auberon looked curious.

"Just like in the mural, she was there helping him at the end. Apparently, she'd been waiting for Gravis to join her."

Auberon looked down at the tattoo on his arm. "Maybe everyone is."

Seven days later, Hadrian watched the arrival of Hanson and Son's stagecoach from a stool at the Drunken Sailor. He sat backward with his elbows on the bar.

The coach came to a stop at the statue of Andvari Berling. The sun of another beautiful day made the coach's filigree shine. Customers dressed in wool and clutching cloaks and blankets stepped out, grinning at the warmth. They wandered toward the docks in awe, staring at the ocean as if they'd never seen water before. Hadrian continued to sip his coffee, a brew that was both richer and fruitier than anything he'd known in Avryn or Calis — it was also free.

Everything was, now.

Royce had destroyed the Falkirk diary, ruining his chance of ever obtaining a permanent key to the city, and yet having one was no longer necessary. No matter where they went or what they asked for, every merchant, craftsman, donkey-wagon driver, street vendor, and danthum owner refused payment, as those who had stayed didn't feel they could ask any more from them. At first, Hadrian thought it was nice, but soon he found it awkward, then finally unpleasant when he discovered the generosity wasn't always voluntary. Those who hadn't lived through the night of the full moon were *made to understand* that anyone failing to treat the city's saviors with the proper reverence and respect would become pariahs. Hadrian began leaving tips, only to have them promptly handed back. One fellow went to the effort of chasing him down to return four copper coins, accusing Hadrian of trying to ruin him.

Holding the last cup of coffee he wasn't allowed to pay for, which was served by a man who couldn't afford not to charge, Hadrian was thrilled to see the stagecoach. The golden sunshine of paradise had grown too bright to endure. The time had come to return to the comforting indifference of the cold gray world that waited beyond the horizon. He hoped that after a few years, new people would come to Tur Del Fur and the old ones would forget what Riyria had done because Hadrian would like to come back — but only if he could pay for his own drinks.

By midday, Shelby and Heath had unloaded the last of the luggage, and the four travelers — a young couple and an older one, whom Hadrian imagined might be the wealthy parents of newlyweds — had hired a donkey wagon and were off climbing Berling's Way. Shelby folded back all four doors and went right to cleaning the interior of the coach, and Heath put feed bags on Jack and Rabbit.

"Good day, sir!" Shelby called out, finally spotting Hadrian.

"Hello, Mister Hanson. Heath." Hadrian waved, then drank the last of his coffee and dropped a stack of coppers on the bar before walking across to the coachmen.

"Ready to go home?" Shelby asked.

Hadrian nodded. "Got room?"

"There are five of you, correct?"

"Nope. Just three: Gwen, Royce, and myself."

"What happened to the other two fellas?" Heath asked.

"They went back on the *Ellis Far* nearly a week ago," Hadrian replied.

Shelby's eyes showed a troubled squint.

"Had nothing to do with the *Flying Lady*. They were just in a hurry to leave."

Shelby nodded. "We heard there had been some trouble down here." Shelby looked about at the boardwalk, which was littered with homemade noisemakers, random bits of clothing — including a pair of shoes that hung from a pole — and discarded mugs of metal and wood. Hadrian suspected the cups were less abandoned and more lost. All rules, formalities, customs, conventions, and even quite a few laws had been ignored as the city celebrated its continued existence. The party that began just after the venting of Drumindor had continued unabated ever since, but the passion, and mortal endurance, was finally fading, and the celebration had dwindled to briefer periods of ebbs and flows. "Doesn't look so much like trouble as it does a celebration."

"Narrowly averted trouble," Hadrian explained. "So, do you have room to take us back?"

"We do indeed."

"It will take us a few minutes to get our luggage down," Hadrian said. "Is that all right?"

"We are at your service."

"You're certain you won't come back with us?" Hadrian asked Rehn as they stood beneath the lemon tree in the Turquoise Turtle's courtyard.

"The church is still a threat," the young man said. He looked like his old self again, his wound hidden by new clothes. "And according to Professor Arcadius, growing stronger every day. It isn't safe. But if you need me, I —"

"No." Hadrian held up a hand. "Stay and be safe. It's enough to know you're . . . that you're alive and doing well."

"That remains to be seen," Auberon said, as he appeared, wearing his straw hat with the blue feather and holding pruning shears. "I have my doubts that an ex-Avryn noble can learn to do real work."

"I will have your head spinning with my energy and dedication!" Rehn declared.

"We'll see." Auberon gave Hadrian a wink. "If you impress me, then when I take my long-delayed trip to see my family again, you will be responsible for all my holdings. They will be yours to care for."

"How many places do you own?" Hadrian asked.

"Including the slip my *Lorelei* docks in?" He closed one eye as he calculated. "Thirty-five."

"You own thirty-five rolkins?"

"Only twenty-eight are rolkins. The rest are shops I rent out, and I'm half-owner in a danthum."

"You must be rich," Rehn said, astounded.

Auberon shrugged. "Don't know, don't care. But it is a fair amount of work." He eyed Rehn. "So, you'd better get well fast. I've a lot to teach you in a short time, and I don't want everything I've built falling apart once I'm gone. You do what I say, work hard, and stay out of mischief, and one day the name of Rehn Purim will be known far and wide as a successful landowner and Tur Del Fur businessman."

Apprehension revealed itself on Rehn's face, and he began to shake his head. "I don't think that is such a good idea."

"You don't want to be successful?"

"I don't think it is healthy for *Rehn Purim* to be known far and wide — especially if I am seeking to stay out of mischief. I have enemies."

The old dwarf nodded and smiled. "You're not alone. That's how I ended up here. You might be surprised to learn Auberon isn't my real name. When I came here, I left the old one up north along with everything it stood for. I planned to make a new life — one that included living — and that required a new name. Perhaps you might consider doing the same." He clapped the young man lightly on the shoulder. "Just make sure it's a good name — something memorable, easy to say, and one you can be proud of."

Rehn looked up at Hadrian, and that long-lost smile of Pickles returned.

Royce was late getting back. He hadn't expected the meeting to take so long. And while he wasn't concerned about the stagecoach leaving without him, he didn't like making Gwen worry. He still couldn't believe she had stayed behind. She said it was her idea, but Royce couldn't help believing Arcadius was the real culprit.

The way Royce envisioned it, Arcadius was following the tried-and-true Rule of Three when he faked Rehn's death for the second time. Arcadius bet that no one, especially not Hadrian, would believe the boy had died. So to ensure his deception, he had had the dwarven doctor administer a drug that simulated death before letting Hadrian see the *body*.

Gwen likely believed that the end justified the means, so she was willing to participate in the ruse, but only for so long. She wasn't about to let the professor get away with it. She likely surmised that Hadrian would need proof, and a living, breathing Rehn would be the only evidence he would accept; as such, she stayed behind with Rehn.

None of this was at all astounding. That Arcadius had lied and manipulated the entire party for his own mysterious motives could have been anticipated and expected. If Royce hadn't been so masterfully distracted, he would have realized the doddering professor was up to something; the full extent of *exactly* what that was remained a mystery. One thing was not in question; the old man's desire to read Falkirk's diary was a driving force, and Royce enjoyed the knowledge that he had deprived the professor of that pleasure.

The truly crazy thing was that Gwen had stayed. She knew both the risks and the odds. And while it was one thing to *say* you believed in someone, it was a whole different world to push in all the chips and roll the dice. Gwen had a ticket to safety, but she had trusted Royce and bet her life on him, and, miraculously, he had somehow managed to reward that faith.

No, he didn't want Gwen to worry. Not anymore. She deserved better.

By the time Royce returned, the last of the luggage had been hoisted up and secured to the top of the coach. Auberon, Sloan, and Rehn were there to see them off.

"Well?" Sloan asked.

"They accept — or rather, Cornelius does, and the others agreed with him."

"Only took nearly losing the bleeding city ta open their eyes."

"As of now, all dwarfs are granted full citizenship. A dwarven council will be created, and its president will join the Triumvirate in running not just this city, but all of Delgos. Also, after seeing the error of removing Gravis from his position, the administration of Drumindor will be awarded to the dwarven council, who will choose Lord Byron's successor. The Trio will go over all this with you tomorrow in a meeting where you can work out the details. Then next week, I think, they plan to hold a parade to celebrate the rebirth of Tur Del Fur. The procession will march down Berling's Way to the statue here. Supposedly Cornelius DeLur will walk out and give a speech declaring all this."

"Supposedly?" Auberon asked.

Royce smiled. "Does anyone here think the man can actually walk?"

"So, it's really gonna happen?" Sloan asked.

Royce nodded. "DeLur isn't a fool. He realizes now that he needs you to keep his city working. This event gives him the perfect opportunity to make a change without conflict or embarrassment."

Auberon looked at Sloan. "You did it, lass. You made them see us for who we really are."

"*We* did it," she replied. Then she narrowed her eyes sternly. "And don't be thinking yer done."

"I am done. I finally helped make things better, and maybe this seed will bear fruit that can grow and spread."

"Sure, sure, but I'll need yer help. I can't be relying on the likes of Baric and Trig ta set up this council. And who are we gonna pick ta run Drumindor?"

Auberon stared at her. "You're just trying to keep me alive."

"I'm trying ta make the world a better place fer all Dromeians."

"You had to put it that way, didn't you? Go right for the soft meat. Hit me when I'm all exposed and vulnerable."

"Winning the peace isn't the hard part," she told him. "Keeping it is."

Auberon sighed, then he nodded. "Sloan, my sweet Bel"—he put his arm around her—"I think this is the beginning of a beautiful friendship."

The two waved their farewells and headed up Berling's Way toward what Royce assumed would be a celebration at Scram Scallie.

"Is that what Cornelius wanted? Is it why you were called to a meeting?" Hadrian asked.

"No," Royce replied. "He heard we were leaving and wanted to offer me a job."

Gwen, who had fashioned an overstuffed snack bag from a discarded patch of Auberon's fishing net, set it on the seat inside the coach. "Doing what?" she asked.

Royce hesitated, then said, "What I used to do."

"Oh?" Gwen smiled, then her eyes widened. "Oh!"

Royce nodded. "Says he'll set me up here. Give me a small palace on the First Tier and a staff of servants to manage it. He also offered a generous salary. I was promised the life of a noble, a member of the landed gentry, a vassal to his lordship. I'd have prestige, power, fine clothes, and my own carriage."

Both Gwen and Hadrian stared at him. They looked worried. The helpful family that had taken in the wounded wolf saw it looking out the open door, listening to the howls of its peers calling from the dark woods.

"What did you say?" Gwen asked, her voice weak.

"Told him I already have a job: watching out for the two of you. Turns out that's a full-time occupation. Also, that sunshine and ocean waves don't agree with me. I like my cloak and my independence. From now on, if I kill someone it's because *I* want them dead."

"Oh-kay." Hadrian looked at Gwen and nodded approvingly. "I suppose we can chalk that up as a win, right?"

Gwen smiled at Royce.

"We're all set to go," Shelby announced. "Hop in, folks."

"You're riding on top again, right, Hadrian?" Royce asked.

"What?" He looked baffled. "There's only three of us. Coach seats four."

"But you're riding on top because of how nice a day it is. You want to take advantage of the sunshine and blue skies before we hit the cold, cloudy weather of home. Isn't that right?"

Hadrian glanced at Gwen, who said nothing. She merely grinned and rocked forward and back from her heels to her toes like an excited child.

Hadrian sighed. "Fine. But I'm coming in at the first sign of snow. And save some of those snacks for me, and not just the ground peas. There's some good stuff in there."

Royce opened the coach door for Gwen as Hadrian climbed up behind the driver's seat.

"Nice to have you aboard again, sir." Heath extended an arm and helped pull Hadrian up.

As he did, Hadrian noticed a ring on Heath's hand. "That wasn't there before."

Heath grinned. "I finally found a girl with most of her fingers."

"It's only been a month!"

Heath shrugged. "When you know, you know."

"She's a wonderful young lady," Shelby declared. "An absolute princess."

"Meaning she's got four limbs, two eyes, and most of her fingers, right?" Hadrian asked.

"Meaning she said *yes*," Shelby corrected.

"She's much more than all that," Heath said. "Her name is Winifred Plinth — but don't ever call her that. She goes by Winnie. Her father is a dairy farmer along our route. We stop there frequently for milk, cheese, and to water the horses. She thinks my life riding up and down the road is exotic and exciting. To her, I'm a worldly adventurer, a hero."

"Well, congratulations. She sounds wonderful."

"How about you, Hadrian?" Shelby asked as he released the brake. "Any rings in your future?"

Hadrian frowned. "For a while, I thought there might be, but I was wrong."

"Didn't have all her fingers?" Heath asked with a smile.

Hadrian thought about it and shook his head. "No. She just wasn't the one."

"No one is perfect, son," Shelby said as he turned the coach around. "Don't be so picky, and don't wait too long. Time is a funny thing. One minute it seems you have forever, then the next you think it's too late. But it's never too late, Hadrian, remember that. The world could be coming to an end, and it still wouldn't be too late."

"Oh, it's too late, I'm afraid." Hadrian laughed. "The world as we knew it already ended—Royce Melborn finally kissed Gwen DeLancy. I'm surprised there is still a sun in the sky."

"I heard that," Royce said.

"I know."

Shelby drove the team up Berling's Way toward the highland, to the north, toward that thin gray line on the horizon where color faded to a dull gray and men faced the consequences of bad decisions. Riyria was going home.

Afterword

Greetings all! Robin here. I'm thrilled to be back with my two favorite rogues for hire. And because we exceeded a Kickstarter stretch goal, I'm going to share my thoughts about *Drumindor*. For those who may not know, I'm Michael's wife, and I take care of a host of the behind-the-scenes activities to produce his works. Doing this frees up his time to write more stories, which I think is good for all of us.

Before I start "dishing," I just want to thank all the people who have mentioned me and my afterwords when writing to Michael (which you can do at **michael.sullivan.dc@gmail.com**). Honestly, I thought writing these might be a waste of time, but after hearing the positive feedback, I'm glad I took the plunge. So thank you for all the kind words.

As I start to write this afterword, I'm hearing Helen Hunt's character from the 1997 movie *As Good as it Gets* when she says, *"What I needed, he gave me great!"* That's exactly how I feel after finishing this book. Don't get me wrong, *Farilane* is probably my single favorite book of Michael's, and *Esrahaddon* was fabulous because of all the backstory in it. But let's face it, these books had world-ending stakes which meant they were "packed with drama" and less "a fun romp." So it was great to get back to a story where the tone is lighter and the risks smaller. In many ways, I think of *Drumindor* as a "cozy, slice-of-life" fantasy where I knew I was going to laugh, and I didn't have to worry about a key character dying. After all, these are prequels to Revelations, so I think it was safe to assume that Royce and Hadrian would be around at the end of the book.

As some may know, Michael wrote The Riyria Chronicles as a gift to me, since I missed Royce and Hadrian so very much. But when he started writing *The Crown Tower*, I had some trepidation. At that time, it had been years since he'd written The Riyria Revelations, and being away from the pair for so long, I wasn't sure if he could capture the same "magic" of their personalities and their unique relationship. I shouldn't have doubted. The pair were as wonderful as ever. This time, however, the time in-between had been even longer. Still, I wasn't concerned. These days I no longer doubt Michael's writing ability, but I couldn't have been more thrilled when I reunited with Riyria and discovered they hadn't changed a bit. I grinned from ear to ear whenever they were together.

The discussion of Monty Mousey wine and Hadrian falling off his horse were "quintessential Riyria." It's quite possibly my all-time favorite Royce and Hadrian scene of any book. Reading "drunk Hadrian" dialog I was reminded of Dudley Moore from the 1981 film, *Arthur*, a family favorite that we often quote from. If you haven't seen it, you might give it a try.

For years, I've seen fan mail that proclaim statements such as, "I would read any story with Royce and Hadrian in it. They don't even have to do anything special. I'd listen to them as they create a shopping list." I couldn't agree more. In many ways, scenes where I was simply "hanging out" with the pair became the ones at the top of my list. Like "drunk Hadrian," other favorites include eating fish shawarma, Royce asking for romantic advice (like the angstiest of all pimple-faced teenagers), and the two of them trying to decipher the combo to get into *Drumindor*.

It would be boring (and repetitive) for me to go through each of these scenes, but here's what I considered to be the best exchange with the two.

> "What's going on, Royce?"
> "I wish I knew."
> "Can I have a hint?"
> Royce pointed at the light on the pole. "Look at all those moths."
> Hadrian gave it a glance. "Can I have a better hint?"

In many ways, this book was an opportunity to see the pair in a different light. For the most part, they weren't battling dragons with complicated names, or saving the world of Elan from destruction, they were on VACATION, and that was just fine with me. In fact, thinking about that brings to mind the 2021 movie *Barb and Star Go to Vista Del Mar*. Do yourself a favor and watch it this winter when the cold wind blows and you need a two hour mini-vacation. You'll thank me later. It is a quirky film that no one ever seems to have heard of, but I've yet to watch it with anyone who wasn't thoroughly entertained. During much of this book, I couldn't shake the feeling of Royce and Hadrian go to Vista Tur Del Fur.

Whether the above movie was an influence for Michael when writing *Drumindor*, I can't say. But one movie's influence is undeniable. Did you notice? If not, here are some clues: The Blue Parrot, a casino, a fat man, a freedom fighter, the name Ugarte, the singing of a national anthem in a crowded bar, and a murdered courier who was robbed of something everyone is looking for. Yep, it was 1942's *Casablanca,* and just as you should read "drunk Hadrian" with the voice of "drunk Dudley Moore," you should picture any scene with Royce and Cornelius DeLur as being played by Bogart and Sydney Greenstreet. And here is a little behind the scenes thing. I asked Michael to add the following line just to cement the connection: *"I think this is the beginning of a beautiful friendship."*

Both *Casablanca* and *Barb and Star* have a setting that is similar to *Drumindor's*, and I absolutely LOVED visiting Tur Del Fur! I so didn't want to leave it by the time the book was over. I kid you not, the final night at The Blue Parrot brought a tear to my eye. Especially when Calvary Graxton says, *"Go forth, all of you, and tell the tale of Tur and fishermen, the Unholy Trio and the Yellow Jackets, the dwarven towers and of the place where dreams came true, and most of all of parrots of blue and a way that was new, that hopefully one day might be again. A toast to Tur Del Fur!"* Even thinking of it now, I lament the loss of that city and its people.

Speaking of tears, how emotionally heartbreaking was it to see Royce Melborn cry? That's another top moment for me. There is so much wrapped up in *that* character having *that* reaction. Royce has really grown since *The Crown Tower* and I can't help but think that if he stays the course, he might become "a real boy" someday! And yes, that's a shout out to Disney's 1940 movie *Pinocchio* because I'm on a movie association roll.

Another thing that tickled me in this book is how Michael made me smile with nothing more than Royce and Hadrian's re-naming of people: Prematurely

Pardoned Pete, Future Corpse Number One, the Gingerdead Man, unusually friendly cloakroom lady, and Bull Neck and Orange Tunic (who Hadrian immediately recognized as Brook and Clem from Dulgath). These nuggets were immensely entertaining.

But perhaps my favorite thing of all about this book is how it interconnects to the larger tale. With the publication of the fourteen books that came out after The Riyria Revelations, it's apparent that Michael's debut series was just one small corner of a much larger tapestry — one whose enormity is almost beyond my comprehension. When Michael mentioned in his Author's Note that *Drumindor* became so much more, he wasn't kidding. I even see connections to books yet to be written, as mentioned by TEC's announcement of The Cycle.

To what do I refer? Well, another movie quote comes to mind. This one from the 1987 classic *The Princess Bride* when Inigo Montoya says, *"No, there is too much. Let me sum up."* A partial list includes, Falkirk de Roche, Mister Hipple, Beatrice, Pickles, Mileva Hitartheon, Bernie DeFoe, Virgil Puck, Bran, Brin, Dulgath, Genevieve Winters, King Mideon, Villar, Rain, Neith, Trilos, the Martel diary, Typhons, Brotherhood of Maribor, Arcadius's meddling with Gwen and Royce, an old fortress on the sea, a lack of rain, the Morgan, Hadrian's mention of the color blue, Kile and the White Feather, Millie, the three creatures trying to escape from deep underground, Avempartha, Tur, the game of Ten Fingers, Merrick Marius, Manzant, the Gur Em, the tiger, Dibben, Death by Steps, Gwen's insistence that the singer is not "the one," people's faces being eaten, Gwen's four gold coins, and most important the panels on the wall inside Drumindor. There were even a few things that weren't explicitly mentioned, but I'm sure my guesses are correct about topics such as: Farilane, a certain individual who goes by multiple names, Mawyndulë, Ruby Finn, and the missing Second Book of Brin. Michael is spinning a lot of plates in this book, and I'm amazed at his prowess of telling a standalone story and yet one that is an integral part of a much larger tale. As much as I would love to go into detail about the things listed above, I can't because for those who haven't read the other books, anything I would say here would be riddled with spoilers. Which gave me a brainstorm, and something for me to spend my time on over the next few years while Michael is writing The Cycle. I'm going to create a YouTube channel called Sullivan's Spoils where I'll be able to talk freely about the books in Elan and how each fits into the whole. You can learn more about Sullivan's Spoils in the next section.

Since I can't talk about the spoilers, it's time for me to wrap up. I'm hearing a song from the 1965 movie, *The Sound of Music,* and I'll bid you, *"Adieu, adieu, to yieu and yieu and yieu."* But before I go, I just want to thank you for all the incredible support you've given the stories, and the love you've expressed for my afterwords. As Michael has alluded, it may be quite some time before we can chat again, but hopefully you'll stop by and visit me at Sullivan's Spoils. Until then, I remain a humble servant in helping Michael get more stories out into the world. I'll do my best to keep them coming.

Robin Sullivan
September 2024

Sullivan's Spoils

Welcome to a new feature for peering inside the world of Elan by Michael J. Sullivan. I'm Robin Sullivan, his wife and number one fan.

With the release of *Drumindor,* Michael's 3,000-year epic is essentially complete. One of the things I've enjoyed the most about the series is that while each book is more or less self-contained, they are all part of a "series wide" story arc, which itself is a portion of an even larger "multi-series" saga.

While Michael is working on The Cycle Project (the fifth and final series), I'll have some time on my hands, and for my own edification, I plan on combing through each of the books to gather the breadcrumbs that Michael has left for us. I'm going to start with *Drumindor* and then go through the other books based on order of publication.

The venue I'm going to use for this is YouTube, because talking is so much easier than writing, and I'm hoping to have Michael come on from time to time, and even invite fellow readers to be a guest if they like.

As the name implies, ALL of these videos will be filled with spoilers, so only come and visit the site if you've read the entire set of books.

As I write this, the channel isn't yet set up. But here are links where you can get more information as it becomes available:

- **bit.ly/sullivan-spoils** - website where new videos will be posted
- **bit.ly/sullivan-spoils-discord** - discord server
- **bit.ly/sullivan-spoils-guest-signup** - form to sign-up to be a guest

I hope you'll join me there!

Have you read any of The Legends of the First Empire novels? If not, you probably aren't aware of the vast number of lies that Michael has told throughout The Riyria Revelations books. After all, history is written by the victors, and myths and legends are created by those in power who wish to suppress the truth for their own benefit. Here is a peek into the initial chapter of *Age of Myth*, the first book of this six-book series.

CHAPTER ONE
Of Gods and Men

In the days of darkness before the war, men were called Rhunes. We lived in Rhuneland or Rhulyn as it was once known. We had little to eat and much to fear. What we feared most were the gods across the Bern River, where we were not allowed. Most people believe our conflict with the Fhrey started at the Battle of Grandford, but it actually began on a day in early spring when two men crossed the river. — THE BOOK OF BRIN

Raithe's first impulse was to pray. Curse, cry, scream, pray — people did such things in their last minutes of life. But praying struck Raithe as absurd given that his problem was the angry god twenty feet away. Gods weren't known for their tolerance, and this one appeared on the verge of striking them both dead. Neither Raithe nor his father had noticed the god's approach. The waters of the nearby converging rivers made enough noise to mask an army's passage. Raithe would have preferred an army.

Dressed in shimmering clothes, the god sat on a horse and was accompanied by two servants on foot. They were men, but dressed in the same remarkable clothing. All three silent, watching.

"Hey?" Raithe called to his father.

Herkimer knelt beside a deer, opening its stomach with his knife. Earlier, Raithe had landed a spear in the stag's side, and he and his father had spent most of the morning chasing it. Herkimer had stripped off his wool leigh mor as well as his shirt because opening a deer's belly was a bloody business. "What?" He looked up.

Raithe jerked his head toward the god, and his father's sight tracked to the three figures. The old man's eyes widened, and the color left his face.

I knew this was a bad idea, Raithe thought.

His father had seemed so confident, so sure that crossing the forbidden river would solve their problems. But he'd mentioned his certainty enough times to make Raithe wonder. Now the old man looked as if he'd forgotten how to breathe. Herkimer wiped his knife on the deer's side before slipping it into his belt and getting up.

"Ah . . ." Raithe's father began. Herkimer looked at the half-gutted deer, then back at the god. "It's . . . okay."

This was the total sum of his father's wisdom, his grand defense for their high crime of trespassing on divine land. Raithe wasn't sure if slaughtering one of the deities' deer was also an offense but assumed it didn't help their situation. And although Herkimer said it was okay, his face told a different story. Raithe's stomach sank. He had no idea what he'd expected his father to say, but something more than that.

Not surprisingly, the god wasn't appeased, and the three continued to stare in growing irritation.

They were on a tiny point of open meadowland where the Bern and North Branch rivers met. A pine forest, thick and rich, grew a short distance up the slope behind them. Down at the point where the rivers converged lay a stony beach. Beneath a snow-gray blanket of sky, the river's roar was the only sound. Just minutes earlier Raithe had seen the tiny field as a paradise. That was then.

Raithe took a slow breath and reminded himself that he didn't have experience with gods or their expressions. He'd never observed a god up close, never seen beech-leaf-shaped ears, eyes blue as the sky, or hair that spilled like molten gold. Such smooth skin and white teeth were beyond reason. This was a being born not of the earth but of air and light. His robes billowed in the breeze and shimmered in the sun, proclaiming an otherworldly glory. The harsh, judgmental glare was exactly the expression Raithe expected from an immortal being.

The horse was an even bigger surprise. Raithe's father had told him about such animals, but until then Raithe hadn't believed. His old man had a habit of embellishing the truth, and for more than twenty years Raithe had heard the tales. After a few drinks, his father would tell everyone how he'd killed five men with a single swing or fought the North Wind to a standstill. The older Herkimer got, the larger the stories grew. But this four-hooved tall tale was looking back at Raithe with large glossy eyes, and when the horse shook its head, he wondered if the mounts of gods understood speech.

"No, really, it's okay," Raithe's father told them again, maybe thinking they hadn't heard his previous genius. "I'm allowed here." He took a step forward and pointed to the medal hanging from a strip of hide amid the dirt and pine needles stuck to the sweat on his chest. Half naked, sunbaked, and covered in blood up to his elbows, his father appeared the embodiment of a mad barbarian. Raithe wouldn't have believed him, either.

"See this?" his father went on. The burnished metal clutched by thick ruddy fingers reflected the midday sun. "I fought for your people against the Gula-Rhunes in the High Spear Valley. I did well. A Fhrey commander gave me this. Said I earned a reward."

"Dureyan clan," the taller servant told the god, his tone somewhere between disappointment and disgust. He wore a rich-looking silver torc around his neck—both servants did. The jewelry must be a mark of their station.

The gangly man lacked a beard but sported a long nose, sharp cheeks, and small clever eyes. He reminded Raithe of a weasel or a fox, and he wasn't fond of either. Raithe was also repulsed by how the man stood: stooped, eyes low, hands clasped. Abused dogs exhibited more self-esteem.

What kind of men travel with a god?

"That's right. I'm Herkimer, son of Hiemdal, and this is my son Raithe."

"You've broken the law," the servant stated. The nasal tone even sounded the way a weasel might talk.

"No, no. It's not like that. Not at all."

The lines on his father's face deepened, and his lips stretched tighter. He stopped walking forward but held the medal out like a talisman, his eyes hopeful. "This proves what I'm saying, that I earned a reward. See, I sort of figured we"—he gestured toward Raithe—"my son and I could live on this little point." He waved at the meadow. "We don't need much. Hardly anything, really. You see, on our side of the river, back in Dureya, the dirt's no good. We can't grow anything, and there's nothing to hunt."

The pleading in his father's voice was something Raithe hadn't heard before and didn't like.

"You're not allowed here." This time it was the other servant, the balding one. Like the tall weasel-faced fellow, he lacked a proper beard, as if growing one were a thing that needed to be taught. The lack of hair exposed in fine detail a decidedly sour expression.

"But you don't understand. I *fought* for your people. I *bled* for your people. I *lost three sons* fighting for your kind. And I was promised a reward." Herkimer held out the medal again, but the god didn't look at it. He stared past them, focusing on some distant, irrelevant point.

Herkimer let go of the medal. "If this spot is a problem, we'll move. My son actually liked another place west of here. We'd be farther away from you. Would that be better?"

Although the god still didn't look at them, he appeared even more annoyed. Finally he spoke. "You will obey."

An average voice. Raithe was disappointed. He had expected thunder.

The god then addressed his servants in the divine language. Raithe's father had taught him some of their tongue. He wasn't fluent but knew enough to understand the god didn't want them to have weapons on this side of the river. A moment later the tall servant relayed the message in Rhunic. "Only Fhrey are permitted to possess weapons west of the Bern. Cast yours into the river."

Herkimer glanced at their gear piled near a stump and in a resigned voice told Raithe, "Get your spear and do as they say."

"And the sword off your back," the tall servant said.

Herkimer looked shocked and glanced over his shoulder as if he'd forgotten the weapon was there. Then he faced the god and spoke directly to him in the Fhrey language. *"This is my family blade. I cannot throw it away."*

The god sneered, showing teeth.

"It's a sword," the servant insisted.

Herkimer hesitated only a moment. "Okay, okay, fine. We'll go back across the river, right now. C'mon, Raithe."

The god made an unhappy sound.

"After you give up the sword," the servant said.

Herkimer glared. "This copper has been in my family for generations."

"It's a weapon. Toss it down."

Herkimer looked at his son, a sidelong glance.

Although he might not have been a good father—wasn't as far as Raithe was concerned—Herkimer had instilled one thing in all his sons: pride. Self-respect came from the ability to defend oneself. Such things gave a man dignity. In all of Dureya, in their entire clan, his father was the only man to wield a sword—a *metal* blade. Wrought from beaten copper, its marred, dull sheen was the color of a summer sunset, and legend held that the short-bladed heirloom had been mined and fashioned by a genuine Dherg smith. In comparison with the god's sword, whose hilt was intricately etched and encrusted with gems, the copper blade was pathetic. Still, Herkimer's weapon defined him; enemy clans knew him as Coppersword—a feared and respected title. His father could never give up that blade.

The roar of the river was cut by the cry of a hawk soaring above. Birds were known to be the embodiment of omens, and Raithe didn't take the soaring wail as a positive sign. In its eerie echo, his father faced the god. "I can't give you this sword."

Raithe couldn't help but smile. Herkimer, son of Hiemdal, of Clan Dureya wouldn't bend so far, not even for a god.

The smaller servant took the horse's lead as the god dismounted.

Raithe watched—impossible not to. The way the god moved was mesmerizing, so graceful, fluid, and poised. Despite the impressive movement, the god wasn't physically imposing. He wasn't tall, broad, or muscled. Raithe and his father had built strong shoulders and arms by wielding spear and shield throughout their lives. The god, on the other hand, appeared delicate, as if he had lived bedridden and spoon-fed. If the Fhrey were a man, Raithe wouldn't have been afraid. Given the disparity between them in weight and height, he'd avoid a fight, even if challenged. To engage in such an unfair match would be cruel, and he wasn't cruel. His brothers had received Raithe's share of that particular trait.

"You don't understand." Herkimer tried once more to explain. "This sword has been handed down from father to son —"

The god rushed forward and punched Raithe's father in the stomach, doubling him over. Then the Fhrey stole the copper sword, a dull scrape sounding as the weapon came free of its sheath. While Herkimer was catching his breath, the god examined the weapon with revulsion. Shaking his head, the god turned his back on Herkimer to show the tall servant the pitiable blade. Instead of joining the god's ridicule of the weapon, the servant cringed. Raithe saw the future through the weasel man's expression, for he was the first to notice Herkimer's reaction.

Raithe's father drew the skinning knife from his belt and lunged.

This time the god didn't disappoint. With astounding speed, he whirled and drove the copper blade into Raithe's father's chest. Herkimer's forward momentum did the work of running the sword deep. The fight ended the moment it began. His father gasped and fell, the sword still in his chest.

Raithe didn't think. If he had paused even for an instant, he might have reconsidered, but there was more of his father in him than he wanted to believe. The sword being the only weapon within reach, he pulled the copper from his father's body. With all his might, Raithe swung at the god's neck. He fully expected the blade to cut clean through, but the copper sliced only air as the divine being dodged. The god drew his own weapon as Raithe swung again. The two swords met. A dull ping sounded, and the weight in Raithe's hands vanished along with most of the blade. When he finished his swing, only the hilt of his family's heritage remained; the rest flew through the air and landed in a tuft of young pines.

The god stared at him with a disgusted smirk, then spoke in the divine language. *"Not worth dying for, was it?"*

Then the god raised his blade once more as Raithe shuffled backward.

Too slow! Too slow!

His retreat was futile. Raithe was dead. Years of combat training told him so. In that instant before understanding became reality, he had the chance to regret his entire life.

I've done nothing, he thought as his muscles tightened for the expected burst of pain.

It never came.

Raithe had lost track of the servants—so had the god. Neither of the combatants expected, nor saw, the tall weasel-faced man slam his master in the back of the head with a river rock the size and shape of a round loaf of bread. Raithe realized what had happened only after the god collapsed, revealing the servant and his stone.

"Run," the rock bearer said. "With any luck, his head will hurt too much for him to chase us when he wakes."

"What have you done!" the other servant shouted, his eyes wide as he backed up, pulling the god's horse away.

"Calm down," the one holding the rock told the other servant.

Raithe looked at his father, lying on his back. Herkimer's eyes were still open, as if watching clouds. Raithe had cursed his father many times over the years. The man neglected his family, pitted his sons against one another, and had been away when Raithe's mother and sister died. In some ways—many ways—Raithe hated his father, but at that moment what he saw was a man who had taught his sons to fight and not give in. Herkimer had done the best with what he had, and what he had was a life trapped on barren soil because the gods made capricious demands. Raithe's father never stole, cheated, or held his tongue when something needed to be said. He was a hard man, a cold man, but one who had the courage to stand up for himself and what was right. What Raithe saw on the ground at his feet was the last of his dead family.

He felt the broken sword in his hands.

"No!" the servant holding the horse cried out as Raithe drove the remainder of the jagged copper blade through the god's throat.

Both servants had fled, the smaller one on the horse and the other chasing on foot. Now the one who had wielded the rock returned. Covered in sweat and shaking his head, he trotted back to the meadow. "Meryl's gone," he said. "He isn't the best rider, but he doesn't have to be. The horse knows the way back to Alon Rhist." He stopped after noticing Raithe. "What are you doing?"

Raithe was standing over the body of the god. He'd picked up the Fhrey's sword and was pressing the tip against the god's throat. "Waiting. How long does it usually take?"

"How long does what take?"

"For him to get up."

"He's dead. Dead people don't generally *get up*," the servant said.

Reluctant to take his eyes off the god, Raithe ventured only the briefest glance at the servant, who was bent and struggling to catch his breath. "What are you talking about?"

"What are *you* talking about?"

"I want to know how long we have before he rises. If I cut off his head, will he stay down longer?"

The servant rolled his eyes. "He's not getting up! You killed him."

"My Tetlin ass! That's a god. Gods don't die. They're immortal."

"Really not so much," the servant said, and to Raithe's shock he kicked the god's body, which barely moved. He kicked it again, and the head rocked to one side, sand sticking to its cheek. "See? Dead. Get it? Not immortal. Not a god, just a Fhrey. They die. There's a difference between long-lived and immortal. Immortal means you can't die . . . even if you want to. Fact is, the Fhrey are a lot more similar to Rhunes than we'd like to think."

"We're nothing alike. Look at him." Raithe pointed at the fallen Fhrey.

"Oh, yes," the servant replied. "He's so different. He has only one head, walks on two feet, and has two hands and ten fingers. You're right. Nothing like us at all."

The servant looked down at the body and sighed. "His name was Shegon. An incredibly talented harp player, a cheat at cards, and a *brideeth eyn mer*—which is to say . . ." The servant paused. "No, there is no other way to say it. He wasn't well liked, and now he's dead."

Raithe looked over suspiciously.

Is he lying? Trying to put me off guard?

"You're wrong," Raithe said with full conviction. "Have you ever seen a dead Fhrey? I haven't. My father hasn't. No one I've ever known has. And they don't age."

"They do, just very slowly."

Raithe shook his head. "No, they don't. My father mentioned a time when he was a boy, and he met a Fhrey named Neason. Forty-five years later, they met again, but Neason looked exactly the same."

"Of course he did. I just told you they age slowly. Fhrey can live for thousands of years. A bumblebee lives for only a few months. To a bumblebee, you appear immortal."

Raithe wasn't fully convinced, but it would explain the blood. He hadn't expected any. In retrospect, he shouldn't have attacked the Fhrey at all. His father had taught him not to start a fight he couldn't win, and fighting an immortal god fell squarely into that category. But then again it was his father who had started the whole thing.

Sure is a lot of blood.

An ugly pool had formed underneath the god, staining the grass and his glistening robes. His neck still had the gash, a nasty, jagged tear like a second mouth. Raithe had expected the wound to miraculously heal or simply vanish. When the god rose, Raithe would have the advantage. He was strong and could best most men in Dureya, which meant he could best most men. Even his father thought twice about making his son too angry.

Raithe stared down at the Fhrey, whose eyes were open and rolled up. The gash in his throat was wider now. A god — a real god — would never permit kicks from a servant. "Okay, maybe they aren't immortal." He relaxed and took a step back.

"My name is Malcolm," the servant said. "Yours is Raithe?"

"Uh-huh," Raithe said. With one last glare at the Fhrey's corpse, Raithe tucked the jeweled weapon into his belt and then lifted his father's body.

"Now what are you doing?" Malcolm asked.

"Can't bury him down here. These rivers are bound to flood this plain."

"*Bury* him? When word gets back to Alon Rhist, the Fhrey will . . ." He looked sick. "We need to leave."

"So go."

Raithe carried his father to a small hill in the meadow and gently lowered him to the ground. As a final resting place, it wasn't much but would have to do. Turning around, he found the god's ex-servant staring in disbelief. "What?"

Malcolm started to laugh, then stopped, confused. "You don't understand. Glyn is a fast horse and has the stamina of a wolf. Meryl will reach Alon Rhist by nightfall. He'll tell the Instarya everything to save himself. They'll come after us. We need to get moving."

"Go ahead," Raithe said, taking Herkimer's medal and putting it on. Then he closed his father's eyes. He couldn't remember having touched the old man's face before.

"You need to go, too."

"After I bury my father."

"The Rhune is dead."

Raithe cringed at the word. "He was a *man*."

"Rhune — man — same thing."

"Not to me — and not to him." Raithe strode down to the riverbank, littered with thousands of rocks of various sizes. The problem wasn't finding proper stones but deciding which ones to choose.

Malcolm planted his hands on his hips, glaring with an expression somewhere between astonishment and anger. "It'll take hours! You're wasting time."

Raithe crouched and picked up a rock. The top had been baked warm by the sun; the bottom was damp, cool, and covered in wet sand. "He deserves a proper burial and would have done the same for me." Raithe found it ironic given that his father had rarely shown him any kindness. But it was true; Herkimer would have faced death to see his son properly buried. "Besides, do you have any idea what can happen to the spirit of an unburied body?"

The man stared back, bewildered.

"They return as manes to haunt you for not showing the proper respect. And manes can be vicious." Raithe hoisted another large sand-colored rock and walked up the slope. "My father could be a real cul when he was alive. I don't need him stalking me for the rest of my life."

"But—"

"But what?" Raithe set the rocks down near his father's shoulders. He'd do the outline before starting the pile. "He's not your father. I don't expect you to stay."

"That's not the point."

"What *is* the point?"

The servant hesitated, and Raithe took the opportunity to return to the bank and search for more rocks.

"I need your help," the man finally said.

Raithe picked up a large stone and carried it up the bank, clutched against his stomach. "With what?"

"You know how to . . . well, you know . . . live . . . out here, I mean." The servant looked at the deer carcass, which had gathered a host of flies. "You can hunt, cook, and find shelter, right? You know what berries to eat, which animals you can pet and which to run away from."

"You don't pet any animals."

"See? Good example of how little I know about this sort of thing. Alone, I'd be dead in a day or two. Frozen stiff, buried in a landslide, or gored by some antlered beast."

Raithe set the stone and returned down the slope, clapping his hands together to clean off the sand. "Makes sense."

"Of course it makes sense. I'm a sensible fellow. And if you were sensible, we'd go. Now."

Raithe lifted another rock. "If you're bent on sticking with me and in such a hurry, you might consider helping."

The man looked at the riverbank's rounded stones and sighed. "Do we have to use such big ones?"

"Big ones for the bottom, smaller ones on top."

"Sounds like you've done this before."

"People die often where I come from, and we have a lot of rocks." Raithe wiped his brow with his forearm, pushing back a mat of dark hair. He'd rolled the woolen sleeves of his undertunic up. The spring days were still chilly, but the work made him sweat. He considered taking off his leigh mor and leather but decided against it. Burying his father should be an unpleasant task, and a good son should feel something at such a time. If *uncomfortable* was the best he could manage, Raithe would settle for that.

Malcolm carried over a pair of rocks and set them down, letting Raithe place them. He paused to rub his hands clean.

"Okay, Malcolm," Raithe said, "you need to pick bigger ones or we'll be here forever."

Malcolm scowled but returned to the bank, gathered two good-sized stones, and carried them under his arms like melons. He walked unsteadily in sandals. Thin, with a simple strap, they were ill suited to the landscape. Raithe's clothes were shoddy — sewn scraps of wool with leather accents that he'd cured himself — but at least they were durable.

Raithe searched for and found a small smooth stone.

"I thought you wanted bigger rocks?" Malcolm asked.

"This isn't for the pile." Raithe opened his father's right hand and exchanged the rock for the skinning knife. "He'll need it to get to Rel or Alysin if he's worthy — Nifrel if he's not."

"Oh, right."

After outlining the body, Raithe piled the stones from the feet upward. Then he retrieved his father's leigh mor, which still lay next to the deer's carcass, and laid it over Herkimer's face. A quick search in the little patch of pines produced the other end of the copper sword. Raithe considered leaving the weapon but worried about grave robbers. His father had died for the shattered blade; it deserved to be cared for.

Raithe glanced at the Fhrey once more. "You're certain he won't get up?"

Malcolm looked over from where he was lifting a rock. "Positive. Shegon *is* dead."

Together they hoisted a dozen more rocks onto the growing pile before Raithe asked, "Why were you with him?"

Malcolm pointed to the torc around his neck as if it explained everything. Raithe was puzzled until he noticed the necklace was a complete circle. The ring of metal wasn't a torc, not jewelry at all — it was a collar.

Not a servant — a slave.

The sun was low in the sky when they dropped the last rocks to complete the mound. Malcolm washed in the river while Raithe sang his mourning song. Then he slung his father's broken blade over his shoulder, adjusted the Fhrey's sword in his belt, and gathered his things and those of his father. They didn't have much: a wooden shield, a bag containing a good hammer stone, a rabbit pelt Raithe planned to make into a pouch as soon as it cured, the last of the cheese, the single blanket they had shared, a stone hand ax, his father's knife, and Raithe's spear.

"Where to?" Malcolm asked. His face and hair were covered in sweat, and the man had nothing, not even a sharpened stick to defend himself.

"Here, sling this blanket over your shoulder. Tie it tight, and take my spear."

"I don't know how to use a spear."

"It's not complicated. Just point and stick."

Raithe looked around. Going home didn't make sense. That was back east, closer to Alon Rhist. Besides, his family was gone. The clan would still welcome him, but it was impossible to build a life in Dureya. Another option would be to push farther west into the untamed wilderness of Avrlyn. To do so they'd need to get past a series of Fhrey outposts along the western rivers. Like Alon Rhist, the strongholds were built to keep men out. Herkimer had warned Raithe about the fortifications of Merredydd and Seon Hall, but his father never explained exactly where those were. By himself, Raithe could likely avoid walking into one, but he wouldn't have much of a life alone in the wilderness. Taking Malcolm wouldn't help. By the look and sound of the ex-slave, he wouldn't survive a year in the wild.

"We'll cross back into Rhulyn but go south." He pointed over the river at the dramatic rising hillside covered with evergreens. "That's the Crescent Forest, runs for miles in all directions. Not the safest place, but it'll provide cover — help hide us." He glanced up at the sky. "Still early in the season, but there should be some food to forage and game to hunt."

"What do you mean by *not the safest place?*"

"Well, I've not been there myself, but I've heard things."

"What sorts of things?"

Raithe tightened his belt and the strap holding the copper to his back before offering a shrug. "Oh, you know, tabors, raow, leshies. Stuff like that."

Malcolm continued to stare. "Vicious animals?"

"Oh, yeah — those, too, I suppose."

"Those . . . *too?*"

"Sure, bound to be in a forest that size."

"Oh," Malcolm said, looking apprehensive as his eyes followed a branch floating past them at a quick pace. "How will we get across?"

"You can swim, right?"

Malcolm looked stunned. "That's a thousand feet from bank to bank."

"It has a nice current, too. Depending on how well you swim, we'll probably reach the far side several miles south of here. But that's good. It'll make us harder to track."

"Impossible, I'd imagine," Malcolm said, grimacing, his sight chained to the river.

The ex-slave of the Fhrey looked terrified, and Raithe understood why. He'd felt the same way when Herkimer had forced him across.

"Ready?" Raithe asked.

Malcolm pursed his lips; the skin of his hands was white as he clutched the spear. "You realize this water is cold — comes down as snowmelt from Mount Mador."

"Not only that," Raithe added, "but since we're going to be hunted, we won't be able to make a fire when we get out."

The slender man with the pointed nose and narrow eyes forced a tight smile. "Lovely. Thanks for the reminder."

"You up for this?" Raithe asked as he led the way into the icy water.

"I'll admit it's not my typical day." The sound of his words rose in octaves as he waded into the river.

"What was your typical day like?" Raithe gritted his teeth as the water reached knee depth. The current churned around his legs and pushed, forcing him to dig his feet into the riverbed.

"Mostly I poured wine."

Raithe chuckled. "Yeah — this will be different."

A moment later, the river pulled both of them off their feet.

About the Illustrations

One of the stretch goals for the Drumindor Kickstarter was to add illustrations to the book. Our daughter Sarah Sullivan provided the artwork for the depiction of The Blue Parrot and Royce and Gwen strolling the streets of Tur Del Fur. The map has been revised and was created by Michael. In addition to the black-and-white version for all the books, a full-colored map is provided on the back end sheet for the deluxe edition. There are also a few "doodles" that Michael had in his notebook, so we threw those in as well.

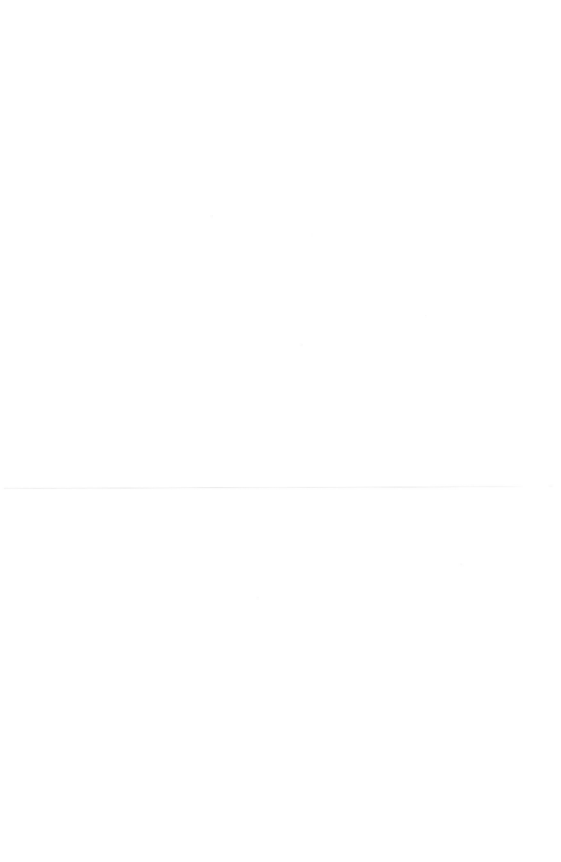

About the Author

MICHAEL J. SULLIVAN is a *New York Times*, *USA Today*, and *Washington Post* bestselling author who has been nominated for nine Goodreads Choice Awards. His first novel, *The Crown Conspiracy,* was released by Aspirations Media Inc. in October of 2008. Michael has been published by the fantasy imprints of Penguin Random House (Del Rey) and Hachette Book Group (Orbit). He has also been a pioneer in the indie publishing movement. As of 2024, Michael has released twenty-one novels (twenty set in his fictional world of Elan, and one standalone sci-fi thriller: *Hollow World*). His series include:

- The Riyria Revelations: 6 books – completed
- The Riyria Chronicles: 5 books – ongoing
- The Legends of the First Empire: 6 books – completed
- The Rise and Fall: 3 books – completed

These days, Michael has returned to his indie roots while still providing his novels through retail bookstores. Each novel is launched via Kickstarter (thirteen projects and counting), where his campaigns are among the most-backed and highest-funded fiction projects. Doing so provides his most-ardent fans with unparalleled author access, deluxe limited-edition hardcovers, exclusive perks, and the ability to read the story months before its official release. Michael always enjoys hearing from readers, and you can email him at **michael@michael-j-sullivan.com**. He is currently working on a new series tentatively titled The Cycle.

Works by Michael J. Sullivan

THE LEGENDS OF THE FIRST EMPIRE
Age of Myth • *Age of Swords* • *Age of War*
Age of Legend • *Age of Death* • *Age of Empyre*

THE RISE AND FALL
Nolyn • *Farilane* • *Esrahaddon*

THE RIYRIA CHRONICLES
The Crown Tower • *The Rose and the Thorn*
The Death of Dulgath • *The Disappearance of Winter's Daughter*
Drumindor

THE RIYRIA REVELATIONS
Theft of Swords (*The Crown Conspiracy* • *Avempartha*)
Rise of Empire (*Nyphron Rising* • *The Emerald Storm*)
Heir of Novron (*Wintertide* • *Percepliquis*)

STANDALONE NOVELS
Hollow World (Sci-fi Thriller)

SHORT STORIES IN ANTHOLOGIES
Unavowed: "The Storm" (Fantasy: The Cycle)
Grimoire: "Traditions" (Fantasy: Tales from Elan)
Heroes Wanted: "The Ashmoore Affair" (Fantasy: Riyria Chronicles)
Blackguards: "Professional Integrity" (Fantasy: Riyria Chronicles)
Unfettered: "The Jester" (Fantasy: Riyria Chronicles)
When Swords Fall Silent: "May Luck Be with You" (Fantasy: Riyria Chronicles)
Unbound: "The Game" (Fantasy: LitRPG)
Unfettered II: "Little Wren and the Big Forest" (Fantasy: Legends of the First Empire)
The End: Visions of the Apocalypse: "Burning Alexandria" (Dystopian Sci-fi)
Triumph Over Tragedy: "Traditions" (Fantasy: Tales from Elan)
The Fantasy Faction Anthology: "Autumn Mist" (Fantasy: Contemporary)
Help Fund My Robot Army: "Be Careful What You Wish For" (Fantasy: Contemporary)

STANDALONE SHORT STORIES
"Pile of Bones" (Fantasy: Legends of the First Empire)